Readers can explore the full collection of colour character illustrations on the author's personal Facebook page here:

https://www.facebook.com/profile.php?id=61581325000577

Contents

Chapter 1: The Interrogation

In a side hall of the Jiangnan Weaving Bureau, wisps of incense curled languidly through the air. The faint rustle of parchment was barely audible.

His tone was calm—too calm.

Each word landed with the quiet precision of a knife.

He sat upright at the magistrate's bench, his face impassive, austere. That gaze held not a shred of familiarity—only the chill focus of a hunter sizing up his prey.

Smoke hung heavy in the still air. The silence pressed in.

Through the soft crackle of documents, Xiao Lingyu heard the brush tip descend—

a quiet stroke, yet one that seemed to seal her fate.

Then, he spoke.

His voice was neither loud nor soft, but each word pricked like a needle: "The Xiao family's business is thriving. So is their boldness."

Instinctively, Xiao Lingyu raised her eyes, casting him a nervous glance—yet she dared not speak.

"Do you know the penalty for tax evasion?"

Suddenly—slam!

The sound shattered the stillness. She flinched.

Fear coiled tight in her chest.

He had hurled his brush onto the desk in restrained fury, displeased by her silence.

Xiao Lingyu stood beneath the dais, her hands hidden in her sleeves, fingers pale from tension. Though her head remained bowed, she could feel it—the sharp, icy gaze slicing down from above.

The man on the judge's seat wore dark robes embroidered with cloud motifs.

His bearing was refined, his presence unshakable — yet his eyes gleamed with a coldness that pierced the bone.

She had thought this was a minor correction to a weaving report— three formal petitions just to be granted this meeting.

Yet the moment she stepped into the hall, one look froze her in place.

Those eyes.

She remembered them.

Cold. Deep. Unrelenting.

Eyes that could see straight through to the soul.

Just one glance—and she knew.

It was him.

And only now, after all these years, did she learn his true name:

Lu Zi Chou.

Deputy Minister of Revenue.

The Emperor's confidant.

A man who held the reins of military stipends and tax oversight in the capital,

controlling the empire's purse strings — a man at the very apex of power.

He had once told her, with a rare tenderness, "Call me Ziyuan." A name not lightly given, kept only for kin and kindred souls.

That, she now realized, was not his name, but his courtesy name.

And – he should not have recognized her.

Back then, they had parted without ever exchanging real names.

She had vanished without a trace, as if she had never been.

Before she could utter a word, his voice cut through, cold as frost: "No need for defence, Madam. Did you not come to confess?"

Her heart dropped.

This was no investigation.

This was judgment already passed.

In his eyes— she was already condemned.

A low, bitter laugh curled from his lips, the smile he wore cold as tempered steel.

"If Madam Xiao insists on pleading innocence… then once I find even a single silken thread of truth, I shall pull until the whole veil unravels.

The full weight of the law shall fall—seizure of assets, and disgrace upon your house."

That storm-lashed night, the vows murmured beneath moonlight, the three fleeting nights of stolen tenderness—each remained etched in memory.

But he was no longer the penniless scholar hidden away in a quiet mountain lodge.

Now, he came as the Imperial Inspector of Silk Affairs, the man whose word could decide the rise and fall of every weaving house in Jiangnan.

And she? Merely a merchant, her name laid before him like a case awaiting judgment.

The brazier burned bright in the hall, but gave no warmth.

He laughed—a faint, hollow sound, dry and sharp, scraped from the depths of silence.

"Back then, you wouldn't even grace me with your real name," he said, voice light as wind, yet sharp with scorn.

"And now? You come willingly to my table—bearing your family business, your craft, your entire fortune, all tethered behind.

Madam, your courage is… truly admirable."

"It is but a humble atelier," she replied softly, lowering her gaze. "I only ask that Your Excellency judge with fairness…"

"You are far too modest," he said. "The secret artistry of Jin Hua—the double-sided, dual-coloured embroidery—none in Jiangnan can rival it."

Her lips drew taut; beneath the flickering lamplight, her lashes quivered—

veiling memories too bitter for words, a sorrow long buried in silence.

Two years past, her elder brother, Xiao Yuan, disappeared along a merchant road and never returned.

The tidings shattered her father—since that day, he had not uttered a sound, limbs frozen like carved jade, breath shallow as winter ash.

Her mother had long since returned to dust.

From that moment on, the weight of blood and name settled upon her.

Light in form, but heavy with all the world could not spare.

Jin Hua Hall weathered wind and ruin, propped up by the slender strength of a woman no one thought worth remembering.

Kinsmen turned cold, the world jeered.

To them, she was merely a cloistered girl behind a loom — a silken blossom, all show, no root.

Who had ever spared her a second glance?

That year, her clan conspired to wed her to Zhang Erlang — a brocade-clad fop with idle hands and greedy eyes, eager to seize the family trade through vows and silk.

All because she was a girl, not a son — unfit, in their eyes, to bear the Xiao name forward. To guard her family's name, she chose danger over disgrace.

——As they wished, she would bear a child as an heir—without a husband!

So the chance came—sooner than she dared dream.

As if the gods themselves had hearkened to her unspoken wish.

Southbound to survey the mulberry groves, she was seized by a sudden tempest.

Blinded by wind and rain, she sought shelter in a lonely mountain lodge.

Inside sat a man in blue linen robes, his brush pen dancing across scrolls, ink blooming like mist.

His brow was calm as still water, his gaze cold and distant.

His bearing, quiet and poised—a man cut from silence, untouched by dust.

She had never believed in love at first sight—until now.

At a single glance, her breath caught. Such rare grace—hidden in the hills?

A thought rose, bold as lightning: If fate must be borrowed, and why not from the one—

whose very form seemed shaped for her alone?

She returned, again and again, cloaked in pretence.

Smiles sweet as spun silk, steps soft as moonlight.

With Suxin's silent help, the moment was arranged.

At last, the incense of Hehuan lit the path—its fragrance gentle as mist, yet potent enough to unmoor the will and awaken desire.

That night, anger warred with shame.

By dying lamp, he vowed: "I will answer for what is done. I will wed you and give you a name."

She wept, then nodded.

Three nights of tenderness passed— and at dawn on the fourth, she vanished.

A note lay on his desk: "Part we must. The bond is but dew at dawn. I dare not long for a dream never mine to hold."

She returned to her world, carrying his child without anyone knowing it.

Months later, she gave birth to a daughter— eyes the shade of ancient bronze—darker, deeper, unlike the usual black of others.

She named her Baor, meaning treasure.

She believed the past buried.

But fate remembers what we wish to forget.

When they met again, he had risen to become the Deputy Minister of Revenue and Imperial Inspector of Weaving.

And she — a merchant, with no name left to defend.

Lately, her embroidery hall had come under siege.

Orders withdrawn. Dye houses shuttered.

Cloth merchants avoided her like plague.

All had begun after that one tribunal.

She had sent three letters of request.

At last—during a factory survey—she finally saw him again.

* * * * *

Five years since that parting.

He stepped from the crowd—robed in black, silver edging glinting in the sun.

Light flashed along his sleeve; his voice, cold as frost, rang clear:

"So, Madam Xiao graces us as well?"

She turned.

At the sound of his voice — all warmth in her blood turned to ice.

He smiled. But his gaze was colder than ice.

"Or perhaps… Madam Li would be more fitting?"

Her head lowered, sleeves trembling. Words lodged in her throat.

He let out a soft, contemptuous laugh.

"Once, a lesser daughter of the Li clan—born of a concubine, raised in the shadows."

A lie she once told him—crafted to shield the truth, now returned to bind her. "Now, the famed head of Jin Hua Hall—Xiao Lingyu. Tell me—how should I address you without offense?"

Pain lanced through her fingers.

Still, she managed a reply.

"So judged by Your Grace… I dare not argue."

Another cold laugh.

His eyes held no trace of the man she once knew.

Once, she had dared to reach for his heart.

Now, she could not even speak her name.

She bowed low.

"In recent days, the weaving hall has met with difficulties.

I dare approach to seek Your Grace's guidance—"

"Guidance?"

He cut in, voice laced with irony.

"Your family reaches to the firmament. What need have you for my counsel?"

She drew a breath, steadied her voice.

"The autumn shipment has been detained ten days. Without the Inspector's seal, the capital delivery may fail. I beseech Your Grace—"

"Delay?"

His voice swept past like winter wind.

"When you chased your goal all those years ago, did you ever once consider whose years you shattered?"

Her face went pale.

"With such talent—to rise from Li to Xiao— surely you can clear your own name.

Why stoop to plead with me here?"

Then his tone shifted, light as silk, sharp as a blade. "Or perhaps… that farewell in the rain still clings to you? Have you come to repay a debt of affection?"

She bit her lip and her throat burned. "I only wish to have a fair investigation…"

He let out a quiet laugh, low and laced with scornful irony.

"And where in this world do you imagine such a thing still exists?"

She opened her mouth — but he had already turned away, voice falling like stone.

"If there is nothing else… Madam Xiao may leave now."

Once again, he asked her to leave, without giving her any opportunity for her explanation.

She bowed once more, sorrow and reluctance woven in her every movement, then turned to leave—graceful, yet with no room for refusal.

Outside, sunlight scorched the courtyard stones.

Yet all she felt was a cold that seeped to the bone.

Chapter 2: Verbal Duel

She had spent the night sorting through three years of the workshop's ledgers—accounts, orders, every shipment that had ever left the gate. By the following morning, she came again to request an audience.

This time, he did not refuse.

And so, here they were—inside the side hall of the Jiangnan Weaving Bureau.

When she entered, she saw the account books already spread open before him, though not a single page had been turned.

He sat in his chair, posture loose, eyes half-lidded, as if every ounce of patience he possessed had been spent before she even arrived.

His gaze lingered on her for a breath, then he spoke, his tone deceptively calm.

"Madam Xiao is diligent indeed. Why not submit a memorial to the Ministry of Revenue and have your workshop registered as a government concern? That way, we can properly lend you support."

His words were soft; his meaning, barbed.

Her face warmed despite herself. "A private workshop must follow the law, my lord," she murmured. "We dare not presume beyond our station."

"Presume?" He laughed once, without mirth. "You call it presumption? And yet here you stand—humble and cautious to perfection. I almost admire the act."

"My lord—" she began, then forced her voice steady.

"If the Xiao family has erred, I ask that you speak plainly. But if there is no proof, I beg for your leniency. We are but small folk. One more blow, and we may not rise again."

His gaze rested on her, unreadable, the depth of his eyes like frozen water. When he finally spoke, the words were low, deliberate.

"A blow?" he said. "That night, in the rain—you left without a word. Tell me, Xiao Lingyu, did you think then of what your leaving cost others?"

Her heart turned cold.

Their eyes met—his sharp as steel, hers wavering. No more words followed, yet the silence itself cut like frost.

She bit her lip. When she finally spoke, her voice trembled.

"If fate could turn back... yes, my lord, in private I was wrong. But now, in public matters—"

He moved not an inch, but a faint smirk touched his mouth.

"Since Madam Xiao admits her fault, tell me—what face have you to speak of public matters now? The world offers no second chances. Surely you understand that."

Her breath caught. There was no use arguing.

She bowed her head in silence, knowing that any further defence would only deepen the wound.
He had no anger left for her—only the colder cruelty of indifference. And she knew, with quiet certainty, that this was only the beginning.

If she broke now, she would only be proving him right.

"If there's nothing else," he said lightly, fingers idly brushing the ledger's edge, "you may leave."

The words struck without force, yet they cut all the same.

Xiao Lingyu stood still, knuckles pale around her sleeve. She knew that if she said even one word more, she would lose the last shred of dignity she possessed. His eyes held no mercy—no warmth, no hatred—only calculation. Not even the anger of old remained. That, she realized, was the most frightening thing of all.

She lowered her gaze and answered softly, "Yes, my lord."

Turning to go, she heard him call out behind her, his tone flat as a blade drawn from its sheath.

"Someone escort Madam Xiao out."

Her lips pressed tight; her spine remained straight. She did not turn back. After three steps, however, she paused, thought once more, and finally spoke—

"If the autumn cloth shipment is found at fault, we will bear the punishment. But if not, I ask only that my workshop—Jin Hua Hall—be cleared of blame."

Then she walked on.

She walked slowly, as though every measured step landed squarely upon his heart.
Yet despite this, she was sent away once again—without being granted a single chance to explain, or to be heard.

Only when her figure disappeared beyond the threshold did he close the ledger—then open it again.

Lines of dense, orderly handwriting filled the pages—her handwriting. Neat, precise, meticulously arranged. Even the smallest discrepancies in each shipment were annotated, every variation accounted for, every length of cloth explained down to the last measure.

He stared for a long while. Then he closed his eyes and let out a low, almost soundless laugh. There was no warmth in it.

"That handwriting…" he murmured. "Still exactly the same."

His fingertips brushed the inked strokes, tracing them unconsciously. He remembered how she once watched him write—how she had pouted when he ignored her, then seized a brush of her own and sat beside him, copying his hand.

"A proper ledger must be clean," she had muttered then. "No wandering strokes. No careless sums. Otherwise, people will take advantage."

He had laughed, teasing her for meddling in men's work, telling her to stick to flowers and patterns instead. She hadn't listened. In the end, he had guided her hand himself, teaching her each stroke—half annoyed, half amused. Back then, her focus had never truly been on the brush.

Now… her writing was flawless. Every number exact. Every line beyond reproach. Even the price difference of a single foot of cloth was clearly noted, with cause attached.

He closed the book, pressing his palm flat against the cover, as though holding something down—a memory, a pulse, or perhaps regret itself.

For a fleeting moment, something complicated flickered in his eyes. Three years, he thought. Perhaps… those years had not been easy for her after all.

And yet—

If that little girl truly carried his blood, how had her mother dared to vanish so completely three years ago? Without a word. Without a trace.

* * * * *

By the next morning, the autumn cloth shipment still remained held at the post station.

The air inside Jin Hua Hall was thick enough to choke on; every thread, every sigh, seemed to tremble with the same quiet dread.

Xiao Lingyu's heart was no steadier than the rest—yet on her face, there was only calm. She understood all too well: this was his test, and his punishment.

If she faltered now, she would only prove him right.

Still, when she looked down at the dwindling silver notes in her hand, and then up at the long list of debts and merchants already offended in his name, the weight pressing on her chest felt heavier than numbers—it was a sentence, and her life hung in the balance.

The bookkeeper paced across the floor again and again, opening his mouth, closing it, his worry written plain.

The master dyer, old and stooped, came forward to whisper, "Madam Xiao… the autumn cloth still hasn't been released.

If it's delayed much longer, the shipment won't make the delivery.

The customers in Jinling are already sending riders to demand compensation."

This was not a matter of one batch of cloth.

It was the face of Jin Hua Hall, its reputation built through years of toil, about to be ruined in a single season.

Xiao Lingyu pressed a hand to the open ledger before her, keeping her tone level.

"I know."

The words were calm—too calm—but beneath them lay iron.

She could not fall.

If she fell, Jin Hua Hall would crumble; her father's illness would go untended; her missing brother would remain lost to the winds; and her daughter… her daughter would be left without a name, without a home. No matter how cold the world grew, she had to stand.

After a long silence, she summoned the shop steward and gave her orders.

"This batch uses the glazed satin dye from last month—the pale lotus shade.

If we delay two more days, the colour will fade and it will become last season's stock.

Have the embroiderers rework the design—replace the crimson and ochre chrysanthemums with

silver thread instead. It will look cleaner, more refined."

The steward blinked.

"That's a new pattern, Madam. The market might not take to it."

"Let them learn to," she said quietly.

"Autumn cloth is meant for the Mid-Autumn festival—lotus silk under moonlight, silver thread like frost. If fortune has turned against us, then we fight it with beauty. Jin Hua Hall was born from innovation; it shall survive by it."

Her words steadied the air. The men bowed and hurried out, the echo of their footsteps scattering like flurries of cloth.

Left alone, Xiao Lingyu stood still for a moment.

Outside, the afternoon light slanted across the dye vats; steam rose from the bronze basins, tinted pink and silver.

She looked at her reflection in the rippling surface—so thin, so calm, and almost did not recognize the woman staring back.

Five years ago, she could never have imagined this— that after leaving him with nothing but silence and a child, she would one day stand before him again, stripped of every defence, and find that he had changed beyond reach.

He had returned not as the gentle scholar she once knew, but as the judge of her fate.

Now, the game was set. Every move from here on would determine not just her survival—but her redemption.

She exhaled slowly and straightened her shoulders.

"Very well," she murmured, half to herself. "If this is the trial he set, then I'll meet him at his own board."

Outside, the wind shifted, carrying the faint scent of dye and iron.

The banners of Jin Hua Hall fluttered in the courtyard like stubborn flames refusing to die.

And within that quiet defiance, Xiao Lingyu took her first step toward turning loss into power.

Chapter 3: Peril at the Embroidery House

Darkened night, the lamps burned low, their wavering flames trembling with the wind. Shadows rippled along the walls, half-light and half-dark.

She sat alone at the desk, eyes fixed upon the open ledger, yet her brush never moved. Her fingers tapped the wood in a slow, hollow rhythm—steady, dull, like a heartbeat muffled beneath stone.

Thought after thought surged and fell, but not one could undo the knot that bound Jin Hua Hall.

On the cover glimmered three faintly gilded characters—Jin Hua Hall.

The gold had long since dulled beneath the wear of years, just as her strength had thinned through nights of toil. That name was all she had fought to preserve: her stubborn faith, her pride, her last fragile courage.

The room was too still.

Only the wind pressed through the window seam, damp and whispering, lifting the loose sheets upon the table. The rustle of paper in the dark was sharp as mockery.

She stilled them with a palm, but her fingertips were cold, and the chill seeped inward like rising tide.

The image of him—of today—remained vivid: He had stood above her, calm, remote, immaculate. Not a single word spoken in anger, yet every one a blade. She had said nothing. Could say nothing.

That night, years ago, she had sinned—reckless, unforgivable. Now he punished her not with fury, but with silence honed to steel. And what could she possibly say against that?

Wax fell from the candle in slow tears, one drop splashing hot against the back of her hand. The brief sting cleared her head. She had survived storms before—three years of hunger and ruin—and still kept the hall alive.

But this time… this time the tide might finally swallow her.

She had once believed endurance was enough.

That as long as she did not fall, as long as she continued to stand, fate would eventually loosen its grip. For three years she had lived by that belief—counting silver until dawn, stitching contracts together with trembling hands, bargaining away sleep, pride, and warmth. Each time she survived another crisis, she told herself she had learned how to endure.

Yet only now did she understand the truth.

Endurance was not strength. It was merely delay.

What frightened her was not that Jin Hua Hall might collapse—but that she herself had already begun to crack, inch by inch, without noticing. The weight she carried had grown so familiar that she no longer felt it pressing down, until her breath came shallow and the ground beneath her feet began to tilt.

She had told herself she could hold on for her father.

She had told herself she could hold on for her missing brother.

She had told herself she could hold on for Baor.

But there were moments—like this one, in the quiet of a darkened room—when she could no longer tell whether she was holding Jin Hua Hall up, or whether it was Jin Hua Hall that had been pinning her in place, slowly crushing the air from her lungs.

Five years ago, her brother Xiao Yuan had vanished while traveling on business; no message had ever returned. The shock felled their father— half-paralysed, speech broken—and the clan closed in, circling like hounds.

They had looked at her, the quiet embroideress, and seen only fragility.

None knew how many nights she had clenched her teeth till her mouth bled, forcing back every cry.

Her fingers brushed the worn pages of the old ledger; the edges were frayed and yellowed, rough against the skin—like the cracks in her heart.

She remembered her father's trembling voice from that sickbed:

"Xiao Lingyu… you must hold it."

Low but firm, the words had settled upon her shoulders like a mountain.

Since then, she had borne it all. To others she seemed gentle, graceful— but inside, her soul had been carved thin by knives.

Jin Hua Hall still stood.

And she—barely.

Yet some prices, she had never imagined she would pay.

The lie she once spun in that countryside house, the deceit that bound one reckless night—now hung over her like a blade, suspended by a single thread.

Still, she did not resent it.

The world had never promised fairness.

If she had not reached for that forbidden thought back then, perhaps today she would not be drowning in its consequence.

But regret, now, was too late.

She closed her eyes and a tightness coiled in her chest.

If only Baor could grow safely, she could bear anything, even shame.

What she could not bear was seeing that child endure so much as a whisper of cruelty.

Today, passing a street corner, she had felt the stares—the whispering, half-mocking, half-pitying looks.

She could pretend deafness.

But if Baor were ever to face those same eyes—she would rather burn herself to ash.

Back then she had said she was Li Meng'er, a concubine-born daughter of the Li family in the capital, sent to the countryside by a jealous stepmother. She had spoken with tears, trembling just enough to stir compassion.

Every word a calculation.

She had only wanted a child—to keep the Xiao family's incense from dying out.

But that small deceit had unravelled into this fatal game of chess.

She had not lied in a moment of panic.

She had lied deliberately.

She remembered clearly how she had chosen each word that day—how much truth to reveal, how much sorrow to display, how deeply to bow her head. She had calculated how fragile she should appear, how broken her past needed to sound in order to be believed. Even the name—Li Meng'er—had been selected with care, common enough to pass unnoticed, pitiful enough to invite mercy.

At the time, she had told herself it was the only path left.

That a woman alone, with a ruined household and no male heir, had no right to hesitate. That as long as she obtained a child, the rest—her name, her reputation, even her future—could be abandoned without regret.

She had believed she understood the cost.

She had been wrong.

A lie, once spoken, did not end when its purpose was fulfilled. It continued to live, to grow roots, to pull unseen threads through the years. What she had thought was a single calculated step had become the foundation of everything that followed—each choice narrowing, each escape closing, until today there was nowhere left to retreat.

This was not misfortune.

It was consequence.

* * * * *

She rose slightly, hand braced on the desk, and the world spun.

"Suxin, fetch water," she heard faintly.

Her maid, Suxin, hurried forward. "Madam, please rest. You've not slept for two nights."

Xiao Lingyu shook her head. Bitterness caught in her throat, sharp as gall.

Then—

"Mama."

A soft, lilting call.

She turned.

At the doorway stood her little daughter, small as a swallow, clutching something in both hands. The child wobbled on unsteady feet, yet carried her prize as though it were treasure.

A single piece of sugar candy, cupped carefully in her palms.

She held it out, smiling—a shy triumph.

Her robe hem trailed along the floor; her lips were sticky with sugar, her eyes bright as lantern glass.

And those eyes— bronze-clear, luminous— just like her missing brother.

In the slant of the candlelight, that bronze clarity struck her with another, darker resemblance—

not hers, not only her brother's… but the man she had seen years ago, in that night's half-light.

For a heartbeat, it felt as though the past had reached through the flame and caught her by the throat.

Her breath caught. A tangle of sorrow and yearning surged through her chest.

Those were Xiao eyes. Her brother Xiao Yuan's eyes—polished bronze in the sun, lucid, unstained.

A quirk of their mother's lineage: somewhere, in each generation, one or two would bear that burnished hue, a remnant of some long-forgotten foreign blood.

Now that same glint looked up at her from her child's face, and her heart ached all the more for the brother who might already be gone.

She remembered his laughter—how he had once teased her: "If ever I have a daughter, may she be as clever as you. It would ease a man's days."

She had laughed then, thinking it jests. Now the memory cut like a blade.

Five years, and no word from him. If he never returned— she feared she could no longer stand.

Baor's eyes were the same as her brother's. Whether it was blessing or curse, she could not tell. But even if what she had done five years ago had been madness, at least the Xiao bloodline—by some twist of fate— had survived through this child.

She forced a smile, faint as candlelight, and reached to take the thin piece of osmanthus candy. Her fingers trembled slightly.

"Thank you, Baor," she murmured.

The candy was sweet—her heart, steeped in bitterness.

"Mama, eat the candy. Be happy, smile big-big!" the girl said with solemn insistence.

Xiao Lingyu nodded, lips curving softly.

"Mm. Mama will eat the candy… and smile big-big."

Their voices overlapped—one high, one low—tender, aching, almost unbearably human.

Her chest warmed.

She took the sweet from Baor's hand, but it crumbled at her touch, fine as dust. For a moment she could not speak. A lump rose in her throat; the air itself felt dry and thin. She knelt and drew the child into her arms, one hand stroking that fragile back.

She gave a bitter laugh, weary and self-mocking.

"I suppose I deserved this."

What she had done could not be softened by intention.

No matter how she dressed it in necessity or survival, she had crossed a line knowingly. She had taken what was never meant to be taken, bound another person into her fate without consent, and walked away believing herself resolute.

If she stripped the act of every excuse, what remained was simple.

She had stolen.

Stolen blood.

Stolen lineage.

Stolen a future that should have been his to choose.

That was why she could not hate him now.

Why she could not protest his coldness, nor resent his silence. If their positions were reversed—if she were the one standing above, with power in hand and truth laid bare—she knew what judgment she would pass.

She might not have spared herself either.

That night, years ago, she had set the trap with her own hands—cast away rank, dignity, name. All for the sake of bearing one child, to keep both her family and Jin Hua Hall alive.

She had thought that even if she left forever, never seeing him again, she could live without regret.

But now, seeing him once more—so high above, so pure in stature, his hand on the levers of power—while she had fallen to dust beneath his feet…

To have stolen his seed, and yet still be breathing— That was mercy enough.

Her voice dropped to a whisper. "In his place… I might not have spared me, either."

The child did not understand.

Baor only wrapped her tiny arms around her mother's neck and whispered, "Don't be sad, Mama. Baor's here."

A quiet laugh escaped her, half sob, half sigh. One tear slid down, catching the light.

"Yes," she said softly. "With Baor… that's enough."

But she knew it wasn't. Some debts could never be so easily repaid.

The door creaked open. Suyue entered in haste, her face pale with urgency.

"Madam—the shop steward sent word from the dye house. The rains haven't stopped. The dyeing materials for the last batch… more than half have already gone to mildew. They're asking what should be done."

The flame wavered, and her heart sank again.

Her arms tightened around Baor, clinging as if to draw strength from that small, warm body.

Her lips moved; she brushed away the wetness at the corner of her eye.

"I see," she said quietly at last. "Tell them I'll decide soon."

She already knew.

Every trial waiting ahead would cut deeper than the last.

Chapter 4: Echoes of a Vow Past

Night deepened. The flame in the lamp wavered faintly; the ink upon the desk had not yet dried.

Outside, the courtyard had long fallen silent save for the slow drip of water from the eaves. Somewhere beyond the bamboo wall, a night bird gave a thin, forlorn cry, then vanished into the dark.

Lu Chou reclined upon the couch, the collar of his robe loosened, one hand resting over scattered scrolls. Between waking and dream he drifted, uneasy, as though the world itself had tilted beneath him.

The pillow was cold, the mat beneath his back unyielding, and his brows knit tightly even in sleep.

Sleep came, but it was not rest—only a slow descent into a dream thick as dusk, a dream that drew him backward, deep into the long, humid years of Jiangnan.

* * * * *

The ancestral compound.

The narrow courtyard beside the family shrine.

That small, austere room where he had once been confined for "quiet study and reflection."

In those days, his half-brother Lu Xiu had already earned minor military honours,

riding in bright armour through the streets while the servants shouted his name.

Their father, seeing Lu Chou's scholarly indifference and refusal to strive in arms or the examinations, had thundered:

"If even the heir of the Lu family achieves nothing, what face have we left to our name?"

To his father, it was not merely disappointment—it was disgrace. What cut deepest was not the punishment itself, but the implication behind it: that as the legitimate son, he had failed the very right of succession. That learning without ambition was indulgence, that withdrawal was cowardice, that choosing quiet over conquest was a betrayal of blood.

In that moment, Lu Chou understood something with painful clarity. In his father's eyes, worth was measured only by conquest and display. Anything else—even restraint, even principle—was weakness unfit for inheritance.

In his fury he had ordered his son to the ancestral estate, to repent before the spirits of his forebears.

At first, Lu Chou accepted the punishment with quiet detachment.

Days folded into days—ancient texts, blue lamps, the faint rustle of silk sleeves against paper. Without his father's shadow or his brother's constant triumphs, the silence of the countryside became almost a solace.

He had always been solitary by nature—believing rank and fame to be illusions, seeking only to live at ease, to paint mountains, to tend a few orchids that bloomed unseen.

But his father would not permit such ease. That winter, after a quarrel at the table, the elder Lu's words had fallen like lashes.

Too proud to bend, Lu Chou was expelled from the main residence and sent to the study by the shrine— a small house with the name Hall of Reflection carved above its door.

The dwelling was spare: a crooked plum tree leaning beside an old well, a single brazier half cold.

Each dawn he burned incense to the ancestors; each dusk he copied sutras by lamplight; and by night he sat before the moon, its pale glow spilling over his hands.

To others such life might have been exile.

To him, it was rare tranquillity.

It was there—amidst that stillness—that he first met her.

A stranger, drenched by sudden rain, seeking shelter.

Then another visit, and another.

Excuses upon excuses, until her presence became a thread of warmth woven into his solitude.

He treated her first with courtesy due a guest—until that night, when courtesy shattered.

He would never forget it.

Rain lashed the eaves; thunder shook the shutters.

She burst through the door, hair unpinned, breath uneven, garments clinging like mist.

Before he could speak, she pressed him backward onto the couch, eyes bright with a resolve fiercer than the storm itself.

He thought—perhaps—it was a dream.

But when dawn came, the storm had passed and the couch was empty. Only the faint fragrance of her hair lingered on the pillow, and upon the coverlet lay a single fallen hairpin.

Then he knew—it had not been dreaming.

* * * * *

Even then his heart had begun to turn.

He knew she was but a concubine's daughter, and that his father would never permit such a match.

Yet he resolved to plead her case, even to defy command if need be.

He never expected that when morning came, she would be gone— leaving behind nothing but a square of embroidered silk and a trace of scent.

Would she return?

She had not said farewell, not even given her name.

From that day forward he understood: the feeling had been his alone, a fever with no cure.

And yet, beneath that certainty, doubt gnawed at him.

Had she come because she chose him—or because circumstance had cornered her into recklessness? Had he been the one desired, or merely the one available? The questions circled endlessly, unanswered.

What unsettled him most was that he had accepted her closeness without asking why, had welcomed intimacy without demanding truth, and in doing so, had willingly stepped into a dream whose terms he did not fully understand.

He sat long, shaken by unspoken thoughts— why she came, why she left, why she had chosen such reckless closeness—he would never know.

Yet one conviction took root within him: if she had dared so bold a choice, how could he let her bear its burden alone?

That evening he prepared the small pavilion beside the moonlit pond.

He lit incense, poured two cups of wine, arranged a pair of offerings.

When dusk deepened, she came again. He breathed out, softly, as though fearing to break the illusion.

She had changed into clean robes, her face still faintly flushed, her steps light as drifting petals.

Standing before him, she lowered her gaze, a tremor of shyness softening her voice.

"You came," he said quietly.

She only nodded.

He placed the fallen hairpin back into her palm.

"I do not know why you did what you did," he said,

"But since fate began thus, let there be no regret."

She bowed her head, voice small and trembling.

"Last night's folly was mine alone. If you despise me, I—"

"I do not despise you," he interrupted, steady and low.

"I only wish to ask—if tonight, beneath this moon, I pledge my heart to you, will you accept it?"

Her eyes lifted, startled, then shone with sudden brightness.

He saw that light and felt his heart shift.

The moon that night was flawless; osmanthus fragrance drifted through the courtyard.

They knelt together before the altar, lit three sticks of incense, and bowed as one.

No witness. No registry. No matchmaker.

Yet to him, it was the truest vow of his life.

"Let the moon bear witness," he murmured.

"Should the world ever ask of this night, I will never betray what was sworn here."

She smiled faintly, eyes lowered, fingers tightening around his hand.

* * * * *

And then—the dream broke apart like mist.

He woke with a start.

The lamp still burned; the room lay silent.

She was gone.

Beside his pillow rested the same old hairpin. He lifted it, thumb tracing the loosened thread of gold, whispering to the dark:

"If you had not left… what might we have become?"

He did not finish.

For in the dream, she had reached for him, fingertips brushing his own— and he had not drawn away.

The wind stirred.

The flame trembled.

Fragrance and moonlight mingled, their shadows stretching long across the bamboo floor— two young silhouettes beneath an ancient moon, bound not by name or promise,

but by a single shared heartbeat.

He woke again.

This time the air was real, cold, and empty.

No trace of her remained.

Upon the table lay a small embroidery box.

He opened it.

Inside lay the handkerchief she had left, the edge stitched with tiny words:

Wish made beneath the moon—let it never be betrayed.

Now, which of them had broken that vow?

And which still wandered within the same dream, unable to wake?

* * * * *

He laughed softly hoarse, without mirth.

"That night… whom did I truly wed?

A woman, a spirit, or only the ghost of my own folly?"

The laugh faded.

The candle guttered low.

Footsteps sounded beyond the door, followed by a hesitant knock.

"My lord," came a voice, "Chief Zhang of the Weaving Bureau begs urgent audience."

Lu Chou frowned.

"At this hour?"

"He says it concerns Jin Hua Hall."

At those words, the drowsy haze drained from him.

"Admit him."

Moments later, a man in a blue robe entered, forehead beaded with sweat.

He bowed deeply.

"Reporting to Your Excellency—an hour past, a fire broke out in the dye workshop of Jin Hua Hall.

It has been extinguished, but the cause appears… suspicious.

Your subordinate dared not act without orders."

"A fire?"

Lu Chou's tone remained even, fingers tapping twice upon the desk.

"Any casualties?"

"None, my lord. It was caught early."

Zhang wiped his brow, then, lowering his voice, produced a folded letter stained with smoke and oil.

"There is… another matter.

Madam Xiao attempted to send this to Lord Xie for aid.

I intercepted it and brought it here."

Lu Chou took the letter. The ink was still fresh.

Her name—Xiao Lingyu—was signed clearly at the bottom.

For a long moment, even the candlelight seemed to hold its breath.

His eyes traced each stroke of her handwriting. A cold gleam stirred there.

"So—she seeks another's protection."

The words tasted bitter on his tongue.

It was not jealousy that stirred within him, nor wounded affection—but something colder. Authority bypassed. Judgment evaded. The unspoken understanding between them quietly set aside.

She had not come to him.

She had chosen a different shelter.

That, more than the fire itself, unsettled him.Zhang dared not speak.

After a silence, Lu Chou said quietly,

"Suppress this matter. Tell no one.

As for the fire—investigate quietly.

Find whether it was chance… or intent."

"Yes, my lord."

When the man withdrew, stillness reclaimed the hall.

Lu Chou sat unmoving, fingertips resting against the edge of the letter.

Then, slowly, he laughed—a sound thin as steel against stone.

"Xiao Lingyu," he murmured, "you've learned far more cunning than before."

The candle guttered once more.

On the desk, the forgotten hairpin trembled with a faint metallic chime—a whisper light as breath, reminding him:

Some debts do not end in dreams.

Chapter 5: A Shadowed Lineage

In the capital, whispers spread like wildfire. The weaving trade was abruptly placed under sweeping review: account audits, surprise inspections, ledgers seized at speed by stern-faced officials who moved like thunder.

Several embroidery halls were dragged into scrutiny one after another, the atmosphere turning skittish overnight. Among them all, Jin Hua Hall stood at the centre of the storm, taking the first blow and the heaviest glare.

* * * * *

Behind the hall, at the narrow door of the accounting room, Suxin entered in haste. Her expression was grim as she handed over a folded decree.

"Madam… this came from the Inspectorate," she said, voice tight. "It bears the seal and personal order from the Minister's office itself. They will investigate our accounts from the past three years in full, and they name you directly. They claim you've evaded inspection multiple times. This time, you must appear in person for questioning."

Xiao Lingyu's fingers trembled as she took the letter. She read the lines once—then again—until the ink seemed to sting.

Her lips curved faintly—half a smile, half a sigh that carried no warmth. "Evaded?" she said softly. "Jin Hua Hall has never turned away an official inspection. Only… the summons never came. Not once did we receive notice."

Suxin bit her lip, hesitating before murmuring, "I fear, Madam… someone may have withheld those notices on purpose, pressing the slips down and letting them rot in silence—just to give them cause later. So that when the knife falls, it looks 'proper.'"

Xiao Lingyu lowered her gaze, and the corners of her mouth tightened in a bitter, restrained smile. "Then it is my own doing," she said. "Had I not left that letter behind… he'd have no reason to remember me at all."

She had once thought she could simply disappear—walk away cleanly, erase herself from his sight, and let the past die without a trace. Now, it seemed he intended for her to pay—debt by debt, memory by memory—pressing closer with each step, as if determined to make her settle every old account with her own hands.

Three days later, she went herself to the ministry to plead her case, carrying her written response and the copies she had prepared through sleepless nights. But the guards barred her at the gate—once, twice, thrice—each time with the same impassive faces and the same cold phrasing, as if reciting a rule carved in stone.

"Lord Lu is occupied with affairs of state," they said. "Without a summons, no one enters."

Xiao Lingyu's jaw tightened. She held out her petition again, knuckles white, forcing her voice steady. "This is my written response to the audit order," she said. "I ask only to explain in person. If he refuses to see me today, I shall wait here—until nightfall if I must."

They had ordered her to "appear in person," yet now denied her entry at the door. Anyone with eyes could see this was no bureaucratic mix-up. It was deliberate humiliation, laid out in broad daylight, meant to grind her patience down inch by inch, to make her stand outside a public gate like a beggar, so the whole street could look and whisper.

Only when dusk began to fall did a young clerk approach in haste, breath thin from running.

"Madam Xiao," he said quickly. "His Lordship has granted an audience. You are to present yourself in the library within the next quarter-hour."

At last, she exhaled—whether relief or the tightening of her throat, she could not tell—and entered.

He was already there, seated behind the desk. Black robes bound with a gold sash, severe as iron; his belt clasped tight, his posture straight as a sword. The lamplight caught the hard lines of his face and made them sharper. He did not lift his gaze when he spoke, as if even the courtesy of looking at her was something he could ration.

"Sit."

She obeyed, lowering herself opposite him. Her eyes fell to the open files before him—ledgers from Jin Hua Hall, spread in perfect order, every page aligned, every label neat, as if he had arranged them with his own hands just to show her how thoroughly she was being stripped.

He turned a page, and only then raised his head. His eyes were clear and cold as frost.

"Three years ago," he said, voice even, "when you registered your household under the name Xiao, your recorded birthplace was Xuanping County. Yet there is no record of your clan among the registries there. No clan roll. No ancestral entry."

He paused just long enough for the words to settle, then continued, each phrase falling like a measured hammer.

"And furthermore—" his voice deepened slightly, "it appears you reported yourself as Xiao, not Li."

He tapped the corner of the page—each sound deliberate, heavy as iron against wood.

"There are also… rumours," he said. "That you were once married. And that you have a daughter—four years old."

The final words lingered in the air. His gaze darkened, a shadow moving behind the stillness. He reached for another document and unfolded it with measured calm, as though he were merely reading out weather.

It was a memorandum from the Ministry's secret office, a complete record of her household changes, business licenses, and merchant filings. And there, at the bottom—

Married. Husband: Li Dashan (deceased). One child, female, aged four.

Lu's eyes lingered on those lines. The porcelain edge of his teacup cracked beneath his grip—soundless, but visible—an injury so fine it looked almost unreal.

"You are skilled at concealment," he said softly, voice coated with ice. "A prosperous Madam of trade—running a hall in splendour for years. A husband, a daughter. Enterprise and household both kept in hand, neither delayed."

Then, at last, he looked at her, and the faintest curl of a smile ghosted across his lips, brittle and cold.

"So that moonlit vow meant nothing to you after all," he said. "And yet you come here now, seeking leniency from me? Seeking a sliver of 'consideration'?"

His gaze fell again to the name.

Li Dashan.

The clean, square strokes stabbed at his eyes. Who was this man—what background, what origin—who had taken her name, her child, the place that once was his? And that child—whose blood ran in her veins?

Rage surged within him, fast and sharp, but he forced it down until it became a colder, clearer thing. He tapped the report against the table, each motion crisp.

"Tell me, then," he said. "How much of this tale have you woven yourself? How many layers are there still beneath it?"

Xiao Lingyu opened her mouth to speak—then closed it again. The room felt suddenly airless.

He drummed his fingers once more, feigning nonchalance, though his voice lowered by a degree.

"This daughter of yours," he said, "she bears the name Xiao. If your husband was Li Dashan, why does she not carry his name?"

A pause. His eyes, cold and clear, flickered once with something else, a quiet, dangerous hope that he could not fully bury. The question slipped out, light as if it were nothing, as if he were asking about a trivial filing error.

"Is she…" His voice dropped to a whisper. "Is she mine?"

It sounded like passing curiosity. But within him, something tightened—sharp and painful—so tight that even his breath seemed to hesitate.

If she were his, then perhaps the past could still be redeemed. Perhaps that one night, that one vow, had not been entirely reduced to ash. Perhaps the ruin between them might yet be bridged—if only by blood.

He waited, eyes fixed on her, as though willing her to break.

But Xiao Lingyu only lowered her lashes. Her fingers twined together, trembling faintly, and when she spoke her voice was low, slow, and final—as if she were cutting something off with her own hand.

"…Baor is not of Your Excellency's blood."

Her voice faltered for a heartbeat, then steadied with quiet dignity.

"I was once married," she continued. "My husband was a refugee—an outsider, without family or record. He never lived long enough to enter the registries. He gave his name as Li Dashan. We were wed only a few months before plague took him. I bore my daughter alone and have raised her since."

Her tone was calm, almost detached—the composure of someone too weary for pleading, and too proud to beg.

"Baor has nothing to do with you, my lord. I beg that you do not trouble yourself with her."

Lu's gaze hardened. The last sliver of softness in his chest died cleanly, as though crushed into powder.

Not his.

He let out a low, bitter laugh. It was quiet, but it carried the sting of a blade drawn slowly from its sheath.

"…Good. Excellent," he said. "Madam Xiao, you are more accomplished than I imagined."

He said nothing further, only lowered his eyes and turned another page of the files before him—as though she had ceased to exist.

Xiao Lingyu raised her head slightly. She met his eyes once, and her voice—when it came—was calm, level, almost unnervingly steady.

"If Your Excellency still doubts, you are free to investigate," she said. "I have nothing to hide."

The words were flawless—tidy, composed, devastatingly final. And with them, she shattered the fragile hope he had refused to name, striking it down as if it had never deserved to live.

He exhaled through his teeth, a cold sound like laughter without mirth.

"So many coincidences," he said. "A false registry, a vanished husband, missing audits—truly remarkable fortune. One would almost admire such… completeness."

Xiao Lingyu straightened her spine.

"Every point has reason and record, my lord," she said, neither servile nor defiant. "My grandfather moved our household once—no one remembers the original registry. The gossip is mere rumour. And as for the ledgers, I have sent copies each season without delay. Jin Hua Hall has never refused an audit."

He smiled—slowly. The kind of smile that made the room colder.

"Is that so?"

He stood, circling the desk, his shadow falling across her. The sound of his steps was light, but the pressure of his presence was heavy. When he stopped beside her chair, he leaned just enough for his voice to drop to a near whisper.

"You speak well," he said. "But I am not a man who believes words without proof."

Her heartbeat stumbled, yet she forced herself to remain still. "If proof is what you require," she said softly, "then let the law judge me. I fear no verdict."

For a moment, he said nothing. Then he smiled again—too lightly, like a feather brushing skin, gentle only in appearance.

"I only fear, Madam Xiao," he murmured, "that when that verdict comes, you will lose not only your hall but your freedom."

Her face drained of colour. And in that instant she understood—this was not justice. This was vengeance, dressed in official ink. He did not want a ruling; he wanted her to kneel. Not for law, but for mercy. He meant to press her down until she had no voice left except to beg.

Xiao Lingyu bowed low, gave thanks, and withdrew. Her palms were slick with cold sweat by the time she stepped beyond the threshold.

Behind her, silence closed in once more.

Lu Chou remained seated, fingers still pressing the report flat against the desk. Outside, the wind moved softly through the eaves. In the candlelight, the fracture in his teacup gleamed faintly—like a thin, stubborn wound that refused to heal.

Chapter 6: Fire in the Dead of Night

Outside the door, Suyue had already been waiting for a long while. When she saw the colour drained from Xiao Lingyu's face, she rushed forward, her hands trembling with worry.

"Madam—how was it?"

Xiao Lingyu gave the smallest shake of her head. Bitterness rose from her throat like something long pressed down, and her fingers quivered faintly, as though her body had not yet escaped the invisible weight of that suffocating room.

"Madam…"

For five years now—ever since she had declared herself a married woman—everyone in the Xiao household and throughout the network of shops had called her "Madam" or "Proprietress." The title sounded so proper, so grand, yet every syllable felt like a veil laid over her face, something she could never truly lift away.

She let Suyue take her arm, and together they began to walk down the rain-dark corridor. Moist air pooled in the courtyard; the apricot branches still held trembling beads of water, each droplet clinging to the petals as if unwilling to fall.

A few fallen flowers lay against the blue stone steps, their pale colour dulled by rain—exactly like her heart in that moment, faint, bruised, but refusing to fade.

At last, Suyue could not help herself. She leaned closer, voice lowered to a whisper. "Lord Lu… he knew, didn't he?"

She had been Xiao Lingyu's personal maid since the beginning and knew too well the tangled, painful thread between her Madam and that man.

She had been the one, years ago, who went out under cover of night to buy that medicine—the single thing that had changed the course of two lives.

Xiao Lingyu did not answer. Her gaze rested on the rain pooling in the cracks of the stones. When she finally spoke, her voice was soft and steady, almost detached.

"We must first steady our suppliers. The embroiderers' wages cannot stop. If they stop, the whole workshop scatters."

Suyue frowned, unable to restrain the worry rising in her chest. "Then why doesn't Lord Lu simply cut us down in one stroke, Madam? Why draw it out like this?"

Xiao Lingyu's lips curved into a faint smile—lighter than wind, gone before it reached her eyes.

"Perhaps he wants to see me collapse inch by inch," she said quietly, "to see me fall apart, yet refuse to fall."

Suyue's chest ached. She pressed her lips together and said nothing more.

When they reached the main house, the lamps beneath the eaves swayed in the damp wind, casting a restless shadow across the wall.

Upon that wall hung an unfinished embroidery of peonies—bright threads halted mid-stitch. Xiao Lingyu stopped there, lifted her hand, and let her fingertips trace lightly over the loose silk strands.

Her voice, when it came, was little more than a whisper.

"Even beneath a weight, one must still live. Only by living can we wait for the turn."

The thread glinted faintly under the flickering lamp, and she looked at it for a long moment, as though the pattern before her was also the map of her own fate—stalled, incomplete, yet still holding the promise of continuation.

This cat-and-mouse game between them—she could only brace herself and keep playing her part. There was no other way.

Because she still had her treasure—her child, her Baor.

Outside, the wind stirred; the lamplight trembled. She turned her face toward the rain veiling the windows, and for a fleeting instant, something sharp flared behind her eyes.

Five years ago, it had also rained like this. She remembered the cold sweat soaking her back, her arms wrapped tight around the small, crying bundle in her embrace. She had believed that if she could survive that one night—just one—she would be safe.

Now she finally understood that single night had stretched into half a lifetime.

* * * * *

Night deepened. Wind combed the lattice, and the flame in the lamp guttered—dying, not yet dead—casting restless, mottled shadows upon the walls.

Lu Chou had fallen asleep over his desk, his brow faintly furrowed and his breathing unsteady. As the candlelight trembled, he slipped once more into an old dream—the one memory he least wished to recall, yet the only tender place left within him.

She had entered his life in a spring rain.

The bamboo window had been half open, and through that thin veil of mist, a pale figure stumbled into view—a woman in soaked robes, breathless, her cheeks flushed from the cold.

She said she was a concubine-born daughter of a wealthy family from the capital, driven south by misfortune, seeking a night's shelter.

Her voice trembled faintly, yet her eyes—so bright, so clear—held seven parts calculation for every three of fear.

He had not seen it then; he only saw the tremor in her fingers, the way her lashes quivered when she spoke.

And still, he believed her.

In the dream, she sat upon the edge of his narrow bed, wrapped in an old cloak, humming a nameless tune as the rain drummed against the eaves. The melody was faint as the scent of plum blossoms, winding softly through the room, through his heart.

He had never been a man of many words, but she spoke to him as though they were long acquainted—of her childhood spent under another's roof, of the mother she saw each night in her dreams, bent over a needle's thread.

She told him of her small, impossible wish: that one day she might have a home where someone waited for her to return, where the soup was kept warm upon the stove, and two people could read side by side beneath a single lamp.

That night, she leaned against his shoulder and whispered, "My name is Li Meng'er."

The sound of it—light as breath—seemed to loosen something in his chest. He smiled faintly and asked, "Meng'er—as in a dream?"

She laughed, soft and clear, eyes curving like the crescent moon. "Mm. And if this truly is a dream," she said, "then I do not wish to wake."

Later, as the rain deepened, she had brewed him medicine, tucked the quilt about his shoulders. Then came her voice again, low, trembling:

"Ziyuan, I wish to bear you a child… one with your eyes, your calm, your gentleness. May I?"

The words had struck through him like thunder. Even now, the echo of them trembled somewhere inside his ribs.

He dreamed that he took a red thread, tied it to a family jade pendant, and looped it gently around her wrist. "No one sees us beneath this moon," he whispered. "This vow is simple, but it is true. If you accept it, I will not fail you."

But dreams cannot last.

The scene shattered. The rain was gone. When he awoke, she had vanished without a sound. Only a slip of paper lay upon the pillow, written hastily, her handwriting hurried and cold.

He had read it a hundred times. The ink had faded, but he still remembered the chill of each word.

The last image that haunted him: himself running across a narrow ridge between flooded fields, calling her name again and again, snow unmelted upon the riverbank. Her figure flickered ahead of him, vanishing into mist—never once turning back.

"Li Meng'er!" he cried, his voice raw, desperate—

—and woke.

Sweat soaked his undershirt. His palms were clenched tight, his breath ragged. The lamp had burned itself to ashes.

Slowly, he opened his fingers. There, in his palm, lay the jade pendant. The red cord was worn thin, but he could not cast it aside.

Li Meng'er.

She had given him more than folly—she had given him a hope he should never have dared to hold.

Who was she now?

Xiao Lingyu, Madam of Jin Hua Hall?

Or simply an actress behind a different name, smiling as she deceived every ounce of trust he had offered?

Lu Chou stared toward the darkened window, his eyes as still as tempered glass. At last, he spoke, voice low and final:

"Dreams should wake."

He rose and dressed. The gentleness once in his eyes was gone, replaced by something sharper, forged in the cold hours before dawn.

She would not acknowledge him; he would not acknowledge her.

And from this moment on, he would seal her path—inch by inch—until there was nowhere left to run.

* * * * *

The rain had only just cleared, but the air still smelled of smoke and damp.

In the back courtyard of Jin Hua Hall, the scent of char and wet ash hung thick in the air. Water pooled over the flagstones, reflecting shivering lantern light. The corner of a wall, blackened by flame, still breathed faint white vapour.

A few workers stooped to sweep away the cinders; bucket water splashed across the stones with hollow sound.

Xiao Lingyu came quickly, the moon-white cloak upon her shoulders still damp, her hair clinging in fine, wet strands to her temples.

She said nothing.

Her gaze swept the courtyard—the blackened wall, the sodden bundles of cloth laid out to dry. When she finally spoke, her voice was calm, yet beneath it lay a chill that could slice through bone.

"How great is the loss?"

The head accountant hurried forward, bowing low. "Madam, we were fortunate. The fire was found early; it didn't spread to the main workshop. But one full rack of cloth awaiting dye has been burned, and two vats of indigo glaze have spoiled in the water. Thankfully, no one was harmed."

Xiao Lingyu looked down at the heap of ruined cloth. The fabric was charred and heavy with soot; thin threads of smoke still rose from its seams, curling faintly in the light. The mist brushed her face, draining what little colour remained.

"How did it begin?"

The steward swallowed hard. "They say the night boy fell asleep. The lamp beside him tipped over, and the flame caught the rack. If not for the embroiderers in the next room who woke in time, the whole dye house might have gone up."

All around, people stared at the ground. The courtyard echoed only with the slow dripping of rainwater from the eaves.

Xiao Lingyu's face did not change. Her voice, though low, carried across the yard. "Asleep?"

The single word dropped like a shard of glass. It barely touched, yet every heart trembled.

Another steward could hold his anger no longer. He stepped forward, voice thick with outrage. "Madam, I cannot believe this was mere accident! That boy may be timid, but he is cautious—he has never failed a single night's duty. This fire—someone must have done it!"

He glanced sharply around, lowering his voice. "I suspect the collateral Xiao branch. They have coveted our business for years, sent spies to pry and learned nothing. This time, they mean to ruin us—to force you to surrender your share of the trade."

At his words, a low murmur rippled through the workers. A gust of wind swept through the courtyard, making the lanterns flicker wildly; one flame flared high, throwing everyone's faces into uneasy gold.

Xiao Lingyu listened, her eyes half-lidded, her expression unreadable. When she finally spoke, her tone was even and deliberate.

"This will not be pursued."

The words fell light as dust, but there was no mistaking their weight.

"No one was harmed. Losses can be repaired. We end it here."

Discontent flashed across the stewards' faces. Someone began to protest, but she turned her gaze on him—cool, steady, unblinking—and the man fell instantly silent.

Her eyes shifted toward the scorched wall at the far end of the yard. "From tomorrow," she said, her voice flat as still water, "night duty will change. Two guards to a shift."

The men exchanged glances. Then, in that same calm voice, she added, "So that each may watch over the other."

A pause—then the faintest edge of meaning: "And keep the other in check."

The night wind moved again, brushing through the damp courtyard. The flame wavered. As she turned away, the hem of her cloak stirred faintly, as though to hide the exhaustion slipping through her poise.

Suyue hurried forward, raising the oiled-paper umbrella above her Madam's head. Xiao Lingyu looked up once at the sky.

The clouds still clung together, moonlight pale and veiled. Behind her, the last embers of the fire glowed a dull red—like anger smothered but not extinguished, waiting for breath enough to flare again.

She knew clearly what it meant: whether accident or intent, the fire had exposed the shadows beneath—the greed, the fracture, the waiting hands.

If it truly had been the Xiao family's collateral branch that moved first, then the contest for power had already begun.

But she—she no longer had strength for war.

"No one was hurt—that is enough," she murmured, so softly that the wind nearly swallowed the words. "At least Jin Hua Hall still stands."

She closed the umbrella, turned, and walked away. Her figure receded into the post-rain mist, thin as a wisp of smoke.

Behind her, the courtyard grew quiet once more. The fire was out, yet its scent lingered—burnt cloth, wet stone, the sharp tang of iron. Only the blackened walls and the heavy damp remained, pressing upon the night like the weight of unspoken sorrow.

The darkness said nothing.

Jin Hua Hall waited—silent, breathless—as though the next storm was already on its way.

Chapter 7: A Gathering Storm

Late spring in Jiangnan, fine rain fell without end, darkening the stone steps before Jin Hua Hall. Xiao Lingyu stepped out from the inner hall, a newly delivered memorial-fold clutched in her hand; the envelope had been pinched into creases by her grip. On the small red-clay brazier, the tea had already gone faintly cold.

"Proprietress, this is the third cloth merchant who has refused us," Deputy Steward Chen Miaomiao said. Her brows were knitted tight, and she kept her voice pressed low. "They say the bolts have all been taken by Yongchang House. They won't say it openly, but they are making it clear. They mean to shame Jin Hua Hall."

Xiao Lingyu did not speak at once. Her knuckles tapped the tabletop lightly, once, then again, a restrained and patient sound. Her gaze sank onto the ledger's incoming-supplies column. It was blank. So blank it looked impossible. The page was a harsh, snow-white glare, like a mute humiliation burning into the eyes.

"Is the Ministry of Revenue still investigating tightly?" she asked. Her voice was even, so calm it was nearly cold.

"Still very tight," Chen Miaomiao replied. "I heard this case was personally approved by Lord Lu. He even pulled it forward by three days on the schedule. This morning someone already came to copy our accounts."

Chen Miaomiao bit her lip, the worry in her throat turning sharp. "I recognized the man. He is Lord Lu's confidant, Secretary Chen. He specializes in inspecting embroidery workshops and ornament houses. If he determines our goods are 'inferior quality at high price,' they start the punishment at a three-month suspension."

Xiao Lingyu closed her eyes briefly. A wave of vexation rose in her chest and she forced it down, swallowing it whole. When she spoke again, her tone was set like a blade placed flat on a table. "Starting tomorrow, the hall suspends all high-end bespoke commissions. We switch to popular patterns and ready-made pieces. If we cannot clash head-on, then we go around."

"But Madam…" Chen Miaomiao faltered. "If we do that, the profits will be cut in half…"

"Better than closing the doors," Xiao Lingyu cut in, final as a verdict. She lifted her hand, signaling them to withdraw.

After they left, the room held only her and Suxin.

Suxin was one of Xiao Lingyu's most trusted maids, second only to Suyue. Her features were plain, but her eyes were unusually quiet; she had followed her Madam since childhood and could read her moods as if they were written on paper. Tonight was no different.

"Madam…" Suxin lowered her voice, worry tightening it. "Does Lord Lu know about Miss Bao, that she is…"

Suxin had not followed them to the countryside back then. She had not gone with her young Madam and Suyue to buy the medicine by the mulberry fields. Yet as a close attendant, she knew what had happened in these past years. She knew the household's seams and hidden stitches. She knew which errands were spoken and which were swallowed.

Xiao Lingyu forced her eyelids steady, as if she had not heard. She only said softly, "Do not speak nonsense. Bao has not the slightest connection with Lord Lu. In five short years he has risen to high rank. Of course he will draw the admiration of many noble daughters."

Once, she had allowed herself a thought. If he were willing to enter her household, if he were willing to take the position of a son-in-law, perhaps marriage would not be unbearable.

But in the end, she retreated.

She was afraid. Afraid that if he became like those clan kin who circled her with greedy eyes, if he too coveted her workshop, her trade, her child, then she would be stripped down to nothing. She would not even have a road left to retreat upon.

In the silence, the papered window sounded twice. Spring rain tapping, drip by drip, as if echoing the rain that had once fallen outside a wooden village house. For a moment she was dazed, as though she saw him again, brows and eyes like a painted scroll, saying to her, "If there is a future, I will marry you properly."

The future never came. The dream had woken far too quickly.

Suxin did not answer. Both women understood what these days of harassment and obstruction meant. His rise had been swift, and his cruelty had been swift as well.

"Mama, eat sugar!" A small voice burst through the quiet.

Baor pushed open the door and ran in, a tiny shard of rock sugar in her palm, her smile bright as a flower. She wore a coarse cloth shirt, and her eyes shone, the same kind of brightness, the same shape, as that man's eyes in those years.

Xiao Lingyu froze for the briefest instant. She took the sugar and placed it in her mouth. It was sweet, and yet on her tongue it turned bitter as well.

Baor looked up at her, innocent and puzzled. "Mama tired?"

"Mama deserves it," Xiao Lingyu said. She finally smiled. The curve of her lips was gentle, but the fatigue behind it could not be hidden. Her fingertips stroked the child's hair lightly.

"Mama once did a wrong thing," she murmured, her voice soft with something like confession. "Now… the retribution has arrived."

She lowered her head and kissed Baor's forehead. Then she spoke even more quietly, as if she feared the words might break if she raised them. "But even if it is punishment, Mama accepts it gladly, because with you here, Mama still has a life. Mama can still endure. You are why Mama can keep going."

She held the child tightly, as though she could hide every hardship, every sacrifice, every bitterness inside her embrace, keeping that small life clean of even a single speck of dust.

Outside the window, the spring rain did not cease. Wind whispered on, like the storm inside her heart that had never once truly ended.

* * * * *

Inside the Weaving Bureau, the surroundings were silent, yet the atmosphere was like facing an enemy line.

Lu Chou flipped through the memorial reports concerning Jin Hua Hall, his face expressionless. His brows drew in slightly, and his knuckles struck the desk twice with heavy force.

"Recheck this account and make it clear," he said. His voice was cold, and his eyes were deep as ink. "Since they asked us to investigate, we will not go soft."

Deputy Commissioner Liang Jin hesitated, uneasy. "Lord Lu… Jin Hua Hall is run by women. If we pursue too harshly, it will harm reputations. Jin Hua Hall has been favored by people within the palace before. If this touches a woman's household affairs, it may not be convenient to press too quickly."

"Having a reputation does not mean being innocent," Lu Chou replied, his tone like blades striking. He said it lightly, but each syllable was edged.

Then he lowered his gaze again and turned to a newly attached detailed workshop list. His fingers paused, almost imperceptibly.

It was a fresh page added to the supplementary file, more detailed than the version he had previously read. In the corner, there was even a handwritten official annotation.

Row by row it recorded the hall master, the stewards, the laborers. Then, at the end, in stark characters that struck the eye:

Xiao Baor, female, four years old, daughter of hall master Xiao Lingyu.

In the remarks column below, four newly added words:

Bronze-coloured irises.

Lu Chou's gaze tightened, as if he had been hit by lightning.

Bronze. Eyes.

He remembered the previous file clearly. It had only stated that Xiao Lingyu had a young daughter, with a recorded father named Li Dashan. There had been no mention of any unusual feature.

This new record, however, cut into his chest like a knife. Bronze eyes were not a color that could belong to Lu blood.

The child did not take the name Li. She did not take the name Lu. She took the name Xiao, and she had bronze irises.

His heart jolted hard, as if someone had driven a fist straight through him. The faint warmth that had inexplicably remained in him these days, that thin strand of softness and indulgence, was doused cold in an instant. For a breath he almost felt unsteady on his feet.

So it was true. If the child's eyes were bronze, then the fact matched what she had said. That child was not of his blood.

"File her information," he said. His voice was very light, yet the cold in it pressed outward. "Investigate her origins, her birth date, her registration. Not a single stroke missed."

Liang Jin blinked, uncertain. "Lord Lu… you mean investigate the Xiao child?"

"Her," Lu Chou repeated coldly, and there was no room for question.

At that moment, a thought rose uncontrollably, sharp and impatient: he wanted to see for himself what those so-called bronze eyes looked like.

He pulled on his outer robe, rolled the page and tucked it into his sleeve. He turned as if to leave, then stopped abruptly at the doorway. He lowered his eyes to his own clenched fist. His knuckles were white. His sleeve cuff trembled.

Inside his chest, anger surged and churned, slamming again and again against the last of his reason.

Her child was truly not his.

Then what were his recent hesitations, his softening, his faint, ridiculous stirrings? What did they amount to?

He was the imperial Weaving Commissioner. He measured cloth and power for the empire, weighed workshops and households, controlled life and livelihood. And yet he had been toyed with, made a fool, led by the nose like some naive youth?

Humiliation and unwillingness swept up together, tearing at the thin seam of restraint he had left.

"Go," he said, his voice low and murderous, like a blade still in its sheath but already gleaming. "Bring Xiao Lingyu's daughter to me."

When he turned, he stood under lamplight tall and cold, his shadow heavy as iron. His sleeve hid a fist clenched so tightly it seemed ready to split skin. Something violent boiled up, close to breaking free. He knew he was on the edge of losing control.

He hated this sudden absurdity. He hated the unasked-for humiliation. He hated Xiao Lingyu, and even more, he hated himself.

For a moment, a darker, more brutal urge flashed through him, so sharp it made the air go thin. He almost wanted to crush mother and child alike, to crush this dream, this scheme, this suffocating pressure in his chest, and be done with it.

But he only added, colder still, "Do it quietly. Do not make noise."

He drew in a long breath and looked straight at Liang Jin, his gaze deep as night.

I will make Xiao Lingyu understand. Deceiving me, tricking me, it will not simply pass.

I will make her understand what the word 'price' truly means.

Liang Jin lowered his head and accepted the order, not daring to say more. Yet he understood. In this moment, Lord Lu's anger had already kindled into fire.

Lu Chou's eyes lifted, and the only thing left in them was ice.

She had ruined his entire youth. Then he would have her repay it with the rest of her life.

Chapter 8: A Fractured Bond

In Jiangnan, at the seam where spring turns into summer, cold and heat refuse to settle. The air shifts without warning, and children are the first to suffer. Baor was no exception. For days her appetite had thinned; that night, a sudden high fever took her. Fine sweat covered her brow, and her small face was so hot it was frightening.

At that moment, Xiao Lingyu was still out, running Jin Hua Hall's affairs from shop to warehouse and back again. Inside the hall, only Suxin and two nursemaids remained to keep watch.

Suxin was frantic, yet her mind moved quickly. She ordered wet cloths and pressed them over Baor's forehead. She sent a nursemaid to the kitchen to simmer a fever-reducing decoction, and in the same breath she rushed someone out to fetch Physician Liu, whose name carried weight in these lanes.

Night felt low; the rain had not yet truly spent itself. Inside the room, the lamp burned no brighter than a bean, turning the window paper a pale wash of yellow. Physician Liu entered under a cloak with his medicine chest, breathing a little hard from haste, a sheen of sweat at his temple.

He took Baor's pulse. After a moment, his focus tightened and the crease between his brows deepened. In a lowered voice he said, "The child's fever will not subside. Her pulse is floating, rapid, and urgent. I fear it may injure the heart and lungs. Ordinary remedies may not suffice. She must be moved to my residence and treated in my medicine pavilion. There is a cold spring there that can suppress the heat. With borneol to open and disperse, only then can her life be preserved."

The nursemaids turned pale at once, and Suxin's heart fell into disorder. She bent over the child and saw Baor's lashes damp, her lips cracked dry, a thin, faint hum in her throat, as if she could only endure in fragments. Suxin clenched her teeth and said, "If that is the case, we must trouble Physician Liu. Please leave at once. I will carry her there myself."

Physician Liu nodded and cautioned gravely, "Do not linger on the road. It must be quick."

Outside, fine rain continued to fall. The bluestone steps were slick and shone under the wet. A carriage was already prepared. Suxin wrapped Baor in a thin cotton quilt, held her tightly to her chest, and as she climbed aboard she could not help bending down to kiss the child's forehead. In a whisper she said, "Baor, get better quickly…"

Hoofbeats broke the rain-wet alley. Wheels rolled through pooled water, scattering a string of tiny droplets. After they passed the eastern lanes beyond the city, the mist ahead grew thicker and the streets fell more and more quiet. At the far end of a narrow alley, a blue-canopied carriage was already waiting, perfectly still. Only a single point of lamplight was lit inside, like a star held low, as if it had been waiting for something.

As they approached the tightest stretch of the lane, Physician Liu suddenly said in a low voice, "The road ahead has been temporarily sealed. Turn into the side alley. Hurry."

Suxin believed him without doubt and signaled the driver to turn.

The moment they rounded the corner, several large men in black surged out of the shadow along the wall. Their movements were as fast as a cutting wind. One seized the driver's wrist. Two pinned the nursemaids. The man in front grabbed Suxin's arm in a single brutal yank.

"You—" Suxin barely forced out one syllable before pain burst through her wrist. In the same instant, Baor was taken from her arms with practised precision.

The movement was too rough. The child startled awake. Her fever-flushed little face shifted; she made a blurred, hoarse sound, "Mama…" and then, as if the fever dragged her back under, she sank again into heavy sleep.

"Baor!" Suxin lunged forward as if she had lost her mind. An elbow slammed her aside. She fell hard onto the wet, cold ground, her skirt hem soaked through at once.

The man in front spoke in a hoarse, low voice. "We're taking Miss Baor. Go back and report to your Madam. Say that Heaven wills it so."

Before the last word fully settled, they had already carried the child into the blue-canopied carriage. The wheels turned. The whip cracked down. A horse screamed, the sound tearing through the bottom of the alley. The blue canopy cut once through rain and mist, the lamplight flickering bright and dim, and then, in a blink, it vanished.

Suxin stumbled to the mouth of the lane and screamed until her throat tore. "Baor! Baor!" The echo scattered layer by layer along the damp walls, and still she could not catch up.

Shaking, she forced herself upright and picked up from the ground a small shoe that had been thrown aside. The toe still held the child's heat. Suxin's vision blackened for an instant; she braced herself against the wall, panting, forcing the collapse down by sheer will. Through clenched teeth she rasped, "Go back… go back and report to Madam!"

* * * * *

At the same moment, the lamps in the Weaving Bureau had not gone out.

Liang Jin stood below the steps, his robe marked with rainwater that had not yet dried. He cupped his hands and reported in a low voice, "My lord, the child has been brought back and placed in the side hall. We did not alarm her."

Lu Chou sat behind the desk. His knuckles tapped the tabletop without a sound, his gaze deep and heavy. "How was it done?"

Liang Jin recounted the movements and the route, then added, "As my lord instructed earlier, the physician has been properly handled. We left him a redemption note and silver sufficient to seal his mouth. The carriage was changed twice. We did not disturb the night patrol on the way."

The case file suddenly snapped shut. The sound was crisp.

Lu Chou rose and threw on his robe, his tone low and cold. "Take me to see her."

The side hall was lit in a faint yellow. Baor lay in a small, tight bundle on the couch, her breathing weak, her forehead burning, her cheeks a fierce red. Her fingers gripped the quilt corner as if it were the last thing she could depend upon. From her throat came a broken, intermittent cry, thin as thread. "Mama… Baor hurts…"

Lu Chou stood at the edge of the couch and looked down. Cold shadow pressed over his brows and eyes. This small face bore traces of that woman's outline. The resemblance was not complete, yet where it did match, it was like a needle-thin thorn that slid beneath flesh and slowly pricked into the heart.

He had thought that what he would feel at this moment was only resentment and rage. He had not expected that one word, "Mama," would strike his chest first, tight enough to choke his breath.

"She's sick?" he murmured, so softly the lamplight almost swallowed it.

Liang Jin kept his head lowered. "These days the weather is disorderly, hot then cold. Many children fall into such illness. I have ordered a fever-reducing formula and prepared borneol to disperse. We will stabilize her through the night. Two nursemaids are in attendance and watching carefully."

Lu Chou gave a slight nod, his eyes sharpening. "The morning after next, summon Xiao Lingyu to the Weaving Bureau. If she does not come, I will send a coffin back to her."

Liang Jin's heart tightened. He answered and withdrew at once.

The room returned to silence. Only the scent of medicine remained, and the damp chill after rain. Lu Chou lowered his eyes and looked once more at the child. Her tiny breaths brushed the quilt. The heat of her body seemed to burn into the air and make the mind restless.

At last he shifted his gaze away and spoke in a low, hoarse voice. "If she is not my blood… then let us see how she can still beg me."

* * * * *

When Suxin stumbled into the inner courtyard, the edge of dawn had only just begun to pale the sky. She was soaked with mud and water; her hair was in disarray. She clutched that single small shoe as if it were her last proof she had not dreamed the night.

"Madam, something terrible has happened! Miss Baor… she is gone!"

Xiao Lingyu had been half-drowsing, leaning against the couch. At the cry, her eyes flew open. It was as if someone had seized her chest and yanked hard. Her breath caught. "What did you say?"

Suxin dropped to her knees, and her tears fell like a snapped thread. "Last night Miss Baor had a high fever. Physician Liu came and said she must be taken to his residence, to use the cold spring to suppress the heat. But when I went after at dawn, his house was empty. The neighbors say he moved away overnight… Madam, what do we do?"

The brush slipped from Xiao Lingyu's fingers and struck the desk with a sharp sound. Ink splashed into a black bloom. She gripped the edge of the table so hard her knuckles turned white, forcing herself upright. "Last night, did you see any unfamiliar figures?"

Suxin sobbed and shook her head. "No one was seen entering or leaving. But outside Jin Hua Hall there were strange faces lingering, and someone was asking about Miss Baor's illness…"

She raised the small shoe with both hands, choking on the words. "This was picked up at the alley mouth…"

Xiao Lingyu lowered her gaze. Her fingertips laid lightly over the tiny shoe. The toe still carried the faintest remnant of warmth, but her heart felt as if a bucket of ice water had been poured over it, freezing into bone.

She shut her eyes and breathed out two very soft words. "I know."

Her mind flashed through countless possibilities, fast as lightning: the collateral branch of the clan, jealous rival houses, a hidden hand within the palace. Every path was possible, and yet each path also fell away, as if rejected by the same invisible force.

At last, one name remained, clear enough to sting.

Him.

Other than him, who would dare to act so openly and still retreat whole?

She remembered those eyes that cut people like blades. She remembered the audits that had tightened step by step, the notices suppressed, the goods sealed, the supply lines choked. She was not naïve. She knew he hated her.

She had simply never imagined that hatred would stretch as far as a four-year-old child.

Suxin's eyes were red and raw; her voice shook. "Madam, if Lord Lu intends harm to Miss Baor…"

"He won't," Xiao Lingyu said suddenly, lifting her gaze. Her voice was low but steady. "He will not let Baor die."

As the words left her mouth, her throat tightened. What if he truly knew? What if he knew that Baor's relationship to him was not what he currently believed?

No. He should not know. She had been cautious step by step, and covered every word. She had never allowed an outsider to catch a flaw.

But he was not an outsider. He was Lu Chou. Cold slid into her palms; her nails bit into her skin to force back the dizziness.

"Do not panic," she said, drawing a long breath and pressing down the surge in her chest. "This matter must not be spoken of. First keep the hall stable. Wages are to be paid as usual. Suppliers are to be soothed one by one. Suxin, prepare the sedan chair. I will go to the Weaving Bureau myself."

Suxin froze. "Madam, go now? But if he…"

"The more it is this moment, the more I must go." Xiao Lingyu tucked the small shoe into her sleeve, as if hiding a heart still burning. "He wants to see me. Then I will see him. The account to be settled will be settled face to face."

She turned and instructed the steward, her tone calm, her steps quick. "Bring the night duty roster, the gate watch log, the register of names and comings and goings. Also withdraw every hand we left at Physician Liu's residence, all of them. Do not leave anyone a chance to frame us."

Suxin followed at her side and did not dare ask more. Xiao Lingyu's back was straight as a drawn bow.

Outside, wind carried the damp smell of rain. Water dripped from the eaves and struck the bluestone with a clear, relentless sound.

Xiao Lingyu lifted the curtain to step out, then glanced back once at the desk. The ink blot was spreading slowly, a black flower opening in silence like a dark plum blooming underwater. Her chest tightened, but she only let the curtain fall.

Baor, wait for Mother, she said in her heart. No matter what lies ahead, she would bring her child back.

* * * * *

In the side hall, the scent of medicine had already risen.

A nursemaid wiped the sweat from Baor's forehead with careful hands. The heat had eased by a fraction. The child's lashes trembled, as if in her dream she searched for someone.

Footsteps stopped outside. Lu Chou stood at the threshold for a moment, as if he were pressing something down inside himself, inch by inch.

At last he turned away, leaving only a flat, quiet instruction. "Change the lamp. Do not let her catch cold."

The wick was raised slightly. The room became brighter, and somehow colder.

Liang Jin escorted him beneath the corridor and ventured cautiously, "My lord, the Xiao household…"

"She will come," Lu Chou replied. His voice was deep and cold. "When she arrives, bring her to the side hall first."

Liang Jin bowed and answered.

They walked side by side under the eaves. Rainwater ran into a single line from the roof edge. Night was like an icy net, silent and unseen, yet it drew tighter and tighter all the same.

Chapter 9: The First Glimpse

When Baor drifted back to waking, a slow heat still pooled at her brow and a weariness tugged at every limb.

She blinked into a room she did not know. Not her mother's face, not Aunt Suxin's—only the kindly features of an older matron bending over her, wiping her sweat with a warm cloth and murmuring, "Good girl, Miss Baor. Let the fever loosen and go."

Her small heart clenched. She tucked herself a little deeper under the quilt.

She glanced around. A carved screen half-closed the chamber. A bronze lamp on the table breathed a mild, amber light.

By the window, a tall figure sat very still. With the window behind him, his outline was thrown into a cut of shadow, all breadth and height.

Baor's eyes went wide. She stared, frightened, fingers pinching the quilt's edge without sound. She wanted to call for her mother, but fear pressed the voice in her throat into silence.

The man moved at last, as if sensing she had woken. He turned slightly, his gaze fell on her face, dark and cold as a winter pond.

Baor held her breath and tried to make herself small, a little animal in its burrow, only the glimmer of two wet eyes showing as she watched the tall stranger.

Lu Chou looked down into those eyes—their strange bronzed hue startlingly clear under lamplight, nothing like the black irises he had seen in dreams, nothing like the eyes he had pictured a hundred times with a hunger he loathed to name.

A cold swept him, as if frost had formed beneath his skin.

So—she had not lied.

This child had nothing to do with him.

A corner of his mouth lifted in a bitter shape. His voice came out low and rasped, as if he spoke only for himself.

"What was I hoping for? To be deceived the way I wanted? To find she had kept my blood?"

He could not say what drove him—only that he had to see with his own eyes what the record had so clearly declared: bronze-coloured eyes.

Self-inflicted, needless pain.

The cold in his gaze hardened. He jerked his eyes away, as if to refuse this small creature even a second look, furious with himself for the ridiculous flicker of hope that had dared to lift its head.

She had fooled him once. Would he grant her a second chance to do it again?

Under the quilt, Baor watched the great, dark shape. A small sob slipped out before she could stop it.

"I… I want my mama…"

The voice was fine and soft, thick with fever—like a frightened kit gone astray.

Lu Chou's fingers stilled. He looked up at her again, then spoke, cool and even. "Your mama?"

Baor nodded the smallest nod, eyes water-bright. She was careful not to cry aloud; some instinct warned her that this cold man would not like it.

"My Mama says I must not go with bad people… b-but I…" She bit her lip, the words barely there. "But I had a fever… Mama said she would find a doctor… You—you aren't a bad person, are you?"

His brow twitched; the pressure in his fingertips sharpened. The lamp threw a brief depth of shadow across his face.

That word—bad—cut cleaner than any blade.

"Am I a bad person?" His tone held winter in it, though, without knowing why, he let the words slow for her. "What do you say?"

Baor stared, solemn with effort, as if the meaning were a knot she could untie if only she thought hard enough.

"I… I don't think you're a bad person," she whispered, testing each syllable. "Bad people scold. They hit. But you… you only have a very fierce face."

He paused, caught off guard; something lodged for a breath in his throat.

"A fierce face?" he echoed, a scrape of mirthless sound in the words. "You are bold to say so."

Baor flinched and pulled the quilt up to her chin, then hurried to add, "But I'm not afraid of you… only a little."

She widened her eyes, trying to look brave.

"Uncle... do you... dislike me very much?" she asked at last, mustering all her courage.

The question closed his hand and darkened his gaze.

Dislike? If only it were that thin. There was anger—shamed, smothered, and rank after being fooled, played, led by the nose. Yet when he looked into those bronze eyes and saw the small fear and the plain innocence living there, some portion of the heat inside him lost its footing.

"Why should I like a child who has nothing to do with me?" he said, the ice in his tone returning to its proper place.

"What is... 'nothing to do'?" she asked.

"It means a child one cannot bring oneself to like," he answered, without mercy.

Baor went still. The colour left her small face. "Then... then Baor did something wrong?" Her voice trembled.

Baor waited, her small chest rising and falling too fast, as if the answer might strike her if she breathed too loudly.
When none came, she lowered her head, lashes clumping together with the tears she refused to let fall.

"My Mama says..." she whispered, searching for the words as though they were rules she had learned by heart. "If Baor listens, and is very, very good... then people will like Baor."

She pressed her lips together, afraid the rest might slip out.
That if she were quiet enough, obedient enough, useful enough—she would not be abandoned.

The thought settled over her like a thin blanket that did not warm.

He said nothing. His gaze pinned the child's eyes—afraid, reddened around the rims, holding. The bronze of them was a thorn that refused to break off.

"My Mama says," she murmured, head bowed, "if I mind and am very, very good, people will like Baor..."

The words were fine and mild like little needles, one by one under the skin.

He turned aside suddenly. His throat worked once. "Why are you crying?" he asked, voice roughened low.

He had not even done anything to her. And still the tears hung, stubborn, ready. That look—wilful, vulnerable—was her mother's look exactly…

Baor sniffled and swallowed the rest of the tears down, her voice still shaking. "My head hurts. C-can I sleep here? Will my mama come to find me?"

He pressed his mouth into a line, then finally said, flat as iron, "She will."

Her daughter lay in his house; he could think of no force that would keep Xiao Lingyu from coming.

He rose in a single motion and let his sleeves fall. "See to her," he told the matron, the words cutting cold.

He left without a backward glance. His sleeve brushed the bronze lamp and a tiny wind quivered the flame. Within, only Baor's small, broken breaths remained, and the matron's quiet words.

Outside, night wind slid along the covered walk. Lu Chou stood in the shadow, fingers locking hard around the rail. He could hear the faint, swallowed sobs from within. An old, unfamiliar emptiness opened in him. He made a low sound that might have been a laugh if it had not tasted so bitter.

An official of rank, and here he was, measuring himself against a child. How ridiculous he had become.

* * * * *

The lamp's flame trembled and steadied. The matron tucked the quilt around Baor's shoulders and touched her brow with two careful fingers. At the first coolness she exhaled.

"Ah. It's eased. A little, but it's eased."

She turned to the maidservant beside her and lowered her voice. "Warm the decoction again. We'll feed her in half a quarter-hour. The physician was plain—we keep the hours, even if the fever falls. No lapses."

The girl bobbed her head and went. As she lifted the curtain she glanced, involuntarily, back at the small figure on the bed.

Baor's lashes were still wet; her face was pale, but no longer burning. Timidly she looked up at the matron. "Did the big lord leave?" she asked, very small.

The matron blinked, then smiled gently. "He's gone. Don't be afraid, Miss Baor. His Lordship isn't a bad man. Only—his temper runs cold."

Baor blinked. She was not sure she understood, but she made a faint sound of assent and asked again, "Will my mama… truly come?"

The matron's hand paused. Then she smoothed the child's hair and said with a smile, steady and light, "She will. Your mother will certainly come. Drink your medicine, sleep a good sleep; when you wake, who knows—you may see her."

Her voice held the even, lilting patience of one who has soothed many small bodies through many hard nights.

Baor softened under it. Her eyelids grew heavy, but she still whispered, "Then you mustn't trick me…"

"I won't trick you," the matron answered, blotting the sweat at her temple with tender care. "I never deceive children."

Soon the maid returned with the porcelain cup; the room filled with the pale, bitter smell of herbs.

The matron tested the heat, blew across a spoonful, and tipped it to Baor's lips. "Come. Be good and drink. Else your mother won't be easy in her heart."

Baor wrinkled her nose, but opened it all the same and swallowed, mouthful by mouthful.

The matron set the bowl back on the tray and closed the door partway. Only a thin seed of light burned in the lamp.

The maid moved quietly, gathering spoon and cup. She held her question until she could hold it no longer, then let it slip out, hushed. "Nurse… whose child is she? For our lord to bring her here himself— and care so… so particularly…"

The matron set her lips and flicked a wary look toward the corridor. The gallery lay still. Only then did she murmur, "Do not speak wildly. It isn't even a thing I dare ask. I heard only that it was done suddenly— and we were told to keep watch by turns, day and night, and to keep our mouths shut."

The girl frowned. "But His Lordship—such a man has never shown such concern for any child. And the way he looked just now—it was like… and yet not like… liking."

The matron sighed. "Like? What can we know of such a one's mind? His rank is high; we are small. Still—"

She broke off, lowered her voice. "When he entered, I thought I saw anger in his eyes. Just for a breath."

The girl's eyes widened. "Heavens. His Lordship angry—what a frightening thing!"

The matron shook her head. "The heart is a hard country to map. The child resembles… someone, a little, if you look long enough—but her eyes…" She hesitated. "That colour is rare."

The matron did not finish the thought. She did not need to.
In houses like this, some things were never spoken aloud—not because they were unknown, but because knowing them was dangerous.

A child brought in by the lord himself.
Watched night and day.
Named in no announcement, explained to no one.

"If there is truly such a tie," she said at last, voice barely more than breath, "then this will not remain a quiet matter."

Her eyes moved, instinctively, toward the corridor—toward the wider house, the wider court beyond.

"The wind has already begun to turn."

The maid leaned in, whispering, "Nurse means… that Miss Xiao?"

The matron's face changed; she rapped the girl's brow with a gentle knuckle. "Hush! Would you say such things aloud? If anyone hears you, I couldn't save you."

The girl shrank and mumbled, "I only guessed. But the look… there is a likeness…"

The matron was a moment silent. "And if there is?" she said at last. "There are many mirrors in the world. But this child… I fear she will not be simple."

Her gaze went back to the small sleeper on the bed. Her next words were scarcely more than breath. "If there is truly that tie… this household will see rough weather."

The maid shivered, gathered the tray fast, and whispered, "I heard nothing. I'll say nothing."

The matron waved her off and kept her attention on the lamp's slight sway. She sighed, very quietly.

Outside, the wind made a thin sound along the eaves. The light's shadow rocked on the wall. When at last the child's breathing eased and lengthened, the matron let out one more breath and told the girl, still under her voice, "Keep watch. If her heat climbs, call at once."

They looked at each other, and neither added another word. In such a still night, even breathing wanted quiet.

Readers can view the full collection of colour illustrations here:
https://www.facebook.com/profile.php?id=61581325000577

Chapter 10: To Return My Daughter

The search ran like headless flies through lanes and courtyards. Rain had fallen the whole night through and into the day; a damp breath soaked every alley of the city.

At the first grey of dawn, Xiao Lingyu finally received a message from the Lu's temporary quarters in Jiangnan. The paper's edge had curled with wet; she clenched it in her palm until her knuckles went cold.

So it was his men who had taken Baor.

She had not slept. The corners of her eyes were red, yet she forced herself to dress with care. Her hair, black as lacquer, was coiled and pinned; she set a single pale flower, neither showy nor plain, above the ear.

Her moon-white over-robe lay smooth and proper; a belt stitched with gold thread held it close. She lifted the weight of "Proprietress Xiao" onto her shoulders. She would not permit herself to break. She dared not.

At the steps of the Lu's temporary quarters, guards stood in the rain with halberds. When her name was announced, a cool male voice drifted from within the side hall, as if it had rolled along the edge of a sword. "Let her in."

She had waited so long her heart had already gone to ash. As she crossed the threshold, the wet on her soles slipped a little—yet her heart had dropped first, striking bottom without a sound.

The side hall was still and lamplit. Lu Chou sat in the seat of Honor, black robe wide-sleeved, cuffs spilling over the table's edge. Files and ledgers were stacked before him like a small mountain.

His lips were pressed thin. In the light, his bronze-dark eyes were mirrors—were knives—catching her figure and cleaving it coldly in two.

He looked nothing at all like the cool, austere scholar she remembered.

A tremor ran through her. She pressed a palm to her ribs to quiet the stab beneath them, and lowered her head. "I, Xiao Lingyu, pay respect to Lord Lu."

"So you still remember your surname is Xiao?"

"I beg Your Lordship's pardon. I have come only to bring Baor home. I entreat Your Lordship's mercy." Her voice was level, neither servile nor sharp, but the hoarseness in it betrayed the tremor beneath.

Common woman. Your Lordship.

Hearing her meek, careful address—left 'common woman,' right 'lord'—each word smoothed and proper, Lu Chou's temper only roughened.

He turned a page, then another, and at last lifted his gaze. "And Baor is who's?"

The question was tossed like a feather, as if nothing hung on the answer.

"Lord Lu, Baor is my own child. This may all be most improper, yet she is young and frail and cannot bear such a fright. I beg you to return her to me."

He let out a short laugh, shut the dossier with a slap, and sat straighter, his glance traveling from head to toe with chill indifference. "Proprietress Xiao, you made sport of me then cast me aside like worn shoes. And now you come rehearsing the figure of a good mother? If I dare not lay a hand on your darling child, will that make it my fault in the end? Will I be the one who has wronged you?"

Every word was cold, barbed, honed to cut.

She startled and raised her head.

What waited there in his eyes was not strangeness, not even detachment—it was hatred, towering and black as storm.

He came down the steps toward her, one measured stride at a time, and stopped before her.

The colour left her face. She pressed her lips together and bent her head. "What happened then… was my fault. Baor is innocent. She has nothing to do with you, nor with that past."

So—no more "common woman," no more "lord."

"Nothing to do with me?" Lu Chou straightened to his full height and closed the distance, his voice so cold it showed his teeth. "Xiao Lingyu, you ought to seek treatment for your memory. In the mountains—under that moon—who bowed with me before heaven and earth? Where is your conscience?"

She flinched; at last she raised her eyes, reddened at the rims. "I was wrong, Ziyuan—"

"Silence!" The word cracked like thunder. "I am not the 'Ziyuan' you once presumed to call!"

She stared at him, stunned, and said low, "All guilt is mine. But Baor has no part in it. I beg you—do not drag her into this—"

Blood surged and churned in his chest; the cold climbed and climbed. He laughed once, without warmth. "No part in it? Then tell me—who was this husband you 'married'? How did you, by chance, give birth to a daughter with the surname Xiao? Am I blind?"

She lowered her head and gripped her sleeve. Her reply was almost soundless. "My husband… died of the plague. Baor was born after he was gone. If there is half a false word, I—"

"Good. You do know how to swear." He cut across her without patience, advancing another pace, gaze like a drawn knife. "Do you know why I kept the child here? The debts you owe will be repaid account by account. And she is where it begins."

Then the tears broke from her eyes. She fell to her knees; her voice splintered. "Baor is blameless. In this life and the next, punish me as you will, humiliate me as you please—I will take it sweet as syrup. Only—spare her…"

Watching her undone like that tore him—sharp and sudden—yet roused his fury all the more. "Do you know," he said, voice raw with cold, "that I should have forgotten you long ago—and cannot? Why come to beg me? Why force me to look at you?"

"Years ago you stood before me and said your surname was Li. Li Meng'er. A pitiable concubine-born girl, forced to the countryside. No kin, no harbor. You asked only for a roof."

"You said those days were the only peace in your life."

He gave a laugh that flashed like steel. "Did you ever say a single true thing?"

Her lips trembled; no defence came.

He drew a long breath, and when he spoke, each word fell slow and heavy. "You said you wished you could stay by me your whole life. And then? A note. And gone."

His face went blank and cold. "After making a fool of me, you married another and brought a daughter into the world?"

She swayed; it nearly took her feet out from under her.

"Baor... where is she?"

"What does it matter?" His voice was very light, and colder than snowmelt. "Aren't you skilled at spinning tales? Why not finally speak plain—who fathered that child?"

Her eyes widened. Her mouth moved. No words came.

"What? Is truth so hard?" His sneer was soft and sharp.

"No, I only..."

"Just now you were 'common woman' and I was 'lord.'" He took a long stride nearer. "How is it you are 'you' and 'I' with me now?"

"No, I... you..."

"Stop stammering." He straightened to his full height above her, gaze locked on her blanching face, every syllable a chip of ice. "Proprietress Xiao—by what right do you speak to me as 'you' and 'I'?"

Under the force of his words and the unrelenting press of his will, the colour drained further from her cheeks. She bit down on the inside of her lip and answered nothing.

He stepped in again, the low weight of his voice crushing. "You want to see her?" A short, cold laugh. "Then let's see how much sincerity you possess."

She nodded, teeth set; her knees had begun to thrum with weakness.

"I beg Your Lordship..."

"Beg? With what?" His voice slid quiet and sharp through the room, a knife through cloth. "You've always been clever, haven't you? A fine reckoner. Then you know the price."

He turned and clasped his hands behind him, speaking almost idly. "Kneel and beg this official one hundred times. Perhaps, if I am in a temper to be generous, I will let you look on her."

He himself did not know whether he meant to punish her—or to see how far she would bend.

Her body swayed; something squeezed tight at her heart. But at last her knees went soft and she sank.

Head bowed, she whispered, voice shaking, "I beg Your Lordship—return Baor to me..."

He did not turn. He looked outward into the rain-blurred distance. His back was iron.

He had expected to feel satisfaction.

But the rustle of her falling to her knees, and the tremor in her plea—at that instant, something clutched hard at his chest.

No pleasure. No savour of revenge. Only a weight, heavy and more complicated than before.

After a moment, hands still locked behind him, Lu Chou turned, slowly, and looked down at her kneeling form. His gaze cut like a blade.

For that child…for the child she had borne with another—she would abase herself so far?

His throat burned with refusal.

He did not speak of Baor. He asked instead, "You claim your husband died of pestilence?" He gave a small, dry laugh and went on. "I searched the registers top to bottom. All I found was a 'Li Dashan.' Everything else is blank."

His tone carried a clear note of scorn. "What manner of man could marry Xiao Lingyu—and be hidden so cleanly?"

Her lips had gone bloodless. She did not answer.

He set another step between them; when he spoke, his voice was low. "That year, under the moon, you swore yourself to me—said your life was mine to keep. Then you turned and went and would not even leave your true name."

Her head bowed. Her reply was as thin as rain on tile. "I wished only to live."

"Heh." His laugh held no heat. "Even your lies were pretty."

"If not for danger, then," she said, teeth set, voice so soft it was almost a thread, "I would never have changed my name; I would never have lied. The offense is mine and mine alone. But Baor is only a child. Whatever I did then has nothing to do with her. Let any punishment fall on me. Send her home."

"What a neat abacus," he said, coldly amused. "Your mouth won't give me a single plain word, yet you ask me to hand your child back without condition?"

"Your Lordship is wise. I have spoken nothing but truth." She bent lower; a pin-prick of sweat beaded at her brow.

"I do not believe you." His brows drew together; the hardness in his eyes spread like ink in water. "What tale will you spin next, Proprietress Xiao?"

His voice darkened. "Do you know how much I have hated you in this life?"

She lifted her face at last. Tears glassed her gaze. She sighed once, broke and quiet, and after a beat said, hoarse but steady, "Then hate me. I have no strength to turn back. Only—give me back my child."

Silence fell like driven snow, smothering air and thought.

At length he flicked his sleeve. "See her out," he said in cold voice.

Baor was not returned.

Beyond the windows the rain did not stop. The air was wet and clinging, like a nightmare that would not end.

Chapter 11: A Deepening Game

Lu Chou returned to the guest manor set aside for the Weaving Bureau's officers. The moment he stepped across the threshold, damp air still clinging to his sleeves, he caught sight of three nursemaids crowding about Baor.

The child's laughter rippled through the hall—a clear, bell-bright sound that pierced the hush.

Her smile was unguarded as dawn itself; the soft lines of her brows and eyes mirrored her mother's grace exactly, that same mingling of gentleness and quiet fire.

A coil of heat snapped awake inside him. Hatred rose from the pit of his stomach and wrapped about his ribs like a living snake.

His brows tightened. "All of you—out." The words were flat, cold iron.

The nursemaids froze for half a breath before scattering.

One cried a soft protest, but Lu Chou's lifted sleeve dismissed them like a gust sweeping dust. The doors thudded closed behind their retreat. Silence rushed in their wake.

Startled by the suddenness, Baor shrank upon herself, small shoulders drawing up under the weight of that silence.

Her face crumpled, tears swimming in the corners of her eyes, yet she clutched at the quilt and bit them back. She would not cry.
Her small body curled inward despite herself, shoulders drawn tight, her face crumpling for a breath before she forced it still.

They faced each other—his shadowed gaze and her wide, uncertain one—half a long moment, and even the candlelight seemed to hold its breath. Only the faint tremor of her breathing stirred the air.

They stood so for the space of half a quarter-hour, eyes locked in silence, until even the candle flame seemed to tire of breathing.

His fury did not subside, yet his eyes kept returning to that fragile face. The conflict inside him was a blade sawing bone; hate and ache met and fused until it burned.

He pressed two fingers to the bridge of his nose and exhaled, the sound nearly a groan. A Deputy Minister of Weaving Bureau he thought bitterly, arguing with a child of four.

Absurd.

He could not tell what he was truly angry at—her mother's calculation, or the weakness in himself that would not be silenced.

Still, the thought of her mother—of years spent tangled in lies—ignited the cold fire anew, creeping through his chest, licking the edges of restraint.

He was still weighing what punishment, what distance, when his gaze fell again upon that tiny figure curled upon the couch. "You," he said abruptly. "What is your name?"

He knew. Yet he asked—as if testing her, or himself.

She lifted her head. The long lashes trembled; her voice came like a flute note, sweet and small. "I'm Baor."

His fingers pressed harder to his temple. "Your full name," he said, rough with impatience.

"Full name?" She blinked, puzzled. "What does that mean? I only have one name. It's Baor." She paused, then added with sudden brightness, "But sometimes Mama calls me sugar. It means I'm very, very sweet."

For an instant her innocence disarmed him completely. His mouth twitched—half a laugh, half a breath—and the warmth of it startled him. The next heartbeat he forced the expression away, the air between them icing over.

"And your surname?"

"Surname Xiao. I'm Xiao Baor."

She said the word Xiao clearly, proudly. His brows drew tight; his eyes locked on the faint bronze gleam in hers. A soundless impact struck deep within him.

Bronze eyes.

He swallowed the rising storm and asked, voice like stone, "Where is your papa?"

She pondered the question with comical seriousness before shaking her head. "I don't know. Mama says I'm her very own little treasure."

She spoke it with no sorrow—indeed, with quiet pride.

That small, pale-flour face, so soft and clean, tugged something raw inside him. His throat constricted. If she had never left, he thought, if this child had truly been mine—what then?

The vision flickered and died. He laughed once under his breath, low and bitter, stamping the thought to ashes. "No papa?" he asked. "Did your mama say that?"

Baor shook her head gravely. "I have a Papa Xie. And Mama says she can do everything. She can raise me all by herself."

Papa Xie?

Xie Huaici?

The darkness behind his eyes deepened. The corner of his mouth bent into a line as thin and sharp as frost. "Indeed. She can do anything—even turn a lie into gospel."

Baor didn't understand, but she felt the air turn hard. Her voice dropped to a whisper. "Why do you keep asking about my papa? Do you… know where he is?"

Every syllable pricked like a fine needle into his chest.

He turned sharply, hands clasped behind him. "That Xie is not your father," he said, low and cutting. "You need not know who your father is. And you will never ask again."

The little girl stared up at him, eyes reddening, her hands twisting the hem of her skirt. Still she did not cry.

With his back toward her he drew a breath that refused to fill his lungs. He knew better than to pity—but the thought came anyway, wild and unwanted: if only she were mine.

He crushed it with a soundless laugh—harsh, self-scornful. Ridiculous.

"Go," he said. "Fetch two nursemaids. Attend to Miss Baor carefully." His tone was glacial. "Food, clothes, sleep—nothing is to be neglected."

The servants bowed and hurried off. He stood unmoving, his shadow tall across the tiled floor.

What was he angry at—her cunning? Or the fool within himself?

Perhaps both.

He stood there without moving, unable to answer himself.

* * * * *

Rain had dragged across Jiangnan for three endless days. The dawn had not yet broken, but already the Weaving Bureau's seal fell before the morning bell. An urgent dispatch, carried through wet roads from Suzhou to Hangzhou, cracked open a nest of suspicion over the local silk tax.

Lu Chou drew on a robe, the fabric cold against his skin, and sat before his desk. Memorials rose in ordered towers, the ink still glistening. For days he had been combing ledgers from three provinces, following thread after thread to a single name—Jin Hua Hall.

Xiao Lingyu's Jin Hua Hall.

His lips pressed thin; a tremor passed through his fingers. The black lines of figures crowded the paper, heavy enough to crush the breath from a man's chest. This year's remittance was sharply below last year's—three years in decline, with neither drought nor flood to blame. With calamity ruled out, what remained could only be the designs of men.

He touched a column with one finger. "This silver—where did it go?"

A scribe stepped forward. "Last year the silkworms were blighted, my lord. Funds were diverted to buy new stock and distribute them among the larger looms, hence the shortfall. The remaining tax was conveyed north by Lord Zhou Ming."

"Zhou Ming?" Lu Chou looked up, his tone quiet and cold. "A man of Xie Huaici."

Xie Huaici. Again.

Papa Xie— the man mentioned by Baor yesterday?

No one dared breathe.

He closed the scroll with a muted snap. Something within him rolled darkly, unspent.

This was not merely about silk or silver. Someone, somewhere, was watching him—testing how far he would lean toward the central court, and how far from Xie.

He said, evenly, "Issue orders. Within three days, seal and audit the accounts of Zhi Yuntang, Ruichun Embroidery, and Jin Hua Hall. If questioned, say it is by imperial command to investigate the silk-tax abuses."

The guards saluted and withdrew. Wind pushed the door ajar; the lamp flame thrashed and shrank again.

He sat long after the sound of footsteps had faded. At last he replaced the brush—too sharply. Ink splattered, spreading across the blank page like a black blossom opening in silence.

By afternoon the storm of rumour had begun along the embroiders' quarter.

In the back hall of Jin Hua, a steward came running, breath short. "Proprietress—the Bureau men have arrived. They say they come by decree, to check the accounts."

Her heart drew tight. Still, her voice held steady. "Invite them in. The ledgers are kept in proper order. There is nothing we need hide."

So, she said—yet her fingertips, resting on the table, whitened. She knew well what shadow walked behind this inspection.

If any other officer had come, she would not have feared. But if he had sent them—this was no audit. This was an opening move.

Wind rose outside, rattling the lattice frames.

Suyue bent close, whispering, "Madam, Lord Lu will not let go easily. Should we—tell him Miss Baor's true birth?"

Xiao Lingyu's voice was almost gentle. "Never."

Suyue frowned. "But—"

"Even if I did, he would not believe. Those eyes…" Her words trailed into a sigh, thin as silk thread.

The words ended in a soundless breath, more wearied than afraid.

Before her, a phoenix pattern lay half-stitched upon the silk square. The threads were unanchored, lifting at the edges whenever the breeze passed. The bird's wings were half-spread upon a painted paulownia bough—neither taking flight, nor finding rest.

* * * * *

Night descended, soft and damp, when Xie Huaici arrived at the Bureau.

"Lord Lu." He saluted, voice smooth as still water. "This southern circuit was meant to survey the silk tax. Why then have three houses been sealed? And why is Jin Hua Hall, which has always been proper, counted among them?"

Lu Chou raised his eyes from the papers. "If Lord Xie wishes to discuss official matters, the memorials are open. If he wishes to discuss the private, I have no answer."

Xie smiled faintly, gaze limpid. "Then permit me bluntness. Jin Hua Hall trades with the Bureau but does not handle tax silver. To strike at her may stir unnecessary talk."

"Talk?" Lu's answering smile was a blade in winter. "If there is no guilt, what harm in scrutiny?"

They stood opposite beneath the lamps, neither man yielding half a step.

Outside, the wind moved through the bamboo, drawing long breaths through hollow stems. The light of the lanterns tightened inward, a slow collapse of flame.

Jiangnan that night was utterly still—still as water before the breaking of a storm.

Chapter 12: The Hall of Judgment

Xiao Lingyu, at this moment, was seated within Xie Huaici's study. Her countenance was composed, and her manner displayed a settled disposition. Although anxiety was concealed within her eyes, her tone remained restrained and measured.

Xie Huaici was her former childhood acquaintance, a person once bound by an ancient pledge. Now serving as the Censor of Jiangnan, he held a weighty position in the region. Though the two had not met for many years, their intellectual connection had never been severed.

"Lord Huaici, the reason I impose upon you this time is because Lu Chou forcibly took Baor away." Her voice was steady, yet every word was distinct and clear. "This matter, I am capable of investigating and handling; yet, at this juncture, I am isolated in power and meager in strength. If I wish to retrieve her safely and smoothly, I must borrow the strength of your arm."

Xie Huaici frowned slightly, his expression grave: "Lu Chou... you know clearly who he is, the Deputy Minister of the Board of Revenue, with Minister Lu still supporting him from behind. Do you comprehend what complications this action might potentially draw forth?"

Hearing this, Xiao Lingyu offered a faint smile and replied coolly: "It is precisely for this reason that I came to see you first, rather than immediately tearing apart this net. I am not one who is unaware of propriety, nor am I a soft persimmon that anyone can knead at will. However, Baor is my daughter; I cannot sit idly by and ignore this."

Her tone was neither servile nor overbearing, carrying a trace of resolute firmness within her composure, which caused Xie Huaici's gaze to shift.

"You have always kept your counsel deep and have never revealed your full hand, single-handedly carrying the Xiao family and the Jinhua Embroidery Workshop for five years, conducting matters with meticulous care, and never associating with the high nobility. Yet, allowing Lu Chou to take Baor is uncharacteristic of your style." Xie Huaici asked, probing her intent.

Xiao Lingyu's expression paused slightly, yet she did not retreat: "The fault in this matter lies in my own momentary misplaced trust, which allowed him to exploit a weakness. But I will not allow Baor to suffer harm, nor will I allow the Lu family to easily succeed in their aims."

Her tone cooled slightly, a flash of sharp light passing through her eyes. "Huaici, my purpose in coming today is not to beg you to take the lead, but merely to hope to borrow the authority of your office as Censor, to provide me and the Jinhua Workshop with a justifiable and legitimate statement."

Xie Huaici gazed at her for a long moment, then suddenly offered a low laugh: "Lingyu, I fear your elder brother is currently powerless to assist you. It is only because I am low in official rank and insignificant in influence."

"Huaici, you are overly humble. I..."

"No, it is not so." He paused, then said with solemnity: "In truth, your elder brother has already exchanged words with Lord Lu, but this man is impervious to oil-tongued persuasion. Hence, your elder brother can only offer you one piece of advice: If this matter is truly tangled with old grievances involving Lu Chou, resolve the entanglements that need resolution soon, lest Baor becomes a bargaining chip between the two of you."

Xiao Lingyu nodded slightly, her gaze clear: "I would never use my daughter as a stake to wager. I never imagined that he would actually order men to abduct Baor."

The two sat facing each other, the atmosphere calm, yet both held deep, concealed intentions.

The lamplight in the study was dim. A fine wind stirred the candle flame through the window.

Xiao Lingyu sat beside the writing desk, gently stroking the corner of her handkerchief, her voice so low it was almost a soliloquy: "If my elder brother were still among the living, I would hope he could return early... Thus, I would not have to bear many family matters alone."

Hearing this, Xie Huaici raised his eyes to look at her, a thread of pity flashing in his gaze. His voice was gentle and warm: "The search for him has lasted nearly five years without any news. Lingyu, you must also prepare yourself mentally."

"I... I understand."

Seeing the desolation in her expression, he sighed lightly and then offered further solace: "Recently, I have also ordered men to re-investigate the old merchant route case from five years ago. Should there be any tiny clues or traces, I will certainly inform you early."

Xiao Lingyu raised her eyes to look at him, a slight dampness in her gaze, yet holding a hint of tenacious smile: "Thank you, Huaici... These past years, had you not occasionally lent your assistance, I fear I would have collapsed long ago."

Xie Huaici smiled faintly, yet his tone was extremely restrained: "Lingyu, if there is any place where you require my help, speak plainly. However, my official rank is not high, and my capability is limited."

Her expression shifted slightly upon hearing this, and she whispered: "Huaici, you are too courteous. Lingyu understands propriety... It is just, this time... if Baor truly suffers misfortune, I..."

The phrase remained unfinished, choked back.

Tears welled in Xiao Lingyu's eyes, and she said emotionally: "Huaici, this profound friendship, Lingyu will etch it into her heart. Thank you for always extending a helping hand in my most troubled times."

Xie Huaici sighed softly: "Do not lose heart. The Lu family is indeed outwardly glorious, but deep undercurrents surge fiercely.

Lu Chou, as the only legitimate son of Minister Lu, is destined to control the great power of the family in the future." He paused, his gaze cooling slightly: "But he has a half-brother, Lu Xiu, whose character is sinister and whose ambition is vast. These two brothers are locked in endless conflict, with hidden and open blades constantly clashing."

Xiao Lingyu frowned slightly: "Therefore? What has this to do with us?"

Xie Huaici tapped his fingers lightly on the desk, his tone sinking slightly: "The Emperor dispatched Lu Chou, the Deputy Minister of the Board of Revenue, personally to Jiangnan this time, ostensibly to investigate taxes. In reality... he may not be merely focused on money, grain, and silver. "

He raised his eyes to look at Xiao Lingyu, his voice slow and cold: "Rumours circulate widely in the court—behind the Jiangnan silk industry, the flow of silver is unclean, and corruption cases are numerous. Did those funds flowing into private coffers ultimately end up in the residences of certain imperial princes? Did they contribute to the struggle for the succession? This is the matter that His Majesty truly desires to investigate."

Xiao Lingyu's heart skipped a beat upon hearing this, faintly realizing that the situation was far more complicated than she had imagined. Yet, she still suppressed her fear and asked: "But... how does this concern Baor?"

Xie Huaici sighed softly, his gaze darkening slightly: "Lingyu, Lu Chou is a rising star in the Board of Revenue, arriving under a secret imperial edict, and his investigation is extremely detailed and ruthless. His repeated attempts to make things difficult for you may stem from public duty, or private grievance—but I suspect this tax investigation is primarily an act to kill the chicken to frighten the monkey."

His gaze fixed intently upon her, his tone slow and grave: "You, a woman, preside over the Jinhua Workshop, with its vast silver flow, and maintain dealings with several major banking houses. Such a background, in Lu Chou's eyes, makes it extremely easy for you to be deemed a target for him to 'establish his authority.' Furthermore... you and I both know that his old grievances with you remain unresolved, which only heightens his ruthlessness."

Xiao Lingyu's face suddenly turned pale, her fingertips trembling slightly. She muttered softly: "...So that is the truth."

Xie Huaici's gaze softened slightly, yet his tone remained serious: "Therefore, Lingyu, this is not merely a simple private feud. It has entangled itself with the political turmoil of the court. You must exercise extreme caution. A slight misstep could lead to complete ruin."

Hearing this, Xiao Lingyu did not know how to react, stammering: "How could it be involved with... the imperial princes?"

Xie Huaici nodded: "Precisely so. Lu Xiu and his father belong to the Third Prince's faction, while Lu Chou inclines toward the Fourth Prince. This struggle for power causes the three of them—father and two sons—to serve their respective masters, leading to continuous disputes."

His tone was heavy: "The internal conflicts of the Xie family have not ceased; your elder brother still struggles to protect himself. Yet, I cannot bear to see you single-handedly manage this situation, especially since the Lu family is a hundred times more complex than ours."

The sound of rain outside the window grew denser. The wind stirred the copper bell hanging from the eaves, ringing clearly.

Xiao Lingyu remained silent for a long time, gently rubbing her knee with her fingertips. She finally spoke in a low voice: "If that is truly the case... then do we, the Jiangnan silk merchants, stand no chance whatsoever, merely destined to be pawns in the hands of the high nobility?"

Xie Huaici's gaze shifted slightly: "What do you intend to do?"

She raised her eyes, her gaze clear and resolute: "I shall personally rectify the account books and submit the clean ledger to the Imperial Weaving Bureau myself, to prevent others from using this as leverage. Rather than being passively investigated, it is better to proactively request an audit."

Xie Huaici was stunned for a moment, then gave a bitter smile: "Lingyu, over these years, you have always been brave and resolute. But if Lord Lu is intent on making things difficult, I fear this measure will still be of little help."

Xiao Lingyu returned a smile that carried a trace of desolation: "Apart from sorting the ledgers to prove my innocence, the Jinhua Workshop and I have no other recourse. If we do not establish a firm footing, this world will crush us into dust."

She rose and straightened her clothes, her voice steady: "Tomorrow, I shall go to the Imperial Weaving Bureau and face Lu Chou in person."

Xie Huaici watched her retreating figure, a trace of deep worry surfacing in his eyes.

He slowly rose and walked to the window, watching the rain that had not ceased since nightfall. He murmured softly: "Lingyu, you do not understand a man's heart. Lord Lu's intention this time, I fear, is not benign."

As his voice faded, the candle flame suddenly trembled, casting the entire study in an unreliable pattern of light and shadow—as if foreshadowing that an even greater storm was slowly closing in from the direction of the Capital.

Chapter 13: The Ledger of Innocence

Lu Chou stood before his writing desk, a sealed intelligence report spread open upon the lacquered surface. His fingertip tapped lightly at one corner of the sheet; his gaze rested on a single line and did not move for a long while.

—"You are telling me that Xiao has lately gone frequently to Lord Xie's residence, apparently to seek aid."

Xie Huaici.

The name tore open an old wound across his chest as if by invisible hands. His eyes darkened, though his face remained without ripple; only the fist hidden within his sleeve had gone white at the knuckles.

"She went to beg him?"

The murmur slipped from his lips; the edge of his mouth was as cold as a blade of snow. He walked slowly to the window, pushed it a finger's width, and let a strand of spring chill pierce to the bone.

Outside, all things were hushed; only the lamplight quivered—like her swaying silhouette the night she left, passing and passing again through his dreams.

He closed his eyes. Something in his chest went off like a muted thunderclap—so cold it bordered on loss of control.

"She cast me aside, and now she turns to another?"

How could he not know who Xie Huaici was? A clean and proper gentleman, upright and high-minded; her childhood companion; their two families once pledged by an old betrothal.

Now he stood in high office, trusted by the Son of Heaven, his reputation unsullied. He was precisely the sort of man a woman ought to admire.

His heart stalled, then he gave a thin, frost-bitten smile. And she? Did she remember the incense-lit vows of those years? Or did she now prefer a lord so polished and resplendent beneath the sun?

If she had ever spoken a single true word—one!

If she had not smiled and said, "I am a concubine's daughter, alone in this world," when her methods were sharper than any man's.

Those ten days of coaxing, that cup of medicated wine, the "bowing to Heaven and Earth beneath the moon" in the storm, the brief, ruthless letter of farewell—each a step in a trap. A web of her weaving.

His palm struck the lattice. Splinters leapt; his fingertips came away bloodied.

"What did she take me for?" he ground out between his teeth, voice honed to a vicious edge. "Once she had what she wanted, she turned straight into another man's gate. Such cruelty—how is a man to trust even a single word?"

Something caught at his throat; the tide of fury snagged upon it and faltered.

Those eyes.

When she turned away that night, there had been tears in them.

And that face… Baor's face now bore its echo.

He should not think of it.

He turned back to the desk. The ink was ground, dark and ready, but not a single stroke would set to the page.

She dared to seek Xie Huaici.

Did she take him for a man without feeling or loyalty? Or imagine he would stand idle and watch her rise again?

For one instant the urge to kill her washed over him so cleanly it left no aftertaste.

End it. End it cleanly.

He laughed once, low and joyless, a sound like steel grating under ice. "If she intends to borrow another's hand to lift herself," he whispered, "then I will show her what it means to be cast into utter ruin."

He turned and called, "Attend me. Bring the tax ledgers of the six great silk houses of Jiangnan—Jin Hua Hall's old books among them— starting three years past."

Hands clasped behind him, he stood at the window as cold wind threaded the curtain's edge and made the flame waver. The fragrance of ink rose and curled; tax rolls and secret notes lay scattered upon the case.

His fingertip slid across them; blood dampened the pad of his finger, and he did not seem to feel it. Outside, rain began—fine as needles, pricking the lattice—like the tears that had filmed her eyes the night before she left.

He lowered his gaze to that line of secret script. A shadowed gleam turned in his eyes; his voice dropped to a breath. "So, you would rather seek Xie Huaici? In that case, Xiao Lingyu—do not blame this officer for forgetting old ties."

The candle jumped. His sleeve trembled once. Heavy ink splashed across the paper, a surge of night poured onto white silk. In that instant his expression was cold enough to be cruel; and yet there was the briefest hesitation.

It sank almost at once—pressed down, smothered like the last gasp at the bottom of a well, swallowed by the dark.

* * * * *

In recent days the Jiangnan Weaving Bureau had become a place of rumour and sharp wings; the silk-tax case had pulled in several great local houses, and already two deaths were whispered through the streets. Everyone was afraid.

Under imperial order, Lu Chou audited the silk levies, calling up accounts of correspondence between the Bureau and the local guilds; many threads pointed toward private collusion between provincial magnates and ministers at the centre.

As Censor of Jiangnan, Xie Huaici's very charge was to investigate corruption and malfeasance in the provinces. Lately a stack of denunciations and reports had been delivered to his desk.

If true corruption lay within the Bureau's case, the Censorate could not shirk its duty. If, on the other hand, Lu Chou's pursuit ran too fierce and cut down honest merchants with the guilty, the Censorate must likewise defend the interests of those who traded in good faith.

Thus, when Lu Chou summoned several merchants for examination that day, Xie Huaici went personally to the Bureau—notionally to "sit in on the proceedings," in truth to gauge the matter's substance and to prevent anyone from using the occasion to crush reputable houses such as Jin Hua Hall.

He had come up through the upright civil path and had long kept company with the clean-trading firms of Jiangnan. His manner was modest, but he carried an ease that belonged to men born to law and text—quite unlike the officers the Ministry of Revenue had dispatched to the Weaving Bureau.

Within a side room in Bureau, a breath of sandalwood burned. The front curtains stirred faintly. It was the very chamber used for routine inspection of levies and review of commercial accounts.

That morning, several heads of the great houses had been called within: the Ministry's inspector was present to review the particulars of the silk tax.

When Xie Huaici arrived, clerks were already posted to either side.

At the centre desk, Lu Chou stood with hands behind his back—tall, exact—his dark-indigo official robe cutting him to a cold, chiselled grace.

"Lord Xie," said Lu Chou, lifting his eyes. His tone was clear and smooth yet carried an authority as unshifting as a mountain. "By imperial command the Ministry has come south to examine the silk tax. The irregularities of Jiangnan's levies are of long standing. Today, with your leave, I will use your hall to review the detailed books."

"In matters of the Ministry, Lord Lu acts rightly," Xie Huaici answered, voice warm and courteous. "If there is anything lacking on our side, I, Huaici, will assist to the utmost."

Lu Chou gave the faintest smile, devoid of warmth. "Very good."

He touched his long finger to several stacked ledgers and turned the pages one by one; then his nail came to rest upon a line. "Here—the Jiang Weaving House's autumn accounts of last year—intake of cocoons does not match the tax remitted. Would Lord Xie be aware of this?"

Xie's gaze cooled, though he did not reply. A subordinate at once bowed his head and explained, flustered. "These were two shipments entered under different dates—there was no concealment of tax, my lord. We will present the supplemental sheets for cross-checking."

Lu Chou's smile said nothing. His eyes, however, returned to Xie Huaici. "Errors in bookkeeping are not grave by themselves. But if someone uses them as a cover for private dealings, the fault will not rest with your bureau alone."

The air chilled in an instant. Breath stilled. Even the cicadas beyond the eaves seemed to fall silent.

Xie inclined himself with composure. His voice was bright and even. "If there has been any violation, I will investigate with rigor; I dare not shield so much as a hair. And I ask that Lord Lu, in examining to the root, remain just and unmoved by other entanglements."

"Other entanglements?" Lu Chou's head lifted sharply; his eyes flashed like a drawn blade. "To what does Lord Xie refer?"

Xie smiled without haste and met his gaze. "Jiangnan has been wild with rumour of late. I dare not repeat idle talk. I only hope Lord Lu will keep the state foremost and not let private matters spill into public duty—lest the innocent be harmed."

"Innocent?" A shard of cold glinted in Lu Chou's eyes, though his tone remained polished. "I will remember Lord Xie's words."

He paused; then his voice turned iron at the edge. "There is one more thing. Certain merchants have lately spread talk that a woman of the trade in Jiangnan has unlawfully colluded with the Imperial Household's supply route. Has Lord Xie heard such a thing?"

A small ripple passed through Xie Huaici's gaze. He answered in a low, steady voice, "If you mean the proprietress of Jin Hua Hall, Madam Xiao—then I know her to be an honest person. As for the routes of trade, I have heard no error named. If Lord Lu has proof, let it be presented in open hall for us all to judge. It would not do to place faith in whispers."

Silence fell like a dropped screen.

Lu Chou's eyes were winter-cold as he closed the ledger, each word as fine as a knife tip. "Let Lord Xie not forget—Jiangnan is a vital artery of the realm.

If any man chooses to be a talisman for crooked traders, he will invite guilt of the same cloth." He flicked his sleeve and shut the book with a whisper. "You know these waters better than I. See that private friendship does not veil a public heart."

He did not wait for reply. His robe swept as he turned and descended the steps. The hem of black silk skimmed the threshold.

All eyes dropped away. The pressure within the hall made the breath catch.

Xie Huaici stood with his gaze deepened, saying nothing. He knew well what had been done today: Lu Chou had wielded public office to serve private aim, had sounded a warning—keep your hands from Xiao Lingyu and Jin Hua Hall.

He looked down and spoke so softly that the words were barely the brush of wind across a teacup. "Lu Chou—are you truly so without mercy?"

Chapter 14: Confrontation in the Shadows

This day, Xiao Lingyu emerged from Xie Huaici's study, her spirit deeply unsettled and troubled.

Scarcely had she reached the corner of the street when a small retainer, neatly dressed, approached her.

He performed a courteous salute and said: "Madam Xiao, my Master requests that you proceed to the Fu'an Teahouse. He has prepared a secluded, elegant chamber and invites you to rest there briefly."

Her heart shifted slightly. She faintly surmised the identity of the requester and hurriedly asked: "Might this be Lord Lu?"

The small retainer nodded and smiled, offering no further discourse. Xiao Lingyu's heart clenched.

She had been troubled, uncertain how she might obtain an audience at the Lu Residence, yet unexpectedly, the other party had taken the initiative to summon her.

She gently squeezed the corner of the handkerchief concealed within her sleeve, smoothed her robes slightly, forcibly suppressed the anxiety in her heart, and followed the retainer quickly towards the teahouse.

Fu'an Teahouse was highly renowned within the city of Jiangnan; it was customarily a place of refined assembly for officials and wealthy merchants.

As soon as she entered the establishment, she was guided to an unadorned, elegant chamber on the second floor that overlooked the street. Upon pushing the door and stepping inside, she saw that familiar, tall, lean, and heart-stirring figure already seated by the window.

Lu Chou was draped in a pale moon-white everyday robe, leaning languidly against a bamboo chair. He gently stroked his teacup but did not sip.

His gaze was cold and clear as water yet carried a degree of profound inscrutability. Seeing her enter, he merely lifted his eyes and said coldly: "Madam Xiao is quite sensible; you have arrived sooner than this Official anticipated."

Xiao Lingyu held her breath and concentrated her focus, suppressing the surging emotions within her chest.

She performed a graceful, low salute and said softly: "I naturally comes when she hears Lord Lu's summons."

She bit her lip, finally unable to resist raising her eyes to look at him, her voice holding a degree of imploring sincerity: "Baor is young and utterly ignorant of affairs. I only fear her crying and restlessness will delay Lord Lu in his official duties. I humbly request that the Lord show mercy and allow Baor to return home as soon as possible."

He remained still as a mountain. The tea in his cup trembled minutely, yet he seemed unwilling to offer any reply.

His thin lips slowly curved into an arc that was impossible to discern, as if he had not even heard her plea.

A pot of tea had already been prepared upon the desk. The porcelain-white cup held a pale jade-coloured liquid. Heat gently misted the air, but the fragrance was extraordinarily clear and crisp, carrying a thread of fleeting coldness.

The moment Xiao Lingyu entered, she caught the scent of the tea, and her mind shifted slightly.

She had never encountered this fragrance before. It was like the first melting of accumulated snow on a high mountain, or the slightly damp frost clinging to leaves in a forest, carrying a chilling coolness that pierced her heart and soul.

"Be seated."

His tone was faint, neither warm nor cold, yet it involuntarily induced a sense of chill.

She slowly took her seat. Just as she was about to speak, the celadon cup was pushed toward her. The curling steam and the verdant colour of the tea liquid wafted towards her.

She inhaled lightly, feeling a sense of familiarity, but remained silent.

He smiled faintly: "What? Are you unwilling to drink it?"

She shook her head: "If it is merely for this one cup of tea, Lord Lu raises this humble woman's status far too highly."

He did not speak. He frowned, his eyes deepening in colour, and his tone suddenly turned cold and severe: "Drink it."

She lowered her gaze. Finally, she picked up the cup of tea and drank it in one motion.

The tea liquid was bitter and slightly cool upon first entering her mouth, then a faint sweetness returned at the back of her tongue, and a lingering fragrance arose—it actually possessed an unspeakable familiarity.

She was startled.

Lu Chou set his teacup down, his eyes meticulously dissecting her expression inch by inch. A cold sneer curved his lips.

"Does it feel familiar?"

She was slightly stunned, her fingertip trembling minutely, yet she still shook her head: "I do not know what affair the Lord refers to."

His gaze darkened further, but his voice was low, like cold iron grinding against stone.

"This tea is named 'Snow Bone of Ming Mountain.' It is cold upon entry but bitter in the aftertaste. That year, when you took shelter from the rain in my small chamber, this was the tea. You said you liked the taste of the solitary mountain after the snow."

She was stunned. Her heart abruptly clenched, yet she still could not articulate a response.

She only felt that familiar taste pressing heavily in her throat, choking her breath. Memories surged like a tide yet were hazy and indistinct like mist.

He watched the complex shifts in her expression, a surge of numbness and irritation boiling in his heart. He knew not if it was anger or mockery.

"Indeed, you have forgotten everything."

He lifted his head, gazing fixedly at her: "You possess quite the ability; even betraying a person, you manage to cut clean the memory without the slightest remorse."

Xiao Lingyu gripped the empty cup tightly with her fingertips, her face pale.

After a long silence, she finally raised her eyes to look at him, her voice pressed extremely low: "It was not entirely without remorse..."

She stopped before completing the sentence.

He sat there, perfectly still. His brows and eyes were carved like swords and knives, utterly different from the thin, handsome scholar in her memory. Yet, those eyes had not changed—they were cold, but exceedingly deep.

Her heart skipped a beat. Her throat felt tight, and she was at a loss for how to respond. After a considerable while, she forced a thin smile: "Lord Lu speaks in jest. This tea... perhaps the common woman has a slight familiarity with it, but it is quite possible I drank it elsewhere."

"Elsewhere?" He gave a soft sneer, his gaze sinking heavily: "Name the place, then."

Xiao Lingyu's fingertips tightened slightly, concealed within her sleeves. That fragrance, cool and clear with a thread of snow, instantly evoked memories that had been sealed away for years.

Five years prior, it was precisely this scent of tea that led her to mistakenly enter that secluded, quiet courtyard. At that time, his robes were unfastened, and he sat alone before his desk, reading scrolls and brewing tea.

The setting sun shone through the window lattice, illuminating the chamber in warm light. And it was this very cup of 'Snow Bone of Ming Mountain' that, across the desolate affairs of the world, stirred her young heart, misguiding half her life.

Now, smelling the old fragrance again, she dared not utter a single word. Affection surging like a tide is the most fatal thing.

She lowered her eyelashes, forcibly suppressing the swirling emotions. Her voice was as placid as ever: "This common woman is ignorant and has never encountered this tea."

She feared that speaking the truth would only add to the weight of past infatuation, causing him to regard her with even colder disdain.

Lu Chou lightly tapped the teacup with his fingertip and said faintly: "This is Ming Mountain Snow Bone. It is harvested only three days each year, made from the tender buds of centenary snow ridge trees. And currently, within the entire Great Jin Dynasty, only a few imperial treasuries and the Lu family's stores possess any ounces."

He glanced at her, a half-smile on his face: "Madam Xiao, even with your extensive travels on merchant routes, this flavour, I fear, is extraordinarily difficult to have tasted."

Xiao Lingyu's heart grew even more panicked; she secretly bit her lip. She prided herself on her extensive knowledge of teas, yet she had never heard this name, much less tasted it personally.

This cup of precious tea was clearly a deliberate display of power, intended to make her realize that the difference in their present identities and methods was vast as heaven and earth.

She lightly lowered her eyelashes and whispered: "The common woman is simply ignorant and ill-informed..."

Lu Chou's brows furrowed in displeasure. "Cease addressing yourself constantly as 'the common woman'; it is tiresome to hear."

Hearing this, Xiao Lingyu's heart grew even heavier. The man before her was utterly composed, yet he had already planned every step of this confrontation.

He suddenly rose and walked towards her, looking down at her. His figure was tall and imposing, his presence domineering. He was virtually unrecognizable from the weak, slender, handsome scholar of those years.

"Then, Madam Xiao, do you remember the night we knelt before the moon, when you wore a plain white dress and said that if there was a next life, you wished to grow old together with me?"

She instinctively wanted to avoid his gaze, but failed to do so.

His voice suddenly dropped low, his tone carrying a slight tremor: "Yet what did you do? You left without a word, without even leaving your name. You said you were a concubine's daughter from some family, banished to a manor by the principal wife, claiming you had no one to rely on... Even this, was a lie."

Her lips trembled slightly, but she knew not where to begin speaking.

"And that letter you wrote was quite succinct: Wishing me a brilliant future, requesting me not to seek you out..." He smiled faintly, that smile carrying the coldness of a blade's edge: "But when I suffered such enormous humiliation, did you truly believe I would not seek you?"

"Did you know that when I later found that manor, the place was long deserted?"

He suddenly leaned down, his voice close to her ear: "You departed with such resolute finality, and I searched for three years."

Xiao Lingyu lowered her eyes. A tear finally escaped and slid down her cheek, yet she forcibly swallowed all words.

She could not offer a defence. The heartless schemes and lies of that year could never be whitewashed.

He watched her anguished appearance, and a greater pain surged in his own heart.

He suddenly retreated half a step, sneering: "Now you have transformed yourself, becoming the famous proprietress of a shop in the Capital. A pity, though—this Jinhua Establishment... I fear it will not last for many days."

Xiao Lingyu finally could not restrain herself. She rose gracefully and performed a slight bow toward him, her voice pressed extremely low, yet every word was distinct and clear: "Lord Lu, the Jinhua Establishment supports over a hundred people, who rely on it for their livelihood. I beg that Lord Lu, in his great wisdom and generosity, refrain from truly implicating the workshop. Otherwise, it will be a complete ruin for the Jinhua Establishment."

She paused, her gaze holding a trace of stubbornness and pleading.

She finally looked up at him: "If you harbor resentment, direct it entirely at me. That year, I... wronged you, and I will accept any punishment you mete out. I, Xiao Lingyu, alone, can bear it. However—those people in the workshop, and Baor, are entirely unconnected to this matter. I pray that Lord Lu will show mercy and ensure that the innocent are not dragged in."

The words faded. She bit her lip, lowering her eyes to conceal the sourness within. Proud as she usually was, her willingness to humble herself this profoundly was for the livelihoods of those hundred souls, for her young daughter, and for seeking one final chance of reprieve for her own desperate situation.

Lu Chou lightly tapped the desk with his fingertip, his gaze falling coolly upon her. His voice was low and cold: "You desire the return of your daughter? I fear... that is not possible yet."

Xiao Lingyu pursed her lips, forcibly suppressing the anger and terror in her heart: "Lord Lu, Baor is unconnected to this affair. Whatever grievances exist, they should be directed at the common woman—"

"Madam Xiao greatly overestimates herself, and... profoundly underestimates this Official." He suddenly smiled, the coldness in his eyes intensified: "The child is now in this Official's keeping. Since she is already involved, do you truly believe that a simple plea will make this Official soften his heart and release her?"

He stood up, looking down at her, his voice pressed extremely low: "Furthermore—do not foolishly imagine that the man surnamed Xie can assist you. The trivial good name of Xie Huaici counts for nothing in this game. Do you truly not understand how deep the waters of the Jiangnan Weaving Bureau truly run?"

He lowered his eyes, his gaze sweeping over her trembling form for an instant. The coldness in his heart deepened. He remembered Baor's pair of bronze-coloured eyes, yet a thread of reluctance and unwillingness could not help but surface.

But the thought vanished instantly. He added a final cold sentence: "Since you have entered the game, do not imagine you can withdraw unscathed. Baor shall remain in this Official's keeping for the time being. As for you... you may leave now."

Chapter 15: The Break

She walked out of the teahouse in a state of absolute numbness. Behind her, the heavy door curtain swayed with a rhythmic, lingering motion. \

The faint, cold scent of the tea named "Snow Bone of Ming Mountain" still clung stubbornly to the tip of her nose, a ghostly reminder of the confrontation.

The rain had already ceased. The puddles scattered across the street reflected the pale, leaden grey of the sky above.

Her foot stumbled for a sudden step, as if she had stepped into some patch of wet mud that threatened to pull her down, yet she did not look back. Not even once.

"Mama!"

From the direction of a street vendor at the far corner, a child's voice erupted, laughing and frolicking in pure delight.

Her entire expression suffered a violent jolt. Instinctively, she quickened her pace, her heart hammering against her ribs, until she turned into a secluded, deathly quiet alley.

There, at last, she leaned her weight against the cold wall and slowly, helplessly slid down until she sat upon the ground.

It wasn't Baor... it was never Baor.

She wrapped her arms tightly around herself, burying her face between her knees. The tears she had forcibly held back with such agonizing effort for so long finally burst their banks, hot and unstoppable.

She had always known in the depths of her soul that this day would eventually arrive, yet she hadn't anticipated it would come so soon, nor had she ever expected it to be so utterly, meticulously cruel.

She had never seen his eyes look like that before.

That was not the simple indifference of a stranger; it was a profound hatred that had been violently torn apart and then forcibly, jaggedly stitched back together. It was a calm so absolute it bordered on a terrifying madness.

She knew very well that he was not a man without heart. If he truly were heartless, he would never have uttered that phrase during that distant year—"I have wronged you; I will personally welcome you through my doors one day."

Alas, that kind of promise was one she had never once intended to see fulfilled.

At the time, her mind was entirely occupied with only one singular obsession: safeguarding her family's legacy and escaping that terrifying, suffocating arranged marriage.

She could not even find the time to look after her own well-being, so how could she have possibly managed the weight of his true heart?

"I deserve this..." she whispered, her voice a broken thread. Her tears soaked the front of her robe, spreading in dark, cold patches.

She had already heard the dark whispers about the mounting troubles of the Jinhua Establishment.

Those few trade routes that had originally been settled with such difficulty had been suddenly and ruthlessly severed by an invisible hand.

From outside the shopfront, news of official government papers spread like a plague; before she could even investigate the details, three entire batches of dyeing materials were seized by the inspectors, who claimed the materials were counterfeit.

Then came the sudden, suffocating tax audit...

She had originally thought it was merely the malicious competition of the marketplace. Only after seeing him today did she realize that every single move had been orchestrated by his hand.

He had already investigated her identity to the last detail. He had already laid out the trap step by agonizing step, waiting for her to walk into the net of her own accord.

"Mother..." she softly murmured into the silence.

She thought of Baor's tender, innocent face. Every smile, every slight frown, every expression was an identical, haunting likeness to his own. She had never dared to tell Baor who her true father was, only telling the child that he had passed away long ago.

That day, Baor had asked her: "Does papa also like to drink tea?" She had remained silent, unable to find a voice. She had merely pressed her lips together and gently, lovingly stroked her daughter's head.

She knew that paper, after all, could never wrap up a burning fire.

But she had truly not expected that this fire would burn so quickly, and with such a fierce, consuming heat.

The sound of approaching footsteps reached her. It was Suxin, who had come searching for her with anxious eyes. Suxin crouched down and reached out to straighten the stray hair at Xiao Lingyu's temples. She asked in a low, worried voice: "Madam... is there any news at all of Miss Baor's whereabouts?"

She nodded slowly. As she attempted to stand up, her legs were actually weak, trembling with a pervasive exhaustion.

On the way back, the street was crowded and clamorous, a sea of voices. Suxin whispered: "Such a commotion. It seems there is some important figure passing ahead..."

She closed her eyes tight and said faintly: "It is Lu Chou."

Suxin paused, her breath catching. "It is Lord Lu, indeed... Does Lord Lu truly intend to make you..."

"Fall into ten thousand tribulations without any hope of recovery." She gave a laugh. It carried a thread of choked, bitter sorrow, yet it was also incomparably, sharply clear-headed.

Suxin saw that distant, hollow look in her eyes. Suxin's own eyes began to redden with distress. She asked softly: "Madam... then shall we return to the Jinhua Establishment first?"

Xiao Lingyu remained silent for a long while, the shadows of the street passing over her face. Her voice was low and hoarse when she finally spoke: "No. We will go to the dyeing workshop first."

Suxin's eyes were brimming with red: "Madam, with Miss Baor away right now, you must hold yourself together even more than before. You are our Grand Proprietress; everyone in the workshop is relying solely on you..."

"Baor..." She looked up, her tone suddenly becoming unnervingly calm: "Repeatedly and many times, I have struggled, and I am weary to the bone. Since he refuses to return Baor to me, then let it be exactly as he wishes."

Suxin was stunned, her mouth slightly agape.

Xiao Lingyu smiled softly, though that smile was tinged with a deathly paleness: "Let's change our way of thinking. Now that the workshop is pressed by internal and external difficulties, I fear I cannot properly attend to her needs or safety. Since he wishes to look after her, let it be as he wishes. Suxin, wouldn't you agree?"

As she turned her body away, the cold wind swept past her temples, as if slicing away the very last vestige of her weakness. She gave a self-mocking, light laugh that didn't reach her eyes.

A soft whisper slipped from her lips and was immediately snatched away by the wind: "All of this... I can only say I deserve it."

* * * * *

With the burden of official business concluded, the night was already far advanced.

Lu Chou set aside his vermillion brush. He raised a hand and rubbed the weary space between his brows. The official papers had been exceptionally taxing and numerous today. But what truly made his heart unsettled and restless was the tense, sharp confrontation with Xie Huaici earlier during the day.

He closed his eyes. He began to pace the floor with his hands clasped behind his back. His thoughts were scattered, disorderly, and sharp. Liang Jin stood in silent attendance at his side.

In his restless, wandering state, he unknowingly walked towards the wing of the manor where Baor was currently lodged.

The night wind was cool and biting. The lantern hanging under the eaves swayed rhythmically, casting dappled, shifting light and shadow upon the wooden corridor.

He was just about to turn and leave, when he suddenly heard a low, muffled sound of sobbing coming from inside the room. It was thin and soft, like a small, wronged animal, whimpering and calling out—

"Mother... Mother..."

The sound was extremely light, yet like a fine, silver needle, it unexpectedly and sharply pierced his heart.

Lu Chou's brow furrowed. He pushed the door open almost without thinking.

The candlelight within the room was weak and flickering. Baor was curled up tightly in the far corner of the bed, her tiny face buried deep in her knees. Her small shoulders shook with deep, continuous sobs; clearly, she had been crying for a very long time. Hearing the sudden sound of the door opening, she lifted her head abruptly. A pair of watery, wide eyes looked over at him, like a startled fawn caught in a light, tears still clinging stubbornly to her lashes.

Lu Chou originally wanted to coldly reprimand her with a harsh voice—"Why are you crying? Has no one ever taught you the manners of this manor?"

But the words reached his lips and were forcibly swallowed back into his throat the very moment his eyes met hers.

Baor saw him standing there, motionless and tall. She shrank back timidly, yet she could not help but let out a small, quiet sob. Her nose was red from weeping, and she looked piteous and small in the extreme.

Lu Chou's legs seemed to move with their own consciousness, then took a few steady steps forward.

His long arm extended slightly toward her. He was subconsciously intending to lift her with one hand, but then he suddenly paused for a brief moment.

"Wuuu..."

His brow furrowed deeper. With a look of irritation, he reached out and scooped the small, soft bundle into his embrace.

Baor was caught entirely off guard. She let out a surprised gasp: "Waa-ooh."

No one had ever held her this high up before!

Her small arms immediately and instinctively wrapped around Lu Chou's neck. She clung to him even tighter. Her tears stopped instantly, as if by a miracle. A brilliant, radiant smile bloomed at the corner of her mouth. Her laughter was like a newly opened flower in spring, crisp, clear, and sweet.

Lu Chou's figure was tall and lean. She was instantly lifted very high into the air. Her vision abruptly widened; even the dim candlelight seemed to become brighter in her eyes.

She blinked. Tears still hung on her flushed cheeks, but she had already completely forgotten how to cry. She only stared at him blankly, her small mouth slightly agape, as if she were astonished in the extreme.

Then, she suddenly let out a small "ya" sound of delight and broke into a wide smile. She had never been held this high toward the ceiling.

Lu Chou froze.

Baor's smile was pure, like snow melting in the first light of early spring, clean and transparent without a single trace of impurity. She even forgot her previous fear.

Her small hands grasped his silk lapels tightly. She began to giggle, as if she had discovered something remarkably novel and fun.

"High! So high!" She excitedly swung her small legs in the air. Her eyes still carried the glint of unshed tears, yet her eyes were already curved into happy crescents.

Lu Chou was frozen in place, his arms still supporting her weight. For a moment, he actually did not know whether he should put her down immediately or continue holding her like this.

He had never held a child in his life.

But at this moment, resting against his palms was Baor's warm, small body. She still carried a faint, sweet medicinal scent. Her fine hair brushed against the sensitive side of his neck, ticklish and soft, like a form of silent, absolute reliance.

He knew he ought to have pushed her away.

But possessed by a strange, inexplicable impulse, he tightened his arms. He supported her steadily against his chest, and even... subconsciously adjusted his grip by lifting her slightly, letting her sit higher and more securely.

Baor immediately laughed again, a sound of pure joy. Her small hands grasped his shoulders. Her eyes were sparkling with brilliance, as if she had just discovered the most interesting thing in the entire world.

"Lord..." she called him softly. Her voice was sticky and soft with a child's lisp, carrying a bit of tentativeness, and also carrying a bit of hidden, bubbling joy.

Lu Chou looked down at her. That inexplicable surge of irritation that had been in his heart, at this moment, actually quietly and completely dissipated.

Her small hands continued to grasp his lapels. She giggled. Her small face was red with excitement. Her eyes were sparkling like stars, as if she had discovered some incredible new thing.

"A bit higher, a bit higher..." She excitedly swung her legs again. Her eyes still carried the moisture of tears, yet she laughed until her eyes were curved into lines of joy.

Lu Chou was stunned.

She looked up at him. In her sweet, baby voice, she asked: "Wow, Lord, you are so amazing!"

Suddenly realizing exactly what he was doing, Lu Chou's body stiffened. He quickly put the small bundle down onto the bed. He said in a low, stern voice: "Go and play by yourself."

He turned his eyes away in annoyance, unable to believe his own brief moment of soft-heartedness just now. What was he doing?

Was he actually coaxing a child?

Baor tilted her head and thought for a moment, her gaze curious. Her small hand reached up and pushed his leg clumsily. "Is the Lord unhappy?"

She smiled again, and her dimples abruptly appeared, bright and deep as stars.

Lu Chou instinctively turned his body away, evading Baor's bright, searching gaze. He strode away from the room as if he were fleeing a battlefield. "I still have urgent official affairs. Go and play by yourself."

Chapter 16: The Zongzi Affair

Night had fallen deeply; the candle flickered, its flame minor and tentative as a bean of flame trembling in darkness.

Baor, having played herself weary, now lay curled within Lu Chou's arms; her small head nodded, inch by inch, as though sleep struggled against her eyelids, yet still she clung steadfast to his robe, as though fearful that the moment she loosened her grip he might vanish entirely.

He lowered his gaze to her, his fingers drifting—almost against his will—to smooth the soft fall of her hair.

She felt small in his arms, a quiet, frightened creature seeking warmth, unguarded and helpless, relying on him for a sliver of comfort.

If, indeed, Baor's father was dead already, as the woman had said…

It was for the first time that such a wild and rash thought had entered his mind—perhaps he could become her father.

His chest felt a blow, sudden and heavy, as though something enormous had struck him, leaving him almost afraid to proceed further.

The notion arrived without warning; it tightened his heart until the breath seemed shallow.

Lu Chou sighed softly and let escape a faint laugh, intending to deride his own folly—but underneath his bowed head he beheld her sleeping countenance, her lips curved in the faintest smile, and his laughter died away.

He had long been cold of heart, reserved, untouched by sentiment and unyielding to emotion. Yet now, in this quiet chamber, he found himself imagining a future he had never allowed himself to conceive.

At that very moment, Baor stirred, half-dreaming, and nestled more closely against his chest; her lips murmured indistinctly:

"… Papa… Baor… play with Baor…"

Those words were as light as a breeze whispering past one's ear, yet they entered his heart with a force that startled him.

His whole body quivered; he stood frozen, unmoving.

Had she truly called him that?

He glanced down: she was sound asleep, her small face pressed against his chest, her breath even and soft, a tear still lingering at the corner of her closed eyelid.

His Adam's apple tightened in a hard swallow, and he forced his breath to steady. Dream-talk—no more than a child's wandering murmur. What weight could it possibly hold?

And yet the sound remained, clinging to the edges of his heart, refusing to loosen its grip or fade.

He meant to set her back upon the divan, to sever this uncalled-for entanglement; yet his hands would not move.

What if she truly had no father?

He found himself unable to deny that, in his heart, he was hoping for that possibility.

Such a thought was madness, wholly beyond the bounds.

He, Deputy Minister of Revenue, high among the court's ministers— could a child's murmured sleep-word unsettle his resolve? And besides—that woman's every word, every sheet of household registration she'd presented, lay steeped in falsehood.

And yet, this soft little life pressed firmly against his chest was undeniable, tangible—so real he could not bear to reject it.

He exhaled a low sigh and drew her even closer into his embrace.

Perhaps… only for this one night, let her lean thus.

Only for this one night.

* * * * *

Twilight lay heavy and muted; the clouds above Jiangnan draped low, as though poised to descend upon the eaves. The long-lingering rainfall had at last ceased, yet the alleys still bore pools of water, and the breeze carried the clear scent of freshly-cut mugwort.

Inside the quarters of the Jin Hua Hall, all was hushed and deserted.

In former years, at this season, the workshop would have long prepared colourful cords, sachets and festival dumplings; the embroiderers would carry on their tasks amid laughter and chatter, and children would cluster about the gate.

But this year was different—the courtyard lay so still one might hear the fall of a needle against the wooden floorboards.

Xiao Lingyu sat within the inner chamber before her ledger-desk, a stack of unclosed account-books spread open before her. Beside her, Suxin held a cup of tea, motionless; at the threshold, Suyue stood counting newly delivered bolts of silk.

"This batch of satin—" Xiao Lingyu's voice was steady.

"Missing six bolts." Suyue replied softly. "Madam, those outside say the officials have detained them for inspection—it must await the official sanction for release."

Xiao Lingyu's expression remained unchanged; she simply closed the ledger. "Send Steward Feng for a report, suspend the dyes for now, and shift to storing the embroidery samples. Any merchant tied to the Imperial Household Department—halt supply for these few days, without exception."

"Yes." Suyue inclined her head and left quietly.

Only Xiao Lingyu and Suxin remained within the chamber.

Suxin regarded her Madam, noting the sleepless lines about her eyes, and at last could not remain silent. "Madam… such a silent Duanwu. Will you not prepare some customary gifts? In years gone by, at this time the workshop was so lively."

Xiao Lingyu paused, her fingers lingering momentarily over a brush. "Indeed… in years past, the embroiderers would prepare their own sachets, and the children would scramble to hang five-coloured cords."

Her tone was gentle, as if speaking of a time long past and already distant.

Suxin lowered her voice further. "Madam, this year is one of the three great festivals—it should be the liveliest. And yet… even Miss Baor is gone."

"Do not speak of her." Xiao Lingyu's fingers trembled slightly; she laid the brush aside and leaned back in her chair, closing her eyes for a moment. Her voice fell to a whisper, barely audible. "Where she is, she at least eats well and sleeps deeply. Better than following me into hardship."

Suxin pressed her lips together, her eyes reddened. "And what of you, Madam? Since young Miss Baor left, you have not sat down to a proper meal. You hold up like this and the people here in the workshop worry."

Xiao Lingyu remained silent a while, then said in a low clear tone: "If I do not hold on, the workshop will collapse. If it collapses, how will the hundreds of souls that depend on it live?"

Outside, the wind rose and stirred the hanging curtains. From a distance came the quiet murmurings of the embroiderers—concerns of tax inspections, missing ledgers, halted work.

She heard them but did not speak. Rising slowly, she smoothed her sleeves.

"Suxin, go to the storehouse and inventory the spices and medicinal herbs. Though we shall not mark the festival as before, since Baor is not here, let us still prepare mugwort and realgar, to distribute among the women for protection from heat and pestilence."

"Yes, Madam."

"Also order sticky rice and red dates—let the embroiderers wrap dumplings. The heart has become unsettled; we must offer them something to steady them."

"When Suyue returns, send her to the apothecary outside the workshop for borneol and musk."

"Yes." She hesitated then added quietly, "But instruct her not to buy too much. Over-rich fragrance is not good for children."

"Shall we make sachets this year?"

"Let us." Her voice softened. "In the past years we refrained for Baor's sake—this year use remaining scraps of fabric, make a few sachets and let them dry in the sun—nothing ornate, only conveying peace."

Suxin wiped her eyes and forced a small smile. "Madam, you always think of everything. Were it not for you, this workshop would have fallen long ago."

Xiao Lingyu lowered her gaze and said softly, "Issue the orders. I too am weary."

She turned toward the window, gazing at the sky where clouds and light shifted uncertainly. The cloud-mass rolled like lead across her chest.

Suxin felt a pang in her heart; words rose but fell unsaid.

Xiao Lingyu bent again to her desk and resumed marking the unclosed ledgers.

The lamplight danced in the room. Her countenance was focused, the very image of one standing firm beneath a gale though she knew the wind might carry her away.

After some time, footsteps resounded from outside.

"Madam, Steward Feng reports that the dye-matter case is confirmed—indeed seized by the Ministry of Revenue, pending the lord's orders."

"Very well—I understand." Xiao Lingyu answered evenly. "Have him visit the Weaving Bureau tomorrow. Should he meet Lord Xie, send him my respects."

"Yes."

The three exchanged glances. None spoke further.

Outside, the daylight waned, and the hum of the looms fell gradually to silence. The wind seeped through the gap in the curtains, damp and chilling.

Xiao Lingyu rose slowly. Her fingers brushed a small sachet—worn, simple. It was the one Baor had stitched last Duanwu (Dragon Boat Festival) —crooked stitches, filled only with coarse salt.

She looked down at it; a subtle curve formed at her lips, too gentle to be called a smile.

"If Baor were here now, she'd pester me to make another just the same."

Suxin and Suyue exchanged glances; their eyes were bright with unshed tears.

"Madam," Suxin whispered, "this year's Duanwu… perhaps the quietest yet."

Xiao Lingyu tucked away the sachet; her voice was calm. "Whether cold or warm, the festival must be observed. Only—"

She lifted her eyes to the sky dyed red by the setting sun, her voice falling to a soft sigh. "Baor will be all right. We will all fare well."

In that moment the entire room stilled.

Only the chime of the eaves-bell remained—a distant echo of some far-off memory.

The next morning, the skies over Jiangnan cleared. The workshop began to thread five-coloured cords and hang mugwort once more. Suyue laid a basket of sachets in the courtyard to dry, her thoughts filled with her young Miss Bao.

Chapter 17: A Sudden Malady

As the Dragon Boat Festival approached, the Lu residence bustled with activity. Freshly cut mugwort lined both sides of the bluestone paths, the clean scent of bamboo leaves and sticky rice wafted from the kitchen, and several young maids gathered together, learning to weave five-coloured cords.

Aside from those who were personal attendants and bondservants who had followed Lu Chou, the others were temporary hands assigned to serve Lord Lu's entourage at the temporary headquarters.

"Baor, come here." In the side courtyard, Nanny Li beckoned with a beaming smile, retrieving a sachet embroidered with the 'Five spieces' pattern from her sleeve. "Nanny made this especially for you. It's filled with realgar, borneol, and musk—it can ward off evil and drive away pestilence."

Baor's eyes lit up. Her small hand reached out to take it, but then she shrank back hesitantly: "Can I?"

Her mother had told her never to take things from strangers, and she was also forbidden from using fragrant things.

A young maid at the side also hesitated: "Nanny, Lord Lu forbids us from using spices…"

"Silly girl," Nanny Li stuffed the sachet into Baor's hand. "The Lord only said his room couldn't have them; he didn't say you couldn't wear them. Look, the other children all have them." She pointed to several children playing not far away—children of the household servants— each with a similar sachet hanging at their waist.

Nanny Li took a yellow sachet shaped like a small tiger's head and, brooking no refusal, tied it firmly to Baor's sash. "Look, isn't this little tiger cute?"

Baor lowered her head and sniffed. A thick, pungent fragrance drilled into her nose. She wrinkled her nose, not particularly liking the smell, but the shape was truly adorable, so in the end, she let it hang there on her belt.

Baor hesitated again, fingers curling against the fabric of her sash. Mama had told her many times that she was not allowed to use scented things, and that she must never accept objects from people she did not know well. The warning echoed faintly in her mind. Yet the little tiger's round eyes and stitched stripes were so vivid that she could not bring herself to refuse outright. She only told herself that this was probably not "fragrant" in the way Mama meant, and lowered her head without another word.

* * * * *

As twilight deepened, Lu Chou was in his study reviewing official documents.

Suddenly, a clamour rose from outside the window, mixed with panicked footsteps and the startled cries of womenfolk.

He frowned, laying down his brush. He had just risen when he heard Liang Jin's urgent knocking at the door.

"My Lord! It's bad! Miss Baor suddenly cannot breathe!"

Lu Chou's heart gave a violent lurch. As he strode rapidly through the corridor, his sleeve swept a teacup off the side table, crashing it to the floor, yet he remained completely unaware.

People crowded outside the side courtyard's wing; seeing him arrive, they hurriedly parted to make a path.

Inside, Baor's tiny body was curled up on the bed. Her face was turning green, her lips tinged with purple. Her chest heaved violently, yet it was as if something blocked the way; she could only make raspy, gasping sounds.

"What happened?" Lu Chou's voice was terrifyingly deep.

"This servant doesn't know," the wet nurse knelt at the side, trembling. "The young miss was fine just a moment ago, then suddenly… suddenly this…"

Lu Chou covered the distance in two strides, scooping Baor up into his arms.

The child was as light as a paper kite, twitching painfully in the crook of his arm. Those eyes, usually full of smiles, were now bloodshot, tears mixing with cold sweat to soak her temples.

Her small hands clawed desperately at his lapels, as if grasping the last straw of life.

And in that instant, a massive terror suddenly spawned within him—what if she truly is my daughter?

The thought struck without warning, raw and violent. He did not invite it, nor did he dare pursue it, yet it spread through his chest with frightening speed.

His arms tightened instinctively, as if the strength of his hold alone could keep her breathing, as if letting go for even a moment would mean losing her forever.

He had faced impeachments, death sentences, and palace intrigue without blinking, yet the weight of this small, convulsing body shattered his composure at its root.

"The sachet…" Liang Jin was sharp-eyed, picking up the colourful sachet from the floor. "It fell from the Young Miss's waist."

Lu Chou took it and smelled it, his expression changing instantly. This pungent mix of realgar, borneol, and other spices was precisely what he had feared most since childhood.

Memories surged like a tide—at five years old, he had accidentally touched a sachet in his mother's room and had suffered this same suffocation, nearly losing his life.

That year, his chest had burned as though filled with fire and thorns. He remembered clawing at the bed curtains, remembered his mother's voice breaking as servants ran in panic, remembered the terror of not being able to draw a single full breath.

Even now, decades later, the sensation returned with merciless clarity, coiling around his lungs and heart alike.

"Everyone gets out!" he shouted sternly, while single-handedly tearing open Baor's collar to help her breathe more freely. "Go get an Imperial Physician! No… this isn't the Capital…"

The Imperial Physicians were far away in the Capital; distant water could not save a nearby fire.

A rare trace of panic bled into his voice. "Liang Jin, where is the nearest medical hall?"

"Answering my Lord, there is a Dr. Xue in the east of the city, said to be highly skilled, only…" Liang Jin hesitated. "The city gates are already closed at this hour, and it is raining outside…"

The wind howled and the rain poured like a waterfall, slapping against the window lattice like a funeral drum.

Lu Chou stood by the couch, his eyes cold as frost blades. Yet deep within those blades lay a panic and helplessness hard to detect with the naked eye.

Even when presenting arguments before the Throne, he had never burned with such panic.

He was accustomed to weighing lives in silence, to deciding fates with a steady hand. Yet now his thoughts scattered, refusing to align. Orders left his mouth faster than reason could follow, driven not by judgment but by a single, relentless urgency: she could not be allowed to die here.

Lu Chou laid Baor back onto the bed. The child was already drifting out of consciousness, her fingernails turning blue purple from lack of oxygen, her breathing rapid, her chest heaving violently.

He pulled the brocade quilt to wrap her tight, and when he turned his head, his eyes were piercingly cold: "Use my official tally to order the city gates opened. Take the fastest horse in the headquarters. Within one stick of incense, this Official wants to see that doctor!"

Baor could wait no longer; his heart was frantic with anxiety.

Liang Jin took the order and flew off. Lu Chou sat on the edge of the bed, using a handkerchief to wipe the cold sweat from Baor's forehead. Every difficult breath she took felt like a knife slicing across his heart.

"My Lord…" Baor called out weakly, followed immediately by a fit of violent coughing.

"Don't speak." He subconsciously grasped her icy little hand, his thumb gently rubbing the back of it. "The doctor will be here immediately."

This soothing gesture stunned even him. Since inheriting the position of family head, he had grown accustomed to decisive slaughter and judgment; when had he ever shown such careful tenderness?

Even stranger, this heart-wrenching feeling was so familiar, as if some instinct deep in his blood had been awakened.

"It is truly strange," said the old Nanny, who had entered with hot water, suddenly speaking up. "Miss Baor's symptoms are exactly the same as the Master's family affliction."

The words exploded like a thunderclap. Lu Chou jerked his head up, staring dead at Baor's purpled lips and the red rash appearing on her neck.

Indeed, not a fraction of difference from his own reaction whenever he touched spices. Yet this constitution was extremely rare; as far as he knew, only his Lu family possessed this allergic affliction.

For a moment, the room seemed to tilt. His gaze snapped back to Baor, tracing every detail he had previously refused to examine too closely. The pallor, the rash, the laboured breaths. Each sign aligned with an accuracy that chilled him to the bone. Coincidence ceased to feel like an adequate explanation.

Among the attendants who had followed him to Jiangnan was this old Nanny from the Lu household.

Nanny He was an old servant who had been with the Lu family since childhood, watching over him as he grew to adulthood, and she knew the Lu family's sickly constitution well…

Outside the window, the sound of galloping hooves arrived. The white-bearded Dr. Xue was practically dragged into the room by Liang Jin.

After checking the pulse, the old doctor immediately took silver needles from his medicine chest, inserting several swiftly into the back of Baor's neck and wrists, and ordered someone to quickly brew a decoction of Ephedra, Apricot Kernel, and Licorice.

(Ephedra, Apricot Kernel, and Licorice all name of Chinese herbs)

"Fortunate that treatment was timely," Dr. Xue said, stroking his beard. "The little girl has a constitution of congenital wind-evil entering the lungs. These types of spices harm no ordinary person, but for them, once used carelessly, it is a death warrant."

Lu Chou's pupils constricted slightly: "Has the doctor seen others with these symptoms?"

"This condition is not common. Only once, three years ago, did this old man treat a family with the same symptoms." Dr. Xue glanced at Baor, still in a deep sleep. "A coincidence, really, otherwise this old man would not have known how to prescribe the remedy today."

* * * * *

In the dead of night, Baor's breathing finally steadied. Lu Chou dismissed everyone, sitting alone in the shadows of the lamp by the bedside.

The candlelight illuminated his profile in half-light and half-shadow, also revealing the clouds of suspicion churning in his eyes.

He reached out, gently brushing away the wet hair sticking to Baor's forehead. The child was about four or five years old, her features delicate and soft, the tip of her nose slightly red, still bearing undried tears.

A terrible conjecture quietly coiled around his heart like a viper—this child, could she truly be… my own flesh and blood?

This was not the first time this suspicion and thought had risen within him. He uncontrollably thought… what if?

He had dismissed it before. Again and again, he had forced the thought down, telling himself that it was absurd, dangerous, born of unresolved resentment rather than truth. Yet each time it returned, sharper than before, gnawing at his composure. What frightened him most was not the possibility itself, but the warmth that followed it, the instinctive tenderness that defied every boundary he had built.

His heart tightened, and even his fingertips trembled slightly.

What startled him even more was that whenever this thought surfaced, a wave of unprecedented softness and pain would surge in his chest, like emotions unknown for years suddenly bursting the dam.

Despite her constant denials!

"It is the child of this common woman and her late husband…" That cold voice seemed to echo in his ears still, every sentence gouging his heart.

But the child before his eyes happened to bear an expression that looked deja-vu, and happened to have that allergic constitution, exactly the same as his own…

Lu Chou's eyes grew dark and deep, his emotions churning like the tide.

Even he could not distinguish whether, at this moment, he should hate, or should… love and pity.

Outside the window, the Dragon Boat Festival moon was half-hidden by dark clouds.

Lu Chou's slender fingers unconsciously stroked the jade pendant at his waist—that was the token of the Lu direct line, said to be made of cold jade.

 It was the token he had left for her back then, but she had left it on the small table before departing, never taking it with her.

Chapter 18: The Parting

Her small body, frail from illness, was curled upon itself like a tender leaf after rain. Her face was pale as paper, her breath still short and uneven.

Lu Chou sat at the bedside, his head bowed, watching her in silence; his gaze sank deep, as though some dark current stirred beneath it.

Between her young lips there slipped now and then the faintest fragments of dream-speech:

" Mama… Mama… Baor is so afraid…"

Each whispered call pricked him like a fine needle thrust into the heart. Without willing it, he reached out a hand and laid his palm lightly upon her brow. It was warm, still fevered, yet no longer searing as before.

Heartache?

He drew back his hand, his brows furrowing; the tips of his fingers trembled slightly.

Again and again, he told himself, with cold and reasoned mind, that this child had nothing whatsoever to do with him—merely another's offspring, nothing more.

But that softness rising from within him would not be stilled; it welled up unbidden, quiet yet unyielding.

He should have returned to the yamen to attend to his cases, yet he could not take a single step away. After a long silence, he drew a heavy breath and called for Liang Jin.

"Go summon Xiao Lingyu. Tell her Baor's fever has not settled. Say that this officer demands her presence."

His voice was cold and formal, but as the words fell, he was dimly aware that his heartbeat had quickened for reasons he could not name.

* * * * *

Night had deepened. Wind swept thin rain across the eaves, and the Jiangnan darkness grew chill as steel.

Xiao Lingyu arrived in haste, dust-laden from the road; she had not changed her plain travelling dress, only thrown on a thin cloak, and beads of sweat still glimmered along her temples.

Her steps shook slightly; by the time she reached the corridor her breath came fast, her heart suspended by a single thread of dread.

Hearing Baor had taken a sudden turn, she had not dared delay a moment.

The carriage raced straight through to the magistrate's compound, wheels striking stones in a breathless dash.

When she entered the room, lamplight burned low. Baor's breathing, though shallow, had steadied somewhat; the faint gasps were no longer as desperate as life and death entwined.

A small part of the weight upon Lingyu's heart loosened; she stepped quickly toward the bed—only to be halted by a sudden, cutting voice.

"Stop."

The sound was low yet edged, a strike of cold iron dropped into the night; it froze her mid-step.

She turned. Her eyes rose—and there by the window stood a tall shadowed figure, light behind him, robe stirred faintly by the wind, his face stern as cast metal, the storm between his brows not yet dispersed.

Lu Chou.

His gaze, cold and fathomless, fixed upon her with unrelenting force, as though to pierce through every secret she had ever buried.

"I pay my respect, Lord Lu," she murmured.

His face remained dark; his sword-like brows knit tight, his eyes unblinking as they measured her submissive posture and lowered head. After a long pause, he spoke, voice low:

"I shall ask you one thing. You must answer truthfully."

The sound was heavy as iron, chilling enough to draw the air itself taut.

Lingyu's heart constricted; her fingertips turned cold. She clenched the hem of her sleeve, pain blooming faintly beneath her ribs.

She knew what he would ask. She drew a deep breath, steadied herself, and though her voice trembled, it did not retreat.

"Please, my lord—ask."

Lu Chou's bronze-dark eyes flashed; the words fell, sharp as steel:

"Who is Baor's father?"

Silence seized the room.

Lingyu's breath faltered, as though struck in the chest by an unseen hammer. The world rang within her skull.

She had long known that this question would come—but not tonight, not so soon, not so nakedly. It struck without warning, leaving no room to hide.

Her fingertips whitened. She lowered her head slowly and answered in a hoarse but steady tone:

"My late husband has been deceased these many years. The matter bears no relation to my lord."

The words were thin as ice over water, trembling yet sealing every path of retreat.

Lu Chou's expression shifted; his gaze turned colder still as he stepped closer, pace by deliberate pace.

"No relation? She shares my ailment, bears five parts of my features—and you still deny it?"

His voice was deep, metallic, quivering with a restrained fury that threatened to break her final defences.

She pressed her lips tight, fingers digging into her sleeve until they pierced the skin. Her tone held firm, though exhaustion trembled through it:

"My lord has asked thrice before, and I have answered thrice. What more would you have of me?"

Her eyes reddened, her voice quivered with both anger and weariness—like a branch of thorns daring to bloom upon the cliff's edge.

"Countless in this world share resemblance. Allergy of body is no sign of blood. If my lord insists on forcing guilt upon me, I have no words left. Baor was born from my own life, guarded by my own hands, and all I wish is her peace—tell me, is that wrong?"

She bit down, eyes bright with defiance, forcing her tears back.

"I will say it one final time—Baor bears no tie to my lord. I beg you, do not drag her into this."

Her voice broke faintly, yet it was firm as a blade; there was no yielding in it.

"You—!"

Lu Chou's breath caught, fury knotting his chest; words failed him. At last he gave a short, bitter laugh.

"Your skill is undeniable: you turn justice to falsehood as though born to the deception. I reckon, Madam, that you will yield no tears until the moment you stand before your own final casket."

The air between them hardened to iron.

She met his stare. Though her eyes were red, they were clear as glass.

"My lord's words are truly absurd. Baor has suffered under your care—her capture, too, was you're doing. You have pressed again and again about her blood. Do you truly believe she could ever be your flesh and bone?"

"Impossible?" He stepped closer, voice cold enough to cut. "If she were truly of my blood—do you think I could ever let her go?"

Her heart convulsed; her lips quivered.

"And what then? Would my lord claim her to the ancestral hall? Take her from me?"

She paused, then gave a brittle laugh.

"The past is smoke, my lord. Why torment yourself? Whose child she is—does it matter? Even if Baor were truly of your blood, could you take her home and name her as a legitimate daughter of the Lu family?"

Their breaths collided; the air itself seemed to pulse with anger and hurt.

Her words struck him deep. For an instant his heart faltered.

If Baor were his flesh—what then?

A child born without match or rite was a bastard, nothing more.

Even so, his reply came cold, self-controlled, edged with pride:

"You need not concern yourself. She will have the rank that is hers by right."

"Her rank?" Lingyu's laugh was a trembling cry. "Then tell me, my lord—what of me? A woman widowed, bearing a lie, clinging to life with a child in tow, burdened with a trade no esteem—what am I to be, in your world?"

He was silent.

Lu Chou's gaze held hers, his fury rising like flame—yet when he met the terror and resolve in her eyes, all his accusations caught in his throat.

After a long pause, his expression darkened to ink.

"Tonight, you may remain—with her."

The words fell flat and cold. He turned sharply, sleeve sweeping the air, and strode toward the door.

He had taken but one step when her voice came, soft yet piercing as a needle dropped upon still water:

"Baor needs no father. She is mine—mine alone."

The closing door sounded like a drumbeat against his heart.

Inside, only Xiao Lingyu and the sleeping child remained.

She reached out, covering her daughter's small hand with her own, her whisper barely more than breath:

"Baor, my precious one… it is your Mama who has failed you, who did not keep you safe."

Lu Chou stopped short outside, his hand clenching until the knuckles whitened. His bronze eyes trembled; anger and pain tangled like thorns across his face.

For a long moment he stood wordless—then, without looking back, he straightened and walked away.

The door closed between them, dividing the world in two.

Within, Xiao Lingyu's tears had already blurred her sight. She bent over her daughter's fragile hand, her voice thick with grief yet firm with vow:

"Baor, fear not—no matter the hardship, I will never let them take you."

Beyond that door, his tall figure receded into the dark, vanishing step by step. His thoughts, however, surged like a storm tide.

From a narrow crack in the window, Lu Chou cast one last glance back at the scene within; a dull ache spread through his chest. He pressed his lips tight, drew a long breath, and turned away at last.

A few paces onward he halted again, arms folded behind him. At the far end of the corridor the lamplight stretched his shadow long and solitary.

He lifted his head slightly, staring at the single lantern above, and set a hand upon his chest where the pain still throbbed faintly.

He could no longer tell—was that pain born of fury, or of heart?

Her face rose before him again, accusing, wounded, proud. He gave a low, mirthless laugh.

How absurd—Xiao Lingyu's tears and trembling words made it seem as though he were the one who had betrayed her.

Chapter 19: The Decalogue of Entrustment

The night wind was cool and carried a damp chill; the sky was dark and heavy as deep ink.

Lu Chou's footsteps were measured and deliberate as he walked out of the wing chamber.

The door was gently drawn shut, insulating the corridor from the low, muffled sobs of the woman and the faint, rhythmic breathing of the child inside.

He stood beneath the long corridor, lifting his head to gaze at the heavens.

The moonlight was frigid and clear as water, yet it could not illuminate the turbulent mass of chaos surging relentlessly within his chest.

Baor needs no father, he thought. She is mine and mine alone...

That single, chilling statement pierced his heart like a fine needle, inch by painful inch, leaving him with a deep, stifling ache.

Rationally, she was merely a woman skilled in stratagems, one who dared to calculate against him.

He should have hated her to the very marrow of his bones and rejected her presence utterly. Yet, why was it that when she spoke that word with tearful eyes, he had a single, terrible moment of weakness... to believe her?

What was more ludicrous was the thought that arose when Baor's large, tear-filled eyes looked up at him: If her father was indeed no longer among the living, perhaps, he could disregard the past entirely and step in to be Baor's father.

Absurd! Laughter-inducing! How could such a presumptuous thought even form in his mind?

Yet, the one point that entirely derailed his calm judgment was that pair of eyes—those distinct, bronze-coloured pupils.

This realization, he could not logically resolve. Reason screamed at him: Do not trust her easily.

Lu Chou suddenly clenched his fist tightly, his knuckles turning stark white. But a more terrifying voice whispered deep within his soul: What if the child is truly and rightfully yours? Are you genuinely willing to surrender that claim?

He closed his eyes, asking the cold question of himself, but found himself unable to provide any answer.

Tonight, he knew that this prolonged battle of vengeance and deeply rooted hatred would likely never find a clean, uncomplicated resolution.

* * * * *

The following morning, as the sky was just beginning to lighten, Xiao Lingyu stood in the corridor of the Lu Residence's side courtyard, gazing silently at Baor soundly asleep in the chamber.

The small girl was curled up deep within the embroidered quilt, her breathing steady and uniform, her face flushed pink with sleep.

In her hand, she clutched the tassel of a jade pendant Lu Chou had casually tucked into her grasp the night before, a piece he often wore at his waist, which she had secretly seized without drawing any attention.

Xiao Lingyu lowered her eyes, her fingertip gently smoothing the paper she had already finished writing in her sleeve—The Ten Maxims for Raising a Daughter.

The page was densely covered with small, neat script, listing ten full articles of child-rearing instructions:

"Avoid fish and shrimp; they readily cause a rash."

"During night terrors, gently pat the back; never stop her sharply with a loud voice."

"Should allergy to spices occur, quickly administer Mahuang Decoction..."

She wrote with meticulous detail, even noting Baor's favourite sweet pastry shops, the specific patterns of dolls she loved to play with, and... the name "Mother" she would occasionally cry out during a nightmare.

Her gaze was gentle, yet concealed a deeply buried, firm resolve.

The morning mist outside the window had not yet dissipated. The low whispers of maidservants and the copper bell of the patrolling watch drifted from within the residence.

The moisture from the previous night's rain had not dried; fine water still pooled on the stone steps, reflecting a dark shadow patrolling back and forth outside the courtyard—a Lu family guard.

Xiao Lingyu's heart trembled minutely.

Her fingers involuntarily tightened around the paper. She had long known that the longer she remained, the deeper this emotional entanglement would become.

She lifted her head, glanced at the heavens, and whispered softly to herself: "Just one more glance, and then I must take my leave..."

Through the swirling mist, she bent low, folded the paper neatly, and gently placed it beside Baor's pillow.

—She had, in the end, chosen to leave Baor behind.

The Jinhua Establishment was currently tossed by wind and rain; accounts were depleted, and several major merchant houses were colluding to suppress them, with the subtle shadow of the government lurking behind the scenes.

She knew clearly in her heart that if she were to fall, Baor would only face greater, unavoidable danger following her.

And Lu Chou...

She looked up, gazing towards the direction of the main residence, a complex, forced smile stretching her lips.

Though he harboured hatred for her, at the very least, he would not mistreat Baor, and he possessed the formidable ability to protect her completely.

"Madam, the carriage has been prepared." Her personal maid whispered a discreet reminder.

Xiao Lingyu took a final look at Baor, turned and walked away, never looking back even once.

The morning wind caught the hem of her skirt, like a silent, definitive farewell.

* * * * *

The morning light was faint. As Lu Chou stepped into Baor's chamber, he immediately saw a piece of paper, folded squarely, resting beside the pillow.

Its opening line proclaimed The Ten Maxims for Raising a Daughter.

He raised an eyebrow, picked it up, and unfolded it. What met his eyes was elegant, small handwriting, though slightly rushed, densely listing ten full articles of detailed childcare instructions, spanning from dietary prohibitions to comforting night terrors, and even meticulously noting, "If crying persists, hum the 'Water Chestnut Gathering Song'—she is particularly fond of this tune."

Lu Chou stared fixedly at the final item, and suddenly let out a low, disbelieving laugh.

"What does she presume this Official is?" He flicked the paper with his fingertip, his tone carrying a distinct sense of the absurd: "A wet nurse? Or perhaps..."

His words were abruptly cut short.

In the bottom right corner of the paper, a faint crimson seal mark was clearly visible—the private stamp of the Jinhua Establishment.

Xiao Lingyu.

His eyes instantly turned deathly cold. The secret guard had only reported her covert departure from the residence last night, yet this entire document now appeared beside Baor's pillow this morning. That woman dared...

"Lord!" Baor rubbed her eyes and crawled out from under the quilt. The moment she saw him, her face broke into a brilliant smile, and her small hands shot up high. "Hug!"

Lu Chou instinctively closed his hand, clutching the paper into his palm.

The little girl, oblivious, already climbed onto his knee, burrowing her fuzzy head into his embrace, directly pressing against the hand that held the 'evidence of her strategic abandonment'. She was warm and soft, like an impulsive young cub.

He looked down at her.

Baor suddenly sniffed, tilting her face up: "Lord, you smell like Mother..."

"Nonsense." He frowned but saw the little girl reach out to grab the paper in his palm and quickly raised his arm to avoid her grasp.

"I want that!" Baor thrashed to grab it, accidentally slipping off his knee. Lu Chou instantly reached out and caught her—

CRACKLE!

The paper fluttered to the ground. Baor seized the opportunity, picked it up gleefully, and pointed to a spot: "Look! Mama drew a little butterfly!"

Lu Chou stared intently. In the blank space of the 'Prohibited Foods List', a butterfly outlined in ink was indeed concealed, its wings meticulously dotted with cinnabar, appearing like a living butterfly that had landed upon the paper.

Baor gently touched the butterfly with her fingertip, suddenly growing quiet, and whispered softly: "Did Mother... not want Baor anymore?"

A gust of wind swept through the window, causing the paper to rustle softly. Those ten densely written maxims now seemed like a silent, final entrustment.

Lu Chou was silent for a moment. He suddenly retrieved the paper, then lifted Baor onto his desk with a single arm.

"How does the 'Water Chestnut Gathering Song' go?" He unfurled a sheet of paper and dipped his ink brush heavily into the inkstone. "You hum, and this Official will record."

Baor's eyes immediately lit up.

* * * * *

Baor nibbled on a piece of candied fruit, taking small bites, the sugar frosting smearing her hands. She swung her little feet, humming the 'Water Chestnut Gathering Song' that Lu Chou had poorly learned a moment ago, her eyes curved like crescent moons.

Suddenly, she choked. A fragment of the candied fruit lodged in her throat, and her small face instantly flushed crimson.

Lu Chou frowned, reaching out almost entirely by instinct.

"When coughing, lightly pat the back three times; never strike hard."

Xiao Lingyu's precise handwriting flashed across his mind.

His hand was already on Baor's back, the force neither heavy nor light, exactly three times.

"Cough, cough—poof!" Baor coughed out a small piece of candied fruit, her eyes brimming with tears as she looked up. She saw Lu Chou staring at his own palm, his expression exactly as if he had witnessed a supernatural apparition.

—He had actually followed that woman's prescription?

What was even more ludicrous was... it actually proved effective.

Baor recovered her breath, completely lacking any memory of the incident. She reached out again for the box of candied fruit: "Want more to eat..."

"I forbid it." Lu Chou coldly closed the lid. "Maxim Three—no more than three sweets per day."

The moment the words left his mouth, he himself froze.

Liang Jin entered with newly brewed tea, and hearing that sentence, his hand trembled, and the tea tray clattered onto the floor.

Lu Chou's murderous glare immediately swept over him.

"L-L-Lord, forgive me!" Liang Jin fell to his knees with a plop. "This subordinate simply did not expect that you would even keep track of how many sweets Miss Baor consumes daily..."

"Get out."

Liang Jin scrambled out the door, only to hear Baor's soft voice from inside asking: "How did the Lord know what Mama wrote for Maxim Three?"

Silence.

A long, drawn-out silence ensued.

Liang Jin peeked through the door crack, only to see his master's ears subtly redden. He expressionlessly unfolded the 'Ten Maxims for Rising a Daughter', now smudged with ink, and began annotating it maxim by meticulous maxim:

"Maxim Five is flawed. Baor dislikes bitterness; Fu Ling must be mixed with honey..."

By the inkstone, the forgotten tax ledger lay, gradually becoming saturated with ink stains.

Readers can view the full collection of colour illustrations here:
https://www.facebook.com/profile.php?id=61581325000577

Chapter 20: A Move in the Dark

The hour was the third watch of the Hare; dawn had yet to lift its veil.

Within the Jiangnan Weaving Bureau the sound of abacuses cracked like a sudden storm.

Lu Chou's fingertip slid across the freshly presented tax register of raw silk; beside his hand a celadon cup of tea had cooled to room temperature on the desk.

Beyond the lattice window hung a veil of April drizzle, faint and grey; within, the air congealed with a chill that no brazier could dispel.

"Last year, Jiaxing Prefecture reported eight hundred dan of prime-grade silk."

His voice broke the hush. The clerks startled as one, their hands freezing mid-count.

"Why," he continued, "does the register record only five hundred?"

The Weaving Inspector Zhou Mian bent low; sweat beaded his brow.

"Your Excellency… there was a blight among the worms — a grievous loss of yield…"

"Is that so?" Lu Chou pushed across a second ledger, its cover still clinging to the cobwebs of last night's seizure.

"Yongchang House of Suzhou," he said evenly, "purchased seven hundred dan from the same prefecture. Tell me, Lord Zhou—did those extra two hundred fall from Heaven?"

At his signal Liang Jin stepped forward and laid evidence upon the table: a bundle of shipping orders bearing the seals of many trading houses, all written by a single hand.

"Forged broker's slips," Lu Chou murmured, stirring the tea-foam with the lid. The faint chime of porcelain against porcelain was colder than his tone. "A clever device indeed, Master Zhou."

"My lord, I am framed!" Zhou Mian collapsed to his knees. "This was… was all…"

"Done at the behest of a nobleman in the capital?" Lu Chou cut in, drawing from his sleeve a folded letter.

The red wax bore half an imprint of a mulberry leaf.

At the sight, Zhou Mian's face turned the colour of ash.

From the courtyard outside came a sudden peal of laughter — a child's bright voice.

For an instant the hand that held the letter stilled; Lu Chou knew the sound. Baor was in the neighbouring wing, learning silk threads from the embroideresses.

Zhou Mian seized upon the pause like a drowning man clutching reeds.

"I heard, my lord, that Heaven has blessed you with a young daughter! I have prepared a little jacket of woven brocade — "

Crack.

The lid of the tea-cup shattered between Lu Chou's fingers.

He arranged the shards upon the desk until they formed a perfect mulberry leaf.

"Tell me, Lord Zhou," he said softly, his eyes lifting at last, bright with sudden frost, "do you know what this officer detests above all?"

He let the pause stretch until even the guards forgot to breathe.

"Those who use children as bargaining chips."

Liang Jin, well trained in the weather of his master's temper, shifted half a step backward. The last time he had seen that look had been during the confiscation of a certain minister's estate in the capital—an affair remembered still by all who had survived it.

"Three days," Lu Chou said at last, rising to his full height.

He tapped the letter once against Zhou Mian's shaking cheek.

"Return the fifty-thousand taels of tax silver you have swallowed, principal and interest. All of it."

"Lord Lu, I am innocent — I swear it!" Zhou Mian's protest broke into a strangled sob. "This silver… this silver has already been — "

"Enough." Lu Chou's tone cut him short. "Excuses are wind. If within three days the funds are not restored, this officer will report directly to the Throne. On the court floor you will find mercy scarce: at best, imprisonment; at worst, confiscation of all and ruin of clan."

"My lord! I beg you—help me! How can a small official raise fifty-thousand taels in three days— "

His pleas dissolved into incoherent keening; his body sagged like a kite with its string severed.

Lu Chou turned from him and crossed the threshold.

Behind him the sound of despair clung to the air.

From the adjoining courtyard Baor's delighted cry rang out, clear as a bell:

"My lord, look! Baor found the golden thread!"

Every guard in the yard froze.

Their commander—whose face moments ago had been carved from stone—had actually stopped, turned, and was walking toward the moon-gate.

As he passed, he plucked a single leaf from the mulberry tree.

"Wrong," he said gently, crouching to the child's height.

He placed the leaf in her small palm. "This is zhè-leaf, not sāng. If the silkworm eats it, it dies."

(This is zhe-leaf (cudrania), not mulberry)

The little girl gasped, wide-eyed, and flung the leaf away as though it burned.

Then, proudly holding up a bundle of gold thread, she said, "For my lord — I'll weave you a ribbon!"

From atop the wall the captain of the dark-guards pressed a hand to his forehead.

Heaven preserves us, he thought. Just a moment ago he was flaying Zhou Mian alive, and now he is teaching the child the difference between mulberry and zhè.

* * * * *

Far to the north, the capital still lay under the dominion of winter.

Spring there was a rumour the snow refused to hear.

The palace walls rose high and blind beneath their white mantles; each glazed-tile roof shone with a light that was cold rather than bright, as if the heavens themselves withheld warmth.

Before the Meridian Gate, guards stood in two perfect rows, spears catching the pallid sun.

Amid that still geometry the Third Prince, Chen Song, paused upon the steps. The wind pressed his cloak against the marble.

He looked up toward the distant eaves of the Audience Hall, the blue-green tiles turned silver in the glare, and the corner of his mouth moved as though at some private jest.

"I hear," he said at last, "that Lu Chou's zeal has shaken the Weaving Bureau. He has stripped it to the rafters."

The attendant behind him bent at once.

"Your Highness, the inspector Zhou Mian took his own life last night. The Deputy Ministry of Revenue reports that the Crown Prince's men were dispatched at once—perhaps to contain the matter."

"Zhou Mian is dead?"

The cup in Chen Song's hand hesitated midway to his lips.

"Yes, Highness."

He smiled, faintly. "Dead men are convenient. They save me the trouble of giving orders."

His gaze returned to the Hall, the sunlight whitening his eyes.

"The Crown Prince's men," he murmured, "are always a half-step slow. They will reach Jiangnan only in time to count the corpses."

He turned and entered the inner chamber. Within waited a court messenger, slender and bowed, the jade of his girdle cold as ice.

The man knelt. "By imperial command I report: Lord Lu has submitted a memorial concerning the silk-tax affair. His Majesty orders him to complete the inquiry without delay and return to court for audience. The Emperor adds—'Is Jiangnan's silk yet cleanly woven?'"

Chen Song inclined his head, neither assent nor surprise.

"The cleanness of silk," he said, "depends on whose hands hold the shuttle."

At that, one of his counsellors, Li Yuan, spoke low.

"If Lu Chou truly exposes the Revenue Faction, Your Highness must be ready. The court will not remain still."

"Ready?" The prince's fingers tapped once on the jade table.

"What is there to prepare? The Jiangnan case will not unravel so easily. Lu Chou will think himself near triumph, yet the skein will tighten before he can breathe. To finish the matter and return by imperial order—too soon."

His voice faded into the vast hush of the palace. Outside, a bell sounded, long and iron-dark; somewhere within the nested courts a white crane rose against the grey, its wings flashing like drawn steel.

The day went on, bright and without warmth.

* * * * *

On the far eastern side of the palace, in the Crown Prince's study, lamplight wavered upon screens of sandalwood and gold.

Chen Gen set down a sealed dispatch; the wax caught the flame and gleamed a dull red. The scent of burnt ink hung between the two men.

"Lu Chou is to return to the capital?"

"Yes, Your Highness," answered his secretary. "Not yet departed—His Majesty has merely pressed for haste."

From the side table, Imperial Preceptor Shen rose, smoothing his beard.

"Your Highness will recall that the Jiangnan affair spreads wide roots. When Lu Chou is summoned to present his report, it may be for merit—or for blame. It depends where guilt chooses to settle."

The prince's smile was calm, almost amused.

"Father calls him back now to remind the ministers that the case is not closed, and to test the man's hand. If the task ends well, the praise reflects upward. A convenient trial for both."

"And if Your Highness's reading proves true?"

"Then the man is of use." He spoke lightly, yet a glint of intent lay beneath the words.

"His name grows swift; half the Ministry already bends toward him. Should he truly possess ability, better to draw him within the Eastern Palace before others think to do the same."

Shen Imperial Preceptor frowned. "Lu Chou is of noble house but difficult temper—aloof, not easily mastered. If Your Highness would employ him, beware that his edge turn backward."

"I am aware." The prince pushed open the lattice.

A scatter of snow light struck his eyes, making them pale and glacial.

"Ambition in a man is no vice; it is the measure of his usefulness. Whether that ambition cuts or serves depends on the bait one offers."

Within the bronze brazier, fire coiled and sank. Its light climbed the wall, half revealing his face, half burying it in shade.

The tutor's voice dropped almost to a whisper.

"Then Your Highness intends… to lend him a push?"

Chen Gen turned from the window. The faint curve of his lips was neither assent nor denial.

"When water runs too clear, no fish remain," he said. "If Lu Chou truly has talent, let the current test him. I fear not his pride—only his purity."

Shen Imperial Preceptor inclined his head. "To rule men, one must first discern their hunger. If he is proud, perhaps he seeks either rank or a name unsullied."

The prince allowed himself a soft laugh. "They say he resists every bribe in Jiangnan—one wonders whether his abstinence is armour or wound. In time we shall see."

"Every man covets something, Highness. When he returns, there will be ways to probe."

"Probe? No. Let the tide do its work." The prince's tone was level, detached.

"This tax case is a double-edged blade: handled well, it brings glory; mishandled, ruin. If he earns his merit through it, I am content to stake a single game upon him."

He rose. The straight line of his back caught the thin gleam of snowlight.

"With Lord Lu in the Ministry, the son cannot easily fail where the father once stood. This match," he murmured, "let us watch how he places his piece."

Within the bronze urn the flame flared blood-red and then sank to ash.

The prince's profile, carved in half-light, seemed forged from the same metal.

Outside, snow descended soundlessly, whitening the lattice until the palace world was sealed again in silence.

Chapter 21: The Turn of Fortune

Three days subsequent, a sudden upheaval surged through the merchant community of Yangzhou.

In the early morning, a runner from the Jinhua Establishment rushed in to report: "Madam, the Yongtai, Longchang, and Furui firms have simultaneously rescinded their commissions,

They refuse even the pre-paid deposits!" Xiao Lingyu's hand, which held the writing brush, paused minutely. Ink spread out, creating a small blotch of shadow on the ledger.

Misfortune did not arrive alone.

Following closely at noon, messengers from the River Transport Guild (漕幫) delivered a message: "Effective immediately, the shipping costs for all Jinhua Establishment cargo will be subjected to an additional thirty per cent levy."

The messenger's eyes were shifty. "The Guild Leader says... this is also unavoidable."

By evening, the matter that most surprised Xiao Lingyu was the delivery of a written document from the Tongbao Bank, a financial institution they had cooperated with for many years: "Due to the current contraction of silver liquidity, all loans are temporarily suspended."

Suyue wrung her hands anxiously: "Madam, this clearly signifies..."

"It signifies that someone is executing a grand strategy," Xiao Lingyu set down the account book, her fingertip lightly stroking the abacus beads on the desk. "Moreover, the plan has been laid for a considerable time."

Outside the window, twilight gradually deepened. Xiao Lingyu stood in the attic, looking out at the shuttle of merchant vessels along the Grand Canal.

She suddenly noted that the cargo ships, which customarily docked at the Jinhua Establishment's pier, had today all redirected their course to the mooring berths of the Yongchang Firm.

"Prepare the sedan chair," she suddenly turned. "We are going to visit the Cheng Cloth Merchants."

* * * * *

Foreman Cheng looked visibly anxious upon receiving Xiao Lingyu, beads of fine sweat forming on his forehead: "Madam Xiao, we sincerely regret this situation..."

"Foreman Cheng," Xiao Lingyu unhurriedly produced a small brocade pouch. "This contains the patterns of Shu Brocade you mentioned last month. I specifically arranged for someone to bring them back from Chengdu."

Seeing the relief in his expression, she continued: "I hear your esteemed son is to be wed soon? The Jinhua Establishment is willing to offer ten bolts of Cloud Brocade as a congratulatory gift, wishing only for our future cooperation to remain unchanged."

Leaving the Cheng Firm, Xiao Lingyu successively visited several other familiar merchants. At every location, she made no mention of her current distress.

Instead, she presented meticulously prepared gifts—either essential samples the other party desperately required, or items known to be favoured by their families.

On the return journey to the residence, Suyue was perplexed: "Madam, why did you not directly discuss the business situation?"

Xiao Lingyu laughed softly: "Few are those who offer timely aid in a crisis; many are those who offer extravagance when times are good. If our Jinhua Establishment were to show weakness now, others would seize the opportunity to manipulate us easily."

* * * * *

At dawn the next day, Xiao Lingyu personally conducted an audit of the inventory in the storeroom. She stroked the smooth, lustrous silk, and suddenly instructed the accountant: "Retrieve that batch of lake-blue cloud-patterned satin from last year."

"But that is..."

"I know it is a treasure item reserved for the bottom of the chest." A look of firm resolve flashed in Xiao Lingyu's eyes. "Now is precisely the time to utilize them. At this moment, we cannot be concerned with profit or loss; minimizing the loss is equivalent to making a profit."

She urgently required sufficient silver liquidity to overcome the immediate crisis.

This prized batch of satin was initially intended to be sold at a premium before the Mid-Autumn Festival.

Now, having just passed the Dragon Boat Festival, she could only sell it at a price slightly above cost, seeking only rapid cash inflow.

That same afternoon, a display stand was erected before the Jinhua Establishment's gate.

That batch of priceless cloud-patterned satin was astonishingly offered for sale at a common price.

The embroiderers of Yangzhou city rushed over upon hearing the news, and a long queue quickly formed before the workshop.

"Is Madam Xiao insane?" Passersby debated amongst themselves.

But discerning individuals noticed that among the queuing crowd were many buyers purchasing for noble households.

It turned out Xiao Lingyu had discreetly released news: this batch of cloud-patterned satin was tribute-grade material specifically prepared for the Mid-Autumn Imperial Banquet.

Three days later, the foreman of the Tongbao Bank personally called upon her: "Madam Xiao, there was a misunderstanding earlier..."

Xiao Lingyu was busy instructing the embroiderers on a new needle technique, and did not raise her head: "No matter. The Jinhua Establishment has no shortage of silver now."

She truly did not lack funds. That batch of cloud-patterned satin not only recouped its cost but also successfully restored the Jinhua Establishment as a hot topic of conversation in Yangzhou city.

What was even more brilliant was that the embroiderers who had benefited from the low price spontaneously began speaking highly of the Jinhua Establishment.

* * * * *

Late at night, Suxin finally could not help but ask: "Madam, how did you know this strategy would succeed?"

Xiao Lingyu looked towards the bright moon outside the window, saying softly: "The merchant path is like a game of chess; sometimes, retreating is the best way to advance."

She withdrew her gaze and let out a light sigh, explaining: "We sell secondary-quality silks now for a price war, aiming to force Yongchang Firm and its partners to follow suit and lower their prices. But price is not the sole key to victory."

Suxin then asked: "Then was the White Deer Academy also for poaching Yongchang Firm's master dyer?"

Xiao Lingyu allowed a rare faint smile to appear, having finalized several commercial tactics. "Indeed. Having poached their master craftsman, Yongchang will likely face significant chaos now."

Suyue smiled: "Oh, truly?"

Xiao Lingyu also showed a rare smile. "Coupled with this paired bolts for the same price promotion, we simultaneously boost cash flow and clear inventory. This blend of sentiment, profit, personnel, and goods, I fear even the old, established Yongchang Firm will suffer considerable losses."

Suxin's smile also broadened. "That truly is excellent! We have long been displeased with the Yongchang Firm!"

"Rest assured, things will continue to improve."

Following this, Suyue seemed to recall something and hesitated to ask: "Madam, if we act this way... will the Yongchang Firm let the matter rest easily?"

Xiao Lingyu gave a laugh, yet her eyes were cold as frost and dew: "We need not fear. The Imperial Weaving Inspector is currently stationed here. The Emperor's eyes and ears are present. Yongchang Firm or any other merchant house will currently be behaving with utmost caution, daring not to employ any illicit methods."

"But the scale of this interference was not small; even the Tongbao Bank was involved—"

"The faster they move, the more it proves their desperation." She dipped her brush in ink, her tone placid: "The chess piece that remains still on the board is often the most fatal."

Suxin listened, utterly captivated, and finally said in a low voice: "Madam, this one game of yours is enough to win back our momentum."

She spread out a piece of letter paper and began to write. The letter was addressed to an old friend far away in Suzhou—a man who specialized in sea transport business and had long been at odds with the River Transport Guild.

"Next..." Xiao Lingyu's lips curved slightly. "It should be Yongchang Firm's turn to suffer a headache."

* * * * *

Xiao Lingyu finalized several plans to counter the Yongchang Firm.

She first arranged for all the accumulated secondary-quality silks in the inventory to be dyed the currently fashionable "rain-washed azure" colour, selling them at half price under the name "Jinhua Special Edition."

Though these fabrics were not of top quality, they precisely undercut the price line of Yongchang Firm's mid-range silks, forcing their rival to follow suit and lower prices.

The accountant stomped his feet anxiously: "Madam, selling at a loss like this..."

Xiao Lingyu smiled faintly: "No matter. Yongchang Firm's silks were all acquired at a high cost. We shall see who collapses first."

Yongchang Firm's most experienced master dyer suddenly announced his retirement and returned to his home village.

Three days later, he appeared inside the Jinhua Establishment's dye workshop.

Xiao Lingyu personally poured tea, treating him with utmost respect. "Master Chen, I hear your grandson wishes to enter the White Deer Academy?" She pushed forward a letter of recommendation. "It happens that I have some old ties with the Academy's headmaster."

She further rolled out a buy-one-get-one-free promotion: purchase one bolt of newly fashionable fabric and receive an older bolt for free.

This boosted sales and increased cash flow while clearing inventory, resulting in a frenzy of purchasing.

Inside the Yongchang Firm's main hall, a teacup was smashed onto the ground, porcelain shards scattering everywhere.

"Xiao Lingyu!" Zhou Yongchang's face was livid. He grabbed the foreman's collar. "Does she truly believe this is enough to overturn the Yongchang Firm? Does she know who she is provoking?!"

The foreman stammered nervously: "Master, our goods have been seized in Guangzhou, our Southeast Asian fleet has been hijacked by Zhao Dongyang, and now even the Imperial Weaving Bureau has begun auditing our accounts..."

"Silence!" Zhou Yongchang kicked over a desk, a look of vicious cruelty flashing in his eyes. "Go, send a message to the Capital—tell them Xiao Lingyu has not only avoided collapse but has actually begun fighting back and auditing accounts!"

He gave a cold sneer, retrieving a sealed confidential letter from a hidden compartment, his fingertip rubbing the wax seal—it bore the distinct mark of the Eastern Palace (Crown Prince's).

"She believes cutting off my supplies, poaching my men, and ruining my reputation is enough to win?" He gnashed his teeth. "She fundamentally does not know that this game, from the very beginning, was never a mere commercial war!"

Chapter 22: Two Nights of Standoff

The night rain fell endlessly—thousands of silvery threads weaving together a muted, mournful rhythm upon the eaves of Jin Hua Hall.

Within the accounting room, the lamplight flickered against ledgers and paper rolls. Xiao Lingyu, draped in a thin cloak, sat bent over her desk, cross-checking accounts.

Ink had smudged her fingertips, yet her gaze could not hold steady. The wick burned too bright; its pale light carved the weariness upon her cheek with cruel precision.

The door slid open; a gust of damp wind swept in.

Suyue entered, breathless.

"Madam, word just came—the Yongchang House has dispatched men to the capital—tonight!"

The brush halted mid-stroke. A droplet of ink spread slowly upon the page, blooming like a black flower.

"Which route?"

"The canal. The fast courier boats. Three days at most."

Silence settled again. The rain outside struck the roof-tiles like a thousand tightened strings, each note falling clear, cold, deliberate.

At length, Xiao Lingyu spoke, her voice roughened at the edges:

"So hasty? Then the man behind Zhou Yongchang can no longer sit still."

She rose, dimmed the lamp, and crossed to the cabinet in the corner.

From within she drew a locked ledger—its cover worn soft by years of touch.

Turning to the middle, she paused. Her fingertip hovered above several faint lines—entries she had paid dearly to obtain, copied from Yongchang's private accounts.

Her finger traced the uneven ink, her eyes turning hard.

"For three years their trade in silk and silver has flowed smoothly through Jiangnan," she murmured. "Only these few large transfers stand apart—the silver went out, yet never returned."

Suyue leaned close.

"All sent to the capital?"

"Yes."

Her tone was calm, yet anger shimmered beneath its surface.

"And the sums are staggering."

She closed the ledger and went to the window. The rain blew slantwise with the wind, striking her sleeve and soaking through the thread.

For an instant her eyes darkened; she understood she had already been placed at the heart of the storm.

"Madam, shall we lie low for a while?"

Xiao Lingyu shook her head. Her voice steadied into iron.

"One may hide for a night, not from the game already begun. They mean to use Jin Hua Hall to make an example. If I retreat now, there will be no ground left to stand on."

She turned, took up her cloak, and said softly:

"Have the carriage prepared."

* * * * *

The rain did not cease.

The streets lay deserted, slick as mirrors; the only sound was the patter upon tile and stone. The lamps outside Jin Hua Hall guttered in the wind, flames trembling like candle-souls.

From the far end of the lane approached the sedan of Lord Lu Chou.

The bearers, bent beneath oiled umbrellas, had nearly reached the crossroads when a pale silhouette appeared ahead—still as marble amid the downpour.

"Who goes there?" one called.

The figure did not move. The rain blurred her features; only the edge of a white sleeve quivered faintly in the wind.

"Stop."

The order came from within the sedan—low, even, unmistakably his.

The bearers halted. The curtain lifted slightly, revealing a corner of dark silk; droplets gathered at its hem and fell, one by one, into the open palm of the woman outside.

Xiao Lingyu raised her head. Her hair clung to her cheeks; her eyes glimmered with cold light. She held no umbrella—she might have been carved from the rain itself.

"Lord Lu," she said. Her voice, thin against the storm, trembled only at its edges. "Might I beg a word—in private?"

For a moment, there was only the rain.

Then a calm reply:

"Come in."

* * * * *

Inside, the air smelled of damp wood and ink.

The space was dim; silence pressed close around them.

Xiao Lingyu sat upright, hands folded upon her knees. Her gown was soaked through, darkening at the seams. The slow sway of the sedan made her pulse beat louder in her ears.

"My lord is charged with investigating the silk and embroidery guilds," she began, her tone calm yet taut.

"I bear no resentment.

But in recent days—Yongchang withdrawing its orders, the canal guild raising its tolls, the money house recalling its loans—every move, they say, was under your command."

She drew several papers from her sleeve, offering them with both hands.

The sheets were wet, the ink blurred, but the official seals could still be discerned.

"I know," she went on, her voice almost lost to the rain, "that you still bear hatred for what happened five years ago."

Her tone faltered, but her posture did not; her hands remained neatly folded before her.

"Yet within Jin Hua Hall, there are more than a hundred mouths—embroiderers, dyers, porters—who live by this trade.

If the orders truly came from the Bureau, I will accept it without complaint.

I only beg, my lord, that you leave them a way to survive."

By the end, her fingers trembled, though she fought to keep her voice composed.

Lu Chou studied her in silence. The only sound was the hush of rain and their breathing, two faint rhythms interwoven. His expression was unreadable, calm to the edge of cruelty.

"So," he said at last, his tone almost indifferent, "you come to surrender all your fortune and property?

Or"—his lips curved faintly—"is this your way of advancing by retreat?"

"No." Her lashes lowered, her voice soft yet firm.

"I only wish to keep my people fed."

The silence returned. Rain tapped upon the roof in a slow, deliberate cadence.

"And you believe," he asked after a pause, "that it was I who ordered this?"

His voice remained calm, yet something cold coiled beneath it.

Xiao Lingyu lifted her gaze. His eyes were deep, reflecting her disheveled, rain-soaked image. She did not answer; the bite of her lip was answer enough.

He looked at her, then noticed the faint burn mark along the back of her right hand—a thin red welt glimmering in the lamplight.

"What happened there?"

"An accident."

He gave a sound that was not quite a laugh, then turned away, spreading the damp documents across his knee. The deputy seal of the Weaving Bureau shone red—but it was not his.

"I have never ordered the suppression of any merchant," he said, voice level, each word struck like iron.

"If someone has acted under my name, that is the one who must be investigated."

Xiao Lingyu froze, her eyes lifting to his. There was no anger in his tone, no heat—yet something within it tightened her chest, as though she had just realized she might have wronged him.

A small, bitter smile touched her lips.

"I understand, my lord," she whispered.

She rose, bowed, and reached for the curtain—but hesitated. Her hand upon the frame trembled slightly.

"May I ask…" she said at last, voice soft as mist, "how is Baor these days?"

"She's well," Lu Chou replied at length, turning his face slightly aside. His tone was even, yet the edges softened.

"Two days ago she learned to braid a flower cord. She said she would weave it for—"

He stopped. The rest of the sentence faded into the steady murmur of the rain. His gaze dimmed, as if the words themselves had turned to ash before they could reach her.

Xiao Lingyu listened in silence. In her eyes, the faintest glimmer passed—something gentle, sorrowful, and gone before it could form a smile.

"That is good," she said quietly. Her lashes lowered; her voice was light, almost dissolved in the sound of rain.

"Thank you, my lord."

The curtain lifted, and the roar of the storm surged in. She stepped down from the sedan without a backward glance.

The pale-blue gown clung to her frame, soaked through, yet her back remained straight as a blade.

Lu Chou watched her walk away until the darkness and rain swallowed her shape. His fingers, still resting on the damp papers, closed slowly.

Tracing the deputy seal of the Bureau, his eyes darkened.

Someone had acted in his name.

Outside, the rain fell harder, slanting like whips across the flagstones.

A guard's voice came muffled through the storm:

"My lord, shall we return to the residence?"

Lu Chou's reply was low but firm.

"No. Back to the Bureau."

He paused, his tone dropping to a murmur almost devoured by the rain.

"If hands have moved in secret, what must be uncovered goes far beyond trade."

The bearers lifted the sedan again. Wheels rolled through the flooded street, cutting faint ripples into the water. The sound of rain drowned all else—the shouts, the footfalls, the city itself. In the corner of the seat lay a forgotten handkerchief.

Its edge was embroidered with a single hibiscus blossom, each stitch fine as breath, each thread nearly invisible in the dim light.

It was her work—her mark.

Lu Chou lowered his gaze.His fingertip lingered at the petal's edge, tracing it once, twice—then stopped.

He did not move for a long, long time.

Chapter 23: The Sword of Legitimacy

In the Capital, rumours had been spreading fiercely in recent days—

"Have you heard? The Jinhua Establishment has offended none other than Lord Lu, the same man investigating the silk taxes!"

"No wonder! Lord Lu is known for his iron-clad impartiality. Madam Xiao, this time, I fear, will find it difficult to recover..."

These rumours were not groundless.

The people from the Eastern Palace had long since been operating in the shadows, ensuring that all directives aimed at suppressing the Jinhua Establishment appeared, on the surface, to follow the pretext of Lu Chou's tax investigation mandate.

Foreman Zhou of the Yongchang Firm spoke to everyone he met, saying: "If not for Lord Lu's strict audit, why would we need to be so cautious?" Even when the River Transport Guild raised their freight fees, they added: "This is done in cooperation with the government's inspection!"

Upon returning to his residence, Lu Chou immediately sensed something was amiss.

All the way back from the Imperial Weaving Bureau, several minor Jiangnan merchants had subtly attempted to pass him petitions requesting an audience, their words veiled and obscure, all stating their willingness to "present a modest profit, only requesting the Lord show leniency."

Scarcely had he entered the study when he immediately summoned Liang Jin, saying coldly: "Go, quickly investigate who dares to operate using this Official's name."

Outside the window, the wind whistled mournfully. The lamplight flickered. He lightly tapped the desk with his fingertip, meticulously reviewing the secret reports that had just arrived.

"Master, it is not only the Jinhua Establishment; six major merchant houses in Jiangnan have all been affected, and the actors involved are all proceeding under your name." Liang Jin reported in a low voice, his brow deeply furrowed. "This servant has investigated closely. The mastermind behind this operates with extreme secrecy, but appears to be connected to the Crown Prince's secret network."

Before even half an incense stick could burn out, a black-clad guard crawled in, reporting softly: "Master, this subordinate investigated throughout the night.

This morning, six major merchant houses have already been forced to withdraw orders or suspend supply. Rumours circulate through the streets that these actions are all instructed by you."

"Six firms?" Lu Chou's sword-like eyebrows furrowed further, his voice cold to the bone marrow.

The guard swallowed, continuing: "And it is not limited to the Jinhua Establishment alone. According to the rumours, this entire campaign of rectification targeting the Jiangnan merchant community is entirely the Lord's intention, saying you are acting upon Imperial will to make an example of disobedient merchants."

Lu Chou gave a cold laugh. The mirth did not reach his eyes, making the expression only more chilling: "The Third Prince certainly calculates a masterful game."

—Borrowing this Official's name to intimidate the Jiangnan merchants, forcing them to contribute silver into the silk tax black coffers.

—Then, using the charge of 'colluding with merchants and disrupting the silk market,' to ensure this Official's Southern tour ends in utter failure.

—If this further incites His Majesty's rage, then seizing the opportunity to strip me of the Deputy Minister of the Board of Revenue position, would that not achieve two ends with one stone?

His finger moved slightly, and his tone darkened: "Does my father know of this matter?"

Liang Jin shook his head: "We have received no reports from our spies, thus far, indicating that the Master is secretly colluding with the Eastern Palace in this scheme. Perhaps it is the Third Prince privately instructing the Crown Prince's secret agents to act. Elder Brother Lu has recently been associating frequently with the Third Prince; I fear he may be implicated."

Who would have imagined that the three men of the Lu family serving as officials at court—Master Lu, the Deputy Minister, and his eldest son—presented a façade of harmony, heralded as "Three Pillars of Virtue, Father and Sons United," a celebrated anecdote in the city?

Yet, if someone could truly perceive the turmoil beneath, they would know that behind this great renown lay mutual calculation and efforts to restrict one another. Lu Chou's eyebrows shifted slightly, his gaze cooling.

Although his father is a key minister to the Emperor and the Third Prince, he has always valued the family's reputation. If he knew this scheme intended to drag the Lu family into the murky waters, he might not have initiated it lightly.

His father might not be aware, but his illegitimate elder brother has likely played a hand.

Lu Chou lowered his gaze in deep thought, a flash of cold light in his eyes.

"The Crown Prince's scheme goes beyond mere profiteering; I fear it is also a test of the Lu family's true allegiance."

After all, the three of them—father and two sons—held differing loyalties.

His fingertip struck the surface of the desk heavily, the sound like cold iron.

"Issue my command, covertly investigate all the Eastern Palace's secret commercial routes in the south. Find out who acted using this Official's name. Focus first on the Yongchang Firm."

Liang Jin received the order and withdrew, his footsteps gradually fading.

Since this game has commenced, only he who can break the stalemate can ascend using the momentum.

Liang Jin received the order and departed.

Lu Chou sat back at his desk, remaining motionless for a moment.

The Third Prince has lost his patience and begun setting the board. If this scheme is thwarted, the Board of Revenue's influence will strengthen, and the Third Prince will lose a vital arm. If it cannot be thwarted... Lu Chou's future career will be stained.

Thinking of this, his gaze subtly hardened, and his thoughts surged intensely.

* * * * *

The afternoon sun warmly cast its light upon the small courtyard. As a gentle breeze passed, the treetops swayed, rustling softly.

In the courtyard, several small maidservants and two young junior attendants were gathered in a circle, kicking a shuttlecock adorned with coloured feathers, their laughter clear and crisp.

The shuttlecock was kicked back and forth between the children, fluttering like a butterfly of many colours.

Baor stood within the circle, clad in a pink lotus-root coloured gauze skirt. As she lightly turned while kicking the shuttlecock, her skirt hems layered and fluttered, like blooming flowers.

Her small face was slightly flushed, and the fine sweat on her forehead had not yet dried.

She kicked with her slender little legs forcefully yet always missed by just a hair's breadth. Each time the shuttlecock fell, the little girl would stomp her foot in frustration, then immediately giggle with delight, utterly undeterred.

"Axi, you kick too fast! I don't have time to chase it!" she protested in a sweet, childish voice, her large bronze eyes sparkling.

Axi, about eleven or twelve years old, chuckled and coaxed her softly: "Miss Baor, you must kick the shuttlecock lightly. Do not rush. Here, I will go slower."

An elder nanny watched from beneath the corridor, unable to suppress a smile, yet feeling somewhat troubled. Since Baor came to stay at the Imperial Weaving Bureau, her days had been unusually quiet.

Baor was young and lonely, confined to her room, and her spirits were low. After seeing her several times staring blankly out the window, the nannies, feeling pity, allowed her to play with the servants' children to relieve her boredom.

Just as the courtyard was filled with happy noise, the door creaked open, and Lu Chou, tall and jade-like, stepped in.

The expressions of everyone in the courtyard instantly changed. The kicked shuttlecock froze mid-air, and everyone stopped in silent terror.

Baor, still oblivious, was giggling as she leaped to catch the feathered shuttlecock. Only upon landing did she sense the shift in the atmosphere.

She turned her head and saw the man standing at the doorway, his blue robe like jade, his expression cold and stern, his gaze sharp as a blade, quietly watching her.

Coldness surged in Lu Chou's eyes—

How could a dignified young lady mingle with the children of servants? Furthermore, with her delicate body, sweating profusely and panting heavily, this was utterly inappropriate!

Rage surged within him. He shouted in a deep voice: "Stop that!"

Like a thunderclap, the courtyard instantly fell silent. The maidservants and junior attendants retreated in panic, standing with their heads bowed.

Baor's pair of bronze eyes stared blankly at him, her lips slightly parted. She looked confused, not knowing what wrong she had committed.

The nannies rushed forward in panic, explaining repeatedly in low voices: "Replying to the Lord... Miss Baor is still young, and she has been very bored these days. We dare not discipline her casually when she is idle during the day. We were just... We simply did not know whether Miss Baor should be provided for as a master's daughter, or treated as a guest, or... well, how we should attend to her. We truly have no clear protocol."

Their explanation was hesitant and cautious, conveying both their difficulty and their lack of guidance.

Lu Chou's chest constricted—

Indeed. What was his original intention when he abducted Baor?

Ah—he intended to strangle her with his own hands!

And now?

She uses the finest dining ware, wears the latest embroidered robes tailored in the Capital, sleeps on a superior zitan wood (luxury sandal wood) couch, and has nannies and maids attending to her constantly. She looks nothing like a hostage; rather, she is being provided for as a young Madam.

How is it that now, looking into those clear bronze eyes, filled with confusion and innocence, he was utterly unable to utter a single word of reprimand?

He bit down on his jaw, suppressing the irritation in his heart, and coldly swept his gaze over the crowd: "From now on, Baor is strictly forbidden from mixing with the servants."

Having spoken, his gaze flickered, holding a hint of evasion. He turned and strode quickly away, his pace even faster than before.

Behind him, the nannies softly consoled the little girl: "Miss Baor, do not be afraid. The Lord did not truly intend to scold you."

Baor tilted her head, her pair of bronze eyes still staring blankly at the receding figure. She asked in a tiny voice: "Why is the Lord angry? Baor only wanted to play..."

The nanny froze, gently hugging her tightly, unable to utter a single word in reply.

Chapter 24: The Weakening Guard

Returning to the study, Lu Chou threw himself heavily into the grand Master's chair. State papers were piled high on the desk, the wax seals yet to be broken, yet he found that not a single scroll could capture his full attention.

Outside the window, the cicadas buzzed with irritating noise; the wind carried a gust of summer heat, rendering his heart restless and irritable.

He raised a hand to rub the space between his eyebrows, gazing for a long period at the half-cold tea resting on the desk.

He had originally sought to settle his spirit and review the state papers. Yet, conversely, he found himself utterly incapable of absorbing a single written character.

What surfaced repeatedly, time and again in his mind's eye, was the image of that dazzling, piercing pair of copper-coloured eyes.

They were clear, they were innocent, and yet they carried a disturbing, unsettling familiarity. Those eyes were strikingly similar to the gaze of her mother during her youth.

However, they possessed fewer lines of worldly experience and carried a greater abundance of pure, untainted spirit.

His knuckles lightly knocked the tabletop, the sound dull and heavy.

—But why, of all things, must they be copper-coloured pupils?

If not for that specific colouration, he would almost be willing to believe that the child was indeed his own bloodline.

Even that extremely rare allergic constitution was identical; to claim they were utterly unrelated was logically impossible to reconcile.

Yet, the copper pupils were like an unyielding iron lock, fiercely securing all his nascent weakness and any shred of hidden hope.

"Damn it," he cursed in a low voice, his tone rough and almost hoarse. The brush in his hand was snapped by his grip, ink splattering across the crevices of his fingers.

He seemed unaware of the damage. He felt only a painful, suppressed irritation and a heavy, stifling ache in his chest, as though something substantial was lodged there, blocking his breath entirely.

At this moment, a light, subtle knock sounded outside the door.

"Enter."

Even he himself could fully detect the profound sense of irritation in his tone.

A young attendant carefully pushed the door open, his hands slightly trembling as he held a tea tray.

"My Lord, your tea..."

"Set it down and leave immediately." Lu Chou did not even lift his eyes; his tone was cold enough to genuinely chill a person.

The attendant fearfully placed the teacup down and was about to retreat when a low, deep "Wait" halted his steps.

A small, compact oil-paper packet had appeared on the desk, upon which a crooked little flower was clumsily drawn. The lines were awkward, but the colours were bright and clear.

"What is this thing?" His brow furrowed slightly.

"Replying to the Lord," the attendant lowered his head, his voice barely audible, "It is... it was sent by Miss Baor. She said... this is a medicinal tea to treat headaches, and that she personally prepared the ingredients."

He paused, his fingertip resting on the paper packet for a moment. That paper still bore fine, distinct finger smudges, clearly the work of a young child.

The attendant hesitated, then opened his mouth again: "She also instructed the kitchen to decoct the tea according to her own recipe... saying that if the Lord drank it, he would not be so angry anymore."

Lu Chou lowered his gaze, his chest tightening subtly.

He slowly unwrapped the oil-paper packet. Inside were a few pieces of dried chrysanthemum and mint leaves, mixed with a thread of clean, fresh fragrance.

The chrysanthemum petals showed slight scorch marks, clearly having been unevenly dried; the mint leaves were folded into small pieces, carefully layered and wrapped with great caution, as if she feared they would break.

"What else did she say specifically?" His voice was low and husky.

The attendant quickly replied: "Miss Baor said... she will not play shuttlecock anymore, and requested that the Lord stop being angry with Baor."

The room fell into an immediate, terrible silence. Only the incessant noise of the cicadas outside, stirred by the hot wind, pulsed in intensity.

Lu Chou stared fixedly at the clumsy little flower. After a long silence, he finally let out a soft breath and waved his hand: "You may leave now."

The attendant, as if granted a great pardon, bowed and quickly retreated from the room.

The study returned to profound quiet.

He looked at the packet of medicinal tea. The suppressed anger and irritation in his heart, somehow, slowly dissipated by several degrees.

Guided by an irrational impulse, he took a pinch and placed it into the tea receptacle, pouring hot water over it. Amidst the rising white mist, a faint aroma emerged, the cooling scent of mint wrapped in the slight bitterness of chrysanthemum.

He picked up the cup and took a sip—it was first bitter and astringent upon the tongue, then turning sweetly refreshing. It was bitter enough to sober the mind, and sweetly gentle.

He leaned back against the chair, letting out a long, deliberate sigh.

Outside the window, the setting sun cast an oblique light, bathing the study in a uniform orange-red glow.

In that precise moment, he suddenly felt a dizzying sense of déja vu—

seemingly transported back to that rainy night, where Xiao Lingyu brewed medicine for him, and he complained of the bitterness.

She had laughed and said: "Quickly, it is bitter, but a truly good medicine."

"Absurd," he murmured self-mockingly, setting the cup down, yet he immediately felt an uncontrollable urge to take another sip.

That specific hint of bitterness tasted just like her.

* * * * *

Night slowly began to descend. The cicadas in the courtyard ceased their noise, leaving only the distant, rustling shadows of the trees.

Lu Chou finished reviewing the last imperial memorial, put down his brush, and rose.

His cloak hung by the screen; he casually draped it over his shoulders, intending originally to walk directly back to his room.

However, as he walked past the small courtyard, his footsteps involuntarily slowed.

This was the courtyard where Baor resided.

The internal lights were extinguished, leaving only a single lantern hanging beneath the corridor, swaying lightly with the night wind.

In the faint, weak light and shadow, a low sound of weeping seemed to emanate.

He frowned slightly and pushed the door open.

The courtyard was utterly silent, save for the movement of the lantern light. Following the sound, he saw Baor curled up on the rocking chair beneath the corridor, her small figure trembling ceaselessly.

Her face was buried in her arms, the crying suppressed and muted, as if she were desperately trying to prevent others from hearing her grief.

"Baor."

The sound startled her into a violent shudder.

She quickly raised her head. Her small face was still streaked with tears, the corners of her eyes red like petals of a peach blossom. She frantically attempted to wipe them away with her sleeve, only smearing them more severely.

"...My Lord," she stammered a greeting. The movement was too hurried, and she nearly stumbled.

Lu Chou instinctively reached out to steady her shoulder. Her frame beneath his hand was so thin it felt almost weightless.

"What is the matter here?" he asked in a low voice.

Baor sniffled, her voice thick and soft: "My Lord... I miss Mother, and Auntie Suyue and Auntie Suxin..." She sobbed between words. "When can Baor return to our home?"

In that instant, Lu Chou's breathing almost stopped entirely.

He looked at that small face, feeling as if his heart were being cut by a sharp blade.

The question was simple beyond simplicity, yet it instantly forced all his trained rationality to retreat.

He tried to speak but found that nothing could leave his throat.

The weak light reflected on her wet eyelashes; crystal tears rolled down her cheek, landing on his fingertips, burning with the heat of fire.

His hand trembled, yet he fiercely controlled the urge to gather her into his arms.

A voice deep in his heart was screaming: She is not your daughter.

But another voice, was subtly answering: What does it matter? The way she cries is exactly like her mother.

She was the hostage he had originally taken—the one he planned to use to restrict Xiao Lingyu, the one he had even actively considered strangling with his own hands.

And now?

This child wears the finest fabrics in his residence, uses the most exquisite utensils, sleeps on a carved couch; she is attended to and protected. How was she a hostage?

She was more like a young Madam he cherished in the palm of his hand.

He shifted his gaze, his voice turning cold: "It is late now. Return to sleep."

Baor froze, then nodded lightly, turning to walk back inside. Her small figure was stretched long by the lantern light, lonely like a swaying shadow.

Lu Chou remained standing, watching the door close quietly. Silence returned to the courtyard, leaving only the sound of the wind.

He turned to leave.

The night wind swept by, stirring the hem of his cloak. That familiar scent of chrysanthemum and mint still lingered on his sleeve, so faint it was barely noticeable.

He looked up at the sky; the moonlight was pale white like frost. The suffocating irritation in his heart, far from dissipating, had only deepened.

It was like an unfinished dream—a dream where those bronze eyes stared unblinkingly at him.

But that relentless gaze, it seemed, would grant him no rest.

That night, he tossed and turned restlessly, the candle burning down and being relit. What surfaced in his mind was not the memorial on the Jiangnan tax case, nor the political layout of the succession struggle in court, but the little girl he had personally brought here.

—Whose daughter should she ultimately be regarded as? A dull ache gripped his chest, as if something were taking root within him. Suddenly, he laughed softly, that smile cold and almost devoid of emotion.

"Xiao Lingyu, what exactly do you want this man to do?"

The candle flame flickered, illuminating the half-bright, half-dark contour of his profile. In his eyes, a trace of tenderness, which he had fiercely tried to suppress, faintly shimmered.

Chapter 25: A Father's Glimmer

Three days subsequent, a sudden, heavy rainstorm swept over and engulfed the entirety of the Imperial Weaving Bureau.

Lu Chou was within the deliberation hall, intently discussing critical official matters with several other high-ranking officials. He suddenly perceived a commotion and disorder outside the chamber.

He frowned, signalling the gathered assembly to pause their discussion, and walked over to the window personally to investigate the cause.

He observed several maidservants and nannies running frantically throughout the courtyard amidst the heavy downpour, appearing to search anxiously for some missing object.

"What exactly is the nature of this disorder?" Lu Chou called out, halting a passing young attendant.

The attendant was entirely soaked through, stammering severely: "R-replying to the Lord... Miss Baor is nowhere to be found! She was just playing in the courtyard moments ago; in the mere blink of an eye, she vanished..."

Lu Chou's heart seized up violently.

Without waiting for the attendant to complete his statement, he strode out rapidly in long strides. Rain instantly drenched his robes, but he paid this physical discomfort no heed, heading directly toward the familiar places Baor frequented for play.

"Baor!" he called out loudly in the rain, his voice severely compromised and drowned by the sound of thunder.

Liang Jin rushed forward, bringing an umbrella and following closely. Lu Chou snatched the umbrella away from him instantly yet did not use it to shield himself from the rain.

He continued onward, his voice dropping to a deep command: "Order everyone to join the search immediately. Do not cease until she is located and returned."

"My Lord, please utilize the umbrella. You are completely soaked through."

"Fewer needless words! Quickly dispatch the men to continue the search with greater urgency!"

"Yes." Liang Jin could only comply with the command, mobilizing all available personnel to search through the rain.

After nearly half an hour had passed, Lu Chou finally discovered Baor curled into a small, shivering ball behind the garden rockery.

She was soaked completely through, her small face pale, tightly clutching a similarly drenched kitten in her arms.

"What exactly are you doing here in this state?!" Lu Chou seized her and pulled her up abruptly, his voice filled with barely concealed fury and frustration.

Baor was shivering uncontrollably, yet she still fiercely protected the kitten. She spoke with a trembling voice: "T-the little kitty was wet by the rain. I was afraid it would be cold..."

Lu Chou gazed at her obstinate, unyielding expression and was rendered speechless for a moment.

He quickly took off his outer robe and wrapped Baor in it and picked up both the child and the kitten together and then used his free hand to open the paper umbrella to shield her from the persistent rain. "We shall discuss this unfortunate matter further once we return to the house."

Back inside the house, the maidservants rushed about, their movements frantic, changing Baor's sodden clothes and hastily brewing ginger soup.

Lu Chou stood aside, his face grim and severe, terrifying the onlookers into utter silence, leaving them afraid even to breathe.

He stood sternly, looking at Baor's small face, which was already slightly flushed. A deep, heavy ache constricted his chest.

"M-My Lord, Miss Baor... she has a fever!" Granny Zhao cried out in genuine alarm.

Lu Chou strode to the bed in two large steps, reaching out to touch Baor's forehead. It was indeed shockingly hot.

Baor hazily opened her eyes. Seeing him, she managed to produce a weak, fragile smile: "M-My Lord... the little kitty... is it alright now?"

Lu Chou's throat felt tight and constricted. He turned and shouted commands at the servants: "Go summon a physician! Quickly, without delay!"

"Little kitty... little kitty..."

"Do not be afraid, my child. The little kitty is perfectly well. You must sleep for a while first, and you can see the little kitty when you awaken."

Baor's cheeks were flushed crimson, yet she revealed a genuine smile of happiness: "Truly so?"

"Mm." Possessed by an irrational impulse, Lu Chou gently nodded his head. His large palm gently stroked her hot forehead, his thoughts profoundly complex and unsettling.

That night, Lu Chou, in an entirely unprecedented action, did not return to his own courtyard. He sat by Baor's bedside, personally changing the cold towel on her forehead and feeding her the medicinal draught.

Baor shifted restlessly in her sleep, murmuring the name "Mother" repeatedly. Every single sound was like a sharp needle piercing the very centre of Lu Chou's heart.

At daybreak, Baor's fever finally subsided completely. Lu Chou wearily rubbed his temples, preparing to leave the room, but then heard Baor's weak, faint voice: "My Lord... were you here all night long?"

Lu Chou turned, seeing Baor was awake, gazing at him with those clear, large eyes.

"Mm." He answered briefly.

Baor revealed a sweet, guileless smile: "Thank you very much." She paused. Then, she added softly: "My Lord, you are actually a very good person. You seem just like Papa..."

Hearing this, Lu Chou froze in place, only managing to say stiffly after a long moment: "What gives you cause to say that?"

Baor held out both hands, gesturing for a hug, smiling sweetly: "I see it! A'Xi's father is very kind to them... and the Lord is very kind to Baor too..."

"Sleep now." Then, he left the room almost as if he were actively fleeing the confrontation.

In the corridor, the morning light was faint and soft. Lu Chou stood by the window, gazing at the distant sky gradually brightening.

For the first time, his fixed resolve for vengeance was severely and profoundly shaken.

* * * * *

The night was deep, and the lights of the Imperial Weaving Bureau still burned brightly.

Lu Chou, however, had not closed his eyes for the entire night.

Baor's image continually lingered and revolved in his mind. The copper-coloured eyes he had seen during the day felt like heavy hooks, firmly anchoring and restricting him.

The child's pathetic, repeated calls of "Mother" while sick were agonizing.

When she cried and called for her mother, he felt a distinct, painful ache in his own heart.

He rose in irritation, putting on his long coat, and paced with his hands clasped behind his back to the window, gazing at the oppressive darkness of the night, his heart troubled and fundamentally unsettled.

After a long pause, he called Liang Jin in a low voice, his tone slightly hoarse: "Go, summon Xiao Lingyu. Tell her... Baor frequently looks for her after waking, and this Official permits her to come look upon the child."

Liang Jin was startled, though he did not understand the reason for the Lord's sudden softness. He dared not utter any question, receiving the command and departing immediately.

* * * * *

However, before half an hour had elapsed, Liang Jin rushed back, reporting softly: "Master, Madam Xiao... refused to come."

"What?" Lu Chou spun around suddenly, his gaze sharp as a blade: "What precise words did she use in her refusal?"

Liang Jin hesitated for a long moment, reporting softly: "She stated that the affairs of the workshop are too numerous and complex, making it difficult for her to spare the time.

She also stated... that since the Lord is capable of competently looking after Miss Baor, she requests that the Lord not trouble her to travel back and forth, to avoid stirring up other gossip."

Lu Chou's chest constricted violently, and he laughed in extreme rage, saying coldly: "Good! She certainly knows how to calculate!

Now that she has simply tossed the child here, does she presume this Official is her household's hired wet nurse?!"

He swept his sleeve across the desk, causing brushes and inkstones to scatter and overturn.

Liang Jin lowered his head and remained silent, only feeling that his master was infuriated to the point of external manifestation, yet could not utter how to resolve the situation effectively.

Lu Chou paced restlessly back and forth, almost moving to personally go to the workshop and drag the woman back for a face-to-face questioning.

But the thought stopped him.

—She certainly knows how to grasp the leverage.

She knows that at this moment, it would be entirely inappropriate for him to erupt.

If he truly stormed the Jinhua Establishment, it would only reveal his complete loss of composure.

Furthermore, Baor... He glanced down. The small, delicate figure on the couch was still in profound slumber, her breathing steady, her features relaxed and unfurled.

Just thinking about how she cried for her mother moments ago, yet found comfort and solace in his arms, the tightness of the pent-up rage in his chest was impossible to genuinely release.

* * * * *

After a long pause, his voice was faint and chilling: "Dispatch another messenger to summon her again."

Liang Jin carefully looked up: "If Madam Xiao... still refuses to come a second time..."

Lu Chou's lips tightened into a thin line.

He lowered his voice, grinding the words out with extreme force: "Then tell her this Official shall throw her darling heart onto the street, leaving her to fend for herself! Have her consider the consequences well!"

"Yes, My Lord." Liang Jin respectfully received the command and departed immediately.

Having spoken, Lu Chou turned his back, standing tall with his hands clasped behind him before the window, gazing at the deep darkness of the night.

The flickering lamplight cast dappled shadows onto the window lattice, making his brows and eyes appear even colder.

After a long while, he briefly closed his eyes, his knuckles tightly clenched, his thoughts surging like an overwhelming tide—Why?

She was merely a female merchant.

Why was he so absolutely unable to quell his fury simply because she refused to come?

Was he angry that she refused his command repeatedly, once again defying his authority? Or was he angry that he cared so profoundly, so uncontrollably, whether she chose to come or not?

Logically, he should be sitting coldly, watching her rush back in anxious supplication.

Yet now,

he felt as if she had utterly outmanoeuvred him, holding a suffocating rage that had nowhere to be released.

He suddenly opened his eyes, his gaze filled with dark, intricate complexity.

"Xiao Lingyu..." He let out a low, cold laugh, but his voice carried a trace of bitterness he himself hadn't detected. "If you think you can manipulate this man, we'll see if you have the capability..."

Chapter 26: A Clash of Circumstances

Within Jin Hua Hall, the accounting room was brightly lit.

Xiao Lingyu, dressed in plain garments without any hairpins or makeup, a trace of weariness still lingering between her brows, nonetheless had a cold and focused expression, her fingertips rapidly flipping through stack after stack of tax records.

It was the hour of Zi; most workers in the hall had already retired for the night, only a few trusted aides in the accounting room remained by the lamplight.

With the situation growing increasingly tense these days, she knew in her heart that every single thread within the hall must be handled with extreme caution.

Holding an old account book, she slightly frowned and was just about to mark it when she suddenly heard hurried footsteps outside the door.

Liang Jin entered with a bow, his voice lowered but unable to conceal his urgency: "Madam Xiao, my Lord... my Lord has ordered me to invite you again.

He said Miss Baor has been frequently asking for you since waking, and requests that you visit to see her."

The brush in Xiao Lingyu's hand paused. Her lips moved slightly, but she did not lift her gaze, her voice faint: "Report back to your Lord that the hall affairs are busy now, I truly cannot get away. If Baor is awake, the matrons can take care of her."

A hint of embarrassment flashed across Liang Jin's face. Caught in a dilemma, he spoke again in a low voice: "Madam, Baor is crying terribly, and Lord Lu... rarely speaks like this. If you could go for just a short while, it would comfort the child."

Xiao Lingyu finally looked up, her eyes sweeping over him coldly, her voice as clear as water: "If I make a move, tomorrow Jin Hua Hall will have more faults picked out. My Lord Liang, persuading me is useless. I have my own sense of priority."

Her tone was neither hurried nor slow, yet it carried a sharp edge.

Liang Jin, helpless, gritted his teeth and tried to persuade again: "Madam Xiao, you... please don't blame this lowly one for speaking out of turn. The Lord hasn't rested all night. When Baor woke up crying for her mother, it was heart-wrenching. Lord Lu has ordered me to come for the third time. If I still cannot invite you this time, I'm afraid it will be difficult to account for..."

Xiao Lingyu did not speak, faintly lowering her head to turn the pages of the book, her knuckles lightly tapping the desk, her expression unmoved.

The atmosphere in the room grew stiff and cold.

Seeing no result, Liang Jin finally gritted his teeth and delivered his master's harsh words: "The Lord said, if you still refuse to go, tomorrow he will throw that child out onto the main street, for anyone to pick up as they please."

Before his words faded, Xiao Lingyu's brush tip snapped with a "crack," halting mid-air.

She looked up at him, her voice several degrees colder: "...He said if I do not go, he will throw Baor out onto the street?"

Pressed by her clear, cold gaze, Liang Jin involuntarily bowed his head and took a step back, saying in a low voice: "...Yes, that is what the Lord instructed."

Xiao Lingyu suddenly laughed coldly, threw the vermilion brush in her hand onto the desk with a slap, pressed her palms on the desk, and slowly stood up, her eyes like frost.

"Heh heh, he was the one who took the child away back then. Now, saying he can't manage and wants to throw her back is also him. What principle is behind him being so changeable?"

A sourness rose in her throat, but she still suppressed it fiercely. Remembering how sensible Baor had been since childhood, never crying or making a fuss, and how before that separation she had looked up with her small face and asked—"Mother won't abandon me, right?"

At the time, she had smiled and replied, "How could I?" Thinking of it now, it felt like a mockery. If she were truly thrown onto the street, that child would probably cry herself hoarse.

"Does he take me, Xiao Lingyu, or take Baor, as mere playthings on his desk? Take them away today, grow tired of them tomorrow, and then discard them on the street?"

As she spoke further, her fingertips turned slightly white, her chest heaved, and the anger she had suppressed for so long finally became difficult to conceal.

"If that's the case..." She said through gritted teeth, her voice cold: "Then let him throw her. If he truly dares to throw her out, I'll trouble the Lord to send someone to inform me. I will then send someone to pick her up from the street. There's no hurry for this moment!"

"Ah? Madam Xiao, what kind of words are these? That Miss Baor is your own flesh and blood. Could you really be so hard-hearted..."

"Say no more." Xiao Lingyu, however, refused to speak further, calling to a servant boy nearby. "See the guest out."

Liang Jin, seeing the cold light in her eyes, felt his heart tighten and didn't dare say more. He could only heave a deep sigh.

He thought to himself incessantly, When gods fight, little devils suffer — this saying is absolutely true.

Xiao Lingyu swept a cold glance over him, flicked her sleeve beneath, turned and sat back down behind the desk, spread open the tax records again, and picked up a brush to resume writing. But one could see her fine brushstrokes were already somewhat unsteady.

—With such surging anger in her heart, how could she truly calm her mind to examine carefully?

But she insisted on gritting her teeth and holding on, unwilling to let that man named Lu or the people he sent see a trace of weakness in her.

Liang Jin was taken aback, not expecting her to speak so coldly and resolutely. He felt both alarmed and admiring. He knew in his heart that although the Lord's words were harsh, he might not truly be able to harm the child. But now, this back and forth seemed like both were testing—whoever softened first would lose.

And though he had witnessed countless storms in his days, he had never seen a dispute like this, where one couldn't find a way to intervene.

He cupped his hands in a salute: "This lowly one understands. I will report back now."

Xiao Lingyu set down her brush and said mildly: "I won't see you out."

Liang Jin retreated outside the door, but his heart was heavy. The master had ordered him to invite her three times; now, three invitations had failed. How was he to account for this?

Inside the room, the lamp had not been extinguished. Xiao Lingyu picked up her brush again, her expression slightly tense.

How could her heart not ache for that child? But nowadays, with alarms everywhere, all parties watching like tigers, and even within her own clan, she had no confidence she could fully ensure Baor's safety.

Ai, I can only let Baor suffer temporarily, and take this chance to let that man named Lu taste the hardships of raising a child!

Her mind finally relaxed a little. She set down the brush and leaned back in the chair. The lamplight on the desk reflected in her eyes, half weariness, half coldness.

Outside, the wind and rain gradually ceased, but the sound of dripping water persisted—just like that place in her heart that could not be calmed.

* * * * *

The night rain gradually stopped; water still dripped from the roof ridges of Jin Hua Hall. Inside the accounting room, the lamplight was half-dim. Xiao Lingyu sat back down behind the desk, listless like an eggplant beaten by frost.

Liang Jin had been gone for a long time.

The room had returned to silence, only the low sound of distant embroidery wheels turning could be heard.

Someone outside reported accounts in a soft voice; she instructed mildly: "Open the doors earlier tomorrow. The submissions for inspection from the official bureau need to be reviewed again."

Her voice was even, as if completely unshaken by the earlier exchange.

But after everyone had dispersed, her gaze fell on the water stains by the window, her expression slightly cold.

The Weaving Bureau's audit was growing tighter; the hall's cash flow had been unstable in recent months. The slightest stir was enough to give someone a pretext to cause trouble. She could not take the slightest risk.

These past few days, she had noticed frequent visitors from the official bureau; even the chief recording official had personally inquired about the goods ledgers.

Xiao Lingyu knew in her heart—if Lu Chou wanted to move against her, he need not say it outright; just a single phrase, "routine account verification," would suffice.

She raised her hand, separated a few pages from the account books, and handed them to a trusted aide: "Make a copy of these few silver trails as backup. Delay shipments to Zhennan Cloth temporarily. If anyone asks, say the goods are damp and not yet dry."

The other party accepted the order and hurried away.

The night wind blew in through the door crack, scattering the documents on the table.

She reached out to press them down, her fingertips pausing—it was an old corner of paper Baor had left behind from practicing calligraphy, the faint ink marks not yet faded.

She lowered her gaze, folded the paper, and placed it in a drawer.

"If things still haven't settled down tomorrow," she said in a low voice, "Baor still cannot return to her side. After all, she could barely manage her own affairs at this moment and might face life-threatening danger at any time. She could not let Baor take this risk with her."

She closed the account book and blew out the lamp wick. Outside, the sky was between dark and light, a thin mist enveloping

Jin Hua Hall. In the distance, the sound of horse hooves could faintly be heard, as if official guards were stationed at the mouth of the lane.

The wind and rain had just ceased, but the atmosphere had already changed—a new game was about to begin with the coming of tomorrow.

Chapter 27: A Probe for Status

"What? That woman surnamed Xiao still refuses to come?"

A furious shout burst through the study, shaking the window lattice with its force.

Lu Chou had been simmering with suppressed ire to begin with; upon hearing Liang Jin's quiet report, his temper exploded. He slammed his palm on the desk, sending hot tea splashing from the cup.

"Good. Very good—" he gave a cold laugh, his tone razor-sharp, "does she truly believe this official is powerless against her?"

Murderous intent surged in his eyes. He suddenly stood and strode towards the door, then turned sharply, barking:

"Liang Jin! Go at once—pack that girl up, pack her thoroughly, and throw her straight out of the gates. Let us see whether that woman surnamed Xiao comes to pick her up!"

"Truly… truly throw Miss Baor out?"

"Is there any need to question it?" Lu Chou snapped, voice icy.

Liang Jin trembled, meaning to offer a word of persuasion, but one look at his lord's storm-dark expression forced the words back down his throat.

It really was immortals clashing—while the little ghosts suffered.

Just then, light and hurried footsteps sounded outside the door.

"My lord—" Baor stumbled into the room. She happened to catch the words "...Miss Baor… throw her out" and froze mid-step. Her little face turned pale at once.

She stood there in a daze, her small mouth slightly open, utterly unable to believe it.

"You… you want to throw Baor out…?"

At that, her milky voice broke. Her tiny body tightened all at once, and tears spilled down like strings of beads.

"No… no… does my lord not want Baor anymore? Baor will be good, Baor will listen…"

Crying as she spoke, she rushed forward and clung to the hem of Lu Chou's robe, sobbing without pause.

Lu Chou was stunned. The harsh words he had just uttered lodged in his throat like a stone.

"…"

He lowered his gaze to the tiny bundle clutching him so desperately. A strange ache flooded his chest—he could not tell whether he was angry at himself or angry at Xiao Lingyu.

Her small shoulders trembled violently. He should have scolded her coldly, yet the words simply would not form.

After a long moment, he furrowed his brows, crouched down, and awkwardly wiped the tears from her cheeks. His tone was stiff and blunt:

"Mn… what this official meant to throw out was… was that little cat. Not Baor."

Baor sniffled and lifted her swollen, reddish-brown eyes to look at him, half disbelieving:

"The little cat… must not be thrown out either…"

Lu Chou fell silent, jaw tightening slightly. He finally twisted his expression aside and muttered in a low voice:

"…Fine, fine. None will be thrown out. Not the little cat, not Baor. Satisfied now?"

Only then did Baor's sobs begin to subside. She wrapped her arms around his neck, still pitifully aggrieved, her mouth twitching as tears clung stubbornly to her cheeks.

Lu Chou felt a surge of vexation, his expression shifting between dark and darker shades.

What was this situation?

Moments ago, he had sworn to throw someone out; now he was completely disarmed by a small bundle of tears. He silently cursed himself a thousand times over.

From the corner of his eye, he noticed Liang Jin standing stiffly nearby, wearing an awkward expression while desperately holding back a laugh. At once, Lu Chou's temper flared anew.

"What are you looking at?" he snapped, his cold gaze sharp as a blade. "Too idle? Shall I throw you out as well?"

Liang Jin shuddered hard, bowed hastily, and replied:

"This humble one shall withdraw at once!"

He spun around and fled as though escaping for his life—yet inwardly he could not help complaining:

Their lord clearly treated Miss Baor like a little ancestor, yet insisted on pretending otherwise.

With the steward gone, only the two of them remained in the room.

Lu Chou lowered his gaze to the child still clinging tightly around his neck. At last, he let out a silent sigh and shifted his arms to hold her more securely.

—Forget it. Dealing with that Xiao woman can wait. For now, calming this little one takes priority. Otherwise she'll cry endlessly… and he'll end up with a pounding headache.

Inwardly, he made a quiet decision:

Since she refuses to come collect the child, then from this day on… he would not return her.

* * * * *

Only then did Baor's sobs gradually quieten.

She lifted her tear-streaked face, eyes still swollen and shimmering, and whispered with a trembling, nasal voice:

"Then… my lord mustn't be angry anymore…"

Lu Chou's heart twisted in a way he had not prepared for.

He had endured countless storms on the battlefield with a steady mind, yet at this moment—faced with a small child clinging to him—he found himself utterly at a loss.

After a long silence, he let out a faint sigh, lowered his voice, and asked:

"Baor… on ordinary days, who usually stays with you?"

Baor rubbed her eyes with the back of her tiny hand, leaving faint streaks across her cheeks. Her voice was soft as cotton:

"Grandpa is sick… he lies in bed and doesn't move. Mama is always very busy. Auntie Suyue and Auntie Suxin play with me. And the brothers and sisters in the courtyard…"

At this point, her head dropped slightly.

Her little hand pinched the corner of her clothes.

"Sometimes… sometimes I see Mama arguing with people. Great-uncles are very fierce to Mama… I was scared, so I didn't dare speak."

A cold shadow crossed Lu Chou's eyes.

Pieces of past suspicions slid neatly into place.

His voice unconsciously gentled:

"Then… have you ever met your father?"

Baor nodded seriously. Her bronze-coloured eyes seemed to glow:

"Baor doesn't have a papa. But Uncle Xie visits me. He brings toys. This year's Lantern Festival, he gave Baor a big bunny lantern…"

Lu Chou's heart lurched—painful and abrupt.

His expression darkened at once, a faint ache tightening beneath his ribs.

—Uncle Xie.

If he were truly the father…

A child would never add a surname.

A child would simply say Papa.

This "Uncle Xie" could only be Xie Huaici—

the man who had been by Xiao Lingyu's side for far too many years.

Before he could chase the thought further, Baor suddenly tilted her face up at him.

Her eyes sparkled through the remaining tears, her smile soft and bright:

"My lord… can you also be Baor's papa? Please?"

One soft plea—papa—

and Lu Chou felt something explode inside his chest.

A shock, sharp and unguarded.

He froze.

Completely unable to respond.

"Please? Please...?"

Baor wrapped her small arms tightly around his neck, her voice pleading and sticky with childish affection.

He swallowed.

His voice came out lower and rougher than he expected:

"...Why does Baor want me as your papa?"

"Because if Baor has more papas... there will be more people to give Baor presents."

Her deep bronze eyes shone like two warm glass beads—clear, earnest, impossibly trusting.

Despite himself, a helpless laugh slipped out.

"Please? Pleeaseee?"

She leaned closer, her cheek brushing his collar, wheedling in the way only a small child could.

His throat tightened painfully.

And before he could stop himself—

"...Very well."

The moment it left his lips, he stiffened—

too late to take it back.

Baor's joy arrived instantly and explosively.

She clapped her hands, eyes curving into two bright crescents:

"Waaah—wonderful! Baor has another papa now!"

She bounced twice on his knee, giggling breathlessly as she hugged him tightly.

Lu Chou, however, sat frozen.

His expression stiffened, his mind tangled into a hopeless knot.

He, who had always been sharp, cold, and unyieldingly rational was now addressed as papa by a child he had taken as leverage.

A child who, paradoxically, now had him firmly within her tiny grasp.

—This situation is becoming more dangerous than any battlefield.

He lowered his gaze.

The child nestled against him, still smiling through her lingering tears and an odd, stinging warmth spread painfully beneath his stern ribs.

Just then, Liang Jin peeked from the doorway.

He happened to hear the crisp, innocent shout—

"Another papa!"

—and froze stiff.

"My lord…" He barely uttered half a word before a frigid glare pinned him to the spot.

Lu Chou turned his head; his voice, though cold, carried a strange new softness:

"Pass down my order. From this day forth… treat Miss Baor exactly as this official's own daughter. None shall neglect her."

Liang Jin blinked, stunned, then bowed hastily:

"Errr–yes, my lord."

Chapter 28: A Gathering Storm at the Revenue Bureau

Within the Imperial City walls, the winds of change had already begun to surge. Within the Ministry of Revenue's offices, several officials were gathered around a table, their voices low and hushed.

"The matter of the Jiangnan tax silver still remains unsettled to this day. I fear the Imperial Weaving Bureau is likely to incur a grave charge this time. This affair... will probably drag the Ministry of Revenue down as well."

"Hmph, Lu Chou, the Deputy Minister of Revenue, has always been known for his iron-clad impartiality. Yet, if his hand reaches so far now, it is likely not possible for him to act without a special edict from the Emperor."

"I hear the Emperor has inquired three times recently, and each time, his questions concerned the affairs of Jiangnan—"

Before his voice finished, a clear, cold voice drifted from outside the door: "The matters of Jiangnan concern the very foundation of the state. Chou shall certainly not fail to uphold the Sacred Mandate."

Upon hearing the voice, the assembled officials immediately rose. They performed their salutations one by one. The man who entered was precisely Lu Wenqian, the Minister of Personnel.

He wore a robe of deep black. His temples were slightly grey, yet his expression did not diminish in authority.

He strode into the hall. His gaze swept across the room. His voice was like polished steel: "Lu Chou is the son of this Official, but he is still a man of the Ministry of Revenue. If he makes a single investigative error, not only will he himself be difficult to protect, but this Official cannot escape responsibility either. Regarding this matter, all of you must speak and act with extreme caution."

The cohort of officials exchanged glances. They immediately fell silent.

Lu Wenqian raised a hand, signalling them to withdraw. He only kept his closest personal assistant within the chamber.

He remained silent for a moment. He slowly opened his mouth: "Send word to Jiangnan. Instruct the Master Chou to return to the Capital immediately.

The matter of the tax silver concerns the foundation of the state. The Emperor has inquired three times in succession. This matter must be thoroughly investigated without delay, and he must return to report on his duties."

The personal assistant hesitated and asked: "Master, if the Master Chou has not been able to conclude the investigation fully, what then should be done?"

Lu Wenqian's expression subtly changed. He gave a cold sneer: "There is no need to investigate every detail thoroughly. What the Emperor truly seeks to investigate is not the corrupt officials, but... hmph."

* * * * *

Within the Eastern Palace, at the very same moment.

The Crown Prince Chen Gen was draped in a thin cloak, standing beside the railing outside. The wind swept from the Imperial Lake, rustling the remaining withered lotus leaves.

Imperial Preceptor Shen stood to one side, his voice low and deep: "Your Highness's prediction was not mistaken. The Jiangnan silk tax case implicates the silver network of several prefectures.

If Lord Lu Chou holds substantive power, and if we can bring Lu Chou into our fold, it is equivalent to the Eastern Palace gaining control over half of the Ministry of Revenue."

The Crown Prince smiled faintly, yet the coldness in his eyes was sharp as a knife: "Both he and his father know how to read the times. But if we do not add fuel to the flames of the Jiangnan situation, how will we know who will be the first to get burned?"

Imperial Preceptor Shen was slightly startled: "Your Highness intends to—"

The Crown Prince turned. His folding fan swayed lightly in his hand. His tone was gentle, yet seemingly laced with venom: "Send word to the Third Prince's residence. Tell him the Eastern Palace is willing to observe this situation jointly with him. We shall see what the Third Brother plans to do next."

"The Third Prince's side also seems to be waiting and observing. It appears he also intends to bring Lu Chou into his fold."

The Crown Prince's thin lips curled slightly. "It is not only Lu Chou in the Lu family. Do not forget, Lu Chou has an illegitimate elder brother, Lu Xiu, who is young and has already begun to distinguish himself in the military."

Imperial Preceptor Shen frowned slightly. "He is merely an illegitimate son. Your Highness overestimates his importance."

The Crown Prince raised his hand and shook it. "Although he is an illegitimate son, he is the eldest illegitimate son of Minister Lu. At a young age, he has already achieved minor military merit. He also appears to be a capable individual. This person should be included among those under observation. We must not underestimate him merely because of his illegitimate birth."

"Your Highness is wise and discerning."

Following this, the Crown Prince's tone remained level: "Minister Lu certainly has a knack for having capable children.

The Lu family not only has Lu Chou, but also the eldest illegitimate son, Lu Xiu, both of whom are capable, clever men.

Especially Lu Xiu, due to his illegitimate status, may harbor greater ambition for power. If this man is not secured carefully, he may become an unpredictable variable in the future. He must absolutely not be underestimated."

This final phrase scattered on the wind outside the hall, like a covert line of influence. No one knew that this 'unpredictable variable' would truly become the crucial pivot point in the subsequent political game.

Imperial Preceptor Shen cupped his hands: "Your Highness speaks correctly."

The Crown Prince's smile was faint. His voice was almost inaudible in the wind: "The rain in Jiangnan should become heavier still."

* * * * *

As summer approached, the Yangtze River waters rose. At the Yangzhou dockyard, thousands of sails formed a forest. Silk, porcelain, and tea bricks flowed northwards, and merchant ships returned fully laden.

However, the atmosphere at the dockyard today was heavy with an eerie silence.

Since the Chen hour (7-9 AM), three large ships fully laden with new Jiangnan silks had been jointly detained by the Imperial Weaving Bureau and the Salt Administration, ostensibly to inspect for anomalies in the silk tax silver notes.

The goods were sealed and the manifests audited on the spot, leaving many merchants in constant dread.

One merchant knelt before the cabin, ceaselessly kowtowing and begging for mercy, only to be kicked aside by a government soldier, who said coldly: "This is by new order of the Deputy Minister of the Board of Revenue. Violators will be charged with tax evasion."

The river wind carried moisture, disturbing the silks within the cabins, which billowed white like waves. The porters, tea vendors, and boatmen along the pier dared not speak, only watching from a distance. Several foremen gathered secretly behind a tea stall, whispering their concerns.

"This affair will likely lead to great disaster."

"I hear the target of this audit is the Jinhua Establishment's cargo."

"Jinhua? That truly means someone has been grievously provoked!"

"Who can say no? If this has truly touched Lord Lu's bad fortune, not even a celestial being can guarantee protection."

The Deputy Minister of the Board of Revenue and Circulating Weaving Inspector? The merchants of Yangzhou were all suspicious.

The Ministry of Revenue had recently seen a new appointment— precisely that cold, impartial official, Lu Chou, who, having been transferred from the Capital less than half a year, had employed thunderous methods, overturning several local tax offices.

Even the Yongchang Firm was apprehensive.

Someone whispered: "If one truly offends Lord Lu, I fear their family fortunes will be overturned completely."

The rumour spread quickly, like fire, reaching a fever pitch, as if the entirety of Jiangnan was holding its breath in the stillness preceding a storm.

* * * * *

Within the Imperial Weaving Bureau, Lu Chou reviewed the warehouse manifests submitted that day. His fingertip lightly tapped the desk.

His voice devoid of any change in tone: "Investigate thoroughly within three days. If a single ounce of tax-evaded silver is found, immediately seize the family assets and charge them with a crime."

Liang Jin reminded him in a low voice: "Master, if you strike so fiercely, I fear it will incur dissatisfaction from various factions at court, and even... Master Lu (his father) might take notice."

"I, conversely, wish to see who dares to use this Official's name to carry out such deeds," Lu Chou gave a cold laugh, killing intent faintly showing in his eyes.

Recently, rumours had grown thick. His aging father in the Capital sent a private letter, intending to counsel him to 'act with caution' and 'return to the Capital immediately.' Various powerful factions were subtly moving, all waiting for him to stumble and fall from power.

He closed his eyes briefly. The scene of the Jiangnan mists and the thousands of sails lined up surfaced in his mind. Beneath the seemingly calm surface of the water, dangerous undercurrents surged.

Someone seeks to launder silver via the silk tax, and the Yongchang Firm is merely one link visible on the surface.

Concurrently, inside the Jinhua Establishment.

Xiao Lingyu assembled her weavers, urgently ordering an audit of the accounts. Steward Wu's expression was grave: "Madam, three major clients withdrew their orders today, the bank refused a loan, and the dockyard seized our cargo. Someone clearly intends to cut off our means of livelihood completely."

"It is nothing; endure it for now." Xiao Lingyu knew the situation well, yet her expression was extraordinarily calm.

She retrieved the old ledgers from three years past, meticulously checking page after page: "Inform the staff below that regardless of the rumours, they must continue what should be done and guard what should be guarded. Do not concern yourselves with anything else."

The foreman hesitated: "Madam, should we not... request assistance from Lord Lu?"

"No." Xiao Lingyu shook her head, her gaze clear and cold as water: "When I politely declined the overtures from the Capital before, it was in the hope that our innocence would protect our lives. If we now cling to Lord Lu, it will only confirm the charge of 'collusion.'"

Having spoken, she looked up towards the low, oppressive clouds outside the window. She knew in her heart that this was not a commercial war, but a political struggle in the court. The blade hung over their heads, and one wrong step meant complete ruin.

Lu Chou listened to the report, his fingertip pausing, and then suddenly gave a cold laugh: "The mastermind behind this possesses extremely ingenious methods. They both force Xiao Lingyu into a dead end and simultaneously push this Official into the eye of the storm. What is more ingenious—if this Official now steps in to assist her, it will perfectly confirm the charge of colluding with merchants."

Liang Jin bowed low: "Master, has the identity of the person behind this already become clear to you?"

"There is no need to act pre-emptively. Merely toss out the fuse, and the snake will inevitably reveal itself."

Having said this, he raised his hand and struck the desk. Cold light surged in his eyes: "Go and conduct a covert investigation. Find out if the Yongchang Firm has recently held any secret meetings with figures from the Capital. Then, send word to the Jinhua Establishment, telling them... if they can hold their ground, they should hold their ground. If they cannot hold their ground, they should not bother coming to seek my help."

"This... you will not help Madam Xiao?" Liang Jin looked surprised. He privately thought the Lord would immediately order assistance for Madam Xiao.

"Help her?" Lu Chou sneered.

Liang Jin paused: "Master, you will simply... let go?"

A trace of complex emotion flashed in Lu Chou's eyes: "If I do not let go, she will perish even faster."

He finished speaking. Silence reigned for the time it took to drink half a cup of tea. The wind blew in through the curtains. The lamp flame flickered. His expression was cold and severe as iron. The thread of unease in his heart was finally suppressed into the deepest depths.

"Have the horse prepared," he instructed softly. "We return to the headquarters."

Outside the window, black clouds churned, and thunder rumbled faintly. The case of the Jiangnan Silk Merchant Contribution had begun. A battle of invisible blades had just commenced.

Chapter 29: A Blade Borrowed

The Capital. Prince Jing's Residence — Side Hall.

Soft cloud-patterned drapes hung low, layers of gauze falling like drifting mist. Incense smoke coiled quietly through the still air.

The Third Prince, Chen Song, reclined upon a couch, clad in a long robe of blue silk woven with muted silver cloud motifs. In his hand, he idly stroked a warm, lustrous jade pendant. His gaze appeared languid, yet beneath it lay a trace of cold detachment.

Only one man stood before him—Lu Xiu, the Lu family's eldest son by birth, though born of a concubine.
Courtesy name: Ji Heng.

"How does the situation in Jiangnan progress?" Chen Song asked. His voice was gentle, yet carried an authority that brooked no refusal.

Lu Xiu lowered his head and replied, "In reply to Your Highness, the six major silk houses are already under pressure. The canal guilds and the money banks are cooperating as arranged. Outside, it is widely believed that Lu Chou, under the pretext of inspecting the silk tax, has begun a sweeping campaign of accusations.

The board has been set. Of the six great silk houses, five have already shifted their stance and are willing to cooperate with tribute. Only Jin Hua Hall remains isolated."

"So smooth a course?" Chen Song's tone retained a hint of indolent skepticism.

"Your Highness's fortune is boundless," Lu Xiu replied.

Chen Song's brow lifted slightly, the corner of his lips curling into a half-smile that was neither amusement nor warmth.

"Heh. Clever indeed. When silver and survival are placed side by side, who still wastes breath on loyalty? In this way, at least the funds have found their source."

His fingers tapped lightly against a jade cup. The Third Prince narrowed his eyes, his voice lowering.

"Father has grown increasingly attentive to the Crown Prince of late. Yesterday's Jiangnan tribute tea was granted to him alone."

The words were light, but carried a chill beneath.

He lowered his gaze, tracing the rim of the cup, as though speaking to himself—or testing the man before him.

"If we do not plan ahead, once the Crown Prince's momentum swells and Father lends him full support, I fear it will be our turn to be utterly crushed."

A flash of cold light crossed his eyes, as if further words remained unsaid.

Lu Xiu gave a slight bow. "The six silk houses have already moved. The people I arranged, acting under Lu Chou's name, have applied pressure to Jin Hua Hall and several other major firms. At present, five have expressed willingness to lean toward the Eastern Palace. Only Jin Hua Hall stands apart."

"Mhm." Chen Song smiled faintly, fingers tapping the jade table. "This time, we act under the Eastern Palace's name. As long as Father believes it, the Crown Prince—"

The sandalwood incense lingered. Chen Song reclined half against the couch, his words trailing off, fingers slowly tapping the cup's rim, leaving the sentence unfinished.

"Father's favor toward the Eastern Palace grows daily. The matter of the exclusive tribute tea, in my view, was merely a test. But if we allow the Crown Prince's influence to grow unchecked, we shall become fish trapped in a jar."

Lu Xiu stood respectfully at his side, head lowered. "As Your Highness planned, I have already instructed men in Jiangnan to coerce wealthy merchants and silk houses into offering tribute under the name of the Eastern Palace. The momentum has been fully established."

"Then I shall simply sit and wait for the net to close." Chen Song lifted a small jade cup toward his lips, a cold curve forming at the edge of his mouth. "Once Father harbors true doubt toward the Crown Prince, the day of our success will not be far."

Lu Xiu's gaze remained lowered, his expression unchanged. "Your Highness speaks with reason. His Majesty dispatched Lu Chou south precisely because he does not fully trust the Eastern Palace. He seeks to trace the flow of Jiangnan silk tax silver—particularly whether funds have entered the private coffers of princes.

At this moment, His Majesty already harbors suspicion toward the Crown Prince. This is precisely the opportunity for Your Highness to bring him down—acting in the Eastern Palace's name…"

"Exactly." Chen Song gave a low chuckle. "Borrowing a knife to kill."

He paused, his gaze darkening. Then, turning his head slightly, he asked, "Your brother Lu Chou has now been pushed to the forefront of the storm. Do you harbor any resentment?"

At this, Lu Xiu's lips curved faintly. His expression was like ripples across an icy lake—no true emotion stirred.

"I was born of a concubine, yet the elder; he is born legitimate, yet younger. Since childhood, I have been told I am inferior and should yield to him. Now that we stand in the court, it is only fitting to contend by merit.

Brotherly affection? I have never dared to expect it. If he blocks my path, I will block him in turn. If he loses within this scheme, it is not by my blade. He may only blame his own insufficiency—where, then, would guilt arise?"

He continued calmly, "So much the better. This time, let him become the scapegoat for this rotten affair. If His Majesty is enraged, neither the Eastern Palace nor Lu Chou will escape unscathed."

"Your Highness is wise," Lu Xiu said with a respectful nod.

Chen Song lightly stroked the jade cup, his gaze distant. "Ji Heng… if this breaks your brother's edge, it clears an obstacle from your heart. Do not soften your hand."

Lu Xiu smiled faintly, his tone neither servile nor defiant. "I understand. My legitimate brother and I have always walked separate paths. I bear no guilt."

"Yes," Chen Song said slowly. "If Lu Chou falls, you will become the Lu family's sole successor. This opportunity must not be wasted."

"Your Highness speaks truly."

Chen Song studied him for a moment, then smiled with faint amusement. "Heh. So utterly devoid of familial sentiment—truly ruthless. That is the kind of man capable of great deeds. And such talent is precisely what I require."

"Thank you for Your Highness's praise," Lu Xiu replied, bowing.

"Good." Chen Song narrowed his eyes, his voice turning cold. "Beyond the Crown Prince, I have also sensed Father's increasing favor toward Consort Yi and the Fourth Prince. The situation cannot be treated lightly. We must cultivate influence, grease all channels, and raise private forces. Silver is indispensable. Jiangnan's offerings are one of the foundations.

If we can use the Jiangnan merchants to amass wealth for ourselves, who will dare move against me in the future?"

Lu Xiu lowered his head. "This humble servant first congratulates Your Highness on achieving eternal success."

"So," Chen Song said slowly, "we are bound to the same vessel, Ji Heng. Do not forget—should I ascend the throne in the future, you shall have a place beside me. I will not fail to repay today's assistance."

Lu Xiu replied calmly, "I thank Your Highness for your patronage."

For a moment, silence reigned within the hall. Incense smoke rose gently, illuminating the two men, each harboring separate designs.

Though the tone remained mild, a sharp glint passed through Chen Song's eyes.

"This matter must be handled with utmost caution. Success or ruin hinges upon this single move. Should your brother truly uncover any traces in Jiangnan, implicating our hidden arrangements, and report them to court—once Father hears of it, neither you nor I may escape unscathed. Our very lives may be forfeit."

Lu Xiu's expression did not change. He lowered his gaze and answered, "Your Highness may rest assured. Since I have boarded this vessel, I understand the wind is fierce and the waves high. I do not seek safe retreat, nor do I fear utter ruin."

He paused, then lifted his eyes to meet the Third Prince's gaze directly. Within them burned a trace of cold resolve and battle intent.

"As for my legitimate brother… if he truly uncovers the truth, Your Highness need not worry. I will not show mercy. From birth, we were divided by legitimacy. We were never of the same path. This time, let him learn—within court politics, there is no room for brotherly sentiment."

Chen Song chuckled softly, approval and darkness mingling in his eyes.

"Good." He nodded slowly. "With those words, I am at ease. Still—this borrowed-knife scheme, conducted under the Eastern Palace's name, is no small matter. A single misstep could result in the crime of exterminating an entire clan."

Lu Xiu clasped his hands. "This humble servant understands."

Chen Song sat back, sleeves folded, the cold light in his eyes unextinguished.

"What of the Crown Prince?" he murmured. "Before the summit is reached, who can say who the final victor will be?"

The game remained unsettled. Victory and defeat were yet unknown. Every chess piece must be placed with care.

That night, the Prince Jing's residence glowed faintly with lamplight. Curtains swayed. Wind murmured softly. The two men concealed their thoughts deep within. The machinery of power had only just begun to turn.

A crystal lamp cast reflections over scrolls embroidered with golden dragon patterns upon the desk. Beneath the eaves, bead curtains chimed softly in the wind.

Within the hall, both men stood composed as still water.

Chen Song reclined upon a carved zitan chair, wide sleeves draped loosely, his features refined and calm, his bearing steady and composed. He lifted a cup of freshly brewed osmanthus wine to his lips—yet did not drink, as though weighing an unresolved game upon the board.

Below him, Lu Xiu stood respectfully. A white jade crown bound his hair; his dark robe lay smooth and orderly. His expression was mild, yet within his eyes lurked a trace of vigilance and calculation.

The lights flickered in the hall, casting shifting shadows that made the expressions of the two men appear even more unfathomable.

Readers can view the full collection of colour illustrations here:
https://www.facebook.com/profile.php?id=61581325000577

Chapter 30: A Commoner's Resolve

The night deepened. In a corner by the side gate of the Prince Song's Residence, the rusted, dark-green gate quietly opened.

The moonlight was cold as water. It reflected softly upon the blue paving stones. The distant barking of dogs was swallowed by the wind and sank into silence.

The street was so still that only the swaying shadows of the trees remained.

Lu Xiu slowly stepped out, his hands clasped behind his back. His cloak lifted slightly in the wind. The conversation, which had been like a game of chess, left aftershocks lingering in his mind.

He knew he need not have entered this political game. Yet, unfortunately... In his father's eyes, he was perpetually the "eldest son by a concubine," while Lu Chou was the legitimate branch, the true heir to the Lu family's legacy.

His father might never have vocalized it, but Lu Xiu understood this distinction from his youth.

What did that ultimately matter?

In this imperial game of power, who ascends to the top and who crashes to the ground is fundamentally a gamble where fate is undecided. If one desires to live higher and longer, one must fight for one's own path.

He walked out past the mansion wall. The night wind blew against his face, dissipating some of the suppressed frustration in his heart.

The wind passed the bamboo shadows, creating a soft rustling sound. It was as if someone was whispering in the darkness.

A figure emerged from the shadows. It was He Qi, his personal guard, who walked closely at his side, asking softly: "My Lord, the Prince's words today were placid, but he may not be entirely truthful. Ought we to dispatch someone... to subtly explore his hidden intentions?"

Lu Xiu's steps paused slightly. He cast a faint glance at his guard, a thread of coldness contained in the corner of his lips: "There is no need to probe. Nothing substantial will be revealed."

He Qi's expression tightened. He immediately lowered his voice: "My Lord, since we cannot reveal anything substantial, should we at least send men to monitor the movements inside and outside the princely residence more closely?"

Lu Xiu heard the question. His lips curved slightly. His voice was low and indifferent: "The princely residence is a place of great importance; how can we arbitrarily probe? This game has just begun. If we act with excessive haste, we will easily leave traces."

"My Lord speaks correctly." He Qi saluted respectfully.

Lu Xiu raised his hand and smoothed his sleeve. His tone was calm: "Currently, I still need to utilize the Prince of Jing's influence. If I carelessly fail to conceal my intentions now, I will ruin the entire situation myself. He Qi, remember this clearly: we only do what we must do now. Since we have boarded the Third Prince's ship, we must heed his instructions and make no rash moves."

He Qi lowered his head in compliance, secretly admiring his master's composure and deep reserve.

The night wind brushed his profile. The candlelight flickered in his eyes. That expression was no longer the fierce ambition of a young military officer, but the stillness of one who has successfully concealed his blade.

Lu Xiu's gaze deepened. He resumed his steps, murmuring softly: "The situation of this Empire, who is the true King and who is the false King, has not yet reached the moment of revelation—I, for one, am not in a hurry."

He Qi said in a steady voice: "Although that is true, the Prince, in normal times, relies heavily upon your Lordship..."

"Relies heavily?" Lu Xiu scoffed softly. He turned his head to gaze at the distant, dark sky. His words were interwoven with coldness: "Though I am the eldest illegitimate son, my entire life has been barred from ascending the hall of the legitimate lineage. During the time Father held that small child, the one with the nickname Chou'er, in his arms, did he ever once recall that I, too, was his eldest son?"

That voice was faint, as if swallowed by the night.

He suddenly gave a humourless laugh, whispering even softer: "Some measure of a father's favour was always reserved for the legitimate son. If an illegitimate son desires to leave his name in history, he must earn it through his own struggle."

His voice scattered far away. The wind swept down the long street. The lamplight shook, casting light on his profile, making his contours appear heavy and resolute as iron.

"Now, who will win and who will lose is yet unknown." Lu Xiu's tone was stable and cold: "The Prince views me merely as a useful piece on his chessboard. Since that is the case, I shall assume the role of that piece—but remember this: when to move, when to retreat, when to act as the general, and when to act as the pawn, all reside in my own heart, not in the hands of others."

He Qi bowed his head in affirmation.

Secretly alarmed: The Master's mind is clearly not comparable to that of common military officers.

Lu Xiu inhaled lightly. His gaze turned cold. Having finished speaking, he paused slightly. A thread of dark, indistinct light flickered in his eyes: "It is you, however, He Qi, who has spoken excessively today— are you perhaps afraid?"

He Qi was slightly startled. He immediately smiled, bowed, and said softly: "Since this subordinate has pledged himself to the Master, I will follow you to the very end. Fear or no fear, those two words do not exist in my vocabulary."

Lu Xiu heard this, and his expression softened slightly. He gazed at the sparse starlight in the night sky and suddenly let out a low chuckle: "So be it then." "Now that my legitimate younger brother has found his path, and I have found my own chosen path, we have entered the game, and we will not be led by the nose by others."

He Qi lowered his head in assent: "Yes."

Lu Xiu resumed his steps, his voice low and deep: "This game in the Capital, I fear, will be far more difficult to navigate than the troubles in Jiangnan. If I succeed, I will secure my own position. If I fail—it may not necessarily be worse than the situation I am in now."

"This subordinate swears to follow the Master until death."

Lu Xiu waved his hand dismissively: "Let us go now. Find a place to drink."

The moment the words ceased, the figures of the two men merged into the darkness of the night. A sliver of the waning moon hid behind the clouds.

The wind swept down the long street, and the lamplight on the eaves flickered, as if shadows were moving in the darkness.

He Qi gripped his sword and followed closely. His eyes moved slightly.

He knew his Master's disposition had only deepened further after leaving the Third Prince's residence today—if they were truly to proceed against the current in the future, this version of Lu Xiu might not be without opportunities to seize the throne.

The long street was cold and still. The lamplight was dim.

A distant bell sound drifted from the Imperial Palace, the tolls echoing, as if narrating a silent opening move. The game of power had just begun to unfold silently.

* * * * *

The afternoon light was soft and still. The wind from outside the curtain carried the humidity of early summer. Xiao Lingyu gently pushed open the door of the chamber. The scent of medicine and herbs immediately greeted her.

On the bed, the elderly Master Xiao leaned against the pillow. Half of his face had lost expression. His gaze was scattered.

Since that stroke, his speech was impaired, and his hands and feet trembled slightly. He could only respond with his eyes.

The nursemaid by the bed quickly rose to perform a salute, saying softly: "Madam, the Master's colour is slightly better today. However, he did not take any porridge this morning."

Xiao Lingyu nodded slightly. She placed the food container in her hand down. Her voice was extremely light: "It is fine. We will proceed slowly. Has the medicinal decoction been administered on time?"

"It has been administered twice. The physician warned that he must avoid anger and damp cold recently." The nursemaid answered fearfully.

She walked close to the bed and quietly looked at that face, now marked by fatigue. The once dignified head of the family could now only raise his hand with difficulty and slight trembling.

Her throat tightened.

Yet she still forced a smile: "Father, your daughter has come to see you."

Master Xiao seemed to understand. His eyes moved slightly. He raised his finger minutely. That movement was so subtle it was almost invisible, yet it brought a sourness to her eyes.

She sat down, retrieved a handkerchief, and poured a bowl of warm water, carefully wetting the corner of the cloth.

As her fingertips touched his rough palm, the warmth in his hand trembled slightly, as if separated by the coldness of time.

"Father, please do not worry. I have arranged everything for the family and the workshop. You only need to recuperate well and recover quickly."

"Uh... uh..." Master Xiao's eyes turned, his mouth and eyes slightly twisted. He could only let out whimpering sounds.

"Your hands are cold again." She murmured softly, slowly and meticulously wiping between his fingers, washing away the faint yellow medicine stains on his palm.

The nursemaid attempted to approach, but Xiao Lingyu raised her hand, signalling her to retreat.

Only she and her father remained in the room. It was so quiet that she could hear the sound of the bamboo shadows swaying outside the window.

"Please do not worry," she said softly, her voice pitched low as if afraid of waking someone. "The Jinhua Establishment is doing well. The embroiderers are still working, and business has not been cut off. Mother, if she knew this from heaven, would certainly be relieved. As for my brother's whereabouts, your daughter is still searching. I will not give up searching for my brother for a single day."

Master Xiao's fingers moved slightly, as if attempting to grip her hand. She paused, then covered his hand with her own, her touch gentle yet firm.

After a long while, she carefully wrung the handkerchief dry and covered her father with the blanket before saying softly: "Father, once your health is restored, perhaps Brother will have also returned. At that time, I will take you everywhere to see the sights. The scenery outside the city is lovely in the spring."

Her voice was soft, yet subtly conveyed a suppressed sob.

As she rose, her peripheral vision swept over the dim light outside the window. A faint pain gripped her heart—in former years, her father stood in the hall, reprimanding officials. Now, only silence remained. And she had no path of retreat, forced to support the remnants of the Xiao family with her own sole strength.

Chapter 31: Resolve at the Precipice

Outside the government offices of Jiangnan, the night was profound and heavy, with only a faint, flickering glimmer of lamplight bleeding through the window paper.

Lu Chou stood before a mountain of dossiers, draped in a slightly worn, indigo official robe. His expression was grim as the silk tax ledgers were spread out before him, their dense thickets of numbers reflecting in the depths of his eyes.

He had worked through three consecutive nights without rest; his eyes were shot through with crimson veins, yet he felt no exhaustion whatsoever.

"My Lord".

A soft double-knock sounded at the door. Liang Jin entered with a bow, cradling a black-edged private ledger in his hands. He reported in a low, hushed whisper, "We have found it. This is a duplicate of the shadow accounts for the Yongchang Firm and the Jinshun Money House from the past six months. It appears an internal source risked their very life to transcribe it; it was only delivered tonight".

Lu Chou's gaze sharpened instantly. He reached out to take the volume, spreading it across the desk to scrutinize the entries with meticulous care.

After a few moments, his brow furrowed deeper and deeper. His knuckles absentmindedly tapped the corner of the desk, producing a hollow, low rhythmic thud.

"...To think there was such a convoluted transfer of hands," he murmured to himself, his gaze as piercing as a blade.

The records in the ledger were explicit: tens of thousands of bolts of Southeast Asian silk, which should have been subject to the silk tax, had been fraudulently reclassified on the books as "Imperial Tribute Silk" during transit. This allowed them to evade heavy duties, and beneath certain manifests, six characters were shockingly annotated: *Direct Supply for the Prince Jing Estate of the Capital*.

Direct supply for the Prince Jing Estate?

For a moment, Lu Chou could not discern whether this evidence was a definitive, iron-clad proof of the Third Prince and the Prince Jing

Estate's embezzlement, or a calculated frame-up by a rival intended to smear them.

A sudden gust of wind whistled outside, causing the eaves-lantern to flicker erratically; the dancing shadows moved across the ledgers in a fitful, unstable rhythm. Liang Jin remained silent, not daring to utter a sound, hearing only the faint, scratchy rasp of a trembling brush. In that moment, the entire room seemed swallowed by the night, leaving only the sound of Lu Chou's breathing intertwined with the scent of guttering candle wax.

The instant he finally looked up, his eyes held no trace of a civil official's calm. Instead, they burned with a fierce, unwavering determination—the kind of resolve born from being driven into an absolute corner.

He tapped the desk again and looked at Liang Jin, his voice low and deep. "Where did this ledger come from? Who would dare surrender the shadow accounts of Yongchang and Jinshun?"

Liang Jin bowed slightly, his tone steady and composed. "My Lord, it was discovered by Commander Ye's undercover network. Previously, you ordered Commander Ye to investigate the unusual flow of silver at the money house. It so happened that an accountant there was expelled due to a personal grudge. To protect himself, he fled with this duplicate and attempted to sell it to foreign spies. Fortunately, we received word first and intercepted the man, allowing us to obtain this volume".

Lu Chou nodded slightly, his brow arching. "A decisive fellow, indeed".

"Commander Ye is currently holding the accountant in secret," Liang Jin added in a low voice. "We have not alerted anyone else. We await your orders on how to proceed".

Lu Chou's eyes darkened. After a moment of contemplation, he said coldly, "Keep him steady. Make him divulge more of the internal truth. If there are secret contacts between the Eastern Palace, the Prince Jing Estate, and the Jiangnan operatives, we must identify every single one. Not a breath of this must leak out".

"Your subordinate understands".

Lu Chou lowered his gaze, his thumb slowly tracing the edge of the ledger. The chill in his expression deepened by several degrees.

As he turned the page, his finger suddenly stopped. His eyes locked onto a cryptic, hidden annotation in the accounts.

After reading further, a cold, mocking smirk curled his lips. "The Prince Jing Estate..."

—*By personal decree of the Eastern Palace Envoy, ten thousand taels of New Year congratulatory silver are to be offered, along with pearls, jades, and woven brocades, all to be delivered to the inner treasury of the Prince Jing Estate.*

The Prince Jing Estate—the residence of the Third Prince, Chen Song.

"...Heh." His thin lips parted in a low, cold laugh that betrayed a trace of irrepressible, bitter cynicism.

The Third Prince had actually used the Crown Prince's name to carry out this extortion, forcing the wealthy merchants of Jiangnan to pay tribute. Once the transactions were cleared, the wealth and goods flowed entirely into the private coffers of the Prince Jing Estate.

As he parsed the logic, a tremor of shock went through his heart—this was a ruthless and deadly gambit.

If the Jiangnan merchants did not know the truth and saw the visitors claiming to be envoys of the Eastern Palace, they would naturally view the silver as an act of fealty to the Crown Prince. Should the matter be exposed later, and the Emperor learn that the great magnates of Jiangnan were privately funding the Crown Prince, a single charge of "forming factions for private gain" would be enough to destroy him.

Meanwhile, the Third Prince would have secured a massive fortune while watching the Crown Prince's reputation be ruined—a perfect masterstroke of achieving two goals with one stone.

Lu Chou's knuckles rapped against the desk like stones falling into a deep well. He suddenly recalled the Third Prince's jade-like, gentle smile at court months ago. In this world, the most terrifying thing was never the blade, but the smile.

"The Third Prince... such ruthless methods".

Lu Chou's voice was icy, half-muttered to himself. A frost-like murderous intent surged in the depths of his eyes.

He had always held to a middle path, unwilling to lightly condemn the faults of the imperial brothers. But what he saw today suggested that the Third Prince's game was no longer about the succession—it was an intent to annihilate his rivals invisibly.

If the Third Prince dared to siphon such sums into his private treasury, ten thousand taels would not suffice his greed. He likely coveted not just the wealth of merchants, but the capital required to seize the throne in the future.

Lu Chou sat sideways at his desk, his knuckles tapping rhythmically. A dark aura of suppressed fury settled between his brows.

"Since you wish to use the Crown Prince's name to play this game, do not blame this official for following the vine to the root. I shall spread these rotten accounts out beneath the sun, one by one".

Seeing this, Liang Jin asked softly, "My Lord, shall we report this to the Capital immediately?"

Lu Chou shook his head, his voice deep and ghostly. "We cannot".

"Eh? Why not?" Liang Jin asked in confusion. The Emperor, the Court, and even the elder Master Lu were all urging Lu Chou to return to the Capital.

"What we have uncovered is merely the tip of the iceberg. Reporting it now would only alert the enemy. Furthermore, the Emperor's intent in sending me to investigate was to see if the Eastern Palace and the various princely estates were clean. If I point my finger at the Third Prince without complete evidence, and the Emperor intends to protect him, we will find ourselves charged with the crime of slandering a prince".

A cold sweat broke out across Liang Jin's back.

Lu Chou's gaze was shadowed, his voice like cold iron. "Moreover, if the Third Prince dares to take such a risk, he may already have other shields in the Capital. The Emperor has always detested his sons privately seizing tax sources. If this turns into a major scandal, it will cause a political upheaval that may not favor me".

"Then when do we strike?" Liang Jin whispered.

"Interrogate the man first. We will discuss this in the Capital once the evidence is ironclad." Lu Chou closed the ledger, his voice frigid. "In the meantime, continue the investigation in secret. Send a covert message to the Jinhua Establishment: tell them to hold their ground".

"Understood". Liang Jin took his orders and withdrew.

Silence returned to the room.

Lu Chou stood before the desk, his eyes dark. He had thought this trip was merely to excise a black hole in the silk tax, but he now realized this web of silk was a chessboard for the imperial princes' struggle for the throne.

He did not fear danger; he only feared the trap was too deep, and that he might fall into the net, bringing shame upon the entire Lu family.

At this thought, his gaze shifted slightly as a certain person came to mind.

"Xiao Lingyu..." he whispered softly.

Though she was calm and fierce, she might not know of the deeper game within the game. If she were dragged too far into the depths, she might not be able to save herself.

His fingers paused. He finally murmured, "So be it. Now that the game has begun, I must move with calculated steps".

Lu Chou did not pick up his brush for a long time. In the flickering candlelight, it was not just the intricate accounts that flashed through his mind, but her—the woman who could remain calm at the brink of disaster, yet carried everything alone. He had never asked why she left all those years ago, nor why she insisted on staying now. The current situation was no longer something she could sustain on her own. He... perhaps he ought to act.

With that thought, he set down his brush and gave a low command: "Liang Jin, prepare a secret scroll. I wish to write a letter personally". Finally, he closed the dossiers, his gaze clear and cold as a blade.

"Yes, My Lord".

The night grew deeper, but the lights remained burning. The ledgers were spread out once more, and the soft scratch of the brush resumed.

He dipped his brush in ink and wrote with swift, staccato strokes. Once this letter was sent, his intentions would be exposed to *that* person.

If the other party responded, he could turn the tide. If rejected, he could only fight to the death. He knew that he had long since ceased to be a mere bystander in this game.

The secret scroll was finished. Lu Chou handed it to Liang Jin to be dispatched, then called out coldly, "Summon Commander Ye at once".

Lu Chou would find no sleep this night.

Chapter 32: A Scheme Woven with Names

The night had not yet turned; the stillness in the rear hall of the Jiangnan Weaving Bureau's temporary office was dense as black water.

Inside a narrow chamber, the curtains hung half-lowered; the air pressed with the weight of unshed words.

Lu Chou entered, the hem of his indigo robe brushing the floor, his expression a quiet blend of fatigue and frost.

The rustle of ledgers ceased only when Liang Jin bent forward and said softly,

"My lord, that accountant, Li Wu, is still held in the side room. He refuses to confess further."

Lu Chou's eyes sharpened. "Bring him in."

Moments later, Captain Ye arrived with two guards, dragging in a man bound hand and foot, blood staining the corner of his mouth.

It was Li Wu of the Jinshun Bank—the keeper of the double ledgers.

The brazier beside them glowed dully; the iron tongs within were red-hot, and the air smelled faintly of burnt ash and fear.

"Untie him."

The ropes fell away. Li Wu collapsed to his knees, sweat running down his temples.

Lu Chou did not question at once. He leaned against the desk, unrolled a yellowed ledger, and turned the pages with unhurried grace.

His voice, when it came, was level as still water.

" Wu, you are a clever man. You have kept books for half the province; you know what ink can buy and what it can bury.

But you also know that by dawn, a man who keeps silent may have no tongue left to use."

Li Wu trembled, lips pale.

"Your Excellency, I… I know not what you mean. The accounts follow the old regulations—nothing more."

"Old regulations?" A faint laugh escaped Lu Chou.

He flicked open a page stamped by order of the Crown Prince's Office and let it fall upon the desk with a sharp crack.

"Is this also an old regulation?"

The accountant's pupils shrank; his breath came ragged, yet he clung to denial.

"I—I only copy what is decreed. The orders came from above…"

"Above?" Lu Chou's tone turned to iron.

"From Deputy Zhang? Adviser Yu? Or someone within The Third Prince's household?"

Li Wu's face drained of colour. He quivered, jaw tight as though to keep his teeth from chattering.

At last he bowed his head and whispered,

"I dare not lie. Your Excellency… I was forced—"

"By whom?"

The man's restraint cracked. Tears and sweat mingled on his cheeks.

"It was The Third Prince's men, my lord! They threatened to ruin my family if I refused. The order came through the Jiangnan gentry themselves."

Liang Jin gave a cold laugh and clapped his hands. "Good loyalty. Bring his wife and children here, then—we shall let him explain in front of them, so they may all die knowing why."

The threat struck like thunder. Li Wu jerked upright, crying out,

"No! Please—spare them! My Mama is old—my children—"

"So you do fear something," Lu Chou said quietly, his gaze cutting through him.

"Then hear me once more. Why was Jin Hua Hall singled out? Who gave the order to crush its trade and install another in its stead?"

The men will broke. He threw himself forward, forehead striking the floor, voice hoarse with despair.

"It was Deputy Zhang and Adviser Yu, my lord! They said a woman must not head a merchant house—that a proper family man would be easier for the capital to manage.

They claimed if Jin Hua Hall were not destroyed, other guilds might follow its example and refuse bribes—then the entire design above would collapse!"

"Above?" Lu Chou's brows drew tight, his voice cold enough to burn.

"Who—exactly—is above?"

"…I don't know… I only know that Adviser Yu sent word from the capital, saying the orders came from some high person in the capital. I dared not ask further…"

Lu Chou's laugh was dry and thin; his eyes went colder. He cut the air with a single, lethal sentence. "Speak plainly. Is it the Prince Song's household? The Crown Prince's? Which gentry families?"

"I…I truly do not know…" Li Wu trembled, sweat beading at his brow.

Lu Chou stood with his hands folded behind his back, his face dark as a storm. He ceased the blunt torment and, in a voice that had turned quietly ruthless, asked, "You claim ignorance on the left and ignorance on the right — then are the ledgers you copied even true?"

"I—"

Lu Chou snorted; his expression hardened into something like a judge's. "If you answer with nothing but 'I don't know,' what use are you kept for? Bring them — bring Li Wu's whole family out here at once—"

At that, Li Wu screamed in horror. "My lord! My lord! I'll speak, I'll speak—"

Liang Jin kicked him. "His lord commands you to speak — are you still thinking to hesitate?"

Li Wu cried out from the pain, then broke into a new confession: "The Cui family, the Zhang family… and the Liu family. The patrons instructed: Jin Hua Hall's steward is a woman, surname Xiao — headstrong and refusing to take bribes. How can others be expected to follow if she will not yield? If she is left to run things, other guilds will imitate her insolence and refuse the customary gifts. So they said we must press hard in the silk taxes, disrupt her shop's trade, force her to submit or step aside, and put a male family manager in her place so the patrons can control things."

The room fell suddenly silent.

Li Wu's forehead hit the floor; blood trickled from a gash.

His voice was barely audible, shaking: "My lord, I did not dare ask more… I only heard that there are people in Prince Song's household who have secret lines into the Imperial Household Office. If the Jiangnan guilds do not pay, their books will be quietly inspected, or the tax bureau will look for faults. Jin Hua refused, and so they drew their ire… I thought that man was merely using Jin Hua Hall's name for an official quarrel — never did I imagine it would reach as far as a prince's mansion!"

Silence held the hall. Liang Jin's face went hard. "So, Prince Song's household, and this phrase 'they were afraid' — charming."

Captain Ye spoke in a low voice: "My lord, if Prince Song's household is involved, this is no small clerk's doing. Li Wu risking copying out these secret ledgers was already a desperate act; I suspect there are scapegoats buried deeper yet."

Lu Chou's expression darkened further. The pen in his hand paused; the nib tore the paper and the ink bled like a small wound.

He rose and stood in the centre of the chamber, looking down at Li Wu. His voice dropped to a level that left no room to hide: "You knew this reached far. Why then did you risk copying the books? Who told you to copy them?"

Li Wu trembled so that even his whisper was a mosquito's buzz: "…Someone at the bank whispered that if the genuine ledgers were delivered out, my family would be spared."

"Who?" Lu Chou's tone was an ice-break.

"They said… they said it was from someone claiming to be of Jin Hua Hall."

The little room felt as if wind had swept through it; the candle flames shuddered. Liang Jin's eyes widened. "Jin Hua Hall?"

Lu Chou's face did not change; his gaze fell, his knuckles went tight.

The lantern threw hard shadows across his features; his mouth pressed into a thin line.

He recovered his calm with the speed of a blade sheathing. "Nonsense. Xiao Lingyu would not stoop to such tricks. If you cast about and accuse recklessly, you will find what justice can do to those who speak falsely."

For a moment an image flashed across his mind — Xiao Lingyu in court that day, pale but forcing herself to meet his eyes.

She could bend when needed; she could be stubborn and proud; but she was not the sort to gamble her name on such a risk.

He had seen the truth of her temper and her spine; she would not have endangered herself in that way. If she had, she would not have tormented him for five years with that absence.

He drew a long breath and his voice lowered: "Li Wu, one last time. If you spread slanders and falsely finger a woman — tomorrow, you may find you cannot even afford a coffin."

Li Wu flung himself face-down, babbling in terror. "I… I do not know the truth! The man only left a letter at night, saying he would save Jin Hua Hall. I dared not disobey… after the letter, that man disappeared!"

Captain Ye and Liang Jin exchanged looks; their expressions shifted.

Lu Chou felt a tempest rise, but he forced it down. After a pause he gave the order in a thin, cold voice: "Keep this man under strict guard. Do not allow any visitors. Captain Ye — find who delivered that letter. Find the body, if there is one; find who buried it."

"As you command."

Liang Jin hesitated, then voiced the doubt that had been burning him: "My lord… if this truly ties to Jin Hua Hall?"

Lu Chou closed his eyes for a heartbeat. When he spoke, his voice was slow, steady, and resolute: "If it is tied to her, I will question her myself. If not, then someone is using her name to set a trap."

He turned to the window; the night outside was a hard black, stars thinned to pinpricks. The Jiangnan wind crept across the eaves, smelling of river salt and ink, and turned the pages of the ledgers on his desk. The paper whispered like a tide.

He understood at last — the silk-tax inquiry had grown teeth of its own. Behind it lay princely contests and courtly measures, and innocents were being conscripted into a game of knives. Xiao Lingyu might already be pushed into the storm's eye.

Lu Chou murmured, almost to himself: "If someone has set her up — I will not forgive it."

He turned, the chill back in his face. The resolve had knitted itself into something edged and immovable.

Chapter 33: The Resolve to Investigate

Lu Chou lowered his gaze; a cold, coiled light churned under the lids, like steel smouldering beneath frost.

Xiao Lingyu truly stood alone at the eye of the knife. No shield. No allies. Only the thin thread of her own resolve keeping her upright amid the storm that had been spun to cut her down.

It was not merely that the Third Prince had been skimming wealth beneath the pretext of the Crown Prince's seal.

There was something uglier beneath, a shadow stitched beneath the first design—an intent to use the capital's noble patrons, the high-born women who ruled salons and charities with hidden hands, to choke the slow, quiet rise of women merchants in Jiangnan.

They feared imitation more than rebellion. If housewives and widows began following her example—if the women of the merchant clans learned to manage their own ledgers, to hire and dismiss, to buy and sell—then the old families would lose their hidden channels of favour and control.

And if Jin Hua Hall established itself as an independent, self-sustaining force in the South, it would grow into something that no patron, male or female, could bend to their will.

No wonder the sudden summonses, the false audits, the sealed cargos, the whispered accusations of fraud—every one of them pointed toward Jin Hua Hall.

Each blow was meant to frighten her, to break her hands, to remind her that the empire was not built for women to own its silver.

Liang Jin's expression changed; anger trembled behind the careful discipline of his face. "For greed's sake," he muttered, voice rough, "they cannot even tolerate a woman who earns her coin by skill alone. These people…"

"Cui. Zhang. Liu."

Lu Chou spoke the names like a string of blades striking stone. "A fine nested plot."

He brushed his sleeve and sat again, voice returning to a flat calm that was more dangerous than rage. "Have Prince Chen Song's men come in person to oversee the operation here in Jiangnan?"

Li Wu's sweat rolled down his temples. His answer came thin and frayed.

"Yes, my lord… the Prince's adjutant, Zhang, came often to review the ledgers, and there is a staffer surnamed Yu who liaises with the guild masters."

Lu Chou's tone sharpened. "And how did you know this?"

The man trembled, his throat constricting. "Such matters cannot stay hidden long," he stammered. "At first the bank received an order from an 'East Palace messenger'—to help move coin, to urge the merchants for donations. The papers bore the seal of a Crown Prince's attendant. Everyone believed the funds went to the Eastern Palace itself."

"So, when did you discover it was the Jing Prince's design?"

Li Wu went pale as paper. "Three nights ago. I overheard Master Qin of the bank speaking privately with Staffer Yu. Yu said the East Palace seal was only a mask—the true command came from the Jing Prince's own circle in the capital. The wagons that carried the coin bore not the Eastern Palace's insignia but the muster marks of the Prince's cavalry."

He dropped his gaze lower. "And once, a ledger recorded 'East Palace messenger escort,' but that day I saw with my own eyes the man who led the convoy—Huang Yao, deputy steward to the Jing Prince's household. He gave orders freely; no one else would dare. I could not mistake him."

"How do you know this Huang Yao?" Lu Chou's tone cut quiet and deep.

"Three years ago, Huang came south under the Prince's orders. I saw him then. He never forgets a superior's rank but forgets every servant beneath. I dared not speak; I only wanted my life." The clerk's breath broke into a ragged sob.

"Good." Lu Chou's reply was almost formal, almost kind—and therefore far colder. "Keep the man under guard. No eyes, no tongues near him. We will question him again."

"Yes, my lord." Liang Jin gestured, and the guards dragged Li Wu away. When the door shut, silence fell so thick that the air seemed to pulse with the rhythm of the lamp.

Lu Chou rubbed the corner of the ledger with one fingertip. His eyes were winter iron. As he had suspected: the Third Prince's scheme was not only to gather coin but to reshape the balance of Jiangnan's commerce—to crush those who would not bend and replace them with hands easily bought.

Xiao Lingyu… If she ever learned the full scope of this, she would fight with all she possessed—and that would only tighten the snare.

He rose suddenly, the light in his eyes flaring like struck flint.

"Have Li Wu write out every word he has said. Not a syllable omitted. Keep him under guard; no whisper of this leaves the compound. When all is ready, he goes to the capital with us."

Captain Ye bowed. "At once, my lord."

When the men were gone, Liang Jin lingered near the threshold. "My lord," he said quietly, "if the grandees in the capital and the Jing Prince move together—if we press too hard—what if the knife turns toward us?"

Lu Chou let out a short, cold laugh, more breath than sound.

"We are already on the board, Liang Jin. Who plays chess staring only at the surface? I will see this through. We'll drag every rotted ledger into daylight so these jackals cannot hang their filth on the Crown Prince's name."

He stood before the desk; the lamp cut his profile into edges of bronze and shadow. The fluttering pages sounded like waves breaking far away.

When he spoke again, his voice was smooth, deliberate, merciless.

Outside, the Jiangnan night breathed against the eaves; the scent of the river carried through the shutters. Within, another move was already being shaped—not by merchants or clerks but by princes who turned silver into crowns. Lu Chou's face in the lamplight was the colour of tempered steel.

The newly uncovered ledgers fanned a quiet storm within him. The killing intent in his heart sharpened, cold and clear.

This was no simple theft. It was a net drawn wide—to blacken the East Palace under the guise of reform, to cripple the new commerce of women, to fold every stream of southern silver back into the Jing Prince's hands.

And Xiao Lingyu—she was the first name written into the trap.

Someone would move against her soon. He felt it as surely as breath.

He closed his eyes and exhaled, the motion slow, precise, like sheathing a sword. His fingers tapped the desk—steady, deliberate.

He had never desired the throne's quarrels, but Jin Hua Hall, and she with it, had been thrust onto that same chess board.

If he turned away now, she would stand alone, without shield or ground.

Not now. Not when every step was balanced on a knife-edge.

The cold between his brows deepened, yet his resolve burned harder than iron. A faint, sardonic smile touched his lips.

Yes—he had once hated her. Hated the calm cruelty of her farewell letter, the silence sharper than any betrayal.

He had wanted to see her fall, to see that proud composure crumble into dust.

But now…

If Jin Hua Hall fell, the Jing Prince's net would tighten; the treasury of the South would pour into his vaults, and the East Palace would bleed out, piece by piece.

Lu Chou gave a quiet, rasping laugh in its bitterness.

"So be it. If she is to fall, it will not be before I have razed their board."

The words were cold as tempered steel, yet beneath them ran a fierce, silent vow. Since he had stepped into this game, retreat was death.

He looked toward the window's dark reflection. A memory flickered there—her at her counter, brush poised, eyes bright and precise, like sunlight on the edge of a blade.

His fingers struck the wood again, the sound rising from somewhere deep within his chest.

He looked down at the ledger but saw beyond it: the river roads swollen with trade, the ships heavy with silk, the invisible hands of nobles squeezing every coin dry.

And now, at the faintest sign of women daring to claim their earnings, the court cried corruption, as if competence itself were sin.

He shut his eyes, fury winding through his lungs like smoke.

The noble wives preached virtue to chain their sisters; the princes preached reform to steal their silver. Each used righteousness as a noose.

Liang Jin lifted his eyes; the light caught Lu Chou's face—serene, flawless, yet his gaze burned like the flash of a blade drawn across frost.

He understood then: his lord's fury was not truly for the trembling prisoner, but for the woman who dared to stand against a rotten world.

Lu Chou laughed once, quietly—a sound of steel over stone.

"Tax to break trade, trade to break women… what a perfect game."

He lifted his gaze to Liang Jin, voice low, final, glacial.

"This is no mere corruption," he said. "It is the rewriting of Jiangnan itself—a chain to bind it once again beneath the nobles' hand."

Chapter 34: The Emperor's Deliberation

The night had deepened.

Yet within the Violet Hall of the Imperial Palace, the lamps still burned bright—silent flames trembling beneath a dome of shadow.

On the imperial desk lay several memorials from Jiangnan, their ink still fresh, their words entangled like roots beneath silk: the tax case—unravelled, yet never clean.

Emperor Jingyuan sat behind the dragon desk, eyes half closed, fingers idly tracing the edge of a jade tablet.

The faintest crease marked his brow—fatigue, yes, but beneath it, a sharper glint of thought.

The doors opened without sound.

Footsteps—measured, soft.

A man in deep-violet robes entered the light, his manner grave yet refined: Grand Chancellor Min Yuanhao.

He bowed low.

"Your Majesty, the night is heavy with dew. If it is not a matter of urgency, this minister begs you to rest the dragon body."

Emperor Jingyuan's eyes lifted—lucid, cutting through the veil of thought.

"You come at the right hour, Yuanhao. Sit. Tell me—have you read the reports from Jiangnan?"

Min Yuanhao obeyed, taking the seat to the Emperor's right.

"I have studied them closely," he said softly. "Lord Lu's investigation is precise and unrelenting. Yet what lies beneath spreads far wider than any ledger. This is not an affair to end in days."

A cold smile crossed the Emperor's lips.

His fingers tapped lightly against the folded memorials.

"Precisely why I cannot sleep. The silk-tax affair appears a matter of corruption—but already it draws the names of the Crown Prince and The Third Prince. The truth remains buried, but the current beneath is that of a struggle for succession."

Min Yuanhao's gaze shifted, his voice low:

"Your Majesty, the winds from the south carry strange scents. The silver flows restlessly among the great merchants, and rumours gather in the streets.

I fear there are those who would stir this case anew, use the silk tax to cloud judgment—and turn suspicion toward the Crown Prince."

Emperor Jingyuan turned the jade tablet between his fingers.

A faint smile touched his lips—cold, amused.

"Whether the tide runs against the East Palace is yet uncertain. I know my son well. The Crown Prince is gentle, upright—beloved by his ministers. Yet virtue alone does not make a ruler."

His tone dropped, the words slow, like a blade being sheathed.

"To be emperor, one must wield both grace and thunder. The Prince holds compassion, but lacks the will to strike. If there are indeed those who bait him with the Jiangnan affair, I would see how he chooses to break the snare."

"Your Majesty is most discerning," said Min Yuanhao, bowing again.

The Emperor paused, tapping once more upon the memorial. A shadow of wry amusement crossed his features.

"Curious, is it not? Lu Wenqian—so steady, so cautious—and yet his two sons could not be more unlike. One, Lu Xiu, the bastard son, already commands troops as Right Commander of the Five Armies— headstrong, dangerously sharp. Were it not for birth, he might rise beyond the rank his blood permits."

Min Yuanhao's eyes flickered upward.

"It is true, Your Majesty. Lu Xiu's talent in arms is notable. To reach such station at his age shows uncommon courage."

"Courage," Emperor Jingyuan murmured, "and a mind too quick for comfort."

Then his gaze shifted.

"And Lu Chou—ah. That quiet one.

I had thought him cautious, mild, a scholar of the desk rather than the field. I sent him to Jiangnan merely to test the edge of his restraint. Yet now—he unravels the web thread by thread, waits while his enemies collapse of their own fear. Such patience... such precision. It is not caution—it is command."

"Indeed," said Min Yuanhao. "He writes with clarity, speaks with weight, and governs with an even hand. Properly guided, he may prove fit for far greater office."

Emperor Jingyuan inclined his head but did not answer.

His gaze lingered on the inked memorials, his voice low, almost to himself:

"When both sons bear talent, the struggle ceases to be of a household—it becomes the reflection of the court itself.

I seek not obedience alone, but the measure of a man's heart, the depth of his ambition.

"This affair in Jiangnan," he said with a faint smile, "has brought both Lu brothers to the surface."

A breath of silence, then:

"The case is yet unresolved. But Lu Chou... that one bears watching. He is steady, bold, and unafraid to dirty his hands for a clean result. Not the makings of a mere bureaucrat.

The question is—how he will stand between the Third Prince and the Crown Prince, and whether he will hold his balance."

The Emperor's tone cooled to frost.

"My third son," he said softly, "has grown clever, yet too eager. His brilliance is not his own—it smells of another's design. He moves quickly, too quickly, and those who move thus often fall by their own step."

Min Yuanhao bowed his head.

"Your Majesty speaks true. The Third Prince's renown has risen swiftly—his alliances spread wide. Yet he is young, and youth is tinder to manipulation. This affair in Jiangnan—if his name be used by others, his ruin may precede his triumph."

Emperor Jingyuan's fingers stilled.

He gazed toward the wavering flame.

"This is no shallow game, Yuanhao. And so, I speak little of it. I will watch.

If the Crown Prince can clear his name and still his house, he is worthy.

If the Third Prince Chen Song dares to scheme beneath heaven, then let him play. The river will show whose reflection lasts."

The night within the Violet Hall had thickened to velvet silence.

Beneath the towering, coffered ceiling, the lamplight burned steady— thin and gold, trembling upon jade and memorials.

Emperor Jingyuan's gaze lingered on the southern reports, their edges still damp with ink.

A faint smile curved his lips, cool and unhurried, though the depths of his eyes were sharp as obsidian.

"The heir's seat is yet unsteady," he murmured, voice as calm as still water.

"The court moves like a nest of serpents. It is time to place one piece upon the board—see who stirs, who schemes—and strike when the hour ripens."

Grand Chancellor Min Yuanhao inclined his head, his tone measured and low.

"Your Majesty, beyond the Crown Prince and the Third Prince, the Fourth has lately shown promise. His manner is restrained, his conduct precise; he has won the quiet favour of the clans and ministers alike."

Emperor Jingyuan's smile deepened by a thread.

"Ah, my little fourth. The stillest waters often run the deepest. Even as a child, he quarreled least, spoke least—yet I have never doubted the depth of his ambition. His silence hides more than obedience."

"Your Majesty knows your sons as only a father—and an emperor— can."

"The struggle for the throne is a visible storm between the Crown Prince and Jing," Emperor Jingyuan said softly, "but if the Fourth chooses to mask his edge, he may yet serve as the balance I require."

He paused, then shifted the current of thought without a ripple.

"As for the Crown Prince— though he has a consort-ranked concubine to assist him, the matter of the Crown Princess can no longer be delayed. The empire is unsettled; an heir without issue is a fault in the order of Heaven itself."

Min Yuanhao bowed again, his eyes glinting beneath the lamplight.

"Your Majesty's foresight is just."

The Emperor placed the jade slip upon the desk, its surface reflecting the dance of flame.

"The Eastern Palace stands steady yet lacks its Madam. To postpone the appointment invites whispers of hesitation. The noble houses already watch, testing the winds. I have in mind two or three candidates—but I shall observe longer."

He paused, then added with a trace of iron beneath his tone:

"The Liangdi (Crown's prince's side consort) may be virtuous, yet her birth is low. To leave the throne's consort unfilled is disorder; but to let one of humble lineage preside over the Eastern Palace is worse. The law must hold."

Min Yuanhao bowed, understanding the unspoken.

"Indeed. The Crown Prince Chen Gen requires a consort of fitting blood—one who may strengthen his standing and fortify the House of the Heir."

He understood perfectly.

The Emperor's impartiality was but artifice; his preference for the Crown Prince was plain as light through silk.

To wed the Prince into a high house would be to shield him from the encroachments of the Third and Fourth Princes—a move of balance disguised as affection.

The message was clear: the Crown Prince's position, for now, still held.

Emperor Jingyuan said nothing. His gaze returned to the memorials, eyes dark and fathomless.

After a pause, Min Yuanhao ventured carefully:

"If Your Majesty permits, this minister dares offer one name for consideration."

The Emperor's brow lifted slightly, a glimmer of curiosity in his tone.

"Speak."

"The daughter of the Imperial Preceptor, Lord Shen Qing-Yuan—Lady Shen Zhaoru."

The hall fell to stillness.

Only the low crackle of the lamp filled the air.

Emperor Jingyuan's fingertips stilled upon the memorial; after a long breath, he said,

"Shen Qingyuan… a venerable man. Steady, incorruptible. His daughter—what of her character?"

"Graceful and composed since childhood," Min replied, voice firm.

"She is praised for her poetry and decorum, her learning unmatched among the young ladies of the capital. The Shen clan is righteous, unaligned with any faction—an ideal house for alliance."

Emperor Jingyuan's gaze deepened, the weight of thought sinking through silence.

"I recall seeing her once or twice," he murmured. "A calm face. A gentle bearing. A poise that complements the Crown Prince's side wife steadiness."

"Indeed," Min continued. "To unite the Crown Prince with the Shen family would still the murmurs of court, and silence the talk of Jing and his kin. Lady Shen is modest, yet learned; she would temper the Prince's household, bring harmony within and reputation without."

The Emperor Jingyuan did not reply. His hand traced the lacquered desk, slow as the passage of time.

After a long stillness, he said quietly,

"This matter shall be considered carefully… there is no need to rush."

"Your Majesty's wisdom shines through."

The lamps flickered. The walls of the Violet Hall breathed with shadows.

Between Emperor and Chancellor, words thinned into quiet—yet from that quiet, a new strand of power wove itself unseen.

The web was already spreading, its threads drawn fine as silk—across court and clan, across love and ambition—ready to tighten with the coming dawn.

Chapter 35: The Consort's Opening Move

Xiao Lingyu stepped into her Papa's inner courtyard with footsteps light as breath, as if even a cough might shatter the stillness that hung like water in the air. She pushed the door open gently. Inside, the lamplight burned dim and yellow, soft yet suffocating.

Upon the couch, Master Xiao sat slumped against the pillow, his gaze vacant and unfocused on a slice of window beyond the curtain. His hair had turned entirely white; one corner of his mouth hung slack, his hands lay lifeless upon his knees, trembling now and then as though searching for something invisible that forever eluded his grasp—yet never finding where to settle.

"Papa."

Her voice came as a whisper, lighter than the rustle of wind brushing through silk. She seated herself beside him and called again, and he turned his head slightly, eyes dull, no spark of recognition stirring there—only a confused, empty stare, as though the world in front of him could no longer hold a shape he could name.

An old nurse and a longtime steward had been keeping watch. At the sight of their Madam, they began to bow, but she lifted a hand in quiet dismissal. They obeyed, retreating soundlessly, leaving the room to silence.

Xiao Lingyu pressed her lips together, swallowing the ache that rose behind her eyes. She forced a small smile, smoothing the quilt around him with gentle fingers.

"You look a little better today. The physician said if you keep taking your medicine, if you rest… perhaps, one day, you might improve."

The old man gave no answer—only a hoarse murmur deep in his throat, dry and broken like an old hinge.

Her gaze fell. She spoke softly, "Your daughter is tired, Papa. Please, get better soon—will you?"

At those words her hand trembled, the brittle shell of composure wavered. She looked into his hollow eyes, and her voice rasped faintly, stripped of strength.

"I know you still worry for Brother. I haven't stopped searching, Papa— I'm still trying to find him." She paused, breathing unevenly, then continued:

"Though Jin Hua Hall struggles now, the Xiao family cannot stand on me alone. If Brother were still here—if he hadn't vanished on that return journey—it would never have fallen upon me, a woman, to step out into the open, to face the markets and the yamen, to bow and bargain with men who mock behind their fans." The words tightened as if caught on bone. "It would never have been left to me to carry the weight that should have been shared."

Her teeth caught her lip; tears welled, clinging to her lashes. "Sometimes I think… I cannot go on, Papa. I am so tired." Her breath shook once. "But when I remember you lying here, ill, and Brother lost without word, I cannot rest. Even if I'm only keeping up a hollow shell, I must keep it standing—otherwise, the Xiao family will fall. Truly fall."

Still, he stared at her without understanding. Then, suddenly, his fingers moved—only slightly, as if reaching for her hand.

She froze, then caught his cool, unsteady fingers in both of hers. "Papa… do you still remember me?"

His lips worked; a rough, slurred sound emerged, shaped almost like her childhood name—blurred, broken at the edges, yet unmistakable enough to strike straight through her: "A…yu."

That faint echo broke her last restraint. She bent her head, tears spilling freely. She pressed her forehead to the back of his hand, voice trembling.

"Give me a little more time, Papa, please. I will rebuild Jin Hua Hall. I will find Brother. Then—then, when you're well again, the three of us can sit beneath the old veranda and drink tea together, just as before."

The lamp wavered. Curtains swayed.

The room fell into such perfect quiet that only the sigh of wind and the small, stifled sound of her breathing could be heard. She did not sob aloud. Her shoulders quivered in silence, as though she were finally letting go of what had been swallowed for too long—grief with no place to speak, loneliness that had never once been permitted to become a sound.

That night, she remained at her Papa's side for a long time, until the wick burned down to ash and moonlight spread across the floor like frost.

* * * * *

By the hour of Chen (7–9am), the long street outside Jin Hua Hall had already awakened. Perfume shops, silk merchants, and rouge pavilions opened their doors one after another. Carriages rattled past, voices rose and tangled in the morning air—a scene of effortless prosperity, ladies and wealthy merchants coming and going, wheels and hooves threading the street without pause.

No one foresaw the sudden thunder that would shatter it.

Hooves struck the stones in furious rhythm; armour clanged like iron hail. Down the main street surged a column of black-armoured officers, banners snapping—flooding the road as if the city itself had been ordered to make way.

At their head rode Lu Chou, Deputy Minister of Revenue, his dark robe whipping in the wind, the jade girdle at his waist flashing cold light. His expression was winter—hard, colourless, and without mercy.

The gates of Jin Hua Hall had not yet been fully opened. Inside, the Madam was instructing porters, telling the clerks what to carry and where, when someone looked up—and froze.

Dozens of officers had already blocked the entrance, sealing it tight in full view of the street.

One unfurled a scroll and shouted, voice booming down the road:

"By Imperial command, Jin Hua Hall is hereby seized and sealed! All within are forbidden to enter or leave—disobedience will be punished as complicity!"

Gasps rippled through the crowd. The street erupted in whispers.

"What's happened? Jin Hua Hall, of all places?"
"But Manager Xiao's no common trader—how could she fall into trouble?"
"Must've kicked a hornet's nest in court… Heaven help her."

Within, the air froze solid.

Xiao Lingyu had been in the storeroom reviewing accounts when the uproar reached her ears. Moments later, a house servant stumbled in, face drained of blood.

"Madam—it's bad! Soldiers—soldiers have broken in!"

The account book slipped from her grasp, striking the floor with a crack that sounded far too loud in the suddenly tightened air.

Before she could rise, the study doors burst open with a heavy crash.

Boots struck the stone in measured rhythm. Several guards in black stepped in, one after another—and at their head, tall and grim, stood the man she knew too well.

Lu Chou.

He wore dark blue brocade, his figure straight and austere. Sunlight glanced across his shoulder, but the chill about him swallowed all warmth.

"Lu Chou!" Her eyes widened; she shot to her feet, voice trembling with shock. "What is the meaning of this?"

His face was iron, expression unreadable. His gaze touched hers for an instant—brief, almost cutting—before turning away.

"By decree," he said flatly, "the Ministry orders a full investigation of Jin Hua Hall. I expect your cooperation, Madam Xiao."

"Investigation?" A bitter laugh escaped her lips, bright and sharp as glass. "My family's trade is clean as spring water. This 'decree' of yours—whose mouth did it pass through? Who ordered you to come and seal my doors like this?"

Lu Chou's jaw tightened; his lips did not move. He gave no answer— only lifted a hand.

"Search."

"Stop!" She stepped forward, blocking the shelves. Fury blazed in her eyes. "These records and manuscripts are my Papa's life's work! You have no right to trample them!"

At last his gaze locked with hers. His voice came deep, almost toneless.

"Defiance of command is rebellion. The punishment is doubled."

At a gesture, two guards started forward. But Lu Chou's eyes flickered—sharp, warning. He raised his hand.

"Stand down."

They halted immediately.

Under the weight of countless eyes, he walked toward her. Stopping close, he looked down, his voice low and steady:

"Madam Xiao, don't make this harder than it must be."

She gave a sudden, bitter smile. "Lord Lu storms into my shop with troops, seals my doors, and now instructs me not to resist? Tell me, sir—what name does that bear, if not tyranny?"

She moved again, as if to throw herself between the men and the shelves. His expression hardened. In one swift motion he caught her wrist.

His palm was cold, unyielding—a manacle forged of restraint. He pulled her aside, half shielded, half restrained, keeping her out of the worst of the disorder while also making sure no one else could put hands on her.

"Xiao Lingyu," he said, voice harsh, almost gritted, "do not shame yourself in the street. If you make a scene here, do not blame me for what follows."

She strained against his hold, hair falling loose, spine rigid as a drawn bow. Her glare burned through the thin space between them.

"Lu Chou, you abuse your power! Cloaking personal vengeance in public duty—what kind of man are you?"

His grip tightened imperceptibly; he could feel the faint tremor beneath her skin. His eyes darkened, but his tone remained icy.

"Personal vengeance? I act on Imperial order. If you continue this defiance, I will take you myself."

Then, turning slightly, he half-shielded her with his arm and spoke aloud to the men and bystanders, his voice carrying with clear finality:

"Madam Xiao is a woman. Any man who shows her disrespect will answer to me."

The soldiers drew back at once. The watching crowd fell silent.

Her heart jolted violently; anger still surged, but her limbs were pinned by his iron hold, and the street's gaze pressed in on all sides.

She glared up at him, eyes bright with rage and unshed tears.

"So, this is how you treat me, Lu Chou? Do you think I, Xiao Lingyu, have no one left to protect me?"

For a heartbeat his expression faltered, a fleeting crack in the mask—so fast it could have been imagined. But when he spoke again his tone was frost itself.

"Take her away."

Two guards stepped forward, seizing her arms. She struggled, her embroidered shoes scraping the bluestone, sliding through mud; her skirts soaked in the puddled courtyard. Around them lay toppled chests, broken porcelain scattered in sharp fragments, servants and maids kneeling in terror, not daring to speak.

"Let me go! Lu Chou—why are you doing this to me?"

Her cry rang sharp in the morning air, but he did not answer.

He stood in the shade of the veranda, unmoving, his gaze as deep and still as a frozen lake, taking in every ruin without letting a single trace reach his face.

"Lu Chou!" she shouted again, her voice trembling with fury and grief. "If this humiliation is what you came for—then take it! From this moment, Xiao Lingyu owes you nothing. Our debts are done!"

He remained beneath the eaves, face unreadable, robe stirring faintly in the breeze.

"Madam Xiao," he said, voice low and cold, "you would do better to worry for yourself."

His gaze lingered a fraction too long upon her face—then dropped, concealing the unrest buried deep behind his composure, as though he had forced something back down where no one could see it.

And outside, under the weight of watching eyes, the once-proud banners of Jin Hua Hall hung limp in the rising wind.

Chapter 36: Detained in Brocade Hall

Just then, a commotion rose beyond the front gate, swelling suddenly like a wave striking the outer walls.

Voices overlapped—hurried, restrained, edged with command. Boots crossed one another on the stone. The crowd gathered at the entrance parted instinctively. A figure in white cut through the line of guards with measured urgency, a dozen armed men following in tight formation. The jade pendant at his waist chimed softly with each step, the sound crisp and controlled.

It was Xie Huaici.

"Lord Lu, what is the meaning of this?"

Xie Huaici's tone was mild, polished, perfectly courteous—yet beneath that calm ran a blade-thin edge. His gaze swept the courtyard in a single, assessing arc: the overturned chests, the shattered porcelain, servants kneeling with heads bowed, skirts soaked dark with mud. Then his eyes fell on Xiao Lingyu, disordered and restrained all at once, and his brows knit sharply.

Seeing him, a thin thread of hope flickered in Xiao Lingyu's eyes, fragile as spun glass.
"Huaici…"

Lu Chou watched that moment—the way her gaze lifted, the way her breath caught—and something in his eyes snapped cold, immediate, as though a lamp had been extinguished behind them.

"Lord Xie," he said evenly, "I am executing an Imperial order. Do not obstruct official duty."

Xie Huaici stepped forward, placing himself—quietly, decisively— between Xiao Lingyu and the drawn steel. The movement was unshowy, precise, protective without spectacle.

"The Xiao household is a reputable merchant family," he said. "Even if there must be a search and seizure, there are established procedures. Your conduct, Lord Lu—so abrupt, so forceful—surely it is… ill-advised."

"Huaici!" Xiao Lingyu clutched his sleeve as if to anchor herself, her voice unsteady despite her effort to keep it level. "They came without cause, overturned everything, trampled the accounts—this is clearly—"

Lu Chou's gaze dropped, slow and deliberate, to the fingers curled tightly around Xie Huaici's sleeve.

A shadow passed through his eyes—brief, dark, unmistakable.

"Madam Xiao and Lord Xie are… close."

The words were neutral on their surface, yet the air tightened instantly, as if the sentence carried a weight it refused to name.

Xie Huaici smiled faintly—gentle, composed, immovable.

"Madam Xiao has been frightened," he said calmly. "Lord Lu, without ironclad proof, I ask that you exercise restraint. If there is any misunderstanding, why not wait until you return to the capital and address it before the Court? Acting thus, here and now, only deepens the disorder."

"Wait?" Lu Chou gave a low, mirthless laugh. "I fear this matter does not afford us the luxury of waiting."

He moved in a blur.

Before Xiao Lingyu could step back, his hand closed around her wrist, firm and unyielding.

"Madam Xiao stands suspected of falsifying accounts and of entanglement in factional strife," he said coldly. "She is to be taken at once for interrogation."

"Lies!" Xiao Lingyu struggled violently. Her nails raked across the back of his hand, leaving livid red marks. Her voice broke sharp and hoarse. "Lu Chou—coward!"

Xie Huaici's expression hardened at once.

"Release her, Lord Lu. Without evidence, this is an abuse of office."

Lu Chou did not answer him.

His grip tightened almost imperceptibly as he drew Xiao Lingyu closer, positioning her away from the guards yet fully within his control.

"If Lord Xie is dissatisfied, he may submit a memorial," Lu Chou said. Then his gaze swept the courtyard—glacial, lethal. "Until then, any who interfere will be charged as accomplices."

Pulled forward, Xiao Lingyu stumbled. Her balance broke, and she nearly fell into his chest.

She looked up, fury blazing—only to catch, for a heartbeat, something else in his eyes.

A complicated light. Pain, restraint, something forcibly buried.

It was too familiar.

Memory struck without mercy: a boy beneath a plum tree years ago, breaking off a branch and thrusting it toward her with awkward pride, eyes burning with something he did not yet know how to name.

"Lu Chou…" Her voice dropped despite herself, unsteady, confused. "What are you—what are you doing?"

"Take her."

He turned his face aside. The warmth vanished. His tone returned to iron.

Xie Huaici's restraint finally frayed.

"Lu Chou! If you insist on this today, then do not blame me—"

"Huaici!" Xiao Lingyu cut in sharply. She drew a long breath, forcing the tremor from her limbs. "Enough. I will go with him."

Xie Huaici stared at her, disbelief plain. "Lingyu…?"

She twisted free of Lu Chou's grasp and straightened on her own. Her robe was crooked, dust-stained, her hair in disarray—but her back did not bend.

"The innocent need not fear," she said steadily. "Since Lord Lu insists on taking me, I will go and see whether the law still stands in this world."

She turned to Lu Chou. Anger still burned in her eyes, but now it was sharpened by something else—scrutiny, wariness, resolve.

"After you, Lord Lu."

His eyes flickered. His throat moved once, as if swallowing something that would not go down.

Then he strode forward. His dark cloak surged behind him; the jade at his belt struck the scabbard with a clear, ringing sound that cut through the murmurs.

"No need to trouble the guards," he said coldly, his right hand closing around her slender wrist again—hard enough to make her wince. "I will escort her myself."

Xie Huaici moved to intercept at once.

"Lu Chou! Madam Xiao is a gentlewoman—"

"Lord Xie." Lu Chou cut him off.

His thumb, almost involuntarily, brushed once across the delicate bones at Xiao Lingyu's pulse—a fleeting, unconscious gesture so slight that no one else noticed it.

Except her.

"I bear His Majesty's direct charge to investigate Jiangnan," he continued evenly. "Your opinions are neither requested nor required."

An autumn wind lifted the loose strands of Xiao Lingyu's hair; several clung to her pale lips. Lu Chou's gaze darkened.

Abruptly, he released her wrist.

"You—" she began.

Before the word could form, warmth descended.

Lu Chou unclasped the black fox-fur cloak from his shoulders and draped it over her in a motion that looked rough, almost brusque—yet his hands avoided her disordered hair with meticulous care. He wrapped the cloak tightly around her slight frame, fingers lingering for a fraction of a second at the ties before pulling them into a hard, final knot.

The cloak carried the faint scent of sandalwood.

Heat seeped through the brocade, slow and relentless, while the weight pressed against her chest, making her breath hitch.

Xiao Lingyu stared, stunned, understanding dawning too late.

She lifted her chin to speak, but saw only his lowered lashes and tightly pressed lips—severity etched deep, and beneath it a line of pain forced into stillness.

"There's no need to—" Her voice trembled and broke.

"Don't move."

He spoke so low that only she could hear. It was not a command.

It was almost a plea.

Her heart lurched, thrown into chaos by the contradiction—tenderness buried inside violence.

"Take her."

In a single motion, Lu Chou swept her into his arms—one arm beneath her knees, the other at her back. She gasped, startled, the humiliation burning hot behind her eyes. His hold was iron; even through the cloak, his body radiated heat like banked fire.

"Lord Xie," he said sharply, "attempt to stop me again, and I will charge you with obstructing an Imperial investigation."

Xiao Lingyu struggled in his arms; an emerald hairpin slipped free and shattered against the blue-stone paving with a sharp crack.

"Put me down! Lu Chou, you—"

"Be quiet."

He lowered his head, his breath warm against her ear, his voice pitched so low that only she received it.

"If you don't want to fall, don't struggle."

Six words—soft as illusion.

Then, louder, clean as steel:

"Men! Inventory every document in the Xiao household. Leave nothing unrecorded!"

Xie Huaici reached out to block their path, but a guard levelled his blade across the way. He could only watch as Lu Chou carried the still-struggling Xiao Lingyu toward the carriage.

For the first time, true fury burned in his usually gentle eyes.

"Lu Chou—put her down!"

Lu Chou did not turn back.

"Will Lord Xie share her guilt as well?"

"Lord Lu," Xie Huaici said, meeting his gaze without yielding, "enough."

"Enough." Lu Chou's voice cracked like thunder. "Xie Huaici—one more word, and I will open an inquiry into the Xie household."

Xie Huaici's expression changed.

Lu Chou did not slow.

As he set Xiao Lingyu into the carriage, he used the shadow of the doorway to mask a fleeting movement—his fingertip brushing away the tear trembling at the corner of her eye. The touch was so swift that even the nearest guards failed to notice.

Yet Xiao Lingyu flinched as if struck.

"My lord..." Liang Jin edged close, voice low. "There's movement from the Third Prince's faction. Among the onlookers—we've identified several watchers."

"Good." Lu Chou cut him off. His voice was dark, steady. "Proceed as planned."

"Hyah!"

The whip cracked. Wheels jolted over shattered jade and broken porcelain. The carriage surged forward and disappeared.

Through the narrow slit of the window, Xiao Lingyu looked back.

Amid the wreckage of her courtyard stood Lu Chou—black-robed, unmoving, like a blade at the instant before it leaves the sheath.

She did not know that his gaze remained locked on the departing carriage until it vanished around the bend. Only then did he murmur, so faint the wind nearly swallowed it:

"Lingyu—better your hatred than your blood."

Had she remained at Jin Hua Hall, the assassins would likely have come before nightfall. Under his custody, she was now a "witness" named in an Imperial investigation—untouchable by lesser hands.

Lu Chou swung into the saddle and followed, dark-blue official robes snapping in the wind. His eyes never left the swaying curtain, as though sheer will might pierce silk and shadow to reach the woman within.

A breath of wind lifted the hem of his robe—and carried away the words no one else would ever hear.

Chapter 37: A Debt Unsettled

Outside the window, the shadow of a parasol tree spilled across the blue-brick floor like ink, spreading slowly as dusk deepened. The light shifted, stretched, then settled, as if the day itself were reluctant to leave.

On the desk sat a bowl of rice porridge, long gone cold, a thin film of oil glazing its surface. The faint sheen reflected the lamplight in dull ripples, untouched.

Xiao Lingyu sat silently by the window, her posture straight, unmoving. Her fingers absently traced the faint red marks circling her wrist, following the outline again and again, as though trying to confirm their reality. The skin there was still tender, the pressure of earlier restraint lingering like an afterimage.

Her gaze drifted toward the courtyard, where a withered plum tree stood motionless in the wind. Its branches were bare and brittle, twisted like exposed bones. She watched it without blinking, her expression just as pale, just as still.

A maid slipped in, footsteps light as a whisper, carrying a tray with a fresh bowl of lotus-seed porridge. Steam coiled upward, pale as mist, briefly clouding the air before thinning away.

"Madam," the girl murmured carefully, eyes lowered, "you barely touched your morning meal, and at noon you only drank half a cup of tea. Please, take a few bites."

"Leave it there," Xiao Lingyu said quietly, her eyes still fixed on the tree beyond the window lattice.

The maid hesitated. Her lips parted as if to plead again, fingers tightening around the tray. After a moment, she swallowed her words, sighed softly, and stepped back.

The room fell utterly still.

Only the sound of dripping water from the courtyard jar marked the passage of time—steady, patient, indifferent. Each drop landed with a faint, hollow note, as though counting something down.

After a long moment, Xiao Lingyu finally lifted the porcelain spoon. She scooped a small mouthful and brought it to her lips. The porridge was lukewarm, tasteless. She swallowed without flinching, her face unreadable, as if even her senses had grown weary of protest.

"Madam—" the maid began again, unable to stop herself.

"That's enough," Xiao Lingyu interrupted, setting the spoon aside with controlled precision. The bowl was still nearly full.

The maid dared not press her further. She cleared the dishes and retreated in silence, closing the door so softly it barely stirred the air.

Evening deepened. Shadows thickened along the corners of the room. The lamplight wavered, then steadied.

By the time the maid replaced that same bowl for the third time, now chilled once more, the door swung open with a sudden creak.

Lu Chou stood framed against the lamplight.

His dark official robe was damp with night dew, the hem darkened where it brushed the threshold. In one hand he held a small green-porcelain vial, its glaze catching the light in a muted gleam.

The faint scent of herbs followed him in, mingling with the stale chill of untouched food. His gaze fell immediately on her wrist, on the faint discoloration still visible despite the dimness, and his brows drew together almost imperceptibly.

"I hear you haven't eaten," he said, stepping over the threshold. His boots crushed a fallen leaf that had somehow been carried inside, the sound sharp and jarring in the silence.

Xiao Lingyu's eyes did not lift. She stared instead at the lattice shadows cast upon the floor, diamond-shaped patterns fractured by the uneven bricks.

"Does Lord Lu also inspect his prisoners' appetite now?"

A faint edge crept into his tone, sharper than before. "What's this? Have you stopped eating and taken to chewing gunpowder instead?"

Her lips tightened. She turned her face away, deliberately breaking the line of sight between them.

"Medicine," he said curtly, coming closer.

She looked up at last, her expression calm as ice, eyes clear and distant. "You needn't trouble yourself."

Without another word, he reached out and caught her wrist. The grip was firm—neither brutal nor gentle—but it left no room for refusal, the pressure exact and unyielding.

She did not struggle. She only watched him coolly, the corner of her mouth curving in a bitter, mocking line.

"So, the mighty Lord Lu finds time to fuss over trifles?" she said softly. "After confiscating my shop, will you now take inventory of my bruises as well?"

Lu Chou said nothing.

He dipped a finger into the ointment and began to smooth it over the dark mark at her wrist. The motion was controlled, precise, as if he were suppressing some deeper force beneath the surface.

Her skin was cold. His fingertips burned.

The faint scent of musk and medicine mingled between them, heavy and close. For a brief moment, neither of them spoke.

"Does it hurt?" he asked quietly.

She gave a low laugh, the sound dry and humorless. "Compared to the humiliation you gave me before half the city, what is this?"

His hand paused. His eyes darkened, something tightening behind them.

"Xiao Lingyu," he said, voice low, "must you always speak like this?"

"And how would Lord Lu prefer I speak?" she countered, voice soft yet cutting. "With gratitude? Or in tears?"

His jaw tightened until the veins at his temple showed. For a heartbeat it seemed he might say something more—but instead he resumed dressing the wound, movements slower, more deliberate.

Suddenly she drew her hand back.

The small jar slipped from his grasp and struck the floor. A splash of dark balm stained the blue bricks, spreading outward in an uneven blot.

"That's enough," she said flatly. "After today, any debt between us is paid. From now on, we owe each other nothing."

He stared at her.

For an instant, a storm gathered behind his composed face—anger, disbelief, something sharper still. Then he let out a cold, mirthless laugh.

"Nothing?"

"Yes." She met his gaze steadily, refusing to look away. "When I left that letter behind years ago, I knew I earned your hatred. I accepted it.

But now—you've ruined my workshop, dragged my name through the mud. Is that not vengeance enough?"

He leaned forward suddenly, one hand braced against the desk beside her. The force of the movement sent a faint tremor through the surface. His shadow swallowed the lamplight, casting her face into half-darkness.

"You think this is revenge?" he said, voice low and rough, each word pressed flat.

She did not flinch. "What else would it be?"

The small vial struck the table with a sharp crack. Somewhere behind them, a startled maid dropped a spoon. It clattered across the floor, spinning in a tight circle before finally falling still.

"Why?" Xiao Lingyu asked, her voice trembling for the first time. Her pale fingers brushed the faint groove on the desk left by a rope, tracing the shallow scar as if it, too, were a wound. "Where are my seamstresses now? My women—where have you taken them?"

Lu Chou toed a stool toward him and sat, movements measured, controlled. He twisted the vial open again with slow precision.

"Does it matter?" he asked.

"It matters to me." She seized his wrist, nails digging through the leather bracer at his sleeve. Her grip was tight, desperate. "If I were truly guilty, why not send me to the imperial prison? Why this charade—this grand spectacle?" Her eyes searched his face, candlelight flickering in their depths. "It's almost as if—"

"As if what?" he said, catching her hand in his.

"As if you're performing for someone," she said with a bitter half-smile. "For which noble in the capital? Or…"

Her voice faltered as he leaned in suddenly. The scent of sandalwood closed around her, heavy and unmistakable. His jade belt struck the edge of the table with a clear metallic click.

"Clever as ever," he murmured.

The finger that had touched the balm pressed hard against her bruised skin. She winced despite herself.

"Then guess again," he said quietly. "Why you?"

Outside, the night watch beat the third watch drum. The sound rolled through the darkness, distant and hollow.

"Because…" Her voice was thin. She drew her hand free, smearing a faint amber line of ointment across the air. "…because you still hate that I left you."

The vial rolled from his hand and hit the floor, spinning to rest beside the cold bowl of porridge.

In a single motion he caught her chin, thumb pressing lightly over the split at her lip.

"Wrong," he whispered, breath rough as gravel. "Because in all Jiangnan, only you can embroider a twin-winged butterfly in two colours."

Her pupils widened.

That pattern—the secret of her family, the soul of Jin Hua Hall.

He swallowed, throat working. The fury in his face broke into something rawer, darker, almost pleading. But when he spoke again, his voice was steel.

"If you promise to apply your medicine every day," he said, "I will let you see Baor tomorrow."

Her breath hitched. A tremor passed through her fingers, through her shoulders. For a long time she said nothing.

Then she slowly extended her wrist again.

"…Fine."

He exhaled, the sound barely audible, and stooped to retrieve the vial. He dipped his finger once more. His touch was slower now, more deliberate—almost gentle.

The wind outside sighed against the shutters. The candle wavered, throwing their shadows together and apart, overlapping and then separating again.

She watched his hand move, watched the careful way he avoided pressing too hard this time. Then she asked softly, "Lu Chou… you hate me, don't you?"

He said nothing.

A faint smile curved her lips, thin and weary. "Then I suppose… I truly owe you nothing anymore."

His hand froze for an instant.

Then it resumed its steady motion. He did not look at her.

When he finished, he straightened, voice cool and controlled. "The medicine's done. Tomorrow—you'll see the child."

He turned toward the door, his figure tall, the line of his shoulders like the edge of a drawn sword. Yet at the threshold, his step faltered almost imperceptibly, as if something unseen had caught at his heel.

She watched him go.

Her fingertips brushed the lingering scent of medicine on her skin, and for the first time that night, fatigue blurred her gaze. The weight she had been holding finally settled into her bones.

The door stood half-closed. The candlelight stretched their shadows long upon the floor. A gust slipped through the crack, stirring the faint glimmer of spilled balm until it gleamed like a ghostly stain.

Her chest tightened.

Beneath her cold fingers, she could still feel the warmth of his touch.

For a heartbeat she saw another winter long ago—a young man tying a cloak around her shoulders beneath falling snow, his eyes unshadowed by the bitterness of years.

She closed her eyes.

And in the hush of the night, a single thought rose within her heart, unheard by anyone:

"If there could ever be such a thing as being even, I would rather never have owed you—nor ever loved you."

The fragrance of herbs thinned. The flame trembled.

The night seemed endless.

Chapter 38: The Game of Wealth and Power

Prince Jing's Residence

The news arrived far sooner than anyone had imagined.

Chen Song had just finished a poetry gathering. He was still accompanying several gentlemen scholars through the bamboo garden, their sleeves brushing the leaves, their laughter and lingering couplets floating among the green shadows, when his confidant Jiang Yue slipped close without a sound and leaned in to whisper a few lines by his ear.

Chen Song had been lounging lazily against a bamboo chair, half-reclined, his posture relaxed to the point of indolence. But the instant he heard the seven words—"Jin Hua Hall has been raided and sealed"—his body straightened a fraction, as if a hidden spring had snapped taut. His eyes lit, not brightly, but with a thin, sharp gleam. The corner of his mouth lifted into a faint curve that was almost too light to be called a smile.

"Is it true?"

"Reporting to Your Highness—confirmed."

"Heh." Chen Song let out a small laugh through his nose. The sound was soft, almost amused, as though he had just heard a pleasing line of verse. "So she finally couldn't hold out."

His folded fan tapped once, lightly, against his palm.

"To think it went so smoothly," he said, voice still mild, still unhurried. "Lu Chou actually did exactly what I wanted. He truly did. Jin Hua Hall—searched, seized, confiscated."

Jiang Yue bowed with practiced respect. "Congratulations, Your Highness. Your wish has been fulfilled."

Chen Song's eyes narrowed into a long, lazy slit, as if smiling without smiling. "This congratulations is far too early."

His tone was gentle, almost courteous, yet every syllable carried a colder edge beneath, like silk wrapped tightly around steel.

"Now," he continued, the fan still tapping his palm in an idle rhythm, "those Jiangnan merchants who live by reading the winds—who change sails the moment they smell a shift—finally have a reason that sounds righteous, sounds proper, sounds beyond reproach, to cast themselves before a new master."

Jiang Yue lowered his voice. "Your Highness, I have already sent men to approach several major merchant houses and guilds. They all expressed willingness to contribute silver—large sums—so long as they receive protection under the banner of the Eastern Palace."

He paused, then added, even more quietly: "This is precisely the snare Your Highness laid. The message from the hidden guard also arrived—there has been unrest among the Crown Prince's faction these past days. They are shaken. And as for Lu Chou… if this matter is pressed through the court, he may not be able to keep his hands clean either. He will find it difficult to preserve the appearance of innocence."

Chen Song gave a low laugh. It was slow, unhurried, yet something within it rippled with an unmistakable chill.

"Good," he said.

"Ah, Jin Hua Hall," he murmured, as if savoring the name. "Who would have thought—of all things, it would become the bait that draws silver into my treasury?"

Jiang Yue bowed again. "Congratulations, Your Highness."

Chen Song's lips curved a little more. "They believe they are throwing themselves at the Crown Prince's feet. They believe they are 'supporting the Eastern Palace.' But the silver they offer—before it even touches the surface of that banner—has already fallen into my hands."

His eyes flickered with a predatory satisfaction. "Such a plan—truly makes one's heart glad."

He rose, unhurriedly, and placed his hands behind his back. The folded fan rested against his knuckles. His gaze drifted beyond the veranda toward the dense sea of bamboo, where the leaves swayed, wave upon wave, as if hiding unseen currents beneath their calm surface. His voice dropped lower, intimate, like a purr spoken into the dark.

"One stone, two birds," he said. "First, I slap the Crown Prince's face and make the Eastern Palace lose standing. Second, I sever Lu Chou's arm—cripple him where it hurts, cripple him in influence."

He let out a soft laugh, almost pleased with his own phrasing.

"And if, while the wound is still fresh, I borrow the court's hand to strike again…" His smile deepened. "Heh. That second son of House

Lu—this upright, annoying paragon—may not walk away whole. He may not even be able to leave the board intact."

He turned, candlelight catching the sharp lines of his face.

"Push it harder," he ordered calmly. "Spread the rumours wider. Let them swell. Let them become so loud that every corridor of the court vibrates with doubt."

He paused, then spoke with deliberate cruelty, each clause set down like a chess piece:

"If Lu Chou tries to clear himself, he must argue, defend, explain—each word will drag him deeper into the mire of his own defence. If he refuses to clear himself, then the court will say he is guilty by silence. Either way, suspicion will hang him."

His eyes half-lidded, he spoke the last line with quiet relish:

"This game has only just opened."

Jiang Yue bowed deeply and withdrew.

Chen Song, left alone, wandered slowly through the bamboo shadows. The night breeze brushed the hem of his robe. His mood was unexpectedly light—almost buoyant—like a man savoring the first move of a long, exquisite match.

The more he played, the more marvelous the board became. He found it endlessly entertaining.

* * * * *

Night fell. The bamboo garden banquet dispersed.

Chen Song did not return to his main hall. Instead, he went to the back chambers and summoned Jiang Yue again—this time in a sealed inner room, a private space meant for whispers and knives.

A single lamp burned faintly. Its flame was thin, trembling, and incense smoke curled upward into the darkness.

Chen Song had changed into plain attire. Standing by the window with his hands behind his back, he looked almost like a scholar at rest— almost. Yet his eyes gleamed with calculation; nothing about them was restful.

He spoke with a calm interest that sounded almost conversational, but carried command in every word:

"Among the great merchant houses of Jiangnan—especially the six great silk firms—who dares to step forward first? Who will be the first to declare loyalty?"

Jiang Yue bowed. "Aside from Yongchang, the houses of Jin Yuan Ji and Wan Feng have already begun to stir. But they still watch and hesitate."

He added, careful, precise: "They fear that once Lu Chou's 'search and seizure' fire begins at Jin Hua Hall, it will not end there. They fear it will spread—burning onward into other merchant houses."

Chen Song let out a low laugh. He turned, the folded fan tapping the table once, lightly.

"Then give them courage."

Jiang Yue leaned closer, voice dropping to a whisper meant for walls and lamps.

"I have already released word that this raid was planned and directed by Lu Chou himself, in secret—not an imperial decree. I have also arranged for people to say that the Eastern Palace has received the news and is displeased. There are already murmurs inside the Crown Prince's residence."

He paused, then delivered the dagger with a soft tone:

"They say Lu Chou is arrogant, overbearing, acting beyond his station. They say his future is doubtful. They say his prospects are dim."

Chen Song's expression shifted—briefly bright, almost delighted.

"Is that so?" he said, genuinely amused. "Then that is truly excellent."

He looked toward the candle flame. The light and smoke cut his face into alternating shadow and clarity, as if he were a man with two masks.

"Lu Chou," he said slowly, almost thoughtfully. "I never placed him in my eyes. But unfortunately—his little bit of clear-minded, righteous temperament wins Father's favour."

His voice remained mild, but each word carried frost.

"The Emperor likes sons who appear bright and upright. Honest. Clean."

His lips curved again, a colder curve.

"If the Crown Prince truly trusts him," Chen Song said, "then the Crown Prince invites humiliation upon himself. At court, loyalty has always been twofold. One loyalty is said to be for the realm. The other loyalty is truly for the throne."

He let the words settle, then smiled more deeply.

"The Crown Prince cannot distinguish the two."

He leaned slightly forward, voice lowering into something almost intimate, almost poisonous.

"And I—need only make the world believe that the Crown Prince and Lu Chou are conspirators together. That they move as one. That they share one intent."

His eyes narrowed into a thin slit.

"Then Lu Chou becomes a thorn in Father's heart."

Jiang Yue bowed. "This subordinate understands."

"Good." Chen Song brushed aside a bit of ash on the table, tone light, but the meaning chilling. "Father fears private sentiment interfering with governance more than anything."

He lifted his gaze.

"If the Eastern Palace dares to protect Lu Chou, then the Eastern Palace itself will not be safe."

He closed the fan with a sharp snap.

"Send word to the censors in the capital—those who owe us favours," he said. "At tomorrow's court audience, I want to hear the words 'Eastern Palace faction abuses power' echo throughout the Golden Throne Hall."

"Yes, Your Highness."

"And another matter," Jiang Yue added, voice dropping even further, the calculation in it unmistakable. "As Your Highness ordered, the rumours have been spread according to plan. All of Jiangnan now believes the raid was Lu Chou's act of personal revenge. Even in the Crown Prince's residence, there are those questioning his abuse of authority."

Chen Song's smile widened.

Jiang Yue continued: "There is also talk that Jin Hua Hall's former gold-thread embroidery will be placed under the Crown Prince's control. If Your Highness steps forward under the name of the Eastern Palace—

claiming to 'protect merchants, stabilize trade, soothe the people'—then those old merchant foxes will see the trend clearly."

He paused, then sharpened the point:

"At that time, to handle them—Your Highness will find it as easy as turning your hand. They will come carrying silver to you, begging, before you even summon them."

Chen Song's eyes half-lidded. "Continue."

"As for execution," Jiang Yue said, glancing toward the distant patrol outside, voice sinking lower still, "in no more than three days… Your Highness need only issue 'protection orders' in the name of the Eastern Palace."

His hand made a gathering gesture.

"In secret, we will take in Jin Hua Hall's former people—its old craftsmen, its old hands. And those merchants who have been frightened out of their wits…"

His palm closed as if grasping something.

"They will bring contributions and plead for shelter." Chen Song clapped softly, once. He looked satisfied—at ease.

"Good," he said. "Do it cleanly. Let the merchants mistakenly believe they are turning to the Crown Prince. Let them keep that belief."

He smiled. "The silver will come obediently."

Then his expression cooled. His voice turned hard.

"Lu Chou," he said, slow and precise. "This move must break him. He must not carry this step without injury."

He lifted his eyes, the gleam like steel.

"At court, push two or three censors to impeach him. Once the momentum rises, once the sound becomes a tide—let's see how he dares defend himself."

Jiang Yue bowed. "This subordinate has already contacted several censors. They only wait for tomorrow's audience."

Chen Song's smile deepened. His eyes were cold as stars.

"Very well." He spoke as if granting a reward. "Jiang Yue, return to Jiangnan personally. Whisper to the merchants that to avoid this calamity, there is only one path—seek refuge under the Eastern Palace."

Jiang Yue's lips curved into a thin smile. "Understood. They will believe they serve the Crown Prince—when in truth, they serve Your Highness."

"Precisely." Chen Song's gaze was steady. "Time does not wait. Leave tonight. Ride through the night if you must."

"Yes, Your Highness." Jiang Yue bowed and withdrew. The secret chamber returned to silence.

For a long while, Chen Song stood before the wavering flame, unmoving. The folded fan rolled slowly between his fingers. His gaze was deep and unreadable, as if he were already watching the next moves unfold in the dark.

"One stone, two birds?" he murmured to himself, lips barely moving. "Not necessarily."

His smile sharpened.

"If this chess is played well… it may be three birds, four birds…"

The candle flickered. Bamboo shadows swayed across the wall like restless water.

He let out a soft laugh, then spoke again—almost gently, yet each word carried a chill that sank to the bone:

"The Crown Prince is too benevolent. Father is too suspicious. Lu Chou is too upright."

He paused, eyes narrowing. "Until the final step, who can say who will ascend?"

His voice remained soft, but the cold beneath it was unmistakable.

"This time, the chance must not be missed. We must use this to topple the Crown Prince."

Slowly, he opened the fan. Mountains and mist unfurled across the silk, mirroring the sharp gleam in his eyes.

"If even this Jiangnan game can be leveraged to push into the court," he murmured, "then the struggle for the heirloom seat… may need to be spoken of differently."

He stepped out of the chamber. Outside, only a few official lanterns lit the corridor; wind poured through, making the flames tremble. The night was so dark it seemed as if ink could drip from the sky.

Bamboo leaves rasped against one another—like the whisper of an approaching storm.

Chapter 39: First Meeting Under the Lamp

The night before the Imperial Consort Selection was as dark as spilled ink, yet the city was ablaze with a magnificent radiance.

With the Qiqiao Festival approaching, Emperor Jingyuan's sudden decree for the selection of imperial consorts had struck like a thunderclap across a calm plain, upending the carefully laid plans of many noble houses. Throughout the palaces and manor houses, subtle schemes were set in motion.

Under the guise of the festival's lantern fairs, grand banquets for launching water lanterns and offering prayers were held on this eve—in truth, these were orchestrated opportunities for brilliant young talents and noble young ladies to cross paths.

Thousands of lanterns shimmered upon the water, and the silver moonlight melded with the golden glow of the lamps, each enhancing the beauty of the other. Within the Imperial City, the lantern banquet in the Royal Gardens was a spectacle of extraordinary bustle.

Myriad colourful lanterns were reflected upon the lake's surface, their ripples glittering as if the stars themselves had tumbled into the mortal realm. Upon the decorated pavilions at the heart of the lake, guests toasted one another, and the air was thick with the sound of laughter and clinking cups.

Deep within the Royal Gardens, an exquisite gallery with upturned eaves sat perched at the water's edge, providing a place for noble ladies to rest and admire the view.

On this night before the grand ceremony, the princes sat upon high platforms in the central courtyard, while the titled ladies and young socialites of marriageable age were scattered among the floral paths, pavilions, and terraces.

From the upper floors, merry voices drifted down, and from behind silk curtains came the rhythmic chiming of jade ornaments.

Shen Zhaoru, the legitimate daughter of the Grand Preceptor, wore her hair in a half-up knot and was dressed in an orange-red silk skirt embroidered with a hundred butterflies. She leaned against a railing, chatting and laughing with two of her closest friends.

As she peeled and ate fresh white lotus seeds from her palm, she murmured a soft complaint: "This selection for the Crown Princess is far too dull. I thought they would at least let the young ladies show off their talents—writing a poem or something of the sort."

The girls sat in a circle, unable to stop chirping as they discussed the matter of the Crown Princess.

"Zhaoru, who knows? Tomorrow, the Emperor or the Crown Prince might set their sights on you, and you'll become the Crown Princess!" one girl teased with a giggle. "That would be far better than us marrying some ordinary gentleman."

"Being a secondary consort to the Crown Prince would be wonderful as well."

"Indeed, indeed! And besides, there are several other princes."

Shen Zhaoru shook her head gently, her eyes bright and clear as water. "I only want what my parents have—to have only each other for a lifetime, never to be parted."

Hearing this, the girls nearby couldn't help but cover their mouths and laugh.

"Oh, Zhaoru, you are far too naive!" a more composed girl teased. "Where in this court exists a one-husband, one-wife arrangement? Having a wife and several concubines is the norm."

Another chimed in, "Men like your father, the Grand Preceptor, who devotes his life to scholarship and takes only one wife, are as rare as a phoenix feather or a unicorn horn!"

Listening to them, the corners of Shen Zhaoru's mouth quirked upward. Her smile held a trace of determination and innocence; she had no desire to share a husband with other women.

A warm breeze drifted through the pavilion, carrying the light scent of fragrant tea. As the girls admired the lanterns, their laughter grew more spirited.

"To be honest, regarding this selection, our Zhaoru may have no interest, but if the Emperor decrees the marriage, she must obey. After all, who else is as well-read, well-mannered, and heavenly beautiful as she?" a smartly dressed girl said with a wink, her eyes full of playfulness.

"Never mind the Crown Princess; which young lord in the capital wouldn't hope to marry her? Just the other day, my third aunt was secretly asking me about Zhaoru's current situation!" another girl added mischievously.

Shen Zhaoru's face flushed red, and she shook her head hurriedly. "Why are you all making fun of me? You wicked girls."

"And you say you aren't that wonderful?" an older girl said, lightly patting the back of her hand. "You have a charming look and a gentle temperament; you are educated and know how to please others. Most importantly, you have the upright Grand Preceptor Shen as a father. Which noble lady wouldn't praise you as the finest catch?"

"Exactly!" a refined girl giggled. "When we play together, Zhaoru is the kind of person who makes everyone look at her first. And once they look, they can't bear to turn away."

"Listen to that! It sounds like poetry!" another laughed. "But in all seriousness—my mother often says we daughters of official houses must choose our husbands carefully. One must marry a man of talent who can grant his legitimate wife proper dignity. We cannot be led astray by those poor noble families who only care about status, and certainly not by those lowly concubine-born sons."

"A man who can grant his legitimate wife dignity and has enough talent to not rely solely on his family's shadow is already a superlative match," another girl agreed with a smile. "Even if he has one or two concubines, the inner household would still remain peaceful and quiet."

"So, finding a man worthy of Zhaoru is truly difficult. He must cherish her in his heart, let her be coquettish, possess both talent and courage, and his family background goes without saying. Alas, I fear there are few young lords in the capital who meet all those marks!"

As they spoke with excitement, they exchanged glances, their tones a mix of envy and affection.

Shen Zhaoru listened, her cheeks slightly crimson, but a stubborn light flashed in her eyes. She said softly, "In the future, if someone is willing to place me at the very center of their heart, just like my father does for my mother, only then will it be a good marriage. If he is merely all show and no substance, I want nothing to do with him."

"What a spirited girl!" the others laughed. "We truly admire your resolve!"

As she turned her head, a lotus seed accidentally slipped from her hand, falling into the pond and creating a circle of ripples. To retrieve the fallen seed, she leaned over precariously, nearly tumbling into the water.

Just as she was about to fall, a powerful arm suddenly reached out from behind, steadying her and preventing her from plunging into the depths.

"Oh, Zhaoru!" her two friends cried out in alarm.

"Oh, that was close." Once steadied, she patted her chest, her heart still racing and her small face flushed.

A deep, low voice resonated from behind her: "Be careful, My Lady."

She turned around and met a pair of deep, silent eyes—it was **Lu Xiu,** standing in the side gallery of the gallery.

He held no place of honor today, standing instead beyond the gaze of the crowd, like a quiet shadow that didn't belong in such a space. He wore a set of black gauze robes with silver patterns—plain attire without official seals—yet he possessed an undeniable air of stability.

Shen Zhaoru gazed at him for several heartbeats before suddenly smiling. "And who might you be, sir?"

"I shall take my leave." Lu Xiu had no intention of revealing his name; he gave a slight bow, preparing to depart.

"Wait, I haven't thanked you yet." In her haste, Shen Zhaoru caught the edge of his sleeve.

"It was a small matter. You need not trouble yourself, My Lady."

She asked in a low voice, "From which house do you come?"

"The concubine-born son of the Lu family, **Xiu.**"

Concubine-born?

"Lu?" she repeated the name, a flash of curiosity and confusion in her eyes. "Are you not..."

The eldest concubine-born son of Minister Lu?

"I am neither a relative of the royals nor of the legitimate line. I am not worth mentioning." Lu Xiu curled his lips in a self-deprecating smile and lowered his head. "It is best if Lady Shen does not remember me."

"So it is Commander Lu." A young lady in a yellow dress nearby recognized him and introduced him to Shen Zhaoru. "This is the eldest concubine-born son of Minister Lu; he works alongside my elder brother."

"I see." Zhaoru gave him a faint smile. "Why is Commander Lu here alone? Why not go to the front and join the other young lords?"

Lu Xiu bowed his head slightly. "My status does not warrant a high seat. I am merely here awaiting orders."

Shen Zhaoru was stunned. Looking at the lake behind him, illuminated by the lanterns, she felt a faint sense of loneliness in his words. She suddenly felt that a man like this, standing on the edge of the crowd, was more unforgettable than the high-ranking youths.

She said in a low voice, "But if a man truly has talent, why must his seat determine his honor or baseness?"

Lu Xiu froze, a glimmer of light flashing in his eyes before he lowered them with a smile. "Lady Shen is exactly right, but the world seldom thinks that way."

Her eyes sparkled like the light upon the water. "What do you mean, 'not warrant'? Commander Lu is as elegant as a jade tree; even among these lords, you stand out like a crane among chickens."

He did not reply. His deep eyes gazed at her as he said simply, "If My Lady enjoys lotus seeds, there is a Sweet Osmanthus Pavilion not far along the shore. There are sugared lotus seeds and tea prepared there. Perhaps you would like to try them."

Shen Zhaoru was taken aback. "How did Commander Lu know I love sugared lotus seeds?"

He lowered his eyes, his voice very low. "A guess."

Shen Zhaoru, who had been speaking with a playful tone, suddenly paused. She was a pampered, willful daughter of a high official, and she had never met someone like this—neither humble nor arrogant, calm and restrained, yet capable of making her heart skip a beat in an instant.

Just as she was about to say more, the voice of another noble lady rang out: "Come quickly and launch the lotus lanterns!"

"Coming..." Shen Zhaoru's friends began to move toward the water's edge.

To avoid being left alone, Shen Zhaoru had to follow. The group exchanged simple bows and took their temporary leave of one another.

Readers can view the full collection of colour illustrations here:
https://www.facebook.com/profile.php?id=61581325000577

Chapter 40: Shadows Crossed in Lamplight

At the lake's centre rose a high platform; jade steps lay under moonlight like pale silver. Silk-and-bamboo music echoed through the night wind, and the scent of wine mingled with flowers.

Crown Prince Chen Gen wore plain gauze robes, with a dark-gold dragon pattern embroidered along his cuffs. His features were gentle, his manner composed, his gaze calm. Beside him, Third Prince Chen Song half leaned against the jade balustrade, a smile held at the corner of his lips; his tone was light, almost lazy.

"Royal Brother's elegance has not diminished tonight," Chen Song drawled. "Even at a consort-selection banquet, you sit so steady. Don't tell me your heart is already set."

Chen Gen lifted his cup and smiled. "Set is too strong a word. Since Father has said he will choose the virtuous and refined, it is only right to value virtue and talent above all. As for who will be chosen—"

Before he could finish, a Hanlin tutor seated nearby spoke in a low voice, as though offering a careful answer rather than intruding.

"If one speaks of virtue and talent together, then among the capital's daughters, Lady Shen of the Grand Preceptor's estate should be the foremost choice. Lord Shen's scholarship crowns the age; his daughter is gentle and proper, and her name in letters is widely praised. We have heard it often."

Chen Song gave a soft scoff and cast a sidelong glance. "The Grand Preceptor's daughter… Shen Zhaoru. The capital's first talented woman. Even if I am a prince, I would still be reaching too high."

Chen Gen smiled faintly. "Third Brother, do not speak so carelessly. Lady Shen is known precisely for her quiet purity of heart. She is not one who clings to power. Do not make her the subject of jest."

Chen Song's thin lips curved. "Royal Brother speaks reasonably. After all, Lady Shen and Royal Brother might even be called childhood companions—did you not once study under the Grand Preceptor's roof together? Naturally her talent and character are lofty. It seems we have spoken too freely."

Chen Gen set down his cup. His expression remained even. "To speak is harmless. If one is fortunate enough to find a good companion, to support each other through wind and rain, rumours will stop on their own."

Chen Song smiled with amusement. "Brother's words sound like a scholar's. But what a pity—this world holds more than poetry and books. It also holds blades and power. A Crown Princess is weighed not only for her own talent, but for the strength of her family."

Chen Gen did not answer directly. He poured a full cup and handed it over, his voice warm as polished jade.

"Third Brother overstates it. If the Crown Princess is truly virtuous, she should steady the hearts of the realm—rather than become a tool for power."

The two princes looked at one another for a heartbeat; the air above the wine cooled slightly.

In Chen Song's heart, a cold snort rose. He was unconvinced. His Crown Prince brother always wore the right mask.

Not a tool for power?

If it were not for Grand Preceptor Shen's influence over scholars across the realm—and if it were not for the fact that marrying into the Shen family carried no threat of dangerous imperial in-laws—would Chen Gen truly be so devoted to virtue?

A moment later, Liang Yunqing—the Censor's son—laughed and stepped in to smooth the air.

"I hear the young ladies are setting lanterns afloat by the lakeshore tonight. Besides Miss Shen, the Minister's second daughter of the Chen family has also been praised as the night's finest—her smile catches every eye. And although the Du family's daughter has not appeared, her literary name is also well known. Even the palace ladies say that, among those who might be compared—if only slightly—to Lady Shen, only the Chen and Du daughters are worthy of mention."

Chen Song toyed with his fan and chuckled. "Second Miss Chen is indeed pretty—when she laughs and speaks, her eyes gleam. If she entered the Eastern Palace, she would bring amusement every day."

Chen Gen's brow tightened faintly, though his tone remained slow and even. "Amusement is not the proper way. In the inner palace, what is most needed is steadiness."

At those words, several young lords exchanged glances and smiled, not daring to add anything.

Fresh tea was served. The night wind carried the glow of water lanterns. From afar, the lake was crowded with floating lights, and the laughter of young women drifted in and out like mist.

Chen Gen's gaze passed over the water, and without intending to, landed beneath the shadow of an osmanthus tree—where a faint figure in pink seemed to stand, delicate and clear.

His eyes shifted. Then he only smiled faintly and drank.

Chen Song noticed and laughed softly. "Royal Brother's heart truly has its owner."

"It is only a festival. How can one speak of ownership?" Chen Gen's tone did not change. Then, slowly, he turned his eyes and said, "But I have heard that the Jiangnan weaving case has begun to show its outlines. Lu Chou has recently been ordered south on imperial business. Has Third Brother heard anything?"

Chen Song paused; a flash crossed his eyes. "I have heard a little. The court's winds are not yet clear. Brother need not trouble himself."

Chen Gen looked at him and smiled without speaking. After a moment, he turned back to the lake, his expression faintly thoughtful.

In the distance the lanterns drifted with the current. A pink lotus lamp swayed, and by chance floated right up to him.

He reached out and caught it. On the lantern base, a single character had been carved with delicate care:

昭.

He froze for the briefest instant—then smiled.

Chen Song saw it and murmured, low and amused, "Shen Zhaoru… truly an interesting figure."

Moonlight poured down. The brothers' gazes crossed, their smiles not the same.

On the lake, ten thousand lanterns shone like stars—yet beneath that still night, dark tides surged soundlessly.

After nightfall, the strains of silk-and-bamboo music by the lakeside gradually faded, yet the water lanterns had not fully dispersed. Palace attendants conducted their routine night patrols, moving along the covered corridors and quietly passing down instructions, reminding the guests at each seating to withdraw in stages. Lantern shadows were stretched long by the wind, cast across the blue stone paving in mottled patterns like rippling water. The high platform that had only moments ago been filled with laughter and conversation was now left with uncollected cups and dishes, the scent of wine mingling with cold dew.

Several Hanlin scholars walked side by side, their steps slowing, their voices lowered to near whispers.

" This gathering tonight was livelier than in previous years " one of them murmured.

" Liveliness is superficial. The real matter is the direction of the wind " another gave a quiet snort. " The Crown Prince scarcely spoke from beginning to end, yet his name was invoked at every turn. That is what truly invites reflection. "

" Well, of course " a third replied lightly. " The Crown Prince is a dragon among men. When is he ever not the subject of discussion? You may as well be stating the obvious. "

The speaker allowed a faint, meaningful smile to surface, his gaze flicking sideways toward another figure. " Look there. Grand Preceptor Shen's bearing—truly beyond our reach. "

" Oh? You mean the Shen household? "

" Not only the Shen household " the man said, tilting his head slightly, his tone layered with implication. " Grand Preceptor Shen's disciples are spread throughout the Six Ministries. Among the ranks of the clean-stream officials, seven out of ten trace their origins to his tutelage. If the Crown Prince were to take a Shen daughter as consort, it would be the same as drawing the entire force of scholarly opinion to his side. "

The others fell silent for a moment before one of them spoke again. " In my view, His Majesty likely holds the same intention. But those few remarks from the Third Prince just now were clearly a reminder—being Crown Princess is not only about virtue, but also about the ability to 'steady the board.' "

" And that " the first man said with a low chuckle, " is precisely what makes it interesting. One speaks of virtue, the other of power. Which stands higher has yet to be decided. "

The youngest official walking at the rear suddenly interjected, " Did any of you notice the pink lotus lantern on the lake? "

The group halted.

" The one carved with the character 'Zhao'? "

" Exactly " he nodded. " At first I thought it mere coincidence, but I saw the Crown Prince take it into his own hands—and pause for a moment. "

At once, the expressions of the others subtly shifted.

" Zhao… " someone murmured under their breath, tasting the sound. " Shen Zhaoru? "

" In the capital, how many could that character possibly point to? " the man replied calmly, his certainty unspoken but clear.

" That would be Miss Shen of the Grand Preceptor's household " another said quietly. " She has known the princes since childhood— especially the Crown Prince. Calling them childhood companions would not be an exaggeration. "

A night breeze swept through, stirring the palace lanterns beneath the eaves. Flames wavered, casting light and shadow across their faces. No one spoke further, but each had already begun weighing matters in his own heart.

Not far away, two palace eunuchs conversed in hushed tones.

" Miss Shen of the Shen household—her talent is renowned throughout the capital. Being placed so prominently at an occasion like this… she is all but certain to be the future Crown Princess. "

" Indeed, "the other let out a soft laugh. " Some people need only sit quietly to the side, and it's as though an immortal has descended among mortals. "

Before the words had fully faded, a duty-ranking palace lady emerged from the shadows, her expression cool and severe. The two eunuchs immediately fell silent, lowering their heads in salute.

Her gaze swept across the lake, lingering for a brief instant on the water lanterns that had yet to drift away, before she turned and departed.

Deeper within the palace walls, lights still burned.

Inside a study, a night-duty attendant moved with great care to replace a spent candle. The figure seated at the desk did not lift his head, merely tapping his fingers lightly against the tabletop to signal dismissal.

After a moment, he spoke in a low voice. " Has there been any movement from the Shen household? "

A voice answered from the shadows. " None as yet. The Grand Preceptor attended the banquet tonight with his daughter. He spoke briefly with several officials, then took his leave early, citing poor health. "

" I see, " The man replied evenly. " Quite restrained. "

Restrained—yet anything but ordinary.

As the night deepened, currents within the palace quietly shifted. No one stated it outright, yet a shared understanding had already taken form—

After tonight, the name Shen Zhaoru would be spoken with even greater frequency, now increasingly bound to the title of future Crown Princess.

Chapter 41: Walk Steady, Walk Far

By the time Shen Zhaoru returned from the Qiqiao Festival, the moon hung exceptionally high and solitary in the sky, casting long, silvery shadows across the ground. She removed her pearl hairpins, changed into her comfortable everyday garments, and stepped into the back courtyard. As she walked, she noticed the lamp shadows within the study remained unextinguished, and through the thin window paper, the lean, slightly stooped silhouette of Grand Preceptor Shen was clearly reflected. A gentle breeze brushed through the bamboo blinds, bringing with it the familiar scent of ink and a sudden, soft, dry cough.

"Father, have you not yet retired?" she called out in a low, concerned voice.

"Your father has been correcting the memorials submitted by the Hanlin Academy these past few days; no matter how I plead, he refuses to rest early." Madam Shen, hearing her daughter's voice, emerged from the inner room and said with a gentle smile: "By the way, you attended the banquet tonight; did everything go smoothly?"

Upon hearing those words, for reasons she could not explain, the tall, lean, and aloof figure of a man suddenly leaped into her mind—Lu Xiu, the one who had saved her twice this very day!

Zhaoru walked to the side of the couch and performed a formal kneeling bow, her voice tender and composed: "It was nothing particularly special. An elegant banquet of poetry is, after all, but a bustling scene; everyone was bound by rigid etiquette, merely maintaining their respective appearances to the fullest."

Madam Shen let out a soft sigh: "Zhaoru, you are the only child of our Shen family, and you have always been a comfort to us since you were a small girl. It is only a pity that I could not provide you with a brother. In the future, when your father and I are no longer here, if others seek to wrong or bully you, who will there be to stand behind you and provide support?"

Hearing this, Grand Preceptor Shen's brush paused mid-stroke. He lifted his eyes to look at her, his voice gentle yet firm: "Mother, you worry overmuch. Wealth does not last three generations, and power does not span ten years. If we place all our hopes and expectations on male heirs, it will ultimately be difficult for the family to endure for long. We scholars must take education as our root, establishing virtue and words rather than establishing mere power and influence."

Having spoken, he offered a smile, though he could not stop himself from breaking into a series of two sharp, involuntary coughs.

"Father!" Zhaoru hurried forward, lightly patting his back, her eyes full of undisguised anxiety. "Please, rest early. There are so many new policies in the capital now; why must you attend to every single matter personally?"

Madam Shen also hurried to pour tea and hand it to him, advising in a soft, persuasive tone: "The weather has turned cold these past few days. You do not even consider your own age; do not push yourself anymore. The rumors in the capital are growing chaotic; our Shen family need only keep to our duty. Your disciples are numerous; let the younger generation contend over the affairs of state."

Grand Preceptor Shen shook his head with a faint smile: "Many contend, but few guard. The social atmosphere is superficial and flamboyant; court officials struggle for power and status, yet they forget for whom they serve. If there is no good teacher to guide the Emperor's heart, where shall the people of the world turn?"

His words were calm, yet they resonated through the room like the low tolling of an ancient bell. Zhaoru lowered her head, quietly watching the oil lamp on the desk. The light reflected on her father's face—lean, clear, and bearing a scholar's characteristic blend of austerity and resolve.

"You, you have been lost in your books your whole life. My daughter and I are but women; we do not understand your grand principles. I only wish for you to rest more and not be so exhausted." Madam Shen gave him a dissatisfied, yet affectionate look.

"And you, you have been nagging for half a lifetime and still cannot stop. I shall rest in a moment."

"I understand my father's ambitions," Shen Zhaoru said, watching the affectionate way her parents interacted with a trace of envy in her heart. She whispered, "It is only that the world does not always go as Father wishes. Loyal and upright officials all take you as their paragon; even I take you as my model. In the future, if I am to marry, I must find someone who is as devoted to me as you are to Mother."

Grand Preceptor Shen was startled for a moment, then laughed heartily. "That sounds exactly like something your mother would say."

Madam Shen gave him a sidelong glance and said softly: "My Lord, it is not that I do not understand your principles, but I am merely a woman who does not comprehend the affairs of the court. I only hope you look after your health. Now that Zhaoru is growing older, I often think at night—if she marries into a powerful family in the future, with her temperament, she might suffer."

Grand Preceptor Shen fell silent for a moment, his tone softening. "A person's fate lies with Heaven; no one can protect another for an entire lifetime. It is better to teach her to understand reason and her own heart, to know when to advance and when to retreat. In this way, even if she encounters storms, she can stand on her own without fear."

Zhaoru smiled, pursing her lips: "I have taken it to heart. It is just... if someone could truly understand even half of my mind and be willing to share a simple, ordinary life with me, that would be a true blessing."

Madam Shen caught the faint tenderness in her daughter's voice and teased lightly: "Did someone at the banquet catch your eye? Was it the Crown Prince?"

Zhaoru's face flushed slightly, and she murmured: "Nothing of the sort... what has this to do with the Crown Prince?"

Grand Preceptor Shen coughed twice more and took a sip of tea to moisten his throat before saying: "The Crown Prince is gentle and kind; you two are childhood sweethearts. He is a good man."

Madam Shen nodded. "Zhaoru has no brothers to lean on. If she could become the Crown Princess, she would finally have someone to rely on."

Shen Zhaoru nodded hesitantly: "Brother Crown Prince is certainly a dragon among men, but I..."

"What? You seem less than pleased?" Madam Shen easily perceived her daughter's hesitation.

"It is not that. It is just that I feel Brother Crown Prince might not necessarily set his heart on me. So, I thought, perhaps..."

"Do not overthink it. A good marriage is destined by Heaven; when the time comes, it will happen naturally," Grand Preceptor Shen comforted her softly.

Madam Shen hesitated, but ultimately only sighed: "You, with all your books, do not know the dangers of the world. If our daughter is to find a good husband, she must see if he has the ability to protect her. I think the Crown Prince is quite good. If it were other royalty or nobles, I fear what they value might not be our daughter's talent, but your prestige as the Grand Preceptor."

Looking at her parents, Zhaoru felt a sudden pang in her chest. She said softly: "What Father and Mother say is right. I only feel that if a heart is sincere, what does status matter? In this world... the rarest thing is a true heart."

Grand Preceptor Shen's gaze grew soft, and he reached out to pat the back of her hand. "Good child. To have such a heart is better than ten thousand volumes of classics. But the distinction between legitimate and concubine birth is still the law of etiquette. One must never hold it in contempt; the legitimate is the primary, and the concubine-born is the secondary—they cannot ascend to the grand hall..."

He was about to say more when he was interrupted by a violent fit of coughing. Tea splashed, and the brush rack tilted. Zhaoru and Madam Shen hurried to steady him. Amidst the chaos, they heard him say hoarsely: "It is nothing, just an old ailment recurring. Lately, the winds in the court have been fierce; the Emperor has repeatedly asked about the Crown Prince's affairs, and I am worried as well."

Madam Shen frowned: "Lu Chou and Xie Huaici are both busy in Jiangnan, and now the rumors have reached the capital. If more waves arise, I fear the Crown Prince's faction will find no peace."

Grand Preceptor Shen shook his head: "Right and wrong will eventually become clear. You need not worry."

The wind outside grew swifter, and the lamp flame flickered. Watching her father's lean and slightly stooped shoulders, a wave of unspeakable sorrow surged in Zhaoru's heart. She suddenly felt that the brilliance and laughter of the banquet were so distant and hollow compared to the solitary lamp before her.

She lightened her voice and said: "Father, it is late; please rest. Mother, you should sleep early as well. Father still has the early morning court session tomorrow."

Madam Shen adjusted his cloak and answered softly: "Very well. You should also rest early. Do not ponder too much."

Zhaoru nodded and was about to turn and leave when she heard her father call her name: "Zhaoru—"

She turned back to see Grand Preceptor Shen smiling beneath the lamp, his tone gentle yet profound: "The glories of the world are like smoke. I only wish for you to remember: if the heart is upright, there is peace; if the path is steady, one goes far."

Zhaoru performed a light bow and turned to walk into the long corridor. The night breeze brushed her face, carrying the distant scent of sweet osmanthus. She looked back at the study; the lamp was still there—its light faint but unextinguished—much like the clarity her father had guarded all his life.

Chapter 42: A Restless Reunion

Night had thickened into a deep, velvety hush.

The Jiangnan air was heavy with midsummer heat; even the lotus leaves outside hung limp and motionless, glistening faintly beneath the moon. Only the faintest breath of wind slipped through the gauze curtains, carrying with it the scent of pond water and a fragile trace of coolness.

Xiao Lingyu had been confined within the quiet pavilion for many days—cut off from sunlight, her world reduced to muted shadows and the slow ticking of the incense clock.

She wore plain linen instead of the bright silks once befitting her station. Her hair, once dressed with gold pins and flowers, now hung in a simple knot; her face, pale and thinned by exhaustion, was calm as still water—serene, almost detached, yet beneath that calm something fragile trembled unseen.

Then—footsteps, faint as moth wings—brushed against the silence beyond the door.

Her heart stilled, then began to race.

"Mother—!"

A small, bright voice pierced the stillness. The gauze curtain stirred, and in the next instant a child burst into the room—a tiny whirlwind of joy. Bare feet, the scent of milk and sun-warmed skin, eyes glimmering like twin stars.

"Baor—"

The composure she had fought to maintain splintered in a heartbeat.

She dropped to her knees and gathered the child into her arms, clutching her so tightly that Baor squeaked in surprise. The world blurred; tears spilled unchecked down Xiao Lingyu's face, hot and blinding.

"Baor… were you frightened? These days, Mother—Mother could not come to you…"

Outside the curtain, Lu Chou paused mid-step. His brows drew together slightly, though his expression remained unreadable.

The child looked up, her round face full of brightness. She reached up with her tiny hands, wiping her mother's tears with clumsy care.

"Don't cry, Mother! Baor's fine, truly fine!"

And then, with all the solemn pride of a four-year-old, she began to chatter—voice clear as bells:

"Papa Lord told me so many stories! He taught me to write my name, and how to ride a pony! He even made osmanthus cakes just for me! He said I'm the best girl in the world!"

The word Father struck like a blade drawn too suddenly.

Xiao Lingyu stiffened. Her arms slackened slightly as she echoed the word under her breath, barely audible.

"…Papa?"

The little girl's eyes curved into crescents, her tone full of certainty.

"That lord, of course! He said I can call him Papa. He paints with me and takes me to see the lantern boats. Sometimes he sings the Picking Water Chestnuts song, the one you used to hum! He said if I'm good, Mama will come get me soon."

For a moment, Xiao Lingyu forgot to breathe.

A dull ache bloomed behind her ribs, spreading outward until every breath hurt. She pulled Baor close again, hiding her face in the child's soft hair.

"Truly?" she whispered, though her voice trembled.

Baor nodded hard, delighted. "Truly! Then… can Lord Lu always be my papa?"

The words fell like a stone into still water.

Xiao Lingyu's lips parted; no answer came. Her throat tightened. After a long silence, she managed a faint smile and stroked the girl's cheek.

"Baor, be good… we'll talk about that later, all right?"

The child's smile faltered; her small shoulders drooped. "Can't we?" she asked softly. "Baor already has a father…"

Xiao Lingyu froze. "…Lord Xie?"

Baor nodded with perfect innocence.

"…Yes," Lingyu said at last, voice barely above a whisper. "Yes, him."

Her face turned aside; guilt and sorrow welled up like a rising tide.

"Oh." The sound was small and disappointed—yet it pierced deeper than any cry.

The words hung in the air, slow and heavy.

The anger she had carried these many days—against Lu Chou, against fate, against herself—dissolved like salt in water, leaving only a quiet, unbearable ache.

She looked down at her daughter's trusting face, saw the reflection of her own helplessness there. Tears welled again, silent and endless.

Baor, she thought, it is I who wronged you. I let you meet your father, yet must keep the truth veiled. I let you call him "Papa," yet cannot give you a home with both your parents beneath one roof.

Her heart constricted, the sorrow too tender to name.

The child, sensing her mother's stillness, reached out and patted her cheek.

"Don't be sad, Mother. Baor loves you most."

Outside the curtain, Lu Chou stood motionless.

The sound of that small voice—Can Lord Lu always be my father?—made something deep within him falter. His hand, resting at his side, curled slightly.

But when Xiao Lingyu's answer came, hesitant and distant, the faint light in his eyes dimmed.

A shadow crossed his face, and his lips curved in a slight, bitter smile—more pain than mirth.

Without a word, he turned and left, his footsteps soundless, his dark robe whispering like a passing wind.

In the end, he thought, he was never the one she chose.

And perhaps he never would be.

* * * * *

Night hung low—

not yet fallen, yet already close enough to taste the weight of it.

Lamplight spilled across the study's walls, stretching the shadows of scrolls and memorials like thin, wavering bars.

After a day of endless dispatches, the table before Lu Chou was still stacked high with sealed documents. The dust had not yet settled, and fatigue pressed behind his eyes. But he did not read.

His finger tapped the bronze paperweight—slow, steady, deliberate—as though tracing the pattern of an invisible game.

Liang Jin entered swiftly, bowing low.

"Your Excellency, the merchants have begun to stir. Two or three houses have already sent agents toward the capital to test the wind. Word is—they intend to increase their tribute in the name of the Eastern Palace."

Lu Chou's expression did not change. Only the corner of his mouth lifted faintly—somewhere between irony and weariness.

"Proceed," he said, voice low as ash. "Exactly as planned."

Liang Jin bowed again, hesitating.

Lu Chou reached for the teacup on his desk; the liquid inside had long gone cold. He drank anyway, then frowned, the bitterness lingering on his tongue.

"The Third Prince," he murmured after a moment, "truly plays well. Two birds with one stone—almost perfect. Such mind and measure are rare."

Liang Jin ventured cautiously, "Shall I add fuel to the fire, my lord? Stir the waters, make them cloudier still?"

"Do it," Lu Chou said softly. "No blades, no blood. Enough to bruise, not to break."

His smile returned—a thin line that never reached his eyes.

"The Eastern Palace… and these merchants still believe the tale. Let them."

Just then, the faint flutter of wings broke the silence.

A page entered hurriedly, bowing low, a white pigeon cradled in his palms.

"Message from the capital, my lord."

Lu Chou took the bird, unfastened the bamboo tube, and drew out a sliver of paper—folded with care, bearing three lines of concise script. His eyes passed over it once, and his expression hardened.

Without a word, he reached for brush and ink. The slip was no larger than his palm, yet each stroke he wrote was sharp, measured, deliberate—like carving words into stone.

When finished, he rolled the note tight, sealed it within a new tube, and handed it back to the boy.

"Send it by the same bird."

Liang Jin hesitated. "Shall I send men to follow its flight, in case—"

"No." Lu Chou's tone brooked no question. "It is meant for one man only. If he cannot receive it, no escort will change its fate. If he can, he will know what to do."

He rose, tall and composed, and moved to the window. The shutters were unlatched; night air drifted in, stirring the papers on his desk until they rustled like whispers.

For a long time he stood there, silent.

The lamplight fell across his face, cutting the sharp lines of his jaw and cheek; yet beneath the calm exterior, something subtle and human stirred.

He saw again those small arms clinging around a mother's neck,

heard the innocent lilt of a child's voice: Papa, can you always be my papa?

The sound replayed in his mind until it became a quiet ache, deep as bone.

He closed his eyes.

For years he had believed himself long past such weakness—beyond desire, beyond longing, shaped wholly by duty.

But when it came to her, nothing remained still.

She had said - We are even now.

Even—was it?

Then why did the echo of her tears refuse to leave him?

Why did the memory of her trembling shoulders burn sharper than any battlefield wound?

He exhaled slowly, pain folding into resolve. This battle was no longer for the court alone, but for something smaller—and far more dangerous:

the single, ruinous thought—If only we could begin again.

Outside, the white pigeon leapt into the dark. Its wings cut through the air like a blade, glinting once in the lamplight before vanishing into shadow.

No one would ever know what that letter carried.

But from this quiet night onward, the balance of the empire began—imperceptibly—to turn.

Chapter 43: Spiralling Out of Control

The night deepened further, and the lamplight trembled faintly.

The light within the room was dim and yellow, vaguely illuminating the outline of case files piled beside the desk like a mountain. Lu Chou leaned against the window, gazing into the oppressive darkness outside. The stars were sparse; half a waning moon hid behind drifting clouds. All around was so still it felt soundless.

Baor's innocent words still echoed in his ears—"Papa Lord, can you stay my Papa Lord forever?" That pure, untainted innocence tightened something in his chest.

Yet Lingyu gave no answer at all. She only shifted the topic lightly, as if the question had never landed. The distance in her movements—cool, restrained, faintly indifferent—was like an invisible blade, cutting deep into his ribs. His brows knitted hard; a wave of anger rose, tangled with a profound, wordless loss.

Alienation. Indifference.

Like a basin of cold water poured straight over his heart.

Lu Chou let out a cold sneer, his features sunk into shadow.

"Truly heartless… and stupid to the point of absurdity," he muttered, his voice so low it was nearly a grind of teeth. "Does she not comprehend even what I have done? In this world, what man would dare court universal condemnation—would dare put his own hands into the fire— to shield a woman who could be silenced at any moment?"

He flicked open the folding fan hidden in his sleeve—pa—then snapped it shut again. He turned sharply, his steps steady, yet threaded with suppressed fury.

Perhaps the fool was himself.

"Liang Jin."

"Present, my Lord."

Lu Chou stood with his hands clasped behind his back, turning away from the window. His voice was as frigid as the night wind.

Moonlight cut along his profile, the outline sharp as a blade—yet stained with a heat he could not entirely press down. He stared out into the dark for a long time, as if wrestling with someone in silence and losing, inch by inch. At last, he yielded—and the words slipped out, cold and harsh:

"Tell me… is that Xiao woman truly so foolish? She is on the cusp of the storm, her life hanging by a thread—yet does she genuinely believe herself invulnerable? At this critical juncture, every eye in the court and the city is fixed upon her. Anyone who sends an assassin could make her die without a sound, without a trace. And she insists on rushing forward to be the one who sticks her head out first—does she truly tire of living?"

He rarely spoke of emotion to a subordinate. But tonight was too quiet, too cold, and too turbulent. Once the words began, they did not stop. His tone grew heavier, as if the murky air that had been pressed in his chest all night finally found a crack—finally found an outlet.

"Tell me—she sees the situation churning like this, and still wears that naïve face. Does she not understand that one slight misstep, and she will be the next pawn to be erased? The next piece silenced?"

Liang Jin stood rigid, head bowed. Sweat beaded on his brow. A torrent of denials—*I don't know, don't ask me*—clamored in his chest, yet not a single word escaped his lips.

Lu Chou let out a cold laugh, the chill sharpening.

"And that Xie Huaici," he said, voice edged with displeasure. "His manner, bearing, learning, conversation—indeed, he is a superior choice."

He gave a snort, his brows and eyes unmistakably dark.

"The day her shop was seized, she stood before this Official like a hedgehog with its spines raised—fur bristling, ready to bite. Yet before Xie Huaici, she lowered her head and became meek, obedient as a kitten."

Another cold snort.

"And Baor calls him 'Papa Xie.' It is simply preposterous."

"……"

Liang Jin remained bowed, expressionless—his inner self already collapsed into mud.

—My Lord, listen to what you are saying.

—You led soldiers to surround her doors and seize her shop. The woman showed supreme benevolence by not chasing you out with a broom. If it were anyone else, they would only dare speak calmly and softly before the gentlemanly Lord Xie.

But could he say any of that?

He did not dare.

Liang Jin only wished he were mute, and forced himself into silence, still as stone.

"Hah." Lu Chou's laugh was colder still. "Look at her—baring teeth and claws. It truly makes one want to throw her outside and let her fend for herself. So foolish she cannot even tell friend from foe."

His voice pressed down, biting.

"Those wealthy merchants and powerful nobles are wishing for her clean, swift death—so that no evidence remains, so that nothing can be traced back. And she still deludes herself into thinking she can stand on 'purity' and keep herself safe?"

Cold sweat ran down Liang Jin's neck, soaking the collar. His master usually spoke with immaculate precision, never leaking a drop. Yet whenever the Xiao Madam was mentioned, it was as if he meant to tear open his own chest and spill everything out.

If he did not speak now, he feared he would become a punching bag.

Liang Jin gritted his teeth, forced a look of cautious prudence, and chose his words with painful care.

"My Lord is discerning. Madam Xiao is blessed by Heaven. Now that you are personally safeguarding her—personally watching over her— there will surely be no worries."

Having been chosen for close attendance, Liang Jin's ability to read eyes and wind had long been honed into something sharper than most men's.

Sure enough—at the phrase "you are personally safeguarding her," Lu Chou's expression eased by a single line. Only a line. But the rigid peak of his brow loosened a fraction.

He did not speak. He only stared out the window again, for a long time, as if forcing himself to swallow back what remained.

At last, he said, low and flat, "Prepare the memorials. In a few days, we set out for the Capital."

Liang Jin felt as if he had received a great amnesty. He answered quickly and withdrew.

Only the lamplight on the desk remained in the room, flickering once—twice—casting over Lu Chou's outline: quiet as iron.

Lu Chou returned to his chair. His eyes were calm as an undercurrent beneath still water—silent, yet surging.

He understood: this return to the Capital was not an ending. It was a beginning.

He would clear away every pawn that should not exist. He would sweep the board clean.

Whether that woman hated him or feared him, she would remain obediently within his game.

Because he never permitted loss of control.

He would not allow anyone—ever—to escape his grasp a second time.

* * * * *

Liang Jin had only just retreated into the corridor. With his back against a pillar, he finally dared to wipe cold sweat from his palm, hard and fast.

The courtyard lamplight swayed. His heart had not yet fully settled—his lord's outburst still rang in his ears, and the command to "prepare the memorials" felt like a heavy burden dropped back onto his shoulders again, crushing down as soon as he'd managed to breathe.

He was just gathering his thoughts when an administrative manager from the headquarters hurried forward. The man's steps were chaotic, as if he were treading on broken tiles; his face was twisted with bitterness and distress.

Liang Jin adjusted his attire, cleared his throat twice, and straightened his back. In an instant he donned an air of superiority, nothing like the cramped, stifled version of himself that stood before his master.

"Ahem. It is so late. Manager, what urgent matter brings you here?" he asked, voice cool and aloof.

The manager, seeing someone who could make decisions, leaned in and whispered urgently. "Lieutenant Liang—may I ask how Madam Xiao is to be settled? Public discussion is already boiling. We cannot simply leave the matter unattended."

At once Liang Jin's temper flared. Sweat bloomed again in his palm.

He spun around and, with a crisp rap of his knuckles, struck the manager on the head—an unmistakable, sharp knock.

"Have you no discernment!" he snapped. "And you're a manager? Do you not understand what 'arrange with the utmost favour' means?"

The manager jolted, clutching his head, half indignant, half pained. "Lieutenant—this humble one only thought… she is an involved party. By regulation, she should be detained and questioned later. Why was she not 押 to the yamen—instead of being brought into the headquarters?"

Liang Jin glared at him, fury cold and clean.

"Involved party?" he barked. "Which of your eyes sees her as an involved party? You think she deserves to suffer? Can you even distinguish between a witness and a criminal?"

His voice sharpened further.

"Madam Xiao is, at present, merely a key witness. Mishandle her, and you stir the entire case—hand our enemies a weapon, overturn the situation for the Capital's people to laugh at. This headquarters lacks precisely this kind of insight. You do not even think—how are we to report upward? How are we to explain ourselves to those above?"

He lowered his voice, but the suppressed anger in it was more frightening for its restraint.

"Remember this: for a witness, the first thing we do is secrecy and protection. In other words—feed her well, house her well, and treat her like a distinguished guest. If you dare let her suffer the slightest grievance, do not blame me for being merciless."

Liang Jin's eyes narrowed.

"Believe it or not—if Lord Lu finds out, he will strip you down to the bone."

The manager's face flushed scarlet. He nodded frantically. "Yes—yes, Lieutenant. Rest assured. We will handle it as you instruct. We will arrange everything with the utmost favour."

Only then did Liang Jin stop. He turned away, fingers rubbing silently along the inside of his sleeve. Beneath the lamplight, weariness flickered in his eyes.

He understood: this game was not only his master's. It was a weight he would have to shoulder step by step.

And with each step he bore, another measure of heaviness settled in his chest.

Chapter 44: To Guard a Name, Set a Trap

The night was deep in the Capital, and the lamps inside Chengming Hall stood in an eerie stillness.
On the desk, the lampwick burned with a soft, steady hiss; its shadow swayed. Beyond the window, the wind howled—thin and taut, like the keening notes of a zither drawn tight.

Crown Prince Chen Gen remained bent over the desk, not yet risen. His brush moved as swiftly as the wind—yet he had already dipped it in ink three separate times, and still not a single character fell onto the paper.

Warm yellow light spilled across the lacquered desk, throwing the vermilion and black annotations of the memorials into a blur of mottled colour—brilliant yet indistinct, as though the words themselves were floating. Chen Gen was dressed in informal robes, a silver-grey crane-patterned cloak draped over his shoulders. He sat hunched over, long fingers resting against the paper, stroking it in slow, unconscious motions.

A faint sound of footsteps came from outside the hall. The Crown Prince did not lift his head—yet he had already recognised who it was.

"Enter."

Du Qian stepped into the hall, performed a salute without drawing attention, and reported in a low voice: "Reporting to Your Highness, news has arrived from Jiangnan. The confidential dispatch states—Lord Lu Chou submitted a memorial this morning, requesting an Imperial decree to return to the Capital. He is to set out within three days. He will be escorting key witnesses from the Jiangnan case—Madam Xiao Lingyu among them, as well as several others—and he is carrying several crates of case files."

The tip of Chen Gen's brush halted. Ink bled across the paper, blooming into an irregular dark blot. He did not change expression. He merely set the brush back beside the inkstone, gently—his voice still even.

"Understood."

Du Qian paused. He lowered his voice further, and a trace of apprehension flashed through his eyes. "Your Highness… Lord Lu's tax investigation in Jiangnan has, in these past months, implicated many. Not only the six great textile houses, but also newly risen merchant factions…"

His tone sank. "If Lord Lu presents the evidence in full before the Sacred Presence—and states plainly that someone obstructed the official investigation, colluded privately with the grain-transport routes, and even coerced wealthy merchants into 'donations'… if all such proof points directly toward the Eastern Palace… then His Majesty—"

Chen Gen raised his eyes, calm as ever. He did not speak.

"Your Highness," Du Qian continued, carefully, "your servant knows well that Your Highness and Lord Lu share a bond that is not shallow. Since Jiangnan began, Lord Lu has manoeuvred among many parties and has indeed relieved Your Highness of much strain… Yet this time, if he truly lays those crates of files directly before the throne—what is implicated will not be one person, nor one matter."

The Crown Prince did not look up again. His voice remained faint.

"Are you reminding this Prince that if he turns his heart, he may turn and bite this Prince instead?"

Du Qian's face did not shift. "Your servant dares not presume to speak of another man's heart. It is only that… men change. In years past, Your Highness and Lord Lu studied side by side for many years, under the same Imperial Preceptor; your friendship was firm as metal and stone. But now…"

At last, Chen Gen's brush descended—but the ink only spread wider, saturating the sheet, as though the page itself could no longer bear restraint. He lifted his gaze slowly to Du Qian. His voice dropped, heavy and low:

"Now you fear that Lu Chou will sit beside the Third Brother— recruiting men for him, drafting his memorials, speaking to attack this Prince's achievements, urging the Imperial Father to cut away this Prince's authority. Is that it?"

Du Qian bowed his head and did not answer at once. After a long moment, he said: "It is precisely because the human heart is hard to measure that Your Highness must watch the present situation. The Third Prince has moved frequently of late. Several men have already been turned by him. If even Lu Chou is drawn under his wing… then after Jiangnan, more measures will follow—one after another."

Chen Gen's expression remained mild, yet a thin chill gathered in his eyes.

He lifted a jade pendant from the desk and let out a soft, cold laugh. "If one of mine can be swayed by him… then why can this Prince not sway one of his?" He paused; his words fell like a blade set down with care. "To answer a man with his own methods—this much stratagem, this Prince still possesses."

"Your Highness." Du Qian took half a step forward, voice lowered. "This contest cannot be judged by affection alone. If Lu Chou remains loyal, Your Highness may rely on him. If he changes…"

He stopped—hesitating.

But Chen Gen had already risen. He smoothed the hem of his robes, his tone unchanged, as placid as moonlit water.

"In this world, there has never been anyone truly reliable—only hearts that shift. If this Orphan cannot stand on his own, cannot save himself, then the position of Crown Heir will sooner or later become an empty shell."

Du Qian swallowed the unease in his throat and continued, more softly: "Your Highness… the journey from Jiangnan to the Capital is long. Of late, bandits have appeared often along the roads. And within court— there are rumours…"

His voice turned probing. "If, on the road, Lord Lu's party were to encounter… a misfortune. If those witnesses and that evidence were all to vanish at once—then the Jiangnan case would end in Jiangnan. And if Lord Lu returns to the Capital only to lend strength to another—"

He did not finish.

Another.

For a breath, the hall fell silent.

Both men knew exactly whom it meant: the Third Prince.

Du Qian's voice sank to nearly nothing. The stillness was so complete that even the faint crackle of the lampwick could be heard.

Chen Gen's knuckles tapped the desk—slowly, evenly, unhurried. His voice was level, almost indifferent:

"You mean… Lu Chou's party should not be able to make it back to the Capital."

Du Qian paused. He lowered his head. Cold sweat beaded at his temples—half fear, half a cautious test.

"Your servant would not dare speak presumptuously," he murmured. "It is only that Lord Lu carries the case files in his hands. If someone on the road were to covet them… then truth and falsehood would be hard to distinguish. The rivers and roads from Jiangnan are long; bandits are rampant. Should an accident occur—court and city would simply call it Heaven's decree."

Chen Gen said nothing. He only looked at him—his gaze light, almost calm, yet cold enough to pierce into the deepest part of a man's heart.

Du Qian felt his chest tighten and lowered himself another inch. "Your Highness… your servant is but mediocre. I know only this: if Jiangnan is pursued to its root, it will surely implicate those around Your Highness. If Lord Lu insists on submitting his memorial—he may not withdraw unscathed. If we can move one step ahead—"

"One step ahead?" Chen Gen's voice was very soft; a faint smile touched it.

"Du Qian. Are you advising this Orphan to walk the edge of danger?"

Du Qian dropped to his knees at once, his forehead nearly to the floor. "Your servant has no such intention! It is only that the world is perilous, and men's hearts are fickle. Lord Lu is rigid by nature; if another man provokes him, it is hard to say he will not grow a different will. Your servant fears only that Your Highness will be dragged into slander— thus I dared to speak."

Chen Gen watched him. The corner of his lips lifted slightly. "You plan thoroughly for this Orphan."

He picked up the brush by the inkstone, turning it slowly between his fingers; the tip caught the lamplight with a cold gleam.

"However—" His voice paused, and he set the brush down, gently. "In all things, men must leave themselves room. If he remains my old friend… I do not wish to see blood."

Du Qian answered softly: "Your Highness is benevolent; we are in awe. Yet if he truly turns to another faction—when His Majesty questions it, it will be even harder to answer."

Chen Gen smiled faintly—cold as iron in winter.

"If this Orphan is not benevolent, will others be?" he said lightly. "In this world, only profit can truly be relied upon." His gaze sharpened by the smallest degree. "Du Qian, remember this—this Orphan does not let blood stain his own hands. This Orphan only lets the board itself close its mouth."

Du Qian froze.

That calm tone was more frightening than any explicit order. He understood at once: the Crown Prince had not refused. He merely would not say it aloud.

He kowtowed and withdrew, cold sweat soaking through his back.

Chen Gen watched him leave, his eyes still mild. He took up the jade pendant again and rubbed it for a long time, then let out a quiet sigh.

"Whether they can return to the Capital… will depend on Heaven's will."

After all—there were many who did not wish Lu Chou's party to reach the Capital.

"Your Highness," Du Qian could not help adding, voice strained, "your subordinate is only afraid you will be implicated and smeared. You are clearly innocent, yet—"

Chen Gen's fingers traced the dried ink stain on the desk. His expression did not change, as though he were tasting tea—yet also as though he were weighing a calculation. He neither agreed, nor rejected. After a moment, he said flatly:

"Enough. It is late. Go and rest."

"Crown Prince—"

"Enough. Withdraw." Chen Gen waved his hand; his tone turned slightly harder.

Du Qian lowered his head. "…Yes."

He knew this manner well: no stance spoken, no restraint given. As with many unspeakable matters before, it would be permitted in shadow— and judged only after success or failure.

At the threshold, Du Qian looked back once.

Inside the hall, the lamplight burned dim and deep. The Crown Prince still sat behind the desk, head lowered over the scrolls. The slanting light cut his handsome face into two halves—one in brightness, one in shadow.

Behind him, Chen Gen lifted a hand.

A hidden guard knelt as swiftly as wind. "Crown Prince. Please command."

Chen Gen fell silent for half a beat, then said coldly: "Send a small team… to Jiangnan."

"Yes!" The hidden guard received the order and vanished at once.

Night pressed down like ink.

And so did the human heart—impossible to measure.

Chapter 45: The First Undercurrent

Xiao Lingyu stood beneath the eaves, watching the figures weave through the front courtyard. Coachmen and retainers moved back and forth, transferring trunks, wicker hampers, and crates from one place to another.
Occasional fragments of conversation drifted into her ears—every one of them mentioning "escort," "setting forth," and "returning to the Capital."

Xiao Lingyu lowered her gaze. Her tone was unhurried, steady on the surface, yet the faint tremor at the very end of her voice could not be suppressed.
"Returning to the Capital?"

Servants darted through the courtyard, busy binding luggage, tightening ropes, and securing the carriages; the sounds of discussion reached her in broken, intermittent snatches.
She stood beneath the corridor, her gaze fixed on the distant corner of an eave—almost as if she had not understood what she had heard, and almost as if she were weighing something in silence.

A matron sent by the Lu Residence stepped forward to salute, replying with a smile: "Indeed. The Lord gave the order this morning. The journey back to the Capital will commence within three days. He said that the public affairs of this Jiangnan trip are concluded, and he also wishes to take… Madam and Miss Baor along for the departure."

She was startled. The fingers hidden in her sleeve curled up imperceptibly, tightening once, then loosening again. After a moment, she asked softly, as if confirming a thing she already knew was unreasonable:
"Baor and I are returning to the Capital together?"

"Yes. The Lord instructed that we prepare Madam's and Miss Baor's personal effects as well," the matron replied with outward respect, yet there was an unconcealed trace of triumph in her brows and in the set of her mouth—as though she took secret satisfaction in speaking these words aloud.

Xiao Lingyu smiled faintly, her expression as placid as ever: "So that is the case."

She did not say anything more, turning to re-enter the room, her steps still steady, her skirt hem unhurried.

However, reaching the doorway, she paused for an instant. Without fully turning around, she asked in an even tone, as though the question were merely procedural:
"If I wish to see the Lord, may I send word?"

"This…" The matron hesitated. "The Lord has gone out to attend to official business and is not within the residence. However, he did instruct before leaving that as long as Madam does not leave the residence, she is free to walk as she pleases within the grounds."

"Anywhere? Including the kitchens?"

The matron's eyes flickered. She hesitated for the briefest moment—then still nodded: "That is also permissible."

"Then I understand."

She replied softly and turned to enter the room, still revealing no emotional disturbance on her face.
But as the door was quietly closed, she leaned against the door-frame. Her long eyelashes lowered, casting a thin shadow across her eyes. After a moment of silence, she whispered, so lightly it was nearly swallowed by the darkness:

"What scheme is he devising now…"

Xiao Lingyu walked slowly along the long corridor, neither hurrying nor hesitating. Her footsteps fell extremely lightly upon the blue bricks, as if fearing to disturb anything at all. Although the maidservants and matrons of the residence did not accompany her, she knew—without needing to look—that the eyes watching from the shadows had not once moved away.

She paused before a door. It was Lu Chou's temporary study.

On this visit to Jiangnan for official business, he was residing in the official quarters attached to the Jiangnan Textile Commissioner's office, and this small courtyard had been specifically designated for officials temporarily lodged here for duty—an administrative compound that carried the quiet severity of a yamen even when no yamen sign stood outside.

The door was ajar; the curtain hung lightly, and the faint scent of ink drifted out.

She raised her hand and pushed the door. The wood felt cool beneath her palm. A junior attendant was inside, sweeping.

Seeing her enter, the attendant did not try to stop her, but instead bowed to pay his respects. "Good day, Madam."

Xiao Lingyu nodded, glancing briefly around the room.

The study furnishings were utterly simple: a desk, a bookshelf, stacked files, and a weapon rack—everything arranged in calm, disciplined order, as if even dust would not dare settle where it should not.

She did not rush to examine anything. Instead, she walked slowly around the room first, one object at a time, one glance at a time, as though memorising the placement of every detail. Her fingertip brushed over a bamboo-carved paperweight; then she lightly touched the inkstone on the desk. Her gaze deepened slightly.

A memorial had not been cleared from the desk; its spine was straight, and the ink marks were fresh—fresh enough to suggest it had been handled recently. She did not open it. She only glanced at the cinnabar annotation, and in that single glance, she already understood what it signified.

—It was intended for the Emperor.

Her gaze shifted. On a side table against the wall lay a rolled-up paper map; its corners were slightly creased, as though it had just been unfolded and refolded. She walked over and opened it.

It revealed a Jiangnan water map.

Pressed beneath it was a letter.

The paper was thin and smooth. There was no signature, yet the handwriting was familiar—it was Lu Chou's script.

Her hand paused.

She placed the letter back where it was, exactly as it had been, neither a fraction higher nor lower, and a flicker of extremely faint perturbation passed through her eyes—so faint it might have been mistaken for lamplight shifting.

After a long while, she took a book from the shelf and flipped through it casually, asking the matron standing by the door in an off-hand manner, as if she were merely commenting on tidiness:
"He never instructed that these things be put away?"

"The Lord instructed that Madam is free to enter and exit, and he never ordered anyone to tidy them."

"...He trusts me implicitly, it seems."

The words sounded like a murmur to herself—yet also like a thinly veiled barb. She closed the book and replaced it.

Before leaving, she took one last look at the calligraphy on the wall—

"Uphold Rectitude, Maintain Balance."

The brushstrokes were sharp and forceful; the ink was stern and cold, carrying a severity that did not soften even in decorative form. She did not know whose hand had written it.

She smiled imperceptibly and turned to depart, yet in her heart, ripples began to stir like a darkened mirror.

—This journey to the Capital, I fear, is not solely for the sake of files and charges. By bringing her along, is his purpose revenge, or is it a lack of resignation?
He never undertakes a pointless action; nor does she.
It appears he has made up his mind that she and Baor must return to the Capital with him. So be it. She will follow him through this ordeal.

* * * * *

In the Capital, inside the Hall of Eternal Peace.

The afternoon sun penetrated the palace hall through the patterned windows, scattering light upon the green-jade tiled floor.
Amidst the shimmering liuli (glazed) light and shadow, the Third Prince, Chen Song, leaned against a couch, toying with a gold-threaded silk ball. His posture was languid, his expression unhurried, and yet in that ease there lay a careless arrogance—as though nothing in the world could truly surprise him.

Jiang Yue stepped quietly into the hall, leaning down to whisper: "Your Highness, the confidential report has arrived. Lu Chou has requested permission to return to the Capital, departing within three days, and is escorting Xiao Lingyu and the other personnel along with all the case files."

A sharp glint flashed in Chen Song's eyes, and the corner of his mouth curved into a meaningful smile:
"Oh? He is returning so soon…"
He exhaled a soft laugh, half amusement, half approval. "Truly— even an honest man has his moments of ferocity."

He twirled the silk ball, rotating it slowly between his fingers: "This is excellent. Before this Prince has even made a move, our Crown Prince will have already lost an arm."

A hint of excitement also appeared in Jiang Yue's eyes, and he continued: "Furthermore… several merchants have already agreed to the gold contribution. The silver has been accounted for, sufficient for Your Highness to continue training troops and preparing horses."

Hearing this, Chen Song gave the silk ball a light shake, his smile widening:
"Heh. This stirring up of Jiangnan has instead provided this Prince with the silver needed to raise troops."
His tone turned faintly mocking, as though he were balancing a ledger.
"I should truly thank that Madam Xiao— and Lu Chou— for clearing this account for this Prince."

Jiang Yue considered for a moment, then whispered again: "However… Lu Chou has always been on good terms with the Crown Prince. If he recalls their past affection and chooses to conceal the case files… what then should be done?"

Chen Song's gaze darkened upon hearing this, yet his tone remained an understatement, light enough to be dangerous:
"Recalls past affection?" He smiled faintly. "Recalling past affection also depends on the timing."
"Should he dare to hide the truth regarding this situation, this Prince will memorialise the Emperor to punish him for the 'crime of deceiving the Sovereign'—let us see whether he prefers a lifetime of unsullied reputation, or to be buried alongside the Crown Prince."

He slowly rose, his gaze like a blade, his tone low yet sharp: "This game has been played for long enough. It is time to collect the profit from the opening move."

Having said this, Chen Song stood fully, tossing the gold-threaded silk ball in his palm. It dropped to the floor with a soft sound. He gazed down at the golden flash rolling twice across the tiles. His smile did not change—yet the chill in his eyes deepened by a degree.

"Go and give the order: instruct our people to monitor the entire length of the Jiangnan road. Should there be any incident…" His voice paused, unhurried. "Do not rush to intervene."

Jiang Yue was startled—then immediately understood. He bowed his head in assent.

The wind from outside swept through the long corridor; the curtain shadows trembled slightly. Chen Song stood by the window with his hands clasped behind his back, gazing at the sky over the outskirts of the Capital.

The afternoon sunlight had long been swallowed by the clouds. A shadow slowly slid past the edge of the palace wall, covering his profile and slicing his originally handsome features in half.

"In three days, they will enter the Capital via Meiling Crossing, will they not?"

"Yes."

"Very well." Chen Song's voice was low and slow, as if speaking to himself—almost indulgent. "There should be some rough weather… to rouse the Capital awake."

He picked up the silk ball again, brushed off the dust, and tossed it into the air casually. The gold thread traced an arc in the light and shadow, flashing like a sword-gleam—

and vanished without a sound.

Chapter 46: Peril on the Road to Capital

The first light of dawn was faint and hazy.

Before the official residence, a carriage with a pale green canopy stood ready. Its embroidered curtains hung low, and delicate wisps of smoke curled from an incense burner within. The rhythmic clip-clop of hooves and the low rumble of turning wheels melded into a dull, restless din. A troop of men and horses stood prepared for departure, their bearing stern and imposing.

Lu Chou stood on the steps, clad in sable robes. His gaze swept over the crowd, his brows and eyes as cold and unyielding as iron. At the very rear of the procession, a heavy prison cart bound in thick iron chains sat in somber stillness. Inside, several men were draped in shackles and yokes; their clothes were stained with blood and their faces lacked any luster—these were the key criminals dredged up from the depths of the Jiangnan case.

Xiao Lingyu stood beside the steps, watching the prison cart ahead. A slow, mocking sneer curled at the corner of her lips, her gaze as sharp and sardonic as a blade.

"How interesting," she spoke in a measured, slow tone, her eyes flashing with irony. "Since these men are already in the prison cart, shouldn't I—this female convict 'burdened by heavy charges and iron-clad evidence'—be locked away alongside them? We mustn't leave anyone out."

At her words, Lu Chou's brow sank abruptly. He turned to cast a cold glance at her, his voice neither hurried nor slow, yet laced with thorns: "If we were truly to weigh your crimes, do you think you would be sitting in this small carriage? I fear there wouldn't even be a place for you in the prison cart; you would be thrown directly into a water dungeon instead."

She gazed quietly at the modest carriage canopy, her voice flat yet hiding a sharp irony: "Since I am a criminal, why go to the trouble of preparing a carriage? It would be better if Lord Lu simply sent me into the prison cart as well, if only to save others from the misunderstanding that I am unrelated to this case."

Lu Chou paused, his expression shifting subtly. He replied coldly: "If this official truly intended to handle you in such a manner, do you think you would still be standing here to speak?"

A faint, chilling smile flickered through Xiao Lingyu's eyes, a laugh that was cold and detached. "In that case, I suppose I should thank the Lord for his mercy."

"Do not try to be clever with me," his voice dropped, his gaze burning with intensity. "The only reason I am ensuring your safe passage into the capital is that this official considers..."

"Considers what?" she interrupted him. Her tone was not sharp, but carried a trace of weary, cold self-deprecation. "Considers that little Baor is still young and requires a mother?"

His expression faltered for a heartbeat. He said nothing.

She lowered her eyes, watching the carriage curtain sway slightly. Her voice was so soft it was nearly stolen by the wind: "I am not a person who fails to understand the gravity of the situation, nor do I deny my initial faults. But these past days, you have neither clarified your stance nor cleared my name, allowing me to be imprisoned here... Does Lord Lu know how many people the Jinhua Establishment supports? A single day without a voice from me leaves dozens of people in a state of panic."

"And so you should rush to the front, offend the powerful, and invite calamity upon yourself? Only to end up with a reputation in tatters and a mountain of dossiers against you?" He sneered. "If you cherish your life so little, what 'long-term plans' can you possibly speak of?"

She looked back at him. There was no anger in her eyes, only steadfastness and endurance: "It is precisely because I cherish life that I must protect my foundation. If the Jinhua Establishment collapses, this lowly woman will not survive either."

For an instant, he was speechless, feeling a stifling tightness in his chest. Their eyes met, and the atmosphere grew taut with an undercurrent of cold hostility.

Just as their words were crossing like clashing blades, little Baor came running over. Her eyes were bright as stars as she asked: "Mother, are we really going to the capital? I heard there are so many sugar-men and candied haws there, and even actors wearing masks!"

Xiao Lingyu froze, looking down at her daughter's radiant face. Her heart stirred. But just as that smile began to rise, Baor leaned in closer and whispered a soft, small admonition: "Mother, don't argue with Father anymore... whenever you start fighting, I feel so sad..."

As these words reached her ears, Xiao Lingyu's expression shifted. She leaned down, her tone turning a few degrees colder: "He is not your father. Stop talking nonsense."

Baor was stunned. Her eyes reddened instantly, and large, pearl-like tears began to well up and swirl. Her lip trembled; though she tried desperately to hold it back, she looked as if she were about to burst into tears.

At that moment, a servant in grey led forward a tall, magnificent horse. Lu Chou was about to mount. Seeing the scene, his brow furrowed. He reached out and scooped up the nearly-crying Baor in one swift motion, settling her securely in front of his saddle. He coaxed her softly: "Who has been fierce with you again? If you shed tears before we set out, people will laugh at you."

Baor sniffled and nodded reluctantly. Her tiny body leaned into his embrace, and in a flash, she was all smiles again: "My Lord, I want to sit on your horse! I want to sit right at the front!"

"Why aren't you calling me 'Father' anymore?"

"Mother won't let Baor call you that..." Baor replied, looking piteously aggrieved.

"Don't listen to her."

"Then, Father, can I ride with you?"

"Yes." Lu Chou smoothed the hair at her temples, his tone exceedingly tender.

This scene fell into the eyes of the followers in the procession. Several exchanged glances, and a maidservant couldn't help but stifle a giggle behind her hand: "Look at that. The Lord and Madam bicker, yet they truly look like a family of three. It would make anyone envious."

An old nurse-maid also smiled: "That little Miss Baor has the same bright eyes as the Lord. Her features look as if they were stamped from the same mold."

"It's just that her eye color is different from the Lord's, alas..." the others lamented softly.

Xiao Lingyu's face flushed slightly, but she was at a loss for words. She could only lower her head to hide the flicker of disordered emotion in her eyes.

The company set out as the first light of dawn spilled across the land. The wind kicked up dust along the wheel tracks as the grand procession began its journey on the long road to the capital.

* * * * *

Dawn had just broken, and the mountain mists had not yet fully dissipated. The wheels ground over the damp bluestone road with a low, heavy sound.

Xiao Lingyu lifted the curtain to look out. The official road ahead was straight, flanked by weeping willows. In the distance, several cavalrymen led the way, their banners vaguely visible. Her gaze swept over the figures and landed on the lead horse—Lu Chou's back was ramrod straight, the hair at his temples moving slightly in the wind. The morning light fell upon his shoulders, yet it failed to melt the aura of coldness surrounding him.

Baor grew tired of riding the great horse after a short while and returned to the soft carriage. She sprawled by the window, half-drowsy, pointing outside: "Mother, how long will we be traveling?"

"Seven hundred *li*," she answered flatly.

"How far is that?"

"We must travel for seven more days."

"So far..." Baor sighed, then whispered: "Will the Lord-Father get tired?"

Xiao Lingyu's fingers paused, her smile extremely faint: "He won't get tired. He is a man who attends to great affairs."

Before her words had even faded, several low cries of birds were heard outside, as if a flock had been startled. Lu Chou 回首, his gaze sweeping the surroundings. He immediately lowered his voice to command: "Have everyone on high alert. The forest path ahead—do not slacken for a moment."

The wind gusted between the horses' hooves, carrying a damp, cold chill. Xiao Lingyu lifted her eyes to the distant mountain pass, her heart tightening. She knew that place—it was the Meiling Ferry. It was whispered to be the place where bandits were at their most rampant.

She lowered the curtain. The fragrance inside the carriage was light, but it could not mask the sliver of unease in her heart. The wind grew stronger, and the mountain mist pressed low. From afar came the sound of several horses neighing. She stroked Baor's hair and said softly: "Sleep for a while. The road is still very long."

Baor obediently leaned into her embrace and fell asleep shortly after. Xiao Lingyu gazed at that innocent face, her expression dazed for a moment. Outside, light and shadow flickered by. Her gaze fell once more upon that black warhorse—Lu Chou's back remained straight, his hand steady on the reins, his expression never relaxing for even a heartbeat.

In that moment, she suddenly felt that the most terrifying thing in this world was never the wind, the rain, or the road—it was the human heart.

Suddenly, a black bird startled from the mountain pass ahead, circling several times before flying swiftly away. The guards beside the carriage looked up, taking it for a common bird. Little did they know that the bird's direction was straight toward a ruined temple by the roadside.

Inside that ruined temple, several shadows clad in night-traveling gear were looking over a map. One spoke in a low voice: "By the hour, they will pass through Meiling by noon. We strike there."

Chapter 47: When Blood Spills Sudden

Late summer turning to early autumn—the evening wind carried both the stored warmth of the hills and a thin thread of chill from the low gullies.

Wild grass leaned along the post road, its tasselled tips brushing at boot and stirrup, and the chorus of cicadas, loud all afternoon, was fading into a hesitant hush. Fine dust hung in the air like smoke and glowed in the slanted light.

After days of hard travel, they were finally nearing the post station.

Helmets loosened, throats dry and salted with dust, the escort eased their shoulders; one guard, grinning with relief, rode forward to report, breath steaming faintly in the cooling air:

"Five li ahead lies the post inn, my lord. The light has not yet gone—we can rest before dusk."

Among the procession, Baor rode gleefully before Lu Chou on a tall iron-grey horse. She twisted about with the unsteady bravery of a child, calling toward the carriage:

"Mama! Look—the clouds there! That one looks like a rabbit!"

Xiao Lingyu lifted her gaze. Her lips curved faintly; fatigue softened about her eyes, yet warmth moved there. She was just about to nod.

When suddenly, the rhythm of hooves shattered into chaos, like a drumline breaking time.

"Movement ahead!" someone cried.

A single shrill whinny split the forest air. Before the station's tiled roof could crest into sight, the orderly skein of carriages and horses unravelled into confusion. Harness bells clanged. A wheel skidded and bit the gravel.

From the dense trees, shadows burst forth—black-clad figures, swift as ghosts, a dozen men with long blades catching the dying light and throwing it back in cold flashes, driving straight for the convoy's heart.

"Protect the lady and the young miss!"

Lu Chou's voice cut through the tumult like an arrow. In the same instant he wrenched the reins; steel whispered from its sheath—his sword already drawn in a single clean motion that spoke of long practice.

The guards snapped into a ring around the carriage, shields up, shoulders meeting. Baor screamed, small and piercing:

"Lord Papa! Mama!"

A man in black lunged from the flank, feet sure on the churned earth, his blade angling straight for Xiao Lingyu beneath the horse's shoulder!

Lu Chou's stallion reared as he dragged it sharply across her path; iron shoes struck sparks. Steel met steel with a shriek that stung the teeth.

The attacker's knife skittered aside—but the short blade of another slid in close and kissed across Lu Chou's shoulder, tearing cloth and skin, staining his sleeve a bright, wet crimson.

"Are you mad!?" Xiao Lingyu cried, her voice trembling despite herself.

"Silence! Guard Baor!"

His shout burned like a brand through the din. He did not give an inch.

The guards roared and met the charge; swords clashed, spear utts thumped, and sparks flew like a handful of stars flung into dusk.

The ring of iron and the human throb of breath and cries filled the trees. Within moments, bodies were already falling, thudding into the roadside scrub.

Lu Chou dropped from the saddle. His sword moved like wind over water—each motion spare, exact, merciless; nothing wasted, nothing showy. He stepped inside a swing and answered with the shortest killing line.

"One squad—hold him! The rest, take the woman!"

The leader's command cut through the din. Several assassins peeled away from the knot, sweeping toward the carriage with the ruthless economy of men who had rehearsed this very route.

"You'll touch her only over my corpse!"

Lu Chou's blade answered before the last word left his mouth—three strokes that sealed every path forward. One attacker barely lifted his knife before the steel point pressed his throat and went clean through.

Another came in low from the side, a smear of motion.

Lu Chou twisted, letting the killing edge spend itself on air, yet a second knife still ripped his sleeve and carved a hot line across the flesh beneath.

The sting sharpened his mind; his strikes turned brutal, relentless—the rhythm of survival when one is outnumbered and responsible for more than oneself.

A shadow rose behind him. He spun; the blade flashed in a single arc and sheared the oncoming knife at the haft. His elbow drove back on instinct and found a face; bone cracked with a dull, decisive sound.

At the carriage front, Liang Jin fought with blood running down his temple, stinging his eye.

"Not a step closer to the lady or the child!" he bellowed, cutting down one assailant with a stroke that started at the hip and finished at the collarbone.

From the distance, a short whistle shrieked—thin, metallic. More shadows burst from the forest edge.

Steel rang against steel. Dust rose thick as fog, muddied with the scent of trampled grass and iron. Vision dimmed beneath the haze of sweat and blood.

The formation wavered. A scared horse screamed and went to its knees.

And still the black-clad men pressed on.

They fought with intent—with design. A knot held Lu Chou at bay, testing, measuring, while two slipped like water around a rock, veering toward the carriage's weaker side.

Xiao Lingyu had nowhere left to run. She gathered Baor into her arms, crushing her close until the child's breath panted wet against her collarbone.

"Mama—!"

In that breathless instant, Lu Chou moved. He threw himself forward, body a blur, sword leaving his hand in a tight spinning throw that sang, struck, and bit; in the next heartbeat he was there in flesh—between the carriage and the killing edge—using his own body as the shield he could not forge for her.

"Lu Chou!"

Her eyes widened in disbelief as the blade found him.

A dull, terrible sound—steel cutting into living quiet. His body jolted once, and then steadied, upright as a spear driven into earth between her and death. The assassin's shock came a fraction too late.

Blood welled from his side, warm and dark, soaking cloth and palm.

For a moment she could neither move nor breathe. Shock, pain, fear, each wave rose in sequence and crushed her reason flat.

He had taken the blow for her.

He could have stepped aside—

He should have stepped aside.

Wasn't he always the cold one, the one who kept feeling at a distance the way a swordsman keeps his measure?

Then why—

Why this?

At that instant, she thought she heard something give within her chest— a fine, soundless fracture spreading outward like a crack through ice.

A ribbon of blood slid down from his shoulder, fell across her vision like a veil, and sank straight through to the place that would not harden again.

"Lu Chou…"

His name left her as a thread of breath, hoarse and broken.

Tears came without warning—spilling quick and hot, soaking her sleeve, darkening the hem of his robe where her hand braced him. Her breath snagged; her body trembled as if the cold had finally found her bones.

Then—

From the other side of the mountain road a hiss of arrows rose, cutting the air like shards of glassy wind.

Another squad of black-clad figures surged out of the woods, their steps measured, their formation tight; blades crossed mid-stride with the first attackers. Arrows struck—throats, brows, hearts—each finding its quiet home.

Within moments, the new arrivals—swift, silent, precise—had joined the fray.

But their blades turned not against Lu Chou. They turned with him, slotting into his rhythm as if they had trained beneath the same hand.

The forest erupted into a second chaos: two tides of shadow colliding in the dim. Commands snapped. Steel answered. Men fell and did not rise.

And then, as swiftly as it began, it ended.

The first wave broke and scattered in splinters; the second melted back into the trees, the way night does at dawn—leaving only the churned ground, the stink of blood and sweat and frightened horse, and a silence too loud for comfort.

Smoke, dust, and iron choked the air.

Liang Jin ran forward, dropped to one knee beside Lu Chou to check the wound, then stooped automatically to the trampled verge where something small had flashed.

When he rose again, his face had gone grave.

In his hand glinted a small iron token, edges nicked, the characters stark beneath the blood: "Eastern Palace."

"My lord," he said tightly, voice clipped to hold itself steady, "this was found among the dead."

Xiao Lingyu's face drained of colour.

"Them?"

Liang Jin hesitated, then let his voice fall to a murmur meant for his lord alone.

"It seems so. This should belong to the first group… The second were our hidden guards—only for precaution. Yet their timing was too exact… almost as if someone knew we would need them here."

He offered the token to Lu Chou.

"My lord, please look."

Lu Chou's hand—slick with blood, veins standing—closed around the iron. His knuckles blanched.

"So," he said with a low, mirthless laugh that held no joy, "they've grown impatient at last."

Xiao Lingyu turned to him. Sweat beaded at his temples; his pallor was a paper thin white. He was still forcing himself upright out of sheer habit.

"You've lost too much blood. Don't move."

She passed Baor—still shaking—to the waiting nursemaid; then she wheeled toward Liang Jin with a steadiness that surprised even herself.

"Help your lord into the carriage. Now."

"I—" Liang Jin froze, caught between rank and common sense, unused to taking orders from the Madam of the workshop.

Her brow tightened.

"What are you staring at? Do you want him bleeding to death?"

"Y-yes, ma'am."

Sense returned like a slap. Within moments Lu Chou was lifted into the carriage, and Liang Jin's voice rang out beyond, cracking like a whip:

"Forward to the post station—hurry!"

Inside, the small space reeked of blood, damp leather, and the resinous bite of the travel-chest medicine. The wheels lurched; the walls shivered with each rut.

Xiao Lingyu tore a strip of linen, pressed it hard against the wound. Her hands were firm, but her tears fell again, hot and ungoverned.

He said nothing. His jaw locked; breath came thin and measured; sweat traced the fine line at his temple and pooled at the edge of his ear.

Blood seeped between her fingers and threaded down his sleeve in slow, dark trails that would not stop.

His eyes remained steady—yet beneath that calm, a faint mist trembled and went away, as if he had ordered even pain to obey.

"Why?" she forced out, fingers working, voice breaking. "Why would you shield me like that?"

She had braced herself for a wall of silence—or for that cool, efficient indifference that had once cut her to the bone and taught her to leave first.

But he spoke. The sound was low and rough, scraped from some place that did not often open:

"If anything happened to you… what would become of Baor?"

The words were soft—almost weightless—yet something within them gave him away.

"You're a fool," she whispered, still binding, still shaking, her tears falling faster because she was trying not to. "A hopeless fool."

His lips tightened. In his eyes, a storm gathered and held its rain.

"Don't cry," he murmured, and the gentleness of it hurt her more than the sight of blood. "I'll be fine."

But watching her weep made his chest ache in a way no blade could touch.

And she knew—looking at this man who had stepped into a blade's path as if that were the obvious choice—that something inside her had shifted, not a step but an axis.

Her heart clenched painfully, as if some long-sealed truth had snapped its seal and filled her ribs with light and hurt.

Only then did she understand.

She had cared for him far more deeply than she had ever dared allow herself to think.

Five years ago, in those brief days they had shared—

she had already fallen for him, and all this time she had only been struggling with the knowledge.

Chapter 48: A Thaw in Frozen Feelings

Wind brushed against the carriage curtains, stirring the stench of blood that thickened in the narrow space and clung to the tongue.

The wheels jolted over ruts; the ceiling ribs creaked like old bones.

Xiao Lingyu's hand still pressed against his wound.

The cloth beneath her palm was soaked through—hot, slick, unwilling to stop and yet she dared not loosen her grip for even a heartbeat.

"Where's the gauze—quickly!"

Her voice shook despite herself.

The nurse beside her fumbled the medicine powder and bandages from the travel chest, her own hands trembling hard enough to rattle the tin lid.

Lu Chou's breathing was shallow, his chest rising unevenly; sweat beaded, gathered, and broke again across his forehead to trace down the curve of his temple.

"Hold still," she whispered through clenched teeth, as if command could steady the tide.

She poured the powder into the gash.

His brows knit tight at the sting, muscle jumping beneath her palm, but he uttered not a sound—only the faintest tremor ran through his fingertips, a quiver like a plucked string.

The lamplight inside flickered with each jolt; their shadows swayed upon the curtain—one still, one moving—two lives suspended by a thread that could snap with a wrong breath.

In the nurse's arms, Baor cowered and wept soundlessly, cheeks wet, tears sliding one after another like beads slipping a string.

Hearing that fragile sob, Xiao Lingyu's chest tightened until it hurt to breathe. Her eyes burned, but her hand steadied, turned sure.

"Don't be afraid. Mama's here."

She said it softly to comfort the child, and perhaps to keep herself from breaking.

Suddenly, Lu Chou's breath snagged on something sharp. His body convulsed once, pain scattering his awareness like startled birds.

She panicked, tearing open his robe to see how far the red had gone.

The white cloth beneath was drenched to the hem; the wound under his ribs gaped wider with each breath, bone glinting through torn flesh like a pale shard in a red sea.

"Heavens, this must be stitched!" the nurse gasped, already rummaging for the kit.

Liang Jin thrust a needle and thread toward them through the curtain, then hesitated at the threshold. "Madam, it should be sterilized—by flame—"

"Then light the lamp—heat the iron!" she cried, her face gone ghost-pale and fierce.

Fire flared, small and urgent. The glow reddened her cheeks as she threaded the needle; her hands trembled so that the silver glimmer of the thread shivered in time with her breath.

She bent over him and began to sew, one stitch at a time, dragging edges together with stubborn care. Tears fell soundlessly onto his robe, darkening cloth where they landed.

When the needle pierced flesh, Lu Chou finally flinched. A muffled groan escaped his throat, rough, unwilling.

Her hand jerked; the needle slipped, and fresh blood welled hot and bright.

He caught her wrist, his voice rough but somehow tender. "Don't shake."

She froze. His grasp was firm, steady, utterly unlike the chaos outside or the quiver inside her.

She looked up at him; the heat of his hand travelled through her skin, struck something deep and unguarded.

For a breath their eyes met. Something wordless moved between them, quieting the storm that had been beating at her ribs.

"Endure it," she said hoarsely.

"I will," he murmured. "Just… don't cry."

Her gaze quivered; her lips pressed tight. She bit down until she tasted iron, forced her stitches to true speed.

"I'm not crying," she whispered. "Say that again, and I'll sew crooked."

A breath of a laugh slipped from him, there and gone, quickly swallowed by pain.

Moments later the final stitch drew closed beneath her fingers. She wiped the sweat from his brow with the back of her wrist, but his eyes had begun to lose their focus, pupils darkening like deep water at dusk.

"Lu Chou—you are not allowed to sleep!"

He seemed to try to answer but only breathed two barely audible words: "Don't… worry."

The whisper was thin as mist—yet it carried a strange calm, an assurance that stung her eyes anew for no reason she could name.

Her throat constricted; she reached and pulled him into her arms, heedless of the blood that soaked through. "If you die here," she choked, "then I… I'll owe you my whole life."

The words startled even her; she had never spoken to him like that before, not even in old days when truth felt less costly.

Outside, hooves thundered closer. Liang Jin's shout cut through the wind:

"Two miles more—the post station's ahead!"

But she did not hear. All she could feel was the faint, fading warmth of the man in her arms. His breathing was a thread, his pulse a whisper.

She clutched him tighter, bent to his ear, her voice breaking into pleas she could not have imagined making a day ago:

"Stay awake… Don't you dare sleep. You said you still wanted revenge, didn't you? I'm begging you—don't you close your eyes.

If you die here, who will I scold?

You said I still owe you—well, the debt isn't paid."

A tear slipped from her lashes and fell onto his lips.

He seemed to hear the shape of it. His mouth moved, barely.

And in a voice softer than breath, he answered:

"Then let it be… a debt for a lifetime."

* * * * *

The Capital Trembles

In the northern quarter of the capital rose the ninefold palace walls, their gilded eaves layered like clouds upon clouds, bright even beneath a gauze of autumn haze.

Bell towers caught the morning sun; shadow pooled blue beneath the vermilion gates.

To the south sprawled the merchant wards—streets woven like a chess board, markets thrumming like veins beneath the skin of the empire.

Hawkers sang prices; porters shouldered bales; sedan chairs nodded like boats in a busy harbor.

Between the morning bell and the evening drum, the city roared with life—officials in debate, clerks bent over inkstones, commoners in haste, a world bound by protocol and dust.

Now, as the first gold of autumn brushed the air and osmanthus sent sweetness down the lanes, the drums before the palace had fallen silent.

The vermilion gates were closed and guarded at double watch.

The affair of the southern tribute had already stirred ripples through court and city alike, yet the deeper currents of power remained veiled: none dared guess which prince would rise the final victor; everyone pretended not to guess.

Within the Yushi Office (Censorate), censors worked by lamplight through the night, brush tips nicked to needles.

From the Ministry of Justice, secret agents galloped through the streets at odd hours. Every faction sent eyes toward the post station or waited, sleepless, at the city's edge for a dust plume that would tell them how the wind blew.

Even the palace itself quivered in small, careful ways.

The old retainers of the Crown Prince's faction moved like startled birds; they gathered and dispersed, never in groups of three.

The Third Prince's manor burned with light into the small hours—there was talk of a private meeting, talk of lists, talk of promises that sounded like threats when repeated.

Lu Chou's return to the capital was nothing less than a stone hurled into an already storm-tossed lake.

In the court, the Third Prince Chen Song stood in full ascendance. His ties with the Ministries of War and Works ran deep; southern merchants and shipping guilds quietly sent him silver and letters of pledge, each a strand drawn into his net.

Rising through military merit, He was known for swift, decisive strikes—no gentle heir, but an edge honed to conquer. Though not the Crown Prince, his momentum shook pillars and loosened old loyalties.

As for Chen Gen, heir of the Eastern Palace—his memorials to the throne had slowed; his allies were stripped of rank one by one; his confidants investigated with an excess of courtesy. His strength waned by the day, and the silence around his halls grew thick.

He had not shown his face in court for a fortnight.

Then, one pale dawn, a dispatch arrived from the south:

"Lu Chou has returned to the capital."

The words fell like thunder across tiled roofs.

Two rumours swept the city at once, running along teahouse benches and down yamen corridors like wildfire.

First—he had escorted secret documents and witnesses northward, survived an ambush at Blossom Ridge, and though grievously wounded, had completed his mission. His loyalty and courage, they said, might yet steady the throne.

Second—he carried proof, it was whispered, that could upend the succession itself, that names were written which should not have been written, that silver had flowed where it should not have flowed.

Before he even crossed the palace threshold, an imperial edict arrived:

Lu Chou and his escort were to return home and rest until summoned.

At the gate, the Emperor's favoured eunuch, Lu Jiabao, waited half a day for the wounded party to appear. When he finally saw them, he stepped forward, smiling with narrowed eyes and a voice full of silk:

"Lord Lu, His Majesty is deeply moved by your service. He bids you return to your estate and recover. When your strength returns, the throne will hear your full account."

Every official present heard the message beneath the courtesy: the Emperor's words carried more soothing than command. The court would breathe, then speak.

Lu Chou did not enter the palace that day. He sealed his gates and received no visitors. He sent his men to ground. He said nothing—yet all of Capital City whispered his name and built towers of inference upon silence.

That very night, the Crown Prince sent word, inviting him to a private banquet at Rongyang Hall, "to welcome an old friend home."

The reply was brief: "I am still recovering from the injury. I beg His Highness's forgiveness."

The Crown Prince read the message, smiled faintly, and asked no more aloud.

Three days later, another invitation came—again politely refused:

"The scar is unclosed. My movement unsteady. I shall disturb His Highness on a later day."

The Prince Song's expression did not change, though his aides exchanged uneasy glances in the lamplight. Paper rustled like distant rain.

Three days more, and a third invitation was sent. This time the messenger bore the Crown Prince's personal seal and message: "His Highness has arranged a small gathering at the hot springs. No outsiders, only old companions to share the evening."

This time, Lu Chou did not decline—he simply replied:

"I have already promised an audience to the Third Prince. Regretfully, I cannot attend. I ask His Highness to forgive the discourtesy."

The envoy stood stunned, mouth opening and closing on the air.

By dawn, the news had spread through every tavern and yamen of the city:

Three invitations. Three refusals.

"Lord Lu declines the Crown Prince thrice—this is no mere grudge," people whispered over cups that went cold. "It is allegiance."

Others murmured with their wine half raised:

"The evidence he carries may strip the Eastern Palace of its heir. The Prince begs his silence."

And in the teahouses, bolder tongues laughed aloud, careless of whose clerk sat nearby:

"Lord Lu knows which way the wind blows. The tide has turned!"

All eyes shifted toward Chen Song, and those who had waited on the fence began to measure which side looked less like a fall.

* * * * *

In the Third Prince's residence, Chen Song received Lu Chou with open delight that did not trouble to hide its calculation.

Bronzes smoked with resin; the floor gleamed with oil; a chess board lay arranged at midgame as if interrupted by important news.

The air between them shimmered with hidden edge and measured flattery.

"Lord Lu," the prince said, tone smooth as polished jade, "you understand the times. That alone sets my mind at ease." He gestured toward the seat at his right, the place reserved for a counsellor who mattered.

Turning toward Lu Xiu, he added with an easy smile that showed a hint of teeth:

"You brothers are pillars to this house. Should fortune ever favour me, I will not forget the bond between us."

Lu Chou merely smiled, silent.

He lifted his teacup and let it turn once in his fingers, the dark liquid trembling like shadowed water beneath a lantern, his eyes as deep and unreadable as night, as if the tea's surface and the city's surface both concealed the shapes that truly mattered.

Chapter 49: Hidden Blades at the Banquet

The capital's most opulent establishment, the Pavilion of the Drunken Moon, was ablaze with lights. Within a classically elegant private suite, three men sat around a single table, the banquet already in full swing.

Inside the Celestial Chamber, three tiers of glazed skylights reflected the night, and the shadows of silken curtains drifted in the breeze.

Prince Chen Song, the Third Prince, had arranged this intimate gathering, where jade vessels lined the table and the air was thick with the scent of fine tea and warmed wine.

Lu Chou and his elder concubine-born brother, Lu Xiu, sat to the Prince's left and right. Both possessed a superlative bearing, yet at this moment, their faces were masks of cold indifference.

There was no trace of the joy one might expect from a reunion between brothers. One was composed of cold jade, like the unmelting snow of a high mountain ridge; the other had soaring brows and sharp eyes, like spring winds giving life to wild grass.

The Third Prince noted inwardly that in terms of presence and visage, it was truly difficult to rank one above the other. Yet, by the laws of heaven and man, one was legitimate and the other concubine-born; one was a civil official and the other a military man.

Who led and who followed had long been dictated by fate.

During the meal, Chen Song brought up the matter of the assassins in Jiangnan, his voice laced with feigned concern.

Lu Xiu caught the opening and raised his cup with a flashing smile. "I heard that during my brother's trip to Jiangnan, he barely had a few days to admire the scenery before he became entangled in a murder case. His Majesty's order for you to return to the capital to recover is quite merciful. And yet... for a dignified official of the court to encounter frequent assassinations, how can one not suspect that he brings the wind and rain upon himself?"

He laughed with easy grace, but his tone was like a flowing spring stream hiding jagged ice beneath the surface. Lu Chou did not offer a direct rebuttal, answering only with a faint, chilling smirk.

Lu Xiu poured more wine, swirling the liquid in his glass as he observed its color. His voice was as light as a drifting cloud, yet it carried an irrepressible hint of mockery.

"I heard the journey through Jiangnan was elegant and unobstructed, the mountain scenery as beautiful as a painting. My brother's mission seems to have been quite leisurely. With the flowers in full bloom, boat trips on the lake, and tea houses tucked away in the alleys—it is truly a fine vista. To act as an investigator while enjoying the sights... such pleasure found amidst work is enough to make anyone envious."

His words clearly painted the turmoil in Jiangnan as a mere sightseeing excursion, every syllable a barbed insinuation that Lu Chou had neglected his official duties for personal amusement.

Lu Chou did not flare up in anger. He did not even rush to reply. He merely lifted his cup to his lips and took a shallow sip, his eyes devoid of ripples and his tone placid. "Jiangnan is wealthy and prosperous, but beyond the glamor, there are hidden perils. If a man's character is not upright and his spirit not firm, it is indeed easy to lose one's ambition to trifles and lose one's footing to the current. This is precisely why the ancients said—only integrity can anchor one's foundation. Without integrity, how can a man stand? Without a foundation, how can he stabilize affairs?"

His tone was level, yet every word landed with the weight of a stone. He moved with silent precision to seal off every one of his brother's jibes, turning the phrase "losing ambition to trifles" back on Lu Xiu as a sharp counter-irony.

Hearing this, Lu Xiu's smile turned cold. Anyone with a modicum of wit could hear that his younger brother was striking back, likely using the very act of Lu Xiu's defection to the Third Prince as a way to mock him for having no moral "integrity."

Lu Xiu's smile did not fade, but a glimmer of sharp light appeared in his eyes as he spoke in a measured pace: "My brother speaks with some reason, but if that 'integrity' is too rigid and fails to recognize the timing of the world, it is like a withered branch. It looks stiff and unyielding, but in truth, it cannot withstand a single snap. My brother's reputation is currently at its peak, and he is the focus of all expectations; he, more than anyone, should know the way of advance and retreat. Otherwise... I fear that for every step taken, the very roots will tremble."

Lu Chou's expression remained unchanged as he quietly set down his wine cup. He understood perfectly. His elder brother, alongside the Third Prince, was extending a co-conspirator's invitation—half-luring and half-threatening him to join the Third Prince's camp.

Seeing the tension, Chen Song interjected with a laugh, "I heard that during Lord Lu's trip to Jiangnan, he grasped a great deal of evidence regarding the Crown Prince's acceptance of illegal contributions. I wonder if there is any truth to this?"

He was merely probing casually, not expecting Lu Chou to actually respond.

"It is true," Lu Chou replied.

"Truly?" Chen Song's voice rose in shock, his posture straightening significantly.

"Yes."

Chen Song instinctively glanced at his surroundings. Ensuring they were alone, he leaned in and whispered, "This matter must not be spread, or it will be a capital crime."

"Heh, I imagine that given the many years of friendship between my brother and the Crown Prince, he wouldn't necessarily present such evidence to the Emperor," Lu Xiu remarked, taking a lazy sip of wine.

To his surprise, Lu Chou's expression turned solemn. His voice was low but as clear as the ring of struck metal: "My brother is mistaken. The moment I entered the capital, I ordered my men to present the relevant evidence to His Majesty in its entirety. Only then did His Majesty order me to return to my manor to rest, awaiting a future summons to the palace to report on my duties."

"Truly?" Chen Song's delight grew even more pronounced. At this rate, how much longer could the Crown Prince hold his position?

Lu Chou lowered his gaze and spoke with gravity, "When the tree seeks to stand tall, the wind will surely try to break it; when a man seeks to be upright, the words against him will be many. If the Crown Prince breaks the law, he is no different from a commoner. If I were to remain silent, I would be unworthy of the Lu name and a traitor to the Emperor's grace. If one must measure the wind's direction before walking, then the path is no longer the original one."

The two brothers went back and forth, their words never devolving into crudeness, yet every syllable was a clash of blades. On the surface, it appeared to be a toast and casual family talk; in reality, dark tides were surging violently.

Both men offered a faint smile, but neither bowed his head. They merely clinked their cups together—swords hidden in the wine, the resonance lingering. "Thank you for the reminder, *elder concubine-born brother*," Lu Chou said, his tone as steady as ever but sounding like the soft grind of a sword's edge. "The road is treacherous, but I walk it with resolve. If one fears a fall, does one not stop walking for a lifetime?"

Concubine-born brother?

Heh. No one at the table was deaf; every word Lu Chou spoke was a deliberate assertion of his own legitimate status.

Chen Song, seeing the gunpowder-heavy atmosphere between the brothers, hurriedly smoothed things over with a laugh: "The two of you—one civil, one military; one stern, one spirited—are like the finishing strokes on a dragon painting. Today, this Prince has set this banquet; let us not turn debate into combat and ruin the pleasure of the wine."

"We thank the Prince," the Lu brothers replied in unison, raising their cups.

"Both of you are pillars of our dynasty. Today, let us speak not of the wind and rain, but only of the elegance within the cup."

Lu Xiu and Lu Chou raised their vessels once more. Smiles remained on their faces, but within their cups was a confrontation as irreconcilable as fire and water. An aura of slaughter flowed beneath the fragrance of the wine.

Lu Chou's brow remained icy, his tone carrying an indiscernible distance: "Your Highness, the rumors have been chaotic lately, and everyone in court has their own tale. For Your Highness to invite me at such a time... Ziyuan toasts to you in thanks."

Lu Xiu gave a cold laugh and followed: "Rumors are but noise. Your Highness naturally has your own calculations, though not everyone has the wit to grasp them."

Lu Chou arched a brow in a sharp retort: "If everyone could grasp them, they would know who the enlightened master is. If that were the case, how could there be conflict in this world?"

The words between the two brothers seemed to spark with fire as they stared each other down. The atmosphere grew heavy in an instant.

Seeing this, Chen Song's heart blossomed with joy. Wasn't Lu Chou plainly stating that he, Chen Song, was that enlightened master?

He raised his cup and laughed: "Alright, alright. You two are my most relied-upon left and right hands. Why look for unpleasantness? At today's table, let us set aside our grudges and drink this cup together."

The corner of Lu Xiu's mouth hooked slightly, still unwilling to show weakness: "Your Highness must be joking. We brothers have always walked our own separate paths; what grudges could there be?"

Lu Chou added flatly: "That may be so, but it is merely a matter of mutual restraint."

Hearing this, Chen Song's smile hid a sharp edge. He slowly swirled his cup and said: "Restraint is fine, and balance is fine, as long as there is one person who can steady the situation. If the court has no North Star to set the scale, no one can avoid being overturned by the waves. Lord Lu, what do you think?"

Lu Chou lifted his eyes, meeting the Prince's meaningful gaze. His tone was like frost: "The Third Prince is wise."

Lu Xiu gave a light laugh and clinked his cup against Lu Chou's, his voice carrying a hint of disdain: "The waves have not yet settled; who dares speak of taking the helm?"

Chen Song was overjoyed, waving his hand for the attendants to pour more wine: "Drink! We shall not return until we are drunk!"

The laughter of the three men rose. On the surface, there was harmony, but the dark undercurrents surged relentlessly between their cups.

Readers can view the full collection of colour illustrations here:
https://www.facebook.com/profile.php?id=61581325000577

Chapter 50: Under the Emperor's Grace

Since the banquet concluded, the sky had darkened, and the two brothers, both slightly inebriated, rode back to the residence together in a single carriage.

Lu Chou and Lu Xiu sat side by side inside the carriage, one to the left and one to the right, separated by a space neither too close nor too distant.

The figures of both brothers were tall and straight, yet their temperaments differed.

Lu Chou's expression was as cold and stern as snow; he rested his eyes, silent as a mountain.

Lu Xiu, meanwhile, leaned against the carriage wall, his demeanour relaxed, a curve of a half-smile clinging to his lips.

The carriage was so quiet that only the sound of the wheels crushing the ground could be heard.

Finally, it was Lu Xiu who initiated the conversation, his tone light and faint, as if merely a casual enquiry: "We hear... that this journey back from Jiangnan, Brother, you not only brought back crucial witnesses and evidence, but also a woman and a child?"

His voice was not loud, yet every word was deliberate, landing in the air like a stone dropped into water.

Lu Chou did not open his eyes, merely shifting the wound concealed within his sleeve slightly, his tone indifferent: "The news travels quickly, it seems."

Lu Xiu raised his eyebrows, a half-smile on his face: "The rumour-mill in this Capital is always swift. Rather, one might say that you have always acted entirely as you please. Why not tell us: who is she? And whose child is it?"

Only then did Lu Chou slightly open his eyes, his gaze cold: "Since the illegitimate elder brother is so well-informed, why not hazard a guess?"

Lu Xiu did not grow angry, but laughed instead, naming them directly: "The Madam of the Jin Hua Establishment, Xiao Lingyu, and her four-year-old young daughter, Xiao Baor."

Lu Chou displayed no surprise, having clearly anticipated this long ago: "Since that is the case, why bother asking what you already know?"

Lu Xiu adjusted his posture, his tone still unhurried and measured: "As your elder brother, it is only natural that I must enquire clearly. Since Madam Xiao is one of the witnesses, why did you care for her the entire journey, even going so far as to protect her with your life?"

"It was merely a matter of convenience," Lu Chou replied, his tone unchanged, as placid as water.

"Convenience?" Lu Xiu laughed softly, as if savouring the two words, his tone carrying mockery: "When did you, too, learn to dispense aid to the poor and relieve the distressed? And even personally bring the woman back, feeding her well?"

The atmosphere darkened.

Lu Chou finally looked up, staring at his elder brother, his gaze like a blade, yet remaining calm: "Trouble yourself no further. I shall personally make proper arrangements for the mother and daughter."

The carriage wheel crushed over some gravel, causing a slight tremor.

Lu Xiu turned his eyes towards the flickering light and shadow beyond the curtain, only saying softly: "But if a man holds no sentiment, only schemes remain."

"What do you mean?"

"Hah, regarding the mother and daughter of the Xiao family, whether your motive is sentiment or a scheme, are you clear on it yourself?"

The words ceased, and the carriage plunged back into silence.

The carriage slowly passed through the East Gate of the Capital. One after the other, two pairs of eyes looked through the shadow of the curtain at the winding streets within the city, neither of them speaking.

Yet, within that silence, the undercurrents continued to surge ceaselessly.

Suddenly, Lu Xiu smiled, speaking with profound meaning: "Do you recall when we were young, Brother, you always disliked vying for power, did you not? Do you remember when you were just past ten, the Master said—'The illegitimate son must strive for strength, and the legitimate son must uphold purity.' You argued endlessly with the Master over this, infuriating him to the point he wished to strike your palm. Now you strive fiercely for everything. It seems, rather, that both of us have changed."

Lu Chou dropped a cold sentence in response: "It is not I who changed, but the situation. For the Lu family to survive upon the crest of the wave, we can no longer afford to leave room for others to make a move."

Lu Xiu's gaze sharpened, and he said slowly: "Five years ago, you drastically changed after returning from the ancestral shrine in the countryside. Previously you did not contend with me; now you press hard at every step. The Court of the Imperial Clan, the Ministry of War, the Ministry of Revenue—you have your people everywhere. Did the old family maxims lead you to comprehension? Or... did you meet someone outside the ancestral shrine who convinced you to reveal even your hidden hand?"

Lu Chou's expression was cold and heavy: "Do you presume everyone is like you, whose sole desire is to crawl higher than the legitimate son?"

Lu Xiu smiled, carrying a challenge: "I, for one, am not like you: losing your heart, yet gambling your life."

Lu Chou gave a cold laugh: "That statement is inaccurate. What do you mean by 'losing your heart'? I, for one, would like to know what, precisely, is the stake of your 'gambling your life'?"

"Must I articulate it?" Lu Xiu sneered. "For her sake, you disregard even your own life."

"Nonsense."

"I speak of you," Lu Xiu's eyes were sharp. "You went to the countryside to study arduously in seclusion, and upon your return, you were like a different man. You abandoned forbearance and began to seize power and influence at all costs. This kind of life-gambling that you are pursuing..."

A cold light flashed in Lu Chou's eyes, cutting short his unfinished words: "And what if I gamble my life? So long as I can ascend that high position, even more life-gambling would be worth it."

Lu Xiu sneered: "Your recklessness, like this, will lead you to reap what you sow sooner or later."

"My elder brother had best attend to his own affairs first," Lu Chou replied coldly, still leaning against the chair without moving: "Can it be that you, an illegitimate son, still intend to surpass the legitimate son?"

"You!"

Their eyes met again, a silent confrontation.

Outside the carriage, the sky gradually deepened. Inside, the intent to kill had not ceased. The two brothers, like the opposing sides of a chessboard game, had no path left for retreat.

* * * * *

Deep autumn in the Capital; the wind passed through the streets and alleys. A slight chill had already settled between the red walls and black-tiled roofs.

Lu Chou led Xiao Lingyu and Baor into the rear courtyard of the Lu Residence.

He did not arrange for them to enter the main house, but instead settled them separately in the eastern wing, an area named the Qingfeng Courtyard (Clear Breeze Courtyard).

It was his former residence from his student days, quiet and secluded, separated from the main residence only by a spirit screen—both near and distant.

Xiao Lingyu knew in her heart that his claim was merely a pretext of 'supervision,' but his true purpose was to safeguard her completely.

"This place is remote and quiet. Should anything occur, send for me at any time." His tone was faint, yet he instructed the servants to stock all necessities—firewood, rice, oil, and salt—in full supply.

Baor chased the fallen leaves in circles in the courtyard. The autumn sunlight scattered upon her bronze-coloured eyes, sparkling like water. The old servants in the courtyard whispered in amazement: "This child's countenance is truly the very image of the Second Master when he was young."

"Only those eyes..."

Lu Chou's gaze paused slightly; he did not speak, merely turning to instruct: "Prepare for the journey to the Palace."

* * * * *

Early autumn in the Capital; the light of the sky was steady. The cry of the cranes from outside the Imperial City walls drifted languidly, as if only a single thread of life force linked Heaven and Earth.

When Lu Chou entered the Imperial Study, his robes were not yet fully arranged, yet his expression was composed.

Having travelled a thousand li from Jiangnan, he was summoned immediately upon his arrival in the Capital—such treatment was considered an exception among the assembled court officials.

Inside the Imperial Study, the Emperor's expression was dark and gloomy.

He was flipping through a joint memorial from the Jiangnan merchant guilds, which accused the Crown Prince and the Third Prince of each deploying their own agents to privately interfere with the silk tax collection, thus affecting state expenditure.

"We are still alive, yet these sons are already so eager to divide authority and seize profits!" The Emperor's voice was like a startling clap of thunder.

"What is your view?" The Emperor slammed the memorial down heavily, his gaze like lightning.

Lu Chou cupped his hands and replied in a deep voice: "Your subject believes that the root cause of the merchants' anxiety and the officials' hesitation in this case is the lack of clarity in Imperial Authority; it is not within the ability of a subject to comment upon the conflict between the Imperial Princes."

The Emperor narrowed his eyes: "You are cautious indeed. But which side have you taken?"

Lu Chou pondered for a moment, his tone steady as water: "The Lu family has served as subjects for generations, receiving grace since childhood, and we maintain our duty scrupulously. Your subject knows not the merits of the Imperial Princes; your subject only knows that all matters must place the Imperial Command first, and the foundation of the state foremost."

The moment this phrase was uttered, the Imperial Study was so quiet that a needle could be heard dropping.

A slight light flashed in the Emperor's eyes, and he suddenly let out a long sigh: "Now, with the entire court, civil and military, engaged in favour-seeking, only you still remember that We are the Sovereign."

"Well said. 'Recognising only the Emperor and Imperial Authority'—
We shall remember that phrase."

The Emperor's voice softened slightly, and he asked again: "And what
of Xiao Lingyu? We heard that on this journey back to the Capital, you
brought a widow and her daughter with you."

Lu Chou raised his eyes, his tone still composed: "Xiao Lingyu is the
Madam of the Jin Hua Establishment. Though targeted several times,
she has never been implicated, proving her purity. It is exceedingly rare
for a female merchant of the common people to maintain her integrity.
This time upon returning to the Capital, your subject feared she would
be framed, and thus brought her back for clarification. The Imperial
merchant guilds now require rectification; if such a person could assist,
perhaps a new spirit could be revitalised."

The Emperor remained silent. After a moment, he nodded: "But her
relationship with you..."

"In the past, we met several times in the countryside, but We never
became close acquaintances. Your subject reflects that he is but a
humble official; how would I dare to compromise public duty for
private interests?"

The Emperor pondered for a moment, then said: "Granted. Allow her to
enter the ranks of the Capital's embroidery merchants. The status of
Imperial Merchant shall be bestowed upon her."

By this time, the atmosphere inside the Imperial Study was already
heavy and dark; the lamp shadows flickered upon the golden-lacquered
desk with dragon patterns.

The Emperor sighed deeply, turned around, and stood with his hands
clasped behind his back, his gaze falling upon the stack of memorials,
and he gave a cold sneer.

"The Crown Prince and the Third Prince are quite zealous now, arguing
until their faces are flushed over this matter of contributing gold from
Jiangnan. We, on the other hand, appear to be surplus to requirements."

Lu Chou lowered his head and cupped his hands: "Your subject dares
not speak presumptuously about the struggle for the succession."

The Emperor glanced at him askance, his voice not loud, yet carrying
oppressive pressure: "You dare not speak presumptuously, yet every
step you take is a strategic move on the board."

"Your subject is simple-minded; I am loyal only to the Emperor," Lu Chou's voice was clear and resonant, neither servile nor arrogant. "As for the matter of the succession, your subject has never spoken presumptuously, nor do I dare to speculate."

The Emperor's gaze hardened. He suddenly gave a low laugh: "You are just like your elder brother: full of declarations of loyalty, yet your intentions are deeply hidden. We ask you, if the Crown Prince were to lose his influence, would your Lu family defect?"

Lu Chou remained silent for a moment before replying: "Since the establishment of the court, the Lu family has been favoured with profound Imperial grace, and only thus have our descendants enjoyed peace and stability. What your subject guards is the foundation of the Great Jin Dynasty, and the sacred person of the Emperor, not any particular heir."

Chapter 51: Twin Schemes Close In

Within the Heaven Chamber of the Drunken Moon Tower, layered curtains hung heavy, the air thick with curling incense.

On the red sandalwood table, wine cups and dishes lay scattered, smoke rose in a thin blue thread above the brazier.

Amid the flicker of lamplight stood the tall figure of a man in jade crown and court robe.

Third Prince Chen Song, the third son of the Emperor—half-reclined, a half-emptied cup still poised in his hand. His eyes glimmered darkly, a smile ghosting at the corner of his lips.

Behind him, a shadowed guard knelt and spoke in a low, precise murmur:

"This subordinate witnessed it with his own eyes. After the banquet, the two sons of the Lu family shared a single carriage.

At first, they sat in silence; later, some word was spoken, and the calm turned to fire.

Voices rose—sharp as drawn steel. They nearly overturned the coach.

From what I saw, my lord, they are utterly at odds, no longer brothers in heart."

Chen Song's smile deepened; the chill left his face, replaced by a slow, quiet pleasure—as if, in all the restless dusk of the capital, this alone could soothe his breath.

He raised the cup, drank lightly, and said with a low contentment:

"So, it is true. Since their return from Jiangnan, the hearts of the Lu brothers have truly parted ways."

Outside, the night wind stirred the lanterns; coloured light rippled across the lattice screens.

The guardsman bowed his head, silent.

After a moment, Chen Song rose, drawing a black cloak about his shoulders. He turned toward the window, his gaze slicing through the city's brilliance like a blade.

"At first, I thought they might be feigning discord," he said softly.

"But it seems… they truly are divided."

Jiang Yue bowed low.

"This servant is dull of wit—may Your Highness enlighten me."

The prince waved a hand, his tone measured, unhurried:

"Both sons of the Lu clan are clever men. The Crown Prince's fortune wanes; they know it as well as I.

Each has wagered on a different horse.

Lu Chou has refused the Crown Prince, Chen Gen's invitations three times—that alone declares his allegiance.

Now both brothers have sought favour with me, yet their hearts no longer align.

Two tigers upon one mountain cannot rest.

Their rivalry will serve me well—just as mine serves against the Crown Prince."

Jiang Yue bowed again.

"Your Highness's foresight is unmatched."

Chen Song smiled faintly.

"Brother against brother—one must never let either advance too far.

If we keep the tempo steady, we shall gather the spoils when they fall."

He paused, then turned, his tone lowering to an edge of command:

"Send word again. Keep watch on the Lu brothers—especially the second."

"Yes, Your Highness. We already have eyes upon his estate."

"Not only the estate," Chen Song said, his gaze deepening to black.

"I hear he returned from Jiangnan with a woman and a child—guarded them closely, risked his life more than once to protect them. Is that true?"

"It is. The woman is Xiao Lingyu, keeper of the Jin Hua Hall, and the child her four-year-old daughter, Baor.

She was among those connected to the Jiangnan case—an important witness."

Chen Song paced slowly, then stopped. His voice sank to a near whisper.

"A mere witness… yet worth such devotion? Worth the risk of death?"

"It seems strange to this servant as well," Jiang Yue replied.

"There is no record of prior acquaintance between them."

The prince shook his head, brow drawn in thought.

"No. If she were only a witness, he could have sent an escort.

For him to act thus—it borders on… sentiment."

"Your Highness means…?"

"Find out who this woman and child truly are," he said, voice low and cold as iron.

"Learn whether there was ever any tie between them and Lu Chou.

I suspect there lies a key piece upon the board—one not yet revealed."

He paused, half to himself.

"For a man like Lu Chou to stake his life—no, it is never merely for the court.

It may well be… for love."

"Yes, Your Highness. At once."

Chen Song's gaze sharpened.

"And if he has hidden that woman and child within his own household—watch them closer still.

Every movement, every breath—report it.

Leave no gap."

The guard bowed low and withdrew into shadow.

Chen Song descended the stairs. His robe brushed the polished floor, his pace unhurried.

At the tower's entrance, he paused and looked back toward the glowing tiers of lantern light above. His voice was a quiet murmur against the wind:

"They call the Lu brothers the twin dragons of our dynasty—one versed in letters, the other in arms.

But in truth, their paths have already parted, their backs turned against one another."

He gave a soft laugh—half amusement, half disdain. Then, as he turned toward his waiting carriage, his tone darkened to a whisper:

"Just as I, too, stand against my brothers—against the Crown Prince, against them all.

For in the struggle for an empire, when was there ever such a thing as brotherhood?"

He swept his sleeve and stepped into the carriage.

The door shut with a sharp thud—clean, final.

Above the eaves, a cold moon hung suspended, flawless as polished steel.

Hooves struck the cobblestones in measured rhythm, each echo drawing fainter until the sound dissolved into the night.

Across the capital, a thousand lamps shimmered like scattered gold dust.

Beyond the palace walls, shadows gathered and dispersed, and in the depth of that silent city, the wind began to turn.

* * * * *

The Eastern Palace — Chengming Pavilion

The lights still burned within the Eastern Palace.

Crown Prince Chen Gen sat before his writing desk, half-robed in wide-sleeved silk.

His fingertips drifted slowly across a jade paperweight, yet his gaze lingered upon the sealed letter newly placed before him.

He did not speak.

For a long while, he merely stared at the red seal pressed upon its end.

At length, his voice broke the silence—hoarse, low:

"The Drunken Moon Tower… They were having tea in the Heaven Chamber there?"

The attendant bowed deeply.

"Yes, Your Highness. They entered at the hour of Shan (3-5pm), and left at hour of Yo (5-7pm).

The two Lu brothers shared a carriage afterward. Midway home, they quarrelled.

The argument grew fierce—loud enough for our watchers to hear fragments through the noise. It seemed no mere difference of opinion, but near to blows."

The Crown Prince's eyes sharpened.

"Quarrelled?"

"Yes, Your Highness. Their words were heated; neither would yield.

It is this servant's belief that both brothers have now turned toward the Third Prince."

Chen Gen's expression shifted; a pause hung in the air before he gave a soft, humorless laugh.

"A quarrel? Hah. Just barely a performance, nothing more."

He turned his head slightly, the corners of his mouth curving without warmth.

"I have been brothers with the Third Prince for years, and look how that bond has fared.

What makes anyone think the Lu brothers are bound by anything stronger?"

The attendant bowed his head but ventured quietly:

"Your Highness, the tide of the court changes by the day.

If Lu Chou has truly allied with the Third Prince—and if discord has risen between the two brothers—it may well mean—"

"May well mean what?" Chen Gen's tone cut sharp; his eyes flicked coldly toward him.

"Speak plainly, not in riddles."

"Forgive me, Your Highness. This servant fears the Lu brothers may already have fallen under the Third Prince's sway."

The Crown Prince's brows drew together. He rose, the sweep of his sleeve stirring the candle flame.

He paced before the desk, the gold light shifting across his profile—half in brightness, half in shadow. His face betrayed nothing.

"The Lu brothers may tread separate paths," he said softly, "but if they are wise men, they will know which course to follow.

If they are shrewd, they will know when to bend."

He stopped before the desk, tapping the jade paperweight with a finger.

Each tap sounded deliberate, controlled.

"Three invitations from the Eastern Palace—all declined.

Yet they drink freely with the Third at the Drunken Moon Tower.

It seems they care little for the Crown Prince's face."

"Your Highness speaks true," the attendant murmured.

"Still, rumour says the Third Prince has lately grown close to the generals, to the Ministry of Works, even to certain young secretaries in the Ministry of Revenue..."

Chen Gen smiled faintly, without a trace of mirth.

"My brother has ever been a collector of men's hearts.

If he believes he can shake the Eastern Palace, let him try."

He sat once more, silk rustling softly against the tiled floor.

His tone was cool, even, like the edge of drawn steel:

"Keep watch on the Lu brothers.

Who visits, who departs, who carries messages, record everything.

I do not believe a mere wind from Jiangnan can topple the Eastern Palace."

Then, as though a new thought had come, he turned toward the window.

Through the narrow slit of the lattice, a line of silver moonlight fell across his eyes.

His gaze hardened; his voice dropped to a quiet blade:

"Since they find pleasure in my brother's company, let them have their wish."

Chapter 52: Severing Favor with Cold Words

Qingfeng Courtyard, evening settled over the small compound; lanterns were only just beginning to glow, little moons blooming one by one along the eaves.

Baor sat beneath the overhang, a small cloth rabbit clasped in her arms, counting the first faint stars as if they might answer back.

The flagstones still held a whisper of the day's warmth; from the plane trees a last, drowsy chorus of cicadas rasped and thinned.

From the kitchen came Xiao Lingyu, carrying a bowl of ginger soup whose steam trailed like breath in winter air.

She called softly, coaxing the child indoors, the bowl bright in her hands, the scent of sugar and spice lifting into the dusk—then froze.

By the gate stood a figure she knew too well, half veiled in shadow where the lantern did not reach.

"Lord Lu?"

Her voice was hushed, rough at the edges, as if rubbed by too many sleepless nights.

Lu Chou stepped out of the darkness.

His gaze fell first upon the bowl in her hands, then upon the loose strands of hair brushing her cheek. His expression was unreadable, something between dusk and stone, the kind of calm that keeps its distance to avoid breaking.

"The decree has been issued," he said quietly, as though reporting the weather rather than altering a life.

"From this day forth, Jin Hua Hall bears the title of Imperial Merchant."

She blinked; the heat from the soup misted her lashes. Her breath hitched, and the surface of the broth trembled.

"Why... why would you petition the Emperor for me?"

For a moment he said nothing. His eyes took in the weariness and resolve carved fine upon her face; when he spoke again, his tone was steady, contained.

"Not for you.

You earned it, by standing when others would kneel."

He paused; a faint chill slipped into his voice, like steel cooling after the forge.

"If even someone like you cannot stand firm, then this world truly belongs only to those who buy favour with gold."

He turned slightly away, the angle of his shoulder closing the distance he would not cross. When he spoke again, his tone had thinned to calm indifference.

"From now on, you'll need no nod from any man. You can claim your own footing in this city."

He made to leave, then halted mid-step, as if one last, vexing thread had caught.

"You once owed me," he said, his voice lower, more brittle.

"I hated you for it. But now let it be as you wished. We're even."

A beat; then, barely above a breath, not blessing so much as vow:

"May you never again have to bow your head.

May you keep Jin Hua Hall standing by your own strength."

When he finished, he turned and walked away. His figure receded through the lamplight—tall, solitary, and cold; the shadow he left behind seemed to cool the air.

Xiao Lingyu watched him go.

The night pressed close, the stars brightened, and her heart swayed between gratitude and grief, unable to choose which would break first. The steam from the bowl thinned, and only then did she remember to bring the soup inside.

* * * * *

Drunken Moon Tower

The Drunken Moon Tower—three stories high, carved beams glittering with gold paint—was the favoured haunt of nobles and scholars. Musicians tuned along the galleries; from private rooms came the rise and fall of laughter.

A stream of new laureates gathered that night to celebrate their success; among them, Lu Xiu had been dragged along by friends and good wine.

After many rounds, his head pleasantly light, he stepped out to the back veranda for air.

The corridor there was hushed, shadowed by bamboo; lamps shimmered faintly beyond the garden rocks, casting ripples of gold on the stone floor. A faint breeze cooled the sweat at his temples; the city's noise dwindled to a distant hum.

As he turned the corner, he saw her.

A slender figure in plain white stood by a vermilion column, still as a painting come to life. Her sleeves stirred slightly in the evening breeze as she gazed at the hanging lanterns, lost in thought—an island of quiet in the noise of the tower.

Shen Zhaoru.

He stopped, a smile tugging at his lips, and leaned lazily against the pillar as if chance, not intention, had placed him there.

"So even the virtuous Miss Shen graces the Drunken Moon Tower?

I'd never have believed it."

She turned at the sound of his voice—yes, it was him. Her eyes flickered, the smallest startle, but she forced her composure, replying evenly,

"I came with my cousin. She wished to select musicians for a performance. It's been some time; I stepped out for air."

She should have left at once. Yet her feet refused to move. His presence filled the narrow walkway—light, unhurried, and dangerously alive, like the flame that leans toward a draft.

That night by the river flashed through her mind: his arm seizing hers from the water, his drenched robe clinging to a frame hard as tempered steel; that calm face—utterly composed, yet reckless in its rescue. The image burned still, sharp and bright, as if the river had never dried from her skin.

"I never had the chance to thank you," she said at last, her voice soft, slightly strained.

Lu Xiu laughed lightly, as though the matter were a trivial story told long ago.

"A trifle.

A man's instinct to lend a hand—not worth remembering."

"But I remember," she said quietly, eyes steady on him.

"Even a small kindness deserves thanks. You spared me quite a humiliation."

Something shifted in his gaze. He had stepped closer only in jest—but her sincerity stilled him.

A flicker of curiosity—almost wonder—passed behind his smile, as if he had glimpsed a door he had not expected would open.

"If Miss Shen truly wishes to thank me," he murmured, tone half-playful, half-intent, "then perhaps you might grant me a few words this evening."

The words were gentle, but his eyes caught light, bright and unrelenting, like a paper lantern trembling in the wind: beautiful, inescapable. Somewhere a qin string thrummed and went quiet.

Shen Zhaoru's pulse stuttered; her fingers tightened unconsciously around the embroidered handkerchief in her palm. And the night, between them, grew very still.

He smiled—the kind of smile that left one defenceless.

Though his bearing was careless, even unruly, his eyes held a depth that spoke without a sound, a patience that said he could wait her answer all night.

She had meant to refuse him. Yet he stood neither too near nor too far; the faint scent of wine mingled with his low, hoarse voice, weaving an invisible net that held her still.

"Master Lu… you speak recklessly,"

she murmured, turning her face aside to hide the faint blush rising to her ears. The protest came softer than she intended, more plea than reprimand.

He caught the tremor in her tone but did not press, only said quietly—almost tenderly, as if making an observation for himself,

"Lu has not changed. It is Miss Shen who has."

"Changed… in what way?"

"In the past, you were always cold. Even when you nearly fell into the water, you did not so much as flinch.
But now—"

his smile deepened, subtle as a blade under silk,

"Now you smile… and it is beautiful."

Colour flared at once across her face. She turned sharply.

"Master Lu, that remark is improper."

"Improper?"

His voice remained lazy, but the mockery had faded, leaving only an unnerving calm—and something dangerously sincere.

"If it offends you, then I shall take it back."

For a moment, she had no answer. Then, softly, a truth she had meant to keep hidden:

"I did not know you were of the Lu family. Had I known…"

"Had you known," he cut in, the smile gone, tone dipped low, "you would not have let me save you? There are many in this capital who dislike me already—does Miss Shen wish to join them?"

She hesitated, caught off guard by the quiet sting beneath his words. He stepped closer—not roughly, but with unhurried grace. His eyes met hers; their breaths mingled in the narrow space between, warm against the cool night.

Her heart began to race. She wanted to step back, yet somehow she didn't.

"Miss Shen."

His voice had changed again—no longer teasing, but solemn, the wine burned off and only intent remaining.

"That night, I merely offered a hand. I sought no return.

If you remember it, that alone is enough."

He took a half-step back, as though aware that one more would cross the line he had set for himself.

Shen Zhaoru tightened her grip on the silk handkerchief, face flushed though she tried to steady her tone.

"…Very well."

Then, after a breath, almost in a whisper,

"But others… say you are not to be trusted."

He paused, then let out a soft laugh.

"And what does Miss Shen believe?"

Her lashes lowered, hiding whatever flickered beneath. It took her a long while to answer, the words gathering like dew.

"I… do not always believe what others say."

Something stirred in his gaze—a glint like lamplight on still water. But he did not close the distance again.

"That is enough.

What others say is their concern.

As for when Lu speaks in jest, and when he speaks in earnest." he smiled faintly, almost to himself,

"You will know in time."

She bit her lip, said nothing. Yet her cheeks had flushed deeper, and the tips of her ears glowed like coral beneath the lantern light. Somewhere inside, a toast went up; the sound arrived like far thunder.

He looked at her once more, eyes darkening, then inclined his head in a courteous bow.

"The night grows cold. Return soon, Miss Shen—lest the wind catch you, and your father, the Imperial Preceptor, find reason to blame me."

He said nothing more. A brief, quiet laugh; then he turned and walked away, his steps measured, unhurried, the bamboo shadows swallowing him by degrees.

She stood where she was, unmoving, until her cousin came searching for her. Only then did she realize how late it had grown. The Drunken Moon Tower was alight with lanterns, their red glow rippling across her face. She touched her chest lightly—her heart still beating fast, too fast.

That night, the wind was soft.

But it carried something into her heart that would not leave.

Chapter 53: Court Quakes with Power Shift

Dawn over the Golden Throne Hall.

The first light of morning broke against gilded beams yet brought no warmth. Frost-pale sun washed the coiling dragons and phoenixes into a dull gleam.

Within the great hall, the air was heavy iron pressing upon the heart.

Ministers stood in ordered ranks, silent as stone; only the faint chime of jade pendants, the whisper of breath behind sleeves, and the susurrus of court robes disturbed the stillness.

"Well done, Chen Song!"

The Emperor's fury cracked through the hall like thunder. His palm struck the jade desk.

Memorials flew from its surface, slapping and skittering down the steps below. None dared move to retrieve them. Even the bronze braziers seemed to shrink from the force.

"He dared collude with merchants raise a secret treasury, divert the tribute silver! Were it not for the memorial I read in secret, this deceitful son would still have me blind!"

The court froze, breathless; a hundred spines straightened as one.

"Lu Chou."

The Emperor's voice dropped to a low clang, iron drawn against stone.

"Every word you wrote, is it true?"

Lu Chou stepped out from the ranks, robes sharp and dark as frost. He bowed low, forehead near the cold jade tiles.

"Your Majesty, every statement in my memorial is fact. The Third Prince's faction conspired with silk merchants to transfer silver for private gain. The evidence is complete dates, couriers, ledgers, seals. I have prepared a sealed record, listing each accomplice in full."

The Emperor's gaze cut through him like a blade, holding there for a long moment. At last came a bitter laugh—harsh, wounded.

"Excellent.

Truly excellent.

The son I raised with such care has become a leech upon his country, a disgrace to the throne itself. He plots with courtiers, builds his own power—and thinks I would not see!"

His voice shifted—from rage to a weariness scoured to the bone.

"Such a son is no son of mine."

Then, in a single, shattering command.

"Write my decree!

Chen Song, the Third Prince, stripped of title, reduced to commoner rank, confined within his residence.

All associates to be investigated and their estates seized. His wife and children, if unknowing, may remain within the compound under watch."

"Your Majesty's mercy is boundless!"

A hundred voices fell to the floor in unison. Silence returned, thicker than before.

Crown Prince Chen Gen stood beside the jade steps, back straight, face unreadable. Only his palm, hidden in his sleeve, was damp with heat.

Years of patience, humiliation, calculation—countless nights of swallowing dust—and now he watched his rival fall.

Yet triumph never reached his eyes. He knew too well: the tides of imperial favour were colder than winter water; they lifted and drowned with equal indifference. One misstep, and all would be swept away.

When the court was dismissed, the Emperor remained upon the dragon throne.

"Minister Lu, stay."

Lu Chou knelt again.

"This case was handled with precision," the Emperor said slowly. "You have served me well. But the court is unstable. I must know—where does your loyalty truly lie?"

Lu Chou bowed lower.

"Your Majesty's wisdom knows all. My family has served for generations, untouched by the struggle for the heirship. This servant's loyalty is to the Throne and to Your Majesty alone—never to any prince."

The Emperor's expression eased, though his tone stayed grave.

"I am not ignorant of your family's ties to the Crown Prince. Should the heir lose his virtue—will you speak the truth, even then?"

"I will act for the good of the realm," Lu Chou replied without a breath of hesitation.

The Emperor nodded.

"Remember—what I require are loyal ministers, not partisans."

He reached across the desk and tossed a folded memorial toward him.

"In this silk-tribute affair, you mentioned a woman—the Madam Xiao Lingyu?"

"Yes, Your Majesty."

Lu Chou's tone was steady.

"She held her ground amidst corruption, refusing bribes despite repeated coercion. I believe she is a rare, upright soul—capable of greater responsibility."

The Emperor arched a brow.

"I recall her establishment—Jin Hua Hall, was it not? Its goods are well-spoken of."

"Indeed. Its embroidery and weave are of fine design and favoured even in the Inner Court."

The Emperor mused, fingers tapping once on lacquer, then said:

"Then let her be ennobled as an Imperial Merchant. Her workshop shall supply the palace directly when the inner treasury requires cloth or silk. Let this decree stand—as a reward to the incorrupt."

"Your Majesty's command—this minister shall obey."

A pause.

"One more thing," the Emperor said softly, tone dipping. "You and this woman—there was once… acquaintance?"

Lu Chou hesitated a heartbeat, then answered with measured calm.

"Years ago, our paths crossed a few times. My intervention now is to keep the innocent from being crushed beneath a contest for power."

The Emperor's gaze darkened deep, unreadable. After a long silence, he rose and walked toward the blazing doorway, robe trailing like shadow.

"The Third Prince has fallen. The court will shift again.

You, Lu Chou, your task is not yet done. Root out his remaining faction. Secure the trade routes from Jiangnan. Not one coin of the Empire's silver must go astray."

Lu Chou bowed until his forehead touched the ice-cold jade.

"This servant shall obey."

When he finally lifted his head, the Emperor's figure had receded beyond the vermilion doors. The memorial in his hand felt unbearably heavy, pressing into his palm like a verdict.

He drew a long, steady breath and lifted his gaze toward the pale morning beyond the eaves of the Golden Throne Hall.

The court was a chess board; the game unfinished, the players yet unseated.

He knew the true struggle had only just begun.

* * * * *

By the time Shen Zhaoru returned to the Shen estate, night had fallen. Lanterns glimmered along the corridors, their light swaying upon carved rafters; the painted beams seemed to breathe with each gust of wind.

The moment she stepped past the hanging-flower gate, a young maid approached in haste and whispered,

"My lady, the Master requests your presence in the study."

Zhaoru paused. Her pulse tightened beneath the calm of her face. Her father, the Imperial Preceptor Shen, was a man of great restraint; if he summoned her at night, it could only mean something grave.

Inside the study, the lamps burned bright. The faint scent of ink and sandalwood lay over rows of classics.

The Imperial Preceptor stood in a plain robe before his desk, hands clasped behind his back. He turned only when he heard her footsteps.

"You've returned?"

His tone was soft yet carried the weight of authority that brooked no refusal.

"Good evening, Father," she answered, lowering her gaze.

His eyes moved over her—keen, measuring; a furrow touched his brow.

"Where have you been today?"

"Accompanying my cousin to the Drunken Moon Pavilion," she replied evenly, "to select musicians for a birthday banquet. We waited a while, and… I chanced upon an acquaintance."

She stopped there, trimming her tone to cut off the hesitation that almost followed.

The Imperial Preceptor did not press at once. His voice, when it came, was calm and cutting.

"The Drunken Moon Pavilion is not a place for you. Now is not the safe time for you and our family. The princes' struggle burns hot; the world beyond our gates is rife with peril. A daughter of the inner court must not wander where she pleases."

Zhaoru's brows knit faintly.

"I was not alone, Father. After all, I am merely your daughter, not one of your ministers. What could the struggle for the throne possibly have to do with me?"

Her father's eyes sharpened; the answer rang like a blade struck true.

"Nothing to do with you? You are the Imperial Preceptor's only legitimate daughter—every glance, every step of yours is watched. One misstep, and tongues will turn your name into a weapon."

She faltered, lips parting in silence.

"The Pavilion," he continued, "is a nest of snakes in silk. Schemes are spun there; traps are baited with wine and laughter. The instant a noble lady crosses its threshold, she becomes a story waiting to be written— by others."

He paused, then let the last words fall like a seal on parchment.

"Especially… Lu Xiu."

So he knew. Her heart jolted; the name—his face—rose in memory, edged still in lamplight and wine.

"Lu Xiu, styled Jiheng—born of concubine blood. His fame is shallow charm; his talent, unbridled. Such men are no true match. Cross paths with him, and you imperil not only yourself but the reputation of our house."

Zhaoru lowered her gaze. She knew these truths as well as he. Yet the evening's meeting—his lazy smile under the lantern glow, that teasing 'Miss Shen, you in a place like this?'—still lingered in her ears. He had stood too close; the faint trace of wine and ink clung to his sleeve. His words were light, almost careless—yet her pulse had stumbled all the same.

And that, too, she could not speak.

Seeing her silence, the Imperial Preceptor's tone hardened again.

"Your mother is already considering a husband for you. Every candidate comes from an upright lineage, virtue unimpeachable—not one to be compared with the Lu family's elder son who is of the secondary line."

The words pierced cleanly, severing the fragile thread of warmth that had barely begun to form.

Zhaoru bowed low, voice scarcely above a breath.

"I… understand."

His expression eased slightly. Turning away, he said with quieter gravity,

"You have always been thoughtful and prudent. I ask not to confine you, but to keep you unblemished—for the sake of this family, and for your own."

"Yes, Father."

When she stepped from the study, the moon hung pale above the courtyard. Its light spread like water across the flagstones. A breeze moved the cassia leaves; shadows flickered like pages turning.

She looked down the long corridor paved with cold blue brick and thought, for the first time, how endless and lonely the road of the Shen family could be.

Chapter 54: The Chessboard Splits

The twilight deepened heavily, cloaking the Capital in a somber shroud. Inside the Lu Residence, the lamps shone with a brilliant, artificial light, yet the atmosphere within the study was like being suddenly plunged into a frozen ice cavern.

As Lu Chou stepped across the threshold, he saw Lu Xiu leaning casually—almost insolently—against the edge of the desk. He was idly spinning a jade pendant between his fingers, speaking and laughing with an air of complete self-possession to the old head butler who stood waiting nearby.

"You still find reason to laugh? You have truly excessive audacity," Lu Chou said, his voice dropping into a freezing chill.

Lu Xiu raised an eyebrow at the sound of his voice. He turned around lazily, his smile layered with meaning and edged with irony: "Aiya, the great meritorious subject has finally returned? What—having finished your triumphant report before the Emperor, you still have the leisure to come here and be lectured?"

Lu Chou ignored his taunts, stepping forward into the study. He bowed deeply and formally toward the man seated firmly behind the desk: "Father."

Lu Wenqian's face was livid, a terrifying ashen-green. His gaze, sharp as a hawk's, swept back and forth between the two brothers. He suddenly slapped the desk with a heavy, resounding thud, the force of it making the brushes jump and the inkstones shake on the wood.

"You two brothers have truly acquired great abilities!" His roar of rage split the air like a thunderclap: "The Crown Prince and the Third Prince were locked in a bloody struggle, and you two dared to employ a scheme of sowing discord between them! You even managed to overturn the entire political landscape with one hand—and your father, the Minister of Personnel himself, knew nothing of it beforehand!"

Lu Chou knelt down, his voice low and steady: "Father, please temper your anger. Your son harbors no intent of disrespect, but this matter was of the highest confidentiality, and we could not afford the slightest carelessness."

"Carefulness?" Lu Wenqian laughed, a sound of extreme, bitter anger: "Are you being cautious—or are you wary of my interference? Were you afraid your own father would ruin the secret conspiracy you brothers hatched together?"

Lu Chou looked up, his gaze heavy and unyielding as iron: "Your son would not dare. It is merely that this case involves matters of such depth that the slightest rumor could have made all our efforts collapse at the last step. If Father had known beforehand, you too might have been implicated."

"Hah, so you can still pretend to spare a thought for me?" Lu Wenqian sneered coldly, his fingers tapping the desk with a sharp, metallic rhythm. "One of you is cold, the other slick; neither of you ever truly keeps your father in your eyes. Now you speak with such grand justifications—do you have even a fraction of concern for the Lu family?"

Lu Chou lowered his head and said in a deep, resonant voice: "What your son did brings no shame upon the House of Lu."

Lu Xiu chimed in with a grin, sharpening the air with a casual knife: "Father, those words are unjust to me. I didn't take part at all. Chou never discussed a single word with me from beginning to end—it was entirely his own doing."

"You still dare to speak!" Lu Wenqian glared at him with frigid eyes. "If you had truly no involvement, how did that cloth merchants come to hand their account ledgers to you? You two—one civil and one martial, one cold and one roguish—together, you cooperated so seamlessly it was flawless."

Lu Chou frowned: "It was Lu Xiu who inserted himself; I never invited him."

"Oh?" Lu Xiu retorted with a smirk. "Did you not just say this matter was confidential and not to be publicized? Then my uninvited arrival— as a mere illegitimate son—surely ruined your perfect plan?"

"At least I did not casually fish for words while drinking and keeping company at the Drunken Moon Pavilion," Lu Chou said. "I was collecting evidence."

"And your constant exchanging of glances with the mistress of the embroidery workshop—do you call that 'collecting evidence'?" Lu Xiu shot back.

"Nonsense. It doesn't compare to you playing the fool and feigning madness."

"Oh? Then your daily visits to the Clear Breeze Courtyard—were they truly for inspecting the Imperial Merchant's affairs?"

"I was investigating whether she was implicated in the case."

"You investigated for three days and still haven't found an answer? It seems even the daughter is already eager to claim you as her own father."

"Enough!"

Lu Wenqian's furious shout was deafening. He slapped the desk and rose to his feet in a fit of rage: "What are you two arguing about here! Are you treating a matter of such grave importance as some common marketplace farce?!"

The two brothers instantly fell silent, though they glanced sideways at each other, the sparks of confrontation in their eyes yet to dissipate. Lu Wenqian's anger had not subsided, yet he could not deny that the victory in this high-stakes gamble was ultimately clean and decisive. The Third Prince's faction was ruined, the Crown Prince's position was solidified, and the Lu family's footing was secured.

As a father, he should have been pleased. But the fact that these two sons—one acting without informing him, the other acting with reckless freedom—were both entirely beyond his control was what enraged him most.

"Remember this: this is the court, not child's play." He slowly sat back in his chair, his tone heavy and sombre. "If you miscalculate even a single step one day, not only you, but the entire Lu family, will be buried with you."

Lu Chou and Lu Xiu simultaneously lowered their heads and replied: "Yes."

The cold wind blew outside. The lamplight flickered slightly. The atmosphere between the father and sons finally eased somewhat. Yet everyone understood that the storm had not fully passed; it was far from a time of true stability.

Lu Xiu raised his eyes to sneak a glance at his brother, sneering: "Father need not fret. Chou has an innate, meticulous mind; he likely prepared a path of retreat long ago."

Lu Chou's expression darkened, and he said coldly: "If this matter had a path of retreat, it would not have provoked the Emperor's fury in the first place."

"You still dare to talk back?" Lu Wenqian slapped the armrest heavily, his voice regaining a measure of terrifying severity. "Do you still hold your father in any regard?"

The room fell into a deathly, suffocating silence, the candlelight swaying violently as if about to be extinguished by the wind.

Lu Wenqian's anger persisted. He said in a deep voice: "You two, collaborating to set this trap and inciting the Emperor's rage... Although the final outcome benefits the Crown Prince, the risk was staggering—if a single link in the chain had failed, the whole board would have been lost! Do you truly treat the affairs of state as a frivolous game?"

Lu Chou bowed slightly, his voice neither servile nor arrogant: "Father's instruction is correct. Your son understands the gravity of the matter, but the court situation had reached a critical juncture. If we had not acted, the Crown Prince would have been doomed beyond recovery."

"So, you consider yourself a paragon of loyalty and integrity now?" Lu Xiu sneered, leaning back in his chair. His demeanor remained lazy, yet his gaze was sharp as a blade. "I accept Father's reprimand, but you should stop acting so righteous and grand. If you did not possess that solemn, upright face and the Emperor's personal favor, would it even be your turn to make decisions someday?"

Lu Chou's gaze narrowed slightly, flashing with cold light: "What I do never requires your approval."

"Oh? You still remember you are my elder brother." Lu Xiu's tone was contemptuous, his smile laced with thorns. "When I was beaten as a child, you only buried yourself in books. Now, in the court's struggle, you make decisions alone again. Has the word 'family' ever carried any real meaning to you?"

The atmosphere abruptly turned ice-cold. Lu Wenqian's eyes were heavy and dark as a deep pool. His trembling fingers tapped the tabletop: "Enough!"

The two brothers fell silent at once, lowering their heads in heavy quiet.

"The clouds over the court have not yet cleared. Do you still have the mind to engage in this internal strife?" Lu Wenqian slowly rose, walking to the window to gaze toward the distant Imperial Palace. His back was weary, yet still held a proud, erect posture. "When I established the Lu family's foundation, I endured humiliation and bore heavy burdens, merely so your lives would be less difficult in the future. Yet now, one of you advances with every step calculated, and the other speaks without restraint, and neither is willing to be truly honest and sincere with the other."

After a moment of silence, Lu Chou finally spoke, his tone low and slow: "Father, for this matter, your son is willing to bear full responsibility."

Lu Xiu snorted derisively, but said nothing further.

Lu Wenqian turned around, his gaze resting between the two of them for a long time. He remained silent, then finally said: "Since the moves have already been made in court, do not stir further turmoil. The Lu family's chessboard tolerates no careless misstep."

He paused, then turned specifically toward Lu Xiu: "As for you, it is time to rein in your temperament. What kind of man is Imperial Preceptor Shen? If you are truly smitten with his daughter, cease your jesting and frivolity. She is not some common woman of the pleasure quarters, but one who can stand shoulder-to-shoulder with you in the future."

Upon hearing this, Lu Xiu finally showed a rare, genuine trace of astonishment.

Lu Wenqian said nothing more, only instructing: "Withdraw."

The two brothers bowed and exited the study. Just past the threshold, Lu Xiu glanced sideways at his elder brother, giving a soft, mocking snort: "Do not imagine that winning this single round means you have won the entire game."

Lu Chou continued walking without pausing, only replying faintly: "If you truly wish to win, first learn the art of restraint."

The moonlight slanted down, cold and pale. The two figures walked away in opposite directions, each harboring his own hidden thoughts, yet they remained beneath the same roof—walking paths that appeared divergent, but in truth, converged toward the same destiny.

Chapter 55: True Feelings, Unspoken

Afternoon sunlight slanted through the lattice, scattering shards of gold across the flagstones. Dust motes drifted in the beam like slow snow.

Beneath the wavering shade of parasol trees, the air shimmered faintly with warmth; a faint cicada-saw crept and fell, as if even summer were holding its breath.

At her desk, Xiao Lingyu bent over the account scrolls.

The brush tip touched the paper, paused, then gave the slightest tremor—an almost imperceptible sign of the unrest simmering beneath her composed exterior.

Her gaze kept drifting, unfocused, sliding off columns of numbers she could have read blindfolded a year ago.

Since the day she had returned from the imperial library, she could feel the change in the wind—subtle, undeniable.

The trading routes of Jin Hua Hall had reopened; the dye merchants sent word; old embroiderers returned one by one with hands roughened and eyes bright.

Contracts that had lain cold found ink again.

She knew well whose hand had moved unseen, and dared not think too deeply on it, lest gratitude turn to something harder to hide.

A servant hurried in and bowed, breath tucked behind his teeth.

"Madam Xiao, the Lord is outside the gate. He requests to see you."

She froze—only the brush hair splayed a fraction, a black flower on the page.

Then, setting her brush aside, she rose so quickly she forgot to change her robe, merely tugged her sleeves into order and smoothed a stray wisp of hair behind one ear, as though order at the hem could restore order to the heart. She went out to meet him.

At the threshold, a figure in a dark robe stood against the light—tall, composed, his presence sharp as tempered steel. The late sun made a thin halo of dust around his shoulders.

Lu Chou.

In his hand was a scroll of yellow silk. He spoke before she could, voice low but clear:

"The imperial decree has been issued. From this day forward, Xiao Lingyu of Jin Hua Hall is acknowledged by the Inner Treasury as an Imperial Merchant—granted entry into the Royal Trade Council, authorized to oversee court textile commissions. The seal herein is your warrant."

She stared at the decree as if struck. Disbelief hit first, then guilt, and behind them something dangerously like relief—like gratitude—with a heat that felt perilously close to joy.

For a moment she forgot even to kneel.

"This… why?" she whispered, voice unsteady, the question turning to mist between them.

"Because you deserved it."

His eyes were deep; his tone, coldly measured. Yet a warmth hid in its depths, banked coals beneath steel.

"Not many choose to stand upright when the tide turns foul. His Majesty saw that—and respected it."

She lowered her gaze, fingers trembling as she took the scroll. The silk felt cool at the edges, yet it burned her palms like a brand. She could almost hear the wax of the seal set hard against wood and years to come.

He watched her expression shift, then inclined his head slightly.

"The message is delivered. I'll not intrude further."

He turned to leave.

But her breath caught—

"Lord Lu—"

He paused, half-turned, lamplight catching the fine scar at his temple.

"Madam Xiao?"

Her lips parted; both hands clutched the decree until her knuckles blanched.

"There are words I should have said… long ago."

Something flickered across his gaze—curiosity, and something sharper that passed like the shadow of a wing.

"Then say them."

Her breath came unevenly; she seemed to summon courage from the ground itself.

"I wish to tell you… about Baor.

She—"

The gate creaked open.

Nanny Ma stepped in, leading Baor by the hand.

"Madam, the young one was fussing to see you. I thought I'd best bring her."

Baor spotted her mother and ran forward at once, the small cloth rabbit bouncing from her arm like a pennant. She flung herself into Xiao Lingyu's lap, laughter bright as silver bells.

"Mama! I made a new friend! There's a sister in the courtyard who gave me honey cakes—they're so sweet!"

The words froze on Xiao Lingyu's tongue. From the corner of her eye, she caught Lu Chou's brief astonishment, he looked of a man suddenly seeing the truth he had not meant to find. A thread pulled taut between past and present.

"Honey cakes, hmm?"

His voice softened without thought as he crouched down; the sternness went out of his features like wind from a flame.

"How many did you eat?"

"One and a half!" Baor lifted her little fingers solemnly.

"I gave half to the sister. She said my smile looks like a crescent moon!"

He chuckled, low and genuine.

"And your mother's smile—what does that look like?"

Baor blinked, then turned up at her mother with grave concentration.

"Mama doesn't look like the moon. She looks like a star—bright, and very, very pretty!"

The words struck deeper than the child could know. Xiao Lingyu's heart trembled; she only managed to lower her gaze and smooth her daughter's hair, hiding the shine at the corner of her eye.

"Thank you, Baor. You've made mama very happy."

Baor nestled closer, then turned to Lu Chou again.

"Lord Lu, do you want honey cake too? I saved a little bit for you!"

He raised an eyebrow, the faintest curve touching his lips.

"Not calling me Lord Papa anymore?"

Baor pouted.

"Mama said I mustn't…"

For an instant, he was silent—then laughed softly, eyes warm with a sorrow she could not name.

"Then I won't argue with your mama. Keep it, little one."

The two spoke as naturally as if they had always belonged in the same room—one voice deep and steady, the other bright as morning bells. There was no distance between them, no pretence left—only the gentle fact of being.

Xiao Lingyu watched in silence, her chest tightening, that half-spoken truth still lodged behind her lips. The courage that had risen moments ago dissolved into the still air, leaving only the weight of what was unsaid.

The wind beneath the eaves shifted. Nanny Ma led Baor gently back into the inner room, leaving only two figures beneath the lantern, its light wavering like breath.

Lu Chou turned, his gaze fixed on the look that had frozen upon Xiao Lingyu's face.

"What was it you meant to say just now?"

His voice was calm, stripped of warmth, almost too careful.

She hesitated, eyes lowering to avoid his. Her reply was almost inaudible.

"…It's nothing. Only an old matter, not worth mentioning."

He did not press her. He merely regarded her a heartbeat longer, expression shadowed, unreadable—like a seal whose inscription could only be guessed by touch.

A breeze slipped beneath the roof tiles, stirring the lantern light until it trembled. Xiao Lingyu bit her lip. Her fingers, still clutching the imperial decree, tightened once more, as if pressure alone could keep a life from spilling.

* * * * *

The Studyroom was unnaturally still. From the bronze censer, a thread of incense rose, curling through the faint steam of untouched tea. The lacquered shelves glinted; the jade brush rest shone like frozen water.

Lu Wenqian lifted his eyes toward the tall figure standing before him. The porcelain lid in his hand tapped softly against the rim of the cup—a measured, rhythmic sound that carried its own quiet pressure.

"That woman and her child," he said at last, "where did they come from?"

Lu Chou stood with hands at his sides, his bearing as composed as stone.

"Years ago, while visiting the ancestral shrine, I stayed some months in the provinces. During that time, I made a passing acquaintance. The woman known now as Madam Xiao—she was that acquaintance."

Lu Wenqian arched a brow, a half-smile that did not reach his eyes.

"Only an acquaintance?"

"Yes."

His tone was even, his face cold and unyielding as frost.

"Her life has not been kind. Father and brother both gone early, she has kept her embroidery house alone. In recent years, she has made a name for herself."

"And because of that," his father said softly, "you petitioned the throne to name her an Imperial Merchant? Tell me—are all the clean-handed Madams of the realm to receive such favour?"

Lu Chou met his gaze, voice steady.

"Because she was the only merchant untainted by the tribute-silver affair. I acted for the sake of justice, not sentiment."

Lu Wenqian gave a short, cold laugh, but let the point pass. Instead, his tone shifted, quiet but piercing.

"And the child? I hear the little girl bears some resemblance to you."

For a heartbeat, something flickered in Lu Chou's expression—then vanished like light under a lid.

"She is not of my blood."

Lu Wenqian's eyes narrowed.

"You are certain?"

"If I were to claim otherwise, it would be deceit before the throne. The child's eyes are of a bronze hue—an uncommon trait, likely inherited from her true father. I have never borne such a mark."

His voice was cool, every word precise, his breath even. Only the smallest shadow crossed his gaze—gone almost before it formed.

But he remembered.

Those eyes.

That night in the mountain hut—the rain whispering against the eaves, her pale face turned toward the faint light, a tremor in her voice as she pressed a hand to her belly:

"If he takes after you one day… that would be enough."

The words had buried themselves in his heart for five long years. And now, he could only say—

"No."

It was not the truth.

But it was the only protection left to her.

Lu Wenqian regarded his son in silence, then finally nodded.

"So long as you know your bounds. The court stands on a knife's edge—let no stray thought become a handle for others to seize."

"Yes, Father."

The chamber fell silent once more. Only the incense smoke drifted upward, wavering like the fragile line between duty and desire, the line men bled to keep, and broke to live.

Outside the window, the wind stirred. It lifted the corner of the hanging curtain, a faint whisper as though something long held back was about to break—and didn't.

Lu Chou lowered his gaze.

His fingers, hidden within his sleeve, had long since clenched into a fist. He had spoken with finality, yet the light he denied had already taken root deep in his heart—too deep to be torn out again.

He was about to turn and leave when Lu Wenqian's voice sounded behind him—calm, almost mild, but brooking no refusal.

"One more thing. Now that both you and Xiu have returned to the capital, it's time you took on your share of the family's affairs."

Lu Chou paused and bowed slightly.

"Please instruct me, Father."

Lu Wenqian took a slow sip of tea, his tone casual, almost offhand.

"You know as well as I do—your mother died young, and there has been no Madam of the household since. Your grandmother still oversees the inner court, but her strength wanes with the years. For some time, Xiu's mother has managed the household in her stead; she has been diligent enough.

Recently, she mentioned that both my sons are of age. It is time we considered your marriages. I've given her leave to make discreet inquiries."

Lu Chou's brow tightened. The words escaped before he could temper them.

"I have no such intention."

Lu Wenqian's eyes flashed cold. His voice sharpened like the crack of a whip.

"Do you think this is a matter of intention?"

He set the teacup down with a solid click.

"You are the legitimate heir—the son of the principal line. The Lu family's name rests on your shoulders. To take a wife, to continue the line—these are not whims of affection, but obligations."

"Your son understands, but the court remains unsettled. For now, state affairs must take precedence. I beg leave to delay private matters."

"State affairs?" Lu Wenqian's voice rose, hard as iron.

"Shall the family fall behind while you chase glory in the court? Will you let a son of a concubine steal the rightful heir's place and make the Lu name a laughingstock? If you are truly capable, you should wed a worthy match—one who strengthens your hand, not weakens it. Only then will you deserve that fine talk of' serving the realm with loyalty.'"

Lu Chou said nothing. He merely lowered his head. A faint pain rippled through him—but he understood. This was the cost of being born legitimate. The price of his name.

Lu Wenqian exhaled slowly, his tone easing a fraction.

"Your grandmother's health grows frail. If you still possess a shred of filial piety, you'll know what peace of mind she wishes before she departs this world."

"Yes, Father." His reply was quiet, barely above breath.

"Then no more excuses." Lu Wenqian's sleeve fell in dismissal.

"Go."

Lu Chou bowed deeply and withdrew. His steps were measured—each one heavy, as though he trod upon the very weight of duty itself.

Outside, the air was faint with magnolia bloom. Half the tree had opened, white petals trembling in the wind. The fragrance was light and pure, yet it could not cleanse the heaviness within his chest.

He thought suddenly of that look on Xiao Lingyu's face when she spoke of her daughter—the gentleness in her eyes, quiet as spring water.

If only, years ago—

If only, now—

But no.

He was Lu Chou: legitimate son, heir of the Lu clan, bearer of its honour and its burden. He could shield her from wind and rain.

What he could not do—was take her hand.

Chapter 56: The Illegitimate Son's Resolve

The night grew deep, yet the lamps within the Yuechuan Courtyard remained unextinguished. Even the wind chimes hanging beneath the eaves were stirred by the evening breeze, their rhythmic *ting-ling* striking against Lu Xiu's heart, one beat at a time, fueling a growing irritability.

He shed his outer robe and draped it carelessly over a screen. Inside the room, the lamplight cast a pale yellow glow, illuminating several landscape paintings hung upon the walls—simple, ink-brushed works he had imitated from master artists during his youth. At this moment, however, he had no heart for appreciation. He felt only a stifling tightness in his chest, a breath of suppressed fury that would neither rise nor fall, leaving him in absolute misery.

He had just emerged from the main courtyard of the Minister of Personnel's estate. Lu Wenqian's furious reprimand still echoed in his ears. Although the two brothers had collaborated to set the trap that brought down the Third Prince's faction with clean and decisive precision, the fact that they had not reported it beforehand had deeply offended Lu Wenqian, a man who prided himself on total control. What galled the father even more was that this strategy was executed through the joint effort of his two sons—the eldest concubine-born and the second legitimate son—leaving him blindsided and mired in a complex web of emotions.

Lu Xiu stared out the window and let out a cold sneer. He had never been a virtuous or submissive concubine-born son. If he did not carve out a path for himself, was he truly expected to spend his entire life lingering in the shadow of his younger brother's protection? He refused to accept such a fate.

As he brooded, a soft, tentative voice called from outside the door: "Xiu-er, it is your Auntie."

He froze for a moment, then stood up to open the door. A gust of night wind rushed in, revealing a woman standing at the threshold. She was in her early forties, dressed in a plain silk gown, her expression gentle yet tinged with fear and anxiety. This was his biological mother—Liu Huiniang.

"Come in," he said, his tone flat, though he reached out to take the food box from her hands.

Liu Huiniang stepped into the room. Her eyes swept over his unfastened robes and his tense expression. She let out a soft sigh. "It is so late, and you still have not rested. I had the kitchen brew some lotus seed and lily bulb soup; you have loved it since you were a child."

Lu Xiu set the soup on a low table but did not touch it. He leaned back in his chair and looked up at her, his voice neither warm nor cold. "What are you doing here so late, Auntie? Are you not afraid of people gossiping?"

Liu Huiniang faltered, then gave a faint, melancholy smile. "I do not care what others say. It is only... when you came out from the Master's quarters tonight, your face looked so ill. I could not set my heart at ease."

Hearing this, Lu Xiu lowered his eyes and smiled, though the expression was laced with frost. "That look on his face... he merely blames me for daring to join forces with my second brother without his leave."

"You and the Second Young Master..." she asked cautiously.

"Young Master?" Lu Xiu let out a cold scoff. "In Father's eyes, he is the legitimate son, the son of the first wife, the very face of the Lu family. And I? Even if I am the eldest born, I am but a concubine's son—fit only to be a pawn in his hand."

Liu Huiniang's heart tightened. She could not help but grasp his hand, whispering urgently, "Xiu-er, do not say such things... I know the bitterness in your heart, but your second brother has never truly mistreated you. He... he still finds it in himself to tolerate you."

"Tolerate me?" He stood up abruptly, his voice low but vibrating with suppressed rage. "But what of me? I even have to weigh my words just to call you 'Mother'! In this entire manor, I am a concubine's son; when they look at me, there is never awe or respect, only contempt!"

Liu Huiniang's hand trembled, her face etched with sorrow. "Those are the rules... My status is lowly. Back then, I was but a bedchamber maid; to have given birth to you was already a blessing. The Master allowed me to stay in the manor to raise you rather than selling me off—that was already a monumental grace..."

"But he never once thought of elevating you to a legal wife," Lu Xiu's tone grew even colder. "You bore him his eldest son and have served him with all your heart for all these years. The primary wife passed away long ago, and there is no other legitimate mother in this house, yet

349

he would rather let you manage the household affairs as a 'concubine' than grant you the status of a formal wife."

Liu Huiniang lowered her head, her fingers gripping tightly. "I do not dare to crave such a status. I truly do not. I only pray for your safety and a smooth career... You are doing such great things now, involving the imperial succession. I... I fear that if a single mistake is made..."

"If I do not fight, how can I turn the tide? How can I change my destiny?" He clenched his fist, his tone deep and stubborn. "Is a concubine's son born to be lowly? I simply refuse to believe in such a twisted fate!"

Liu Huiniang looked at him, her eyes brimming with tears yet filled with a steady resolve. "That you can think this way... I am proud of you. But Xiu-er, you must remember to leave room for maneuver in all things. You may be unwilling to submit, but do not let resentment consume you."

Gazing at her red, swollen eyes, a soft spot within Lu Xiu's heart was pricked. Since he was a child, what he feared most was not beatings or punishment, but seeing this woman—who was always so soft-spoken before him—secretly wiping away her tears. She was lowly and weak, yet she was the only person who stood unconditionally by his side.

He turned his face away and muttered, "I know what I am doing. Do not overthink it, Auntie. Go and rest."

Seeing his tone soften, a trace of a smile finally appeared at the corners of Liu Huiniang's eyes. "Then rest early; you must report to the palace tomorrow. I shall not disturb you further."

She rose to leave, but at the doorway, she turned back. "If you have time... come sit in the back garden more often. The osmanthus is in bloom; you loved it most when you were little."

With that, she gently closed the door and departed.

The room fell silent once more. Lu Xiu stood by the window, his gaze heavy, his clenched fingers slowly loosening one by one. He would still struggle; he would still fight. But in this high-stakes gamble of a life, he would remember that there was one person whom he could not loudly call "Mother," yet who remained the deepest concern of his soul.

Lu Xiu sat back at his desk. The tea had grown ice-cold. His knuckles absentmindedly tapped against the wood. What echoed in his mind was no longer his father's lecture on "legacy," nor the sorrowful pleas of Auntie Liu.

Instead, it was—that moment in the back gallery of the Drunken Moon Pavilion, amidst the drifting scent of sandalwood, that silhouette in white as pure as snow.

Shen Zhaoru.

He closed his eyes, and that elegant, upright face seemed carved into his mind, impossible to banish. She was clearly as cold as frost, yet when she spoke to him, she could not hide the ripples of emotion in her eyes. She was the daughter of the Grand Preceptor, born of noble blood, yet when he drew near, even the tips of her ears would flush a quiet crimson.

The corners of Lu Xiu's lips slowly curled into an arc—partly a smile, and partly a mockery.

He knew well that a legitimate daughter like Shen Zhaoru was always reserved for a legitimate son. She was so noble, so precise in her conduct, raised since childhood to be the consort of a high official or a marquis. And yet, it was exactly such a woman who, in his presence, had been moved.

He had originally acted out of a moment's playfulness; seeing her extraordinary composure and how difficult she was to provoke, he had felt a spark of competitive whimsy. He hadn't expected her to truly place him in her heart.

This realization brought him a strange, deviant pleasure.

Perhaps... marrying a legitimate daughter of a high house was another opportunity to break his current deadlock. For a concubine-born son to rise, he could not rely solely on methods and courage; he also needed fortune and leverage. And the favor of the Grand Preceptor's daughter would be enough to allow him to carve out a new path within this capital.

Furthermore—she was not at all unpleasant. Even, for a fleeting moment, he had truly felt his own heart stir for her.

A pity, then, that she was a legitimate daughter and he a concubine's son. She had parents to protect and uphold her, while he? His mother was a mere chambermaid, and he could not even call her "Mother" in a formal setting.

He had never blamed Auntie Liu; she was his only true kin. He only hated his own lowly birth—that no matter how full of talent he might be, he could never truly hold his head high.

If one day, I could walk openly into the Shen Manor, welcoming her as a rightful husband, would those past humiliations be wiped away in a single stroke?

"Zhaoru..." he murmured, his voice as deep as the night wind, carrying an indiscernible trace of restraint and heat.

His gaze shifted. He was no longer the silent, oppressed figure who stood before his father, but a man of deep, calculated foresight. In this game of chess, he had made up his mind: he would take his pieces much, much further.

Chapter 57: Illusions Under the Lamp

Autumn had arrived in the Capital; the sky was high and clear, and the fragrance of sweet osmanthus saturated the winding alleys.

As it coincided with the Mid-Autumn Festival, the Imperial Palace was adorned with lanterns and colourful streamers, while the city marketplaces were bustling with extraordinary vigor.

At dusk, little Baor, her face alight with excitement, tugged at the corner of Xiao Lingyu's sleeve. Her eyes were full of anticipation as she said, "Mother, many people on the street today are saying that the Capital is so beautiful on Mid-Autumn night. Baor wants to go see it; may I?"

Xiao Lingyu was still holding her account ledgers, having just verified the final entry. Hearing this, she lifted her eyes, her expression momentarily dazed.

Lately, she had been calculating when to begin the journey back to Jiangnan to rebuild the Jinhua Establishment.

Being ennobled as an Imperial Merchant had been an unexpected turn of events, and soon, she would have to bid farewell to this Capital.

At this thought, her heart stirred slightly, and she replied in a low voice, "Then let us go. It is well; before we return to Jiangnan, we shall witness the prosperity of this Capital."

Before her words had even faded, the sound of footsteps came from the courtyard gate. Lu Chou pushed the door open and entered, carrying a stack of documents in his hands. "These are the account books and evidence you left behind previously. The Ministry of Justice has finished its review and has authorized their return."

Xiao Lingyu was slightly startled. She accepted them casually, her tone calm: "For such small matters, you could have simply had someone deliver them. It was truly unnecessary to trouble Lord Lu to make the trip personally."

Lu Chou choked on his words, his expression shifting slightly, yet he found himself at a loss for a reply.

He was just about to turn and depart when he heard little Baor clapping her hands. "Lord-Father, we are going to play on the streets tonight! We will solve lantern riddles, look at the flower lanterns, and there are even wonderful performances to see!"

Upon hearing this, his brow furrowed. "The crowds will be vast tonight, and I fear it will be congested. It is not appropriate for the two of you to go alone. I shall accompany you."

Xiao Lingyu originally intended to decline, but her gaze met the sparkling light in Baor's eyes. Her heart softened, and in the end, she did not speak. She simply said, "Since that is the case, I shall trouble you then."

The curtain of night fell low as the three of them stepped into the bustling market. Every street and alley was brilliantly illuminated; lanterns were hung and streamers tied.

Upon the colourful pavilion stages, drums and music rang out in unison. Children carrying revolving horse-lanterns wove back and forth, and the sound of laughter was unending.

Little Baor pulled Xiao Lingyu to guess lantern riddles one moment, then was drawn to a sugar-man stall the next, laughing until she bent over, as joyous as a celestial child.

* * * * *

The Mid-Autumn lantern festival in the Capital had always been extraordinarily lively. Outside the Xuande Ward, the clamour of voices was deafening, and ten thousand red lanterns hung from the eaves of towers and pavilions all the way to the end of the long street. It was a forest of fiery trees and silver flowers, as bustling as the day.

Little Baor wore a pale pink jacket-skirt, with a sweet osmanthus velvet hairpin that Xiao Lingyu had sewn by hand tucked into her hair. Her eyes were shining as she held her mother's hand, looking left and right, her mouth never ceasing its exclamations: "Mother, look! That lantern is a carp, and it can even move!"

"Mother, look quickly! That is a white rabbit lantern-carriage. What a huge rabbit!"

Xiao Lingyu was infected by her daughter's excitement, and her originally restrained expression gradually softened.

She reached out to steady the hairpin at her daughter's temple, saying warmly, "Be careful not to run too fast, and do not bump into people."

A half-step beside them, Lu Chou walked with his hands behind his back, watching the mother and daughter with a smile in his eyes.

"Is this your first time seeing the lanterns in the Capital?" he suddenly asked.

Baor turned her head and nodded. "Before, when we celebrated the festival in Jiangnan, we only lit small lamps in the embroidery workshop. Mother said the Capital was more lively, and today I have finally seen it. My Lord, did you play with lanterns when you were little?"

Lu Chou paused slightly, lifting his eyes to look at the distant sea of lights. His voice was mild and thin: "When I was little... it was not so lively. There were many people in the manor, which made it rather uncomfortable."

As soon as he finished speaking, Baor gave an "Oh," and then said innocently, "Then in the future, you should celebrate with us! My mother makes the best sweet osmanthus cakes."

Hearing this, Xiao Lingyu was slightly stunned, and the corners of her eyes quietly reddened. She looked toward her daughter, then stole a glance at the man beside her.

Lu Chou lowered his head, meeting Baor's gaze. His expression was soft to the extreme; he actually reached out to rub the top of her head, his tone uncharacteristically tender: "Alright, as long as your mother is willing to invite me."

Xiao Lingyu's cheeks heated up slightly, and she hurried to change the subject: "Does Baor want to guess lantern riddles?"

"I do!" Baor cheered.

The three of them stopped before a lantern riddle stall by the roadside. Lu Chou bent over and picked up Baor, allowing her to see the colorful lanterns hanging high above.

Suddenly, Baor furrowed her delicate little brows. "But Baor cannot read..."

"It doesn't matter, I will read it to you. Look, that one says: 'A man sits inside a room.' Can you guess what it is?"

"Ah, someone who doesn't go out... that would be so dull..." Baor wrinkled her little brow. "Baor... cannot guess it..."

Before she had finished speaking, Lu Chou whispered quietly into her ear, "It is a character. It is read as—Qiu (Prison)."

Baor's copper-colored eyes lit up, and she shouted joyfully at the top of her voice, "Is it the Qiu like the embroidered ball? My Lord is so clever... no, it is my Lord-Father who is so clever!"

Lord-Father...

Lu Chou thought to himself that this was another new title the little girl had made up, yet he was happy to accept it. His originally sharp features softened their lines in that moment.

"Not bad at all; this little lady is very clever." The stall owner chuckled and handed over a piece of candy, joining in the praise: "Here is your prize!"

Baor held the candy, overjoyed. "Mother, look! I guessed it right!"

"Baor, don't shout so wildly..." Before Xiao Lingyu could finish, he reached out an arm to interrupt her.

Lu Chou touched her lightly and gave her a look, saying in a low, fine voice, "As long as Baor is happy."

Xiao Lingyu let out a soft sigh and smiled, her eyes turning warm and gentle. "Yes, our Baor is the most impressive."

"My, this little girl's eyes are truly beautiful—amber-colored! Here, I'll give you another piece of candy."

Hearing herself praised by a stranger, Baor became even more delighted. "Wow, thank you, Boss! You are so kind."

Lu Chou signaled with a glance to a personal guard nearby, who immediately handed a piece of silver to the stall owner. The owner's face lit up with joy, and he poured out a basketful of auspicious words as if they cost nothing, throwing out every phrase whether it fit or not.

"Oh, what a celestial family! I wish the Lord, the Madam, and the young Miss peace, joy, and good health—"

That word "Madam" made the tips of Xiao Lingyu's ears turn hot. She had intended to speak and correct him, but Lu Chou had already naturally taken a step to the side, unobtrusively shielding her from the stall owner. He held a piece of crystalline sweet osmanthus sugar before her eyes.

"Want a taste?"

Xiao Lingyu instinctively looked at the piece of sugar. The hand holding the candy was right before her, only an arm's length away. Unaccountably, her heart felt a sudden moment of weightlessness. Dazed, her gaze followed his long fingers upward until it met his expression, which held a faint smile. His features, both steadfast and soft, caused her heart to feel empty once more.

Her cheeks burned, and she instinctively looked away, avoiding his heart-stirring gaze.

"What is it? Do you not like sugar? Five years ago, you loved it dearly..." His voice was low, its edges muffled by the clamor of the crowd, yet it fell only into her ears.

"Give it to me." She took the sugar, her fingertips inadvertently brushing across his palm, sending a wave of slight numbness through her. "It is just a piece of candy; Lord Lu need not bring up the past. People change."

"That is true; people change." His gaze was tranquil as he looked into her eyes, with the ten thousand lanterns of the city behind him. "Yet not everything is so, Lingyu. I know your heart is set on Jiangnan and you do not wish to be trapped in the Capital. But if I said that I have already informed my grandmother of everything—that the main gates of the Lu family will always be open to you and Baor, and that you need not give up the Jinhua Establishment, nor conform to any rigid rules—"

His voice paused, growing lighter yet ensuring every word was clear:

"Would you be willing to trust me this once?"

Xiao Lingyu clutched the cool piece of sugar, but a strange warmth surged in her chest. She lowered her eyelashes and did not answer immediately.

In that moment, the lamplight cast the shadows of the three of them upon the bluestone road—overlapping and intertwining, just like a painting of family bliss.

Chapter 58: Resolving to Part

Not far away, an entertainer set off a burst of fireworks. The firelight shot suddenly into the sky and exploded into a bloom of silver-white brilliance.

Little Baor tilted her head up, clapped her small hands, and cheered in a soft voice. Lu Chou said gently, "Shall we walk to the river? There will be lantern boats to be released."

Xiao Lingyu hesitated for a moment. Just as she was about to speak, Baor had already grabbed her hand in one quick tug. "Mama, let's go, please! Baor hasn't ever seen water lanterns being released in the Capital!" In the end, Xiao Lingyu nodded slightly and replied softly, "Alright."

They walked together into the deeper heart of the lantern light. The street was packed tight, and the voices were deafening, yet she suddenly felt a strange illusion of quiet. With her daughter beside her and him accompanying them, it truly seemed as though everything in the world was secure, as though the years themselves could pass in serene peace.

That serenity, however, was far too brief—so brief it felt like a phantom scene inside a dream. Xiao Lingyu understood this clearly.

Such a sight could perhaps exist only within the lantern light of this single night. She looked at her daughter's smiling face, warmth spreading through her heart, and in that moment, she was stirred by a faint, unwilling thought of leaving.

They reached the willow embankment by the river. Autumn water murmured as it flowed, and the wind carried a slight coolness. Lu Chou said he would go find a lotus lantern for Baor and led the little girl toward a lantern shop not far away.

Xiao Lingyu, accompanied by a maidservant and a guard, stood beneath the drooping willows, quietly watching the moonlight reflect upon the water.

Just as she was about to rest for a breath, she suddenly heard several women nearby whispering in low voices. "I heard that the legitimate daughter of Imperial Preceptor Shen came tonight as well—the foremost talented lady of the Capital.

She has both talent and beauty, and her family background is lofty. She truly makes people envy her." Another replied, "Yes. I've also heard that the Shen family seems to have the intention of forming a marriage alliance with the Lu family. If that is true, then it would truly be a fine match—perfectly balanced, properly matched in rank."

Xiao Lingyu heard every word clearly. Her heart jolted faintly, as though someone had poured a basin of cold water straight down over her head. She instinctively bit down on her lip, a thread of bitterness flashing through her eyes. Without drawing attention, she turned her body slightly aside, pretending to admire the lanterns along the riverbank, yet she did not miss a single word.

Between her and Lu Chou, they had never stood on equal ground. He was the son of a noble house, with real power in his hands.

As for her, she was only the proprietress of an embroidery workshop—a woman who had once borrowed her own body to bear a child. Their reunion, and their walking side by side like this, was perhaps nothing more than an accidental misplacement in time.

The night wind brushed lightly across her face. Xiao Lingyu closed her eyes for a brief moment. The thought of returning to Jiangnan grew even firmer at this instant. She could no longer indulge in this short-lived tenderness, nor foolishly crave a future that did not belong to her.

She stood beneath the willow shade, holding a small, delicate palace lantern in her hand.

The lamplight was dim and subdued, reflecting upon her face and lending her features a tranquil appearance, while beneath that calm lay a surging, restless turmoil of thought.

In the sound of the wind, those words still lingered in her ears—"the Shen family forming a match with the Lu family," "the foremost talented lady of the Capital." The tone carried admiration and yearning, and with painful precision exposed the chasm between her and him.

She had always known it clearly. Over these years, he had climbed step by step toward greater heights, while she remained only a widow supporting an embroidery workshop alone. Even her enfeoffment as an Imperial Merchant was no more than a measure of temporary expediency.

"Mama!" Baor's call broke into her thoughts. "Look at my lotus lantern! It's so beautiful." Xiao Lingyu looked at the pair before her—one tall, one small—and for a moment fell into a brief daze. The scene looked so very much like a family of three.

"Is it?" she said with a faint smile. Yet her gaze, without meaning to, fell into his deep, shadowed eyes, and her heart tightened. Her throat constricted, and the tiny tenderness that had just risen was crushed down by reality, heavy and unforgiving.

"Baor, it is getting late. We should go back," she said softly. Baor pouted. "Mama, but—"

Xiao Lingyu cut her off gently. "No 'buts.' It is time for you to rest."

"Aiya, Mama, I haven't finished looking at the moon yet..." Baor protested unwillingly. "It is not too late to admire the moon after we return,"

Xiao Lingyu replied, her tone gentle yet allowing no argument. If she did not leave now, she feared she would drown in this empty illusion and be unable to pull herself out.

Lu Chou stood just outside the edge of the lamplight, quietly watching her profile. Only moments earlier, she had been smiling as she accompanied

Baor in choosing lanterns, her brows and eyes soft with tenderness, exactly as she had looked that year beneath the misty rain of Jiangnan. Yet after speaking a few words with the vendor, her expression had faded, her smile slowly withdrawn, her gaze lowered slightly, as though she were avoiding something.

He remained silent for a short moment, then finally spoke. "What is wrong?"

Xiao Lingyu started slightly, as though she had only just registered his presence. She turned her head to look at him, her eyes flickering, yet she only replied softly, "Nothing."

His brow moved faintly. His gaze fell on the revolving lantern she held in her hand, embroidered with a phoenix rising through clouds, its light so dim it seemed almost about to go out. "Is this lantern not pleasing?" he asked evenly. "Or did you suddenly decide you do not wish to choose one after all?"

Her fingers tightened, crumpling the paper slightly. "It's not that," she said. "It's just... the time is about right."

His eyes sharpened. "The time for what?"

She pressed her lips together and finally spoke. "I think it is time for me to return to Jiangnan."

As the words fell, even she could feel the tightness in her chest. He froze for a moment, a complicated emotion flashing across his eyes. "Did you not say that you had not decided yet?"

"I never intended to stay long," she replied, her voice pressed very low, almost swallowed by the crowds and the drums. "The case is concluded, and the grievances have been settled. My remaining here would only invite misunderstanding, and it would be of no benefit to you."

Her tone was calm, yet it could not hide the urgency that bordered on flight. He looked at her, and at last his voice turned cold. "Misunderstanding? Who is misunderstanding you? Or what is it that you are fleeing?"

She drew a deep breath, her expression trembling subtly. "Lord Lu, I never foolishly hoped for anything more between us. I have felt guilt over the events of that year until this day. These past days, it was you who ensured the safety of our mother and daughter, and I hold gratitude for that in my heart. But I ought to depart. I ought to return to the place where I belong."

Her words seemed to sting him. He fell silent for a long time before asking coldly, "The place where you belong? What is this place where you belong?"

She lowered her eyes, not daring to look at him. "You speak correctly," he said at last, a faint smile appearing, his voice slightly hoarse. "You never foolishly hoped for anything from me. Those were my own misplaced affections."

"It isn't…" She lifted her eyes abruptly, their rims faintly red. "I only… I'm afraid…" Before she could finish, Baor's laughter drifted over from within the crowd, and both of them paused.

Lu Chou's gaze shifted toward the small figure, his voice dropping suddenly. "Then what of her? Have you considered how you will tell her?"

Xiao Lingyu's hands clenched tightly within her sleeves, her knuckles whitening. "She is still small. She won't remember too much."

"If she does not remember, can you leave with a clear conscience?" His tone was extremely light, yet it pierced like a needle, the veins standing out faintly on the back of his hand.

Xiao Lingyu closed her eyes briefly, her voice almost trembling. "I fear that if I stay longer, I will forget that I must remain clear-headed."

He asked no further questions. He only turned and walked toward Baor, his back solitary, straight, and resolute.

Xiao Lingyu remained standing where she was, her chest rising and falling violently. She looked at the lantern; its light flickered in the wind, the shadows wavering, as if the lantern itself were struggling. After a long while, she reached out and gently set the lantern down upon the stone table beneath the willow tree. It was like setting down a lantern, and also like setting down a dream she dared not continue.

They stood in silent confrontation for a moment. At last, he spoke. "When do you plan to set forth?"

Only then did Xiao Lingyu answer in a low voice. "In three days, I will take Baor back to Jiangnan."

As the words faded, the night wind turned cool, lifting the strands of hair at her temples and disturbing whatever fragile thing had been held in his heart.

Lu Chou remained silent for a long time, then finally let out a soft laugh, his voice cold and edged with irony. "Madam Xiao is indeed decisive in her actions. You always handle matters of personnel with such resolution." In his heart, he added an unspoken sentence—she leaves without hesitation. Five years ago, it was the same. It is the same now.

Xiao Lingyu lowered her gaze and said nothing, only tightening her grip on the lantern. He turned away without looking at her, his tone still carrying his habitual indifference. "If you wish to depart, then depart. Madam Xiao is always resolute in her own mind. You have no need to say more to anyone."

She froze for an instant, her heart clenching. Though she knew his tone was merely defiance, it still pierced her like a needle. When the wind rose, he had already walked away, his back straight as a pine. Yet in that single instant, she saw it clearly—the tension in his clenched palm, as if he had used enormous effort to restrain himself from turning back.

He let her leave, just as he had never truly possessed her.

Chapter 59: Confrontation at Sunset

Three days subsequent, Xiao Lingyu drew the cloak about her shoulders with increased firmness, standing before the courier station in the faint luminescence of the early morning.

The sky had not fully brightened; a thin layer of mountain mist heavily draped the silent official road. A single, prepared carriage was halted beside the blue flagstones.

Baor nestled close to her side, her tiny fingers clutching the fabric of her mother's sleeve, her eyes glistening with the light of reluctance and imminent tears.

Lingyu lowered her head and stroked her daughter's soft hair, struggling intensely to force out a thin, reassuring smile: "Be not afraid, my child. We shall very quickly return to Jiangnan."

Her voice was soft and gentle, yet the undeniable acridity in her throat was difficult to suppress. The normally bustling Capital was at this hour profoundly still, with only their isolated figures standing alone.

Lu Chou had not appeared to see them off—perhaps, he was fundamentally and utterly unwilling to present himself.

At this painful reflection, a dull, heavy ache gripped her heart. Her fingertips trembled minutely, but she could only forcibly suppress the surging sourness deep within her soul.

"Baor, let us board the carriage now." Lingyu urged softly. Tears welled and spun like large beads in Baor's eye sockets, yet she nodded in perfect obedience.

She was carried onto the carriage by her mother, but her head turned back repeatedly with every step taken, still poking her small forehead out of the window to peer intently towards the distant conclusion of the long street.

Beneath the heavy, grey-tinged dome of the sky, that familiar, unshakeable figure did not materialise. Baor pursed her lips, saying in a low, disappointed voice: "Mama, is Papa Lord truly not coming to farewell us?"

Lingyu's heart clenched violently. Forcing back the hot, stinging ache in her eyes, she shook her head and began to speak: "Do not dwell upon it, my treasure. His official duties are numerous and pressing…"

Before she could complete her phrase, she suddenly heard the coachman call out softly from the front: "Who goes there!" Before his voice completely faded, the horse suddenly neighed loudly in panic!

Several dark silhouettes, appearing from nowhere, swiftly and silently encircled the carriage. The leader of the group brandished his blade and swung it, actually striking the coachman down with a single, swift slash!

Blood splattered onto the carriage shaft; the horse neighed loudly in fright; the carriage lurched violently.

Lingyu stumbled severely, nearly losing her footing and falling. She instantly pulled Baor tightly into her embrace, demanding in a sharp, urgent voice: "Who are you all, and what is your purpose?!"

The figures in black did not respond, their gazes as cold and unpitying as polished steel. Several long, gleaming swords were instantly held against Lingyu's throat.

Baor screamed hysterically: "Do not wound my mother!" Her tender, childlike voice trembled severely with sheer fear. Lingyu's heart twisted like metal in a furnace, but she forcibly gathered her wits, fiercely protecting her daughter behind her back.

"Xiao Lingyu, you will accompany us for a journey!" A chillingly cold voice rang out.

That leader slowly advanced, his pair of triangular eyes conveying the deepest sense of sinister ruthlessness. He sneered: "Someone entrusted us to treat you two, mother and daughter, 'well' upon your journey."

Xiao Lingyu's delicate body shook from a surge of cold understanding.

She instantly comprehended the truth: they were the vengeful remnants of the Third Prince's faction!

Lu Chou had, in recent days, thoroughly ruined the Third Prince's source of wealth and utterly sabotaged his treacherous plot for rebellion.

Now, she had been chosen as the prime target for retaliating against Lu Chou! At this painful realisation, her fingernails nearly dug into the very flesh of her own palm.

The leader saw the swift, complex shift in her expression. He gave a savage, mocking grin, wasting no further deliberation, and waved his hand, signalling his subordinates to commence the seizure: "Take them away!"

Several large, brutish men instantly stepped forward to forcibly restrain Lingyu.

Although she had received some instruction in self-defence techniques, she was utterly powerless against the actions of these well-trained death soldiers.

She felt intense, searing pain in both wrists, which were hauled and bound behind her back.

Her shoulder instantly went numb as her acupuncture point was precisely struck, rendering her entirely immobile.

"Baor!" Lingyu cried out in an extremity of distress, yet she could only watch in terror as one of the black-clad men reached out to grab Baor from her frantic embrace.

"Vile villain, dare not touch my daughter!" Lingyu let out a sharp, feral roar, fiercely slamming her body sideways into the assailant! The black-clad man was caught utterly off guard by her desperate collision; he was unbalanced and missed his grasp. Baor took the opportunity to roll out of her mother's arms, falling hard onto the ground.

As Baor fell, her knee scraped and fresh blood began to seep out, but she did not have the slightest time to cry. Like a startled, tiny creature, she scrambled towards the courier road, her small feet stumbling, tears mixing with the dust. Step by painful step, she fled desperately towards the darkness outside.

"Baor, run! Run forward!" Lingyu screamed hoarsely, her eyes on the verge of splitting open from the pressure of her despair.

She struggled violently to impede the two black-clad men rushing toward her, striving to gain a precious few moments for her daughter.

Baor's face was deathly pale with terror. She fell and sat upon the ground. But hearing Lingyu's urgent, desperate cries, she nodded, tears streaming down her face.

She scrambled back to her feet, tumbling and crawling, running with all her remaining might towards the outside of the courier station.

A blade flashed, but the man suddenly checked his movement.

The leader had shouted a cold prohibition: "Enough! She is just a small whelp. She cannot run far; we will capture her later." His sinister gaze swept over Lingyu's face: "The one we truly desire is the darling of Lord Lu's heart."

Lingyu's arms were held tightly. She watched helplessly as Baor's small pink figure disappeared into the fading morning mist, consumed by a terrible mix of grief and towering indignation.

Tears burst forth, wetting her face: "If you dare wound her in the slightest, Lu Chou will never spare any of you—" Before she could complete her threat, she was struck heavily on the back of her neck. Her vision went black, and she collapsed down limply.

* * * * *

After an unknown, protracted duration, Lingyu awakened from her heavy stupor, finding herself inside a ruined temple. The main door was half-open.

The slant of the setting sun illuminated the interior, casting a deep, faded yellow light. The air was thick with dust and the acrid smell of mildew. Her hands were still bound behind her back to a stone pillar.

When she moved her fingers, a sharp, needling pain shot through her wrist bones. Recalling the earlier terrifying scene, her heart jolted violently: "Baor! Where is Baor?"

"Hmph, that little whelp was quite quick-witted; she ran fast enough," A chilling, sinister sneer drifted from a dark corner of the temple hall. "Too bad. Even if she calls for help, what good will it do? Do you truly believe Lu Chou can save you?"

Xiao Lingyu followed the voice. She saw a figure slowly walking out of the shadows.

The newcomer was dressed in a brocade robe, his cultivated, handsome features conveying a chilling coldness, a mocking smile playing upon his lips.

It was none other than the former Prince Song, Chen Song, who had been demoted to a commoner—the once high and mighty Third Prince!

Though his brocade robe was magnificent, the hem seemed to be stained with dust, and his boots were muddied. He was utterly devoid of his former dignified, upright bearing.

He still advanced slowly with his hands clasped behind his back, a smile lifting the corner of his lips, yet a sharp, cold light flickered intensely in his eyes—like a venomous snake, flicking its tongue before launching its final, desperate strike.

Lingyu's heart clenched tightly. She glared at him venomously: "It is you... you, the dignified Third Prince, have personally stooped to this..."

"Personally, setting forth?" Chen Song chuckled softly, pacing two steps closer with his hands behind his back. "If this Prince did not personally undertake this venture, I could only wait passively for ultimate defeat." His voice was an understatement, yet his eyes betrayed a raw, bloodthirsty hatred.

Xiao Lingyu spoke coldly: "You are holding the family member of a court official hostage; your crime is not insignificant! Chen Song, do not imagine you can use me to threaten Lu Chou! He... he will not die for me!"

Despite her brave words, Xiao Lingyu's eyes were already overwhelmed with panic and despair.

Lu Chou had always been reputed as cold-hearted and ruthless.

Even though this whole ordeal arose because of her, would he truly come? Knowing beyond doubt it was a lethal trap... why would he ever venture into such danger?

Chen Song seemed to read her inner thoughts, and the smile on his lips deepened: "Will not die for you? Heh..."

No sooner had he finished speaking than rapid, heavy footsteps were heard outside the hall. Chen Song's brow subtly lifted, and he mocked: "Eh, so swiftly?"

Several of his subordinates retreated into the hall in disarray, their steps stumbling, their faces showing profound shock.

The leader in black, clutching a profusely bleeding wound on his shoulder, said: "Your Highness, someone is forcing entry!"

Chen Song's face instantly turned ashen: "Who is it that dares to intrude?"

Before he could finish, a tall, slender figure swept into the hall like a sudden whirlwind. Lingyu looked—the man was clad in deep black, his robes dusted, his expression cold and deeply anxious. Who else could it be but Lu Chou?

Lingyu's heart violently seized up. She nearly cried out his name: "Lu Chou—" but the sound caught painfully in her throat.

Seeing him arrive alone at this moment, she was simultaneously intensely moved and utterly heartbroken. The bitterness and pain in her chest were unbearable, and hot tears nearly spilled from her eyes.

Lu Chou's eyes instantly fell upon Lingyu, who was bound to the pillar. His pupils abruptly constricted: "Lingyu!"

His voice was hoarse, loaded with barely concealed anxiety and rage. Seeing her robes dishevelled and her face pallid, his heart felt as if it were being sliced by a thousand cuts.

His fingertips trembled imperceptibly, but he forced himself to regain his composure.

He swept his gaze over the hall full of black-clad assassins, his final cold stare landing on Chen Song: "Prince Song, that is indeed a grand and vile scheme you have undertaken..."

Readers can view the full collection of colour illustrations here:
https://www.facebook.com/profile.php?id=61581325000577

Chapter 60: Redemption Through Blood and Tears

Chen Song saw that Lu Chou had truly come alone, just as he had demanded. A hint of pure astonishment flashed briefly across his eyes, only to be instantly replaced by a sharp, mocking sneer.

"I had truly supposed," he began, his voice dripping with derision, "that Lord Lu was a man of cold blood and narrow affection—one who had long ago forsaken all love and discarded all sentiment. I did not think you would ever be foolish enough to deliver yourself into such a transparent snare. Observing you now, standing here alone, it seems this Prince has actually overestimated your legendary ruthlessness."

Lu Chou did not rise to the bait of the barb. He merely began to advance, his steps slow and measured, until he stood at a distance directly opposite Chen Song. His gaze was as heavy and unyielding as a pool of molten iron. "What is it you truly desire?"

Chen Song leaned lazily against the altar table, his posture relaxed as he clapped his palms together in a mocking, rhythmic fashion. "What? Did he not tell you before? He said he would not hazard his life for you! Now, let us see with our own eyes exactly how far his commitment goes, and what he is truly willing to do for your sake!"

"No—!" Lu Chou's pupils seemed to fracture with sudden dread. He let out a primal, gut-wrenching roar, his voice cracking with a fury that was beyond his control. Simultaneously, his body coiled, his muscles tensing as if he were about to launch himself forward in a desperate, lethal charge.

"Halt immediately!" Chen Song shouted, his command ringing out with frigid authority. "Dare to take but a single step further, and this Prince shall instantly sever her throat!"

Beneath the cold, sharp flash of the steel blade, a fine and slender line of crimson had already been drawn across Lingyu's alabaster neck. Her body was forcibly bound against the cold stone pillar, rendered so utterly immobile that she could not even twitch to avoid the blade. She could only clamp her eyes shut in sheer, unadulterated agony.

Lu Chou's figure was arrested mid-motion, coming to an abrupt and jarring stop. It was as if his very breathing had been suspended in that same heartbeat. Every single tendon and vein in his body felt like a conflagration of burning blood and bone. His eyes were turned a stark, visceral crimson; in that second, he wished for nothing more than to fall upon those two executioners and tear them into bloody shreds. However, the threat was immediate and absolute. Lingyu's life hung by the most tenuous and fragile of threads. He had no choice but to forcibly suppress the murderous intent surging within his chest, retreating step by agonizing step back to his original position.

"Cleverness itself," Chen Song remarked, clapping his hands together with a wicked and insidious smile. "Lord Lu, were you not formerly the most adept of men at carefully weighing your options? Were you not the master of executing necessary sacrifices? Did you ever foresee that there would come a day when you would find yourself so utterly bound and helpless as you are now?"

Lingyu forced her eyes open and saw Lu Chou being compelled to hold his ground solely for her sake. Her heart twisted with a sudden, sharp agony, as if it had been grasped and squeezed by a jagged knife. Tears burst forth, streaming uncontrollably from her eyes.

"You ought not to have come..." she murmured between sobs, her voice bitter and profoundly choked with grief. "They are distinctly targeting you... they want your life... why would you ever..."

Hearing her anguished, broken cries, Lu Chou felt a sudden and vicious tearing at the most tender part of his heart. As he met Lingyu's deeply sorrowful and tear-filled eyes, a colossal, suffocating pain gripped his chest, a feeling he found impossible to restrain. At this singular moment, all the grievances, all the resentment, and all the misunderstandings of the past were utterly transmuted into an engraved, bone-deep devotion—and a final, undeniable love for her.

His throat felt tight, constricted by emotion. He slowly shook his head, his gaze never wavering. "Lingyu, for the sake of you, I am willing to do anything. I am willing to sacrifice everything."

Though his voice was hushed and low, every single word was infused with an unshakeable and absolute resolve, as undeniable and heavy as forged steel. Lingyu stared back at him blankly, feeling as though some staunch, ancient barrier of ice in the very depths of her soul had instantly fractured and collapsed into nothingness. A single, pure tear traced its path down the curve of her cheek. She whimpered softly, now entirely incapable of finding the strength to speak another word.

"Tsk tsk, such profound and touching affection," Chen Song lamented with a layer of exaggerated theatricality. "What a pity, Lord Lu. Do you truly believe that a single phrase of devotion can move this Prince's heart? Now—discard the sword you hold in your hand!"

Lu Chou did not spare his weapon even a fleeting glance. He obediently released the long sword, and with a loud, metallic "clang," the blade struck the hard stone floor and skittered away. He spread his palms wide to show he was unarmed and spoke in a heavy, resonant voice: "Chen Song, let all your enmity and all your hatred be directed at me alone. Release her now."

Chen Song raised an eyebrow, a mocking and triumphant sneer widening across his face. "Release her? That is indeed possible. Lu Chou, if you end your own life here and now—tell me, how does that proposition sound? Your death in exchange for her survival."

Lingyu was struck with an immense and paralyzing terror upon hearing this. She cried out anxiously, her voice reaching a fever pitch: "No! Lu Chou, you must not heed him! Do not do it!"

Chen Song laughed, a sound that was both grim and frigid. "What? The target has finally arrived. Let this Prince see exactly how far he is willing to go for you!"

"...This vile woman shall immediately accompany you to the grave!"

Before the declaration was even fully spoken, Lingyu began to struggle with the frantic desperation of a lunatic. She did not even sense the coarse hemp ropes grinding into her wrists until the skin broke and they bled. "No... Chou..." Her beautiful eyes were wide and distended; she was weeping almost to the point of total asphyxiation, staring fixedly at Lu Chou with an expression overwhelmed by appeal and utter despair.

Lu Chou drew a deep, long breath, and contrary to all expectation, he became completely and unnervingly serene. He offered Lingyu a gentle, soft smile, his gaze entirely filled with indulgence and a profound sense of reassurance.

"Do not be afraid," he whispered, his voice low and steady. "I am here with you."

The very instant the words concluded, a flash of cold light erupted through the dim hall. Lu Chou unexpectedly snatched the sharp dagger concealed within the lining of his boot and stabbed it with brutal, final finality directly into his own left flank!

The blade bit deep into his flesh; fresh, hot blood instantly gushed forth in a torrent, staining half of his coat a brilliant and terrifying scarlet!

"Chou—!"

Lingyu cried out a grief-stricken lament, her vision darkening as the world tilted; she felt poised on the very brink of collapse. Her tears had long since become a frantic torrent. She struggled with all her might to move towards him, to reach him, yet the bonds rendered her utterly motionless.

She could only watch him stumble, his strength failing as he sank heavily to one knee. The dagger remained inserted deep in the wound in his abdomen, and blood dripped steadily from the blade's tip onto the dusty, cold ground. Every single drop seemed to strike Lingyu's heart with the force of a heavy hammer.

Everyone in the hall was instantly seized by terror and shock! Chen Song's pupils constricted to pinpoints. He stared at Lu Chou in sheer, unadulterated disbelief. "You—have you lost your mind?!"

Cold sweat streamed profusely from Lu Chou's brow. His complexion was ashen and pale due to the unbearable agony of the wound, yet a determined,決絕 smile appeared at the corner of his lips.

"Why, Your Highness? Was it not my blood you desired?" He struggled with every ounce of his being to keep himself from collapsing entirely, his voice sounding as deep and heavy as iron. "I surrender my life to you. I only ask that you honour your pledge and permit her to depart this place safely."

Chen Song's entire demeanour changed dramatically. He had plainly not anticipated that Lu Chou would inflict such grievous and lethal self-harm upon himself, and for a moment, he remained stunned and frozen where he stood. Not far off, the two assassins who were holding Lingyu exchanged a glance, their grips on their swords involuntarily relaxing in their shock.

It was at this precise moment that confused and rapid footsteps suddenly thundered outside the hall, mixed with fierce, sharp shouts and the unmistakable clashing of armour and weapons!

Chen Song's face abruptly turned ashen. He roared, gnashing his teeth in fury: "Is it the official soldiers?!"

Lu Xiu had finally led his elite troops to the scene. Over ten armoured men surged into the dilapidated temple like an incoming tide. Under a furious cry of "Execute the rebels!", the black-clad death-soldiers instantly collapsed under the assault.

Chen Song saw that the situation was dire and attempted to seize Lingyu once more as a final shield, but a swift arrow from Lu Xiu's bow struck him cleanly in the shoulder. He let out a scream of pain and fell to the ground.

The remnants of the Third Prince's faction were either annihilated or surrendered in an instant. Within moments, bodies covered the temple floor, and the air grew thick with the acrid, suffocating stench of fresh blood.

"Lu! Xiu!" Chen Song screamed in an ultimate, manic rage. His expression was frantic, completely devoid of his former noble and dignified bearing. "I placed my faith in you! You two-faced, double-dealing wretch! It is because of you that I have been vanquished so completely! Ha ha..."

Lingyu had been utterly bewildered and stunned by this sudden upheaval, only regaining her full senses after a long, dazed pause. She found that the iron sword previously held against her neck had been lowered, and the assassins who had seized her were all eliminated.

Lingyu's body went weak, and she slid powerlessly down against the stone pillar, her mind an absolute blank as she began to weep hysterically. In her eyes and in her heart, only that one figure falling into the pool of blood remained.

"Chou!"

Lingyu, forcing herself to ignore the acute and searing pain in her wrists, stumbled and crawled desperately towards Lu Chou. At this moment, Lu Chou, due to the severe loss of blood, had become physically exhausted.

His body, which had been kneeling on one knee, finally began to sink slowly toward the floor. Lingyu rushed forward to pull him into her embrace, crying in a tremulous and broken voice: "Lu Chou, you... you must hold on! I beg you, please hold on..."

Lu Chou managed to open his eyes with great difficulty, looking up at Lingyu's tear-streaked face. His lips trembled, and he seemed to want to raise his hand to wipe away her tears, but he was far too weak to exert even the slightest bit of strength. Lingyu leaned down, tightly gripping his cold hand and pressing it against her own cheek. "Do not speak, do not be afraid... Lu Xiu... he has arrived... We are safe now..."

In the distance, Lu Xiu stood imposing and tall at the temple entrance, surveying the devastation with cold, detached eyes. A mocking sneer curled his lips. "Hmph. A mere woman, and she has reduced you to such a pathetic and miserable state."

He raised his voice, commanding his men with authority: "Take the rebel Chen Song away! Someone, swiftly carry Master Chou back to the army camp for urgent treatment!"

Having finished his orders, he cast one final glance at his brother, his eyes filled with a complex mix of contempt and disdain, as he coldly uttered two words: "Useless trash."

Lu Chou appeared as if he had not even heard the insults. He only gazed intensely at Lingyu, who was sobbing uncontrollably in his arms. A faint, weak smile appeared at the corner of his lips. "Lingyu, do not... please, do not weep..."

Lingyu shook her head desperately, her tears gushing like a spring. She held his blood-stained body close, crying until her voice was hoarse and broken. "Lu Chou, you utter fool... How could you possibly do this..."

Lu Chou's breath was frail and shallow; his eyelids grew increasingly heavy with every passing second, but he still endeavoured to force his lips into a smile, as if wanting to offer her some small comfort. His fingertip gently stroked her cheek one last time before finally sliding down weakly due to his total lack of strength.

"Lingyu... so long as you... are safe and unharmed..."

His voice was as light and ephemeral as a wisp of smoke. Before he could even complete the sentence, his eyes closed, and he collapsed into semi-consciousness.

Lingyu felt her heart convulsed with a profound agony. She clutched him tightly in her embrace, tears silently streaming and falling onto his cold, ashen cheek. The surrounding commotion and the noise of the soldiers seemed, at this instant, to have receded into the far distance. She heard only his faint, shallow breath and the nearly suffocating, frantic rhythm of her own heart.

At this moment, at the precipice of life and death, Lingyu finally understood. Lu Chou had wagered his very existence for her, and in doing so, he had completely shattered the final emotional barrier that had stood between the two of them for years.

The sunset's last ray of splendour slanted through the shattered window frame, slowly engulfing their two figures in a golden light. Lingyu gently stroked Lu Chou's closed eyes, her fingertips trembling and tender as her tears rolled down onto his brow. She sobbed in a low, mournful voice: "Lu Chou... you must, you absolutely must, survive... I still... I haven't even had the chance to tell you..."

Her voice faded away, her tears now a flood. Lingyu bent low, and amidst the veil of her falling hair, she gently pressed her forehead against his, her hot tears sliding silently onto his skin.

In the distance, Lu Xiu observed this scene with cold detachment, his gaze dark and inscrutable. He finally flicked his sleeve and turned away. In the vast, desolate twilight, only the broken walls and residual ruins of the temple remained. As the wind passed through the ruins, it seemed to still echo with the woman's suppressed and mournful weeping.

Chapter 61: Vigil of the Heart

When Lu Chou was lifted onto the carriage by the official soldiers, his entire person had already fallen into a state of semi-consciousness. Blood had thoroughly stained the front of his robes, and his breath was as weak and faint as a dying ember.

Lingyu's eyes were swollen and red; she clutched his hand—which was entirely covered in fresh blood—with trembling fingers. Her voice was raspy and broken: "Do not sleep… you must not sleep, no matter what…"

Lu Xiu gave the order for the carriage to race directly toward the Ever Peace Medical Hall in the west of the city.

This was because, although the Lu Manor was closer, he feared the medicinal supplies there might be insufficient, whereas a medical hall would have a full complement of staff and herbs to immediately address the injuries.

Upon arrival at the medical hall, Lingyu watched with frantic anxiety as several guards supported him inside. His frame was unstable, and he nearly collapsed and fell to the ground with every step.

Lu Chou instinctively moved his feet to steady himself, but as he inadvertently opened his eyes and caught sight of her face etched with anxious worry, his heart softened. His mind began to stir—*if only he could...*

Thus, the corners of his lips twitched with effort as he feigned a weak, ghostly smile.

He whispered in a low, raspy voice: "I am fine… do not weep…" He thought to himself that if she could look upon him with such devotion just a moment longer, even this searing pain would be a price well paid.

Before the words had fully left his mouth, he was suddenly seized by a wrenching cough.

Immediately, a mouthful of blood and foam erupted from his lips. The bloody foam surged out abruptly, winding its way down the corners of his mouth to stain the front of his garment beneath his chin.

"Chou!" Lingyu was on the verge of total collapse. She fell to her knees before the bed, her voice trembling as she called his name. With frantic, clumsy movements, she tried to wipe the blood from his lips, her sobs suppressed in her throat as her entire body shook. "Do not frighten me… do not frighten me so…"

Lu Chou bit back a groan of genuine distress in his heart. He had only intended to win her concern, yet the force of the cough had truly wrenched the wound in his abdomen.

One hand pressed against the injury, his teeth clenched against the unbearable agony, yet he still maintained his facade of composure. He weakly reached out to cover her palm with his own. "Lingyu… do not cry. I… can still endure it."

Several guards deftly moved to carry Lu Chou into the medical hall. Xiao Lingyu was intending to follow them inside, but she was barred at the door by the physician. "Madam, pray wait outside for a short while. The consulting room will be fouled with blood and filth; I fear it would be an affront to your sensibilities."

Hearing this, Xiao Lingyu remained undeterred and insisted on following him into the room. "It is no matter. I am not afraid."

The physician wore a look of difficulty. "Madam, the issue is not whether you are afraid… it is whether Lord Lu will be afraid."

"What do you mean?" she asked.

It was then that the physician explained with a complex expression, "This… Lord Lu's wound lies in his chest. To diagnose and treat it, we must loosen and remove his robes. In such circumstances, if a female guest were to remain by his side… it would truly be a breach of propriety."

Lingyu froze where she stood, her cheeks flushing a deep scarlet in an instant. Her lips parted, and only after a long silence did she whisper, "I am only worried for him..."

The voice was as faint as a mosquito's hum, yet it was saturated with a thousand-fold affection.

The residual warmth of his palm still remained on her fingertips, and her mind was a chaotic tangle.

She knew she should not be so flustered, yet she could not stop the trembling of her heart.

During the jolting journey here, he had leaned heavily against her shoulder in his stupor; that weight had felt as though it were pressing her very soul into the depths of her heart.

She closed her eyes, forcing herself to draw a deep breath as she turned her back to the consulting room door. Yet through the wood, she could still hear the intermittent commands, the *clink* of silver needles hitting the tray—every sound felt like a needle piercing her own heart.

The wind pried through the cracks in the door, cold enough to make her bones ache.

She could not help but murmur softly, "When you wake, you will surely scold me for meddling… but I would rather you scold me than remain this silent." Her voice was so light it was nearly carried away by the wind.

She wiped her tears, straightened her back, and forced herself to stand firm.

Loosen his robes?

Only now did she feel as if she were waking from a great dream, a cloud of crimson blooming across her cheeks. "Uh… my apologies."

This scene was witnessed in its entirety by Lu Xiu, who stood by the entrance.

A brow lifted slightly as a flicker of coldness and mockery surfaced in his eyes. His fingers tightened within his sleeves for a moment before he let out a cold, derisive scoff and turned to depart.

* * * *

Inside the consulting room, the physician and his apprentices hurried in and out. Hot broths, silver needles, and hemostatic medicines were brought in succession, the air thick with the heavy scents of herbs and iron-sharp blood.

Outside, the sky gradually darkened. Xiao Lingyu sat upon the stone steps, her hands gripping the hem of her skirt so tightly her knuckles turned white. She remained motionless, as if abandoned by time itself.

The long night stretched on. Finally, at an unknown hour of the watch, the door creaked open.

The physician stepped out, his robes stained with blood, lifting a hand to wipe the weary sweat from his brow.

She sprang to her feet. "Doctor, may I… may I go in?"

The physician offered a slight nod. "You may, but he has not yet woken. Do not disturb his wounds."

Lingyu stepped into the room. She saw that he had been changed into clean, white inner robes; his face was so ashen it appeared almost transparent.

Cold sweat covered his brow, and his breath was shallow and weak, like a flickering candle in a gale.

She sat at the bedside, reaching out to wipe the beads of sweat from his forehead.

As her gaze swept over the layers of gauze wrapped around his side, her eyes burned once more. Her fingertips were trembling; her heart was aching.

"You fool… truly a fool…" she murmured in a broken whisper. "This is the second time you have been so reckless with your life… how am I ever to repay this debt to you…" Her tears fell silently, dampening the side of his pillow.

The moonlight, cool as water, poured through the lattice window, illuminating the soft yet sorrowful silhouette of her head as she bowed. She kept vigil by the bed, leaning against the couch throughout the night, neither daring to close her eyes nor bearing to leave, until the physician returned to the room.

The figure on the bed remained still, yet those previously shut eyes opened a sliver, showing a trace of clarity amidst the haze. Lu Chou had finally stirred. His lashes fluttered, and though his breath remained weak, his gaze slowly refocused.

"Ziyuan!" Lingyu cried with a mixture of surprise and joy. She leaned closer. "You are awake? How do you feel? Where does it hurt? Are you still in discomfort?"

Lu Chou offered a slight shake of his head but did not speak, appearing unwilling to waste his breath.

At that moment, the physician entered with his medicine chest. Seeing him awake, he was just about to report, "Madam, do not be anxious. Though the wound is severe, in truth—"

Before he could finish, Lu Chou shot him a sidelong glance. The look was like the flick of a cold blade, sharp and commanding. The physician's words caught in his throat; his mouth twitched as he abruptly changed his tone.

"Ahem… in truth… he still requires absolute rest. He must not be exposed to wind or agitation. Emotional fluctuations must be avoided at all costs, lest they damage his very foundation."

Lingyu, her face full of frantic concern, nodded repeatedly. "I understand, I will be careful. But… he will truly be alright?"

The physician cupped his hands, his tone turning solemn. "If he takes his medicine on time and receives meticulous care, there should be no great hindrance. However… during this period, it would be best if someone were to look after him every moment, never leaving his side."

The moment those words were uttered, the gaze of the man on the bed flickered, yet he remained peacefully with his eyes shut as if still in a deep slumber. Only the slight curve of his lips betrayed his hidden thoughts.

The physician sighed inwardly.

This Lord Lu might be injured, but his ability to calculate remains entirely undiminished.

Having practiced medicine for decades, treating everyone from royalty to desperate outlaws, the doctor was far too experienced not to recognize such a signal. At present… his task was clearly to help the man keep the lady by his side.

He coughed again, speaking with heavy sincerity, "Madam, rest assured. The Master needs peace of mind above all else. Having someone at his side—whether to feed him medicine or apply poultices—will greatly assist in stabilizing his spirit."

Lingyu's face warmed. "Then… I shall not leave. I will stay to care for him."

The corners of the man's mouth on the bed curved for a fleeting, imperceptible instant.

The physician wiped a bead of sweat from his brow, thinking to himself: *Alas, these days, it is not enough to merely read a pulse and write a prescription; one must also be skilled at reading faces and understanding the ways of the heart.*

Chapter 62: The Illegitimate Son's Gentle Light

"Papa Lord!"

It was merely a child's sharp cry from outside the hall, yet it made Lu Xiu—who had been lounging idly within—lift a brow in sudden amusement.

"Who is making such a fuss?"

A servant bowed hastily, his voice trembling. "It is… it is the daughter of Shopkeeper Xiao, sir. She has been crying incessantly, demanding to see her mother. No one can manage to calm her, and she keeps shouting something about a 'Papa Lord'…"

The corners of Lu Xiu's lips curved with a trace of interest. "'Papa Lord,' hm? She is likely calling for that blockhead younger brother of mine, is she not?"

The servant did not dare to field such a remark and could only lower his head in silence.

After a short while, Lu Xiu rose, his tone sounding lazy and unhurried. "Bring her in. I wish to see just which family's little girl is amusing enough to create such a scene."

Before long, a small figure was led into the hall. She blinked up at him with a pair of clear, oddly striking bronze-coloured eyes, staring with unabashed curiosity.

Lu Xiu halted—surprised for a fleeting heartbeat—then allowed a faint smile to tug at his mouth. "Well now… those eyes are rather charming."

Upon hearing this, Baor instantly stopped her crying; she broke into a sudden smile, and her little nose even puffed out a small bubble of snot. "Really?"

Lu Xiu leaned down until their eyes were level, studying that unusual eye colour closely.

Then, with a sudden movement of his long finger, he tapped her little nose, which was still red from weeping. "You are quite the clever one—knowing to run toward the post station. And bold, too." His gaze narrowed slightly as he looked her over with a discerning eye.

Baor blinked her large eyes, her curiosity finally overtaking her fear. "Uncle, who are you?"

He did not answer her directly. Instead, he turned to the servants and asked, "Who usually looks after her?"

"It… it is the matron from Lord Lu's courtyard, sir."

"Call her here. She can continue taking care of the child."

The servant hesitated for a moment. "Then… shall we send Young Miss Baor back to Master Chou's Qingfeng Courtyard?"

Lu Xiu let out a cold laugh at the suggestion. He lowered his gaze to Baor and said lazily, "Send her back? Why bother? This little thing seems rather entertaining. Let her stay with me for a few days to help dispel my boredom."

* * * * *

Ever since the little girl was moved into Lu Xiu's courtyard, the entire rear residence of the Lu Manor felt as though a bright, noisy whirlwind of joy had descended upon it.

Baor, that little rascal, was not afraid of him at all. She would tilt her head and stare up at him with her shiny bronze eyes, sparkling and bright.

At first, she had been uncertain and timid, but not even two hours later, her mouth was already calling him by a name sweeter than any servant had ever uttered: "Uncle Lu~~~"

"Call me Big Uncle," he corrected her flatly.

He considered himself Lu Chou's elder brother; according to seniority, the girl ought to address him as Bobo—Big Uncle.

And when she piped out that soft, syrupy "Big Uncle," he felt a ridiculous surge of satisfaction—a pleasure so sharp it completely smothered any thought of his younger brother. He did not understand why—only that it felt inexplicably good.

"Okay! Big Uncle~~" Baor obediently chirped back, changing her address with ease.

Lu Xiu did not even bother waiting for the chance to watch his legitimate younger brother choke on this development. With a flick of his sleeve, he stood. "Come. We are going out for a stroll."

The next moment, the entire Lu household exploded into chaos. Who could have imagined that the eldest son of the Lu family—the coldest and most severe master of the house—would personally take a tiny, milky-voiced child out for a walk in the streets?

He was tall and imposing; with one sweep of his long arm, he scooped Baor up with effortless ease and held her snug against his chest. Just like that—one large, one small—they stepped out of the Lu Manor and onto the long street teeming with shops and bustling stalls.

Even the street vendors stared, dumbfounded, wondering if their ears were playing tricks on them. "This… uh… candied haw… how many skewers would you like, sir?"

"How many?" He turned to look at Baor.

Baor pointed eagerly at the entire basket of candied hawthorn, her eyes sparkling with longing. "I… I want to eat them all…"

"All of them," he said without a blink.

Baor's eyes widened. "Really?"

Lu Xiu lifted a brow. "Do I look like someone who jokes?"

All along the road, Baor received everything she desired. She bounced and swayed, laughing like a little flower in full bloom. Sugar figurines, masks, swings, pinwheels—even a barking clay puppy ended up stuffed into her arms.

He followed behind her at a leisurely pace; though his mouth complained that she was noisy, his hand naturally steadied the candied-haw skewer that was about to tilt out of her grip, and he still remembered to ask, "Hungry? Do you wish to eat something better?"

Baor looked up at him with wholehearted admiration. "Big Uncle is amazing—even nicer to Baor than Papa Lord!"

At this, Lu Xiu paused mid-step. He shot her a sideways glance, and the corner of his mouth lifted in a rare, amused arc. "Oh? How so?"

"Papa Lord won't let Baor eat too much candy. Only three pieces a day. He is just like Baor's Mama…" Baor pouted, feeling deeply wronged.

Lu Xiu set her on the ground and crouched so their eyes were level, his thin lips curling into a faint smile. "Tell me—why do you call that brother of mine 'Papa Lord'?"

"Because Baor wants a papa"

"…Baor does not have a papa?"

Baor frowned seriously, pondering for a moment, then raised two fingers. "Now Baor has two daddies. Daddy Xie and Papa Lord."

In her simple little heart, any adult man who treated her well automatically counted as a "daddy."

At her words, Lu Xiu reflexively took hold of her tiny, raised fingers. His tone softened with a tenderness he did not even notice himself. "Good girl. Whatever Baor wants today—today, I shall buy it all."

"Waaah! Big Uncle is the best! Baor likes Big Uncle the most!" she cheered, hopping twice in place with joy.

"Good. Say it again."

Baor's eyes rounded. "Big Uncle is the best!"

"Better than your Papa Lord?"

"Mm-hmm." Baor had one hand held by him, while the other was busy stuffing candied haw into her mouth.

He let out a laugh. "Little thing, you truly know how to coax people."

After laughing, Lu Xiu suddenly lifted his chin, pointing toward a shop at the street corner. "Over there is the most expensive theatre in the capital. Come, Big Uncle is taking you to hear a play."

Baor still had sugar stuck to the corner of her mouth and looked very puzzled. "What does 'hearing a play' mean?"

"It is singing that sounds almost like crying; ordinary folks simply love spending silver to go and suffer through it," he said casually, yet was already striding ahead with long steps.

Baor hurried after him, her short legs moving as fast as they could, yet she still could not catch up. She could only look up and ask, "Ah?"

"Just follow Big Uncle. I shall take you to see something new." He glanced back with a smile, his eyes carrying a hint of teasing. "Not just watching a play—there will be plenty of good food too."

Baor did not understand the teasing in his tone; she only felt this uncle was capable of anything. She instantly became happy and started hopping beside him.

When they arrived at the theatre entrance, the manager had just opened his mouth to stop them. But the moment he saw even a corner of Lu

Xiu's robe and the jade pendant at his waist, his entire posture stiffened like lead, and he immediately bowed his head.

"For today, stop the performance for the time it takes an incense stick to burn. Clean the private room upstairs. Prepare pastries and fruit. And whatever sweets the little girl wants—have them all ready, and make sure they are easy for her to digest." His tone was lazy to the extreme, yet it carried an oppressive presence that no one dared defy.

Baor stepped into the private room and, at first glance, saw a table overflowing with sweets. Her eyes lit up at once. She whispered, "All of these… can Baor really eat them?"

"Not only can you eat them, but we shall also pack them up and take them back to the manor." Lu Xiu lounged lazily on the couch, holding a piece of milk cake shaped like a little white rabbit. "If you cannot finish them, we shall stock them up. They are all for Baor."

Baor nodded while eating, her tiny mouth so sticky with sugar she could barely speak, yet she mumbled, "Big Uncle is… the biggest uncle!"

He looked at her face covered in sugar, eating with such satisfaction, and it seemed that some place in his own heart was also filled with that same contentment.

He reached out helplessly to wipe her clean, then suddenly spoke: "Since you said you have two dads now, then… if one day you had to choose one to be the real one, who would you choose?"

Baor's mouth was puffed up with food, and for a moment she did not answer.

"Little girl, your life is truly good. You have so many dads taking care of you."

Baor happened to swallow a bite of sweet cake, her bright eyes shining as she innocently asked, "Big Uncle, how many dads did you have when you were little?"

Hearing that, Lu Xiu paused for a moment. The smile on his face faded, and only then did he reveal a slight, bitter smile as he said, "Uncle did not have as good a life as Baor. Uncle had only one dad, and even that one had to be shared with someone else."

Baor stopped chewing. Her small hand reached up to touch the sharp line of his jaw, looking at him with a sweet smile, as though she were trying to comfort him. When her tiny hand touched his jaw, he almost wanted to turn his face away, yet he still could not bring himself to move.

He lowered his head to look at her. After a moment, his smile carried a hint of a joke as he said, "Then how about letting Baor have one more dad? Big Uncle can also be your dad. From now on, I shall buy you candied haw every single day."

Baor looked up at him. After quite a while, she answered seriously, "Then… Big Uncle can be the daytime dad, and Papa Lord can be the nighttime dad. That way Baor has daddies every day!"

When he heard this, Lu Xiu was stunned for a moment, and then he let out a laugh and shook his head, murmuring to himself, "This little thing… truly does know how to take the best of both worlds."

Outside the private room, the autumn wind brushed against the curtains, and from beyond the opera house, the noise of the crowd surged. He had never imagined that one day he would be sitting in an opera house, accompanying a tiny girl whose nose had not even finished running, watching opera skits, and yet actually feeling that life was quite pleasant.

He murmured softly under his breath, "Just where did you come from, little thing… How can a person, at first sight of you, already feel like they cannot bear to let go?"

Chapter 63: Gaze Across the Opera House

The interior of the opera house was a roaring sea of voices, the heavy scents of wine and roasted meat permeating the entire hall.

This was the Cloud Spring Opera House, one of the premier establishments in the capital. The first floor was a vast, open hall facing the stage, with seats arranged in orderly rows where everyone from common tradesfolk to idle scholars could find a place.

Vendors wove through the aisles with trays, laughter and calls rose and fell, and the press of bodies was so tight it felt as though even water could not seep through.

The second floor, however, featured a curved gallery designed in a half-moon shape around the stage, partitioned into several exquisitely carved private boxes.

From this height, one could look down upon the performers—it was a sanctuary for the powerful and the refined to view the theatre, engage in restrained conversation, and quietly exchange greetings with old acquaintances under the cover of lantern-light.

The carved screens and railings were fine enough to display craftsmanship, yet high enough to keep the lower hall at a distance; within the boxes, even a single glance carried meaning.

On the first floor, the hall was packed shoulder to shoulder, cheers rising in overlapping waves.

Above, Baor lay pressed against the carved railing of their box, her tiny hands clutching a stick of candied haws. Her eyes were wide and round, and she remained entirely unaware of the thin threads of sugar stuck to the corner of her mouth.

The performance reached its zenith. Onstage, a troupe was enacting a face-changing play; the performer was clad in a monkey costume, dressed as Sun Wukong, brandishing a golden staff.

With a swift lift of the hand and a sharp turn of the head, he transformed his painted features into another face entirely, drawing a thunderous roar of approval from the hall below.

Lu Xiu leaned against the window, his left hand resting upon the railing as he watched the play in a reclining posture. From time to time, he lowered his head to wipe Baor's mouth, his expression lazy and unrestrained—unbothered by the noise, as though the entire opera house were merely another place he could sit as he pleased.

Looking back down at the lower floor, he saw a crowd so dense even water could not pass; but in the private box directly opposite, a shimmer of pale blue suddenly caught his eye, appearing remarkably familiar.

Onstage, the performance burned with a fierce intensity. The face-changing actor turned with dazzling speed—a sweep of a sleeve, a step and a whirl, and with a shui sound, the fierce Vajra mask was replaced by a gentle, smiling white face.

Silken ribbons danced and masks flickered through the air, drawing thunderous applause from the hall as children clapped their hands and shouted, "Once more!"

Baor sat perched upon Lu Xiu's long legs, one arm hugging her candied haws while the other held a small milk cake he had just pressed into her hand.

Her face was smeared with sweets, yet her eyes followed the movements of the female performers onstage, spinning in their sockets and wide with wonder.

She laughed until she was slapping her own thigh: "Big Uncle, look, look! He changed his face again—!"

Lu Xiu leaned back in his chair, lazily raising his cup. One hand supported the back of her neck to ensure she did not topple over the railing, while the corner of his lips curved slightly: "Is it truly that rare to see?"

"Rare!" Baor answered without a moment's hesitation.

He let out a chuckle and was about to lower his head to tease her further, when his gaze was suddenly arrested by a figure in the box opposite.

It was indeed she—Shen Zhaoru.

She was dressed in a light blue ruqun, sitting upright in silence, her posture composed and unyielding. Inside that box were approximately three or four young women crowded together; the one seated closest to the window was none other than Shen Zhaoru.

She wore a moon-grey short jacket paired with an embroidered skirt; her face bore only the faintest trace of powder, as if she had applied it out of courtesy rather than vanity. Though she wore no elaborate ornaments, her features remained cold and her expression still.

When she conversed with those beside her, she offered only a slight nod; holding her tea cup alone, she gazed unblinkingly at the stage, as though the clamor below had nothing to do with her.

When Lu Xiu caught sight of her, the corner of his lips lifted. He raised his wine cup in a silent gesture across the void, uttering not a single word, yet his gaze swept past like a light brush of wind—flippant, effortless, and impossible to ignore.

Shen Zhaoru paused for a beat, her brow stirring. In the end, she offered a gentle nod in return, though her fingertips unconsciously tightened around the rim of her cup, leaving the porcelain a shade whiter where her fingers pressed.

The women beside her, however, were not nearly so composed.

"Eh, look at the box opposite. That must be the eldest concubine-born son of the Lu family, is it not?" A woman dressed in a goose-yellow gown lowered her voice, her tone laced with interest. "He is indeed exceptionally handsome. I heard that although he is the son of a concubine, he is still the eldest son of the Lu house; several matchmakers have already begun making inquiries about him."

"He is but a concubine-son after all; he merely has a few minor military merits to his name, which cannot be compared to his legitimate younger brother, Lu Chou." Another woman joined in, her voice dripping with ill-concealed disdain, though her eyes could not help but steal several more glances across the way. "But... what is the matter with that little girl beside him?"

"Indeed, I was just looking at that myself. The child's features do not resemble anyone else's, and they are so close... have any of you heard of him marrying?"

"None. In this capital, if a young master of any house takes a wife, how could there be no sound of it? I dare say, she is likely an illegitimate daughter raised in some outside residence." The woman speaking covered her mouth with a handkerchief and laughed softly, her tone full of contempt. "To have the nerve to flaunt such a status in an opera house—he certainly has bold courage."

Having spoken, the women exchanged looks, all revealing a shared expression of disdain, as if a single rumor were enough to pin a person to the ground.

Shen Zhaoru had originally been listening in silence, but at this moment, she set her tea cup down with a shade more force than necessary. She spoke softly: "Nonsense."

Her tone was not heavy, yet it was cold enough to cause those noble ladies to fall silent all at once.

In the centre of the hall, the face-changing act concluded, and the main performance of the day commenced—The Romance of the Western Chamber. The hall's drafts shifted with the crowd's movement; the lantern-flames trembled faintly, and the stage curtains breathed like waves.

After approximately one or two kè of singing, the melody shifted into a particular passage. The actress sang: "Cloud-like tresses, flower-like face, and golden dangling hairpins; the hibiscus bed-curtains are warm as we spend the spring night."

The tea cup in Shen Zhaoru's hand wavered slightly, her fingertips tightening. That lyric was nothing new, yet for some reason, hearing it tonight, every word seemed to land directly upon her heart, leaving her feeling inexplicably melancholy and wistful.

The sentiment was too thick, the vocals too tender; every stroke and word felt as though it were written for someone else—written for a different pair, in a different room, under a different lamp.

Her heart was stirred, but she quickly suppressed it. Her face remained unmoved as she merely shifted her gaze away, as if turning her eyes aside could also turn her thoughts aside.

Lu Xiu remained seated by the window.

Across the distance of the roaring crowd, he slowly let a smile curve his lips in her direction. In that smile, there was a hint of provocation, and perhaps... a shadow of silent waiting—as though he had all the leisure in the world to see how long her composure could hold.

Before long, as Baor watched, her eyelids began to droop. Yawn after yawn followed; the bamboo skewer of the candied haws hung slanted between her fingers, and sugar stains smeared half her face.

Tiny as she was, she slumped against Lu Xiu's shoulder, her breathing becoming steady and soft as she fell into a deep slumber.

Lu Xiu lowered his eyes to look at her, his expression softening by a degree. Setting aside his wine cup, he gathered her up with one long arm, lifting her from his lap while the other hand steadily supported her back and the hollow of her knees.

His posture was familiar and natural—too practiced to be a first attempt—and he did not wake her at all. The child's head nestled against his shoulder, her small hand still curled around the skewer, limp with sleep.

He was about to turn and depart when his steps paused. He looked back toward the box opposite, his thin lips curling slightly as he offered a gentle nod in that direction—light as a courtesy, yet deliberate as a mark.

Shen Zhaoru instinctively looked toward him. Across half the theatre, she found herself caught in those narrow eyes filled with quiet amusement, and her heart gave a sudden, violent thump.

The man stood tall and upright with the child in his arms, his silhouette outlined by the lanterns in a warm, mellow glow; the noise below surged like a tide, yet in that instant, she heard only the beat in her own chest.

 She hesitated for a fleeting moment before finally inclining her head and lowering her lashes, returning the gesture.

He did not stay, turning to depart of his own accord. Behind him, the sounds of the play continued, yet they no longer reached his ears.

In the opposite box, the women who had also been watching the play had noticed the man's nod of acknowledgement, and could not help but break into low whispers once more.

"That eldest son of the Lu family is truly handsome beyond compare..." one sighed, her tone full of infatuation. "Concubine-born or not, one has to look at a husband's face for a lifetime. With looks that handsome, even I would be moved."

"Alas, you look only at the surface!" another said with a curl of her lip. "What is the use of being handsome? Men like him are what I fear most. Look at his manner just now, carrying a child through the streets for all to see."

"Indeed, I was also wondering where that child came from. She does not look so small; no matter how one looks at it, she seems like... a daughter raised in secret outside."

"Ah, with his birth, even if he were to propose marriage, it would be difficult to enter a high-ranking house. To say nothing of carrying such a burden—it is truly..."

As they spoke, their tones grew increasingly flippant, their features full of mockery, as if words cost nothing in the warmth of a private box.

The tea cup in Shen Zhaoru's hand paused, the white porcelain meeting the lacquered wood table with a light clack. Her tone was flat: "Do not mention him again. Are we here to watch the play or not?"

The voice was not loud, yet it was cold enough to silence the women instantly; they dared not utter another word.

In the opera house, the stage continued with the soulful passages of The Romance of the Western Chamber. Amidst the shifting drafts of the hall, it seemed as if someone's gaze had not yet turned away—that silhouette, which had once offered a flippant smile and a silent wait, had already been etched into this night, carried forward with the music, and left behind like a trace that would not quite fade.

Chapter 64: Disturbance in the Heart's Game

Before long, The Romance of the Western Chamber drew toward its close. The melody softened, tapering into a lingering refrain of low, winding lyrics: "May all lovers beneath the sky become true companions; for in this bustling world, only love remains unspoken."

The actress's voice stretched long, the final note quivering before it dissolved; yet it seemed to fall into someone's heart, rippling outward in endless circles.

Inside the box, the lamps were dim, and the tea within the porcelain cups lay heavy and dark. Shen Zhaoru bowed her head, her fingertips tracing the rim of her cup; her palm was a sheet of faint cool.

"All made-up nonsense," one of the young women laughed, clearly unmoved by the sentiment of the ending.

Shen Zhaoru heard her, yet only offered a slight smile, neither agreeing nor refuting. But in that quiet smile lay something fragile and imperceptible, as if it might shatter at the lightest touch.

When the play ended and the crowd began to disperse, the great bell of Yunchun Theatre tolled—slow, lingering strokes that drifted through the rafters and the corridor like a reminder pressed gently yet insistently into everyone's ears: it was time to rise and take one's leave.

Simultaneously, by the theatre's side gate, a servant in blue came quietly forward to meet them.

"Young Master, the sedan chair is ready."

He had come on foot during the day, but now that Baor had fallen asleep, he had ordered a small chair to be brought around.

Lu Xiu nodded. Looking down, he saw Baor sleeping soundly, a small thread of sugar still clinging to the corner of her eye.

He could not help but reach out to brush it away; his gesture was uncharacteristically gentle, though his lips bent in a touch of resignation.

"This little imp… truly knows how to create a fuss."

They left the theatre. Night had deepened. At the mouth of the lane, two drunkards staggered past. Catching sight of his fine attire, they stumbled closer, muttering inane words, eager to crowd up and be rude—yet a bodyguard at Lu Xiu's side barked a warning, driving them back until they scurried away.

Lu Xiu's brows drew together; instinctively, he tightened his hold on the child. In his arms, the little girl shifted, a soft hum through her nose as if searching for something in a dream. He let out a low laugh, but his steps did not slow.

Inside the sedan, soft cushions had been laid thick. After he placed her down securely, Baor remained curled within the small quilt, still gripping the bamboo skewer of the sugar-haws even in sleep, her nose reddened from the chill.

"Return to the manor," he ordered.

As the chair swayed into motion, he glanced through the curtain at the night outside, and suddenly remembered that final verse from the Western Chamber. A quiet, derisive laugh escaped him.

—Only love remains unspoken—

What love, he wondered, could possibly be so precious it could not be named aloud? It was nothing but the self-inflicted troubles of mediocre men.

To him, if there was any affection that could not be claimed, seized, or entreated for—if it was truly something one could neither get nor beg for—then he would cast it aside. He would simply—discard it.

Life is short; why bind oneself to restraints born of illusion? Why shackle oneself and refuse to move?

* * * * *

Elsewhere, Shen Zhaoru had left the theatre and walked home without a word. At the gates of the Shen estate, a lamp-bearing matron stepped forward, intending to help her remove her cloak, but Shen Zhaoru lifted a hand to stop her.

"I will do it myself."

She dismissed the servants with a brief command, and only then entered her chamber alone.

She sat for a moment in silence. The candle flame wavered quietly on the table, its small light reflecting in her dazed eyes. What lingered in

her mind was that look the man had given before he turned to leave—
that single glance over his shoulder. Was it deliberate? Or only idle jest?
She did not know why she minded so much, nor why it refused to be
shaken off.

After a pause, she turned slowly and pushed open the lattice window,
gazing toward the distant night—toward the direction of the theatre. Yet
within her heart, the echo of that song still drifted, soft and unfinished,
as though the meaning of the play had not yet ended, as though some
lingering thread of "drama" still circled and would not settle.

And in this city washed with moonlight, who could have guessed that
today's play—what happened within the play and outside it, the myriad
faces of people and their fleeting passions—had already, in silence,
begun to alter the course of certain lives?

* * * * *

The lights of Ever Peace Medical Hall had dimmed past midnight. Only
in the consulting chamber of the east wing did a single lamp still burn,
the wick trembling with a faint glow that threw shifting shadows against
the corners of the walls. The room was hushed to the point of stillness.

Xiao Lingyu sat by the bedside and sighed softly. Her voice was low as
she asked: "...Are you certain Baor is truly all right?"

Lu Chou reclined against the pillows. His gaze darkened for a moment,
then steadied into its usual calm. "Rest easy. Baor is safe."

She bit her lip, unable to hide the worry in her chest. "Though word
came that she was brought safely back to the Lu manor, she is still so
small. That day was a mess of chaos and bloodshed... I always feel..."

"She will be fine," he said quietly, but with unwavering conviction.
"There are plenty of people in the household. They will not fail to look
after one little girl."

A moment of silence followed. Soon, the bubbling of the medicine pot
broke the hush; the decoction had reached its final draught, the residual
heat still rising. She tested the warmth, cooled it with a breath, and only
then approached the bed.

"You must finish it," she murmured, her tone soft, almost afraid to
disturb the quiet.

Lu Chou's eyes were half-closed; his face remained pale. The wound at his side had been bound, but the loss of blood had left him weak. He lay motionless save for the faint tremor of his lashes, showing his consciousness was still clear.

She leaned closer, supporting his neck, and began to feed him the medicine with care. As the rim of the bowl brushed his lips, he coughed suddenly, turning his face aside with a weak but obstinate frown. "Bitter…"

"You are a grown man and still complain about bitterness?" she arched a brow. "Drink it quickly."

He slowly turned his face back toward her, opening his eyes. A faint light of amusement rippled within them. "You are the one feeding me?"

She was startled, her fingers jolting so that the bowl nearly tipped. After a moment, she forced herself to recover and set the bowl upon the table. "Rest," she said. "I will fetch the physician."

She had just risen when his hand shot up and caught her wrist. The grip was not strong, but it was remarkably steady—as though he were drawing upon the last of his strength to hold onto this single attachment.

"Xiao Lingyu," he called to her softly—yet in the very next breath, the name seemed to press closer, more intimate, as though it had slipped past restraint of its own accord. "Lingyu…"

His voice was gentle, yet it pressed tightly against her heart.

She looked down at him, her mind a tangle of emotions, light flickering in her eyes. At last, she said only: "Rest well. You are not allowed to speak nonsense."

She tried to withdraw her hand, but his grasp only tightened.

"That day… I did not finish what I meant to say," he murmured between breaths. "If not for... if you had not come, I would have..."

Before he could finish, she lowered her eyes and raised her hand to cover his lips.

"Do not speak further," she whispered, her eyes trembling. "If there is anything, wait until you are healed."

For a moment, they faced each other in wordless silence. Only the rustle of the night wind stirred the curtains, bringing a faint scent of osmanthus.

Her hand remained against his lips, and he did not speak again, yet his gaze refused to shift from her even for a fraction.

In that instant, the air seemed to congeal, leaving only their overlapping breaths. She had meant to pull away, but was held deeper by those cool fingertips.

"Lingyu," he breathed, the word spilling almost against her fingertips. "If you had not come, I fear I would have..."

He broke off, exhaling a soft laugh at his own sentimentality. "Forget it. This is fine. At least I can still look at you."

Her heart tightened and her fingers quivered, yet she did not pull away. She only whispered, "You must get well. I will look after you."

"...Alright." His breathing settled, though his eyes still burned with a wakeful will.

She was dazed, her gaze disordered, finally whispering back: "Truly a fool, alas..." But the sound was so light it was nearer to a sigh.

Her fingertips still felt the warmth lingering on his lips; her heart was as chaotic as a stone thrown into a lake.

The silence stretched so long she could almost hear her own heartbeat. Outside, the wind moved and the shadows of the candle flickered. For a moment, she was lost in a trance—if time were to stop here, it would not be such a bad thing.

But just as the thought arose, a soft cough sounded from the doorway...

"Cough."

The sound broke the stillness, shattering the fragile air of ambiguity. Xiao Lingyu snapped back to herself, instinctively pulling her hand away. She turned her head and saw Lu Xiu leaning against the doorframe, arms folded across his chest, watching with a cold, measuring eye—as if he had been there for a moment already, silent, unannounced, and entirely unbothered by the intimacy he had just interrupted.

Chapter 65: Bloodlines and Bitter Truths

"I had thought the physician sent both of you out, but it seems this room has turned into a bedside tryst," Lu Xiu drawled as he stepped over the threshold.

Xiao Lingyu froze, the tips of her ears flushing a deep crimson as she forced herself to maintain a facade of composure. "I only came to feed him his medicine."

"Feed him?" Lu Xiu arched a brow, a smirk of amusement curling at the edge of his lips. "For a mere bowl of medicine, you managed to feed it with such tender affection that you did not even perceive how long I have been standing outside the door. Truly, it is impressive."

Xiao Lingyu's expression changed sharply; before she could speak, Lu Chou had already knitted his brows, his voice cool and dismissive. "Enough with the nonsense. Why have you come so suddenly?"

Lu Xiu did not answer him immediately. Instead, he turned toward Xiao Lingyu, whose face was already burning with heat. His tone shifted—it was flat and polite, yet marked by an unmistakable sense of distancing. "Madam Xiao, if you do not mind, allow Lu to have a few words alone with my foolish younger brother?"

She was stunned for a moment, a flash of embarrassment and panic flickering through her lowered gaze. She dropped her eyelashes and whispered, "…Very well."

She turned to leave; her steps were not fast, but they were visibly stiff. Her receding figure beneath the lamplight carried a subtle air of a desperate retreat, almost as if she were fleeing the room.

The door closed slowly, leaving the chamber in a heavy hush.

Only after the latch clicked did Lu Chou face his brother, who was now wearing a distinctly wicked grin. "You still have not stated the purpose of your visit."

Lu Xiu casually dragged a chair over and sat, stretching out his long legs and propping one carelessly upon a nearby stool. "While you are in here whispering sweet nothings and talking of love, I have been busily playing nursemaid to the both of you for days. Have you no shame at all?"

Lu Chou averted his gaze uncomfortably. "That little girl is not mine."

"Is that so?" Lu Xiu shrugged his shoulders roguishly, wearing an air of utter indifference. "Funny. I happen to think that tiny chin and that tiny nose look remarkably like yours when you were a brat."

"Do not talk such nonsense."

"I have not seen you ask after the little girl these past few days," Lu Xiu continued, his tone half-teasing and half-probing. "Were you so certain that, amidst that day's chaos and the clash of soldiers, I would manage to find her?"

"I trust you."

"Heh. Listen to you. Why is it that when you say it, I somehow trust it even less?" Lu Xiu let out a cold, amused snort, his thin lips curving in a sharp line.

Lu Chou returned the gesture with a frigid glare. "Believe whatever you wish."

After a light chuckle, Lu Xiu spoke again: "That little girl actually had the sense to run all the way back along the official highway—that is how I found her. She is quite clever, and her features are handsome. If she truly is not of your bone and blood, then it is simply your lack of fortune."

"Do not drag other matters into this. You do not show up without reason; speak plainly." Impatience darkened Lu Chou's expression.

"Of course." Lu Xiu's gaze swept over him with cold detachment. "You are an injured man, and it is inconvenient for you to give an account to others. I, as your elder brother, have naturally come to handle it for you. The remnants of the Third Prince's faction have been largely cleared out. His Majesty requires you to write a formal deposition, detailing the beginning and end of this affair with great care."

"My wounds have not yet healed—"

"Have you not performed enough for one lifetime?" Lu Xiu walked up to the bedside, letting his gaze sweep over the man beneath the quilt with a look of indifference. A sardonic smirk played on his lips. "How much longer do you plan to milk this little act of 'harming yourself to prove resolve'?"

At that, Lu Chou allowed himself a rare, almost wicked curl of the lips—a smile charming enough to beguile the masses. He offered no denial, saying only, "The injury remains a fact."

"Oh, it is real," Lu Xiu said lightly. "It is only that this blade miraculously managed to avoid every vital point. It looks severe, but in truth, it is but a flesh wound. Your little trick is only enough to fool naive women."

Lu Chou did not dispute it. "Last time, you said that if a man has no attachments, he relies only on stratagem. I find that statement erroneous now. It is only when a man holds an attachment that he is willing to employ stratagems to reach his heart's desire. Especially in this matter of the Third Prince—would my elder brother disagree?"

Lu Xiu lifted a brow, his tone languid. "Fair enough. In the matter of the Third Prince, you and I exchanged messages by courier pigeon. The world believed the Lu brothers were at odds, and only thus could the Crown Prince regain his footing and win this round. If we are speaking of scheming, the depth of your city-deep mind truly deserves the credit."

A faint, controlled smile touched Lu Chou's lips, his voice remaining steady. "You were not far behind."

"Except you," Lu Xiu drawled, "with your no less than eight hundred hidden schemes, made me use far too many coded phrases. Next time, use simpler ones." He leaned slightly closer, his tone shifting into mock complaint. "Especially that reply you hid within the layers of the account book; I spent half the night puzzling that one out."

"If I had allowed you to understand it at a single glance, that would have been my failing." Lu Chou's tone was neither light nor heavy.

"You are calling me stupid in a roundabout way, aren't you?" Lu Xiu let out a cold laugh. "Do not get too pleased with yourself; it remains to be seen who the true fool is."

He paused, and for once, his tone carried a note of rare seriousness. "When it comes to plotting, I cannot compare to you. You clearly knew reinforcements were arriving, yet you refused to endure a moment longer, choosing instead to let yourself take a blade to seal the act. This 'bitter meat' ruse of yours... tsk, tsk..."

"Have you said enough?"

The two of them met each other's eyes for a moment, neither speaking again—one giving a cold smile, the other a rogue-like grin.

After a long while, Lu Xiu stood up and reached out to pat the wooden rack beside the pillow. "If there is nothing else, raise a few more carrier pigeons. Who knows when they will be needed again."

Lu Chou did not answer; he only closed his eyes and coldly spat out a single word: "Get out."

"I think so too." Lu Xiu let out a laugh, turned back, and swayed step by step toward the door. "You continue pretending to be sick; I shall go report your safety."

The door was gently pulled shut, leaving behind a quiet room, with only the lamp wick flickering lightly and a sigh so faint it was barely audible.

* * * * *

Outside Yong'an Medical Hall, Xiao Lingyu stood beneath the eaves on the outer side of the east wing, waiting in silence.

Before long, the door creaked open, and Lu Xiu strolled out. He was draped in his outer robe, his movements casual and unrestrained as always.

He seemed to have already expected that she had not left; seeing her standing in the corridor, he showed no surprise, merely saying lightly, "The wind is strong at this hour. Why has Madam Xiao not yet gone home?"

She gave a slight nod, her voice not loud but clear. "May Lord Lu be at peace. This humble woman waits here for Lord Lu only to give thanks."

"Oh?" He lifted a brow, smiling but not smiling. "This is truly an honour I did not expect."

She lowered her gaze a little, cupping her hands in a formal salute, her tone carrying a trace of sincerity. "This time, I am indebted to Lord Lu's assistance. Had Lord Lu not led the soldiers and rushed over… this humble woman and Baor might have… never seen daylight again."

He merely gave a light scoff at her words. "If I had not come, that foolish younger brother of mine really would have thrown his life away for you. That the little girl is safe is merely a testament to the fact that your lives are hard to extinguish."

She fell silent for a moment, then added another sentence. "During these days, Baor has disturbed you; I also thank Lord Lu for taking care of her on our behalf."

This made Lu Xiu pause for several breaths. His gaze lingered on her for a moment, then suddenly shifted into something filled with interest.

"Speaking of that little girl..." He stepped forward slowly, his eyes sweeping up and down over her with half a smile. "Her brows and eyes are quite clever, and her temperament lively and cute..." His tone suddenly shifted; he asked extremely directly: "Is Baor of the Lu family's bloodline?"

Regarding Baor's birth and origins, he had long ago secretly sent people to investigate.

The report from his agents had surprised him—it claimed she truly was not that blockhead Lu Chou's child. It was reasonable, yet beyond expectation; after all, no one in the Lu family possessed such a pair of copper-coloured eyes.

Xiao Lingyu froze, her back tensing. She instinctively wanted to hide it; her lips parted, yet no sound came out.

Silence thickened like stagnant water.

Her fingertips tightened inside her sleeves, as though wrestling with some internal struggle. After a long time, she finally lifted her eyes, as if gathering all her courage, and faintly exhaled one word: "Yes."

The moment that word fell, it seemed as if even the wind stopped for a beat.

Lu Xiu stared at her for several breaths, the corners of his lips slowly curving into a light, provocative arc that was both sexy and full of resignation. Her answer had truly astonished him. He raised a long finger to point toward the door behind him, seeking confirmation. "Is she his?"

Xiao Lingyu took a deep breath and lowered her eyelashes. "She is."

"And the little girl... he truly does not know?"

After a stunned moment, Xiao Lingyu gently shook her head.

Thinking for a moment, he still voiced another doubt. "Why those eyes...?"

"It is inherited from my mother's family." Before he could finish, she directly solved the riddle. "My missing elder brother also possessed a pair of copper-coloured eyes."

"Remarkable..." he said softly, as though confirming a speculation he had long held.

The spy's report had been in error; that little girl really was the daughter of that blockhead Lu Chou. That fellow truly surpassed him in everything, making one both jealous and grudgingly admiring… it was utterly infuriating.

Since birth, he had seized all of the Lu family's resources and their parents' affection, and now, he even possessed a child earlier than him—a bond that asked for neither identity nor profit.

And he—remained alone in this world!

"Why tell me?"

"I only hope Lord Lu, for the sake of Baor being of the Lu family's bloodline, will look after Baor's safety with more care. This humble woman would be deeply grateful."

"Heh, how interesting." Having said so, he suddenly let out a laugh, his steps widening as he walked out. As he walked, he continued laughing under his breath, his voice full of teasing amusement. "Fool… fool."

He murmured it, as though talking to himself, yet also as though judging someone else. His figure went farther and farther away, his laughter drifting lightly through the night.

Xiao Lingyu stood where she was, her fingers tightly gripping her sleeve, silent for a long time. She had no other options; danger surrounded her from all sides, and she needed to find a proper place for Baor.

She only hoped that he might, for the sake of Baor being a Lu bloodline, show a little more care for her child's safety.

The wind brushed past the curtain edge once more. She gently closed her eyes and, in a very low voice, murmured—

"I am the fool."

Chapter 66: The Third Prince's Downfall

Inside Qianyuan Hall, the golden lanterns burned with a high brilliance, yet the atmosphere was as heavy and oppressive as the dead of winter.

Below the imperial steps, the court officials were arrayed in rows, kneeling in a posture of deep prostration; not a single person dared to utter a word.

Everyone could see that His Majesty's anger had by no means subsided; his face was as dark as still water, radiating a biting chill that bordered on a palpable intent to kill.

Chen Song knelt at the very centre of the hall, his hands bound and his head lowered. His blue robe was stained with blood, and his complexion was deathly pale.

Not a single supporter stood behind him, and to his left and right was nothing but a void; he appeared like a doomed minister at the end of his tether.

The Emperor said, "I ask you—as a prince, you actually dared to personally lead men to encircle and kill loyal officials, to destroy evidence, and to attempt a desperate gamble with the fate of the realm. Do you admit to this?"

The Emperor's voice was not loud, yet every word pierced like an awl, cold enough to sink into the very bone.

Chen Song rasped, "Your son… your son…"

"Still you dare to prevaricate?" The Emperor struck the jade table with a sudden, violent blow. The inkstone on the corner split apart at the impact, the sound exploding through the hall like a clap of thunder. "If Lu Chou had not carried My secret decree, and if Deputy Commander Lu had not arrived with timely rescue—tell Me, if you were not a prince, do you think you would still be kneeling here speaking to Me?"

As the words fell, the officials bowed even lower, like mountains collapsing, and the entire four quarters of the hall fell into a deathly silence.

"Guards. Announce the decree!"

An inner attendant hurried forward, unfurled the gold-edged edict, and proclaimed loudly: "Third Prince Chen Song, having acted unlawfully, privately mobilised soldiers, disrupted governance, and brought harm upon the people—effective immediately, his princely title is stripped. He shall be escorted to the Western Ancestral Mausoleum to guard the tombs and atone for his crimes.

He is to be confined within the underground palace for three years, and may not leave without imperial command. Should he cause any disturbance, his entire house shall be implicated!"

"Your Majesty, spare him!" Grand Tutor Du Zhongming suddenly knocked his head to the floor, his voice trembling and nearly breaking into a piteous wail. The Du clan was the family of Consort Du Yingxiu, the mother of the Third Prince. "The Du family has been loyal for generations. Though the Third Prince has erred, I beg Your Majesty to consider the bloodline and spare him a sliver of mercy!"

"He is My son—he is not the son of your Du family!" The Emperor cut him off coldly, his voice severe and awe-inspiring. "If the Du family wishes to preserve itself, then remain silent from this moment on. Should you dare, even once more, to plead out of personal sentiment—I will deal with all of you together!"

"…Yes!" Du Zhongming pressed his forehead to the floor, his entire body trembling. He dared not utter another word.

That phrase—'deal with all of you together'—was as cold as severed iron, extinguishing every last vain hope of negotiation or reversal.

Hearing this, Chen Song slowly lifted his head. His eyes were calm, and his expression remained unyielding. He did not argue further; instead, he let out a low laugh and bowed deeply. "Your son… obeys the decree."

The Emperor closed his eyes and flicked his hand in a dismissive wave. "Take him away."

Once the Third Prince was removed, the hall remained sunk in an oppressive, leaden silence.

A moment later, the Emperor opened his eyes again. Though his tone was even, it had turned to a new, decisive sharpness. "The Third Prince being deposed, the Crown Prince's position must now be steadier than ever. I intend to select a Crown Princess to stabilise the hearts of the people."

At those words, the officials were shocked; gazes shifted across the hall, turbulent as a rising undercurrent.

"His Majesty is wise," the officials responded, bowing in unison with cupped hands.

The Emperor swept his sharp gaze across the assembled court before speaking slowly: "The Grand Tutor's daughter, Shen Zhaoru. Her conduct and appearance are exemplary, and her family is upright; she shall be one consideration.

The eldest daughter of the Assistant Minister of the Right, Liu Zhengliang—Liu Yishu—steady in conduct and well-raised, is another fitting choice."

"This matter I will not decide with finality yet." He turned his gaze toward the Crown Prince, his tone carrying an unmistakable deeper meaning. "The Crown Prince shall first meet with both families and make his choice within three months. There is no need to act with undue haste."

The Crown Prince bowed his head. "Your son receives the order."

In that instant, every minister in the court understood: the Emperor's actions were both a warning to many and a move to re-establish authority and stabilise the state. From today onward, the Shen, Du, and Liu families had stepped yet another level deeper into the shifting currents of power.

* * * * *

The night wind was heavy, and the lantern light cast itself against the corners of the eaves. In Lu Manor's Moon River Courtyard, the world was so quiet that only the sound of the wind remained.

Lu Xiu returned earlier than usual, yet he did not enter his study. He simply stood beneath the corridor, his gaze lifted slightly as he looked toward the moon—not yet full and half-veiled behind a thin sheet of clouds.

The door opened with a soft creak.

Baor, dressed in a little jacket with her hair neatly combed, came hopping out from the inner room. When she saw him, her eyes lit instantly—bright as the liveliest star in the night sky.

"Big Uncle! You're back!" She ran over quickly, tilting her head up with a face filled with pure, innocent joy. "Baor waited for you the whole day! I drew a big fish today—really big! Nanny said it looked very, very good!"

Her tiny hand reached toward him, as though wanting to pull him inside to look.

"Who told you to wait?"

"No one. Baor wanted to wait on her own." She looked up at him smiling, her excited eyes curving into the shape of little crescents.

Lu Xiu was taken aback. His gaze fell on those bright, unfamiliar bronze-coloured eyes, and something in his chest tightened abruptly. His feelings were tangled and complex—this clever, lively, adorable little girl unexpectedly turned out to be the bone and blood of the one person he resented most. Heh.

She carried the Lu family's blood. She was the daughter of the younger brother who had beaten him at everything since childhood.

In that instant, the faint warmth he had felt a moment earlier suddenly drew back.

Baor did not notice Lu Xiu's coldness at all. She continued chattering happily: "Come see! The fish I drew is so big, and it's red, and it's really, really pretty—"

"Go to your nanny. It's late; why are you still not ready to rest?" His tone was faint. He turned his face away, stepping back half a pace and shifting his body to avoid the small hand reaching toward him.

Baor froze for a moment. She blinked, her small mouth slightly open, a hint of grievance rising. "But… Baor isn't sleepy yet. Baor was waiting for you. And… waited the whole day."

Her voice grew softer, as though she were a wounded creature. She had always been an extremely sensitive child, and though she didn't understand everything, she could feel this sudden, unguarded coldness. She could feel his refusal.

Lu Xiu lowered his gaze. When he looked at that small, soft face, something in his chest tightened unexpectedly. He had wanted to stay away from this warmth that had nothing to do with him. Yet with just that one sentence—"I was waiting for you"—his composure quietly faltered.

This was Lu Chou's child. This was Xiao Lingyu's secret of five years. This was the line he knew he should not cross, the truth he should not touch—

But it was also the first time… the first time a child had ever waited for him to come home.

Since his youth, he had grown used to cold stoves and empty corridors, used to days when no one waited at the door and no one asked after his return. Even when he returned to this Lu Manor, no one had ever stepped out even half a pace to welcome him.

But today, this little girl said she had waited for him the entire day.

He wanted to say, "Be troublesome no more," but the words caught in his throat. Those bronze-coloured eyes stared up at him without blinking, as though afraid he would grow cold again.

His throat tightened, and his tone finally softened a degree: "I shall look at your drawing tomorrow. It is late; go and rest now."

Having spoken, he turned away, his steps so quick they were almost as if he were fleeing.

Baor stood in her place, staring at his retreating back with a face of total bewilderment, her tiny hand slowly dropping to her side. She did not understand why Big Uncle was different today.

Behind that closed door, Lu Xiu stood in the shadows, his knuckles gripping the edge of the table so tightly the joints turned pale. He shut his eyes and murmured under his breath: "Truly, it is infuriating to the extreme… How does he always get everything good first?"

His tone carried a bitterness he could not quite name—for he was the elder son, born a full year before that legitimate younger brother.

Baor's warm, earnest gaze had carried so much expectation; it could not be denied it had softened him for a moment. But that brief warmth felt like a stolen happiness, something he had taken, even if for a heartbeat, from the one who had always stood above him.

But he knew this softness did not belong to him. He should not touch it, and he must not grow attached.

Chapter 67: Heart's Defences Shattered

The night was heavy and deep, and within the chamber, the lamps burned with a low, flickering luminescence.

From the incense burner, a faint thread of sandalwood drifted, its smoke curling upward in soft spirals—yet even this fragrance could not mask the persistent weeping of the young girl upon the couch.

Baor had buried her face deep within the nanny's embrace.

The rims of her eyes were a raw crimson, the bridge of her nose stung with the heat of her tears, and her small frame shook with jerky, hitching sobs, looking for all the world like a kitten that had just been cruelly bullied.

"Nanny… I do not want to stay here any longer… *hic*… It is no fun here… and no one likes Baor at all…"

She hiccupped through her words, her voice already hoarse from her lamentations. Her small face was flushed as red as a fully ripened jujube; as she spoke, she rubbed her cheek against the nanny's knee, as though trying to hide all her burgeoning grievances within the folds of the woman's skirts.

The nanny, her heart aching with pity, held the child tighter and gently patted her back with a soothing hand. "What is the matter, Baor? Be good now and weep no more. Did you not say that when the Eldest Young Master returned, you were going to show him the great fish you had drawn?"

"Baor does not want to show him anymore!" Baor burst into a fresh wail, tears spilling down in a renewed stream. "He does not like Baor… He would not even take Baor's hand just now… Mama used to hold my hand all the time…"

A maid nearby hurriedly leaned in, proffering a handkerchief to help dab away the tears. "The Young Master must simply be too tired. It is not that he dislikes you… perhaps he is merely burdened with heavy affairs…"

"No, he is not!" Baor choked out, her voice tight with a mixture of anger and hurt. "He clearly does not like Baor. Just now… he even told Baor to go and find Nanny to sleep… he would not even look at the drawing Baor worked so hard on… I waited the whole day… the entire day…"

By the end, her voice had gone utterly raspy. Tears fell down her cheeks again in messy streaks.

"Mama always used to say they were so beautiful… *wuuu…*" Her little mouth turned down; she was on the verge of another outburst but forced herself to endure it, her voice dropping to a dull, low murmur: "Baor wants to go home… I want my Mama… This place is not good at all…"

Before the last word had even faded, the sound of a footfall came from outside the door—steady but not fast, each step measured and incredibly light.

The nanny was startled and started to rise, but before she could stand, the door was pushed open.

Moonlight spilled through the opening, casting a long shadow of a figure standing at the threshold. He wore a robe of deep obsidian, his black hair bound neatly in a crown, his expression obscured by the shifting shadows.

It was Lu Xiu.

He should not have come back—or rather, he ought to have allowed this minor melodrama to subside on its own.

Yet he had stood beneath the corridor for a long time. Those soft cries and childish complaints had somehow made it impossible for him to truly turn away and depart. Not until that sentence—*"I want to go home, I want to find my Mama"*—pierced his heart like a needle for reasons he could not name.

His footsteps had turned back of their own accord.

Baor saw him at once. Her small body turned rigid, and she forgot even how to cry. Her large, mist-filled eyes stared fixedly at him, teardrops still clinging to her lashes. Her little face was wrinkled with misery, looking utterly piteous, yet she instinctively straightened her posture, as if afraid he might see the full extent of her wretched state.

"Master Lu…" she called out in a low voice, the words sticky and soft, still saturated with grievance.

Lu Xiu stood at the doorway. He showed no outward sign of anger, though his brow was knit in a slight furrow.

He took two steps into the room, looking at her swollen eyes and damp sleeves; his tone was not heavy, yet it carried a faint note of reproach: "It was merely a suggestion that you go to sleep early, and yet you weep to such an extent? Truly… you are far too delicate."

He recalled how, in his own seventh year, he too had suffered a high fever and cried until his voice broke—yet he had merely been sent to a side chamber to be looked after by an old servant for the night. No one had ever held him like this; even his biological mother had been unable to care for him personally.

From childhood, he had been forced to learn the rigours of strength… and now this child, merely because he had been somewhat cold, wept herself into such a state. It made his heart twist with an inexplicable pang.

Baor blinked, her tiny mouth opening slightly. She did not know whether she ought to argue or lower her head in admission of fault; she could only murmur in a small, hesitant whisper, "You ignored Baor just now…"

The nanny was about to speak to smooth the situation over, but she saw that Lu Xiu had already walked to the side of the couch. He bent down, extending a long arm, and with a practiced, efficient movement, he lifted Baor out of the nanny's embrace.

The action was not particularly tender, but there was no hint of rejection in it either.

Baor's body tensed for a fleeting moment, then she slowly collapsed against his shoulder, her small hand clutching the edge of his robe. She ceased her crying and made no further fuss; only her small nose sniffled in short, rhythmic hitches.

It was as if all she had been waiting for throughout the long day was nothing more than this single embrace.

Lu Xiu held her, standing in the softly flickering candlelight of the silent room. For a long interval, he did not speak.

He looked down at the child in his arms; her face was flushed and swollen, her lashes still wet, but after the storm of tears, her gaze was now unbelievably meek. There was none of the boisterousness from before.

"Very well. I shall look at it—will that suffice?"

Having been lifted so suddenly into the air, her body rising weightlessly, Baor instinctively stretched out her small, soft arms and wrapped them around his neck, her crying breaking into a sudden smile. "Master Lu is the best."

His heart tightened inexplicably, and his throat felt as though something were lodged there—*was that all it took to coax her?*

"You little girl… you truly know how to feign piteousness," he sighed softly, the chill in his tone finally thawing.

Baor tilted her head up and asked in a tiny voice, "Then… will you still look at the big fish Baor drew?"

Lu Xiu was taken aback. Looking at the expectation and careful hope filling her eyes, she looked exactly like he once did when he sought a single word of approval. He averted his gaze and replied in a low voice, "I never said I would never look at it."

He had intended to maintain a cold distance to teach her to restrain her temper—after all, she was the biological daughter of *that man*—but that soft, syrupy declaration of *"Master Lu is the best"* was like a small claw clutching at the very tip of his heart. He found he could not even pretend to be unmoved.

Baor's eyes lit up with brilliance, and the corners of her mouth finally curved upward.

Seeing this, he gave a bitter smile, shaking his head as he muttered to himself, "How is it you are so skilled at acting spoiled? You are far more… adorable than that father of yours was in his youth."

Having spoken, he sighed again—a sound that seemed to be half self-mockery and half resignation.

Chapter 68: Nothing But Gain

The flame atop the stone lantern wavered in the wind, its wick thin as a bean sprout—a mere smudge of terminal yellow reflecting in the Crown Prince's eyes as a shadow that was neither fully alive nor entirely extinguished.

He stopped abruptly beneath the eaves, remaining motionless. His fox-fur mantle rippled softly in the night breeze.

Around him, the world was so silent it left only the soughing of bamboo shadows, rustling like a muted, persistent breath. Du Qian stood exactly half a step behind him, silent as a shadow.

Then the Crown Prince gave a low laugh, so faint it was almost swallowed by the wind. "But tonight," he murmured, voice slow and even as if to himself, "has not been entirely without its reward."

He spoke in an unhurried manner, his tone hovering between a murmur and a quiet monologue.

"All these years, I could never truly see through what it is he desires in his heart. He climbed upward, pressing closer to me—appearing to be a man enamoured with the allure of power. Yet what makes power alluring is never the hollow title itself, but the immense additional value that trails in its wake."

"He seeks neither fame nor beauty; he forms no faction, offers no tribute, covets neither rank nor silver. Others say he is a man of ice and stone—living only for principle and the grace of his lord—and for a time, I almost believed them."

His voice slowed, shading into dark contemplation. "But however still a heart may be, there must always be a lingering attachment." He paused for a heartbeat, a faint chill flickering across his gaze. "Now, at last, I understand."

Light and shadow crossed within his eyes; a trace of cold irony curved the corner of his lips. "In the end, he is human after all. And all men—so long as they are human—have a weakness."

For years he guarded himself with extreme depth, appearing calm and self-possessed on the surface, but all the while, he hid himself profoundly. To think of it now, all of that was merely to shield the one bond he could not sever."

It was not ambition. It was not the pursuit of lust. But that woman and her child.

The Prince's tone remained mild, yet it was as if a heavy chess piece had just settled firmly into the centre of his heart. "The hardest to guard against are never one's enemies," he said quietly, "but the loyal ministers who believe themselves beyond reproach. Xiao Lingyu and that child—they are the only soft ribs in his chest."

He paused for a long moment, his voice turning colder, sharp as a winter blade. "Lu Chou—calm without, restrained within—appears unassailable. But once a man allows himself to feel, he inevitably loses his balance. And where there is a fracture, there lies a point of leverage; where there is a flaw, there lies the means of absolute control."

When he finished, a flicker of dark, deliberate calculation passed through his eyes, gone as swiftly as it came.

He drew the fox-fur tighter and resumed his measured stride, as if the momentary chill of a murderous intent had never been.

The night was ink-black; the wind hummed low along the galleries and eaves, carrying his voice away into the shadows. Only one final murmur lingered, sharp and cold as a blade: "If he cannot withstand even this much, then he is unworthy of my continued trust."

With that, he swept his sleeve and turned toward the temple gates. Contrasted with the previous heaviness of his spirit, his steps now possessed a certain lightness. "Come," he said idly, "let us return. I would see how my Liangdi fares."

* * * * *

The lamps within the inner chamber still burned low; beyond the thin lattice window, the winter wind whispered and sighed faintly against the eaves.

Xiao Lingyu sat leaned by the writing desk, her fingers turning the pages of the account book, yet not a single line entered her mind.

The faint glow of lamplight traced the edge of her cheek, soft yet cold, as if the quiet itself were waiting for something unspoken to break.

The door creaked—just once, a breath of sound in the stillness as the wind pried through the crack and lifted the hem of her sleeve. She did not turn her head. Thinking it was only her maidservant come to deliver a fresh pot of tea, she spoke in a low voice, "Leave it there. I shall rest soon."

No footsteps followed. No reply came through the silence.

And then, all at once, a familiar presence rose behind her. A pair of hands slid beneath her elbows, pulling her back into a sudden, fierce, and wordless embrace.

She froze, her entire being turning rigid and still where she stood.

The man behind her held her close—desperately close—his brow pressed against the hollow of her neck, his breath heavy and uneven, yet he remained utterly silent.

"Don't turn around," he murmured, his voice so low it carried a faint tremor. "Just… let me hold you for a while."

Her lips parted, but the words lodged in her throat, unspoken.

He leaned into the curve of her shoulder and neck as if the emotions he had suppressed all night had finally collapsed; the feelings he had restrained for so long poured out in the sanctuary of this quiet night.

Her own heart began to race, wild as the wind.

At last, she raised her hand and laid it lightly over his, which clasped her waist so tightly she could feel the thrum of his pulse against her palm.

She did not pull away; she did not ask a single question. She simply stood there, letting him hold her, letting him bury every scrap of panic, silent obsession, and regret into the hollow of her shoulder.

He remained silent against her neck for a long time before finally speaking in a voice raspy with a hidden hoarseness: "I thought you would leave on your own…"

A tremor passed through her heart, and her fingers tightened. Finally, she spoke in a voice no louder than a breath, "This time… I had no thought to hide. But if I were truly to leave, I would not do it in silence."

He made no answer. Only his arms tightened again, as if fearing she would slip from his embrace like a ghost in the next heartbeat.

Outside, the wind shifted and grew harsher against the lattice. The candle flame jumped and wavered; she instinctively moved to turn her body, but his hand pressed against her shoulder with a firm weight.

"Don't turn," he said, his voice a low rumble against her ear. "Just stay like this."

She gave a faint, helpless laugh. "What is it you are truly afraid of?"

His breath brushed the back of her neck, carrying a heavy, sorrowful note. "I'm afraid that if I let go, you'll disappear… just as you did five years ago."

At those words, her eyes burned; the world before her blurred through a sudden, hot film of tears.

His next words came quieter, almost a mere breath. "You mean to return to Jiangnan, do you not? Do not be afraid. This time, I shall go with you."

She went still, her voice uncertain and trembling. "You truly can?"

He gave a low hum of assent, a sound of absolute resolve.

As if unable to help herself, or perhaps wanting to lighten the weight in the air, she gave a faint, light-hearted laugh. "Then… very well."

He bent his head, brushing a soft kiss against her hair and his voice was pressed extremely low, muffled by her tresses. "Bring Baor with us. Last time, I nearly failed to protect you both."

Her eyes grew hot, and she dared not look back. He did not release her, as though wanting to knead all the unspoken remorse and the tender affection of these past five years into this single embrace.

"Lingyu," he called her name at last—a sound deep and gravelly. It was a call that seemed to pierce through to her soul, causing her body to tremble. "Mm?"

"Do not be afraid." His voice was husky against her ear. "I want you to remember this—whenever you look back, I will be here."

She stood in a daze, her heart suddenly racing like a drum, pounding as if it would burst from her chest. Had he not held her so tightly from behind, she might have fallen. Heat spread from the base of her neck, her chest tightening until she felt as though she had been placed in a box without air, every limb trembling.

Never had she seen him like this, never had she heard him speak in such a voice—so close, so raw, and so real. Never had she imagined he would hold her with such absolute lack of reservation.

She drew a long, uneven breath, trying to steady her fluttering heart. "I… I know," she managed to whisper.

He shifted slightly, his cheek brushing against the back of her ear, and a soft, deep laugh escaped him. "I am serious."

She bit her lip, finally unable to suppress the swell of longing in her throat. Her voice came faint and shaking. "Then you had better say it… even more clearly."

His voice dropped lower, his words pressing directly against her skin. "Very well."

"Then listen carefully," he said, his breath warm at the curve of her neck. "I love you. My heart is pleased with you. This did not begin only now—it began from the first time I ever laid eyes upon you. Five years ago, I let that chance slip away into the dark. I have not dared to speak of it since."

Her fingers trembled.

A single, silent tear fell, darkening the back of his hand where he held her waist. She closed her eyes, wanting to laugh but failing to make a sound; she simply raised her hand over his and gently clasped his fingers.

"Then you had better keep your word," she whispered. "If you are no longer there when I look back, I will never forgive you."

She leaned her weight into him, for a moment hardly believing this was real—that the man who had once stood with cold indifference was now the one holding her, speaking so plainly. He had once seemed unreachable, yet now he was close enough for her to feel every rhythm of his heart.

Outside, the wind rose and pressed against the window. The candlelight cast two overlapping shadows across the wooden lattice—one before, one behind—joined together as if bound by fate itself.

She remained silent for a long while before speaking again. "This road will not be an easy one."

He answered with quiet, unshakeable certainty. "If you will but take one step toward me, the other nine, I will walk toward you."

She turned her head slightly to look at him, tears still glimmering in her lashes, yet her smile was more radiant than anything before. "When did you learn to say things like that?"

He looked down at her, his voice low and a little rough with feeling. "Because I fear that if I do not speak them now… it may already be too late."

She said nothing more. She simply turned fully and wrapped her arms around him, holding him tighter than before.

The lamps flickered. The night deepened. From far away came the clap of the watchman's wooden clappers—it was already the third watch of the night.

"When do we leave?" she asked softly.

"In a month," he replied. "Before the Winter Solstice. The imperial edict has been issued. The name of Jinhua Gallery and the title of Royal Merchant will return to Jiangnan—along with you."

She nodded against his chest. "Then let us go." She looked up into his face, her gaze calm and resolute. "Since you said you would not let me go again, then this time, I will not turn back."

He took her hand, his palm closing warmly around her slender fingers. A faint smile curved his lips; his eyes, deep and steady, made him appear even more handsome in the wavering light. "No matter where you go, I shall walk beside you."

* * * * *

Night had deepened further. The side chamber lay hushed and still, every sound withdrawn into the shadows; only the inner room still held a wavering flame.

The bed curtains stirred faintly. Baor sat upright upon the quilt, her arms wrapped around the blanket, refusing to lie down. Her two round eyes—bright as grapes in the lamplight—stared fixedly at the man seated by the bedside.

"I want to hear the end of the third story! There is still one left that you haven't finished!" she protested, her voice soft and sticky with sleep, her little mouth turned down in indignation.

Lu Xiu, dressed in a robe the colour of pale moonlight, leaned against the bedpost with one hand propping his temple, one leg hanging carelessly over the side.

The faint blue shadows beneath his eyes spoke of a man long past the point of weariness.

"You are extorting me," he muttered.

"I am not!" Baor clutched the edge of his robe, tilting her head up with wounded seriousness. "You said you would stay with me tonight. You are the adult here who doesn't keep his word."

Lu Xiu let out a low grunt in his throat—not quite a sigh, as if suppressing something or simply surrendering to her. After a pause, he cast her a sidelong glance. "Why do I feel as if I owed you eight hundred taels of silver?"

"How much is eight hundred taels?" she asked at once.

"…" He was speechlessly silent.

Baor, undaunted, began to bargain. "Then just three more stories and that's it!"

Lu Xiu pressed his fingers to his brow, wondering how he had managed to trap himself in this.

All because, that afternoon, she had come running to him in tears, crying, 'Mother and Papa Lord won't play with me!'—and his heart had softened. He had agreed to keep her company for one night. Now here he was, telling stories until he was nearly asleep himself, while the child was still full of spirit.

He looked down at her—a small, warm bundle, her eyes brimming with trust and expectation. Ah well, he thought. It's my own fault for having a loose tongue.

"Once upon a time," he began quietly, his tone slow, low and mild, "there was a fox who hated nothing more than a clingy little raccoon cat. But one day, it happened to meet one…"

"Was it a pretty fox?" Baor interrupted, eyes shining with delight.

"…A vain one," he corrected her flatly.

"Pfft!" Her laughter burst out; she ducked into the quilt, giggling into the fabric, her small warm body leaning softly against his knee. Lu Xiu reached out, steadying her with a light touch. "When you fall asleep, I am leaving."

"You mustn't."

"…Do you still want to hear the story or not?"

"I do!" she declared loudly, then obediently lay down again—though she kept a firm, tiny grip on the hem of his robe.

He looked down at that small hand, wondering for a moment if something had gone wrong in his head. He was not built for such tenderness, yet here he was, possessed of a patience he had never shown to anyone.

A faint smile tugged at his lips, half self-mockery. "Lu Xiu," he murmured under his breath, "you have no one to blame but yourself."

At last, the child's breathing slowed, her small fingers still curled around the fabric of his sleeve.

He looked down at her sleeping face—soft, tranquil, and utterly trusting—and felt a strange, quiet settle over him. He had never imagined that one day, he would sit wakeful through the night for the sake of a child, and find the act so unexpectedly sweet.

Chapter 69: Brothers Part Ways

The flame atop the stone lantern wavered and flickered in the fitful wind, its wick thin and fragile as a bean sprout. The light it cast was dim and faltering, a mere smudge of terminal yellow that reflected in the Crown Prince's eyes as a shadow that was neither fully alive nor entirely extinguished.

He stopped abruptly beneath the shadows of the eaves, remaining utterly motionless. His fox-fur mantle rippled and snapped softly in the cold night breeze.

Around him, the world had fallen into a profound silence, leaving only the soughing of the bamboo shadows as they swayed, rustling like a muted, persistent breath.

Du Qian stood exactly half a step behind him, an ever-present and quiet companion, existing much like a silent shadow merged into the dark.

Then, the Crown Prince let out a low, dry laugh; the sound was so faint it was nearly swallowed by the swirling wind. "But tonight," he murmured, his voice slow and even, as if speaking more to himself than to the night, "has not been entirely without its reward."

His tone was neither rushed nor slow, possessing a quality of detached contemplation.

"For all these years, I could never truly see through the depths of that man's heart to discern what it is he truly desires.

He climbed upward with such diligence, pressing closer to me at every turn—appearing for all the world like a man enamored with the allure of power and status. Yet, what makes power truly alluring is never the hollow title itself, but the immense additional value that trails in its wake."

"He seeks neither fame nor the company of beautiful women; he forms no secret factions, offers no tribute to curry favour, and covets neither noble rank nor silver.

Others say he is a man of ice and stone—living only for the rigour of principle and the grace bestowed by his lord—and for a time, I almost believed those tales myself."

The Prince's voice slowed further, shading into a dark and murky gloom. "But however still a human heart may be, there must always be a lingering attachment, a tether to the mortal world." He paused for a fleeting heartbeat, a faint and sharp chill flickering across his gaze. "Now, at last, I understand."

Light and shadow crossed within the depths of his eyes; a trace of cold irony curved the corner of his lips. "In the end, he is human after all. And all men—so long as they are human—possess a fatal weakness. For years he guarded himself with extreme depth, maintaining a facade of calm and self-possession, but all the while, he was hiding something profound. To think of it now, all of that restraint, all that silence, every mask he wore—it was merely to shield the one bond he could not sever."

It was not ambition. It was not the pursuit of lust. But that woman and her child.

The Prince's tone remained mild, yet it was as if a heavy chess piece had just settled firmly and irrevocably into the centre of his heart. "The hardest men to guard against are never one's overt enemies," he said quietly, "but the loyal ministers who believe themselves to be beyond reproach. Xiao Lingyu and that child—they are the only soft ribs in his chest, the only vulnerabilities in his armour."

He paused for a long moment, his voice turning colder, sharp as a winter blade. "Lu Chou—calm without, restrained within—appears unassailable. But once a man allows himself to feel, he inevitably loses his balance. And where there is a fracture, there lies a point of leverage; where there is a flaw, there lies the means of absolute control."

When he finished speaking, a flicker of dark, deliberate calculation passed through his eyes, gone as swiftly as a ghost. He drew the fox-fur mantle tighter about his shoulders and resumed his measured, steady stride, as if the momentary chill of a murderous intent had never existed.

The night was as black as ink; the wind hummed low along the galleries and eaves, carrying his voice away into the shadows.

Only one final murmur lingered, sharp and cold as a knife's edge: "If he cannot withstand even a burden such as this, then he is unworthy of my continued trust and heavy use."

With that, he swept his sleeve in a sharp motion, turning toward the temple gates. Contrasted with the previous heaviness of his spirit, his steps now possessed a certain lightness. "Come," he said idly to the shadow behind him, "let us return. I would see how my Liangdi fares."

* * * * *

The lamps within the inner chamber still burned low; beyond the thin lattice of the window, the winter wind whispered and sighed faintly against the eaves. Xiao Lingyu sat leaned by the writing desk, her slender fingers turning the pages of the account book, yet not a single line of the figures entered her mind.

The faint, flickering glow of the lamplight traced the delicate edge of her cheek, soft yet cold, as if the very quiet of the room were waiting for something unspoken to break.

The door creaked—just once, a mere breath of sound in the stillness—as the night wind pried through the crack and lifted the hem of her sleeve. She did not turn her head. Thinking it was only her maidservant come to deliver a fresh pot of tea, she spoke in a low, distracted voice, "Leave it there. I shall rest in a short while."

No footsteps followed her command. No reply came through the silence.

And then, all at once, a familiar and overwhelming presence rose behind her. A pair of hands slid beneath her elbows, pulling her back into a sudden, fierce, and wordless embrace.

She froze, her entire being turning rigid and still where she stood.

The man behind her held her close—desperately close—his brow pressed against the hollow of her neck, his breath heavy and uneven, yet he remained utterly silent, as if any word might shatter the fragile moment he was fighting to hold.

"Don't turn around," he murmured, his voice so low it carried a faint, perceptible tremor. "Just… let me hold you for a while."

Her lips parted, but the words lodged in her throat, remaining unspoken between her teeth.

He leaned into the curve of her shoulder and neck as if the emotions he had suppressed throughout the long night had finally collapsed; the feelings he had restrained for far too long poured out in the sanctuary of this quiet night.

Her own heart began to race, wild and erratic as the wind. At last, she raised her hand and slowly, gently laid it over his, which clasped her waist so tightly she could feel the thrum of his pulse against her palm. She did not pull away; she did not ask a single question. She simply stood there, letting him hold her, letting him bury every scrap of panic, every silent obsession, and every regret into the hollow of her shoulder.

He remained silent against her neck for a long time before finally speaking in a voice raspy with a hidden hoarseness: "I thought you would leave on your own… without a word."

A tremor passed through her heart, and her fingers tightened over his. Finally, she spoke in a voice no louder than a rustle, "This time… I had no thought to hide from you. But if I were truly to leave, I would not do so in silence or without a sign."

He made no answer. Only his arms tightened about her again, as if he feared she might slip from his embrace like a ghost in the next heartbeat.

Outside, the wind shifted and grew harsher against the lattice. The candle flame jumped and wavered; she instinctively moved to turn her body, but his hand pressed against her shoulder with a gentle yet firm weight. "Don't turn," he said, his voice a low, vibrating rumble against her ear. "Just stay like this."

She gave a faint, helpless laugh. "What is it you are truly afraid of?"

His breath brushed the back of her neck, carrying a heavy, sorrowful note. "I am afraid that if I let go, you will disappear… just as you did five years ago."

At those words, her eyes burned; the world before her blurred through a sudden, hot film of tears.

His next words came quieter, almost a mere breath. "You mean to return to Jiangnan, do you not? Do not be afraid. This time, I shall go with you."

She went still, her voice uncertain and trembling. "You truly can?"

He gave a low hum of assent, a sound of absolute resolve.

As if unable to help herself, or perhaps wanting to lighten the suffocating weight in the air, she gave a faint, light-hearted laugh that was tinged with emotion. "Then… very well."

He bent his head, brushing a soft kiss against her hair. His voice was pressed extremely low, muffled by her tresses. "Bring Baor with us. Last time, I nearly failed to protect you both. I shall not let that happen again."

Her eyes grew hot, and she dared not look back. He too refused to release her, as though wanting to knead all the unspoken remorse, all the bitter regret, and all the tender affection of these past five years into this single, crushing embrace.

"Lingyu," he called her name at last—a sound deep, gravelly, and rough. It was a call that seemed to pierce through to the very depths of her soul, causing her body to tremble. "Mm?"

"Do not be afraid." His breath brushed against her ear, his voice husky and low. "I want you to remember this—whenever you look back, I will be here."

She stood in a daze, her heart suddenly racing like a drum, pounding as if it would burst through her ribs. Had he not held her so tightly from behind, she might have lost her footing. Heat spread from the base of her neck, her chest tightening until she felt as though she had been placed in a box without air, every limb trembling with the force of his presence.

Never had she seen him like this, never had she heard him speak in such a voice—so close, so raw, and so real. Never had she imagined he would hold her with such absolute lack of reservation.

She drew a long, uneven breath, trying to steady her fluttering heart. "I… I know," she managed to whisper.

He shifted slightly, his cheek brushing against the back of her ear, and a soft, deep laugh escaped him. "I am serious."

She bit her lip, finally unable to suppress the swell of bitterness and longing in her throat. Her voice came faint and shaking. "Then you had better say it… even more clearly."

His voice dropped lower, his words pressing directly against her skin. "Very well."

"Then listen carefully," he said, his breath warm and intoxicating at the curve of her neck. "I love you. My heart is pleased with you. This did not begin only now—it began from the first time I ever laid eyes upon you. Five years ago, I let that chance slip away into the dark. I have not dared to speak of it since."

Her fingers trembled violently. A single, silent tear fell, darkening the back of his hand where he held her waist. She closed her eyes, wanting to laugh but failing to make a sound; she simply raised her hand over his and gently, firmly clasped his fingers.

"Then you had better keep your word," she whispered. "If you are no longer there when I look back, I will never forgive you."

She leaned her weight into him. For a moment, she could hardly believe this was real—that the man who had once stood with cold indifference at the edge of her world was now the one holding her, speaking so plainly and tenderly.

He had once seemed as unreachable as the moon, yet now he was close enough for her to feel every rhythm of his heart against her back.

Outside, the wind rose and pressed against the window. The candlelight cast two overlapping shadows across the wooden lattice—one before, one behind—joined together as if bound by fate itself.

She remained silent for a long while before speaking again. "This road we take… it will not be an easy one."

He answered with quiet, unshakeable certainty. "If you will but take one step toward me, the other nine, I will walk toward you."

She turned her head slightly to look at him, tears still glimmering in her lashes, yet her smile was more genuine and radiant than anything before. "When did you learn to say things like that?"

He looked down at her, his voice low and a little rough with feeling. "Because I fear that if I do not speak to them now… it may already be too late."

She said nothing more. She simply turned fully and wrapped her arms around him, holding him tighter than he held her.

The lamps flickered. The night deepened. From far away came the sharp, hollow clap of the watchman's wooden clappers—it was already the third watch of the night.

"When do we leave?" she asked softly.

"In a month," he replied. "Before the Winter Solstice. The imperial edict has been issued. The name of Jinhua Gallery and the title of Royal Merchant will return to Jiangnan—along with you."

She nodded against his chest. "Then let us go." She looked up into his face, her gaze calm and resolute. "Since you said you would not let me go again, then this time, I will not turn back."

He took her hand, his palm closing warmly around her slender fingers. A faint smile curved his lips; his eyes, deep and steady, made him appear even more handsome in the wavering light. "No matter where you go, I shall walk beside you."

* * * * *

Night had deepened further. The side chamber lay hushed and still, every sound withdrawn into the shadows; only the inner room still held a wavering flame. The bed curtains stirred faintly in the draft. Little Baor sat upright upon the quilt, her arms wrapped tightly around her blanket, refusing to lie down. Her two round eyes—bright as grapes in the lamplight—stared fixedly at the man seated by the bedside.

"I want to hear the end of the third story! There is still one left that you haven't finished!" she protested, her voice soft and sticky with sleep, her little mouth turned down in a pout of indignation.

Lu Xiu, dressed in a robe the colour of pale moonlight, leaned against the bedpost with one hand propping his temple, one leg hanging carelessly over the side. The faint blue shadows beneath his eyes spoke of a man long past the point of weariness.

"You are extorting me, child," he muttered.

"I am not!" Baor clutched the edge of his robe, tilting her head up with wounded seriousness. "You said you would stay with me tonight. You are the adult here, and you are the one who is not keeping his word."

Lu Xiu let out a low, rough grunt in his throat—not quite a sigh, as if suppressing something or simply surrendering to her logic. After a pause, he cast her a sidelong glance. "Why do I feel as if I owed you eight hundred taels of silver?"

"How much is eight hundred taels?" she asked at once, her curiosity piqued.

"…" He was momentarily speechless.

Baor, undaunted, began to bargain with him. "Then just three more stories and that shall be enough!"

Lu Xiu pressed his fingers to his brow, wondering how he had managed to trap himself in this absurdity. It was all because, that afternoon, she had come running to him in tears, crying, 'Mother and Papa Lord won't play with me!'—and his heart had softened. He had agreed to keep her company for one night. Now here he was, telling stories until he was nearly asleep himself, while the child was still full of spirit.

He looked down at her—a small, warm bundle of a person, her eyes brimming with absolute trust and expectation. *Ah well, he thought, it is my own fault for having a loose tongue.*

"Once upon a time," he began quietly, his tone slow, low, and mild, "there was a fox who hated nothing more than a clingy little raccoon cat. But one day, it happened to meet one…"

"Was it a pretty fox?" Baor interrupted him, her eyes shining with delight.

"…A vain one," he corrected her flatly.

"Pfft!" Her laughter burst out; she ducked into the quilt, giggling into the fabric, her small, warm body leaning softly against his knee. Lu Xiu reached out, steadying her with a light touch. "When you finally fall asleep, I am leaving."

"You mustn't."

"…Do you still want to hear the story or not?"

"I do!" she declared loudly, then obediently lay down again—though she kept a firm, tiny grip on the hem of his robe.

He looked down at that small hand, wondering for a moment if something had gone wrong in his head. He was not a man built for such tenderness, yet here he was, possessed of a patience he had never shown to anyone in his life.

A faint smile tugged at his lips, a look of half self-mockery. "Lu Xiu," he murmured under his breath, "you have no one to blame for this but yourself."

At last, the child's breathing slowed into a steady rhythm, her small fingers still curled around the fabric of his sleeve. He looked down at her sleeping face—soft, tranquil, and utterly trusting—and felt a strange, quiet settle over his own soul. He had never imagined that one day, he would sit wakeful through the night for the sake of a child, and find the act so unexpectedly sweet and fulfilling.

Chapter 70: A Glance That Stirs the Heart

The lamps in the sleeping hall glowed faintly, sandalwood drifting in soft curls, a small red-clay brazier warming freshly brewed tea, its fragrance lightly stirring in the air.

Lady Xu Hui sat by the couch, working delicately on a piece of fine gauze, her movements slow and steady, making not the slightest sound.

She suddenly heard footsteps outside the door. Instinctively, she set down her embroidery needle and rose to greet the person approaching.

She saw the Crown Prince with his cloak loosely undone, a layer of weariness resting in his eyes. His fox-fur mantle was still on, his brows faintly drawn together.

"Your Highness," she called to him gently, her voice soft and graceful.

The Crown Prince's gaze settled on her, as if this quiet composure steadied his mind. He said in a low voice, "Why have you not retired?"

"I heard you were discussing matters in the front hall until late at night, so I did not dare sleep early," she replied with a mild smile, stepping forward to help him remove his outer cloak with gentle hands, then personally warming a cup of tea and offering it to him.

He accepted the cup, his fingers long and well-defined, his palm faintly warm. Yet he did not drink at once. Lowering his head to look at her, he spoke very quietly: "Does your hand still hurt?"

"It is no longer serious," she replied, dropping her lashes. "The imperial physician prepared a salve. It is no longer swollen as of today."

Only then did he give a slight nod, saying nothing more.

Seeing the fatigue pressed between his brows, she guided him to sit by the couch. She herself knelt half-seated behind him, both hands gently pressing his shoulders—not heavily, but with precise, measured strength.

"In a few more days, it will be winter. The southern grounds may soon be sealed. If Your Highness still wishes to go hunting, perhaps..." She faltered for a moment. "...perhaps it must be done sooner rather than later."

The Crown Prince lowered his eyes and remained silent. After a long pause, he suddenly spoke: "My lady."

Her hands paused. She answered softly, "I am here."

His voice was steady, yet carried a rare trace of warmth. "Have you ever… resented me in your heart?"

She stilled for a moment, then smiled gently, not a hint of complaint in her tone. "Resent what? To accompany Your Highness like this is already the greatest fortune granted to me."

The Crown Prince said nothing. He merely lifted his hand to lightly cover her wrist, as though quietly feeling the warmth in her palm.

Lady Xu seemed to understand his intention and continued, "I was born of humble origins. I have long known I am unworthy of any formal title. If Your Highness truly wishes to establish a Crown Princess, that would be a blessing for the Great Jin. I… would not dare harbour presumptuous thoughts."

The Crown Prince's gaze deepened, yet he spoke softly. "The list for the Crown Princess was personally drafted by His Majesty."

He paused, his eyes sinking into shadow. "I had originally intended to place your name among them, but feared you would then be criticised, spoken of behind your back… I have always known that you are the one who understands me best."

She gave a gentle smile, her expression calm. "Your Highness holds the affairs of the state close to your heart. How could I not understand? The position of Crown Princess is no trivial matter. One chosen must serve as model for all under Heaven. Someone of my standing is scarcely worth mentioning. That Your Highness has treated me with such consideration is already a great kindness."

She said it softly and with composure, without a trace of pressure.

The Crown Prince lowered his head and looked at her fingers. After a long moment, he spoke in a muted tone: "My lady, you are my confidante."

The words were not heavy, yet they carried great depth. Her fingertips trembled. She lifted her eyes to him, and her lashes glistened faintly with moisture.

"To be remembered by Your Highness in such a way… I have no regrets."

For a moment, the hall was so quiet that only the soft crackle of the brazier could be heard.

The Crown Prince withdrew his hand and said quietly, "Someone in the temple tonight made me realise certain things. Matters of the heart do not necessarily hinder matters of governance, so long as… one maintains balance."

Lady Xu lowered her head, a slight shift flickering in her gaze. She answered in a subdued voice, "If Your Highness truly meets someone who can stand at your side, I would be glad for you."

The Crown Prince looked at her with a faint, unreadable smile, neither agreeing nor denying.

Outside, the wind rose, and the candlelight flickered against the red walls.

Lady Xu smiled softly, her voice carrying a hint of warmth and unspoken tenderness. "Your Highness, it grows late. You should rest."

He looked at her for a long while before finally nodding, his tone very light, tinged with fatigue. "Very well. Speaking with me… can count as rest."

She answered softly and reached to straighten his robe. Her fingertips brushed his shoulder, her movements as gentle and obedient as always.

But he suddenly caught her hand, his voice low. "You are always like this. It makes my decisions all the harder to make."

Lady Xu's heart gave a slight tremor, yet she merely smiled. "If that is the case, then let time decide for you."

That night, the lamps burned without rest. Neither spoke further, yet within that silence, both understood something.

* * * * *

Late autumn, the sky was clear and the frost was cold.

Morning light had just risen; the grassland shimmered gold like a carpet, distant mountains veiled in pale mist.

A trace of early-winter chill hung in the air, yet it failed to suppress the lively atmosphere around today's competition.

The Crown Prince had arranged a banquet at the Southern Park's Eastern Field, holding a "Wild Riders' Race" under the pretext of autumn hunting.

The participants were all sons of noble families, clad in armour and mounted on horses, galloping through the frosted, golden grasslands.

On the viewing terrace, silk and brocade gathered in abundance; ladies of aristocratic households sat in clusters at the front seats, some hiding their lips behind delicate fans as they whispered, some lifting embroidered veils slightly.

Not a single rider had yet entered the field, and already anticipation ran high.

The grassland stretched wide; the frost had not yet lifted. Ginkgo and maple leaves drifted like brocade. The autumn sun remained warm, and a cool wetness lingered in the air, giving the hunt an air both solemn and splendid.

The Crown Prince, rarely appearing in person, was present upon the viewing platform.

He wore a dark robe embroidered with gold patterns, his expression composed.

Seated beside him was the Minister of Revenue, Lu Chou.

Next to him sat a woman in plain attire, her features gentle and refined. At her knee sat a five-year-old girl, large-eyed with long lashes, her brows faintly resembling Lord Lu's.

The little girl was happily eating a cup of osmanthus cake. She suddenly turned to say something to the woman beside her, and the two exchanged a smile. The scene, falling into the eyes of the others in the viewing stands, drew a few discreet glances.

"Look quickly— that child… is she not the one who sat with Young Master Lu the other day at the theatre?"

"She is. I remember someone even said at the time that she was a daughter Young Master Lu kept outside."

"From the looks of things, she seems more like the Master Chou's child?"

"Not necessarily. Look at the woman— she resembles the child in the brows and eyes. Perhaps she is the mother… But I heard Lord Lu has yet to marry?"

"And those eyes— the colour isn't black…"

The whispers were low, yet they spread like wind sweeping over golden grass, stirring ripples. Behind a curtain on the eastern side, Shen Zhaoru held a scented handkerchief. She gazed at the mother and daughter in the field with a faint, ambiguous smile.

She had heard it.

She kept her expression still as she looked toward the woman in plain garments — the woman had just lifted her hand to wipe a crumb of cake from the little girl's lips, her manner gentle and measured.

Beside her, Lu Chou said something in a low voice.

The woman paused slightly, then her lips curved into a small smile. Baor laughed with her eyes arched like crescents, and with a soft patter of steps, climbed onto the man's knee.

Shen Zhaoru's heart gave a sudden jolt. Her fingertips slowly brushed the corner of her handkerchief — if that child truly belonged to Lu Chou, and not to Lu Xiu… well then, she ought to be pleased.

Just then, a horn sounded in the distance, drawing everyone's attention toward the horse field.

The trial-riding formation, made up of the royal hunting guards and the sons of court officials, rode out in an orderly line.

Cloaks streamed behind them, banners snapped sharply in the wind, and the cold breeze swept frost from the ground, their momentum rising like a rainbow.

Suddenly, a single rider galloped forward from the rear.

He wore no armour, only a jet-black riding coat, his hair bound behind a coronet, revealing a tall and well-built figure.

Gold thread embroidered the hem of his coat, and as it fluttered in the wind, it resembled the sweep of a golden serpent.

He mounted his horse in one fluid motion, clean and crisp, almost as though man and horse were one. Hooves struck the earth like drums, the sound reverberating; the guards unconsciously gave way down the middle.

"Who is that?" a young noblewoman asked softly.

"The Lu family's elder son, a son of concubine, Lu Xiu."

"With such presence… I thought he must be the heir of some great military clan."

"It is a curious thing. He was not trained in the army yet taught himself with no master. Now he serves as Deputy Commandant of the Palace

Guard. In recent years, he has taken first place in every military riding trial."

Shen Zhaoru's hand paused on her teacup. The tea did not spill, but she froze for a moment.

He is here.

Riding out of the wind, out of that silhouette in her dreams that refused to fade.

By now, Lu Xiu had already galloped into the field.

He took bow and arrow, loosed three shots in succession — the strings had barely sounded before the falling targets hit the ground, drawing gasps of astonishment from the viewing stands.

The ends of his hair were slightly damp, yet his expression was cold as a winter star. As he guided his horse to turn, he glanced once toward the viewing terrace.

He did not linger, but the brief look cut through the air like a cold sword-light, striking straight into the chest.

Shen Zhaoru's heart shook violently.

Her handkerchief almost slipped from her fingers; her fingertips trembled, and a faint flush swept across her cheeks.

Was that glance… truly an illusion?

On the viewing terrace, even the Crown Prince let the smile fade from his face.

He turned slightly and spoke to Lu Chou in a low voice:"Your illegitimate elder brother is remarkably handsome, spirited even."

Lu Chou gave a faint smile and did not reply further.

The wind in the field rose again, hooves thundered like rolling storms, yet upon the viewing stands, another silent contest was being waged, some were astonished, some were stirred, and some… began to feel uneasy.

"That Lu Xiu possesses such exceptional talent. It seems he hides himself well in daily life. Hmph, he certainly knows how to seize a moment to draw all eyes."

At her side, someone murmured in agreement:

"He does indeed know how to seize the moment — the nature of a concubine-born son."

The woman who had spoken earlier let her expression turn faintly cold. She brushed the corner of her sleeve and said no more.

Sunlight fell across the man's brows and eyes; his eyelashes lowered slightly, his expression composed and cold.

He competed with no one, yet every gallop, every arrow, landed at precisely the right rhythm. His bearing seemed innate, forming its own aura.

"Far too handsome…" someone whispered, transfixed.

Shen Zhaoru could no longer distinguish the voices around her. Her heart suddenly leapt, as though struck hard.

She had seen him in plain garments, in court attire; seen him half-leaning and half-smiling within Drunken Moon Pavilion; seen him standing in Moonriver Courtyard with cold indifference as he looked back at her.

But she had never seen him—like this.

Never seen him shining so brightly.

Her lips pressed together without her noticing, her chest tightening in waves, a fleeting panic flashing through her eyes.

How can he… so easily make someone's heart stir?

The drums in the field sounded again. The group of riders moved like flying dragons, chaotic yet powerful, wind howling like thunder.

And then that dark figure suddenly surged ahead, a single rider taking the lead. His long whip flashed like lightning, sweeping past the crimson silk target—

Bullseye.

Just as gasps of astonishment rose from the stands like a swelling tide, the figure in the field — the one who stood like the moon surrounded by lesser stars.

Suddenly turned his gaze toward the distant crowd.

His sharp eyes locked onto a figure clothed in pale violet, deep and burning, like autumn fire, looking straight into her eyes.

Their gazes met.

Her heart tightened violently.

She was no longer certain whether his action was intentional — or whether she was merely imagining things.

Shen Zhaoru's fingertips turned pale as she tightened her hold on the corner of her handkerchief.

Behind her, the Crown Prince seemed to notice something and let out a soft laugh.

"This Lu Xiu… so young, yet rather skilled at capturing admiration. Look at that group of young ladies — whose eyes are not stuck to him? Even I am almost turned into a mere backdrop."

She jolted slightly and lowered her gaze.

"His martial skills are exceptional. It is natural that people admire him."

The Crown Prince's smile deepened, his tone carrying a layered meaning.

"Not only admire, I imagine. After today's competition, many hearts will be lost to him."

Shen Zhaoru did not respond.

She only slowly tightened her grip on the handkerchief, a sense of urgency and unsettled trembling rising in her eyes in a way she had never felt before.

Out on the field, Lu Xiu had already dismounted. He cupped his fists in a composed salute.

His expression was as usual, his bearing cold and austere, completely unaware that this morning's single ride into the arena had quietly claimed the hearts of countless young women and also… the quickening beat of hers, which she could no longer control.

Chapter 71: A Hairpin as a Pledge

At the edge of the grassland, the race had only just ended, yet its echoes still hung in the air. The crowd remained loud and buoyant; children darted and chased one another; on the viewing stands the noble ladies' laughter had not yet subsided. Pair after pair of eyes still clung, reluctant to look away, fixed upon the black-clad rider.

Lu Xiu swung down from his horse. An attendant stepped forward and presented the prize that marked the field's champion: a pendant of cold jade. Its colour was gentle and refined, carved into the shape of a phoenix tail and drifting clouds. It could be worn by man or woman alike. At its heart, a faint frostiness still seemed to linger; when held, it chilled the palm at once.

He lowered his gaze to glance at it. His brow did not so much as stir. Plainly, he took little interest in the reward.

"Uncle—!"

A crisp, milky voice rang out. From among the seats of the viewing stand, a tiny figure came running—skirts fluttering, steps swift and fearless. It was Little Baor.

He paused, caught off guard. Before he could even react, the little girl had already thrown herself to the space before him, tilting her face up. Her eyes shone brightly as she stared at the jade pendant in his hand.

"Wah, it's so pretty!" She clasped both hands against her chest, her admiration sincere and unfeigned. "It's like… it's glowing!"

He looked at her, the corner of his lips lifting slightly. He dropped into a half-crouch and held the cold jade pendant out toward her.

"If you like it, then take it."

Little Baor accepted it with both hands. She studied it for a moment, reluctant to part with it even for a breath. Then, as though something suddenly came to mind, she lifted her head and looked toward the viewing stand.

"Pretty big sister!"

Not far off, Shen Zhaoru had been standing behind the crowd all along. She had not spoken, yet her gaze had never truly left this place.

She had not expected the little girl to wave and shout in her direction. She froze, and almost instinctively glanced to the side—as if to confirm the child could not possibly mean her. Yet the little girl was already running toward her, cheerful and unrestrained.

"Slow down—careful, you'll fall," Shen Zhaoru said without thinking, crouching at once to catch the child's wobbling little body.

"Pretty big sister, do you remember Baor?" Little Baor patted her chest with pride. "That day at the theatre! Baor and Uncle were sitting right across from you!"

Hearing the child call him "Uncle" with her own ears, Shen Zhaoru's lips curved into a faint smile before she could stop it.

"Of course I remember. A little girl this pretty—how could anyone forget?"

Little Baor spread her palm and displayed the cold jade pendant like a treasure, holding it up high—so high it rose above her own head. She craned her chin and asked earnestly,

"Pretty big sister, look! Is it pretty?"

Shen Zhaoru blinked, her gaze resting on the pendant—cold as jade, clear as frost. After a moment, she answered softly,

"Mmm. It's beautiful."

"It's Uncle who gave it to Baor! He's the most amazing!" The child's eyes gleamed.

It was the first time Shen Zhaoru had seen, from such close distance, the girl's unusual eye colour.

"Your name is Baor, is it?" Shen Zhaoru said gently. "Your eyes are like agate—so very beautiful."

Praised so directly, Little Baor's grin widened at once. Without hesitation she thrust the jade pendant toward Shen Zhaoru.

"Then I'll give this jade-jade to Pretty big sister!" she declared, utterly satisfied. "Because big sister said Baor is pretty!"

Before Shen Zhaoru could refuse, the child shoved the pendant into her palm with stubborn insistence, patted her little skirt as though pleased with her own decision, then turned and ran straight back toward Lu Xiu.

The cold jade in Shen Zhaoru's hand carried a mingling of warmth and chill, as though it still retained the heat of his palm.

She lowered her eyes to look at the pendant, her expression complicated. Her fingers tightened, then loosened—again and again—

yet the jade's coolness could not temper the heat burning in her own hand. She hesitated, struggled, and in the end could not bring herself to let go.

Her gaze followed the little girl as she ran toward that tall, slender figure dressed in ink-black. When he turned—and, inadvertently, his eyes swept toward her—

Her heart lost the rhythm it had always known.

* * * * *

Lu Xiu watched the child come bounding back. Those large eyes were full of smug triumph as she called out,

"Uncle—! I gave the jade-jade to Pretty big sister!"

His gaze paused for a fraction. One hand went behind his back. His face betrayed nothing. He only asked, as though it did not matter,

"Mmm. Why did you give it to her?"

"Because Baor saw Uncle when we watched the play that day—Uncle kept looking at that pretty big sister," Baor said, frowning as she tried to make her reasoning very serious. Then she added, as if it were an obvious conclusion, "And pretty big sister kept looking at Uncle too."

It was only a child's babble, a child's innocent logic—yet for some reason, at those words, something struck lightly against his chest.

Lightly.

And yet it could not be ignored.

That cold jade pendant was what he had won. It was what she had received.

But it had not been placed into her hand by him.

* * * * *

The afterglow of sunset lay slantwise across a narrow path through the woods. Orange-red light spilled through the silhouettes of bare branches, scattering across the ground where a thick layer of mottled fallen leaves lay piled. A stream murmured beside the path. A small bridge of green stone crossed it in quiet stillness. There was no one in sight—only the wind and the water interweaving at the ear.

The lively horse-racing meet had already dispersed, yet Shen Zhaoru found an excuse to remain behind. She did not return home with the others.

The cold jade pendant was still in her hand.

When she reached the bridge, she slowed, unease rising in her chest. She weighed it again and again, and in the end followed the horse track, choosing this secluded stretch—hoping to meet him where few would come.

Her fingertips traced the phoenix tail and drifting-cloud pattern carved into the jade. The pad of her finger was faintly chilled. Her heartbeat was disordered, skipping and stumbling.

She knew she should not have come. Yet there was a softness in her heart she could not drive away.

Then she heard it—a light sound of hoofbeats behind her.

She turned her head. Lu Xiu was approaching at an unhurried pace.

At the sight of the figure she had been waiting for, she let out a breath without realizing she had been holding it.

He rode through the dying light and the shadows of the trees, man and horse moving as if of one body.

His robes lifted and streamed; the wind traveled with him. Hooves pressed into fallen leaves with a soft, crisp rustle.

When he suddenly saw her standing by the bridge, something like a smile stirred faintly at the corner of his lips. As she had hoped, he tightened the reins, and the horse obeyed, coming to a stop.

He dismounted in one smooth motion and stepped forward with calm ease.

"Miss Shen," he said, "you have not yet left?"

She lowered her gaze. She opened her palm to reveal the pendant.

"What the little girl gave me earlier… it is not proper." Her voice was quiet. "Please take it back."

He glanced at it. The smile in his eyes did not deepen.

"Once it has been given, it is yours."

"Unearned gifts are not to be accepted," she said softly. She lifted her eyes to him. "I cannot simply take a kindness for nothing. I do not even know how I ought to thank you."

His gaze shifted. A low laugh escaped him. He stepped one pace closer.

"If you truly wish to thank me," he said, "then why not… walk a stretch with me?"

She froze, about to answer, yet he had already turned slightly, leading his horse.

Lu Xiu extended one hand, and with a small bow offered it toward her. His tone sounded casual, almost offhand, and yet beneath it lay sincerity that was hard to refuse—along with a trace of teasing warmth.

"This road is not short. Walking would be tiring." He tilted his head. "Shall we ride together? One horse. Is that all right?"

The wind swept through the treetops. Leaves whispered. Light fell on his brows and eyes like an accidental gentleness.

Shen Zhaoru's fingers tightened around the cold jade pendant. Her heartbeat abruptly slowed by a half beat. Standing by the bridge, she lifted her face to look at him, and felt as though even the air had thinned.

In that moment, heaven and earth were quiet.

At last, she nodded—lightly.

He did not speak further. He mounted with brisk efficiency, then reached down and held his hand out to her.

She looked at that hand—long, clean, knuckles defined. She drew a deep breath and placed her hand in his.

With one pull, he drew her up and settled her before him. Hooves moved again; wind returned. He gathered the reins, turned the horse, and said softly,

"Hold steady."

She answered, her voice so faint it was nearly inaudible.

In that instant, she had no idea that this short journey would become the heart's trial of her entire life.

Later, she would think back often to that autumn day: yellow leaves covering the bridge, the woodland path, the two of them upon one horse.

He steadied her with practiced ease, then swung up behind her, seating himself close. Under the afterglow, the horse walked at an unhurried pace. Their sleeves stirred in the wind. Their thoughts rippled faintly. The mountains and forest bore witness; light and shadow wrote the record.

Dusk deepened. The long wind turned cool, sweeping through the trees. The reddened sky spilled a whole earth of mortal colour, casting it upon the horse they shared.

Shen Zhaoru sat in front. He held the reins with one hand; with the other, he let his palm settle slowly at her waist. Through the layers of cloth, he did not press hard—yet the contact was steady, close, leaving no way to flee.

"Miss Shen said earlier—one does not accept unearned gifts," he murmured, his voice low and threaded with the faintest smile. "Then let that cold jade pendant… be my token of thanks for Miss Shen sharing this ride with me today."

Shen Zhaoru shifted, trying to draw a little distance between them, yet his arm held her in place with quiet firmness. She forced herself to remain composed.

"I am not worthy of such a courtesy," she said. "It is I who should thank Lord Lu for carrying me."

"Miss Shen is too polite," he replied, the tone unchanged—light as drifting clouds, calm as the wind.

"Miss Shen is talented and refined, with a cold clarity of bearing. In the Grand Tutor's residence you are known as a true jewel. For me to have such an opportunity today—it is only because Miss Shen deigns to look kindly upon me."

Shen Zhaoru startled. She turned her head; their eyes met.

High on horseback, the wind lifted a few strands of hair by her ear, and also stirred a hidden turbulence in the depths of his gaze—something that flashed and vanished before it could be grasped.

She lowered her voice.

"Lord Lu… do not joke."

"I am not joking," he answered softly.

His eyes darkened for an instant. His voice suddenly grew very light, very slow—and he changed both the way he addressed her and the way he referred to himself. In a heartbeat, the air turned hot, teasing, and dangerously intimate.

"Zhaoru…" he said. "If I told you I once had a thought—of borrowing your name, using your standing, to climb over the high walls I, a concubine-born son, cannot enter—would you believe me?"

Shen Zhaoru shuddered. She turned fully, her eyes filled with shock.

He looked into her stunned gaze and gave a short laugh—bitter at the edges.

"I am not a gentleman," he said. "When I first met you, I thought: if you were willing to look my way, then why not borrow the momentum and climb? You are the Grand Tutor's legitimate daughter. A power house at court. For a time, the voices calling for you to become Crown Princess were louder than for anyone else."

"Lu Xiu—you—how can you…!"

"But later," he cut her off at once. His voice fell, sounding like self-mockery—and yet also like confession. "Later I realized you were not like the noble daughters I imagined. You look at people truly. You believe truly."

His breath brushed near her ear as the horse continued on.

"You ask whether I regret it." He let out a quiet, low laugh. "I regretted it too early. If I had awakened a little later, perhaps… I might have managed to deceive you into a moment of heart-movement."

Something struck Shen Zhaoru as if with a heavy hammer. Her breath caught; her face flushed, she did not know whether from shame or alarm.

His voice sank even lower, nearly against her ear.

"And now—what if I told you that it is no longer about weighing identities, no longer about calculating status…" He paused, and the next words fell like a slow, hot brand. "What if it is simply… that I like you. You, as a person."

The wind seemed to stop. The world seemed to hold its breath.

Shen Zhaoru bit her lip. Both hands gripped the saddle before her so tightly her knuckles paled. Her heartbeat was chaos—yet she forced her voice hard, red-faced, as if scolding him could anchor her.

"Lord Lu speaks like this—how can you not be called frivolous!"

He did not argue. He only said softly,

"Very well. Then remember this: the first time I was frivolous with you—was this moment."

He freed one hand. Without asking, he reached up and plucked a pearl-inlaid gold hairpin from her hair—so domineering it was almost outrageous. Heat surged to her face.

"Did you not say you wished to thank me as well?" he said, perfectly calm. "Then in exchange—this hairpin shall be mine."

"Hey—you—how could you…!" Shen Zhaoru's face burned through, and she thought, at least he sits behind me on horseback—at least he cannot see how helpless I look right now.

He said no more, soon, he tightened the reins and rode on, careful to steady her within his hold. Gradually, the horse emerged from the woods. An orange-red sun lay slantwise upon the ridge ahead.

He drew the reins in, holding her securely—as though he had already decided he would not let her slip farther and farther out of reach again.

And in his heart, he knew it with brutal clarity.

Shen Zhaoru was light.

Moonlight he, a concubine-born son, should never be allowed to possess—yet could not help but draw near.

He wanted her.

He wanted her so eagerly, with nothing hidden, with nothing ashamed.

Chapter 72: The Illegitimate Son's Ambition

The wind had turned colder; night was slowly deepening.

Lu Xiu dismounted in a smooth, practised motion, his steps light, though something within him was still faintly unsteady, as if the day's earlier stir had not yet settled.

The horse race earlier that morning had been loud and lively, a spectacle that drew countless eyes.

Under the watch of the entire crowd, he had taken first place—becoming the focus of every gaze. When he won that piece of cold jade, he had thought nothing of it.

But when Baor came bounding over, her eyes sparkling as she exclaimed, "It's so pretty!"—he had simply handed it to her without a second thought.

Who could have guessed that the child would turn around and, without the slightest hesitation, give it away.

—Give it to her.

When Shen Zhaoru accepted it, she had lowered her gaze with a quiet, gentle smile. That smile still lingered in his vision now, like autumn water catching the glow of sunset, its ripples yet to fade.

He had thought the day would end there. Yet she had come—alone, with that pendant in hand, saying only "I cannot accept without merit"—and that single sentence had exchanged for a shared ride through the forest, a span of solitude, and a confession he had never imagined he would speak aloud.

He had escorted her all the way to the lane before the Shen residence, careful not to let the horse's hooves make a stir.

He only said, "Your residence is close from here. Better if you walk the rest, so as not to invite idle talk."

She nodded lightly, said nothing more, but before turning away, she looked back at him once.

That glance—gentle with a quiet glow—fell upon his heart like lingering dusk upon still waters, the ripples slow to still.

He replayed the events of the day over and over on his way back, each detail vivid, and by the time he returned to the Lu estate, night had fully settled.

The gates were half-closed. As soon as he stepped past the shadow wall, a young servant hurried towards him.

"Master, the Lord has been waiting in the study for some time. The Master Chou is there as well."

"This late?" Lu Xiu lifted a brow, casually removing his cloak and handing it to the servant, a trace of amusement still lingering on his lips. "What now? Did my dear younger brother displease Father as well?"

The servant bowed his head carefully. "This servant dares not speculate, but… the Lord does not look to be in a pleasant mood."

Lu Xiu smoothed his robe with an idle hand and walked on.

As he neared the study door, he heard from within the faint sound of a teacup being knocked askew, as if something had been upset.

He pushed the door open.

Smoke curled faintly through the room; lamplight flickered in unsteady patterns across the walls.

Lu Chou was already standing on the right side of the main hall, his expression calm and unreadable.

Their father, Lu Wenqian, stood before the window with his hands clasped behind his back, saying nothing, his posture rigid.

This lineup… was clearly more than just "waiting for him."

"Father. Younger Brother." He cupped his hands in greeting, his tone as mild and composed as ever.

Lu Wenqian turned, his gaze sweeping once across both sons before he finally spoke in a low, grave voice.

"Good. You're both here. Saves me the trouble of calling you one by one."

He pointed at the list placed on the desk.

"This matter should have been overseen by the household's Madam, but this manor has only concubines, and your grandmother is ill and unfit to exert herself. Thus, I can only make the selection myself for the two of you. Especially since, in recent days, whispers from the palace speak of shifts in the struggle for the heir apparent—East Palace grows steadier.

The Crown Prince's residence sent word, hinting they intend to choose a marriage to assert their standing. I made inquiries. There are names you know on this list."

His tone shifted sharply, and he fixed his gaze on Lu Chou.

"It is the Second Princess. His Majesty intends to match you with her, to solidify the Crown Prince's faction."

Lu Chou replied in a steady voice,

"Your son already has someone he holds in his heart."

A cold laugh escaped Lu Wenqian.

"You think I do not know your every action? Your 'beloved'? Do you even understand who she is? A Jiangnan merchant woman. A widow with a child."

"This does not hinder anything. What your son values is her steadfast nature—"

"Silence!" Lu Wenqian's fury burst forth, impossible to suppress.

Hearing this, Lu Xiu lifted a brow.

So this blockhead truly still hasn't realised that Baor is his own blood daughter? Unbelievably slow.

His father's scolding had barely fallen when Lu Xiu, already lounging comfortably in his seat, lazily ran slender fingers along the rim of a teacup and drawled,

"Father, don't stop Second Brother. I've met that little girl several times—quite adorable, quick-witted too. And she looks rather a bit like him…"

Lu Wenqian slammed the table, rising abruptly.

"You stop your flippant remarks! I was planning to choose a marriage for you as well. There is a list for you here too—several noble houses, their illegitimate daughters—"

Lu Xiu's idle look vanished; he straightened slightly, answering with unexp

Lu Chou was already standing to the right of the main hall, his expression calm.

Lu Wenqian stood before the window with his hands clasped behind his back, saying nothing at all.

This posture… clearly meant this was not as simple as merely waiting for him.

"Father, Chou." Lu Xiu cupped his hands in greeting, his tone as composed as usual.

Lu Wenqian turned, his gaze sweeping over his two sons, before finally speaking in a low, heavy voice:

"Good. You are both here. Saves me the trouble of calling you one by one."

He pointed to the list laid out on the desk.

"This matter should have been handled by the Madam of the household, but the Lu family has only a concubine, and your grandmother is ill at present and unfit to labour. Therefore, I must choose on your behalf. Especially as word from the palace these days speaks of movement in the struggle for the heir apparent—the East Palace grows steadier. The Crown Prince's residence sent a message, hinting they intend to choose a marriage to assert their standing. I asked around. There is someone familiar among the names."

His tone shifted, and he abruptly fixed his eyes on Lu Chou.

"It is the Second Princess. His Majesty intends to match you with her, to stabilise the Crown Prince's faction."

Lu Chou replied quietly,

"Your son already has someone in his heart."

A cold laugh escaped Lord Lu.

"You think I do not know your every movement? Your so-called beloved? Do you know who she is? A Jiangnan merchant woman. A widow with a child."

"This does not hinder anything. What your son values is her resilient character—"

"Silence!" Lu Wenqian's anger rose uncontrollably.

At those words, Lu Xiu lifted a brow.

This fool truly still hasn't realised that Baor is his own child? He really is slow beyond belief.

Lu Wenqian had not yet finished, when Lu Xiu leaned back in his chair with perfect ease, long fingers idly tracing his teacup as he said,

"Father, do not stop Younger Brother. I have met that little girl several times—she is quite adorable, clever in temperament, and she even resembles Younger Brother a little…"

Lu Wenqian slammed the desk and rose abruptly.

"You keep your frivolous remarks to yourself! I was planning to select a marriage for you as well. There is a list for you here too—several noble households, their illegitimate daughters—"

Lu Xiu's idle expression tightened; he straightened slightly and answered with rare seriousness,

"No. Your son also has someone in his heart."

"Which family?"

Lu Xiu gathered his thoughts, allowing a faint smile to appear, and spoke words that stunned the room.

"The Shen family's legitimate daughter, Shen Zhaoru."

When he finished, no one answered. For a brief moment, the air itself seemed to freeze.

A moment later, Lu Chou's lips curved slightly, as though he had heard an amusing joke.

"The Imperial preceptor's legitimate daughter, the capital's foremost talented lady—Shen Zhaoru?"

Lu Xiu nodded, his expression unchanged.

"Yes."

Lu Chou said nothing further. He merely let out a quiet snort, one eyebrow lifting as he looked at him. The smile did not reach his eyes. He really dares to say it.

"You—"

Lord Lu Wenqian raised a trembling finger at his elder son.

"I truly did not realise your ambition had grown this large."

He flipped open the booklet in his hand.

"The Imperial preceptor's household is absolutely impossible. There are still several noble families with legitimate daughters suitable for you—"

The air stalled for a beat.

Lu Chou turned back towards him, his gaze cooling in an instant, like snow-laden wind pressing down on branches.

Lord Lu's chest rose and fell sharply with anger.

He pointed at him and shouted,

"Are you mad? Do you know who Shen Zhaoru is? The Imperial preceptor's only daughter, listed as a candidate for the Crown Princess! And you dare harbour such thoughts? Outrageous! If even a whisper of this spreads, the entire Lu family will be dragged down!"

Lu Xiu let out a slow, unhurried laugh, though there was not the slightest hint of retreat.

"I only ask one question—if I truly can marry her, will Father permit me not to marry any other woman?"

"Ridiculous!"

Lord Lu's anger flared into a disbelieving laugh.

"You two brothers—one the legitimate son, wanting to marry down to a merchant widow with a child and raise her to the main wife's seat; the other wanting to marry up into the Crown Prince's future marital home—do you think the Lu family has no rules?"

The tension tightened further.

The lamplight flickered within the study, falling across their faces, scattering shadows; the situation stretched taut like a bowstring.

Lu Xiu slowly rose to his feet, hands clasped behind him. There was a hint of a smile in his eyes, though it did not reach his heart.

"In that case… why don't we both refrain from marrying? That way Father need not trouble himself."

"What nonsense—"

Lord Lu jabbed a long finger back and forth between his two sons, chest heaving.

"One is twenty-four, the other twenty-three, and neither intends to marry—what does this look like?"

"Father, pray calm your anger. Your son will soon depart for Jiangnan by order of the Crown Prince to carry out the purge of corruption. This matter can be discussed again when I return to the capital."

Having spoken, Lu Chou cupped his hands in a formal salute and made to rise and leave.

Seeing this, Lu Xiu naturally felt the moment could not be wasted. He followed at once, saying,

"Father has taught me to be cautious and restrained since childhood, but he never taught me how not to be moved."

He, too, cupped his hands, turned, and walked out, leaving behind only a single sentence that lingered faintly within the study:

"I will marry her—Shen Zhaoru. My intention will not change."

* * * * *

The study door creaked open.

Lu Chou walked ahead, expression cool. Lu Xiu followed behind, his manner relaxed, a faint, ambiguous smile playing at the corner of his mouth.

The two descended from the moonlit platform, and just as they stepped past the covered corridor, they saw a matron in plain satin standing at the foot of the steps.

When she saw them, she immediately stepped forward and said respectfully,

"The Old Madam requests the Master Xiu to come to her couchside."

At these words, Lu Chou's steps halted. He turned instinctively to look at the matron.

Lu Xiu raised an eyebrow and paused as well, speaking in a lazy tone,

"Did you perhaps misspeak, Matron? Should it not be the Master Chou?"

But the matron smiled steadily, her voice firm,

"The Old Madam said the Master Xiu. This old servant's ears are quite sound—how could I mistake such an instruction?"

A faint flash of surprise crossed Lu Chou's eyes, but he said nothing.

He merely lifted a hand to dust his sleeve, then turned and walked away without a word.

Lu Xiu, however, was momentarily stunned. He quickly put away his smile, cupped his hands, and said,

"Then I shall trouble you to lead the way."

* * * * *

Within Huichun Hall, the lights were soft and warm, sandalwood burning quietly in the air.

The Old Madam reclined slightly on her couch, wrapped in a grey-blue crane-embroidered cloak, her white hair pinned meticulously without a single strand out of place.

She did not raise her head; she only spoke in a soft tone. "Come sit."

Lu Xiu obeyed, stepping forward and kneeling on the cushion before her couch, his expression calm.

The Old Madam slowly lifted her gaze to him, her eyes sharp as a blade, though tempered with a trace of compassion.

"Your father has shown you the list, has he not?"

He feigned ignorance. "What list?"

The Old Madam gave a cold snort, her gaze sweeping sideways at him.

"Playing dumb in front of me?"

Seeing this, he withdrew the hint of playfulness, his tone still gentle yet without the slightest retreat.

"He gave it to me, but I did not look at it."

"Why?"

Lu Xiu lowered his head and said nothing.

The Old Madam remained silent for a moment before letting out a soft sigh.

"You child… ever since you were young, you have kept your words locked tight. Even now, you refuse to speak?"

The corner of Lu Xiu's mouth moved faintly before he finally opened his lips.

"Grandson is well aware that, as a son born of a concubine, I cannot easily ascend high halls. And being flesh and blood, it is likewise impossible to command one's affections. The young lady I admire… I admire her because she is exceptional, and my heart bends. She is a high branch, and I entertained thoughts… I simply did not expect that after everything today, I would find myself all the more reluctant to let go."

The Old Madam coughed lightly twice, raising a hand to cover her mouth, though her gaze did not leave him for even a moment.

"Your mother has endured much hardship in this household over the years. I, your grandmother, have not been blind to it. Do not blame me for never lifting her to a higher status. After all, she was only a maid when she first entered the family…"

She paused briefly.

"With your status, reaching where you stand today is already something to be proud of. But you must remember—whatever thoughts you have, you are still a son of the Lu family. Even as a concubine-born son, you are still the elder son of your father, the Honourable Minister Lu."

She paused again, her tone deepening.

"Do not make yourself too small, and do not let yourself grow too wild."

Lu Xiu lifted his eyes to meet his grandmother's, his expression steady and sure.

"Grandson has never dared harbour desires for things that do not belong to me. Since childhood, I have known clearly what should or should not be mine. But… if she is willing to walk towards me, then grandson will not retreat even half a step."

The Old Madam paused for a brief moment, then gave a faint smile.

"I had not expected you to be able to say such words. Since that is the case, I will not stop you, but neither can I shield you. What you wish for is not something I can secure for you. If you truly have the ability, then go and obtain it yourself."

Her tone cooled slightly.

"The Lu family does not lack clever sons; what it lacks are those who can shoulder responsibility."

Lu Xiu bowed low in acknowledgement.

"Grandson understands."

The Old Madam studied him for a moment before her voice softened slightly.

"But you must remember this—if, in the end, that young lady gives her hand to another, then you must… by no means take her by force."

Lu Xiu lowered his gaze and answered,

"If that day truly comes, grandson will naturally sever all thoughts."

After the eldest grandson withdrew, the Old Madam let out a long, heavy sigh. The attendant matron beside her immediately offered a cup of hot tea.

"Old Madam, pray do not trouble your heart further. Sons and grandsons have their own fortunes. Both young masters are grown now and capable of bearing matters."

The Old Madam turned slightly and said,

"You tell me—this child resents me for not raising his mother to the position of principal wife, leaving him to carry the name of a concubine-born son his whole life. But tell me again—are we the sort of family to be heartless? Look at all the other households—what family allows a maid girl to bear the eldest son of the house? Which of them does not resolve such matters with a single bowl of medicine to remove the trouble?"

Seeing her Madam growing agitated, the attendant matron hurried to gently pat her back.

"Indeed so. That the Master Xiu still stands here unharmed is entirely due to your kind heart, Old Madam."

The Old Madam let out a weary breath.

"Ah… I only hope he knows how to advance and retreat, and does not resort to force. Otherwise, the Lu family…"

Chapter 73: Able to Abandon, Unable to Confess

Little Baor stood upon the steps outside the hall, wearing small shoes embroidered with floral clusters. One foot was on tiptoe while the other swung back and forth, her rounded little face pressed against the doorframe as she watched the maidservants bustling to and fro inside, her eyes shining as bright as crescent moons.

"Is Mama going back to Jiangnan?" she suddenly turned and asked, her copper-coloured pupils reflecting the flickering lamplight in the wind, sparkling brilliantly.

Inside, the room was a hive of activity. Xiao Lingyu was leaning over, instructing Suyu to pack away brocade boxes and ledgers; hearing her daughter's voice, her movements faltered slightly.

Before she could even speak, little Baor was already clapping her small hands in delight, saying gleefully, "Back to Jiangnan! I want to see the big boats and eat osmanthus cakes! And, and... the smell of fish when it's being grilled—" As she spoke, she stood on her toes, her gaze appearing as if she could already see the water alleys, the blue bricks, and the ponds full of lotus leaves.

Xiao Lingyu let out a chuckle; the journey had not even begun, yet this little person's heart had already flown a thousand miles.

Yet in the next heartbeat, little Baor's eyes suddenly widened as if she had just remembered something, her gaze shining even brighter than before.

She raised her voice several measures, her tone filled with innocent rapture and surprise: "Then... then is Papa Lord coming with us too?"

"Yes." She nodded gently, a trace of sweetness surfacing in her heart.

Baor's tone was as if she had discovered some monumental piece of good news. Her tiny body spun in a circle where she stood, her hands clasped to her chest and her little face flushed crimson, her eyes curving like a pair of crescents.

"That is wonderful! Papa Lord and Mama, and Baor, all going together—that is the best!"

As she reached the final words, she gave a light stomp of her foot, the irrepressible joy in her voice bubbling up like froth.

Xiao Lingyu had originally intended to merely watch her with a smile as she prattled on, thinking it no more than a child's fantasy to be coaxed away. But at this moment, she felt as if she had been struck violently by something; her heart suffered a heavy jolt.

She gazed at little Baor, who was smiling like a spring peach blossom in full bloom, yet she found herself unable to utter a single word.

That phrase—"Papa, Mama, and Baor going together"—was simple and plain, yet it was like a needle being driven slowly, yet with unerring precision, into the depths of her heart.

Baor did not know.

Baor knew nothing at all.

She was too well-behaved, so good that it made one's heart ache—an ache that left one speechless.

Xiao Lingyu suddenly found it difficult to breathe, her throat feeling as though something were wedged there; if she spoke, it would turn into a sob.

She slowly leaned down, reaching out her hand to touch her daughter's face, but she paused halfway. Her fingertips hung suspended in the air, just as that sentence in her heart remained suspended, not daring to fall to the ground—*He is Baor's biological father!*

But if she did not speak, how could she do justice to this child's heart full of expectation and innocent trust?

The voice that spoke next was gentle and steady, carrying an irresistible composure.

"Baor," her voice was so soft it nearly dissolved as she lightly brushed away that stray lock of hair from her daughter's forehead, her gaze brimming with deep meaning, "Do you know that 'Papa Lord'... he, in truth, is..."

Just as she was about to part her lips, a light knock suddenly came from outside the door, cutting the words short.

"Lingyu, is it convenient for me to enter?"

—It was the voice of Lu Chou.

Today, he was not dressed in his ordinary robes, but in a plain green brocade gown, untouched by the dust of the world; his complexion appeared even more refined than usual. The coldness of the past and his customary mockery were entirely restrained now, and his eyes held a hint of light, lingering tenderness.

"I just passed the street corner and saw the weather was fine; I thought to take you and Baor out for a stroll."

His tone was extremely light, as if he feared disturbing someone.

Xiao Lingyu was startled; just as she was about to refuse, little Baor had already lunged forward in a single stride, hugging his leg and looking up to say in a milky, childish voice, "Then can I go buy candied haws? I want osmanthus cakes too!"

Being embraced by this soft, dough-like little person, Lu Chou's eyes instinctively softened. He leaned down to pick her up, then turned his head to look at Xiao Lingyu: "You surely wouldn't have the heart to let the child be disappointed, would you?"

The words Xiao Lingyu had intended to say were utterly interrupted by this moment of tenderness; she could only nod with a slight touch of wariness: "Only for a short while."

Who could have known that this "short while" would involve riding a carriage across three alley entrances to arrive at a tranquil neighbourhood. There, stone lions stood before the gates, the courtyard walls were washed snowy white, and between the entrance and exit, the upturned eaves were delicate and exquisite.

Lu Chou pushed open the door and entered; Baor had already run into the courtyard in high spirits, chasing a butterfly.

Before Xiao Lingyu could even ask, he spoke of his own accord: "This residence was recently renovated. I asked someone to look for it two days ago; it is not far from the Lu manor, a place of quiet amidst the bustle. Today, the deed has already been transferred into your name."

She was stunned, her eyelashes trembling slightly as she turned her head to look at him, her eyes filled with even more bewilderment.

Lu Chou, however, merely gave a faint smile. His gaze was no longer as sharp as it once was; instead, he spoke in a warm voice: "Lingyu, this is not for the sake of currying favour, nor is it to trap you. I only wish... for you to know that in my heart, you and your daughter are worthy of this house, and worthy of me providing a place for you to settle in peace."

The wind passed over the corners of the eaves, and the plum branches swayed slightly.

the residence was silent and wordless; only that touch of autumn light was spilled into the depths of his eyes, reflecting an emotion called fulfillment.

"This house... you are giving it to me?" She looked on with utter disbelief while Baor was already darting back and forth in the garden.

"Wow, it's so beautiful here."

"Yes."

"Why?"

"Because my heart is pleased with you, and I hope to be closer to you."

"But we are all returning to Jiangnan; why waste money on property in the capital?"

He gave a light laugh and explained in a soft voice, "Who can say for sure what will happen in the future? Perhaps one day you and Baor will return to the capital; at least you will have a place to stay."

Though he explained with a smile, Xiao Lingyu's heart sank. She had originally felt a surge of joy, but now it was a bitterness difficult to swallow. She understood that between him and her, it would ultimately be difficult to grow old together.

"To suddenly buy a house for me... I fear the elders of the Lu family do not agree to the matter between us, do they?"

Lu Chou lightly drew her to him, coaxing her in a low voice: "Rest assured, leave this matter to me. I certainly shall not let you and Baor suffer any grievance."

Xiao Lingyu was slightly dazed, her fingertips lightly stroking the mottled wood grain of the doorframe. After a long while, she said in a low voice: "Why... why do you trouble yourself so."

She stood there, her thoughts surging; for a time, she did not know whether to be grateful or to feel heartache.

It was also at this moment that she suddenly felt fortunate that she had not yet had the chance to tell Baor those words.

Certain truths, once spoken, can never be taken back. If they ultimately could not grow old together, could not stand side-by-side through the wind and rain, then the one to be hurt in the future would not be her alone—

What she feared was not failing to win a formal status, nor being looked upon with cold indifference by others; rather, she feared giving Baor hope only to have her spend her life carrying the regret of "being unable to reunite with her biological father." That kind of fracture and deficiency—she was unwilling to let her daughter taste it even once.

That little girl, who called him "Papa Lord" every day, would one day understand that the kinship that was once so close could also become so distant.

What she feared was never the gossip and rumours, nor supporting their lives alone; it was letting her daughter grow up with hope, only to have to learn how to accept loss in the end.

She lowered her eyelashes to hide the flash of bitterness.

The corners of her lips curved into a very slight, faint smile, appearing like resignation and also like self-consolation—things were fine as they were now. Baor could still laugh without worry or fear, still innocently call him "Papa Lord"—that would be enough.

At this moment, the little girl who had been running wildly through the garden stopped, her little face flushed. "Mama, are we going to live here from now on? Then I want Mama to hold me to sleep every day."

The corners of her lips moved slightly, but in the end, she only smiled and said: "...Alright."

* * * * *

Shen Zhaoru lightly set down her brush and inkstone, turning to look at that dark-coloured nanmu cabinet by the bed. After a moment, as if she had made some resolve, she rose and walked to the cabinet. Bending down to open the fine lock, she slowly drew an object from the very bottom—

The object was wrapped securely in layers of brocade, feeling soft and warm to the touch, seemingly a most precious thing. She moved the Sichuan lamp a little closer, and then beneath the light, she carefully opened that layer of brocade inch by inch.

The moment the brocade was unfurled, three words fell quietly amidst the lamplight—*The Romance of the Western Chamber*.

The book cover was somewhat old and the corners slightly curled, yet it had been kept by her as clean as new, as if she feared it catching even a speck of dust.

She sat down with her lips lightly pursed, her fingertips softly stroking those three words. She did not move for a long time, finally parting the pages. *"Night the First: Zhang Junrui First Meets Cui Yingying."*

The ink marks were still fresh, the handwriting neat, and the pages emanated a faint fragrance of books. She lowered her eyes and read in silence, her gaze sinking inch by inch into the spaces between the words. Her throat was slightly constricted, and her breathing became light and slow.

She read to the line—*Since our parting, I recall our meeting; how many times in soul-dreams have I been with you...*

Her fingertips trembled.

The lines of the play from the theatre that day were still echoing in her ears. Between her and him lay a performance, a moment of looking at one another across the balconies; a single lyric had quietly stirred her heart into turmoil.

"Cloud-like tresses, flower-like face, and golden dangling hairpins; the hibiscus bed-curtains are warm as we spend the spring night..." She suddenly slammed the book shut, recalling the lyrics of the actress that day. Her thoughts were in disarray and the skin behind her ears felt hot, as if she were back on that woodland path sharing a single horse, with him behind her, softly telling her in her ear that his heart was pleased with her...

His hand had reached from behind her to help her hold the reins. At first, he had called her "Miss," but later he had directly called her by her given name, "Zhaoru." That low, raspy voice—she remembered it all with perfect clarity.

Now, every line in the book was like that day's gaze in the theatre or the wind passing through the treetops, stirring the tremors hidden in the depths of her heart inch by inch.

She lowered her head, opened the book once more, and read on in secret. The corners of her lips curved in a silent, slight smile, yet her heartbeat gradually grew disordered. Her features sank into the lamplight, reflecting a layer of hazy, soft light.

On this night, without a sound or sign, she tucked a storybook—and the affection within its pages—into the deepest recesses of her heart.

* * * * *

The theatre remained as bustling as ever; as the gongs and drums sounded upon the stage, the entire hall became vibrant.

Lu Xiu had originally been passing through this place today on business. Who could have known that just as his carriage turned the corner of the alley, he would hear the familiar sounds of strings and woodwinds emanating from the theatre, the noise reaching the heavens. The page asked if they should take a detour, but he suddenly lowered the carriage curtain and raised his hand to stop the vehicle.

The page lifted the curtain to ask: "Master, shall we take another road?"

"Wait."

He stepped down from the carriage and gazed up at the theatre's plaque for a moment. His gaze flickered, appearing as if he had fallen into a brief trance. Then he began to walk, following the crowd into the venue.

He did not enter a private box but merely stopped at one side of the side corridor, standing silently as he leaned against a carved wooden pillar. Below, the gongs clanged and the pipes and flutes were clamorous, yet his ears heard only a single line—

"Only affection is difficult to voice, as dreams are severed where the fragrance fades and the jade perishes..."

He was suddenly taken aback.

He had heard this play before. That day he and little Baor had sat in a second-floor box; in the box opposite, he had seen her sitting by the railing with several of her young friends, the curtains swaying in the light breeze. He remembered that at that time, the stage was singing: *Only affection is difficult to voice, as dreams are severed where the fragrance fades and the jade perishes...*

At that time, he had not taken it to heart, thinking only that the lyrics suited the occasion. Now, hearing this line again, it felt as if his chest were being pulled by a thin string, drawn tight.

He instinctively looked toward a certain place upstairs—that private box had been draped with red curtains that day, yet tonight it was utterly empty, leaving only a single lamp that had not been extinguished, swaying lightly in the night wind like a flame.

He suddenly broke into a chuckle, murmuring a line in a soft voice:
"...Only affection is difficult to voice?"

How had he put it back then?

— Is there truly any affection in this world that cannot be voiced? It is nothing more than the self-inflicted troubles of a mediocre man. To him, if there was truly an affection that could not be obtained or entreated for? Then he would—abandon it! Life is short; why should one stick to old ways?

He let out a low laugh, his voice raspy, as if he were laughing at himself. He had clearly spoken with such ease and detachment, yet now even a single line from a play could make his heart feel stifled.

How ridiculous.

He turned to leave, but after taking only a few inches of a step, he paused again. That line of the play was sung once more, the vocal style vast and lingering, as if coming from a great distance, passing through the boiling din of voices to fall into his ears alone.

He stood in the depths of the shadows cast by the lamps, unmoving for a long time. His gaze was steady, his brows lowered.

— Is there truly an affection that can be abandoned the moment one says it is to be abandoned?

He suddenly felt that the person in the play might not be the foolish one; the foolish one was the person outside the play.

Chapter 74: Wounding Oneself to Prove Resolve

In a side hall adjacent to the Ministry of Revenue, Minister Zhou Shuo sat hunched over his desk, scrutinizing the ledgers of the silver treasury.

Lu Chou had arrived on imperial orders to discuss official matters.

Clad in his formal court robes, his appearance solemn and his gaze settled, he cupped his hands in salute and said: "Lord Minister has been toiling with great hardship of late. For these past twenty days, the Ministry's audit of the Jiangnan silver taxes has been exceedingly meticulous, drawing much praise from the court."

Upon hearing this, Zhou Shuo gave a bitter smile. Flicking his sleeves as he took his seat, he remarked: "I dare not accept such praise. These accounts appear to show a bountiful sum, but in truth, it is merely a superficial shimmer. The Crown Prince's grand wedding is imminent, and the Ministry of Rites' budget is like a bottomless pit; the silver vanishes the moment it enters."

He tapped his fingertip lightly against the corner of a ledger: "To say nothing of the fact that the small disturbances at the frontier have not yet subsided, and there are frequent unusual movements in the North. If war truly breaks out, I fear the imperial treasury could scarcely sustain the effort for even three months."

At this point, he turned a page, his brow furrowing slightly: "Look at this entry—reported by the Court of Imperial Sacrifices for the incense and sacrificial rites of the Prince's wedding. And this one, hidden silver quietly disbursed from the Inner Treasury, prepared for... the Great Occasion of State Funerals."

Having finished speaking, he lifted his eyes to look at Lu Chou, his gaze gaining a measure of gravity: "The Emperor's dragon body has been unwell for more than just a day. Though the Imperial Household Department conceals it tightly, you and I know full well in our hearts that it is best to prepare early. Once the Crown Prince ascends the throne and the new policies begin, the grand wedding, the new rites, and the enthronement ceremonies—every single thing will consume silver like water."

Zhou Shuo paused, lowering his voice even further: "...When I entered the palace in the first half of last year, I saw the Emperor's gait was unsteady and his complexion pale; even the imperial physicians dared not linger. Now, one no longer hears of him summoning the doctors at all. The Imperial Household Department... I fear more than half of it has already been taken over by the Crown Prince."

He lowered his head and tapped the corner of the desk, his eyes dark and murky. "It is the way of the world that tea grows cold once the guest departs. A single imperial decree can change the dynasty; a shift in the wind overnight can decide the fate of a thousand souls. But if a true upheaval occurs within the Heavenly House, there will be no more room for manoeuvre in the court's affairs."

Lu Chou's expression did not waver. Smoothing his robes as he sat, he replied in a low voice: "This subordinate understands. What the Ministry of Revenue requires now is not merely routine disbursements, but the reservation of funds for sudden contingencies."

"Precisely." Zhou Shuo offered a slight nod, his gaze deep and profound. "The court appears calm and tranquil on the surface, but in truth, a storm is brewing. With the Third Prince fallen, the Second and Fourth Princes have begun their secret maneuvers. Recently, they have been frequently active within the inner court, attempting to win over the external officials."

Lu Chou's features remained serene, his fingertips lightly brushing the hem of his robe upon his knee as he said: "It is for this very reason that the journey to Jiangnan cannot be delayed. The remnants of the Third Prince's faction appear swept away on the surface, yet their silver veins still lie dormant in the shadows. If the roots are not pulled out, once the wind rises in the future, they may well strike back with a vengeance."

Zhou Shuo gazed fixedly at him for a long while before finally nodding: "...This mind of yours truly possesses much of your father's legacy."

He paused, his tone shifting: "However, they are ultimately not as composed as you. During your last southern inspection of taxes, your methods were steady and appropriate—neither overstepping propriety nor falling into negligence. It truly made me look upon you with new respect."

Lu Chou's gaze darkened slightly; he cupped his hands but remained silent.

Zhou Shuo glanced at him, a smile touching his lips: "Your family's character is upright and proper. Now that both brothers of the Lu clan are pillars of the state, do not allow those with ill intentions to sow discord between you."

He paused, his voice dropping several measures: "The Crown Prince relies heavily upon you; naturally, there will be those who find it an eyesore."

"This subordinate shall keep it in mind."

Zhou Shuo sighed lightly, his voice carrying a hint of reluctance: "The Crown Prince has ordered you south once more to eradicate the remnants of the Third Prince's faction. I, for one, shall be losing a most capable helping hand..."

* * * * *

In the western wing of the Shen manor, the morning light was just beginning to rise, causing the thin gauze at the window to sway.

Shen Zhaoru had not yet put away last night's copy of *The Romance of the Western Chamber*; the pages were half-spread, lying quietly upon a low table. S

he sat before her dressing table, the residual warmth of the book's paper still lingering on her fingertips, her brow slightly knit as if she were still lost in thought.

She finished murmuring the verses to herself, her fingertips clutching the corner of the page tightly.

At that moment, she thought of him—the lingering scent of sandalwood in the theatre, and him standing outside the curtain, his gaze sweeping over her with a seemingly indifferent yet lingering look.

The spring day in the forest, the flower shadows falling at an angle, and him holding the reins as he turned back to say: *"My heart is pleased with you..."*

Suddenly, a thin voice announced from outside the door: "Miss, the Madam has arrived."

Startled, she hurriedly rose to put the book away, hiding it at the bottom of a chest before turning to offer her salutes: " Mother, what make you come so early? I was on my way to see you." Zhaoru forced herself to appear composed, rising to take the tea tray and pouring a cup of warm water for her mother.

Madam Shen had already entered the room, wearing a smile and walking with graceful steps. Her attire and jewellery were all exceedingly magnificent. Though she was all smiles, a trace of unquestionable sharpness was hidden in the corners of her eyes—it was the majesty cultivated over many years as the matriarch of the Shen family, a silent authority that pressed upon others by its mere presence.

She carried a small, carved wooden box in her hand, her sleeves trailing upon the floor as she sat upon the k'ang bed and beckoned her daughter over: "Mother has come specifically today to bring you an addition to your bridal dowry."

"An addition to the dowry?" Zhaoru was stunned for a moment.

Madam Shen, dressed in a moon-white robe embroidered with cloud patterns, could not hide the joy between her brows. She smiled and said: "Is it not heard that the Palace already intends to select a consort for the Crown Prince? Your age is appropriate, and your character, appearance, and learning are all beyond reproach. Our family should also make preparations early."

As she spoke, she placed the small carved box upon the table and opened it gently.

Lying quietly within the box was a bracelet of mutton-fat white jade; it was warm, delicate, and entirely flawless. It emanated a soft glow, with a faint, milky-white aura shimmering around it.

Madam Shen took the bracelet out, cradling it in her palm to examine it closely for a moment before lightly sliding it onto her daughter's wrist. With a face full of smiles, she said: "This was left behind by your grandmother. When she married into the Shen family years ago, the Old Great Madam gave it to her as part of her dowry. I originally thought I would pass it to you in the future as well."

She paused, her eyes brightening slightly as she continued: "Now is the perfect time. Once the imperial decree is issued, when people see this bracelet, they will know how much our Shen family has set its heart upon and valued this marriage."

Filled with exuberant joy, Madam Shen smiled again: "Such a monumental blessing is something our Shen family hasn't encountered in several generations..."

Shen Zhaoru gazed blankly at the bracelet, yet she did not reach out her hand.

Seeing her silence, Madam Shen's brow furrowed slightly: "What is it? Do you not like this bracelet? Or do you feel...?"

Shen Zhaoru pursed her lips and said in a low voice: "...How can Mother be so certain that the chosen one must be your daughter?" After all, for the position of Crown Princess, there was another candidate.

Madam Shen's tone was soft yet possessed a cutting edge: "The Empress Dowager herself has sent a letter; can there be any falsehood in it? You are not unaware of the recent movements in the Grand Secretariat. This marriage is not merely a betrothal, but an investiture of a consort. Currently, all the factions in the Grand Secretariat are watching. If this step is taken steadily, our Shen family will have established a firm footing. In the future, you are destined to be the Mother of the World!"

As she spoke, her tone grew slightly heavier: "You should also restrain your temperament. Stop reading those storybooks and listening to *The Romance of the Western Chamber* all day.

Once you are in the Eastern Palace in the future, the consorts and palace maids will be like clouds. If you do not steady your heart, how will you establish yourself?"

Hearing this, Shen Zhaoru felt a constriction in her chest. Her fingertips tightened, and she actually felt the bracelet upon her wrist grow heavier with every moment it was worn.

"...Does Mother know that His Royal Highness the Crown Prince has not expressed his stance?"

"Ai, in such matters, where is there room for a man to speak? To say nothing of the fact that he is the future master of the country?" Madam Shen gave her a reproachful look. "As long as you maintain your status, what is yours to have will naturally come to you. Do not indulge in further idle thoughts, lest you ruin your own future."

"Mother, what future? I am but a daughter of the inner chambers. I do not sit for the civil examinations, nor the military ones, and I have no brothers. Why must I contend for some future?"

Upon hearing this, Madam Shen's face darkened. "It is precisely because you have no brothers behind you to act as your support. Since you and His Royal Highness were childhood friends, you must rely even more upon the Crown Prince. Only he can ensure your peace and safety for a lifetime."

"Mother, after Prince Brother ascends the throne in the future, there will be the Three Palaces and Six Courtyards..."

Madam Shen interrupted her with displeasure. "No matter what is said, you will be the Mistress of the Central Palace, and that is enough!"

Shen Zhaoru lowered her eyes in silence and spoke no further. She knew that her parents had already made up their minds, seeking every possible way to make her the Crown Princess; there was no need to say anything more.

Seeing this, Madam Shen's tone became gentle yet remained firm: "My foolish Ru'er, do you think I have been making inquiries these past days for nothing? The people around the Crown Prince have privately probed for our views multiple times. The Empress Dowager has also said she likes a gentle and steady girl like you. Besides, other than you, which noble daughter is worthy of this future seat in the Central Palace?"

"But..." She pursed her lips, her voice so low it was almost inaudible: "What if your daughter does not wish for it?"

"What nonsense are you speaking!" Madam Shen's face changed, and her voice grew several degrees colder. "You are the Di daughter of the Shen family; you ought to undertake the responsibility of choosing the fortune of the clan. Could it be that you harbour other intentions in your heart?"

Shen Zhaoru remained silent for a good while before saying in a low voice: "Mother, I am simply... a little tired. Can we discuss this matter another day?"

Seeing her cold expression, Madam Shen found it difficult to press her further, saying only: "Keep that bracelet and think it over well. Once the decree to enter the palace arrives, do not wear this look again, lest people see it and think you are unwilling."

Madam Shen continued to talk to herself: "When you go to the Empress Dowager's palace to pay your respects tomorrow, remember to dress appropriately. That purple-blue surcoat would be quite good..."

The voice was like a silken thread, winding and entangling. Shen Zhaoru felt a tightness in her scalp, and a few beads of fine sweat broke out at her temples. She gazed blankly at the bracelet on her wrist, suddenly feeling that the milky-white luster was actually heavier than iron.

A monumental blessing felt, instead, like a monumental cage.

Shen Zhaoru finally endured until Madam Shen departed; a line of maidservants filed out, and the courtyard gradually returned to silence.

She sat upon the k'ang for a long time, the jade bracelet on her wrist resting heavily, as if it weighed a thousand pounds. After a long while, she rose and walked to the dressing table, looking down at the person in the mirror—

That face was clearly only sixteen years of age, yet it had early on learned how to remain unmoved and how to cope with circumstances beyond one's control.

But no matter how she learned to be steady and calm, was she truly to spend her entire life living within the arrangements of others?

She stared at herself in the mirror, suddenly finding that face somewhat strange.

She lowered her eyes and removed the jade bracelet from her wrist. At that instant, the coldness sliding past her fingertips actually carried a bone-chilling sensation.

She placed it gently back into the brocade box and locked it at the bottom of a cabinet, as if what she had locked away was not merely a jade bracelet, but the path of destiny she was originally meant to walk.

She turned back and sat down, then drew out the copy of *The Romance of the Western Chamber* she had carefully hidden last night. Holding it with both hands, she slowly unfurled it.

The pages were yellowed, and the ink marks were quiet.

She turned to that page—*Since our parting, I recall our meeting; how many times in soul-dreams have I been with you.*

Her lips moved slightly as she read the line in a low voice, her voice trembling as if she feared disturbing the name in her heart that she dared not proclaim.

It was him. That unintended look exchanged in the theatre that day, it was him. The one who rode a single horse with her on the woodland path that day, holding the reins and whispering to her—it was also him.

She was habitually calm and never easily moved her heart, yet it happened to be him, entering her heart bit by bit, like that page of the book which, once turned, could never be returned.

She suddenly let out a low laugh, her eyes downcast, yet her voice carried a trace of bitterness: "My heart is pleased with him... but what can be done?"

She remembered her mother saying "such a blessing" just now, remembered the weight of that bracelet pressing upon her wrist, remembered the letter from the Empress Dowager, and remembered the winds and clouds of the imperial court...

She murmured softly: "If I truly had to choose, I would rather..."

The sentence was not finished; she forced herself to swallow it down.

The lamplight flickered. She sat alone in the silent room, holding the storybook in her hands, yet there was not a hint of lightheartedness or jest in her eyes; there remained only a deep, unshakeable gloom.

Her hand tightened, and that page of the book was slammed shut. The corner of the paper was sharp, and it sliced open her palm. A trickle of blood seeped out, shockingly red, yet it was shallower than the mark left upon her heart.

Even if it could not be spoken, even if it could not be made clear, at least—at this moment, she could still quietly read this book, and still secretly think of that person.

Chapter 75: Testing the Heart with a Game of Chess

Outside the Hall of Xuande, slanted shadows of bamboo fell across the stone steps, and the summer cicadas droned in low, lingering tones.

Lu Xiu had entered the palace with several officials by imperial order to report on military affairs.

When the matters were concluded, the Crown Prince Chen Gen did not command his attendants to dismiss the guests. Instead, he spoke softly, "Lu Xiu, remain."

Lu Xiu inclined his head slightly and stood to one side, his gaze composed—neither servile nor arrogant.

"Sit. Keep me company for a round of chess."

Lu Xiu could only obey and took the seat opposite the Crown Prince.

Chen Gen held a chess piece in one hand and lightly brushed the lid of his teacup with the other before asking, "Do you know that urgent reports have arrived from the northern frontier?"

Lu Xiu's expression shifted faintly. "I heard that His Highness Chen Xu dispatched troops to reinforce the defence, drawing upon two camps from Yunbei."

"What do you make of it?" As he spoke, the Crown Prince placed a piece upon the board, his manner unhurried.

In speaking of "not forcing," his tone remained mild, yet the authority beneath it did not soften in the slightest. It was the kind of gentleness that allowed no refusal—like a hand resting lightly on a sword hilt. In that moment, the line between Crown Prince and sovereign seemed to blur, and the weight of the throne pressed down invisibly upon the board.

"If this subject speaks strictly from a military standpoint, then the Fourth Prince's mobilisation was timely enough. However… altering troop deployment without the Ministry of War's directive may not convince the court."

"Hm." The Crown Prince nodded—or almost did. After a brief pause, he shifted the subject. "Since my third brother's fall, the fourth has gained quite some momentum in court. I would not mind it ordinarily, but if he begins harbouring other intentions, it becomes no small matter."

Lu Xiu lowered his gaze. "Your Highness sees clearly."

Silence lingered in the hall for a moment. The Crown Prince personally picked up a black stone and set it down, his tone indifferent. "You have grown as well. Your manner is unlike your elder brother's. He is meticulous, while you are sharp-spirited—sometimes taking an oblique path, yet never losing your edge."

Lu Xiu paused slightly before replying softly, "This subject thanks Your Highness for the praise."

Chen Gen lifted his gaze to him, a faint smile that did not fully reach his eyes. "There is no need to be tense. I have long held friendship with your father, and I think highly of both you and Lu Chou. The Eastern Palace carries heavy burdens at present—if I have capable men at my side, that is precisely what I desire."

A faint tremor moved through Lu Xiu's chest, but his smile remained reserved. "What does Your Highness intend?"

"Lu Xiu has always been keen-minded. You should know that although I am already the Crown Prince, this position is not yet secure. I still require the strength of the… Imperial preceptor."

Upon hearing this, Lu Xiu could hardly fail to understand the Crown Prince's unfinished meaning.

His expression did not change; he forced down the turbulence within his chest, bowed with clasped hands and said, "If Your Highness deems this subject trustworthy, then I shall naturally do my utmost to share the burdens of the Eastern Palace."

Shen Zhaoru… in the end, she is not someone I am able to contend for…

The Crown Prince gave a soft laugh when he heard this and placed another piece on the board. "Truly quick-witted. Then I shall speak plainly. You have been frequenting the western side of the city lately and have had no small amount of contact with the Shen family. There are some rumours outside… What is your view?"

His expression did not shift, though inwardly every string had tightened to its limit.

He bowed slightly. "This subject would not dare make careless claims. But the Shen family's legitimate daughter is dignified and poised, with uncommon discernment. If she were to serve Your Highness, she would indeed be an excellent choice."

The Crown Prince halted the movement of the chess piece in his hand and looked at him lightly.

"An excellent choice?" His tone sounded calm, yet a faint weight pressed beneath it. "You yourself have never entertained such intentions?"

Lu Xiu lowered his gaze and answered in a deep voice, "This subject knows his status is limited, and has never dared to aspire above his station, moreover…" He paused, pressing his voice lower still. "If Your Highness has such intentions, then this subject will naturally yield by three parts, and would never presume to overstep."

"That is good. You must know that the Imperial preceptor's disciples fill the court from top to bottom, their influence far-reaching. He was even tutor to me in my youth, and one day may be the master of the future Emperor. And the Imperial preceptor has only one legitimate daughter, no sons, and prides himself on upright conduct…"

Before he finished speaking, the Crown Prince Chen Gen turned his gaze sharply upon him, studying him for a long moment before saying, "Lu Xiu speaks well at this moment. But in this world, if merely 'yielding three parts' were enough to cut something cleanly away, it would not be called 'feeling'."

A shock moved through Lu Xiu's chest, though his face remained as calm as water.

The Crown Prince suddenly curved his lips in a smile, his voice carrying a hint of amusement. "The Imperial preceptor is steady and seasoned in his conduct. That young lady of the Shen family was raised from childhood with utmost care—virtue and appearance both outstanding… If she were to enter the Eastern Palace, it would indeed be a fine affair. I… am not someone who fails to appreciate a fine jade."

These words neither declared nor denied anything, yet every implication was unmistakable.

Lu Xiu's fingertips tightened slightly, something inside him sinking heavily. He bowed his head and replied in the same tone as always, "Your Highness is wise."

"You truly think so?" The Crown Prince looked at him coolly. "I believe that you… harbour a particular feeling toward her."

Lu Xiu fell silent for a moment before finally lowering his head and saying, "This humble subject, being born a concubine's son, knows well his lowly standing, and does not dare harbour desires for someone—or something—beyond his allotted measure."

The Crown Prince stared at him for a long time without speaking.

Outside the window, the wind brushed through the willows, and a single leaf drifted down.

Chen Gen suddenly let out a quiet laugh. "Lu Xiu, you have always been perceptive and quick-witted. When speaking with you, one must always keep three parts of caution. Yet I, for one, happen to appreciate your sense of measure."

"You should not belittle yourself too much. Though you are a concubine-born son, you are still the elder concubine-born son of Minister Lu. And Shen Zhaoru is a good young lady; she and I may be considered childhood companions. If she becomes my Crown Princess, I shall naturally treat her with generosity. If she is unwilling… I will not force her."

Chen Gen paused, turned back to glance at Lu Xiu, the corners of his mouth carrying a faint smile. "But in this world, there are certain unions—where only the right person can match."

His tone held considerable meaning.

Lu Xiu bowed with lowered head, the corners of his lips drawn tight. "Your Highness's benevolence… this subject feels it to the depths of his being."

The Crown Prince said no more and merely continued placing his pieces swiftly, saying in an even tone, "Go. The Eastern Palace is short-handed these days, especially in matters of the capital's defence. Moreover, the border has been unsettled of late. Others may not trust you, but I am willing to give you a chance."

"Thank you, Your Highness."

He withdrew, saluted, and walked away with steady steps. Only when he reached the threshold and stepped out of the hall did he finally exhale a long breath.

Outside, the daylight was bright; bamboo leaves quivered lightly, and a breeze swept past his ear, bringing with it a trace of chill.

He stood upon the stone steps, lifting his fingers to lightly brush the faint red mark in his palm—the mark left from that day when she let fall a handkerchief from the upper floor, its embroidered corner grazing his fingertips as it passed.

It had been so slight a touch—barely more than a brush of thread against skin—yet it had lodged itself in him like a splinter. Even now, when his finger traced that place, the memory rose with humiliating clarity, as though the warmth of her presence had never truly left.

Now, he finally understood.

She was not his.

He slowly closed his eyes, and after a long while, the faintest smile surfaced at the corner of his lips.

For no reason, he thought again of that line from The Story of the Western Wing:

—Feeling is hard to speak—

If even the old plays said as much—if "feeling" was truly hard to speak—then what else was there to do but swallow it whole?

Since that is so, reason told him that he should abandon it…

But why did his heart hurt so much?

Lu Xiu stepped back several paces. Before turning away, he saw that the Crown Prince was still standing before the palace doors, gazing at the willow branches in the courtyard, his eyes deep and unreadable.

In that instant, Lu Xiu could not tell whether he had been released… or enclosed.

He turned and walked out of the Hall of Xuande. His knuckles tightened; his palm was already damp.

He had thought he could abandon it, yet only now understood—on the imperial court, even the right to abandon required the Emperor's grace.

* * * * *

Late at night, the lamps were quiet. In the study, only a faint trace of incense lingered from the bronze burner, the lamplight wavering softly.

Lu Xiu leaned against the desk, his left hand propping his brow, his right hand turning the jade-inlaid brush shaft, scarcely moving at all.

Several volumes lay stacked on the table, yet he had not written a line. His gaze rested on the blank page before him, lost in thoughts he could not name.

He did not know how much time passed before he finally reached for the brush, dipping it in ink without a sound.

Stroke by stroke, the characters came out steady—uniform and upright. Yet when he finished an entire line and lowered his gaze, he froze abruptly.

—"Cloud-soft hair and a blossom face, gold hairpins swaying; beneath the warm hibiscus canopy, they spend the spring night."

His hand halted; the brush tip trembled slightly.

After a moment, he let out a quiet laugh. The sound was very soft, like speaking to himself—yet also like mocking himself.

"…Truly an illness not lightly cured."

He tossed the brush aside and pinched the edge of the paper, lifting the slip on which the theatrical verse was written.

Each character was clear, line by line—and there was even a small note: First night—Zhang Junrui first catches sight of Cui Yingying.

Staring at that marginal note, his pupils contracted. A short, sharp laugh escaped him—he had even written down which act it was from.

As if fearing he might forget— as if he truly meant to keep a scholar's record of the exact moment his heart first went astray.

"Excellent. Lu Xiu, sober you write memorials, muddled you write love verses. What sort of besotted scholar do you take yourself for?"

He lowered his head and laughed for a moment. The laughter faded quickly, and his expression grew sombre.

Recalling the conversation over chess with the Crown Prince earlier that day, a bitter smile slipped out of him.

Not long ago, he had vowed so firmly that he would marry her; moreover, the memory of sharing a horse with her beneath the autumn trees remained vivid—

Yet now, not much time had passed, and between him and her… such a thing could never happen again.

And added to this was Grandmother's reminder to him that day—if she were promised to another, then he must… by no means force it.

And he had, in turn, given Grandmother his assurance—if that day truly arrived, he would sever all thought of her himself.

His fingertips curled, lifting the sheet of paper and placing it into the bronze brazier at the side.

The fire rose lightly; the edges browned first. As the flames licked over the four characters "hibiscus canopy warm", he watched for a moment without moving.

Only when the paper turned into a thread of ash did he shift his gaze away.

"Feelings that cannot be obtained—once burned, then let them be."

He spoke softly, his tone light, as though commenting on an official document with a misplaced character, carrying no emotion at all.

Yet within his sleeve, the faintly clenched joint of his finger was bloodlessly white.

* * * * *

Shen Zhaoru stood beneath a row of maple trees, her fingertips gently brushing the edge of her sleeve.

She had quietly made inquiries for several days, and only after much effort had she learnt his schedule for today.

She had waited early at a teahouse along the road he must pass, and after waiting an entire hour, she finally saw a figure slowly approaching from the far corner.

Lu Xiu had arrived. Clad in pale blue, his brows and eyes were as they had always been, his steps still composed. Yet for reasons she could not name, she felt there was something slightly different about him today.

"Lu Xiu…" She hurried forward and called out softly, lowering the brim of her hat.

He stopped a few steps outside the pavilion and gave a slight bow. Recognising her voice, he paused for a moment before regaining his composure. His tone was respectful, yet distant: "Miss Shen."

She froze for a moment, her voice hesitant. "…Why have you suddenly changed the manner of address?"

"Since you are soon to enter the Eastern Palace, Xiu does not dare to exceed propriety." He inclined his head slightly, avoiding her gaze.

In that instant, it felt as though a drop of water had fallen into the lake of her heart, sending out quiet ripples.

"The matter of His Highness the Crown Prince… is not yet decided." She spoke softly, as if explaining, yet also as though reminding him.

"Since there are already whispers in the palace, it would be best for you to make early preparation." he said. His tone remained even, yet his words carried a faint sense of distance—as though deliberately keeping others a thousand li away.

She grew slightly flustered.

"What is wrong with you today?" she asked in a low voice, her tone carrying a trace of urgency. "That day you clearly still…"

Still stood across from me at the opera house and looked at me through the window, still rode back with me on the same horse, still said you held affection for me…

Yet today, he would not even spare her an extra inch of his gaze.

She instinctively stepped half a pace closer, and through the veil, her eyes looked straight into his. "Are you avoiding me?"

He lowered his gaze, the corner of his lips seeming to pull with effort. "It is nothing more than official matters weighing on me of late."

"Why are you telling me these formal empty words?" Her voice was very soft, yet a faint mist rose in her eyes. "I know myself… I am not just anyone…"

A breeze rose inside the pavilion, scattering the hair at her temples. Mist shimmered faintly in her eyes, yet she bit down hard on her lip, refusing to let herself cry.

At this point, with her intelligence, what else was there she did not understand?

He… regretted it.

He finally lifted his eyes to look at her. His gaze was so complicated he almost could not speak.

And had he not felt pain himself?

But in his mind echoed the Crown Prince's words in the hall: "If she becomes my Crown Princess, I shall naturally treat her with generosity. If she is unwilling… I will not force her…"

What a claim of not forcing. What a retreat that advanced instead. Someone the Crown Prince desired—what power did he have to contend?

And there was Grandmother's earnest reminder that night, every sentence urging him to put the Lu family first.

As a subject, as the elder concubine-born son of the Lu family, he could not gamble. He was not worthy to gamble.

He turned slightly to the side, forcing himself into calm. "You should return early. The weather is hot; Miss should go back quickly, so as not to harm your health."

When the words fell, he bowed his head, saluted, and turned to leave, his steps slightly unsteady.

Shen Zhaoru stood in the pavilion, her eyelashes faintly trembling. Her throat felt blocked by a heavy breath—unable to speak it out, unable to swallow it down.

Behind her, blossoms fell one after another, landing silently upon the ground like rain—just like her at this moment, standing in the pavilion with nowhere to place herself.

She clenched her palm tightly, her fingertips cold. After a long while, she finally turned to leave, her steps unsteady as she trod upon fallen maple leaves scattered across the ground.

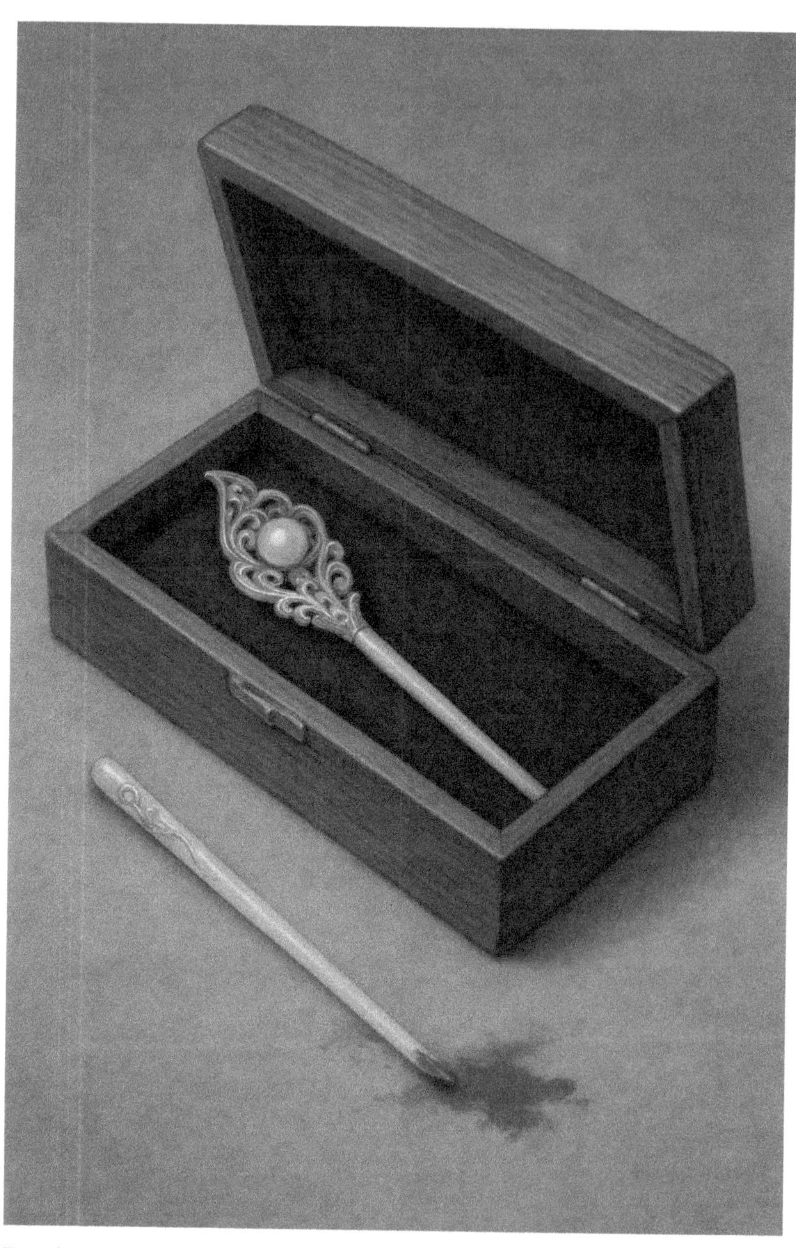

Readers can view the full collection of colour illustrations here:
https://www.facebook.com/profile.php?id=61581325000577

Chapter 76: Affection and Glory

The weather had turned suddenly cold, and in the forecourt of the Shen manor, the plum blossoms were beginning to bloom. Dots of snowy white clung to the branches; as a light breeze brushed past, their fragrance permeated the entire alley.

Shen Zhaoru, dressed in a plain white padded jacket, paced the courtyard for a long time before finally gathering her courage to head toward the Lu manor.

She told no one; wrapped only in a white cloak against the biting wind and wearing a hooded veil upon her head, she stood alone at the street corner, waiting in silence.

She could wait no longer.

Since their parting that day, he had become as cold as if they had never known each other, leaving her to toss and turn through sleepless nights, finding no taste in her food or tea. Her already delicate frame appeared even more wasted and thin now, yet the suspicion, dread, and indignation in her heart accumulated day by day until they were finally more than she could bear.

It was not until that tall, slender silhouette she thought of day and night appeared outside the Lu manor gates that she hurried forward. However, her body, which had gradually grown numb and stiff from the cold, nearly failed her; she called out in a soft voice: "Master Lu," her tone carrying panic and urgency.

Hearing her voice, he instinctively turned back and saw her swaying form. With a stride of his long legs, he moved swiftly forward to catch her, his brow suddenly knitting tight.

Taking advantage of his supportive stance, she leaned against his chest. Lu Xiu froze for a moment; his limbs seemed as frozen as the air, and he did not push her away from her leaning position.

He looked down and saw her dark hair drawn up neatly. Having removed her hooded veil, her face was plain and without powder, yet her features were as beautiful as a painting, and the depths of her eyes could not hide her profound affection.

"I have words I wish to speak to you," she said softly.

Lu Xiu turned his head. Seeing her standing at this cold, snowy street corner in the early morning and knowing not how long she had waited for him, his throat tightened and his heart grew heavy, yet he maintained a feigned composure and nodded: "Follow me."

Then, without allowing for argument, without an explanation, he swept her up against his chest and entered the Lu manor through a side gate, proceeding directly to the front of his study before finally setting her down.

The two were silent throughout the journey. Once she had regained her footing, she followed him into the study, but he immediately lowered his gaze and pulled shut the door behind her.

Standing behind him and watching his busy movements, Shen Zhaoru could not help but murmur: "These past two days... have you been avoiding me on purpose?"

The hand Lu Xiu used to turn a page faltered. After a moment, he spoke in a flat tone: "I have indeed been busy of late."

She did not speak, only gazed at him with an indescribable sense of grievance and trepidation: "I thought that after we rode together in the forest that day, our hearts were already in accord."

His hand remained resting upon the door bolt, his fingers inadvertently tightening. He did not turn to look at her, yet the tension in his heart made breathing a difficult struggle.

That day sharing a single horse, that day when he softly called "Zhaoru" in the wind, that moment of looking at one another in the theatre—how could he not remember?

But he also remembered the Crown Prince's casual remark to him: "I intend to take Shen Zhaoru as my Crown Princess..."

And his grandmother, looking at him, had said: "If she is ultimately promised to another, you must... by no means take her by force."

How could he not know—this affection should not be born, nor should it be dwelled upon.

She took a step forward and reached out to tug at his sleeve, her voice trembling slightly: "Do you not wish to see me?"

He raised his eyes to look at her, his gaze dark and profound, like a lamp hidden under the cover of night—flickering yet concealed. He opened his mouth, but his throat felt obstructed, yielding only a low, hoarse: "It is not that I do not wish to."

She pursed her lips, her chest heaving violently. Her fingers clenched at her side and then released; finally, as if she had summoned a great resolve—she suddenly embraced him from behind.

Having not expected her to take such a sudden action, his entire body grew even more rigid, and even breathing became a difficult task.

Though several layers of clothing separated them, he could still feel her breath against his back; it was so scalding it nearly made it impossible for him to support himself.

"Do not ignore me..." Her voice was choked with sobs, as if she were on the verge of tears.

It felt as though a mouthful of blood were lodged in his throat. Only after a long while did he manage to force out a low, raspy sound: "...I am sorry. It is I, Lu, who have failed you; it is I who am caught in circumstances beyond my control..."

His three consecutive apologies left her stunned and bewildered.

"Why?" The jade-like arms she used to clasp him tightened once more. "Is it because of the position of Crown Princess..."

"No," he interrupted her coldly. "Do not overthink it. Your status is noble, and it is I, Lu, who am unworthy. My past actions were an impudence; I hope Miss Shen does not take them to heart."

She was dazed, and just as she was about to press him further, she saw him suddenly stand up, his voice dropping several measures: "I still have a memorial that has not been drafted. We shall talk... another day."

He avoided her gaze, the corner of his sleeve trembling slightly. As he bypassed her, his steps were hurried, as if if he looked at her but once more, those words hidden in the depths of his heart would no longer be able to be suppressed.

"It is cold outside. Miss Shen, please wait here for a moment. I am burdened with heavy official duties today and cannot personally escort you, but I shall dispatch a carriage to return you safely to your manor. I shall... take my leave now."

The door was closed softly, leaving her standing alone in the centre of the study. The room was filled with warm fragrance, yet it could not withstand the desolate cold in her heart. Amidst the flickering shadows of the lamplight, she looked toward the desk and saw a piece of paper pressed under the inkstone; upon it was a faint, charred mark from burning, as if something had been quietly destroyed.

She murmured in a light whisper: "You truly are... avoiding me."

Beyond the wall, the wind rose, and the flowers fell without a sound.

And Lu Xiu, after stepping out the door, kept his spine tensed. He walked until he reached the corner of the corridor before leaning against a pillar to catch a breath; his eyes were dark as he forcibly suppressed that word—"abandon"—into the deepest recesses of his heart.

He knew he had fled, but if he did not flee, he feared he would reach a point where—he would never be able to let go again.

* * * * *

News in the palace travelled with extreme speed.

Especially matters of this nature.

By dusk that day, the Ministry of Rites sent word: His Royal Highness the Crown Prince had personally entered the Imperial Presence to discuss the selection of the principal consort for the Eastern Palace. At the hour of the Dragon the following day, the decree would be issued upon an auspicious selection.

For a time, the Shen manor was unnervingly quiet; even the usually talkative nannies had the sense to withdraw.

Shen Zhaoru sat upon an embroidered k'ang bed, clutching a half-finished silken pouch; the silver needle hung in mid-air, yet it delayed its descent for a long time.

She kept her eyes lowered, her eyelashes casting two light shadows. The light filtered through the curtains and cast mottled halos upon the floor like shattered jade in the wind.

"What is this look you are wearing?"

Madam Shen's voice suddenly came from outside the door, carrying her habitual majesty and scrutiny.

As soon as she entered the room, she first glanced at her daughter, her gaze falling upon the unfinished pouch. Seeing the girl's pale face and dazed expression, she immediately understood the situation in her heart.

"Mother," Zhaoru called out softly.

Madam Shen sat down beside her, reaching out to take her hand. After looking at it closely for a moment, she spoke slowly: "You have been raised since childhood with the understanding that you would enter the Central Palace and manage the Six Palaces; this is your destined path. Why is it that as the decree is about to descend, you appear as if... you are unhappy in your heart?"

Shen Zhaoru's fingertips tightened.

She pursed her lips and remained silent.

Madam Shen heaved a sigh, her tone turning heavy: "Do not tell your mother that you are... still dwelling upon that Lu family concubine-son."

"Mother, how did you know..." Before the words were finished, Madam Shen interrupted her.

Madam Shen took a book from the hands of a nearby maidservant and held it out before her. Shen Zhaoru's gaze fixed upon it, and her heart instantly grew half-cold; it was the very book she had so carefully cherished—The Romance of the Western Chamber.

Shen Zhaoru's eyes flickered; she pressed her lips tight and uttered not a word.

This silence carried more weight than any verbal answer.

"Still trying to hide it from your mother? This little thought of yours— one round of questioning those around you made it perfectly clear." A trace of coldness flashed through Madam Shen's eyes, her tone pressing closer inch by inch: "Do you know what kind of matter this is? The Crown Princess is the future mistress of the Central Palace, a position looked up to by ten thousand people. And who is Lu Xiu? What does he possess? He is a concubine-son of the Lu family, with no real power behind him. Though he has a future, he is destined to be unable to stand as your equal."

"...Your daughter knows..." Zhaoru finally said in a low voice; the sound was so faint it was like the wind brushing over the peonies in the courtyard, unable to stir the slightest resonance.

"What do you know?" Madam Shen sighed softly. "That Lu Xiu is indeed a man of talent; even as a concubine-son, he is the eldest son of Minister Lu, and his family standing is not considered low. However, you are different. You have been childhood friends with the Crown Prince since you were small; you have long been the guaranteed daughter-in-law of the Imperial House."

Shen Zhaoru kept her lips pressed tight, her eyes rimmed with red.

"If you know, then you should not harbour such delusions." Madam Shen spoke word by word, her voice carrying a hint of anger. "In the beginning, you said you only wished to live without shame in your heart, and your mother believed you. Now, do the thoughts in your heart do justice to His Royal Highness the Crown Prince? Do they do justice to your own future?"

Shen Zhaoru's eyes grew wet, and her knuckles gripped the embroidered edge of the k'ang so hard they turned white. Finally, she replied in a low voice: "If your daughter truly had a choice... your daughter would rather not be some Crown Princess."

As soon as these words were spoken, the room fell into a sudden silence.

Madam Shen was speechless for a long time, finally letting out a soft, cold laugh.

"This world has never allowed you a choice. You are the only Di daughter of the Shen family; you have no elder brothers to act as your support. You must use your own body to carry the glory of the clan. What you bear is not affection, but the reputation of your house."

Having said this, she flicked her sleeve and stood up, walking out from behind the curtains with a decisive and cold gait.

Outside the curtains, the wind stirred and the peonies fell in disarray, just as the myriad thoughts in Shen Zhaoru's heart were being torn to pieces, bit by bit, in this wind.

She picked up the half-finished pouch; the embroidery thread still hung from the tip of the needle, only one stitch away from being finished.

Yet she suddenly found herself unable to make that final stitch.

Because that thread was something she had personally embroidered for him.

And tomorrow, she would have to accept the destiny of another.

* * * * *

In the greenhouse, the scent of sandalwood drifted. From behind a screen, a eunuch offered a low report before withdrawing.

Chen Gen was leaning by a small table next to the k'ang, toying with a tea cup lid with one hand. His expression was languid, yet his gaze remained fixed upon the memorial that had just been presented. Xu Hui entered with light steps and offered a bow; seeing his unsettled state of mind, she smiled softly and said: "Has Your Highness been sleeping poorly again of late? I have brewed some calming tea here; perhaps Your Highness would care to take a short rest?"

Chen Gen shook his head and spoke in a casual tone: "It is no matter. In a few days, it will be the Empress's birthday; the Ministry of Rites has already made the arrangements. As for the jewels to be presented and the congratulatory scrolls to be submitted, I, as a prince, should still expend more thought upon them."

Xu Hui's smile did not waver as she sat across from him and said: "That is what is required on the surface; I naturally would not dare to overstep. However, I always feel that if everything is prepared by others, it is inevitably a bit dull. I was thinking... of doing something myself; perhaps it would show more sincerity."

Chen Gen arched an eyebrow and offered a smile, seemingly not taking it to heart: "In that case, what do you intend to do? A fragrant sachet? Or perhaps embroider a character for 'blessings'? Even those high-ranking consorts use surrogates for such work; which of them truly does it by their own hand? Besides, you are now my Liangdi; why must you personally labour over such a thing?"

"It is not for the sake of competing in cleverness... it is just that I have recently learned some embroidery techniques and wish to make a headband, or perhaps some knee-guards or the like. They are not precious, yet they can serve to express my heart. It would be cliché if everyone merely presented jade pendants of auspicious beasts; that would be too conventional."

Having spoken, she drew several small embroidery patterns from her sleeve and spread them upon the table. They were all refined patterns with subtle ingenuity: a headband with a flower-picking fretwork design, and knee-guards with a pattern of bird feathers in the light of the sunrise. All were extremely exquisite, and the coordination of the coloured threads was elegant, clearly showing she had exerted effort.

Chen Gen had been indifferent at first, but his gaze faltered slightly as he swept over those patterns. He pondered for a moment, then suddenly said: "These patterns are not common; they possess a certain flavour of Jiangnan. Since you are so skillful and possess such filial piety, it is a pity no one is helping you select the materials and coordinate the colours... why not—"

He paused, his gaze shifting, his tone casual yet saturated with a deep meaning: "Have that Madam Xiao from the Jinhua Gallery come for a visit. She is exceptionally skilled in embroidery and also an expert in the selection and coordination of implements. Let her help you cut some fine materials, fashion a few small items, and incidentally provide you with an embroidery frame that is suitable for your hand. In any case, she is idle."

Xu Hui was startled, then pursed her lips and smiled, saying in a soft voice: "Madam Xiao's reputation has become increasingly resounding of late; I too have long wished to see her handiwork."

Chen Gen gave a grunt of affirmation and lowered his eyes to cover the embroidery patterns on the table, as if unwilling to speak further. Seeing this, Xu Hui asked no more, but within her heart, she already had a plan in place.

Chapter 77: Severing Affection with Cruel Words

The night grew deep as the wind rose like silken threads, casting disordered shadows upon the green-latticed windows.

Inside the study, the candle flame flickered slightly, casting a thinned silhouette upon the wall.

The scroll in Lu Xiu's hand remained unfurled, for he had long been unable to take in a single word. His father's command from their conversation yesterday still echoed in his ears: *"The daughter of the Shen family has already been betrothed to the Eastern Palace; you are to harbour no further thoughts..."* Even his grandmother had warned him in a cold voice: *"If she is to be the mistress of the Central Palace, then immediately restrain all your notions and keep your distance henceforth; there must be no lapse in conduct."*

In his reason, he understood that affection must not overstep propriety. Yet, somewhere in his chest, there remained a stifling ache.

At that moment, a faint sound came from outside the window.

His brows furrowed, and just as he rose, the door was pushed open.

With a surge of wind, a lean figure burst inside, draped in an ink-black cloak. Her hair was disarranged, and her collar was left untied. She stood in the wind, the rims of her eyes slightly red, yet her gaze possessed an unprecedented resolve and clarity.

"Zhaoru?" He gasped in surprise, immediately stepping forward. "Why have you come? Dressed in such a manner—what propriety is there in this—"

He caught sight of Liang Jin peeking and prying by the door and instantly understood that the lad had not reported her arrival but had brought her in secretly.

Lu Xiu's gaze turned cold; the boy shuddered under that sweep of the eyes and hastily shrank behind the door.

"Eldest Young Master, your servant only saw... saw that Miss Shen was so piteous..." Liang Jin defended himself in a low voice outside the door.

"I shall settle accounts with you later!" Lu Xiu barked in a deep voice, then promptly closed the door. He turned to support her as she sat, his throat bobbing twice before he lowered his voice: "Why... why have you come at such an hour?"

"I waited outside for two hours, yet did not see you exit the manor. Just now, that young page saw me and said he could lead me in to find you."

"Why... why must you do this?" Hearing this, Lu Xiu's chest tightened, his tone filled with an irrepressible anxiety.

"I came to see you." She interrupted him, her voice trembling yet every word distinct. "I do not wish to be some Crown Princess, I want no part of the Central Palace's seat. I only ask you one thing—do you dare to leave with me?"

For a moment, the study became so silent that a falling needle could be heard.

The wind snuck through the crevices of the window, blowing the candle flame into disarray, and blowing his heart into turmoil as well.

He gazed at her blankly, a sudden warmth rising in his heart as an unprecedented impulse surged from his chest.

He wanted to say, *"I dare."*

Truly, he wanted to say, *"I dare."*

But before that sentence could escape his throat, the reminders from his grandmother, the expression of the Crown Prince, the lifeblood of the Lu family, and his own status as a concubine-born son flashed through his mind... and then there was her, the Di daughter of the Shen family, the one destined to stand as the head of the Six Palaces.

He abruptly clenched his back teeth, swallowing all his emotions into his belly.

He averted his eyes and said in a low voice: "Zhaoru, you have gone mad."

"Yes, I have gone mad." She drew closer step by step, tears in her eyes but her tone resolute. "You have finally called me by my name again?"

"Do not be like this; it is I who have failed you..."

"No, I do not want you to fail me. You clearly said that day your heart was pleased with me; so, do you want me to wait for the decree to arrive, and then have you say 'Congratulations, Crown Princess' to me? Did you not say that life is short, so why stick to old ways?"

She looked at him, her smile bitter: "Then I ask you, if in this life I am truly destined only to face you in wordless silence, would you ever be reconciled to it?"

His fists were tightly clenched, his spine stiff and upright.

He did not speak of his feelings, but spat out each word with deliberate force: "If I were to follow your wishes now and elope with you, it would be the utter burial of both your life and mine. If you marry the Crown Prince, it is the glory of the Shen family and a lifetime of wealth for you. If you flee with me, you would be nothing more than... an outcast of the Shen family, the mistress of a Lu manor concubine-son."

"I am not afraid—"

"But I am!"

He finally broke out in a loud cry, interrupting her with a voice that carried an unprecedented shattered quality. He turned away, averting his face, not daring to look at her again.

What I fear is not exile—it is you being dragged into baseness by my hand.

She stood frozen on the spot, her tears falling, yet she made no sound.

After a long time, she turned slowly and walked out the door.

The wind made the door creak slightly; that familiar figure gradually receded. He did not give chase.

He merely stood where he was, his fingers trembling as they brushed the corner of the desk. There lay the scorched fragment of *The Romance of the Western Chamber* that he had failed to burn that day; upon the paper, a line of the play was still vaguely visible: *"If one may obtain the heart of a beloved, they shall not part even when their hair turns white."*

He gave a soft laugh—laughing at his own incompetence, and laughing at the piteous state of this world.

He murmured under his breath: "Affection is hard to voice... and even harder to forsake."

* * * * *

The following day, at the third mark of the hour of the Sheep, the decree of betrothal from the Eastern Palace arrived, written by the Imperial Brush itself, with all the ceremony of a grand procession.

—The daughter of the Shen clan, Shen Zhaoru, being virtuous, upright, and possessed of both fine character and appearance, is chosen to be the Crown Princess, to be invested on an auspicious day and proclaimed to all under heaven.

The eunuch held the imperial decree and read it aloud at the Shen manor; amidst the sound of drums and music, every street and alley heard the news, and it spread throughout the capital.

Madam Shen wept for joy, immediately ordering her servants to change into red attire, prepare return gifts, and announce the celebration far and wide.

Yet Shen Zhaoru, at the moment of the reading, stood behind a curtain, her face as white as paper.

She looked at that gold-lacquered imperial decree as if she were seeing shackles locking away her entire life.

She made no sound, only turning to return silently to her bedchamber.

The door was closed, the windows shuttered; all sounds of the world fell still.

She sat before her dressing table, gazing into the bronze mirror. Her eyes were rimmed with red, and her fingertips gripped the edge of the table so tightly her knuckles turned white.

She remembered his evasive gaze from the previous night, remembered him saying *"But I am afraid,"* and remembered the words *"I am willing"* that he could not voice.

She began to laugh, murmuring to herself.

In that laugh there was no joy, only despair and irony.

She slowly opened her cosmetic box and drew a dagger from the bottom layer. The cold light of the short blade trembled slightly; it was a gift from her father and brother in years past for self-defence, and it had never once been unsheathed.

She placed it upon her knees, her fingertips passing inch by inch over the surface of the blade.

Outside the window, the shadows of flowers swayed; the wind passed through the parasol trees, and the autumn light was as cold and clear as water.

She asked herself in a soft voice: "If I cannot be the master of my own life, if the one I love cannot stay... then what is the meaning of my remaining here?"

She gripped the dagger, her hand trembling slightly, her gaze resolute.

In an instant, the sound of hurried footsteps and the startled cry of Nanny Su came from outside the door:

"Miss! You must not—!"

The door was violently burst open; it was Madam Shen rushing in.

She saw the short blade in Shen Zhaoru's hand at once and was seized with immense terror, her voice trembling: "Zhaoru! Have you gone mad? You are now the Crown Princess! You are the future Empress of the Central Palace, destined for glory and wealth; how could you do such a thing!"

Shen Zhaoru uttered not a word, only staring at her with eyes full of coldness. "Which of you ever asked me if I was willing?"

"Mother, if I truly enter the Eastern Palace, there will be no path of retreat in this life. Do you understand?"

"What you and Father love is the Shen family climbing higher. But your daughter does not love the Crown Prince; your daughter only wishes to live a proper life."

Madam Shen shook her head through her tears: "What nonsense are you speaking? The Crown Prince is young and elegant, and he is a childhood friend of yours; in the future, he will be the master of ten thousand people, and you are the chosen of Heaven! How could you..."

"Mother, you and Father only care for status; you do not ask after the human heart."

"No, daughter, you are wrong. Your mother failed to bear you a brother; I am afraid that in the future, after your parents have passed on, you will have no one to rely upon." Madam Shen explained with a hoarse voice, constantly wiping her tears.

"And what of it? Mother, you say that after the Crown Prince ascends the throne, he will inevitably have his Three Palaces and Six Courtyards; will he truly be my future reliance?"

Having finished speaking in a low voice, she abruptly raised the blade toward her own wrist—

At that very moment, a figure broke through the door, travel-worn and with a fierce gaze.

"Zhaoru!"

It was the Crown Prince, Chen Gen!

He snatched the dagger from her hand in one movement and pulled her tightly into his embrace, his voice carrying both harshness and dread: "Zhaoru, do not be foolish."

She gazed at him blankly, her tears finally falling, soaking his collar inch by inch. "Prince Brother..."

He held her close, murmuring in a trembling voice: "Do not cry; how could you do such a foolish thing?"

"I... Prince Brother..." Her voice was so hoarse it was barely recognisable.

"Zhaoru, do not be foolish. One's body, hair, and skin are received from one's parents; if you were to die... have you ever thought how the one who remains alive is to endure??"

She leaned against his chest, her fingertips trembling, as if she finally could not hold herself up any longer; her entire body curled inward.

Chen Gen held her, saying nothing for a long while; he only felt the chill from her body seeping into his chest bit by bit, as if it would freeze his entire ribcage.

The lights in the room flickered, and the sound of the dagger hitting the floor had not yet faded.

He looked down at her, his voice low and hoarse: "Zhaoru, I did not expect you to be so unable to see a way out. Had I not happened to come to the Shen manor today to discuss matters with the Imperial Preceptor, I fear you would have harmed yourself. Why must you be so despondent? You know that if you were unwilling, I would not force you..."

She shook her head, her throat tightening, her voice sounding as if squeezed from the depths of her chest: "It is not your fault. It is I... I should not have believed those words of his; I should not have thought he had the courage to overcome the world..."

"Zhaoru, you and I have been classmates since our youth, and I have always regarded you as my own younger sister. If you have any difficulties, you need not speak; I shall naturally help..."

"No, Prince Brother, it is I who was wrong. It is I who believed in the wrong person..."

Chen Gen's gaze darkened, his fingertips tightening as if he wished to rub her into his very bones and blood: "You believed in the wrong person once; then let me carry this life for you, shall I?"

Shen Zhaoru's form shuddered; she raised her eyes to look at him.

He lowered his gaze, his face full of exhaustion and regret: "I shall not let you face those rumours alone again, nor shall I let anyone use you as a bargaining chip ever again."

"But you are the Crown Prince..."

"Precisely because I am the Crown Prince can I keep you safe."

At that moment, she could finally no longer feign strength. Her tears fell like pearls from a broken string as she threw herself into his embrace without a word.

Chen Gen reached out to brush away the disordered strands of hair from her forehead, saying in a low voice: "Let us go; return to the palace first. For every moment longer you remain outside, my unease grows by another measure."

She nodded gently, as if she had finally surrendered all her strength, standing only by leaning against his arm.

A carriage was already prepared outside. He personally assisted her into the vehicle and commanded his followers: "By my decree, the manor of the Imperial Preceptor is to close its gates to guests for three days, to be guarded personally by the Chief Internal Attendant."

He looked at Shen Zhaoru again, his tone gentle yet firm: "This is not a punishment, but protection. I am unwilling to let you be burdened in the slightest by others again."

The night wind grew sudden and sharp; the carriage curtain was closed. Amidst the sound of horse hooves, a past of grievances and affections finally reached its conclusion.

Once the carriage had moved far off, Chen Gen's thin lips curled slightly, finally revealing a smile of confidence and composure.

Shen Zhaoru, Lu Xiu—as the saying goes, "in war, there is no such thing as too much deception." My move of retreating in order to advance was successful; one can only blame the fragility of the affection between you two, which could not withstand the test.

Chapter 78: I thank you all for your kindness

Night had only just begun its descent.

Within the Golden Throne Hall, lamps were kindled one after another, their glow settling over jade-laid tables and banquet settings.

Young nobles, refined maidens of eminent families, court officials and titled ladies filled the seats in quiet splendour.

Beyond the hall, the sky deepened shade by shade; within, light gathered in soft brilliance, the murmur of cups and voices flowing like a gentle, unbroken stream.

Shen Zhaoru sat among the women's ranks.

The dishes arranged before her were as finely crafted as painted scrolls, fragrant and warm, yet she had not lifted her chopsticks once.

The talk circling around her had drifted from idle palace tales to the shifting winds of court affairs, for reports from the northern border had arrived in swift succession, troubling every mind.

"Rumour says the northern troops are stirring. They have already tested the defence line thrice."

"His Highness the Crown Prince has held private councils with several key ministers who favour decisive action. It seems a great move may soon be set into motion."

She had meant not to listen, nor allow the words to reach her thoughts.

Yet when the phrase "northern border" brushed her ear, her heart faltered with a faint, involuntary tremor.

Her fingertips touched the rim of her wine cup, tapping out the lightest rhythm, barely there, like a note that fades before it is heard.

A small breath caught within her chest.

She raised a hand to her lips, offering a gentle smile.

Madam Han, seated beside her, leaned forward with concern. "Your Highness the Crown Princess Consort appears pale. Is the hall too warm for your comfort?"

Zhaoru steadied herself with quiet grace. "Perhaps the candlelight is too bright. My chest feels somewhat close."

Madam Xiao, nearby, added with a soft laugh, "The weather shifts so quickly between chill and warmth. Your Highness must take great care, lest His Highness the Crown Prince worry."

She lowered her gaze, the curve of her lips faint. "I thank you all for your kindness. A moment of air will suffice."

She rose, speaking softly to her maid. "I feel a little light-headed. I will step out for some air."

Without waiting for a reply, she withdraws quietly toward the side corridor.

Lantern-light brushed against the vermilion palace walls; her steps were slow and measured, the hem of her cloak gliding across the stone floor like a drifting shadow beneath moonlit eaves.

From the distance, a familiar figure approached along the pale path.

It was the Crown Prince's favoured consort, Xu Hui.

Zhaoru had seen her often before: a slender, mild-tempered woman who always stood a respectful step behind her elder royal brother.

Clad in an apricot-coloured palace gown, a sachet held lightly between her hands, Xu Hui paused before her, offering a graceful curtsey and a gentle smile.

"Lady Shen… though now, I believe it is proper to greet you as Your Highness, the Crown Princess Consort."

Shen Zhaoru offered a faint smile. "Your Ladyship jests. Though the imperial edict has been issued, the rites are not yet complete. To address me as Crown Princess Consort at this moment would run ahead of propriety."

"Very well. Until the grand rites are held, I shall continue to call you as before, Elder Sister Shen."

Xu Hui curved her lips in a playful smile.

Zhaoru returned a slight, courteous smile.

The two of them stood beneath the eaves, side by side, saying nothing for a time.

After a brief pause, Xu Hui spoke softly. "Elder Sister… there are some words I do not know whether I ought to speak."

Zhaoru answered her with a polite smile. "Your Ladyship need not stand on ceremony. If you have something to say, please speak freely."

Xu Hui seemed to think for a moment, as though gathering her courage, before she said quietly, "When I learnt that the final choice for Crown Princess Consort was you, I was truly glad."

At this, Shen Zhaoru showed a trace of puzzlement, though she did not question her at once.

Xu Hui continued gently. "You and His Highness the Crown Prince grew up together. You are both graceful and wise, admired for both conduct and talent. And His Highness is young and accomplished. You and he are as well matched as any could hope."

Shen Zhaoru could not help turning to look at her directly. Only after a moment did she speak. "You… truly think so?"

Xu Hui covered her smile with a handkerchief. "But of course."

"To share a husband with others… do you not feel jealousy?"

"Not at all." Xu Hui shook her head. After a moment, she added, "Elder Sister, do you believe a man such as His Highness… could ever be anything but lonely?"

Zhaoru lifted her gaze slightly, taken aback, unable to grasp her full meaning.

A moment later, Xu Hui went on. "Elder Sister Shen, His Highness is a good man. That much, I dare vouch for."

Her smile remained soft. "His Highness carries duty in his heart, but he is also capable of affection. Only, he never forces his will upon others. The position of Crown Prince is one all eyes are fixed upon, yet his solitude is far beyond what common hearts can fathom."

Zhaoru did not reply.

She simply looked toward the sea of distant lanterns, her eyes cool and unreadable.

It was then that a familiar figure approached.

The Crown Prince, Chen Gen, was dressed in dark brocade threaded with muted gold, his steps steady and composed.

Seeing the two women standing together, he paused briefly before smiling.

"So, the two of you converse with such accord. It makes one wonder whether I might be allowed to hear a word of it."

Xu Hui bowed. "Your Highness."

He inclined his head, his tone gentle. "Go on. The night breeze is cool—do not catch cold."

Xu Hui answered softly and withdrew. Her attendants followed in quiet order.

Shen Zhaoru watched the retreating figures for a long while without speaking.

Behind Xu Hui trailed several palace maids and young eunuchs.

Though their number was not small and their steps varied, none made a sound; they faded, one by one, into the distance of the corridor—a silent procession, a quiet performance slipping offstage.

A faint tightness gathered in her chest.

She could not help imagining the near future—

that she, too, would become part of such a silent tableau, only with more attendants, finer robes, more layers of ceremony.

Chen Gen did not know what filled her thoughts. He merely saw her staring after his consort's departing retinue for so long that he turned toward her and said, quietly:

"If you have something to ask, then ask it."

Shen Zhaoru turned back, lifting her gaze, eyes holding a question. "Just now at the banquet, I heard mention of unrest at the border."

"Mm. The border has been unsettled for over a decade. It is nothing new."

"Then… may I ask whether Crown Prince Brother intends to send him to the frontier?"

"Whom?"

Chen Gen gave a soft laugh, deliberately feigning ignorance. His handsome features carried a trace of teasing.

Zhaoru pressed her lips together, saying nothing, but her eyes—clear and luminous—looked steadily at him.

He could not withstand that look. After a moment, he nodded. "He requested the assignment himself."

Neither of them spoke the name, yet the tacit understanding between them was unmistakable.

She stilled, her lips parting slightly, but in the end she did not ask the question that lingered beneath her breath—

why.

"I had thought Crown Prince Brother would mind… about me and him…" she murmured.

"What is there to mind?"

The Crown Prince returned her gaze; it seemed gentle, yet beneath it lay a quiet sharpness.

"A man unmarried, a woman unwed—nothing more than a passing stir of youth. Why should such a thing trouble anyone?"

She paused for a moment, then lowered her gaze with a faint, self-deprecating smile.

"Crown Prince Brother speaks truly. Since there is no attachment to speak of, whether he stays or goes… has nothing to do with me."

Chen Gen's lips curved suddenly, and his tone softened—yet the gentleness struck closer than any sharpness.

"Zhaoru, I have little interest in forcing another's will. To marry you is because you possess discernment, steadiness, and reputation—and because you can also… tolerate her. It is a need of the court, yes, but also a wish of my own."

She looked at him, startled by the straightforwardness of his words.

"But…"

"I am no villain who delights in breaking pairs apart."

His voice was calm, almost quiet.

"You may have held affection elsewhere, yet the difference in station means such a bond was never one that could be fulfilled. If you wish it, after the wedding, in all things I shall not press you. You will have dignity, and you will have freedom. As the Crown Princess chosen by me, no one would dare utter half a word of idle gossip against you. On that, you may rest easy."

He smiled faintly; under the lantern glow, his already handsome features seemed even more composed, more difficult to read.

"As for what comes in the future… who can claim certainty?"

She did not answer at once.

Her eyes drifted beyond the red palace walls—a leaf loosened from a high branch, swirling once before vanishing silently into the night wind.

—Whom could she still love?

—And what courage was left to love at all?

Love was a blade, a fault, a weakness.

She no longer wished to hold it, nor to be wounded by it again.

"…Very well."

Her reply was soft. "I understand."

At that moment, she chose the Crown Prince—not out of affection, but because her heart had already ceased to trust in love.

In that moment, she truly became the Crown Princess. Yet she knew: from this day forward, the door within her heart would open for no one again.

Chapter 79: The Road Home

From beneath the corridors came the rhythmic clink and clatter of copper horse-bells, bamboo food hampers, and soft travel satchels, carried out piece by piece from the eastern wing.

Lu Xiu stood before the steps with his hands clasped behind his back; his expression was cold and detached, a flicker of deep loathing surfacing in the depths of his eyes.

The servants' faces were piled with smiles as they chattered away, exclaiming how "the Young Mistress prefers fragrant felt and soft pillows" or how "the Young Miss's embroidery chest requires a separate wooden case," speaking with such immense bustle as if they were seeing off a pair of harmonious lovers on a distant excursion, or perhaps arranging a new life for someone.

Lu Xiu gazed upon this scene of exuberant joy and found it only an eyesore. It was as if this military expedition were not a matter of life and death, but rather an attendance at a celebratory feast.

He flicked his sleeve with impatience and commanded in a cold voice: "Get far away from me, all of you; the noise is deafening."

Within the manor, the voices of people seethed like a boiling cauldron; armour, travel gear, horse tack, and bows and arrows were all being tallied and packed. Servants hurried to and fro, the atmosphere a mixture of tension and excitement.

But none of that had anything to do with him.

He turned abruptly, his robes fluttering as he exited past the screen wall; before him lay the main thoroughfare.

Who could have known that after turning but a few paces, he would collide head-on with a person—Lu Chou.

the other man appeared in excellent health, wearing a brilliant smile; amidst his fluttering cloak, he even carried a food hamper, possessing an air of leisure and unruffled grace that was truly vexing.

He stood there, unmoving and refusing to yield, his gaze like a blade; clearly, he had been waiting. Lu Chou paused his steps slightly, his eyes betraying bewilderment.

"Second Brother!" Lu Xiu suddenly called out. Before Lu Chou could react, a fist slammed into his face, and a thin trail of blood instantly seeped from the corner of his mouth.

"What madness has possessed you?"

Before the words could even leave his mouth, a second fist arrived head-on—

Bang!

Lu Chou staggered back half a step, then immediately raised a hand to press against his cheek, his expression turning dark in an instant.

Lu Xiu spoke coldly: "It is nothing; I simply find this face of yours truly deserving of a thrashing."

Lu Chou wiped the bloodstains from the corner of his mouth; he did not grow angry, but merely arched an eyebrow with a smile: "What, no reason?"

"There is," Lu Xiu sneered. "These two punches are what I, your elder brother, have wished to deliver for over a decade."

"Then why did you not strike back then? Did you lack the courage?"

These words pierced straight to the heart.

Lu Xiu's expression turned frigid; without a word, he swung another fist, but it met only empty air, for after taking two punches, Lu Chou was now on his guard.

The two entangled in a brawl beneath the corridor, every punch striking to the bone, devoid of any mercy. Servants shrieked and fled; none dared to intervene.

It was not until the head maid from the Old Matriarch's courtyard rushed over that Lu Xiu, who was raising his fist to strike, found his arm gripped firmly by Lu Chou.

"What? Did you think I would let you land a third?"

"And why not?"

The maid shouted sternly to stop them, bringing a group of manservants to force the two apart: "Do the two of you have no sense of propriety? In two days' time, the Eldest Young Master must go to war, and the Second Young Master must go south to investigate a case. Do you intend to make the entire manor a laughingstock?"

Lu Xiu panted for breath, his collar dishevelled and the veins at his temples bulging.

He stared into his younger brother's eyes, which still carried a hint of a smile; suddenly, his chest tightened, and he said in a cold voice: "I do not loathe you; I simply cannot stand it—how you have everything, yet live with such ease."

He paused, then suddenly lowered his eyes and whispered: "The third punch... shall be owed for now. If I do not return, these two punches shall serve as... a sending-off."

Lu Chou's expression was shaken; he looked down at the bloodstains on his palm and remained silent for a long time.

The wind rose, and falling leaves cut like knives.

This was no mere exchange of fists, but the most painful farewell in a brotherhood.

He did not look back.

Because he knew that if he looked back, he too would lose.

Three paces apart, the brothers stood back-to-back, each in his own silence.

Just like the three years to follow—one to the South, one to the North, with no further intersection.

The sunlight outside the corridor was fine and fair, yet the murderous aura in the courtyard was heavy.

The bloodstains gradually dried, yet like an old wound that had long failed to heal, they throbbed with a faint ache.

He suddenly felt that this blood did not sting; rather, it was his chest that felt stifled and swollen—that punch had clearly landed on his face, yet it felt as though it had fallen heavily into his heart.

* * * * *

Lu Xiu, covered in the dust of travel and looking quite wretched, stepped into the Yuechuan Courtyard just as the light of heaven began to slant.

No sooner had he entered the gate than he saw Liu Huiniang already waiting beneath the corridor; the hair at her temples hung loose and unbound, and the rims of her eyes were as red as if touched by rouge. Upon seeing him, she hurried forward, her tears falling with a splat.

"Xiu'er, what are you doing... how have you beaten your hands into such a state?"

She had already heard the reports from the servants; her Xiu'er had, for some unknown reason, suddenly come into conflict with the Second Young Master and fought a fierce battle in full view of everyone.

She sobbed as she reached out to pull at him; seeing his knuckles swollen and red and his collar in disarray, it was clear he had come to blows. She drew a sharp, low breath and asked tremulously: "Did you... did you strike your Second Brother? He is the Di son of the main wife... how could you be so impulsive..."

Before these words were finished, Lu Xiu's expression changed abruptly.

"The Di son?" He gave a cold laugh and suddenly wrenched his hand from hers, his voice carrying a fury never heard before: "Yes, precisely because he is the Di son and I am a Shu son born of a concubine, I cannot marry her in this lifetime!"

Liu Huiniang trembled with fright, her eyes full of panic and heartache, yet she dared not say more, only murmuring: "Her? Who is she?"

Lu Xiu had never spoken to her in such a manner.

He did not answer, turning his back in silence. His spine was ramrod straight and his voice low and taut, as if foul air suppressed for too long had finally exploded.

"I am Shu, he is Di, so I must let him be ahead of me in every matter? I yielded from childhood, and I am still yielding as an adult—yielding until I do not even dare to open my mouth to contend for the person I love! You say I am impulsive... if I do not act impulsively just once, I shall be crushed to death by this status for the rest of my life!"

He spoke with such urgency that the veins at his temples throbbed; for a fleeting moment, a flash of stubbornness and pain crossed his eyes.

The room became so quiet that a falling needle could be heard.

Liu Huiniang had shrunk into a corner beneath the eaves, weeping, not daring to approach further, yet she could not help but whisper: "Xiu'er...

you are going to the Northern Frontier. If... if there is some mishap... how can you... what is your Auntie to do?"

Before the words were finished, Lu Xiu suddenly strode to a cabinet in the corner, opened a locked box, and pulled out a thick stack of banknotes.

He turned back and thrust the banknotes into her hand without allowing for argument; his movements were crisp, yet his tone was low and heavy.

"Mother, keep these safe." His eyes were bloodshot, yet exceptionally determined. "Let me call you 'Mother' one last time, rather than 'Auntie.' If your son does not return, it shall not be said that you raised me for nothing. There is not much here, about fifteen thousand taels; keep it, and do not wrong yourself again, nor live your life in a lowly manner."

Liu Huiniang's tears could no longer be stopped; her trembling hands tried to push them back: "I do not want money, I only want you..."

He looked down at her, his gaze softening inch by inch, until he finally whispered: "Mother, I know that all your life you have not dared to contend or entreat, which is why you made me, your son, live with such endurance. But I am different."

"Once I go to the frontier this time, if I am able to return alive, I shall contend for my own destiny. If I cannot..."

He paused for a moment and actually smiled, though it was a smile of bitter heartache: "Then so be it; let this life... end as it is."

Liu Huiniang lunged forward to embrace him, her tears wetting his collar as she said in a trembling voice: "My son..."

But he did not move, only lowering his eyelashes and letting her weep and hold him, as if he had long grown accustomed to such distance and restraint.

The wind blew in from the window, causing the edges of the papers on the desk to tremble slightly.

That night, the lights in the Yuechuan Courtyard were never extinguished; mother and son leaned by the lamp, remaining silent for a long time.

* * * * *

The warm sun spilled through the window lattices at an angle, falling upon the rosewood table. The Old Matriarch sat upon the k'ang bed, draped in a dark red cloak embroidered with gold thread; the tea cup in her hands had been held for a long while, yet it never reached her lips.

She gazed at the withered branches swaying outside the window, her expression solitary; her gaze lingered for a long time upon the travel gear and horse tack in the courtyard, most of which had already been cleared away. She lightly wiped the corner of her eye, her movements extremely subtle, as if she feared disturbing someone.

"This courtyard," she finally said in a low voice, "is as desolate as an ancestral hall after the autumn sacrifices."

Lu Wenqian, who was standing by the k'ang, stood with his hands lowered; he turned his body slightly, a trace of apology in his expression: "Your son has caused you worry."

"Ai." The Old Matriarch shook her head, her gaze still not withdrawn, saying softly: "Our Lu family has only these two seedlings. One must travel far to the frontier, and the other must go south on official business... tell me, why is this world so chaotic that it must send two brothers to opposite ends."

"The situation at court is ever-changing; this too is beyond one's control." Lu Wenqian's tone was steady, yet it carried a hidden self-reproach. "It is your son's incompetence that he cannot protect the integrity of the family gate."

"Wenqian." The Old Matriarch sighed lightly and turned to look at him. "Mother is not blaming you."

She set down the tea cup, her fingers trembling slightly as she smoothed her collar. Her gaze swept over his official robes, and only after a long while did she speak: "You, since childhood, have always been the one to put one's mind at ease. Now that your two sons are so promising, it would be a lie to say you do not feel proud as a father. But as a mother—I seek only one thing."

She gestured toward her own chest, her tone low and soft: "That they be safe. For the whole family, in peace and safety, to sit down and have a meal, to exchange a few words of idle talk—then Mother shall be content."

Hearing this, a complex expression flashed through Lu Wenqian's eyes, and he immediately nodded: "Your son shall remember."

The Old Matriarch, however, seemed to have long seen through his thoughts; she smiled faintly, yet wiped the corner of her eye once more.

"You, do not just speak fine words. Mother knows you are biased in your heart." Her tone was not heavy, yet every word hit home. "Chou is the Di son, fine in both appearance and character; everything naturally goes smoothly for him. It is inevitable that you, as a father, look upon him more frequently; Mother does not blame you for this."

She paused, her tone dropping slightly: "But you must also remember that although Xiu is born of a concubine, he is your eldest son, and he has never brought the slightest shame to our house. His temperament is so stubborn that he knows not how to act spoiled or curry favour with you, but he is a good child with backbone and ability."

Lu Wenqian's expression shifted, and he nodded in silence.

"This time, he is going to the frontier." The Old Matriarch lowered her eyes, her voice somewhat hoarse. "What kind of place that is, you and I both know in our hearts. Mother does not understand court politics, but I heard your father say that year—if war truly breaks out, it is a place where people are slaughtered on sight."

Speaking to this point, her voice shook slightly, and she added in a low voice: "Both brothers were raised under my watch... though he does not say it, I know that his heart is bitter."

Lu Wenqian's expression grew solemn, and he said in a deep voice: "Your child will provide extra care, dispatching capable hands to protect his safety. The necessary travel funds and equipment have also been prepared in secret."

The Old Matriarch nodded slowly, and only after a long time did she heave a sigh: "Doing this, Mother is at ease. But you must also remember, it is not just to protect him this one time... if there is an opportunity in the future, he too must marry and have children, to form a family. Mother has not said it these years, but it is not as if I do not keep it in mind."

She paused for a moment, her tone slowing: "I do not worry for Chou; he has his ways, and there are people to arrange things for him. Xiu, however, is different... there is always a knot in this child's heart that he cannot bypass. If he truly does not return, or if he returns with a dead heart, then I... how am I to give an account to his mother? His mother has not had it easy these past twenty-some years either."

Lu Wenqian's gaze was shaken; he suddenly said in a low voice: "Mother, rest assured. Your son... will certainly not disappoint you."

Only then did the Old Matriarch nod slowly, a lingering dampness still in her eyes. She gazed at that empty corner of the corridor and suddenly whispered as if talking to herself: " These two brothers, split between North and South, are like kites with severed strings... drifting ever further into the distance. ."

"Mother only hopes that no matter how far they fly, they must still find the road back home." The room was silent; the sound of the wind moved slightly, and the window paper trembled like a breath. The travel gear in the courtyard had been collected, and the sunlight gradually slanted. She slowly sat up straight, adjusted her sleeves, and suddenly asked: "Nothing happened to Chou's face, did it?"

Lu Wenqian paused, finally revealing a bitter smile: "Replying to Mother: it is fine. The bone was not injured, it is just a bit bruised. However... that punch, Xiu landed it with great force."

The Old Matriarch shook her head and raised a finger to point at him: "You, do not ask too much. Between brothers, if they do not fight, they do not become close."

"This fight was well fought." Her voice was slightly hoarse, yet she revealed a rare, aged, but warm smile. "What was struck out was resentment, but what remains is the bond of kinship."

Readers can view the full collection of colour illustrations here:
https://www.facebook.com/profile.php?id=61581325000577

Chapter 80: North and South, Divergent Paths

The intent of snow had not yet dissolved, and the spring chill was sharp and biting.

To the northwest of the capital's outskirts, the Five Camps of the Great Army were arrayed along both sides of the official highway; banners snapped and fluttered in the wind, stretching further than the eye could discern.

The vanguard had already commenced their journey three days prior; today marked the hour for the central army's departure.

Over a hundred armoured warriors stood in formation with halberds in hand, their iron mail reflecting the light, their murderous aura cold as frost.

Lu Xiu, clad in his armour, stood before his steed. His gaze was settled and resolute as he looked afar toward the snow-sealed mountain passes.

Suddenly, the light creak of carriage wheels was heard as a small, ornate vehicle with a flowered canopy emerged slowly from the woods.

The carriage curtain was lifted, a rustle sounding in the wind, and a shimmer of light purple appeared like a layered shadow amidst the snow.

It was Shen Zhaoru, the tassels of the dangling ornaments at her forehead trembling slightly, her robes and cloak fluttering.

Her expression was still and cold, yet she could not entirely mask the surging, restless turmoil between her brows.

This time, she did not come by stealth, nor would she depart in secret.

Instead, she came openly and with full dignity, in her capacity as the prospective Crown Princess, to personally see him off—to escort him for one final stage of his journey.

"The Crown Prince said that as an old friend is travelling far, it is only fitting and reasonable for Shen Zhaoru to bid him farewell on his behalf." *Her voice was soft, yet her inner character remained upright and awe-inspiring.*

Lu Xiu was stunned for a fleeting moment, but ultimately he lowered his head and cupped his hands in a respectful salute, saying in a low voice, "This subject... thanks His Royal Highness the Crown Prince."

His tone was respectful, yet from beginning to end, he did not call her by her given name even once.

She descended from the carriage, her steps slow and steady, holding in her hands a flask of floral wine and a small glaze-glass cup.

Between the two of them stood a tall horse; there also lay a divide of destiny and two distinct sets of identities.

"This was brewed by my own hand during last year's Double Ninth Festival." *Zhaoru proffered the wine, her eyes calm, yet her voice trembled ever so slightly.*

"I originally intended to save it so we might drink together come next spring. Now, if we do not drink it today, I fear there shall never be another chance to drink it."

She held up a single cup of wine and slowly parted her lips: "Today, Shen Zhaoru opens the wine for the Great Army. May the army, on this expedition, find safety and return home in glorious triumph."

He took the wine cup, his fingertips brushing against her slightly cool knuckles; *at that instant, the strings of his heart very nearly snapped.*

He tilted his head back and drained it in one draught, the glaze-glass trembling slightly. *His throat surged with emotion as the words "I thank Her Ladyship for bestowing the wine" finally escaped his lips.*

The voice was incredibly soft, yet it felt as heavy as a thousand pounds.

Shen Zhaoru lowered her gaze, her eyelashes quivering. She tucked her hands into her sleeves and took back the flask, intending to turn and depart, yet she came to a halt several paces away.

—This wine was a parting, not a blessing. This journey was a sending-off, not a reunion.

"You should know... that my coming here was not solely for the Prince."

She kept her back to him, her voice drifting in the wind: "I also wished to personally see you off... simply because I do not wish to have regrets."

Lu Xiu's heart suffered a jolt, and waves surged in the depths of his eyes. He wished to say so much—but he said not a single word.

He only gazed at her silently, his voice low and hoarse: "If I am able to return from this journey, I wish to have no further lingering attachments with Your Ladyship."

The wind and snow suddenly grew heavy. Shen Zhaoru stood amidst the white, her robes fluttering as she responded in a low whisper: "You and I have long been without such attachments. I only hope that Sub-Lieutenant Lu has a safe journey... you must, by all means, stay safe."

She boarded the carriage without looking back. As the carriage curtain fell, it was as if their fates had dropped away, never to intersect again.

He stood before his horse for a long time without moving. The wind and snow became more oppressive, and the light of heaven grew grey and hazy.

"Zhaoru..." *he called out in a low voice.*

The sound of the words was extremely faint, yet it seemed squeezed from his very vitals, abruptly snapping apart in the wind.

He flipped himself up onto his horse, *yet his fingers trembled at that moment. Hidden in a place close to his body within his robes, he concealed an object.*

On that day beneath the sunset, as they rode a single horse together along the woodland path, amidst their playful banter, he had roguishly and forcibly taken the hair-pin from her tresses; a strand of black hair was still entangled at the pin's end. That gold pin inlaid with pearls—he had kept it all along.

Today, he had gripped it in his palm many times, pondering whether or not to return it. Yet every time he moved to take it out, that trace of imperceptible warmth would seep into his knuckles, like her breath—soft yet stubborn—entwining him and refusing to let him let go.

Ultimately, he still did not return it.

He carefully stowed the pin away, hiding it in the most secret inner pocket of his armour—the small pouch where he kept his personal seal and military texts close to his skin. *He never harboured sentiments of the heart, yet today, he had broken his rule.*

He could not take her away, yet he still selfishly wished to keep a small fragment of remembrance.

—Let it be, he thought, the final delusion within his heart.

* * * * *

Suddenly, a thin, childish voice was heard coming from behind the carriage: "Big Uncle~~ Are you really going to leave?"

Lu Xiu was startled. He turned his head to see that tiny little person, who had run out from the other side of the woods at some unknown point; her cheeks were blown crimson by the wind, and her hands tightly clutching a package of pastries.

It was Baor.

She stood in the snowy ground, looking up at him, the rims of her eyes slightly red. *Yet she* exerted great effort to suppress her sobs:

"These are the osmanthus dumplings I made... didn't you say you liked eating sweet things?... My Mama wouldn't let me come; Papa Lord brought me out here in secret... you mustn't tell her..."

His expression shifted slightly, and a ripple of emotion passed through his eyes. Ultimately, he dismounted and knelt to take the pastries from her hands.

"Baor, Big Uncle will be gone for a very long time on this trip. This road... is too far, and the wind is great. You should stay by your Mama's side and take good care of her, alright?"

She nodded her head, yet she pouted: "Then when you come back, will you still carry me and hold me up high?"

His fingertips lightly brushed away the frost and tears from her face. His lips pressed into a thin line as he said in a low voice: "As long as you remember Big Uncle, I certainly shall."

What he did not say aloud was that single sentence: "If I am still able to return."

Having spoken, he handed the pastries to the lieutenant at his side and turned to mount his horse.

Baor tilted her small face up, gazing blankly at his receding figure, when she suddenly murmured a sentence: "Big Uncle... Baor will miss you..."

She did not know why she had blurted it out; perhaps she simply wished to make him stay.

The voice was too light; it might not have been heard in the wind.

But Lu Xiu pulled the reins and paused, his back stiffening slightly. He did not look back, *only the palm of his hand, hidden within his armour, tightened again and again.* He turned his head to meet the man who had remained quiet at the side.

Lu Chou took Baor into his arms and gave a cold snort, saying only: "Go then. Just be sure not to go and get yourself killed."

Lu Xiu followed with a scoff of his own. "Likewise. You, on the other hand, should be sure not to go and court death with your own antics."

Lu Chou: "..."

He felt that for this trip, he really shouldn't have come!

* * * * *

Seven days later, the palace gates swung wide as ten thousand people offered their congratulations. Shen Zhaoru was invested as the Crown Princess. Clad in a phoenix crown and embroidered robes, she stood atop the golden steps; from this moment on, she held a place in the Golden Throne Hall, but the doors to the deep palace were closed to the world.

And that day was precisely the day that he and the Great Army stepped across the Snow-Sealed Pass.

The north wind blew for a thousand miles as the war drums began to roll. She had been crowned a consort, and he had set foot upon the path of war—for the remainder of their lives, there would be no more words between them.

The wind and snow grew more rapid, and the cold gale poured into the armour at his neck, yet he was entirely oblivious to it.

Beneath the horse's hooves, the accumulated snow began to melt, and the splashing water droplets dampened the hem of his garment.

Lu Xiu held the reins with one hand, while the other hand gripped something tightly—the object in his palm was slightly cold, its touch familiar.

That was a gold pin inlaid with pearls; hers...

He had thought that on that day he would hand it back and make a clean break. But at the moment she had proffered the wine cup and said she "did not wish to have regrets," he knew—that he, too, could not bear to break it.

He looked down at that hairpin, his knuckles pale, his fingertips trembling slightly.

It was not for the sake of lingering attachment, but because he did not dare to forget.

On this road of high mountains and distant waters, should he fail to return, he wished to still remember a trace of her features and that soft call before the wind and sand covered his bones.

He closed his eyes, and when he opened them again, there were ten thousand miles of passes and mountains.

The bugle sounded ahead; he surged forward on his horse, his lips pressed tight, finally uttering a low sentence: "Zhaoru, do not forget what you said—that you do not wish to have regrets."

Then he spurred his horse into a gallop, never looking back again.

* * * * *

The spring chill gradually receded; the mountain breeze brushed against faces, and new greenery was born.

Unlike the murderous aura and congealed frost of the Northern City, the atmosphere here was actually somewhat bustling.

Several official carriages were ready to depart, with the Forbidden Guard clearing the way in front and attendant horse-carts following behind.

Passersby cast sidelong glances, thinking only that some imperial kinsmen or nobles were going on an outing, unaware that this was exactly the departure of the Junior Vice Minister of the Ministry of Revenue, Lu Chou, "acting on imperial decree to tour the South" to inspect the silk taxes of Jiangnan.

But looking at this display, how did it resemble official business? It was clearly a springtime excursion to distant lands.

Xiao Lingyu was dressed in lake-blue travelling attire with gold-thread tassels tied at her waist, her eyes clear and bright.

She had not wished to be ostentatious, yet she could not resist Baor's wheedling; she still wore that green jade butterfly pin slanted in her hair, which swayed amidst her tresses, making her appear even more radiant than the spring light.

As for Baor, she had long since burrowed into the carriage, clutching a package of sugared osmanthus cakes, her mouth full of sweet fragrance, not forgetting to wave at Lu Chou upon his horse: "Papa Lord, my seat must be by the window! My Mama sits in the middle!"

Xiao Lingyu was slightly startled and raised her hand to give her a light tap on the forehead: "Sit properly at once, otherwise be careful that I'll punish you by not allowing you to eat snacks."

Lu Chou arched an eyebrow and smiled, his tone extremely casual: "Hmm, well said. This official thinks exactly the same."

Baor cried out: "You can't do that!"

Having spoken, she curled herself into a ball, laughing until she rolled behind the carriage curtain. Her milky, childish voice of protest came from within: "Baor will be hungry; it's so pitiful!"

Xiao Lingyu was caught between tears and laughter. She turned her head to look at Lu Chou.

The man had already flipped himself onto his horse, wearing silver armour over his robes, his blue cloth cloak snapping and moving in the wind. *His features were steady and composed, yet he could not suppress the smile at the corners of his lips.*

"I didn't expect there to be so much luggage; there are as many as two whole carriages."

"Travelling south this time, the weather is gradually warming. It matters not if official business is set aside for a few days; I shall accompany you for a few extra days of sightseeing to ease your mind."

His voice was not loud, yet it fell truly and clearly into her ears.

Xiao Lingyu lost herself for a fleeting instant.

Such words, had it been five years ago, she would never have dared to believe. He had been so cold, so headstrong, yet now he was this warm and doting.

Her heart felt a slight warmth; she pursed her lips and turned to enter the carriage, speaking no more.

At the end of the official highway, a bugle sounded lightly.

The sound of horse hooves rose and the carriage wheels turned. Amidst the spring breeze were the silhouettes of a family of three, receding into the distance toward the fresh green of willows and the gurgling of streams, looking for all the world as if they were stepping into a long-awaited dream.

—The two brothers had departed only a few days apart; one went alone to the mountain passes, while the other went side-by-side with his family toward Jiangnan.

The former was a parting, the latter a homecoming; one side was the sealing of a heart, the other the opening of a door.

Two paths of horses and carriages, one North and one South, one of sorrow and one of joy.

Destiny diverged, and the mountains and rivers were not the same.

Chapter 81: Rallying Aid in Jiangnan

A sudden chill had settled over the capital. Daylight itself looked bleak, as though the sky had been scraped thin. Wind and snow carried urgent war dispatches straight to the palace.

Within the Eastern Palace's study—the Hall of Solemn Counsel—palace lamps swayed beneath their shades. A gust lifted the golden silk drapes, and a wave of cold rolled through the hall. The floor furnace burned, yet it could not defeat the winter wind's bite.

Upon the yellow sandalwood desk lay several military reports, spread open one after another. Cinnabar marks ran across the pages where decisions had been made in haste—and in more than one place, the ink had been smeared by blood.

Since the first snowfall, the He Yan tribes had pressed the border again and again. Skirmishes sparked in quick succession. Reports flew in daily; there was scarcely a single day of true quiet.

Crown Prince Chen Gen stood before a screen of maps, his face composed, yet his gaze growing heavier with each message.

"The He Yan are skilled riders," a general stepped forward, voice low and grave. "They excel at fighting in snow. This year's winter is harsher than usual. The northern snow has already reached two feet deep. Supply roads are hard to keep open. Our army is at a disadvantage."

"At West Pass, we killed one of their deputy commanders," another officer added, "but we lost a hundred elite troops. Two days ago, the snow sealed the mountain route again and fighting broke out anew. There was no clear victory."

"The enemy's intent is obvious," a third said. "They mean to strike at year's end, when our transport is most vulnerable—seize winter stores, raid grain, burn depots. If the outer camps beyond the pass fall, the consequences will be unthinkable."

Chen Gen's fingertips moved once. He reached out and lifted one of the dispatches—its characters blurred where blood and melted snow had soaked the paper.

"This... was submitted by Lu Xiu?" he asked quietly.

A court attendant bowed. "Yes, Your Highness. A report from the central commander. Three days ago, he personally led a detached force and launched a surprise raid on a He Yan supply convoy. Though it was not a complete victory, more than forty were slain, and a portion of supplies was recovered."

Chen Gen lowered his eyes and turned page after page. At the very end, the ink was still fresh, the strokes pressed hard as if carved:

'The northern wind and snow grow ever heavier. Those who go deep alone step into hardship at every turn. We can only fight to the death, to keep the winter granaries of the Central Plains secure. May His Majesty and the Crown Prince remain well. Your subject, Xiu, bows his head.'

The hall fell silent.

For a long time, Chen Gen did not speak. At last, he said softly, almost to himself, "...This battle will not be easy."

He looked toward the wind and snow outside the window. His voice was very light, yet it cut through the dim daylight like something thin and sharp.

"He stayed behind alone, holding the rear. He walked into a blizzard as if walking into a blade. For whom does he keep watch like this?"

For family? For the realm?

Or also… for her?

No one answered. The hall was still as dead water.

Only after a long pause did Chen Gen lift his gaze and speak with decision.

"Order the Ministry of Revenue to release emergency funds. Have the Grand Granary open its stores. Divert a tenth of the preserved meat originally meant for Jiangnan—send it north first."

He paused, calculating, then continued, each number precise.

"Allocate three hundred barrels of oil, one thousand sets of down garments, one hundred sacks of coarse grain, and thirty thousand taels of silver. The rest—hold for now. We observe the battle for three more days."

A courtier hesitated and lowered his voice. "Your Highness, if the enemy uses the snow to press deeper, and our troops are not suited for snow fighting, the border supplies may—"

Chen Gen cut him off coldly.

"I will not stake the empire's reserves on a single bloodstained letter."

His fingers tapped the edge of the desk once. His tone shifted, lower, controlled.

"...But this step, I also want him to keep walking it. If in three days there comes another victory, the Ministry will continue the allocation."

He turned slightly. "Draft another order. Deliver it by word to the general: the frontier is bitter, but the court has not forgotten."

"Yes, Your Highness."

Chen Gen's steps paused. His voice dropped again, quieter than before.

"...And one letter. For him."

Brush and ink were brought.

That letter bore no official seal. No palace stamp. No corded cover.

Only two words—All well.

Yet each stroke was written slowly, with deliberate weight, as if every line had to pass through the heart before it reached the paper.

The attendant, holding the brush with both hands, ventured softly, "Your Highness… shall we mark it with the Eastern Palace's small seal?"

Chen Gen shook his head.

"This letter is not a command," he said. "It is only for him."

He paused, then added, "If he asks whom it is from, tell him—an old friend in the capital."

The attendant startled, then bowed deeply. "Yes, Your Highness."

He withdrew on silent feet.

Outside the window, the snow did not cease.

And across the far northern frontier, for ten thousand li, beacon fires still burned beneath the wind.

* * * * *

On the southern road, spring cold had not yet lifted. It warmed for a day, then turned sharp again, as if the season itself could not decide.

One night they lodged at Linjiang Post Station. Wind howled outside. The tent curtains trembled in their bindings.

Lu Chou rose with his outer robe thrown on. The lamp on the table had not yet burned out; its flame was low, but steady. An urgent dispatch lay spread before him—each character pressed hard, the handwriting harsh and iron.

All of it came from the northern front.

The He Yan tribes had harassed the snow-sealed line for days. Three clashes: some won, some lost. The blizzards were too fierce. Down garments were nearly exhausted. Frostbitten fingers and frozen wounds were beyond count. The forward battalion had not collapsed, yet supply roads lagged and morale sank by the day.

Lu Chou's knuckles went pale. He clenched the paper as if he meant to crush it.

Xiao Lingyu stepped into the tent, a cloak over her shoulders. Seeing the tightness in his brow, she asked softly, "...What is it? Why do you look so strained?"

Lu Chou nodded once. His lips were drawn tight.

"Xiu's battle," he said, voice low. "It will be a hard one."

She sat beside him, calm. "War has never been easy."

He shook his head.

"It's not only the fighting. The north is buried in wind and snow. Supplies cannot reach them. And the court has been tight these days—funds are stretched thin. The aid the Crown Prince can send will be limited."

"How could it come to this..." she murmured.

Lu Chou steadied his breath and handed her the dispatch.

"The He Yan struck in the heart of winter. The northern troops have held, but the cold injuries worsen by the day. The Crown Prince has done what he can. Xiu will not be able to hold for long."

Xiao Lingyu read in silence. Her eyes moved line by line, unhurried, as though she were weighing not only ink but lives.

After a long moment, she interrupted quietly, "Wait."

Lu Chou looked at her. "What?"

"This matter," she said, voice low but certain, "may have an answer in Jiangnan."

He frowned slightly. "What do you mean?"

She did not rush. She let the thought settle, then spoke with steady clarity.

"Then we must reach Jiangnan as quickly as possible. Spring is already touching the south. Trade roads can move. And now that I have been named Imperial Merchant by His Majesty himself… what I can do is carry the burden a little further."

Her tone remained even, but her eyes held a kind of stubborn resolve.

"I know several weaving houses and guilds in Jiangnan. If we can raise funds, gather cloth, down, and medicine, and then send them north by river—no, it will not match an imperial allocation," she said plainly, "but it can fill the gap. It can buy them time."

Lu Chou lifted his gaze to her. For an instant, something complicated passed through his eyes.

She continued, firmer now.

"I bear the title of Imperial Merchant. Why should I not use that name to rally aid? Jiangnan has always been rich in grain and silver. If we can secure down, cloth, and medicine, and ship them north along the canal, then at the very least we can relieve the front—if only for a while."

"That is the duty of the Ministry of War and the Ministry of Revenue," he said, frowning.

"Then why did His Majesty appoint me Imperial Merchant?" Xiao Lingyu's voice remained calm, yet each word landed with bone-deep force. "Was it not for times like this—so I might do what others cannot?"

Lu Chou fell silent. His brows drew together as he weighed the possibility, not with tenderness, but with the seriousness of someone who understood what failure meant.

She added, without flinching, "The nation is in crisis. Even a common man bears responsibility. I am not even common."

At last, Lu Chou nodded.

"If we press the road," he said, "we can reach Jiangnan within five days."

He had wanted to say, This is the court's burden. Why must you shoulder it?

But when he met her eyes—so steady, so unyielding—those words never left his mouth.

Instead, he said in a low voice, "This journey, I will see you safely back to Jiangnan. Once there—do what you must. I will support it."

Xiao Lingyu nodded once. She turned immediately to the table, took up her brush, and began to write—one letter after another.

Each letter was sealed. Each prepared with the proper marks and insignia.

On every envelope was the name of an old, reputable merchant house she had once dealt with in the tides of commerce.

She had survived the market's rise and fall before.

Now, under the name of Imperial Merchant, she would open a different kind of battlefield—one fought not with blades and blood, but with ink, seals, and the weight of what could be moved through human hands.

Chapter 82: A Subtle Shade of Jealousy

Five days later, Jiangnan was steeped in mist and rain.

Xiao Lingyu stood within a side chamber of Jin Yun Hall, the light from the window lattices pale and watery. A stack of letters lay beside her, each one written in her own hand, sealed, and addressed with care.

She had already sent couriers to Xiulan Zhai, Ruichun Embroidery, and the Feihe Trading Guild—old houses with old roots. In Jiangnan, such families did not move lightly; their coffers opened only when the tide of the world forced them, or when someone with enough weight stood before them and made them believe the road ahead was real.

In the past, she had maintained ties with them as a merchant, a craftswoman, a woman who understood that relationships were not ornaments but lifelines. Now, she summoned them under a different name.

Imperial Merchant.

Not a title of vanity, but a banner that carried the court's authority, the realm's urgency, and the unspoken implication that refusal would not remain private.

She did not write long speeches. She did not plead.

She simply said: the north needs aid; the border is bitter; the spring cold has not lifted; soldiers are dying not only by blade, but by hunger and frost.

Within days, three houses responded—promptly, decisively, as though they had already been waiting for someone to give them a reason to act.

Some pledged silver.

Others offered bolts of cloth, crates of medicine, down and fur, sacks of grain—things that, in a war, were not commodities but breath.

Xiao Lingyu looked out at the river beyond the fogged windows. The canal's surface was still grey, still heavy, but it no longer lay sealed; the thaw had begun, slow and stubborn.

"If we can fill one boat with down, another with medicine, and a third with cloth and food," she murmured, voice low yet firm, "then the northern troops might survive this spring cold."

She knew little of warfare.

But she understood human suffering. She understood what it meant to go without. To be cold with no way to warm. To watch a child's lips turn pale. To count days by what remained in the brazier.

A few more days passed. Preparations were complete.

Three ships stood ready at the docks, their hulls deep with cargo. On the sails, embroidered in firm, dignified script, flew the name that would travel before them like a seal stamped upon the wind:

Merchant of the Crown, House of Xiao.

The Grand Canal had begun to thaw. The water beneath the hulls murmured with steady strength, dark and moving, carrying the weight of the south toward the starving north.

Lu Chou stood at the dock in silence, watching as the vessels slipped slowly into the river fog.

He did not praise her loudly. He did not offer grand words that sounded like court rhetoric.

He only turned his head and looked at her once—one glance, quiet and heavy, as though it held what could not be spoken in front of servants, dockhands, and the watching world.

The look in his eyes was too layered to parse: pride, restraint, something like admiration, something like worry, all pressed down beneath a surface made calm by habit.

In the end, he said only, softly, "You've done well."

Xiao Lingyu did not answer. She merely stood beside him, and together they watched the three ships disappear into the fog as though swallowed by Jiangnan's own breath.

She knew this was not a transaction.

It was a long journey undertaken to save lives.

* * * * *

That night, within a side hall of the Jiangnan administrative yamen, a single lamp burned steadily. The faint scent of sandalwood lingered in the air. The rain had quieted, and the darkness outside lay deep as water.

Xiao Lingyu had personally seen off her guests. Her footsteps faded along the corridor; the hall returned to stillness.

Then another figure approached from the covered walkway—unhurried, familiar, as though he had walked these halls before and knew exactly how loud or quiet a man should be in such a place.

"Lingyu," he greeted, a faint smile touching his lips. "It's been a long time. I didn't expect you to be… an Imperial Merchant now."

She turned at once, caught off guard.

"Huaici?"

Xie Huaici.

He wore a plain official's robe, colour subdued, lines clean. His manner remained calm and composed, the steadiness of a man long seasoned by provincial affairs. There was gentleness in his gaze—but beneath it, the cool clarity of someone who saw through motives and pretences.

She gave him a respectful nod, then smiled, the expression polite yet sincere.

"This thanks is overdue," she said. "If you hadn't eased the path behind the scenes—and applied a little pressure—I doubt those Jiangnan households would have been so swift to open their coffers."

Huaici flicked open a folding fan with an easy motion, his tone unhurried, almost mild.

"You were named Imperial Merchant, and you chose to act personally. That alone is rare." His fan stirred the lamplight slightly. "What they handed over wasn't merely coin. It was the price of survival."

His words shifted, subtly, as his eyes rested on her face.

"Besides, Lord Lu wasn't exactly gentle this time." His smile was faint, but not mocking. "The merchant houses once entangled in the Third Prince's case—he placed them at the top of his inspection list. Refusing to contribute would only draw eyes to their books, old and new."

He paused, as if letting the implication settle where it would.

"Jiangnan has a long memory," he added softly. "People remember who once raised funds for His Highness, and who hid behind excuses when the wind turned."

A flicker crossed Xiao Lingyu's eyes. Her voice lowered. "So that's why… things moved faster than I anticipated."

"The accounts were never clean to begin with," Huaici replied. "Donating a portion now, under the banner of 'protecting the realm'—call it penance, call it insurance." His fan tilted slightly. "Lord Lu never needed to threaten them openly. A single letter. A single list. Anyone with sense understood what he meant."

Xiao Lingyu's gaze dipped. Her words were quieter, weighed by honesty.

"So although this bore the name of Imperial Merchant… the pressure behind it still came from him. I wasn't so much persuading as… standing there while the tide pushed."

"Don't belittle yourself," Huaici said mildly, without heat, without flattery. "Had you not appeared in person, many of them would not have dared believe the road ahead was real. And besides—if you hadn't come to me, I might not have acted either."

She looked at him, momentarily startled.

He continued, the smile at his lips gentle, the sincerity in his eyes steady.

"You weren't asking for silver for your own house. You were trying to buy breath and time for the soldiers in the north." His voice was calm. "If I still turned a blind eye, then I've no business calling myself a steward of this province."

Xiao Lingyu bowed deeply, her tone even and resolute.

"I won't forget your aid, Huaici. If ever I can return the favour, I will not refuse."

Huaici watched her for a long moment—then asked, almost casually, as if it were merely idle talk, though the line of his gaze said he was not entirely idle.

"You and Lord Lu… traveling together like this. Is something more on the horizon?"

Xiao Lingyu's eyes widened a fraction; then she let out a quiet laugh. Her voice remained mild, yet not without meaning.

"…I haven't asked what others are saying."

"She wouldn't need to," Huaici replied, his smile light but his eyes sincere. "The way he looks at you leaves nothing concealed." He paused. "You've suffered much these past years. If you've found someone true, it's no small thing."

Xiao Lingyu lowered her gaze with a faint smile and shifted the topic as gently as one closes a door.

"I heard you've married?"

"Just the daughter of a local official," he said simply. "Mild in temperament, well-mannered. Suited for a quiet life."

"You've always been upright, Huaici," she said, warmth quiet in her voice. "You deserve a good lady. My congratulations."

"Thank you."

He closed his folding fan with a soft snap and made a gesture to take his leave.

Xiao Lingyu did not urge him to stay. She merely stood in silence, watching him turn away.

The breeze stirred the eaves; the lamplight wavered slightly. In a world where fortune rose and fell without pause, this quiet accord between two people—light as wind, yet deeply felt—lingered unspoken.

Huaici had barely taken a few steps when a clear, childish voice rang out from the courtyard like a bell.

"Papa Xie—!"

Both of them turned at once, momentarily stunned.

Two figures stepped into the moonlit hall—one tall, one small—each cloaked against the night chill. The child ran forward on quick feet, laughter bright as silver.

Baor.

"Mama said you were here," she exclaimed, eyes shining. "And you really are!"

Huaici—usually composed to the point of austerity—could not help the smile that curved his lips. He stooped and steadied her by the shoulders.

"Why are you still awake at this hour?"

"I wanted sugar cakes!" she declared, tilting her head up. "And Mama said you were visiting, so I begged her to bring me!"

Her words were innocent, artless—yet from behind her, something in the night air cooled.

Lu Chou approached at an unhurried pace. His footsteps were even. His posture was the same as always—upright, controlled, and not a hair out of place.

His gaze swept across the scene—Xiao Lingyu beneath the lamp, Huaici with his fan, Baor standing between them—before finally settling on the child's small hand, still resting trustingly in Huaici's palm.

His face showed no sign of displeasure.

Yet the atmosphere shifted by a degree so slight it could be missed—unless one had lived long enough around men who wore restraint like armour.

Lu Chou bowed slightly, manner impeccable.

"Lord Xie," he said. "Still here, I see."

Huaici returned the gesture with his usual composure.

"You arrive at the perfect time," he said evenly. "I was just taking my leave of Miss Xiao."

Lu Chou's eyes flicked briefly toward Xiao Lingyu, then Baor. His tone remained even, almost mild—yet a quiet chill threaded beneath it.

"We owe you thanks for your help, Lord Xie." He paused, just long enough to let the next words land where they would. "Xiao Lingyu has spoken of you—with much gratitude."

No overt rebuke.

No accusation.

Yet something unspoken tightened the air between them—an edge too subtle to name, too palpable to ignore.

Huaici's smile remained light, unreadable. He did not step back, nor did he step forward.

"No need for thanks," he replied. "When someone sets her heart upon something, it's only natural that someone will lend a hand."

Then, as though refusing to let the exchange harden further, he lowered his gaze to Baor, his voice softening.

"Have you been good, Baor? No more drawing cats on the window lattice?"

Baor's eyes sparkled. "I drew a bird! And Lord Xie too!"

For an instant, the hall went strangely quiet.

Xiao Lingyu gave a soft cough, the sound small but deliberate—an adult's instinctive attempt to smooth the jaggedness of a child's honesty.

Baor blinked, then explained solemnly, as if clarifying a great principle.

"But Mama said I can't write people's names," she said. "So I only drew a fan and a tree."

Huaici chuckled and brushed a gentle hand over her hair. His eyes were kind.

When his gaze lifted to Lu Chou's, however, the hand paused—just slightly. It seemed he meant to speak, but in the end, he pressed his lips together, swallowed whatever words rose, and said quietly,

"It's grown late. I've stayed too long already. I'll take my leave."

He bowed to Xiao Lingyu, smiled once more at Baor, and turned away.

The night wind moved softly under the eaves; lamplight wavered. The fan turned once between his fingers, and the long shadow of his figure faded gradually into darkness.

Lu Chou's gaze followed him until that shadow disappeared beyond the corridor.

Only then did his expression shift—the calm giving way to something harder, more subdued, as though the mask had not fallen, but tightened.

At last, he looked down at Baor, who still clung to her mother's sleeve. His voice was quiet, but cool.

"So—you spoke for quite some time."

"It was business," Xiao Lingyu replied evenly, her tone steady. She did not rise to the chill, nor did she soften it. "Since Baor's here, shall we send her to bed?"

Baor looked from her mother to Lu Chou, head tilted in thought. Then, with a child's disarming innocence, she asked,

"But now that Papa Xie is gone… will my other lordly papa stay and sleep with me?"

Lu Chou raised an eyebrow. For a heartbeat, the edge at the corner of his mouth softened, a rare warmth tugging through despite himself.

He bent, gathered Baor into his arms, and answered in a low voice, warm enough to soothe.

"Of course."

As he turned to leave, his gaze brushed once more over Xiao Lingyu—
still standing beneath the wavering lamplight, her expression calm, her
eyes deep with thoughts she did not speak.

The lamp flame trembled.

The rain outside had ceased.

Yet something in the quiet hall remained unsettled—like water that
looked still, but moved beneath the surface.

Chapter 83: The Bone-Breaking Path to Heaven

The night was deep as water, and the light within the quiet room was faint.

Baor had already fallen asleep upon the couch in the inner chamber, the corner of her mouth still carrying the sweetness of the sugar cake.

Xiao Lingyu tucked the thin blanket over her and had just turned to leave when she saw Lu Chou leaning against the doorframe, his eyes in the lamplight dark and still as the night.

"She is asleep." she said softly.

"I know." His tone was calm, yet he advanced step by step. "You were speaking with Lord Xie… for quite a while."

"Not that long." She was slightly taken aback, then gave a light smile, her voice holding a touch of teasing: "What is it? Is my lord jealous?"

Lu Chou said nothing; he merely clasped her wrist with one hand, lowered his head to her ear, and his voice came out extremely low: "Am I jealous? What do you think?"

She blinked, seemingly unafraid of his displeasure, and only said with a smile: "He is an old friend, and he helped me today. Naturally I owed him a few words of thanks. You, a grand imperial envoy, would grow sour over something as simple as courtesy?"

He gave a cold snort and released her hand, sitting down, though the corner of his eye still held displeasure. "I care not who he is. The way he looked at you—I saw it clearly."

She walked over, poured a cup of warm tea, and handed it to him. "You are overthinking it."

He did not take it, only looked at her.

After a moment of silence, he suddenly spoke: "The matter in Jiangnan has been settled. The wealthy merchants are willing to donate silver, and the military supplies can be transported north. In a few days, I shall depart for the capital."

He paused, his tone dropping, as though repressing a careful trace of expectation. "Come with me."

Her hand trembled, and the tea rippled over the rim of the cup. After a long while, she lifted her gaze to him, her voice calm yet carrying a trace of distance: "Return to the capital… for what?"

He watched her, his tone cautious, probing: "To… marry me?"

"What nonsense are you speaking?" She lowered her eyes. "My trade, my foundation—they are all here in Jiangnan."

"But Baor—"

"Baor was also raised by my own hands. She lives well here. If she returns to the capital—how long can you shelter her from wind and rain?"

"Do not worry. I will see to everything…"

She cut off the unfinished words. "Say no more. It is impossible."

"Why is it impossible? Do you not wish to grow old with me?"

She let out a faint, dazed smile. "Your words, I believe. But what of the Lu family? Will they accept Baor?"

Her tone remained gentle, yet each word pricked like a needle.

Lu Chou's knuckles tightened before he finally said: "Lingyu, do not worry. I know you have little confidence in me for now, but you must trust me. I do not merely wish to shelter you from wind and rain—I wish to hold the same umbrella with you."

Silence filled the room for a brief instant.

Xiao Lingyu gave a low laugh, turned, and ladled half a cup of tea for him, speaking softly:

"I have never asked for an umbrella, nor have I ever sought to hide from the rain. In those days, it was I who chose to remain in the wind. Here lies not only my home, but also my responsibility."

He looked at her back, his eyes seeming to hold countless words, yet in the end he swallowed them, only saying: "I shall ask again—on the day I depart."

She nodded, her tone gentle yet resolute: "And I will give you the same answer."

Outside the window, the wind brushed the eaves and stirred the wavering flame of the lamp. This conversation held no quarrel, and neither turned away—yet it tightened the chest more than any farewell.

* * * * *

In the capital of Great Jin, upon the Imperial Avenue, wind and snow drifted in the air.

Midwinter had arrived; the vermilion gates of the palace were shut tight, and the golden tiles were covered with a fresh layer of snow.

The hour of Chen had just passed; within the Golden Throne Hall, the officials were already arranged in ranks, and the morning court was nearing its end.

His Majesty wore a dark robe, his features wan, leaning against the dragon throne, a trace of weariness showing between his brows.

Since autumn he had suffered bouts of cold, and lately, losing sleep through the night, his spirit had grown further diminished.

Rumours had long circulated in court, yet none dared speak plainly.

At that moment, when an attendant minister of the Ministry of Revenue reported that the northern border was still short of three-tenths of its military provisions and requested additional funds,

His Majesty, who had been resting his eyes, suddenly opened them.

He was about to raise his hand in signal when his arm trembled, his fingers shaking slightly, and his complexion turned deathly pale.

"Your Majesty!" The inner attendants cried out in alarm, and every face in the hall changed.

Before the ministers could react, His Majesty had already slanted slowly from the imperial throne and collapsed straight to the floor.

"Summon the Imperial Physicians—quickly!"

"Close the hall! Call for the Crown Prince—!"

Shouts rose like a surging tide; inner attendants and palace servants fell into confusion, and the chief ministers of the Three Departments and the Six Ministries all turned pale.

Several elder ministers wished to step forward to support him, yet were stopped by the attendants.

Moments later, the palace guards had sealed the Golden Throne Hall on all sides, and heavy curtains were dropped, shutting out the wind and snow.

By the hour of Wei, Crown Prince Chen Gen hurried from the Duangong Hall, his expression grave.

According to the report from the Imperial Medical Bureau, His Majesty had collapsed from long-accumulated exhaustion and disrupted vital energy, and required several weeks of complete rest, unable to attend to state affairs.

That very night, an imperial decree was issued: the Crown Prince was to oversee the realm and temporarily assume the powers of governance.

With this edict released, the court was shaken at once; the struggle for the heir's position suddenly stood in stark relief.

The Inner Cabinet convened urgently, the Ministry of War discreetly activated its northern defence protocols, and the Crown Prince summoned the Privy Commissioner and the two Censors that very night, redeploying all plans for the He Yan front.

He further ordered: "Imperial Envoy Lu Chou is still in Jiangnan—command him to return to the capital at once!"

* * * * *

The night snow had yet to melt, yet Jiangnan lay windless.

Xiao Lingyu had just concluded a discussion with several stewards of the embroidery workshop when an urgent report arrived at the door.

Liang Jin hurried inside and presented a sealed dispatch. "My lord, a letter from the capital—it is an emergency document of utmost urgency!"

Lu Chou took the scroll and unfolded it. Under the lamplight appeared a handwritten command from the Crown Prince himself.

For an instant, his gaze turned as cold as frost, and he tightened his grip on the paper.

Xiao Lingyu stepped forward, saw the gravity in his expression, and asked: "Something has happened?"

He put away the letter, lifted his gaze toward her, and said in a low voice: "There has been upheaval in the capital. His Majesty is gravely ill. The Crown Prince has taken regency—and has summoned me to return to the capital at once to assist in governance."

Xiao Lingyu's heart gave a fierce tremor, and for a moment she found no words.

After a long while, she asked in a low voice: "...When will you depart?"

"Make preparations at once. We set out before dawn tomorrow."

He looked at her, wanting to speak yet stopping short: "Lingyu..."

After a moment, he said softly: "Can you not reconsider... and return to the capital with me?" His tone held a caution he had never shown before.

Her hand paused. At last, she lifted her gaze to him, her eyes calm: "Go." Her voice was gentle, yet clear. "This realm is what you must safeguard. Returning is what you ought to do. You are the imperial envoy—of course you must go back and report to the Crown Prince."

"And you?"

"I... must stay and guard Jinhua Hall. Jiangnan has only just stabilised. I cannot leave."

"Do not push the matter onto the workshop." His tone deepened slightly. "This time, you are not alone. Baor should not remain here either."

Xiao Lingyu said softly: "This is where she grew up, and it is the root of her surname Xiao. Returning to the capital... there are too many eyes, too much conjecture. I do not want her to live in the cracks of such a world."

"But if you refuse to leave, how shall we meet again on the road to the capital?"

She did not answer.

He rose, walked to stand before her, and looked down at her: "When you left that year, you did not utter a single word. And now you would do the same again?"

Her fingers tightened, her voice almost without fluctuation: "At that time, it was for the child. Now, it is still so."

Lu Chou lowered his gaze, his voice hoarse: "And if this time, I am unwilling to let you go?"

She lifted her eyes to him and spoke each word distinctly: "Then it is you who have wronged me."

The air seemed to freeze. The fire and pain in his eyes were crushed by that single sentence, and at last he stepped back, as though granting them both a final shred of dignity.

Neither of them spoke again.

After a long time, she said softly: "Chou… go back. When the situation in the capital has steadied, if there is the slightest opening, I will bring Baor to find you."

Lu Chou slowly turned, walked to the doorway, then stopped again: "You need not search for an opening for my sake. I will sweep aside all the wind and snow for you, and clear a path for you myself."

He did not look back, leaving only one sentence: "Even if I must turn the whole capital upside down, I will not err a second time."

The wind slipped in through the crack of the door, and the lamplight trembled like tears.

* * * * *

At dawn the next day, the carriage stood ready before the provincial office.

Xiao Lingyu brought Baor to see him off in person.

The little girl's eyes were red, yet she bit her lip and did not cry, only shoved a bundle of sugar cakes into Lu Chou's hand: "Mama made these last night. They're for you to eat on the road."

Lu Chou lifted her up and responded softly: "Very well. I will remember you often."

Baor blinked and asked: "Then when will you come back to fetch us?"

His gaze paused, turning toward Xiao Lingyu.

She did not reply.

Only the wind lifted the hem of her skirt as she stood with the light behind her, the shadows in her eyes shifting as though containing the silence and parting of an entire night.

He placed Baor back into her arms, his voice low: "Whether you say it or not, I will return to fetch you both."

With that, he did not look back again and stepped onto the carriage.

Baor lay against her, muttering: "Mama, Baor will learn embroidery, and make a very big brocade handkerchief, with a picture of you and Lord Lu holding hands…"

Her lips moved slightly, yet she did not speak. She only held the child close and watched the carriage procession grow farther and farther away, until it was swallowed by the morning mist of Jiangnan.

Those words, she could not bring herself to say. She knew he would understand them all the same.

* * * * *

The He Yan tribes had taken three cities in succession; the border's food supplies were nearly exhausted, the days and nights were bitterly cold, and the morale of the troops was wavering.

The mountain had been sealed by heavy snow for over five days. In a certain camp on the northern frontier, the wind howled like a beast, and the tent flaps quivered without cease. Inside the tent, the lamp was close to burning out, and the brazier held only the last bundle of dry firewood.

Lu Xiu sat armoured, a sealed letter spread in his hands, bearing neither seal nor name, its content only a few sparse words: She is well.

His fingers trembled faintly. After a long moment, he quietly folded the letter and placed it into his inner garment. Within his breast, he kept another object.

It was a gold hairpin, its tail wrapped in fine gold filaments, and at the base twined a single strand of dark-green hair. He had attempted many times to return it, yet each time withdrew his hand.

He tightened his grip on the hairpin shaft until his knuckles whitened.

Just as well. It'll make it easier for me to leave."

Suddenly, a soldier outside approached at a quick pace and cupped his fists in report: "Vice-Commander Lu, the scouts have returned.

The He Yan tribes have taken Wuqi Valley. If we do not retake it soon, our supply line will be cut!"

The deputy general entered shortly after, speaking in a low voice: "The heavy snow has sealed the mountain.

All paths are blocked. Only one old trail skirts the pass from Eagle Ravine, but the ice cliff has cracked—it is extremely dangerous..."

"Prepare the troops to take the valley." Lu Xiu's voice was like iron, without the slightest hesitation. "If our provisions are cut and no reinforcements can reach us, twenty thousand men will be waiting for death."

The deputy general was shocked. "My lord! That cliff road is perilous. Even travelling light is difficult, let alone leading troops!"

"Which is why we will not lead troops." He lifted his gaze, his tone sharp as a blade. "Select ten men—skilled in archery and horsemanship, light-armoured night riders. They depart with me tonight. The rest will hold the central camp and allow no one to act without orders."

The deputy general was aghast. "My lord, you intend to go personally?"

"If this mission fails, I will bear military punishment myself," he said, his tone without ripple. "But if it succeeds, the He Yan supply line will be severed, and we will still have a chance in this battle."

The deputy general wished to persuade him further but was cut off by his cold voice: "If we remain alive, we shall yet see Great Jin rise with the sun and endure with the moon."

With those words, he rose, donned a black cloak, fastened his sword at his waist.

The cloak billowed sharply, and his steps were resolute.

Outside the tent, the wind and snow had not ceased; the distant mountains looked as though splashed with white ink.

The cliff path known as "Eagle Pass" lay hidden like a serpent's shadow among

The ten light cavalrymen had already assembled and awaited orders, each armoured, none speaking a word.

Lu Xiu mounted his horse in one motion and glanced back once at the tent behind him. Under the cold clarity of the moon, he murmured to himself: "Your Highness the Crown Prince... since she is well, then in this battle, I shall guard it for you—and for her—and return to you both an age of peace and clarity."

With that, he spurred his horse and rode out of the camp, the ten riders behind him following like shadows, treading through the snow.

The snowy night was utterly silent, save for the sound of hooves breaking ice and pressing through snow.

The wind cut like blades, slanted and sharp, glancing against the blood-tinted jade hairpin hidden in his breast, stained upon his cloak.

Like a flame that refused to be extinguished.

The snow fell without pause through the long night.

Within the main camp, no one slept.

The deputy commander returned at dawn, his armour crusted with ice, his breath coming in ragged clouds as he dismounted. He knelt outside the command tent on one knee, snow melting into dark streaks along his greaves, and held out the object clutched against his chest throughout the night.

It was the hairpin.

The gold had been bent, its pearl cracked at the setting, blood having seeped into the fissure and dried there, darkened by frost and time. The warmth that had once lingered was gone, leaving only a cold weight that seemed heavier than iron.

"General Lu... covered the retreat," the deputy said hoarsely. "He ordered us to withdraw. Eagle Pass... has not been reclaimed. He did not return."

No one spoke.

The wind lifted the tent flap slightly, letting in a blade of pale morning light. It struck the hairpin where it lay, casting a dull gleam across the table like a wound reopened.

A sealed letter lay beneath it.

The wax had not yet been pressed. The ink upon it was still faintly damp—an edict written by the Crown Prince himself, meant to be dispatched at first light. Now the corner of the parchment was stained red, the blood seeping outward in a slow bloom, as though fate itself had reached out and marked it.

The commander stood there for a long time, his fingers resting lightly upon the hairpin, his knuckles whitening inch by inch.

"He will not fall here," he said at last.

The words were quiet—neither proclamation nor consolation—yet they struck the tent like a nail driven deep. No one dared contradict him.

Outside, the snow continued to fall.

It fell upon the broken ridge, upon the cliff path known as Eagle Pass— the Bone-Breaking Road—where ice clung to stone like teeth sunk into flesh. There, amid drifts piled higher than a man's chest, blood had frozen into dark veins across the rock.

No trace of him remained.

Only the silence endured.

As though somewhere upon that precipice, a solitary figure still stood— cloak torn, blade dulled, breath shallow yet unyielding—holding the line between collapse and survival, between a realm's retreat and its final stand.

The snow buried everything.

But not the fire.

Not yet.

Chapter 84: Ambush at Eagle Pass

In the Eastern Palace study, the lamplight wavered.

Four palace lanterns stood in a row before the desk; their red velvet shades washed the paper-laden table in a pale, buttery yellow. Outside the hall, wind and snow collided in chaos. Ice pellets pattered against the lattice like thrown beads. Heaven and earth seemed to have sunk into a mute, frozen night.

Chen Gen sat alone behind the desk, clad in a black robe, his brows locked tight.

Two stacks of memorials already marked with vermilion had been piled to one side; the untouched ones, however, had risen higher than his elbow. The faint crease between his brows—since the day the Emperor collapsed—had never once eased.

Four secret reports had come in one after another today.

The first: the He Yan tribes had amassed troops in the northern wastes; scouts reported the enemy's intent to push south.

The second: the Minister of Revenue had submitted a memorial, stating that border pay and provisions still lacked three-tenths; if no funds were released soon, morale would falter.

The third: the Fourth Prince was openly recruiting talented men as "guest advisers" to his residence—no small matter, and with an edge that pointed straight at a single truth: the imperial authority was not secure, and others had begun to covet it.

And the fourth, the most veiled of all, forwarded by a senior palace attendant: rumours within the inner palace were already whispering—if the Emperor remained unable to rise, should a new "supervising commander" post be created, and should the Fourth Prince be appointed to oversee the realm and assist in governance?

Chen Gen gave a short, cold laugh.

There was no mirth at the corner of his mouth—only sarcasm, fatigue, and an anger forced down so hard it tasted bitter.

Four reports, and two involved the Fourth Prince.

Such "Sima Zhao's heart"—did it still need a veil?

He reached out, took up that memorial, and tore it cleanly in two.

He was not ignorant. Over these years, the Emperor's trust in him had always been limited; though the title of Crown Prince sat upon him, it was never a rock that could not be shaken. The Second Prince had hidden himself in deep waters for years. The Fourth Prince was far more skilled at winning men; the marriages and rewards that lay behind military power had long since seeped into the deepest seams of the court.

But he could not fall.

He was the Crown Prince—Great Jin's only Crown Prince.

Outside, the wind rose suddenly, snapping the corner of the hall curtain. The sound was like a wolf's long howl, tearing open the night.

He stood up at once, strode to the window, and pushed open the bronze-hooked lattice.

Snow hung heavy over the Imperial Avenue. Within the palace walls, lines of lamplight circled the pavilions and halls like dragon veins—yet the farther the glow reached, the dimmer it became, until it sank into boundless cold.

A flicker of pain passed through his eyes.

In a low voice, as if speaking to no one, he murmured: "Everyone says the Crown Prince's station is unmatched in honour. Yet on what day—have I ever felt ease, even for half a moment?"

His words dissolved in the room, and fell into dead silence.

Footsteps came.

An inner attendant hurried in and reported softly: "Your Highness, the Minister of War, the Vice Commissioner of the Privy Council, and the two Censor-in-Chiefs are waiting in the outer hall."

Chen Gen turned back, smoothed the hem of his robe, and his voice steadied as it always did.

"Summon them."

The attendant withdrew. Moments later, the ministers filed in, one after another, hands clasped, offering bows.

"The Emperor remains unconscious; as regent, I have not dared to be lax."

Chen Gen spoke neither fast nor slow. His gaze swept across them.

"Tonight I have called you here to discuss three matters."

"First: the He Yan tribes seize winter's cover to advance. The northern border is in peril. Has the Privy Council prepared its response?"

"Second: border funds are still short; the Ministry of War's reports have yet to list the figures in full detail. The inner treasury is empty—how do we raise the silver?"

"And third…"

His voice paused. His eyes turned to a censor seated at the farthest corner.

"There are already voices in the palace—saying I am timid, without authority; that another should be appointed to supervise the armies. Does this talk have any basis?"

The censor's face changed. He dropped to his knees at once, knocking his forehead down.

"Your Highness, forgive me. This minister… this minister has never heard of such a matter…"

"Is that so?"

Chen Gen's tone stayed mild—yet it brushed the hall like a cold blade.

"If there are truly those with treason in their hearts, then while His Majesty has not yet passed, I will first cut down the source of this disorder."

Silence swallowed the hall.

Chen Gen looked at them again. His voice was smooth, without ripple now.

"Tomorrow I will enter the inner palace and petition His Majesty to activate the authority of the Three Departments—full power to deploy military funds and handle state affairs, without further need for imperial vermilion approval."

He held their gaze.

"Gentlemen—if any of you object, speak now."

This was his first step to establish power.

It was also the first step from which there could be no turning back.

No one spoke.

"Since there are no objections," he said, "return and draft your proposals. Within three days, submit your complete border plan and your methods for raising and allocating funds."

The ministers withdrew.

The hall returned to its quiet.

Chen Gen walked back to the imperial desk, and his fingers came to rest on a letter he had not yet opened—an urgent dispatch from Jiangnan, sealed with Lu Chou's personal stamp.

At last, his brow loosened. Something shifted in his eyes.

"So long as Lu Chou can make it back in time," he murmured, "this game can still be held steady."

He thought of the friendship of their youth.

He thought of Xiao Lingyu—the woman who, together with Jinhua Hall, had anchored the southern situation and kept Jiangnan stable.

He thought, too, of that hurried marriage: Shen Zhaoru, the Imperial Preceptor's daughter, a woman quiet as still water after wedlock—so cold that he never knew how to draw near.

This realm—everyone desired to stand against him.

And yet not a single person, at his side, could say: you are not alone.

No… there was one.

His liangdi, Xu Hui—quiet, without contention, gentle, considerate— his only place to rest, if only briefly.

He had once believed he did not need such a person; that he should not have one.

And yet, whenever the night deepened and all sounds died, he still remembered her soft call and her warm gaze—like, in all the world, only she looked upon him without calculation.

He brushed at the fatigue at the corner of his eyes, and the corner of his mouth lifted into a near self-mocking smile.

So be it. Do not think too much.

Then he leaned back into the cushioned seat; for an instant he gave a helpless, quiet chuckle—before, suddenly, his voice came out low and rough, and never had it sounded so firm:

"If I become Emperor one day, no one will be allowed to make me guard this realm alone."

The snow did not stop. The lamps did not go out.

This night was fated to be sleepless.

* * * * *

On the He Yan borderlands, the night wind was a blade, and the snow was fierce.

Between gusts, white covered the mountains; the cold cut to the bone like iron. Lu Xiu led an elite small squad, moving in silence to the southern side of Broken-Wave Ridge. They had meant only to cross the cliff road, to reach a position where allied reinforcements could respond from the flank—

but they were discovered by enemy scouts.

"Bad—enemy vanguard!"

The scout's voice was sharp; before his words even fell, a horn sounded in the distance, deep and muffled as a beast's roar.

Within the snow forest, shadows swept forward.

A volley of arrows burst forth.

"Form up!"

Xiu's shout was low and forceful. He had already drawn his sword and surged into the enemy line first.

Iron hooves crushed snow. Blades struck and crossed.

He wore a pale-ink cloak; his features were coldly carved; his figure flickered like a hawk. With one stroke he brought down the enemy standard-bearer. Blood blossomed on the snow—

and in the next breath, three fronts of He Yan cavalry closed in around him.

"Commander—there are too many! We can't fight on—!"

"You go," Xiu said. "Once you cross Broken-Wave Ridge, the reinforcements are there. If we're all trapped here, the army will have no turn left."

"But you—!"

"I will keep moving to Eagle Defile."

"Commander!"

"Shut up. Obey."

He tore something from himself and thrust it into the deputy's hands.

It was a gold hairpin set with a pearl. Its tail had been soaked by blood mist and snow frost, and yet it still held a faint glimmer—like a trace of warmth that had not yet died.

"If I do not return from this trip… give this hairpin to His Highness the Crown Prince."

The deputy shook, about to speak—

but Xiu's gaze was iron-dark. Without another word, he turned away.

Yet in the instant before he turned, his fingers trembled slightly, and his eyes lost focus for the space of a breath.

He should not have carried that hairpin with him.

He should have forgotten. He should have severed it long ago.

Yet it had remained hidden under his armour, tucked within his collar, pressed against flesh. No one knew: on the day he went to the front, he refused every pain-dulling draught.

Only this hairpin had ever been pressed to his heart.

Shen Zhaoru—she was the lamp in his chest that never went out. He had never dared hope to draw near. He only wished her safe.

That single line—she is well—only a few sparse words in a letter, yet it had slammed into his ribs like a storm tide.

Then it is enough. He asked nothing more.

Now, as he finally handed the hairpin away, it was as if he were severing a fixation he did not even want to admit existed.

"Commander, if you don't go, how can we go!"

"I will hold the rear and buy you time," Xiu said. "Another word, and we all die here."

He turned back.

His long sword swept—

and he charged alone into the enemy ranks.

Wind screamed. Blood splashed snow.

One man, one sword: he forced back wave after wave of cavalry charges. His figure seemed to fuse with storm and snowfall—like a solitary peak that would not fall.

Hooves thundered like drums. Spears and blades crossed—

and still he stood.

The deputy clenched his teeth, turned, and cried until his throat tore:

"Withdraw! Report to the main camp! Go—now!"

The rest did not hesitate again. With tears, they broke through and fled.

Behind them, on the cliff-edge, only Xiu remained: snow on his shoulders, guarding the pass; fighting until the sword broke, fighting until strength was exhausted.

Dawn wanted to split the sky. Blood and snow spread across the entire mountain road.

* * * * *

The lamp-keeper froze. No one dared speak first.

The wind lifted a corner of the tent flap, spilling in a wavering warmth of light—so that the hairpin looked like gold reflected in blood.

That night, the deputy returned through snow, stumbling, drenched in gore, one thing clasped to his chest as if it were his own heart.

The storm had not ceased. He dropped to one knee outside the command tent, voice dark and hoarse:

"…The general held the rear and did not return. He only asked that we bring men quickly to reinforce Eagle Defile…"

He held out the hairpin.

It was a gold pin with a pearl at the end—now broken. Blood had seeped into the crack, webbed through its fissures. Wind-snow and battle dust stained the shaft, and yet it still carried a thread of warmth that had not fully dispersed.

A secret letter written in the Crown Prince's own hand lay on the table, not yet opened—its corner already dyed red by that blood-stained hairpin.

Inside the tent, the commander stood with head bowed. His thumb brushed the pin; his knuckles whitened.

On the desk, another letter lay spread—freshly written by the Crown Prince himself. The ink was not yet dry; it had not been sealed in wax. Now the hairpin lay slantwise across it, staining a corner with a streak of crimson.

He stared for a long time, lips pressed tight.

At last he spoke, low:

"…He will not perish like this."

The voice was light as a murmur—yet it landed like a nail driven into every heart in the tent.

The snow fell for an entire night.

As though someone still stood upon that broken cliff, not yet returned.

* * * * *

Sunlight filtered through carved lattice, dappling the brocade carpet. Pale smoke curled. Silence held.

In the Eastern Warming Pavilion, Shen Zhaoru sat leaning at the side of the couch. A plain-white brocade dress made her look even thinner. In her hands she held a cup of autumn-white porcelain, sipping orchid tea slowly. Her expression was faint, her lips without any hint of a smile, and yet her gaze rested on a few yellow leaves drifting outside the window—her spirit clearly elsewhere.

Opposite her sat Xu Hui, the one the Crown Prince had come to trust in recent years.

She was born to a scholarly family; her father was only a fifth-rank Director of Ceremonial Matters—his rank not high, yet because she was gentle and compliant, her conduct proper, she had won the Crown Prince's favour.

Today she wore a dark-purple jacket with a subtle woven pattern. She sat straight, her brows and eyes full of mild humility.

Without making it obvious, she watched the tea in Shen Zhaoru's hands. A trace of hesitation flickered in her eyes—something she wanted to ask and did not.

At last, she spoke, voice soft, as if casual concern—yet every word was placed like a piece on a board.

"Elder Sister… your complexion lately seems not as it was."

Shen Zhaoru seemed not to hear. Only after a long moment did she answer faintly:

"The cold snow through the nights. Perhaps the dreams are unsettled."

She did not say: in her dreams, there was always that northern snow and soldiers stained with blood; the one who had not returned—standing, and standing, across a thousand mountains of white.

"Once the Winter Solstice passes, the New Year comes," Xu Hui said with a smile, lightly shifting the topic, as if unthinking. "Does Elder Sister have any plans?"

"Festival matters have their precedents. Each office will handle its own. This palace does not need to spend thought," Zhaoru replied, lowering her eyes to sip her tea, tone calm.

Xu Hui was about to say more when fine footsteps came outside. A young eunuch knelt and reported:

"His Highness the Crown Prince has arrived."

Xu Hui started and rose, meaning to withdraw—

but Shen Zhaoru stopped her with a single sentence.

"Stay. His Highness carries the burdens of ten thousand affairs; it is not often someone keeps him company to speak."

The tone was flat, and yet it left no space to refuse.

Chen Gen stepped in at once. He wore ink-blue everyday robes; his figure was straight and tall, but the fatigue in his eyes had not yet scattered.

His gaze swept the room; he gave the two women a slight nod.

"You're both here."

Shen Zhaoru rose a little and saluted with perfect form.

"Your Highness."

"What were you discussing?" he asked, his voice gentle—yet his eyes fell on the pallor of her profile, and the words behind his gaze seemed to halt at his throat.

"Idle talk," Zhaoru said. Her lips moved slightly. Then she turned and offered Xu Hui a small, composed smile.

"This consort is somewhat tired. I won't sit long."

Xu Hui's eyes widened, and she hurried to persuade her.

"How can that be? Just now you looked quite well…"

Shen Zhaoru was already standing. Her figure was long and clean, like a jade plum. Her voice remained warm and mild.

"The tea is still hot. You two talk slowly. Forgive me—I will take my leave first."

She turned and went.

Her sleeve brushed the table edge; the movement was elegant—and unmistakably cool. Until her silhouette vanished beyond the door, she did not turn her head back, not even half a step.

Xu Hui stared at the place she had disappeared for a long while before letting out a quiet sigh.

"She is always like this… The moment Your Highness arrives, Elder Sister leaves."

Chen Gen did not answer.

His fingers lightly traced the white porcelain teacup on the table, and he stared at the fine tea threads floating on the surface, silent for a long time.

It was the cup she had just drunk from—her lipprint still there, her breath not yet gone.

And she—never once stayed for herself, not one step.

Readers can view the full collection of colour illustrations here:
https://www.facebook.com/profile.php?id=61581325000577

Chapter 85: The New Emperor Ascends the Throne

In the capital, within the depths of the Solemn Hall.

The night had not yet reached its deepest hour, and the lamps refused to sleep, their flames burning steadfast against the encroaching dark. A full table of memorials lay piled like mountains, a weight of empire upon his shoulders.

Tonight, four confidential reports had arrived in succession, each one pressing on the same raw nerve.

Crown Prince Chen Gen, dressed in a deep-blue court robe, sat behind the desk, his brows heavy with the cares of state. Several strands of dark hair fell over his brow, catching the lamplight like a dusting of early frost.

Since assuming the regency, he slept only three quarters of an hour each day. Court deliberations, the Ministry of War, the Ministry of Revenue, the Privy Council, the Imperial Clan Court—matters of every sort tangled about him like a fine, unyielding web.

The first report warned that the Helian forces had begun massing troops in the northern desert, their scouts probing southward under the cover of winter storms.

The second came from the Ministry of Revenue: frontier military stipends still lacked nearly a third of the required silver. Delay any longer, and morale would fracture.

The third concerned the Fourth Prince, who had begun gathering scholars and officers into his household as private retainers—too openly, too deliberately.

The fourth, the most insidious of all, came through palace channels: whispers within the inner court questioning whether, should the Emperor fail to recover, a separate regency or supervising commander ought to be appointed.

Two of them pointed, unmistakably, toward the same prince in the shadows.

Chen Gen gave a short, humourless laugh. Fatigue clung to him, but beneath it stirred a restrained, sharpening anger. Four reports, and half of them already circling the same threat. Did they truly think the intent so well concealed?

He picked up the last memorial and tore it cleanly in half.

He was not ignorant of his position. Though named Crown Prince, the ground beneath that title had never been unshakable. The Second Prince had learned patience; the Fourth excelled in alliances. Marriage ties, military appointments, private favour—each had long since seeped into the court's foundations.

But he could not fall.

He was the Crown Prince. The only Crown Prince of Great Jin.

He forced himself to remain clear-headed, relying on the authority of one imperial decree to suppress the gathering storms of the court. He had learned this much already: if he did not cut first, he would be cut.

Outside, the wind rose suddenly, clawing at the window lattice like a wolf's cry tearing through the night.

He stood and went to the window, unhooking the bronze latch. Beyond the palace walls, the imperial avenues lay buried in snow. Lanterns wound through the palace grounds like a dragon's spine, their light thinning the farther it reached, until all warmth dissolved into the endless cold.

Everyone said being Crown Prince was honour beyond measure.

Yet not for a single day had it ever felt light.

Footsteps approached.

"The Minister of War, the Privy Council deputy, and two Censors wait outside," the eunuch reported in a lowered voice.

Chen Gen turned back, smoothing his sleeves, his voice steady once more. "Summon them."

Moments later, the ministers entered in sequence, bowing deeply.

"With His Majesty yet unconscious," Chen Gen began evenly, "I have not dared neglect the duties of regency. I summoned you tonight to discuss three matters."

First: the northern frontier. What measures does the Privy Council propose in response to Helian's advance?

Second: the military stipends. The accounts remain unclear. With the inner treasury depleted, how is the silver to be raised?
Third—

His gaze settled on the censor standing at the far edge of the hall.

"There are voices within the palace," he said calmly, "claiming I lack authority, that another should be appointed to supervise the armies. Are these rumours without foundation?"

The censor's complexion changed instantly. He dropped to his knees. "Your Highness, this servant has heard nothing of the sort—"

"Is that so?" Chen Gen replied lightly. His tone brushed past like cold steel. "If there are those harbouring treasonous intent, then before His Majesty has even passed, I will see the source of disorder severed."

Silence fell.

"Tomorrow," Chen Gen continued, his voice level, "I will petition to activate the full authority of the Three Offices. Military funds and state affairs will proceed without further imperial countersign. Any objections may be raised now."

None spoke.

"Very well. Submit your respective plans within three days."

The ministers withdrew.

Only then did the hall sink back into stillness.

Chen Gen returned to the desk. His fingers came to rest upon an unopened letter sealed with a familiar mark—Lu Chou's personal seal from Jiangnan.

His gaze eased, just slightly.

As long as Lu Chou returned in time, this board could still be held.

He thought of Jiangnan, of Jin Hua Hall, of the woman whose steady hands had anchored the southern economy when the court itself wavered. He thought, too, of Shen Zhaoru—the Shen clan's daughter, now his Crown Princess—so composed after marriage, so distant, a still surface he had never learned how to cross.

In this world, everyone seemed to stand against him. No one stood beside him and said: you are not alone.

No—there was one.

Xu Hui.

Quiet, unambitious, gentle, unguarded. The only place he could rest without calculation.

Perhaps this was enough. There was no need to think further.

He leaned back, a faint, self-mocking curve touching his lips.

"If I become Emperor," he murmured at last, the resolve in his voice colder than iron, "no one will leave me to hold this realm alone."

At that moment, hurried footsteps, sharp and urgent, sounded outside the heavy doors.

"Your Highness, a confidential letter has arrived from the Heyan border force."

He lifted his gaze from the scrolls; his voice was steady as ever. "Present it."

Before the scroll was even fully opened, a small, cold object rolled out from the brocade pouch.

A hairpin.

It was crafted entirely of gold, with a single luminous pearl set into its tail. The shaft was cleanly broken; the pearl was stained with blood not yet fully dried.

Clearly a woman's ornament—and there was no need to ponder whose it was, that he would carry it so close to his person, next to his heart. He should not have carried it—not to the frontier, not beneath armour—yet it had been hidden against his skin all this time.

It was the silent proof of a long-held affection, and now, the stark clarity of a final farewell.

She was the lamp that never went out in his heart. He had never dared to draw near—only to hope she stayed safe.

Chen Gen's fingers halted mid-air.

The accompanying letter held only a few brutal words:

"Breakthrough at Broken-Waves Ridge. Xiu stayed behind as rearguard. Entered Eagle Pass alone. Life or death unknown. Hairpin returned."

His grip tightened around the cold metal, nearly crushing the gold.

After a long silence, he spoke, the words forced through clenched teeth. "Prepare no record of 'killed in battle.'"

He closed his eyes.

"Lu Xiu," he whispered, voice low and absolute, "I have not granted you leave to die. You dare not."

Dusk bled into the palace grounds. The cold rain had ceased, leaving the air heavy with the scent of wet earth and sorrow.

Shen Zhaoru had just seen the stewards of the embroidery workshop away.

Returning to the inner courtyard, she found Crown Prince Chen Gen standing before her chambers, a statue clad in damp court robes.

His expression was carved from stone, so grave it repelled approach.

In his hands lay a slender wooden box, plain and unadorned, yet it seemed to bear the weight of a thousand mountains of snow.

Her heart clenched. Instinct screamed that the contents within were ominous.

"Your Highness?" Her voice was a thread of sound, frayed with unease.

He offered no greeting, only extended the box. His eyes were still waters over drowning depths.

She pressed her lips together and accepted it.

The moment her fingers touched the unvarnished wood, a chill pierced her to the bone.

She lifted the lid a fraction.

A soft creak broke the silence. Within lay a single object—a gold hairpin, its pearl setting stained with a darkness not yet dry.

Her breath caught, sharp and sudden, as if an invisible hand had seized her throat.

She pushed the lid fully open.

There it lay.

The hairpin, its body twisted, blood seeping into the very heart of the pearl. It rested in its coffin of plain wood, as if it had traversed all the storms of the frontier solely for this moment, for her eyes alone.

The box fell. The crack of wood on stone was a shattering in the quiet.

"My lady—!" Her maid rushed forward, catching her as she swayed.

Her legs betrayed her; she nearly collapsed into the servant's arms, her lips drained of all colours. Yet she forced her spine straight, the words a ghost from her lips. "What… has transpired?"

Chen Gen looked upon her, his voice rough, each word dragged over the coals of his own heart. "He… Lu Xiu, led a strike at Suilang Ridge. They were ambushed, cut off. He entered the cliff path of Eagle Pass alone… His fate… remains unknown."

At those words, a tremor seized her body and her gaze went hollow.

"Life… and death… unknown…?" she echoed in a whisper, as if the words held no meaning she could grasp.

He gave a grim nod, the exhaustion and grim finality settling deep into the lines of his face. "The sealed report states only that as he covered the retreat, the pin fell during the fiercest fighting. Before he vanished alone into the cliff-pass, he ordered his remaining men to return it…"

Before he could finish, Shen Zhaoru's fingers had closed convulsively around the hairpin.

It was the very one—the one he had plucked, unasked, from her hair in the sunset glow as they shared a horseback ride…

Now it was bent, stained with blood, lying cold and heavy across her palm like a fractured span of time, a thread of fate severed silently from the day he had departed.

She lowered her head, staring at it. Her fingertips trembled, yet no sound escaped her lips.

After a long silence, she slowly lifted her gaze to the lamp on the table. Within the firelight, the hairpin gleamed with a faint, jade-like sheen, as if it still held the lingering warmth of his hand.

—He had carried it with him.

It was no military tally, no protective talisman—merely an ordinary woman's hairpin. She had once believed that in his subsequent distance, he had cast it carelessly aside.

Now she knew he had kept it, always carried it to the battlefield, into the bloodshed, borne it with him until that final, rearguard stand.

For a moment, she could not tell whether it was grief she felt, or bitterness.

She grieved that he was trapped in peril, and hated that he had never spoken of it—hated that he was ever thus, placing life and death at the forefront, and her at the very end.

Something in her chest felt violently torn open, the pain so acute she could scarcely draw breath.

Yet she refused to let a single tear fall, only clenched the pin tighter and whispered, soft as a breath, "You truly are a fool…"

The words were spoken, her voice light as the wind, trembling, aching.

And the hairpin lay silent in her grasp, a wordless farewell of profound affection, buried now within these palace walls, buried in the depths of her heart, never to be retrieved.

"Has anyone been sent?" she asked, her voice raw.

Chen Gen did not answer at once. Only after a weighted pause did he reply, faintly, "No."

"Then why will you not send them?!" Her voice rose sharply, threaded with choked tremors and helpless dread. "Your Highness is the Crown Prince—you reign in the Emperor's stead, you command the armies and the empire's might—why will you not dispatch men to save him—?"

"…The blizzard at Suilang Ridge has not ceased. All routes are severed. To force reinforcements through now would only bury more men…" His voice was low, pressed flat like a sheathed blade, its edge turned inward. "I cannot sacrifice more lives to follow him."

"So Your Highness would let him die alone in the snow?!" The control shattered; tears finally fell, her voice shaking uncontrollably. "Is he not the one upon whom you rely most? Did you not say yourself… that he was your strongest arm?"

Chen Gen bowed his head, offering no defence.

She bent, retrieving the wooden box from the floor, her fingers clutching the broken pin as if it were a lifeline. Tears soaked silently into her sleeve, leaving no trace but the cold.

"If he does not return… then neither shall I…"

Her voice nearly broke, the final, unspoken word buried deep within her heart, a vow of stone.

He looked at her, his gaze still as midnight—yet within it, a fine crack began to spread.

After a long moment, he spoke, his voice low. "I have already commanded the Privy Council to re-establish lines to the frontier. If there is the slightest news… I will dispatch the Shadow Guard at once."

"It is not enough." Her voice cut through his, cold, hoarse, and unyielding. "This humble one implores Your Highness—so long as he… so long as a single breath remains in him, spare no cost. Bring him back… no, even if it is only his body, you must bring him back… I beg you…"

Shen Zhaoru knelt before him.

Her brow was flushed and swollen; the skin had split, a thin line of blood tracing the curve of her browbone. She spoke no further, only raised the hairpin in both hands, her grip upon it white-knuckled.

"For him… you, the foremost talented lady of the capital… would debase yourself to this? Do you forget you are my Crown Princess?" Chen Gen's tone was tight with a leashed fury.

"This humble one begs you." She remained bowed in supplication, her form trembling faintly against the stone.

Crown Prince Chen Gen gazed at her in a silence that stretched long and heavy, before at last releasing a sigh that seemed to carry the weight of the world. "I ask you—did you not once declare that you had severed all ties with him?"

She lifted her head. Her countenance was pale as frost and snow, yet held not a trace of fear.

"This concubine believed she could," her voice was faintly raw, scraped thin by grief. "But he carried my hairpin to the very brink of death… how could such a bond ever be severed?"

A flicker of pain crossed the Crown Prince's eyes, sharp and immediate, mingled with the bitter sting of jealousy and a colder, deeper irony. "But now," he reminded her, his voice low, "you are my Crown Princess."

"Yes." Her reply was as light as a ghost's breath. "Which is precisely why I beg you… to send men to save him."

She lowered her head, her voice fracturing like fine porcelain. "If he truly dies… then I would be left guarding only an empty title, a hollow name. But he is still out there—he carried my hairpin. As long as Your Highness sends men to bring him back, this concubine will uphold the title of Crown Princess for all her life, and never… never think of anything more."

The Crown Prince looked at her, into the stark desperation and the unyielding resolve, and finally spoke the words. "A thousand soldiers—this I grant you."

A pause, then the cold, pragmatic addendum, the warning of an emperor-in-waiting: "If the entire force is lost, I will not save him a second time."

She bowed her head to the cold ground, the sound of her brow meeting the stone clear and sharp, like jade shattering on marble. "Thank you, Your Highness."

* * * * *

Three months later, the palace at last released the low, far-carried toll of the mourning bell, its sombre voice rolling over the silent capital.

The Emperor of Great Jin had passed away in the Taiji Palace at the age of fifty-six.

The court and the very realm seemed to quiver with the shock; officials entered mourning as one, donning white robes of grief.

On the day the new emperor ascended the throne, a strange thaw came; the snow in the capital melted away, the people stood in solemn, silent ranks, and the great ceremonial bell sounded nine times, its echo passing through all nine gates, proclaiming a new era.

Shen Zhaoru stood beside the Chenggan Hall, watching as Chen Gen, dressed in the full, imposing regalia of the Son of Heaven, performed the intricate rites of accession.

The Minister of Rites called the proclamations in a voice meant to carry through history.

The assembled officials bowed deeply and hailed him wan sui; dust motes drifted through the slanted light as he finally stepped up and took that seat which had, in truth, never truly been empty.

From that day, she became the Empress.

When the decree was issued, it praised the Crown Princess of the Shen clan for her gentle virtue, her composed nature, and her capability in the governance of the inner palace—deeming her fit to be the central consort, the mother-figure of the realm.

Yet her elevation ceremony was nothing like the grandeur of the enthronement: the inner palace held only one modest banquet, and no high banners flew in the outer court.

With war still pressing at the borders, the court entangled in countless affairs, and the imperial treasury strained thin, many of the customary rites were simplified, or quietly postponed.

Some concubines whispered behind painted screens that she had merely leaned upon her father the Imperial Preceptor's towering reputation to climb to the Empress's throne.

Even her procession was overly sparse and lacking in splendour, proof enough she was not truly favoured by the new emperor.

But she paid them no heed.

She had long grown accustomed to the myriad voices that drifted, like insubstantial gossamer, through the palace halls.

The phoenix crown of an Empress—she had accepted it with her own hands, and placed it with finality upon her own hair.

Seated within the Pepper Chamber Hall, dressed in a plain robe intricately embroidered with phoenix motifs, wearing no rouge nor powder to colour her cheeks, she touched her hair lightly before the bronze mirror.

It was a gesture that seemed to smooth away the world's idle rumours—and to smooth, too, the faint, restless unrest that refused to still within the deepest chambers of her heart.

She had not taken this place for power, nor for transient glory.

It was simply the most proper, the most inevitable, conclusion to the silent pact between her and him.

She understood this clearly: before the ascension, Chen Gen had been the man who, in the deep of night, held a blood-stained hairpin with grief heavy in his eyes.

Now, he was the sovereign of a nation, bearing soldiers, rivers, mountains and the fate of an entire dynasty upon his shoulders; he could no longer allow his private joy or sorrow to tilt the balance of the world.

And she was no longer that young girl who once flushed crimson at a single, heartfelt confession.

Yet in the late hours, when dreams rose unbidden from the depths of sleep, she still sometimes dreamt of that hairpin, of that pearl forever stained with a touch of blood, of the man who had once said, with a simplicity that now felt like a lifetime ago, "I am fond of you."

When she woke, she would sit quietly in the lingering dark, straighten the bedding with methodical hands, instruct the attendants in a calm voice to prepare the morning meal, and then rise to don once more the solemn, dignified robes of the Empress.

From this moment on, the state weighed heavy—and the word love weighed the lightest of all.

Chapter 86: Return in Triumph

Another March arrived.

Spring stirred gently over the empire. Willows unfurled their first pale threads of green, but the capital still wore the dim veil of mourning for a dead emperor and the tremor of power newly shifted.

Bells tolled slower than before; even the wind through vermilion eaves seemed to carry the scent of ashes.

Then—like thunder splitting the horizon—came the news from the borderlands:

Victory at Broken Wave Ridge.

The enemy routed.

The head of General Helian of the northern horde taken in battle, his banners burned, his troops scattered to the frozen steppes.

The dispatch galloped through the night and burst into the Central Secretariat at dawn, scattering ash and ink across the jade floor. The court, half-asleep, jolted awake.

According to the letter from the front, Lu Xiu—missing for three long months—had disguised himself as a mute foot soldier, infiltrating the enemy camp under the snow of the twelfth month.

He lay hidden for days and nights without speech or fire, waiting for the wind to change. He endured the cold and hunger like a thing already half erased from the world.

When the enemy commanders grew careless, he struck.

A single blade through the throat.

The head rolled in the snow; the camp fell into chaos. By dusk their formation collapsed, and by dawn their entire host had fled beyond the frontier.

The news spread through Great Jin like wildfire. The bells of the nine provinces rang; taverns overflowed with toasts. Even the old monks of Lingyan Temple beat their drums three extra times in thanksgiving.

In the Golden Throne Hall, beneath the gaze of the newly crowned emperor, civil and military ministers bowed low, crying as one:

"Triumph to Great Jin! Glory to our army!"

Yet while scrolls and sealed reports piled high in the Secretariat, in the quiet Palace of Pepper Chambers, the Empress—Shen Zhaoru—sat before a low desk, paging through a book of medicinal formulas. The scent of sandalwood drifted through gauze curtains; she did not look up when the eunuch burst in, breathless, and fell to his knees.

"General Lu returns victorious! He lives!"

Her hand froze. The paper slipped soundlessly from her fingers.

For a heartbeat she did not move; then the air left her lungs in a single tremor.

The man she had searched for in dreams, thought of by day and night—

He was alive.

Alive—truly alive.

Alive.

Her lips parted, yet no sound came; only her lashes quivered. After a long moment she whispered, barely audible,

"…He came back."

And for the first time in three long months, the corners of her eyes curved into a smile—faint, fleeting, but wholly real.

* * * * *

The palace that night blazed with light.

Lanterns streamed from carved eaves like falling stars; silk banners unfurled in the new wind of spring. The clang of bronze bells mingled with the thunder of drums, carrying across every courtyard.

Civil and military officials lined the marble steps below the golden dais. The new emperor, draped in dark silk embroidered with gold, held the jade register and proclaimed his decrees in a voice that shook the rafters.

The heroes of the northern campaign were named—one by one, their honours read aloud.

Among the consorts gathered behind the screens, Shen Zhaoru stood upon the terrace beside the throne.

Her phoenix crown glimmered under torchlight; crimson robes trailed like flame. She smiled as the court chanted its praise, yet her heart was far from the hall.

When the feast was done and the crowd began to thin, she slipped away through a side passage.

The incense smoke lingered, faint as memory; the red candles had burned low, their wax tears hardened along the bronze stands.

At the far end of the colonnade, half veiled in shadow—

she saw him.

Lu Xiu.

He was turning to leave the hall, cloak dark with travel dust, the gleam of battle armour still beneath his robe.

"Xiu—"

The single word tore itself from her throat.

He stopped. Slowly, he turned. His gaze met hers.

She descended the marble steps, the heavy phoenix robes dragging behind her like a trail of blood and silk. "You're alive," she whispered, the words trembling. "You're… truly alive."

Her eyes shone wet. She took one step closer, almost reaching out—

He bowed. The movement was measured, precise, the bow of a soldier to a sovereign.

" Peace to Your Majesty—the Empress," he said, the title clean and distant, leaving no room for anything else

She froze where she stood.

He straightened, offered no further courtesy, and walked past her. The hem of his cloak brushed lightly against her sleeve—soundless, final.

As if everything between them had been folded shut with the turn of a single page. As though everything they had ever been had already turned to ash.

She stood motionless, her tears caught in the last flicker of candlelight, each one reflecting the ruin of something too delicate to name.

* * * * *

When he returned to the main hall, the banquet was in full tide again. Jade cups clinked; laughter rang bright as coins.

Emperor Gen raised his goblet high, smiling with all the serenity of command.

"Today the frontier stands secure, the realm at peace," he declared. "There is one person this emperor must first thank—the Empress!"

A murmur swept through the hall; all eyes turned upward toward the woman upon the phoenix throne.

"Was it not for her persistence," the emperor continued, voice smooth yet carrying to every corner, "her plea that the Imperial Guard be dispatched in secret—her tireless efforts to raise silver for the northern campaign—how could our army have triumphed so swiftly at Broken Wave Ridge?

With such a worthy consort beside me, what more could a ruler desire?"

Applause and laughter followed.

The emperor's smile deepened as his gaze slid sideways—to the man seated below, clad still in the steel of battle, face composed, eyes dark as tempered ice.

Lu Xiu.

Yes, the emperor thought. You will understand what I mean to show you. He wanted Lu Xiu to hear it—every word, every syllable—clearly and publicly.

That one word—Empress.

That one phrase—her pleas and her tears. That she had knelt. That she had begged.

Each syllable deliberates, each like a dagger turned over in the light.

She is mine.

The woman who once knelt and begged for your life now sits beneath my crown.

He did not love Shen Zhaoru—perhaps he never had. But he knew the truth that had once passed between her and this man of the frontier, and it pleased him to expose it, to gild her devotion as imperial virtue, to turn her tenderness into a spectacle for the world.

This, he thought, was justice.

This was power.

Only an emperor could decide what was fair.

He caught it then—the smallest tremor of Lu Xiu's hand, the wine in his cup rippling before he stilled it again.

And in that instant came a flash of memory:

her tear-bright eyes beneath palace lanterns,

her voice breaking as she whispered his name,

her figure in red silk, trembling before him—barring his path.

And he, answering only with a bow and four cold words: Peace to the Empress.

The hall erupted again in laughter and toasts. Emperor Gen's mirth rang bright as metal.

Lu Xiu sat among them like a man beneath a mountain. It felt as though thorns had been driven beneath his skin. The joy of triumph sounded hollow; something sharp pressed against his ribs.

He bowed his head, forcing the ache down, swallowing what might have been regret—or something far more perilous.

She should never have been the one to beg.

* * * * *

Outside Zhengyang Gate, the last snow had melted into streams along the stone road; early blossoms trembled under the wind.

But within the imperial study, the air remained cold, austere, heavy with the scent of ink and steel.

Lu Chou stood before the emperor's desk, his fingertips resting on a memorial written in his own hand. He already knew the answer before the words left his mouth. He bowed low and spoke :

"Your Majesty, this minister humbly requests reassignment to Jiangnan—to oversee trade levies and the canal transport. The region's commerce may yet—"

"Another petition?"

The emperor set down his jade brush. His voice was calm but cut like glass.

Lu Chou lowered his eyes. It was the fourth petition; the others had all been denied with a single stroke of vermilion.

This time he had dropped all pretext. Jiangnan is peaceful, he had written. A loyal hand is needed there.

"Jiangnan is not without capable men," the emperor said, his tone deceptively mild. "Where I need you most, Lu Chou, is here."

"But—"

"My man Lu," the emperor interrupted, gentler but no less firm. "You are my arm and my blade. The realm is not yet settled. I cannot let you go."

Silence.

Lu Chou bowed lower, submitting, though within him something shut like a door. Something sealed shut inside him, quiet and final.

Beyond that door lay mists and rain—the hum of looms, the fragrance of silk, her hands restoring Jin Hua Hall, the sound of their child's laughter beneath the lamplight.

Since his return, only letters had passed between them. Her writing was graceful as ever, her words kind, never reproachful.

But never once had she written come to the capital.

Nor could he bring himself to write I will return.

She waited for him to bend.

He waited for a mercy that would never be given.

The emperor turned another page, then spoke lightly:

"The Empress Dowager's birthday approaches. I intend a grand celebration—to reassure the people."

"…A grand one, Your Majesty?"

"I have appointed the Ministry of Rites," Gen replied. "But I want you to oversee the entire ceremony. Nothing must go amiss."

"…Yes, Your Majesty."

When Lu Chou left the study, his posture remained perfect, but each step felt heavier than the last. He did not return to his residence.

Instead, he walked to the small pavilion beside the Hanlin Academy—the quietest corner of the palace.

A white pigeon settled on the beam above, cooing softly.

He unrolled the latest letter from Jiangnan. The lines were few, written in her hand:

The peach trees will bloom soon. Baor asked about you today. I told her—you are busy.

He stared at the words until the ink seemed to blur, then smiled faintly—a smile too thin to hold.

Beyond the pavilion, the walls of the city melted into mist. The wind carried a scent of rain and the faint sweetness of peach blossoms.

Spring had come to the capital.

But Jiangnan, within his heart, remained a thousand miles away. No decree could shorten that distance.

Chapter 87: Brother Xiao Returns

Night weighed heavy, dew thick upon the tiles.
In Qingfeng Court, the lamps flickered softly, shadows swaying against the carved screens.
Lu Xiu entered, the scent of cold wind and steel still clinging to him, his cloak still carrying the breath of snow and frost from beyond the walls, as though he had stepped straight in from a battlefield rather than the inner court.

At the desk, someone was already seated—pouring tea with unhurried grace, as though expecting him all along, as if this meeting had been waiting for him long before the door ever opened.
The tea fragrance mingled with the lamplight, curling lazily through the room, crossing and interweaving with the shadows on the walls, as though the stillness itself had known he would come.

"I had thought my elder brother long fallen for the empire," Lu Chou said lightly, swirling the tea in his cup. His tone was languid, casual, threaded with faint mockery that did not quite conceal its edge. "Who would've guessed he'd return a war god?"

Xiu's steps paused.
His gaze, cold and sharp, flicked toward him—brief, cutting, carrying the chill of iron drawn from its sheath.

"Disappointed?"

"Indeed." Chou smiled faintly. "For one brief moment, I feared you might not return."

The smile had not yet fully faded when his fist struck.

It came fast and heavy, without warning.
A dull crack echoed through the study.

Xiu staggered back half a step. Blood spilled from the corner of his mouth, the bruise blooming instantly along his lip and cheek, dark and livid beneath the lamplight.

"That's for the blow you gave me years ago," Chou said coolly, flexing his wrist as though testing the weight of the strike. His voice was low, controlled, carrying a cold satisfaction. "I've practiced this punch a thousand times. You should thank me for sparing your face. After all, I was kind enough to leave you something presentable."

Xiu lifted a hand and wiped the blood away with the back of his fingers. The smear of red only made his grin look more crooked, more reckless. His eyes glinted with a sharp, unrepentant amusement.

"Hard enough," he rasped. "And late enough."

He straightened, rolling his jaw with a faint pop, fingers briefly pressing along his cheekbone as if testing whether anything had cracked.
"The second punch can wait," he added hoarsely. "I came tonight to bring you a gift."

"I don't need it."
Chou's tone turned to ice. His fist lifted again, knuckles tightening, the intent unmistakable.

"Look first," Xiu said calmly, without flinching. "If you don't like the surprise I prepared, hit me after. It won't be too late."

He turned toward the door and flicked his hand outward in a careless gesture.

"Bring him in."

Two attendants entered, supporting a man between them.
He was covered in dust and grime, clothes torn and worn thin, his body marked by long hardship. A strip of black cloth was bound tightly across his eyes.

Chou frowned at the sight.
"What is this?"

"Remove the cloth," Xiu said with a thin smile. Beneath it flickered a trace of satisfaction he did not bother to hide. "And you'll see."

Chou hesitated only a moment.
Then he stepped forward and reached out, fingers closing around the edge of the cloth.

The blindfold came loose.

Under the wavering lamplight, the man's eyelids fluttered, then slowly opened.

Clear.
Bright.

Bronze-flecked, catching the light with an unmistakable sheen.

Exactly like Baor's.

Chou's heart lurched violently, as though struck from within.
His breath hitched. He took an involuntary step back, his voice
dropping low, roughened almost to a whisper.

"Who... is he?"

Xiu leaned back into his chair, posture loose, expression lazy and
faintly pleased, as though watching a carefully prepared play unfold
exactly as intended.

"Didn't you always wonder about Baor's lineage?" he said lightly. "He
is none other than—Xiao Lingyu's long-missing brother, Xiao Yuan."

"Xiao... Yuan..."
The name slipped from Chou's lips in a murmur, stunned, as if lightning
had struck too close for sound to follow.

Xiu waved his hand without looking away.
"See that Master Xiao is given proper rest. Do not slight him."

"Yes, sir."

As the attendants turned to lead the man away, he suddenly spoke, his
voice uncertain and confused.
"Wait—who are you?"

"Friends," Xiu replied mildly. "We're here to help."

With that, he waved again, and the attendants guided the man from the
room.

The study fell quiet once more.
Only the faint hiss of the oil lamps remained, thin and steady.

Chou stood motionless, his expression unreadable. Shock lingered in
his eyes, tangled with disbelief and something far deeper that had yet to
surface.

"When he vanished years ago," Xiu continued evenly, as though
recounting the fate of a stranger rather than a blood tie, "he was sold
into forced labour at a mining camp in the western territories. The
Heiyan garrison once passed through there. When I went to the border, I
found him by chance."

He tilted his head slightly, studying Chou's face. A ghost of a smile
played at his lips.

"Those eyes," he said softly, "were far too familiar to ignore."

Then, meeting Chou's gaze directly, his tone carried quiet, deliberate satisfaction.

"So I brought him back. I thought… you might find him interesting."

Chou's fingers curled slowly into his palm.
The joints of his hand tightened until the knuckles blanched, all colour draining from them. His voice came low, rough, as if scraped raw.

"…You're saying he's really Xiao Yuan?"

"Ask him yourself."
Xiu's reply was light, almost careless, the tail of his words lifting with faint mockery. "You wanted the truth, didn't you? I've given it to you. Now—"

He paused.
The levity drained from his tone, replaced by something heavier, colder.

"It's your turn to decide what to do."

A chill crept down Chou's spine.

Something was wrong.

The young man's eyes—clear and bright as polished bronze—reflected the lamplight, yet held no focus, no spark of awareness.

They shone only with borrowed light, without ripple or response, as though sight itself had been hollowed out and left empty.

Chou frowned.
"His eyes…"

Xiu had already caught his meaning.
His smile grew languid—and cruel.

"Blind."

Chou's head snapped up.
"What?"

"Mhm." Xiu nodded, the corner of his mouth lifting in a lazy curve that chilled the air. "The mines are full of ash and stone. A falling rock struck his head. Since then—no daylight for him. He sees nothing at all."

His tone remained careless, almost amused, yet each word pierced like a needle.

"This gift," he added softly, "is for her—and for you. So? Does this little 'reunion' earn me that second punch?"

Silence fell.

The air in the study turned glacial, heavy enough to press against the skin.

Chou stared down at the man before him—a stranger, and yet not.

Those blind eyes caught the lamplight, and in that glow he suddenly saw another pair—smaller, rounder, bright with innocence.

His throat tightened.
Words failed him.

For a long moment, neither of them spoke.

Chou stood frozen, staring into those bronze-coloured irises—the very shade that had haunted him since the day he first met that child.

The man who had never faltered, never wavered, now looked utterly lost, as though someone had whispered ten truths into his ear at once—and he understood none of them.
It was as if ten sentences had been spoken into his ear at the same time, and not a single one had reached his mind.

Xiu propped his chin on one hand and watched him.
At last, he sighed. The sound carried more weariness than mockery.

"…Idiot," he said quietly. "Baor is your daughter."

Chou's head jerked up.
Shock and disbelief collided in his gaze—followed by something raw, bright, and unguarded.

Xiu smiled, unhurried and deliberate.

"You've wondered about those eyes, haven't you? Now you know. She takes after her uncle. A Xiao family trait—there's no escaping it."

Chou's pupils contracted.

In the next instant, he turned on his heel and shoved the door open with a sharp crack, as if ready to storm south that very moment and seize them both back with his own hands.

Xiu laughed aloud, calling after him,
"Hey! Night's fallen—you planning to ride straight through till dawn?"

Sure enough, before long, footsteps returned.

Chou stood in the doorway, brows drawn together. For once, he looked utterly disoriented—like a man who had lost his bearings entirely.

His voice came rough, uncertain, almost boyish.

"…Then tell me—what am I supposed to do now?"

Lu Chou stood motionless, as though the ground itself had vanished beneath his feet.

Her voice echoed in his mind—every time she had said, *"This child has nothing to do with you."*

His chest rose and fell in uneven rhythm.

For a long, suspended moment, all sound fled the world.
Only the heavy thud of his heartbeat remained—each strike sharp enough to ache.

Images flashed before his eyes—Baor's bright laughter, her tear-stained cheeks, the way she would pout when angry, lips trembling like a tiny blossom in the wind.

So she truly was his flesh and blood.

His throat tightened; breath caught like something torn loose from within.
Before reason could follow, the decision burst free.

"I'm going to her," he said hoarsely, already turning toward the door.

"Wait—where exactly do you plan to go?" Xiu's voice rose behind him, half-mocking, half-concerned. "You'll sprout wings and fly to Jiangnan?"

Chou froze.

The truth struck him all at once—he could not simply appear before her. His thoughts tangled into chaos.

Xiu tilted his head, tone lazy, as if discussing tea rather than turmoil.

"If you run off without a word, won't His Majesty have your hide by morning?"

Chou's jaw tightened.
He said nothing.

"That's easily fixed," Xiu drawled, eyes glinting with mischief. "If you can't go, then have her come here."

He paused, savouring the moment, then added deliberately,
"Rare sight, seeing you this stupid. Truly—tsk, tsk."

For once, Chou didn't even try to argue.

He simply stood there, dazed, as though his thoughts were still struggling to catch up with his heart.

Xiu shot him a sidelong glance of mock disdain.
"What happened to that clever mind of yours? Did the wind blow it away?"

Silence stretched.

Then, slowly, Chou turned toward him.

The frost in his eyes softened.
A faint, genuine smile tugged at his lips—tinged with something like reconciliation. For the first time in many years, the ice in his gaze finally thawed.

"…I owe you one," he said quietly.

Xiu laughed, raising a brow.
"Well, now—to hear that from your mouth? Remarkable. I'll have to think long and hard about how to collect it."

The lamplight flickered between them, gentle and golden.

And on that night—after years of unspoken distance—the frozen bond between two brothers finally began to thaw.

* * * * *

The next morning, court convened as usual.

The great hall was still wrapped in early chill. The gold-inlaid bricks beneath the ministers' feet held the cold of night, seeping faintly upward through layers of court robes.

The Emperor—once the Crown Prince, Chen Gen—leaned lightly against the imperial desk. His fingers traced the edge of a folded memorial, slow and habitual, his eyelids half-lowered. Between his brows lingered a faint shadow of weariness, subtle yet unmistakable.

"The Empress Dowager's birthday draws near," he said quietly. "Preparations must begin early."

At once, the Grand Steward of the Imperial Household stepped forward and bowed.

"Your Majesty, for the Dowager's sixtieth birthday, the initial plan was a modest celebration, in accordance with precedent," he reported respectfully. "However, as the realm has only recently been pacified, the ministers advise otherwise—that this occasion be used to proclaim peace and prosperity to all under Heaven. The Ministry of Works has already fixed the date and rites. Matters of weaving and dyeing have likewise been assigned to the palace embroidery bureau."

The hall remained hushed, breath held between stone pillars. One by one, ministers stepped forward to deliver their reports, voices echoing faintly against the vaulted ceiling.

Lu Chou stood among them, outwardly composed, yet his thoughts drifted far from the orderly cadence of court ritual.
Half his mind weighed how best to renew his long-delayed request for leave; the other half calculated, with careful restraint, how he might lawfully depart the capital and head south.

His brows knit faintly.

Just as he prepared to step forward, the Emperor spoke again.

"This is the first birthday since Our accession, and the Dowager's sixtieth year besides," Chen Gen said evenly. "It must not be slighted. How fare the preparations between the Ministry of Rites and the Household Bureau?"

The Grand Steward bowed lower.

"In accordance with established rites, Your Majesty. However, Her Majesty the Dowager has long favoured the fine embroideries of Jiangnan. She has therefore ordered that a number of folk artisans be summoned to craft her longevity robes, screens, and draperies. Results are expected within ten days."

Lu Chou's gaze shifted almost imperceptibly.

"I heard," he said, voice calm, "that several palace embroiderers have fallen ill of late?"

The Steward hesitated for a fraction of a breath before replying.

"Indeed. A few were stricken with cold and damp and have been granted leave to recuperate. While the delay should be minor, as precaution the Household Bureau has already summoned skilled women from the southern provinces to assist."

Something flickered behind Lu Chou's eyes.

He stepped forward half a pace, sleeves brushing the cold air.

"Your Majesty," he said, bowing slightly, "I have heard of a workshop in Jiangnan known as Jin Hua Fang. Its embroideries are of rare craftsmanship, long praised among the tribute offerings of past years. Their work was once held in high regard within the Palace itself. If summoned, they could surely aid in the preparations."

The Emperor lifted his gaze.

"Jin Hua Fang…?"
It was not a name spoken lightly, nor recalled on impulse, but one long noted and quietly remembered.

Lu Chou inclined his head.

"Yes. Their Madam, Madam Xiao Lingyu, once presented Her Majesty the Dowager with a double-sided embroidered sachet. For that piece, she received explicit commendation."

Recognition lit the Emperor's eyes.

"Ah. Xiao Lingyu," he murmured, memory stirring. "I do recall that name. Last year, Consort Hui herself commissioned her to select the colours for a headband—and even Hui, with her exacting eye, declared that not a single flaw could be found."

Soft laughter rippled through the hall.
The rigid atmosphere eased, tension loosening like a breath released.

Lu Chou lowered his gaze, concealing the brief surge of relief—and something quieter, steadier—that stirred beneath his composure.

The Emperor cleared his throat and straightened, his posture returning to calm authority.

"Very well," Chen Gen said. "Let Our decree be written."

His voice rang clearly through the hall.

"Summon the Imperial Merchant of Jiangnan—Madam Xiao Lingyu of Jin Hua Fang—to the capital at once. She shall oversee the embroideries for the Empress Dowager's jubilee. She is to arrive within ten days. No delay shall be permitted."

"Your servant obeys," Lu Chou replied, bowing deeply.

As his palm pressed to the cold stone floor, he felt a faint heat bloom there—quiet, contained, undeniable.

At last, he had a reason.
A righteous one.
An unassailable one.

A reason to bring her back to the capital.

* * * * *

That evening, the lamps of Jin Hua Hall bloomed one by one against a veil of drizzle.

Spring's chill had returned. The air was thin and damp, carrying the scent of rain-soaked stone.

Inside the hall, Xiao Lingyu sat beside the embroidery table, reviewing a set of bridal robe patterns with several seamstresses. Between her fingers lay a sheet marked with red-ink revisions—lines precise, deliberate—when hurried footsteps sounded from the corridor.

"Madam," Suxin called softly from the doorway, her voice careful, "a messenger from the Imperial Household has arrived. He bears an official dispatch."

Xiao Lingyu paused mid-stroke.
The brush hovered above the paper, ink threatening to pool.

"The Imperial Household?" she repeated.

Suxin stepped forward and handed over the document.
The envelope bore the crimson wax seal of the bureau—not an imperial edict, yet formal in every respect, leaving no room for neglect.

Xiao Lingyu broke the seal and unfolded the letter.

Her eyes skimmed the lines swiftly, accustomed to official phrasing, until they stopped upon the final sentence.

"By decree, the Imperial Merchant Xiao Lingyu is to enter the capital within three days, to assist in the embroidery of the Empress Dowager's ceremonial robe."

Her fingers tightened.
The edge of the paper creased beneath her touch.

The room fell silent. Even the seamstresses sensed the shift in the air and lowered their eyes.

Suxin hesitated, then whispered,
"Madam… will you truly go?"

Xiao Lingyu drew in a quiet breath and folded the document closed.

"It is an imperial summons," she said softly. "How could I not?"

Outside the window, dusk thickened to ink.
Rain glimmered in the lamplight, blurring the mouth of the alley into a
pale haze.

"Have the masters tally this year's accounts," she added after a pause,
her voice steady once more, "and prepare them for handover."

She hesitated, then continued, more softly,

"And… bring the 'Water and Cloud Shadows' inlaid hair-box. If Her
Majesty asks, I shall have something to present."

Suxin nodded and withdrew, footsteps retreating down the corridor.

Left alone, Xiao Lingyu returned to the embroidery frame.

Her fingertips brushed across a half-finished pattern—phoenix and
dragon entwined in silk.
The threads lay unknotted.
The needle rested where it had been left, suspended, unfinished.

Much like the line of fate she had once believed severed.

A quiet smile curved her lips—tender, tinged with sorrow.

"So," she murmured to herself, voice barely above the rain,
"in the end… I must return after all."

Chapter 88: Entering the Palace in Uniform

Before dawn, the courier road outside the capital lay drowned in dense mist that had not yet dispersed.

Lu Chou had already been waiting beyond the city gate for a long while.

People came and went around him without pause—merchant caravans, relay horses, travellers wrapped in cloaks—yet he did not spare a single glance for any of them. His eyes remained fixed upon the long official road ahead, as though within the sound of that wind he could already hear, faintly, the familiar creak of wheels and the laughter he had been missing, stirring his heart into a restless, unbearable tremor.

Only when a carriage he knew all too well drew nearer from the far end of the road did his breath catch. His chest tightened; his eyes, before he was even aware of it, had grown damp.

The carriage came to a stop.

Little Baor immediately poked her head out from the window, and the moment she saw him, her face lit up with dazzling joy.

"Papa Lord—!"

Lu Chou surged forward at once. He reached in and lifted her out, raising her high as if she weighed nothing at all, then pulled her close, kissing and hugging her in a frenzy that made his voice turn hoarse.

"Baor… Baor…"

Baor wrapped her small arms around his neck; her cheeks had flushed bright red from excitement. She blinked up at him and asked in confusion, "Da-ren Daddy, why are you crying?"

"I am not crying," he said quickly, as if the words could steady him. "It is only… the wind is too strong."

Yet the next moment, he held her even tighter, burying his face in her hair and whispering over and over, voice breaking into a rough murmur:

"Daddy missed you. Missed you until I went mad."

No one seemed to notice it—not even he himself at first—yet somewhere in that instinctive outpouring, he had already changed the way he addressed himself. The "Da-ren" was gone. In its place, there was only "Daddy", intimate and raw in a way that could no longer be concealed.

Xiao Lingyu also stepped down from the carriage.

She had not heard the words he had murmured into Baor's hair. She was dressed in plain, pale clothing, without ornament, and when she saw him so visibly undone, she let out a quiet laugh.

"How unlike you," she said softly.

Lu Chou held Baor in one arm, and with the other, he drew Xiao Lingyu into his embrace as well. The joy in his brows and eyes was almost impossible to restrain—yet beneath it, there was also something like remorse, thick and bitter, pressed tightly behind his smile.

He lowered his head to her ear and whispered, each word like a vow forced out of his throat:

"In this life… I will never dare wrong you again."

She stared at him, wide-eyed, stunned.

"This is sudden… What is it? What has happened?"

Lu Chou tightened his hold around her.

"I know everything now," he said, voice low. "Baor is my daughter."

At those words, Xiao Lingyu's heart clenched hard; a dull, swelling ache rose in her chest.

"You… you know…"

"Mhm." He let her lean against his chest. " Xiu told me. You, a foolish girl… you should have let me know sooner."

"It is not that I did not wish to tell you," she said, her throat tight. "I was only afraid…"

"Before I ever knew the truth," Lu Chou cut in, voice steady despite the tremor beneath it, "I had already treated Baor as my own. And now that I know she is my blood—my legitimate kin—there is even less for you to fear."

He paused, his tone turning softer, almost gentling.

"Do not be afraid. From this day on, leave everything to me."

Xiao Lingyu's lashes trembled. The corners of her eyes reddened, and she was just about to speak when Lu Chou's expression shifted. He gave her a faint, almost secretive smile.

"Come with me," he said. "I have another gift for you."

Before she could fully recover, she saw him lift his hand and signal toward the rear.

The next instant, a figure was helped down from behind another carriage.

The man wore a coarse grey robe. His face was thin, his features slightly sunken from hardship, and over his eyes there was a layer of fine gauze.

Xiao Lingyu's pupils contracted violently.

That silhouette—straight as a pine. That familiar angle of the jaw. That way of standing, as if even exhaustion could not bend him—

Her throat seized. She barely dared breathe as she forced out a broken whisper.

"…Brother?"

At the sound of her voice, the man's body jerked as though struck. He turned toward her; though his eyes held no light, his movement did not hesitate for even a fraction. He called, precisely, unerringly, as if he had never lost her at all:

"A-Yu."

That single syllable was like a wheel crushing straight across the years.

All those seasons of ruin and separation, the countless times she had stood by the gate and waited, the old dreams in which she had met him again—everything surged up in a fierce flood.

Xiao Lingyu lunged forward and grabbed his cold hand. Her tears finally burst free.

"Brother… How… how did you only return now… How could you…"

Xiao An smiled gently. His fingertips rose and brushed the corner of her eye, wiping away the tears with a tenderness that made her throat ache.

"Do not cry, A-Yu," he said. "Brother is back. I am home."

"I looked for you for so many years…" Xiao Lingyu's voice broke.

"Do not cry," Xiao An said softly. "Is Father well? Is everyone well?"

Xiao Lingyu lifted her sleeve and wiped her face with a handkerchief, trying and failing to steady her breathing.

"After you disappeared, Father suffered a stroke. He passed away half a year ago," she said, each word heavy. "Now… Jin Hua Hall is held up by my hands alone."

Xiao Yu'an's smile faltered for a heartbeat. Then, very quietly, he said:

"A-Yu… you have suffered."

Baor, who did not fully understand what had happened, only sensed that everyone's eyes were red. She wriggled out of Lu Chou's arms and toddled over, stopping beside Xiao Yu'an with the innocent seriousness of a child.

"Is that Uncle?" she asked in a soft, milky voice. "Baor missed you. Mother said you disappeared."

Xiao Yu'an froze.

Then he laughed—a laugh that carried the warmth of something recovered after loss, and also the release of blood and tears finally set down.

He reached out, gently touch and patted Baor's head.

"Yes," he said, voice gentle. "Uncle came back too late."

Only then did Xiao Lingyu notice something wrong.

"Brother… your eyes…"

Still crying, she lifted a hand and brushed away the rain strands from his forehead. Only at that moment did she see it clearly: his gaze was fixed and unmoving, staring into an empty place as though the world before him did not exist.

Xiao An shrugged, as if it were no great matter at all.

"In the mine pit, a boulder struck my head," he said casually. "I went blind."

"Brother…"

Xiao Lingyu's tears fell even harder.

Lu Chou stepped forward. With one hand he held his wife close; with the other he reached back for Baor's small hand. He faced Xiao An and spoke with quiet seriousness:

"Brother An, do not worry. I will search the world over for physicians to treat you."

Xiao An shook his head. Though he could not see, his face turned precisely toward Lu Chou, as if his gaze still fell in the right place.

"I have not yet thanked Lord Lu," he said. "To have the chance to return home and reunite with family is already a blessing beyond measure. I dare not ask for more."

Baor's bright expression crumpled into worry.

"Uncle… you cannot see?" she asked, voice small. "Then… you cannot see Baor?"

Xiao Yu'an reached out and searched gently until his fingers found her cheek. He smiled.

"Do not fear," he said. "Uncle can use his hands. Our Baor has grown."

At last, dawn broke through the mist, and the light fell upon the four of them.

A reunion long waited for, a family finally gathered. In that moment, they all knew—every storm and every year of endurance had at last met its spring.

* * * * *

Within the inner chambers of the Central Palace, incense smoke curled thickly beneath the lowered curtains.

The spring cold had only just risen, and the candle flames warmed the air into a stifling heat; yet even that warmth could not dilute the silent pressure flowing through the room.

Shen Zhaoru stood quietly, dressed in a pale-blue palace gown, her posture calm as still water.

Behind the desk, the Emperor Chen Gen was turning through memorials. He had not spoken for a long time; the vermilion brush between his fingers hovered in mid-air, halted as though even ink could not easily descend.

Only after a long silence did he lift his eyes.

"These few days," he said lightly, "you seem to have something on your mind."

Shen Zhaoru lowered her gaze.

"This consort would not dare."

Chen Gen's mouth curved faintly, his tone softening by a degree.

"Between you and Us, must you still speak so formally?"

"There is truly nothing," she replied, turning her face slightly aside, avoiding the way his eyes examined her as if interrogating her.

Chen Gen let out a cold laugh.

"The Empress is a clever woman," he said. "You should know why We have come tonight."

Shen Zhaoru's fingers trembled, almost imperceptibly.

"Your Majesty…" she said quietly. "At the beginning, Your Majesty said you would not force me."

Chen Gen stared at her for a long while without speaking. Then he set down the vermilion brush and rose to his feet. His voice was not loud, yet it carried a weight that left no room for evasion.

"At that time you said," he began slowly, "that so long as We sent troops to aid him, you would—thereafter—cease refusing Us. And now, We have already bestowed upon him the title of Dingbei General, with ten thousand upon ten thousand troops under his hand."

His gaze sharpened.

"What is it that you are still not satisfied with?"

Shen Zhaoru finally lifted her eyes. Her manner remained gentle, yet within it there was a stubborn line that would not bend.

"This consort remembers," she said, each word controlled, "that this consort only asked Your Majesty to grant a little more time."

"Time," Chen Gen repeated, his laughter edged with mockery. "Again it is time."

He stepped closer by half a pace, the candlelight cutting his profile into hard lines.

"You always say you need time," he said, voice cold. "Yet Our patience is not without end. Do you truly think that the position of Empress can shelter you forever, allowing you to flee without limit?"

He smiled—a smile without warmth.

"You know what We require," he said. "We need a legitimate heir."

"This consort… knows."

"Then you should also know the duty that comes with being the Empress."

Shen Zhaoru did not answer at once. After a moment, she lowered herself to her knees and spoke with controlled calm:

"This consort begs leave to go to the Detached Palace."

Chen Gen's eyes narrowed.

"To leave the palace?"

Shen Zhaoru's fingers clenched hard against her skirt, knuckles whitening.

"This consort has no intent to break faith," she said softly. "Only… the fruit forced from a twisted branch is of benefit to no one."

The Emperor's gaze cooled further.

Yet in the end, he did not force the matter.

After a long silence, he said:

"Very well. Go."

"The spring cold at the Detached Palace has not yet dispersed. Have them prepare medicines and warming things."

He paused, then spoke with finality:

"We grant you seven days. If after seven days you still do not return, We shall personally go to invite you back into the palace."

Shen Zhaoru bowed deeply to the ground.

"This consort thanks Your Majesty for Your grace."

When she rose, Chen Gen already stood with his hands behind his back, not looking back. His voice fell lightly, yet it struck like a blade.

"Go, then. Think it through."

"You are no longer a Shen daughter who may act as she pleases," he said. "Do not forget your present identity as Empress, nor the worth of this Central Palace seat—how many great families dream of it."

His last words were quiet, almost contemptuous.

"Do not fail to recognise your honour."

"This consort understands," Shen Zhaoru replied, tone still steady. "Your Majesty is benevolent."

At that final phrase, her steps paused for the smallest instant—then she did not stop. She turned and withdrew, slowly, beyond the hall doors.

As the doors closed, there was a soft click.

It was as though a human heart, too, had been sealed behind layered gates.

* * * * *

The night was the colour of ink, and within the Detached Palace of the Imperial Gardens outside the capital, a persistent fine rain was soaking through the tiled eaves and blue stones.

The sound of the rain was a fine, continuous drizzle, flowing from the ridge of the roof all the way to the deepest recesses of the human heart.

Shen Zhaoru arrived from out of the rain, clad in a cloak; she had not used the Empress's palanquin, but merely a carriage fashioned in the style and scale of a wealthy household.

Unexpectedly, the cavalcade became obstructed along the mountain path, and the heavens suddenly unleashed a heavy downpour, forcing the attending eunuch to reluctantly invite her to rest temporarily in a side hall.

"Though this place is small, it is nevertheless clean, Your Ladyship. It is a condescension for you to alight here; may Your Ladyship forgive my fault,"

The junior eunuch said, trembling with trepidation.

Shen Zhaoru smiled faintly and said: "It matters not. We shall depart after resting for a short while."

The palace lanterns were lit one by one; amidst the swirling night mist, she stepped into the empty corridor. The construction of the Detached Palace was simple, without elaborate floral carvings, consisting only of the old colour of stone and wood, which unexpectedly harmonised deeply with her state of mind.

Turning past the corner of the corridor, she suddenly came to a stop.

That person stood within the veil of rain.

His dark armour was not yet unbuckled, his cape was not undone, and the hair at his temples was slightly damp, yet his features were as cold and clear as the first snow. The lamplight cast his handsome silhouette from the side; those eyes still held a coexistence of mockery and restraint, but were a few degrees heavier than in former days.

Lu Xiu.

Their four eyes met, and no one spoke first.

Who was the first to look away was no longer discernible.

"The Empress would actually deign to come to this place,"

His voice was faint, like the cold rain brushing across the stone steps, carrying a subtle and disdainful sarcasm.

"This place is not comparable to the Eastern Palace, and is perhaps somewhat desolate."

Shen Zhaoru raised her gaze to look at him, without a ripple in her eyes:

"This Palace intends to proceed to the Detached Palace, but the carriage was unfortunately obstructed. I am merely borrowing this place for a night's rest. If the General does not welcome this, you may naturally send another court attendant."

He advanced two steps, his boots squelching upon the water.

"May I ask the General, why are you also at this courier station?"

Shen Zhaoru glanced slightly towards him, her gaze falling upon his chiselled profile.

Lu Xiu's gaze was directed towards the veil of rain, and he merely offered two simple words:

"Sheltering from the rain."

"Oh, that is truly a coincidence."

He turned his profile slightly to look at her, his voice deep: "It is a coincidence. Earlier, when the fancy took me, I came to the suburbs for a ride, yet unexpectedly encountered this sudden heavy rain."

"So that is the case."

His gaze rested upon the strand of rain-dampened hair near her temple: "You are in such light attire; are you not cold? How have your serving maids been attending to you?"

She was slightly stunned, then smiled faintly: "I am not cold. I instructed all of them to retire so that I could have some quietude. Moreover, there is never warm wine to comfort the heart in the Palace, and the General is not also laden with cold air, yet is he not still living quite well?"

He stared at her for a long time, then suddenly smiled, though that smile possessed not a fraction of warmth. "Zhaoru, you are still as eloquent as ever."

Shen Zhaoru's expression did not change; she merely said: "Indeed. If I were not eloquent, I would have lost my life long ago."

The two stood beneath the corridor, one in front, one behind, silent with one another.

The sound of the rain was incessant, like broken threads, and the night was evocative.

That kind of entanglement and complexity, unresolved over many years, was now slowly emerging in the damp, cold veil of rain.

The former silence, the desertion, the missed opportunities, all lay hidden silently within this short distance of mere steps.

After a moment, she said softly: "The rain is heavy here; I shall return to my room first."

As she turned, intending to depart, Lu Xiu suddenly said: "Do you know—"

She halted her steps, without turning her head.

Lu Xiu gazed intently at her slender back and said in a low voice: "I have learned... that when I was trapped and holding out in the Northern Frontier, it was you who, in the Capital, prevailed over all objections, defying counsel and resisting the Imperial Edict, to secure reinforcements for me. Zhaoru, this deep affection and righteousness... Xiu is eternally grateful for it."

Shen Zhaoru lowered her gaze for a moment, and softly replied: "The General overstates his case. You donned your armour and faced danger for the sake of the Empire; what Shen Zhaoru did was merely her duty."

She did not linger further, stepping into the deep mist of the rain. Behind her, Lu Xiu watched her retreating figure, his knuckles lightly clenched, his voice as faint as a murmur to himself: "Have you, after all... ever regretted it?"

* * * * *

The night passed the Zi Shi hour (11 p.m. to 1 a.m.); within the Detached Palace, a single, still lamp shone like a bean.

Shen Zhaoru sat before the desk, holding a cup of warm wine between her fingers; the white porcelain lightly touched her lips, yet she had not taken a drink.

The palace attendants had long been sent by her to rest in the side halls, and even her most personal junior court attendant had been instructed to prepare incense and bath linens for her and had not returned for a long time.

She was alone, her robes still on; she had not slept, nor did she wish to sleep.

The incense burner beside the desk emitted a faint aroma, its thin blue smoke curling upwards, just like the layered, persistent turmoil in her heart.

Since entering the Palace, she had never been so distraught. It was not because of the Emperor's words: "After seven days, We shall personally come to invite you back to the palace," but rather—

She knew that this brief stay at the Detached Palace would be the only time in her remaining life when she could act upon her own will.

Suddenly, footsteps drew near outside the window. Before she could call out, the door was pushed open by half an inch.

That person stood outside the door, still in dark robes and a cape, his features cold and grave as frost, yet his expression carried a measure of vigilance and enquiry.

It was him.

Lu Xiu.

Shen Zhaoru did not rise; she merely turned her head to look at him, a faint gleam in her eyes, like starlight beneath the curtain after a night rain, indifferent yet deeply affectionate.

"You have come?" Her voice was extremely soft, yet held no surprise.

"...Someone reported that you coughed twice in your throat; that is why..." His voice was deep and husky, yet the moment he spoke, he knew this excuse was utterly ridiculous.

She smiled softly, her gaze dropping to the water marks beneath his feet: "To wet your boots through the night, the General is indeed attentive."

He frowned slightly, looking towards the space inside the room where no one else was in attendance: "So late, and you are alone? Where are your accompanying maids?"

"I wished for a moment of solitude, and dismissed them all." She raised her eyes to gaze at him, slowly rising, and walked towards him step by step, the distance so close that she could almost hear the subtle rising and falling of his breath. She asked softly, tentatively: "If you do not wish to be alone... General, would you be willing to keep me company?"

He was momentarily stunned, his throat tightening slightly. He subconsciously stepped back half a pace, not using the respectful address: "You... must not make such a jest."

She, however, smiled, her smile extremely slight, and her fingertips were already resting lightly upon his sleeve.

"I am not jesting," her tone was extremely light and steady, as natural as a friend, as if stating something that required no explanation, "Tomorrow I must proceed to the Detached Palace; as for what follows, you and I both know it clearly in our hearts."

She looked at him, saying word by word: "But tonight, I only wish to be myself. Even if only for one night."

Lu Xiu's knuckles tightened slightly, and his eyes surged with restraint and hesitation.

"Do you know what this signifies?"

"Of course, I know... At that time, beneath the setting sun, on the maple-lined path in the woods, you told me from horseback that your heart was pleased with me; has the General forgotten?" She took one step closer to him, the distance now less than an arm's length.

Lu Xiu secretly took a deep breath; his nostrils were completely filled with the fragrance emanating from her body, and his entire body was a boiling torrent of blood. His voice was choked and husky. "It was I who was useless... I failed to protect you."

"I do not blame you; I only blame the impermanence of life." She smiled, yet there was not a fraction of mirth in her eyes: "I, too, comprehend everything, Xiu. But I do not wish... for the person you remember to forever be only an Empress."

He lowered his gaze, as if trying to suppress a thousand words and ten thousand phrases. After a moment, he finally raised his hand and covered her palm.

At that moment, the sound of the wind outside the window ceased, and the lamp's shadow was silent.

She moved close to his ear and whispered softly: "Tonight, I am Shen Zhaoru, not the Empress."

He did not speak; the struggle and desire in his eyes were intertwined, just like that night which faded away before completion many years ago.

Shen Zhaoru did not press him, only watched him quietly, her gaze serene as water.

After a long while, he finally reached out and slowly drew her into his embrace, his voice hoarse: "I lied to you earlier. It was not on a whim that I rode in the suburbs, but... I followed your cavalcade all the way..."

She was taken aback, staring at him with wide eyes. "Why?"

"Because I kept thinking... that to see you from afar... would also be good."

"You truly are... Alas..." Having said this, her body gently leaned towards his broad shoulder.

It was not a passionate embrace, but a hug of extreme restraint and profound pain, like holding onto a dream that was about to sink beneath the surface.

She buried her face in his shoulder, detecting the scent of cold wind and snow still clinging to him, yet still feeling a sense of reassurance.

Her fingers lightly trembled, slowly reaching out and gripping his chest.

"Xiu..."

Her voice was faint, yet it was like a flash of lightning, cleaving the final line of defense between the two of them.

He trembled slightly, as if he had finally admitted to something, and as if he had finally been vanquished.

The next moment, his lips descended.

It carried a deep suppression and a profound hunger; there was no longer any speech, no longer any thought, only their mutual breaths intertwined in the night.

She trembled softly in response, her fingertips tightly gripping his collar, as if seeking to melt him into her very bones and blood.

Her hair at the temples was in disarray, and the air was misty with fragrance.

Outside, the sound of the rain had not ceased, yet inside, there remained only the sound of robes slipping and heartbeats interlacing.

He wished to stop at one point, yet his hands were already beyond his control.

She wished to flee at one point, yet she ultimately took the initiative to untie her sash, her eyes filled with a tenderness and a finality that wished to say no more.

On this night, they spoke no words of love, nor did they make any vows.

He only kissed her brow repeatedly, as if sealing all regret and resentment into this one action.

She, too, only watched him quietly, closing her eyes in that final moment, weeping silently.

The rainy night was silent. Amidst the spring cold, one person finally abandoned all reason, embracing that destined conflagration.

* * * * *

The sky was faintly bright; the fine rain outside the Detached Palace's window lattice had long since ceased, leaving only water droplets silently sliding down along the tile ridge.

The morning mist hung lightly, the light was still indistinct, and within the curtains reigned a profound stillness.

Shen Zhaoru lay against Lu Xiu's embrace, her hair loose at her temples, a smile lingering at the corner of her lips.

Her fingers slowly traced the indentations of his armour upon his chest, just like those gentle yet decisive kisses of the night before, silently narrating a dream that refused to be woken from.

Lu Xiu opened his eyes, gazing intently at her features, his gaze concealing the heat and unrest of a sleepless night. He spoke in a low voice: "Zhaoru, come away with me, will you not? At this very moment, now, I am willing to renounce my office, renounce my army, renounce everything. Shen Zhaoru, so long as you nod your head, to the ends of the earth, I will protect you and keep you safe."

She did not answer immediately, only raised her hand to gently stroke his brow, like coaxing a stubborn child, and chuckled softly: "Do you know? I asked you that very same question all those years ago."

He froze.

She looked at him, saying word by word: "Before the Imperial Edict declared me Crown Princess, I sought you out. At that time, I asked you—could you take me away?"

His Adam's apple moved slightly, yet he made no sound.

"You were silent for a long time before you said: 'I was not my own master.'"

Shen Zhaoru sat up lightly; the quilt slipped from her shoulder, revealing the faint kiss marks upon her skin. Yet she made no attempt to conceal them, merely turning around to face him.

"And now, alas, I have also become that person—who is not her own master."

She was smiling, yet her eyes were moist: "Xiu, neither of us can leave. You have your ten thousand troops, and I have my position in the Central Palace. Our names are inscribed in different chronicles; we can no longer stand side by side."

Lu Xiu abruptly sat up, intending to speak, but only felt a sharp pang of pain in his heart. She reached out and pressed his lips, saying softly: "This night was one that I sought for myself. I have no regrets, nor do I ask you to remember it."

She paused, her tone as light as the wind: "I only beg... that the General never mention this again hereafter."

He watched her, his eyes reflecting the light of dawn, and also reflecting that drop of tear in her eye which had not yet fallen.

She lowered her head and gently kissed his temple for a moment, like a breeze sweeping past.

"Day is about to break; I should depart for the Detached Palace." She gave a desolate smile. "General, let us part here. In this life... may we each find our own peace."

* * * * *

The morning light splashed upon the window lattice of the Detached Palace, mottled and translucent.

Lu Xiu sat alone at the edge of the bed; beside him, the space was utterly empty, with only a brocade quilt still holding residual warmth, as if it retained her body temperature and the fragrance of her hair.

The room was still misty with the residual fragrance of the night, yet not a trace of her figure remained.

The incense had burned down to cold ash, the flowers in the water cup already faded, as though the night had quietly erased itself.

Outside the window, a palace maid timidly tapped on the door and whispered softly: "General, the Empress Ladyship has already departed at the Chen hour (7 a.m. to 9 a.m.)."

He stepped outside the door, and just as he reached the front of the corridor, a gust of wind arose.

The wind lifted the corner of the curtain; in that instant, he seemed to see the residual shadow of her flowing robes fluttering past, exactly as she had looked when they first met, all smiles and beautiful chatter.

But the wind passed silently, the empty curtain hung low, and no one stood in the long corridor.

He stood rooted to the spot, closing his eyes heavily.

He had never regretted loving her, yet he had never truly possessed her.

Last night, she had said: "I am Shen Zhaoru, not the Empress."

Yet this morning, she was already the Empress, and from this day forth, their paths diverged to the very ends of the world.

He lowered his head, his palm gripping the brocade quilt, holding it tightly in his hand.

His knuckles were white, and his heart was gripped by a dull ache, yet there was no one to whom he could tell his suffering.

When the wind rose again, he did not raise his head to look once more.

——This parting truly became the cessation of all paths in this life.

Chapter 89: Love Reaches Its Depths

The Fall of the Preceptor and the Shadow of the Throne

The three strikes of the bronze gong echoed through the Meridian Gate, signaling the officials in their court robes to enter the hall. The daylight that morning was unusually overcast; beneath the imperial throne, rows of purple robes and black hats stood with bowed heads, holding their breath in a heavy silence, broken only by a slight cough from the man high above.

The Emperor leaned half-sideways on the dragon throne. The jade tablets in his hands remained unread, his gaze instead fixed upon a cold, sharp figure within the ranks of the military officials: Lu Xiu, the General of Northern Pacification, commander of a hundred thousand border troops.

His reputation had soared after the recent victory, but even as rewards for his campaign remained unsettled, he had already become the focal point of the court's whispered anxieties.

The Emperor lowered his eyes, his voice steady and calm: "Though the border defenses have been stable of late, we must consider the distribution of military power—the necessity of checks and balances."

As these words fell, the air in the hall grew instantly heavy. The Minister of War bowed in response: "Your Majesty's foresight is profound. Perhaps we should station the Commander of the Right Valiant Guard in the northern camps to assist the General—serving as a measure of mutual restraint."

The Right Valiant Guard was the Emperor's personal force, and its commander had long been at odds with Lu Xiu. This proposal was a blatant attempt to fetter his military authority. Yet, Lu Xiu remained unmoved, his voice as cool as iron: "This servant lives only to serve the frontier and submits entirely to Your Majesty's deployment."

A flicker of an expression, neither a sneer nor a smile, crossed the Emperor's face. After a long silence, he spoke softly: "The General is indeed a man of great composure."

Just then, an attendant hurried into the hall, whispering urgently into the Emperor's ear. The Emperor's brow furrowed, then he spoke in a deep, sonorous voice: "Imperial Preceptor Shen Huaizhong has been gravely ill for months; he passed away this morning. Dispatch the Imperial

Physicians to verify the cause, and command the Ministry of Revenue to arrange the funeral rites. The court session ends here. Dismissed."

The officials cried *Wan Sui* in unison, dispersing like a receding tide. Behind the closing palace doors, the Emperor remained alone, murmuring to himself: "One Shen Huaizhong is gone. Lu Xiu... how much longer can you remain calm?"

* * * * *

On the third day of the retreat at the Detached Palace, before the first light could break the horizon, the dire news arrived: Shen Huaizhong, the Imperial Preceptor, had breathed his last at the hour of *Zi*. He was fifty-three years old. The Imperial Medical Bureau reported: *"A long-standing illness turned chronic; he passed peacefully in his sleep."*

When the report reached Shen Zhaoru, she nearly collapsed beside her couch. The tea in her cup surged over the rim, soaking through her silk sleeves. "Father... your daughter has been unfilial..." she murmured to herself. Her voice was thin, but the choking grief was beyond words as silent tears fell.

Before noon, a grand imperial decree was issued: The Empress was to return to the capital immediately for the mourning rites. The eulogy was to be drafted by the Hanlin Academy, and Shen Huaizhong was posthumously granted the title of "Grand Preceptor Wenzheng." He was to be enshrined in the Hall of Virtuous Sages, and his funeral conducted with the honours due to a prince.

The capital was shaken once more; the scholarly community trembled with grief. Civil officials rose in collective mourning. All who had once been pupils of the Great Preceptor—whether they were Grand Secretaries of the Secretariat, Ministers of Rites, or humble Doctors of the Court of Imperial Sacrifices—donned plain white robes and hempen mourning clothes to attend the funeral. The academies suspended classes for three days. Ten thousand scholars lined the streets, and every alley was draped in white banners.

When the coffin was escorted to the Hundred Flower Tomb in the suburbs, the pines and cypresses bowed their branches, and the white funeral flags fluttered like falling snow. The mournful music wailed without cease, and the Imperial Avenue was so densely packed with people kneeling in grief that there was not a single inch of clear ground to walk upon.

On that day, the new Emperor, Chen Gen, personally donned plain robes and walked three *li* to escort the spirit. With a white mourning band around his forehead, his expression was one of profound sorrow.

The officials watched with reverence; the scholars sang his praises. That night, rumours already filled the teahouses: *"The new Emperor honours his teacher and respects the Way. He kept vigil for three days—how can he not be a monarch worthy of our devotion?"* *"They say the elegiac verses were handwritten by the Empress and polished by the Emperor himself. Every stroke, every character, was imbued with the deepest affection..."*

From that moment, the tide of public opinion began to turn. The past anxieties caused by the princes' struggle for the throne faded. Seeing the new Emperor so elegant and refined, so grateful for his teacher's grace, and so loving toward the scholarly class, the people felt the state could truly be entrusted to him. Suddenly, the policy of *"Restraining the Military and Exalting the Civil"* found its most righteous justification.

* * * * *

On the sixth day of mourning at the Shen residence, the weather was damp and grey. The wind lashed the funeral banners until they snapped like whips, yet the interior of the house remained unnervingly quiet.

In the warming pavilion of the rear hall, He Qi slammed a sealed decree onto the table, his face turning ashen with rage. "Who exactly issued this order? 'Vice-Commander of the Western Defense Circuit'?! This is a demotion! It is not a redeployment—it is an exile!"

Lu Xiu leaned lazily against his chair, one hand propping up his forehead. He did not even lift his eyelids, as if the command written on that paper had nothing to do with him.

He Qi paced back and forth, finally lowering his voice: "Master, how long have you even been back in the capital? You haven't even made your move in this battle, and he strikes first to ship you off to the western defensive line. He calls it 'training the troops,' but in truth, he is purging you from the capital. If even the Empress's pleas couldn't secure you a post here, then you and I..."

"Careful. That is a formal decree," Lu Xiu finally spoke, his voice still indifferent. "If someone sees you throwing it about like that, you will have a bitter price to pay." He cast a fleeting glance at the decree on the table, his eyes devoid of any ripple. "Regardless of who drafted the order, the imperial command lies behind it. The military power never belonged to me to begin with. He let me hold it only as a temporary piece in his game; now that he wishes to take it back, it is entirely within reason."

"The Emperor?" He Qi frowned. "If not for your help in toppling the Third Prince back then..."

Lu Xiu struck him on the back of the head with his palm. "Are you tired of living? How dare you say such things out loud?" He Qi rubbed the sore spot. "I'm only saying... it must be because of the Empress. What happened at the courier station... the Emperor must know. This decree doesn't even bother to hide its true motive with a proper excuse."

Lu Xiu heard this and, surprisingly, let out a faint smile. "This is for the best," he said calmly. "He has finally decided to act." He Qi was stunned. "Master, have you gone mad? You can still laugh?"

"Because I said it before—" Lu Xiu leaned forward slightly, reaching out to retrieve the decree. He folded it neatly and tucked it into his sleeve, his tone steady. "If he did *not* move against me, *that* would be the true trouble." With that, he rose, straightened his robes, and threw on his outer cloak. His voice was low and resolute: "Let us go."

He Qi blinked. "Where to?" Lu Xiu looked back, the corner of his mouth curving slightly, though there was no warmth in his eyes. "—To the Palace."

* * * * *

Early summer had arrived in the capital, the wind stirring the first sounds of cicadas.

Within the inner hall of Jinhua Workshop, shadows of needles darted back and forth. On the looms, piles of colored silk and fabric were stacked high, and the air was thick with the scent of mingled threads and ink-drawn patterns.

Xiao Lingyu stood before the design table, her fingertips tracing the flow of each stitch, allowing no room for error. She kept her eyes fixed on the work while listening to the accountant's low-voiced report on the ledgers. "Pause the Suzhou embroidery batch," she instructed swiftly. "Switch back to double-sided embroidery. The Empress Dowager's palace desires 'delicate elegance,' not excessive gaudiness. Remember that clearly."

An embroideress named Qiaoxin hurried in, clutching a reward ledger sent from the palace. "Lady, the inner attendants are pressing us. If we don't send them in now, we will miss the auspicious hour."

Xiao Lingyu rubbed her brow, her voice slightly hoarse. "Give me another half-stick of incense. I must first inspect this batch of gold thread."

Outside the hall, Suyu ran in, drenched in sweat. "The Ministry of Internal Affairs just reported that our thread colors are incorrect!"

Xiao Lingyu paused. After a moment, she said, "Don't panic. I will go there personally. Qiaoxin, bring me the list of embroiderers I arranged last night and transfer Aunt Lan over there."

Qiaoxin was startled. "But Aunt Lan is the primary stitcher for the palace's base patterns—"

"I will fill her place."

Before she could finish, Xiao Lingyu picked up her embroidery basket and strode out of the inner hall.

* * * * *

Her voice had not even faded when the sound of horse hooves echoed outside, and a familiar figure stepped onto the veranda.

It was Lu Chou.

He was dressed in plain attire, his aura cold and crisp. His gaze swept over the chaotic hall and her disheveled appearance—her robes unkempt, her sleeves stained with loose threads—and he asked in a low, vibrating voice: "Did you miss me?"

She paused in her tracks and turned to look back at him, but her tone did not carry a hint of softening: "Stop your smooth talk. Move aside, I am very busy."

He took two steps closer, his eyes darkening slightly. "Can you not wait for a single word from me?"

She arched an eyebrow, her tone laced with a smirk. "Does Master Lu have any instructions?"

Lu Chou's brow furrowed, his voice deep. "It isn't a matter of instructions."

She suddenly pulled him into a side corridor, her voice lowered, yet carrying a rare trace of exhaustion: "...What on earth is it? Nowadays, you act as if you're here to conduct an inspection."

The air momentarily stilled; even the sound of needles and thread in the workshop seemed to cease at that instant.

He finally stopped speaking. After a moment, he said only: "...I missed you."

She froze, speechless. For a long while, she finally let out a soft laugh.

The tension that had gripped her for days seemed to loosen, inch by inch, within those words. She looked down at the fine brocade in her hand, where a gold thread was still wound around her finger, leaving a faint red mark. She blushed and whispered: "...This slave's heart feels the same."

* * * * *

The night was deep, the dew heavy upon the tiles. Inside the Qingfeng Courtyard, shadows from the lamps wavered and flickered against the carved screens.

Lu Xiu pushed the door open, the scent of cold wind and winter steel still clinging to him. By the writing desk, someone was already seated, pouring tea with an unhurried grace—as if he had been expecting this arrival all along, as if this meeting had been predestined long before the door ever creaked open.

"I had thought my elder brother long fallen for the empire," Lu Chou said lightly, swirling the tea in his cup with a lazy precision. "Who would have guessed he would return a war god?"

Lu Xiu's steps paused. He cast a cold, sharp glance toward his brother. "What? Are you disappointed?"

"Indeed," Lu Chou smiled faintly. "For one brief moment, I truly feared you might not return."

The smile had not even faded when his fist struck like thunder.

A dull crack echoed. Lu Xiu staggered back, blood blooming at the corner of his mouth, a bruise already darkening his cheek.

"That is for the blow you gave me years ago," Lu Chou said coolly, flexing his wrist. "I have practiced this punch a thousand times. You should thank me for sparing your face; at least I left you something presentable."

Lu Xiu wiped the blood with the back of his hand and let out a crooked, reckless grin. "Hard enough," he rasped. "But far too late."

He stood up, rolling his jaw with a faint pop. "The second punch can wait. I came tonight to bring you a gift."

"I do not need it." Lu Chou's tone turned to ice as his fist lifted again.

"Look first," Lu Xiu said calmly. "If you do not like the surprise I prepared, hit me afterward. You will not regret it." He turned toward the door and waved a hand. "Bring him in."

* * * * *

Two attendants entered, supporting a man between them—his clothes were in tatters, stained with the dust of a thousand miles, and a strip of black cloth was tied across his eyes.

Lu Chou frowned. "What is the meaning of this?"

"Remove the cloth," Lu Xiu said with a thin, mocking smile, "and you shall see."

Lu Chou hesitated for a heartbeat, then reached forward. The cloth came loose. Under the wavering lamplight, a pair of eyes slowly opened.

In that instant, Lu Chou felt as if struck by lightning.

Those eyes—clear, bright, and flecked with bronze—were unmistakable. They were exactly like Baor's. His heart lurched, and he took an involuntary step back, his voice low and hoarse: "...Who is he?"

"He?" Lu Xiu leaned back, his tone lazy and faintly pleased. "Didn't you always wonder about Baor's lineage? He is none other than Xiao Lingyu's missing brother—Xiao Yu'an."

"Xiao... Yu'an..." Lu Chou murmured the name as if it were a ghost.

Lu Xiu waved his men away. "See that Master Xiao is given proper rest. Do not slight him." As the attendants led the confused man away, Lu Chou remained frozen.

"When he vanished years ago," Lu Xiu continued, his voice regaining its composure, "he was sold to a mining camp in the western territories. I found him by chance. Those eyes... they were far too familiar to ignore."

He met Lu Chou's gaze directly, adding with quiet satisfaction: "So I brought him back. I thought you might find him interesting."

* * * * *

Lu Chou's knuckles went pale as he clenched his hands. His voice was raw. "...You are saying he is truly Xiao Yu'an?"

"Ask him yourself." Lu Xiu's reply was light, his tone rising with faint mockery. "You wanted the truth, didn't you? Now you have it. It's your turn to decide what to do."

Lu Chou's chest tightened. He looked at the doorway where the man had been. Something was wrong. The eyes were clear, but they held no focus—they reflected the lamplight like polished bronze, yet they remained still, without a trace of response.

"His eyes..." Lu Chou began.

"Blind," Lu Xiu said, his smile turning cruel. "The mines are full of ash and stone. A falling rock struck his head. Since then, he sees nothing at all."

His tone stayed careless, yet each word drove like a needle. "This gift is for her—and for you. So? Does this 'reunion' earn me that second punch?"

Silence fell like an ice floe. Lu Chou stood paralyzed, the image of those eyes etched into his mind. Suddenly, the pieces of the puzzle he had obsessed over for years fell into place.

Lu Xiu watched him, then let out a long, weary sigh. "...Idiot," he muttered, the word carrying more pity than mockery. "Baor is your biological daughter."

Lu Chou's head snapped up, shock and a raw, bright joy flashing through his eyes.

"You've wondered about those eyes, haven't you?" Lu Xiu said unhurriedly. "She takes after her uncle. A Xiao family trait—there is no running from it."

Lu Chou turned on his heel so fast his robes snapped, and he shoved the door open as if ready to ride through the night to Jiangnan.

"Hey!" Lu Xiu laughed aloud. "Night has fallen—are you planning to fly there?"

Lu Chou stopped, his brows drawn, looking for once like a man who had lost his bearings. His voice came rough and uncertain: "...Then tell me—what am I supposed to do now?"

Lu Xiu shot him a look of mock disdain. "Where is that clever mind of yours? If you cannot go, make her come."

Silence stretched—then, slowly, Lu Chou turned toward him. The frost in his eyes finally thawed, replaced by a genuine smile. "...I owe you one."

"Heh," Lu Xiu raised a brow. "To hear that from you? Remarkable. I'll think of how to collect it."

The lamplight flickered between them, gentle and golden. On that night, the frozen bond between the two brothers finally began to melt.

Readers can view the full collection of colour illustrations here:
https://www.facebook.com/profile.php?id=61581325000577

Chapter 90: Preparing the Road for the Exiled

When the three bronze drums struck before the Meridian Gate, the court assembled.

Under the shadowed sky, the light was strangely dim. Row upon row of ministers in purple robes and black caps bowed their heads in silence,

until a single cough echoed from the throne above.

The Emperor half reclined upon the dragon seat, the jade memorial untouched in his hand. His gaze, however, drifted toward the ranks of military officials— to that single sharp, unyielding figure standing among them.

Lu Xiu, General of the Northern Command, commander of one hundred thousand frontier troops— his name now resounded through the realm.

That spring, he had pacified the last remnants of the Western rebels; his rewards had yet to be decreed, yet his growing renown had already become the quiet unease of the court.

Lowering his eyes, the Emperor spoke in a voice smooth and measured: "Though the borders are settled for now, the balance of arms must not be forgotten.

It is time to consider dividing command, lest power rest too long in one hand."

A silence fell, heavy and taut.

The Minister of War stepped forth, bowing low.

"Your Majesty's concern is most prudent.

Perhaps the Commander of the Right Vanguard might be stationed in the northern camp,

to assist— and thus temper—the General of the Northern Command."

The Right Vanguard— the Emperor's own guard.

And its commander, a man known to be at odds with Lu Xiu.

There was no mistaking the intent: a check upon his power.

Eyes shifted among the assembled ranks, yet Lu Xiu alone remained unmoved.

He bowed with perfect composure and said evenly, "Your servant serves only to guard the realm's borders. I obey whatever His Majesty commands."

The words were cold as tempered iron—neither submission nor defiance.

The Emperor's gaze narrowed slightly, a faint curve ghosting across his lips— it was unclear whether it was satisfaction, or the hint of mockery.

After a long pause, he murmured,

"You truly know how to hold your composure."

At that moment, a eunuch hurried in, whispering urgently at the steps.

The Emperor's brow furrowed; then, after a brief silence, he spoke:

"The Imperial Preceptor— ill for months—has breathed his last this morning.

Summon the Imperial Physicians to confirm the cause, and command the Ministry of Revenue to prepare the rites."

He rose slightly from his seat.

"Court adjourned."

The chorus of Long live the Emperor thundered through the hall, then ebbed away like the retreating tide.

When the great doors of the audience hall closed, the Emperor remained alone.

He sat motionless for a long while, then said softly, almost to himself: "One Shen Huaizhong is gone. Lu Xiu… how long can you remain so calm?"

He lifted the jade memorial in his hand.

Upon it were the joint petitions of the frontier generals— urging that Lu Xiu be granted the title of Grand Marshal for Distant Pacification, and that a new military council be established under his command to oversee border affairs.

The Emperor's fingers tapped lightly upon the case-table.

A quiet, mirthless laugh escaped his lips. "Grand Marshal… You dare to dream that high."

The light slanted across the dragon dais, deepening the shadows in the corners of the hall, until even the gold upon the throne seemed to darken.

* * * * *

On the third day of the Empress's stay at the Detached Palace, before dawn had broken, ill tidings arrived—

Imperial Preceptor Shen Huaizhong had drawn his last breath in the hour of the Rat (11pm-1am), at the age of fifty-three.

The Imperial Medical Bureau reported formally:

"A long-standing illness; a natural passing in sleep."

That morning, when Shen Zhaoru heard the news, she nearly collapsed before her couch.

The tea in her cup spilled over, soaking her sleeve through.

Her lips trembled as she murmured,

"Father… your daughter has failed you…" The words were faint, yet choked and halting; tears slid down soundlessly.

Before noon, the imperial edict arrived—

By the Emperor's own decree, the Empress was to return to the capital at once for mourning.

A memorial text was drafted by the Hanlin Academy, posthumously conferring upon Shen Huaizhong the title Imperial Preceptor of Rectitude and Learning, to be enshrined in the Temple of Worthies, and his burial rites were to follow those accorded to a prince of the realm.

The news spread swiftly through the capital. The literary world was shaken.

Scholars and officials alike were overcome with grief.

All who had once studied under the Imperial Preceptor— men of the Secretariat, of the Hanlin Academy, the Ministry of Rites, the Court of Ceremonies— donned white robes and hempen bands to attend the funeral.

The academies suspended classes for three days; poets and scholars filled the streets in mourning; white banners draped every eave and alley.

The coffin was borne to Baihua Hill outside the city walls.

Cypress and pine bowed under the wind; the white streamers fluttered like snow.

The sound of mourning filled the air without cease.

Along the imperial road, throngs knelt in unbroken rows; there was scarcely room to stand.

That day, the new Emperor, Chen Gen, dressed in plain mourning garb, walked three li on foot behind the bier, a white cloth bound across his brow, his expression solemn with grief.

The sight drew whispers among the officials; the scholars began to sing his praise.

By nightfall, the teahouses were already alive with talk—

"The new Son of Heaven honours his teacher, holds to the rites of gratitude—

keeping vigil three nights at the bier! Is he not a ruler of virtue?"

"They say the elegy was penned by the Empress herself, each word refined by the Emperor's own hand, his brush steady, yet touched with sorrow..."

Thus public sentiment began to shift.

The memory of the princes' bitter struggle for succession slowly receded, and with it the unease that had shadowed the throne.

Now, the people beheld a sovereign gentle in manner, mindful of his teacher's grace, gracious to his scholars, and compassionate toward his subjects.

Truly, they said, here was one worthy to bear the fate of the realm.

In the wake of that belief, the new Emperor's policy— to exalt the civil, restrain the martial, and draw the reins tighter upon the armies—

found its loftiest justification.

* * * * *

Shen Zhaoru returned to the capital without adornment— only a plain white robe of mourning silk upon her shoulders. She stood to one side of the Shen family's ancestral hall.

When the gathered disciples, old friends, and former pupils of her late father bowed to her in unison, her throat closed with grief, and no words could rise.

That night, after the funeral rites had ended, the rain finally stilled.

Before the spirit tablet, the air hung heavy with the scent of incense and damp earth.

A voice came softly from behind her. "Your Majesty."

It was the eunuch, come to summon her back to the palace. She did not turn. Her voice was calm, but faintly hoarse.

"My father has only just departed. The palace is ill suited for mourning. Tell His Majesty… that Shen Zhaoru wishes to keep vigil for the full ten days. I beg permission."

The eunuch hesitated a moment, then bowed lower.

"His Majesty has already decreed it. The Empress may observe seven days in mourning.

The Emperor says—Imperial Preceptor Shen's virtue was a model for the age. It is only proper that he himself should abide by that virtue."

At this, she finally lifted her head.

Before her stretched rows of black-and-white mourning banners, their silk edges rippling faintly in the wind.

She looked toward them and murmured, half to herself:

"What he seeks is not merely filial virtue. It is a fitting moment—to gather the scholars, to win the hearts of the learned."

A draft passed through the hall; the white candles flickered, their flames trembling.

At that same hour, within the Ministry of Justice, a file was quietly opened— an investigation begun by the Emperor's Right Vanguard Guards. Its cover bore a single line in vermilion ink:

Records from the Command Tent of the Northern Marshal.

The packet was sealed and sent directly to the imperial desk, for the Emperor's eyes alone.

Under the wavering candlelight, he held the dossier in his hand, his gaze resting on the name inscribed within. A faint smile touched his lips.

"If I do not strip you of your command," he murmured, "how else can this throne secure its name?"

* * * * *

The night had long fallen, yet the candles in the imperial study still burned with steady light.

Scrolls lay open upon the desk, their edges faintly warped with damp, as though once touched by rain.

Chen Gen sat reclined behind the jade-inlaid table, expression composed, his fingers idly tracing one sealed dispatch after another.

The confidential report from the Ministry of Justice had arrived that morning; only now, at this late hour, did he choose to unseal it.

Records of the Northern Marshal's Command Tent.

Line after line attested that no irregularities had been found within Lu Xiu's army—

each entry meticulously dated and numbered, each allocation of pay and movement of troops accounted for, the handwriting precise, the official seals intact, the wax unbroken.

It was, in every respect, impeccable.

Reading to the third page, the Emperor's lips curved faintly, neither smile nor sneer.

"...Indeed," he murmured, "a troublesome man to tame."

Too clean. Too careful. An inconvenience of virtue.

Then his hand stilled.

At the edge of the desk lay another sheet—creased, unsigned, without envelope.

Only its first few words were enough to quicken the pulse.

"Her Majesty the Empress, delayed by rain, took lodging at a roadside post-station.

The Northern Marshal, likewise hindered by the storm, entered by the side gate.

The lights in the inner chamber burned until dawn.

The attendants were dismissed. No one else was permitted to approach."

He lowered his gaze, staring at the letter for a long time. At last, he folded it once, neatly, and laid it atop the immaculate military dossier—not destroyed, merely waiting.

The candlelight flickered, deepening the hollows of his eyes. His fingertips brushed the edges of the sealed scrolls; the knuckles whitened, then curled slightly.

His voice, when it came, was soft but cold enough to still the air: "...So. He could not resist, after all."

Upon the desk, a jade imperial seal had shifted slightly askew.

He reached out, set it square, and rose.

Drawing a plain cloak about his shoulders, he crossed to the window.

The rain had ceased.

Through the translucent paper, the moonlight shone pale and remote; far off, the funeral banners of the Shen household fluttered like ghosts beyond the city walls.

He stood there for a long while.

When he finally spoke, it was almost to himself:

"Seven days of mourning—enough."

Turning back to the desk, he placed both the Command Records and the anonymous memorandum into a black sandalwood coffer, sealing them together.

With a steady hand, he took up his brush and wrote a brief imperial decree.

The words were few. Their weight, immense.

"The Northern Marshal Lu Xiu is hereby reassigned from the capital command.

Appointed Vice Military Commissioner of the Western Garrison Route.

To depart within ten days."

The vermilion seal pressed so deep it nearly bled through the paper.

Replacing the jade seal, he allowed himself the faintest trace of a smile.

"It is time," he said softly. "For him to go."

* * * * *

The sixth day of mourning dawned under a damp, leaden sky.

Wind howled through the courtyard, whipping the white funeral banners until they cracked like whips, yet within the Shen residence all was deathly still.

In the rear hall's warm chamber, He Qi slammed a sealed dispatch onto the table, the paper rattling like a blow.

His face was ashen with fury.

"Who in heaven's name issued this decree?

Vice Military Commissioner of the Western Garrison Route?!

This isn't a reassignment—it's a dismissal! They're sending you away!"

Lu Xiu lounged in his chair, one hand propping his temple, lids half-lowered.

He did not so much as glance at the document, as though the order had nothing at all to do with him.

He Qi paced twice across the floor, then lowered his voice, strained and urgent.

"My lord, you've barely returned to the capital! The game has hardly begun, and he's already shipping your west. They call it military rotation, but it's exile in all but name.

If even Her Majesty's intercession can't keep you here, then we—"

"Careful," Lu Xiu interrupted, his tone mild. "That's an imperial order you just threw. If someone sees, you'll earn yourself a fine flogging."

Only then did he raise his eyes, letting them rest briefly on the decree. There was no ripple of emotion.

"No matter whose hand penned it, the will behind it is the Emperor's. The command of troops was never truly mine. He let me hold it for a while, to test the board. Now he wishes to take it back. Fair enough."

"The Emperor?" He Qi scowled. "If it weren't for you, His Majesty would never have—"

A sharp crack: Lu Xiu's palm struck the back of his head. "Do you have a death wish? Some words are better swallowed."

He Qi rubbed the sore spot, muttering. "Then it's because of the Empress. The post-station that night—His Majesty must have found out.

This decree doesn't even bother with pretence."

Silence.

Lu Xiu's mouth curved, almost into a smile—though there was no warmth in it.

"At least he's finally made his move," he said softly.

He Qi stared. "You've gone mad, haven't you? How can you smile?"

"Because I've said it before—" His voice was calm as still water. He leaned forward, took up the imperial writ, folded it carefully, and slid it into his sleeve.

"If he never moved against me, that would be the real problem."

He rose, smoothed his robes, and reached for his cloak. His tone deepened, steady and clear.

"Come."

He Qi blinked. "Where to?"

Lu Xiu looked back at him, the faintest edge of a smile on his lips, but his eyes were cold as steel.

"—To the palace."

* * * * *

The first breath of summer stirred the capital's air, cicadas humming in the trees.

Within the inner hall of Jin Hua Hall, silver needles flashed between slender fingers; skeins of coloured thread and silk bolts lay piled upon the brocade tables, the air faintly scented with ink and dye.

Xiao Lingyu stood before the pattern desk, her fingertip tracing each line of a stitch-path, every curve precise, leaving no margin for error.

Her gaze did not waver. As the accountant murmured through the ledgers beside her, she spoke swiftly, her tone even but decisive:

"Pause the Su embroidery order. Revert to double-sided stitching. The Empress Dowager's palace requires refinement, not opulence. Remember that."

A young embroideress, Qiao xin, entered in haste, clutching the imperial reward ledger.

"Madam," she whispered, "the palace messenger is pressing again—if we don't deliver this hour, it'll miss the auspicious time."

Xiao Lingyu rubbed the bridge of her brow; her voice was soft, slightly hoarse.

"Give me half a stick of incense more. I'll finish checking this gold thread first."

From outside came hurried steps—Suyue burst in, sweat beading her forehead.

"Madam! The Household Bureau just sent word—the colour of our silk threads is wrong!"

Xiao Lingyu froze for half a breath, then said quietly, "Don't panic. I'll go myself.

Qiao Xin—bring me last night's roster. Move Lan-gu to that section."

Qiao Xin blinked. "But Lan-gu's the chief needle for the palace base sample—"

"I'll take her place."

Before the protest was finished, Xiao Lingyu had already taken up her embroidery basket and strode out of the hall.

Her voice had scarcely faded when the sound of hooves broke through the drizzle of thread and murmurs—

A familiar figure stepped into the corridor.

It was Lu Chou.

Dressed in plain attire, a chill of travel still clinging to him, his gaze swept over the flurry of workshop motion—and came to rest on her: sleeves marked with dye, threads looped round her wrists, hair slightly undone.

His voice was low, carrying a trace of teasing warmth:

"Missed me yet?"

Her step faltered. She turned her head slightly, her reply crisp, unsparing:

"Stop that nonsense. Move aside—I've no time for games."

He came closer, the look in his eyes darkening. "Couldn't you at least wait for me to speak?"

She arched a brow, the corner of her lips lifting. "Then speak, my lord—what counsel have you to offer?"

Lu Chou frowned; his tone deepened. "This isn't about counsel."

She caught him lightly by the sleeve, drawing him toward the side corridor. Her voice dropped—low, edged with weariness rare for her: "What is it then? You sound like a man sent to inspect his own household."

The air between them stilled. Even the faint rhythm of needles in the hall seemed to pause.

For a long moment, he said nothing. Then, in a voice scarcely above a whisper:

"...I missed you."

She stared at him, momentarily unguarded. No words rose; instead, a small, helpless laugh escaped her lips.

The tension she'd carried these past days—tight as gold wire— unspooled with that single confession.

Lowering her gaze, she looked at the narrow ribbon of brocade in her hand.

The gold thread still coiled round her fingers, leaving faint red marks against her skin.

Her cheeks warmed; she bowed her head slightly, voice barely audible—

"...So did I."

Chapter 91: Claiming His Birthright

The early summer brought a slight warmth, the sky was blue with white clouds, and the air was clear, crisp, and refreshing.

The main hall of the Lu Residence was adorned with lanterns and coloured silks, yet there was no festive occasion. It was merely because the Old Grand Madam's persistent cough had recently improved, and she had uncharacteristically agreed to meet outsiders; thus, the household had prepared some refreshments for a small gathering.

The butler was already waiting before the gate. Upon seeing the figures arrive, he quickly stepped forward to salute: "Second Master, the Old Grand Madam is already waiting in the hall."

Lu Chou nodded, then lowered his head to take the hand of the young girl beside him, whose childlike innocence had not yet faded.

"Little Bao, do you still remember what I told you?"

Little Bao looked up, her pair of bronze-colored eyes clear and bright, and she recited in a childish voice: "Entering the door requires a salute, do not run around, do not speak carelessly, speaking requires the nasal sound 'En,' and one must say 'Grand Madam is well.'"

Lu Chou could not help but laugh, rubbing the top of her head: "It is 'En,' not 'Wu.' Practice a bit more."

She puffed out her little cheeks and solemnly mimicked the gesture of an adult by cupping her hands and giving a salute: "Little Bao greets the Grand Madam... En."

He nodded: "Very good. Let us go."

Inside the hall, the incense burner was lit, silver threads of smoke curling languidly. An elderly person, dressed in simple elegance, sat upon the main seat, her expression serene and composed. There were no others present, save for an old wet nurse standing at her side.

When the Old Grand Madam saw Chou enter leading a small girl, her eyebrows lifted slightly. She first smiled and said: "Whose little girl is this? She is grown so handsome?"

Lu Chou bowed his head, his tone steady: "She is called Little Bao."

Little Bao stepped forward as instructed, calling out in her tender, young voice: "Little Bao greets the Grand Madam."

The Old Grand Madam's gaze fell upon that pair of bronze-colored eyes, and she paused slightly: "This child... her eyes are quite unique."

Lu Chou remained silent for a moment before saying: "Her mother found it inconvenient to attend, so I brought Little Bao to pay respects first."

The Old Grand Madam scrutinized her for a few moments, then suddenly smiled: "This child's eyes are truly bright... her hands are fair and her bones are fine, her vitality is not weak; she is a child blessed with good fortune."

Little Bao nodded, saying in a sweet, childish voice: "My mother also says I am a lucky star. I eat a lot, and I sleep early."

Upon hearing this, the elderly woman actually burst into laughter, nodding her head: "Interesting, interesting."

She waved a hand: "Someone, go and fetch that pair of gold-threaded rabbit-patterned boots—the ones Chou kept from when he was small. They will fit her feet perfectly now."

The wet nurse quickly hurried to retrieve them. Lu Chou cupped his hands in a respectful salute: "Thank you, Grandmother."

The Old Grand Madam pulled Little Bao to her side, looking her over from left to right, growing more delighted the more she looked.

"You still haven't said, whose child is this? To grow up so beautiful?"

Chou's voice was low, yet without the slightest hesitation: "She is of our house."

"What?" The Old Grand Madam failed to react for a moment and nearly rose from her chair.

"This old woman must be hard of hearing; whose house did you just say?"

Even the wet nurse beside her was greatly astonished: "Second Master, are you saying... this child is of our house?"

Lu Chou immediately knelt down, taking Little Bao with him, his expression respectful and resolute.

"Yes. This little girl is indeed your grandson's own flesh and blood."

Having spoken, he recounted the old events from beginning to end, telling the story concisely.

The Old Grand Madam's eyes grew red as she listened, her fingers trembling slightly. After a long moment, she suddenly pulled Little Bao into her embrace, old tears streaming down her face:

"I never thought... this old woman would actually have a great-granddaughter... I originally believed that in this lifetime, I would never live to see this day..."

The wet nurse beside her also had reddened eyes: "Old Madam, this is a tremendous joyous occasion. You must not cry and damage your health."

"Yes, yes, it is a joyous occasion, a blessing..." The Old Grand Madam wiped away her tears while smiling, the wrinkles on her face smoothing out like a spring breeze.

Little Bao looked on, bewildered, not understanding why everyone was crying, and said softly: "Grand Madam, do not cry..."

The Old Grand Madam hugged her tightly and planted a kiss on her cheek: "Our Little Bao must change her address. It should be 'Great-Grandmother.'"

"Oh... Great-Grandmother." She obediently complied, her voice soft and sweet like a spoonful of honey.

"Aiya, my darling heart." Having said this, she slipped off a gold chain from her neck, upon which hung a small key. She immediately placed it around Little Bao's neck.

"Aiya, Old Madam, but this is your little private vault!"

"That is right, it is perfectly suited for our Little Bao."

Lu Chou prompted Baor to express her thanks. "Wow, so pretty, thank you, Great-Grandmother."

The Old Grand Madam looked at Chou, her tone low and allowing no dispute: "This is your providence, and also a blessing for our house. This child, and her mother, must both be properly brought home. Do not wait until the day I close my eyes to speak of it."

His expression solidified, and he replied with solemn earnestness: "I shall marry her, so long as she is willing to wed."

The Old Grand Madam was silent for a moment, then looked down at Little Bao, who was nibbling small bites of a refreshment, and suddenly asked: "Does she know who you are?"

Lu Chou paused slightly, then replied gently: "She calls me... 'Lord Papa.'"

The Old Grand Madam was startled upon hearing this, then let out a laugh, seeming to contain both mockery and joy: "A fine 'Lord Papa.'"

"Then let her take her time. Do not frighten the child," she said, gazing at the grandfather and great-granddaughter, her eyes gentle and profound.

"If you have the ability, then ensure that for her entire life, she need only be happy."

Lu Chou lowered his head and bowed deeply.

"Yes."

* * * * *

Inside the deliberation hall of the Lu Residence, a lamp shone dimly.

Minister Lu Wenqian had just returned from the Outer Court and, before even changing his attire, was summoned before the Old Grand Madam. Only a half-censer of tea incense burned in the hall, yet it could not mask the oppressive tension in the air.

"Mother, you mean..." Lu Wenqian stood in the center of the hall, his voice pressed extremely low, yet every word was almost bitten off like shards of ice: "That impudent boy has actually fathered a five-year-old daughter out there?"

"Are you only just realizing it now?" The Old Grand Madam sat at the head of the table, sipping her tea expressionlessly: "I only held her for the first time today."

Minister Lu's face was livid, and he almost ground his teeth: "Without a matchmaker, without betrothal gifts, without any formal arrangement, the child is already five years old! If this were to spread, what would it be counted as? The child would be nothing more than a—"

"If you were about to utter the words 'illegitimate daughter,' then hold your tongue!" The Old Grand Madam struck the armrest heavily, her voice sharp and clear, interrupting him instantly.

Minister Lu's breath hitched.

The Old Grand Madam set down her teacup and spoke coolly: "That son of yours acted improperly; this much I know. But you, as the head of the household, truly believe that everything must be judged solely by family status? Do you know that the child calls me 'Great-Grandmother' with every breath, melting my very heart?"

Minister Lu's face remained grim: "Mother, your affection for her is her good fortune, but this matter is not so simple—what kind of person is her mother? She comes from a brocade workshop. Though she is an Imperial Merchant, she is ultimately no match for our Lu family in social standing."

The Old Grand Madam sneered, a hint of coldness rising in the corner of her eye.

"Family status? You speak of family status? Your son hid his daughter for so many years outside. Is this the style of a noble gentry family? If it were not for the fact that I perceive her mother to be polite and aware of her boundaries, anyone else would have long ago raised a commotion that reached the Court of the Imperial Clan. Could you still stand here speaking so boldly?"

"She is an Imperial Merchant, the head of a brocade workshop currently in the ascendant. The Empress Dowager specifically designated her designs for the birthday banquet, and several consorts in the inner palace utilize her family's scented powders. You despise her status for being low? I think it is your heart that is narrow."

Minister Lu was momentarily speechless, his face alternating between blue and white.

The Old Grand Madam narrowed her eyes at him, her tone turning grave: "I shall not argue this matter further with you. Starting tomorrow, select an auspicious date, and have Chou proceed with the betrothal gifts to the woman's family. The betrothal certificates and the list of rites must not lack a single item. Before this month is out, I want to see them wed, the child entered into the clan genealogy, and her name properly recognized."

"How can it be done so quickly?"

The Old Grand Madam paused, then let out a cold snort: "Then I shall personally send people to carry Little Bao into the ancestral shrine. If you refuse to acknowledge her, I will acknowledge her!"

She rose, flicking her sleeve, her voice low yet decisive and absolute: "This child is my Lu family's great-granddaughter, the bloodline I personally welcomed through the door. Should anyone dare to harm a single hair on her head, this old woman will not spare him!"

Minister Lu was filled with suppressed anger, yet he spoke no further words. After a moment, he said in a low voice: "Your son... obeys."

The Old Grand Madam's expression softened slightly, and she waved her hand.

"Why are you still standing there? Go attend to the matter. The betrothal gifts must adhere to the formal Lu family regulations. I have not met the young woman, but your mother will tell you the truth—"

She paused, and said slowly: "This time, your son has stumbled upon a treasure."

Chapter 92: The Imperial Physician Confirms the Pregnancy

Early summer light had barely ripened; dawn hung pale and tremulous over the vermilion eaves of the Ning Shou Palace.

Through the latticed windows, the gauze curtains stirred with a faint whisper of wind. A cup of tea sat cooling on the table, untouched.

From the incense burner on the low stand, a thin column of calming fragrance curled upward, silver as breath, dispersing into the still air.

Beneath that mist of smoke stood the new Empress Shen Zhaoru, motionless by the window, a memorial scroll cradled in her hands.

Her expression was composed, almost tranquil, yet the faint press of her lips betrayed the effort it cost her.

Her complexion, usually luminous, was bloodless today — pale as frost on porcelain.

The tea on the desk had long gone cold. In the quiet, she felt again the dull sweetness of iron rising at the back of her throat.

She lowered the scroll carefully and turned her back to the room, bracing a hand on the wooden lattice of the window.

Her fingers clenched until the knuckles whitened. Beyond the glass, a ginkgo tree gleamed in the morning light, its new leaves trembling in the wind like tiny coins of gold.

For a long while she simply stared at it and said nothing.

At last, she spoke, her voice low, even, deliberate.

"Bring me some plum-sour soup," she said. "Make sure it is very sour."

The maid who waited on her, a woman brought from the Shen household in her girlhood , paused, hearing something unspoken beneath the calm command.

"Your Grace," she ventured softly, "are you… unwell again?"

Zhaoru shook her head. "It is nothing. I have merely felt tired these few days."

Her tone was tranquil, but her eyes, half-lowered, betrayed vigilance. She would not allow the smallest crack to appear in her mask.

Her father's passing was still within the mourning period; she was, in name, the daughter of a house in filial restraint, and her marriage to the

Crown Prince Chen Gen had been brief. By custom, they had not yet shared the marriage bed.

If the court were to learn that she carried a child now before the mourning term had ended, before the imperial rites had joined them as husband and wife, the scandal would be enough to shred her life apart.

Ritual, rumour, and politics would converge like blades, slicing through her and the innocent being she carried.

This child was the last thread between her and Lu Xiu.

She had planned everything with the precision of desperation.

If she could claim a retreat to quiet contemplation — a season of fasting, prayer, and seclusion — she might obtain leave to reside for a year or so at the South Mountain Convent, where widows and noble ladies sometimes went to "cultivate the spirit."

There, under the pretext of praying for the Empire's peace and her late father's soul, she might bring the child to term in secret.

Afterward, she could find some hidden path — a nursemaid loyal to her, a distant villa, a way for the child to live beyond the reach of court.

Even if she were fated never to meet Xiu again, she could at least protect what little remained of their love.

Her resolve had been quiet but absolute.

The memorial requesting leave was already written; she had planned to send it through the Ceremonial Directorate at the end of the month.

But that day never came.

Before she could set her plan in motion, a summons arrived from the Hall of Heavenly Principle.

Her heart had given a single violent tremor when she heard the eunuch pronounce the words.

Now, as she was led across the marble courtyards toward the vast central hall, she felt the blood draining from her lips.

The sky above the inner court was piercingly clear.

On either side of the imperial steps, peonies were in full blaze, scarlet and carmine, their fragrance thick enough to suffocate.

Each breath she drew tasted of fear.

She walked forward, each step heavy, precise, echoing against the flagstones like a count of fate.

She knew — once she crossed the threshold of that hall, there would be no return.

The new Emperor Chen Gen sat upon the dais, calm as an unmoved mountain.

The folds of his dragon-embroidered robe were arranged with the same careful symmetry as his words. His face held that unyielding gentleness which was, in truth, the most terrible of weapons.

"I hear," he said with mild curiosity, "that the Empress has been unwell of late. I have summoned the imperial physician to take your pulse."

The words struck her like a bell.

Her heart stopped, then lurched painfully.

"Your Majesty," she began, forcing a smile that faltered at once, "this concubine has merely been fatigued a trifling malaise. There is no need to trouble the physician."

The Emperor, Chen Gen's eyes rested on her — unblinking, measuring.

His smile deepened a fraction, neither kind nor cruel.

"Whether the Empress is well," he said, "is for me to decide."

"Your Majesty, I have been occupied with palace duties and have neglected rest. It is nothing serious. Truly, the Royal Physician need not—"

"I said," he interrupted softly, "that your pulse shall be taken."

The words were not loud, yet they fell with the weight of command, ringing through her bones.

Her breath caught. She pressed her fingers against her sleeve, the colour draining from her face.

"Your Majesty… I have taken medicine recently; my pulse may be disordered. If he reads it now, it may mislead his judgment."

Chen Gen's tone remained composed, almost pleasant. "The Royal Physician's skill is beyond question. I trust him."

Even as he spoke, royal physician Wu advanced, bowing low. His hands trembled slightly as he unfolded the silk pulse cushion.

Zhaoru stepped back, her whole body rigid. Her voice wavered.

"Your Majesty, I… my monthly cycle is irregular, sometimes delayed
— it is not unusual. I beg pardon; allow me to return to my palace to
rest."

The panic that flickered in her eyes was naked, though she tried to hide
it behind courtly grace.

She already knew the truth of this encounter: it was no inquiry but an
unveiling.

He knows.

Every breath told her she was walking into a net already drawn tight.

"Your Majesty, the wind is sharp this morning," she said, clutching at a
last, fragile excuse. "If the chill enters, it might disturb the pulse.
Perhaps another day—"

"Stand aside," Chen Gen said without raising his voice.

His mildness cut deeper than anger.

"The Empress's health is paramount. There is no need for further
speech."

At that, the physician approached.

Zhaoru's steps felt weighted with iron.

When she finally sank onto the stool, her hands were like frost.

"Forgive me, Your Grace," murmured Royal Physician Wu. He bowed
again and set his fingertips gently upon her wrist.

The touch was light — a feather, a verdict.

In that instant her body turned to stone.

Her breath was trapped somewhere between throat and heart; her vision
dimmed.

She wanted to pull her arm back, to flee — but her limbs would not
obey.

The world seemed to narrow to that single, terrible silence between the
physician's fingers and her pulse.

Barely a few seconds passed before the man's brows moved.

He withdrew his hand, bowed low once more, and spoke in a voice
pitched precisely to carry.

"Your Majesty, the Empress is with child. The pulse is steady, the foetus well-rooted — approximately one month along."

For a heartbeat, the universe ceased to breathe.

The great hall was so still that she could hear the blood thundering in her ears.

Her pupils contracted; her lips parted in disbelief.

She wanted to speak — to say no, to deny — but no sound came.

Chen Gen's voice broke the stillness like a blade sliding from its sheath.

"The Empress is with child," he said calmly, "and Heaven favours the realm. It is a blessing for the Empire."

The courtiers standing at the edges of the hall bowed in unison. The rustle of their robes was like the signing of a tide.

Zhaoru's heartbeat so violently she could scarcely breathe.

Her knees felt hollow. The words scraped her throat: "This… this child… it cannot—"

Chen Gen's eyes held hers, still smiling faintly, the kind of smile that permitted nothing.

"Cannot?" he echoed, softly amused. "You are Madam of the six palaces. To be with child is a joy ordained by Heaven. Why speak as though it were misfortune?"

Her lips trembled. "This concubine… has been unwell with grief. My courses were delayed; I did not perceive—"

He laughed then, quietly, the sound as smooth as flowing silk.

"The Empress's pregnancy is the Empire's good fortune. Since the child is Heaven-sent, it shall be announced at once, to invite auspicious omens."

Panic surged through her. She stepped forward, falling to her knees in full court bow, the hem of her gown spreading like a white wave across the jade floor.

"Your Majesty, this concubine is still within the mourning period. If word of a pregnancy spreads, tongues will wag; malicious talk will stain the throne's dignity. I beg Your Majesty to reconsider — to delay the proclamation—"

Chen Gen regarded her in silence, and when he spoke, his voice was soft as drifting ash.

"What does the Empress fear? I fear no gossip. Let us see who dares to speak."

His eyes flicked to the chamberlain. "Have it proclaimed. Inform the ancestral temple; select an auspicious day. Let the world know the Empress is with child."

Her breath left her in a rush. She knelt frozen, staring up at him as though the air itself had turned to glass.

In that moment she understood.

The Emperor had always known.

This entire scene — the concern, the physician, the pulse — had been theatre, perfectly staged.

He was not discovering her secret; he was claiming it.

The child, her secret, her guilt — all were now his instruments.

By naming the unborn as imperial blood, he erased its origin and bound her to his design.

The Emperor gained a son; the Empire gained stability; and Lu Xiu lost the last fragment of her that was his.

Her heart broke so quietly that even she could scarcely hear it.

She bowed her head until her forehead touched the floor. "This concubine… obeys the decree."

When she raised her head again, her vision blurred. The scent of peonies seemed to twist around her like smoke.

The Emperor watched her, his face serene, his tone almost kind.

"Let the rites be prepared. The Empress shall rest and nourish the child. As for the mourning—"

He paused, the faintest smile touching his lips.

"You are now the mother of an imperial heir. Life and death, ritual and rule — all bend before the will of Heaven. The rights will be… adjusted."

His words fell like petals from a poisoned flower — delicate, final, inescapable.

Zhaoru bowed once more, her voice barely a whisper. "As Your Majesty commands."

When she left the hall, the peonies outside were still burning red in the sunlight.

Their fragrance followed her down the steps — heavy, suffocating, sweet as sorrow.

And the child within her stirred, small as a secret, silent as fate.

Chapter 93: All is a Game of Chess

The imperial road stretched long and wide beneath the heat of midsummer.

The air was heavy, motionless — a slow suffocation beneath the white glare of noon.

A line of guards stood in formation, their armour dull with dust; cicadas shrilled from the cypress trees, each cry like a thin piece of ice scraping the silence.

Lu Xiu rode alone.

He wore black from collar to hem, the austere hue absorbing the light until he seemed part of the road itself. His boots struck the stone with soundless precision; not a speck of dust clung to his stirrups. His eyes, as always, were calm — cold even.

Today, he was riding toward the palace gates.

He had already decided what must be done.

He would enter, kneel, and offer his life to the Emperor — an open plea of guilt, a surrender meant to buy another's freedom.

He had calculated every path, every possible outcome. Now that his rank had been relinquished, his command stripped away, he no longer feared the empire's will or the Emperor's wrath.

If one broken body could unchain her, then let it be his. If one fall from grace could spare her ruin, then he would fall without hesitation.

That was the thought that steadied him until a voice, low and indistinct, drifted from a cluster of eunuchs ahead.

"Have you heard? Her Majesty is with child, it's been a full month already."

"Indeed. The imperial physicians say her colour is radiant. His Majesty is overjoyed — the edict to announce it to the realm was sent this morning."

The words struck like an arrow.

Xiu's hands tightened on the reins; the horse reared, letting out a shrill, startled cry. Dust rose in a violent burst, blurring the sunlight.

He sat frozen, chest heaving once, then again as though the air itself had turned to ice.

A child.

For a moment, the world receded to a dull, pulsing void.

He heard nothing but the ringing in his ears — like iron clashing under water.

She has a child?

The thought hollowed him out. His mind flooded with images he had fought for months to bury:

Her face, pale beneath the lamplight.

Her silence that night, a silence sharper than any refusal.

Her absence when he left the capital, the absence that had followed him through every mile of exile.

Was it… his? Or—

He could not finish the question. Even his thoughts flinched away from it.

He had ridden here prepared to beg forgiveness, to lay down every ounce of pride and blood in exchange for a single chance to stand beside her — no title, no future, only her.

He had been willing to cast away his sword, to bear the scorn of ten thousand tongues, to die a traitor if it meant she could live as a woman unburdened.

But now—

If the child she carried belonged to the Emperor, then his very presence would be a desecration.

To go before the throne now was not atonement — it was suicide.

And worse than his own death, it would drag her down into ruin, her name forever smeared in the ink of scandal.

His fingers clenched around the whip until the leather creaked, the veins along his wrist standing like cords of steel.

He could feel the pulse in his throat — harsh, uneven, almost painful.

Slowly, he lifted his gaze.

Beyond the haze of heat, the vermilion walls of the palace rose — high, endless, and terrible in their grandeur. The tiled roofs shimmered like molten gold; banners hung motionless in the still air. Behind that wall was the world she now belonged to — the world that would never again be his.

The faint wind carried the scent of incense from within the gates — faint, almost sweet, yet suffocating.

Xiu's lips pressed into a hard, bloodless line.

That world was hers now.

And for him, it would remain — forever — a prison of red walls and shadowed silence.

Her sanctuary.

His hell.

He shut his eyes for a long moment.

The world within him seemed to splinter — a thousand knives drawn through the heart, each one slow, deliberate, merciless.

Yet when he finally opened them, there was no sound, no cry, no word of protest.

The reins turned in his grasp.

The black stallion wheeled around with a sharp breath, hooves striking sparks from the stone.

* * * * *

The sky had gone the colour of old bronze; light in the windows fell in mottled bars from the branches outside, but within the halls of Zhaoning Palace the air felt as if it had been frozen into breath—hard, thin, unbearable.

Shen Zhaoru stood in a plain mourning robe, the linen sober and clean, her face chalk-pale. Underneath that composed surface her brows carried a tremor—an animal quickness of fear braided with a restraint that had the shape of anger.

She had just been told by an inner eunuch what had already been arranged in the palace: from this day forth Zhaoning Palace was to be sealed.

The imperial physicians and the palace maids who tended her would be dispatched by the inner court; no one might come and go at will. She had been—softly, officially—put under house arrest.

She brushed aside the hands of her attendants and cut straight across the court toward the Hall of Heavenly Principle.

An attendant at the gate opened his mouth as if to stop her, then shrank back and said nothing. The steps into the great hall were gilded by slanting sunset; every beam and cornice blazed with gold, opulent—yet the light tasted of ice.

On the imperial dais Chen Gen sat propped against his cushions, idly toying with a jade disc between his fingers.

At the sound of her approach, he lifted his chin and smiled; it was a smile without ripple, placid as a still pool. "Empress, what brings you here? You are with child—shouldn't you rest more? Such movements are not suitable."

Shen Zhaoru stood at the foot of the dais, fingers clenched until the knuckles paled. Her voice trembled as she forced the words out: "Your Majesty—why have you sealed Zhaoning Palace? My child within me…why would you do this?"

Chen Gen glanced at her; his tone slid into something almost solicitous. "What nonsense are you speaking? This is my son in your womb. I must be cautious; I must shield him diligently."

"You know—" she began, the accusation already edged in her throat—

"Empress! Mind your words!" The emperor's voice snapped like a whip. The softness vanished; for a heartbeat his manner tightened into command.

Her restraint ripped. She could not hold herself steady any longer and her words came in a raw, quivering rush. "Your Majesty…you—surely in your heart you know—why then—"

Her steps faltered; the surge of feeling caught her balance and she involuntarily took two quick steps backward, one small hand flying to the soft swell at her belly as if to shield it. For an instant she was a doe driven to the cliff's edge, alert, every muscle taut.

Chen Gen watched that motion and something like a quiet amusement passed across his face—so slight that it seemed almost courteous, but the calmness of it cut to the bone.

He set the jade disc down with the languid gesture of a man folding a letter. "Ah, the affairs of the heart," he murmured, the words half-playful, half-accusatory. "Love—how ruinous it can be."

He rose and descended the dais step by step, approaching her with measured steps.

"Are you afraid of me?" he bent his head as if to examine her, his look unnervingly gentle. "Are you afraid I will harm your child? Or are you afraid I will harm his?"

Shen Zhaoru bit her lip and could not answer. Her eyes were full of dread and helplessness.

"Shen Zhaoru," he said softly—his voice a velvet knife—"I never forbade you your loves. Nor did I ever coerce another. All of this was your own choosing, was it not?"

The insinuation hung there like smoke. Then, softer still, almost confidential: "Whether in this game one wins or loses—who can say yet?"

She pressed both hands to her belly, voice raw: "Your Majesty…what are you going to do?"

He smiled, the kind of smile that polished and chilled at once. "What, indeed?" he said, as if answering a child. "I shall protect you. I shall protect your child. I shall protect the hearts of the people. I shall protect this drama—so that it unfolds without a seam."

"And if he—" she faltered, the word jagged—"if he finds out, what then?"

The emperor's eyes darkened; the smile deepened into an expression that was almost indulgent. "If he is clever, he will not come to disturb you. If he is not clever…" his voice dropped and there was no softness left in it, "then I will teach him. There are some things in this world one simply cannot take."

He turned away; the dismissal was final. "Rest properly. Tend the child. I will make proclamation to the realm on your behalf."

The great doors closed behind him. Shen Zhaoru swayed on her feet as if the floor itself had been stripped from under her; for a long moment she felt as though she had been dropped into an ice cave, the cold pressing inward from every side.

* * * *

The lattice window of the embroidery room stood half-open, the slanting light of dusk pouring through it, golden warmth spreading across the table like a quiet tide.

Xiao Lingyu had only just lifted her head from the account scrolls when Suxin hurried in. For once the maid's composure was broken by excitement; her voice trembled with delight.

"Madam—news has come! Baor has been taken to the Lu residence. Lord Lu himself brought her, and she's met the Grand Madam!"

The brush in Xiao Lingyu's hand stopped mid-stroke. A pulse of alarm struck her chest.

"What did you say?"

She rose swiftly; the hem of her pale robe swayed. Her eyes darkened in disbelief.

"How could you—how could he—take her there without a word to me?"

Before the protest could finish, the faint sound of footsteps crossed the threshold.

A light wind brushed the curtain. The doorway stirred and there he was.

Lu Chou stepped in, still in indigo court robes, the dust of the road not yet shaken from his sleeves. The moment his gaze met hers, her breath caught fear, confusion, and the ghosts of too many sleepless nights flashing through her eyes.

"How could you decide on your own?" Her voice quivered, each word clipped and trembling. She's just a child. The Lu estate is full of eyes and tongues—what if someone—why didn't you ask me first?"

He said nothing. Only closed the distance between them and took her hand in his.

His palm was warm, his grip firm and steady. The simple gesture seemed to draw her back from the edge of all her panic and hesitation.

"The Grand Madam's health has improved," he said at last, his tone gentle but resolute. "For the great-granddaughter to greet her is right and proper. I want Baor's place acknowledged—and I want you to stand upright beside her."

Her head lowered. Her voice, soft as breath upon silk:

"But… they'll talk. They always talk. She's still so small…"

His fingers tightened around hers. His reply came low, steady as an oath:

"Xiao Lingyu—while I live, no one will harm you, and no one will touch her. You and Baor are my life's roots."

He lifted a hand, brushing a stray lock from her brow. The motion was so tender, so deliberate, that for a heartbeat it seemed almost unfamiliar.

"But the Minister—your father—he'll never allow—"

"Don't fear him." His tone remained calm, weighted with quiet certainty. "So long as Grand Madam stands, I stand with her. It will be fine."

Then, in a motion both protective and unhurried, he drew her into his arm and gave her shoulder a light, reassuring pat.

"From this day, you will no longer bear anything alone. No guessing, no fearing. I will guard you, lend you my strength, whatever you choose to do."

She looked up at him, dazed; her eyes glistened though no tear fell. Slowly, she nodded, resting her forehead lightly against his shoulder.

"Don't… don't be this kind," she whispered, her throat tightening. "When you are too good, I fear you'll vanish."

He gave a faint laugh, roughened by emotion yet anchored by certainty.

"I won't. In this life, only death itself could part us."

At that moment, the last of the sun unfurled across the wall, casting their joined shadows long and gold—two figures bound within the quiet warmth of evening, like a painting whose colours would never fade.

Soon after, the nurse arrived, guiding Baor in by the hand.

The child's eyes were quick to notice.

"Eh? Why is your face red, Mother, and Father's ears red too?"

Lu Chou cleared his throat.

"The wind," he said.

Xiao Lingyu dropped her gaze.

"…The sun. Too bright."

Baor blinked, serious in thought.

"Hmm. So, was it the wind, or the sun?"

Both adults froze. Then Lu Chou laughed quietly, and Xiao Lingyu—blushing to the tips of her ears—could only hide her face.

Her cheeks were aflame. He leaned down, his breath brushing her ear, his voice a low murmur meant for her alone:

"We're not hiding, Xiao Lingyu. I'm loving you in plain sight."

* * * * *

In the capital, Drunken Moon Pavilion had always been a gathering place for nobles and courtiers—its balconies gilded, its air heavy with incense and wine.

Tonight, however, it lay unusually still. Only from one private room on the second floor came the faint, uneven clink of pouring wine.

A wine pot lay toppled on the table; shards of jade cups glittered across the floor. The scent of strong liquor mingled with the dust of shattered porcelain, filling the air with a strange, fevered quiet.

Lu Xiu sat alone by the window. His dark robes were still fastened, his collar loosened just enough to betray disorder. His face lay half-hidden in the shadow of the lamp, only his eyes visible—dark as spilled ink, deep enough to drown in.

He raised the cup in his hand—half a measure of osmanthus wine—and drained it in one swallow.

The bitterness lingered on his lips; a faint, helpless smile followed.

The door creaked open. He did not look up.

Heard instead the hurried footfall, and the weary sigh that came after.

"My lord, how many jugs has it been?" asked He Qi, stepping forward.

"I've lost count." Xiu's voice was hoarse, barely above a murmur. "But I'm not drunk. Not yet."

He Qi frowned.

"My lord, you're to depart within ten days. Three have already passed, and you've done nothing to prepare. A royal command isn't something we can bargain with. What is it you intend?"

Xiu gave a low, bitter laugh.

"Depart…?" He tapped the rim of the cup with his knuckles, gaze sinking into the reflection of the flame. "If I go, what becomes of her? Will this city protect her—or swallow her whole?"

A gust stirred the curtain. Footsteps crossed the threshold.

Someone entered—tall, clad in dark court attire, his expression solemn as winter.

Lu Chou stopped at the doorway, his eyes resting on the disarray before him: the overturned cups, the scattered wine, the brother he had never before seen so undone.

"Ah, Lord Lu," He Qi said with a forced smile. "You're just in time. See what your elder brother's turned himself into—"

Lu Chou inclined his head slightly. His tone was calm, almost dispassionate.

"Brother… have you gone mad enough yet?"

Xiu did not look up. His laugh was soft, self-mocking.

"Here to bid farewell? Or to witness the fall?"

"I'm here to end this farce." Lu Chou's brow furrowed. "You know as well as I that staying will change nothing. If you truly want her safe, you need to leave now—clear-headed, alive."

Xiu's lips curved in a soundless sneer.

"You tell me to leave. And if something happens to her while I'm gone—what then? What would you have me do?"

Lu Chou's patience thinned. His gaze swept the wrecked table, the smell of wine thick as smoke.

"What happened?"

Xiu let out a hollow laugh that cracked halfway. "She's with child."

The words struck like thunder.

Lu Chou froze. The colour drained from his face; the air between them seemed to vanish. His fingers twitched slightly before curling into a fist.

"Don't tell me…" His voice was almost a whisper. "That the child is—"

Xiu hesitated. Then, in a voice gone rough and low:

"I don't know."

Lu Chou exhaled sharply, anger and dread entwined.

"Then why are you sitting here drinking yourself senseless? If you don't know, all the more reason to go—now!"

He reached for him, intent on pulling him up by force.

But Xiu was faster. He shoved his hand away, the motion sudden and violent.

"I said I'm not leaving!"

"And if you stay, does that save her?" Lu Chou's voice was flint against steel. "Can you protect her? Protect that child?"

Xiu's head lifted sharply. His pupils flickered with both fury and despair.

"So you know too."

Lu Chou met his gaze coldly.

"If you remain, it won't just be your life. Hers, the child's, the entire Lu family's—will burn with you. You think drowning in wine will keep them safe? If you still have a heart, then stay sober."

Xiu laughed—a sound torn between grief and madness. He slammed the cup onto the floor; porcelain splintered with a sharp crack.

"Sober? I am sober!" His voice broke. "She came to see me that day. I said nothing, because if I asked her to stay—she would have. And that would have destroyed her."

He lowered his gaze, the words thinning into a whisper.

"But I still can't let it go."

He Qi stepped forward, hesitant, reaching to steady him.

"My lord, I understand—"

Xiu shoved him aside.

"You understand nothing!"

He Qi staggered back, anger and pity warring in his face.

"Then wake up, damn it!"

Before Xiu could rise again, Lu Chou moved. One swift motion—his hand cutting through the air—struck the back of his brother's neck.

The sound was barely audible.

Xiu's body went limp, his eyes fluttered once, then closed. He collapsed forward into his brother's arms.

"You actually knocked him out!" He Qi exclaimed.

Lu Chou's face was expressionless.

"If he were sober, he'd never leave. So, I'll see that he sleeps until he's past the city gates."

He bent down, lifted the unconscious man onto his back as though he were no heavier than a cloak, and said quietly:

"Prepare the horses. We ride for North-West Pass at first light. Not a moment's delay."

He Qi followed him out, pausing at the doorway. The night air was cool; the moon shone pale as cut silver.

In the shifting light, the younger brother's silhouette stood tall and unyielding, burden on his back, sorrow in his eyes.

He Qi's throat tightened.

These two brothers—one silent as stone, one fierce to ruin—each breaking himself for the other.

Outside Drunken Moon Pavilion, the wind carried the faint scent of wine.

Lu Chou walked into the moonlight, his shadow long and steady, the weight he bore pressing against him like fate itself.

Behind him, the night closed in—cool, clean, and terribly still.

Chapter 94: Reconciliation Between Brothers

Deep within the palace gardens, lilac and sandalwood twined through the corridors like veiled smoke.

Xiao Lingyu had just completed the final stitches on an imperial robe; a single thread of gold still glimmered beneath her fingertips. She was about to rise when she caught the faint sound of footsteps outside the window—light, careful, almost hesitant.

When she lifted her gaze, Lu Chou was already there.

The moon cast a pale wash across his face, and for once his calm seemed frayed—his eyes shadowed, his composure worn thin.

"Why are you here again?" she asked softly. "Didn't you say your duties were overwhelming?"

He gave a strained smile and stepped inside. The lamplight revealed fatigue beneath his eyes, a faint bruise along his left cheek, and an unhealed weariness in every line of his posture.

"You haven't slept," she murmured, frowning.

He hesitated—just long enough for the silence to press between them— then exhaled.

"That bastard Lu Xiu..." His voice dropped to a rasp. "He and the Empress—"

He stopped mid-sentence, realizing too late that he had said too much. A shadow crossed his face; his jaw tightened.

Xiao Lingyu's heart skipped. She turned quickly, drawing him toward a shadowed corner of the chamber, away from prying attendants. Her voice trembled between disbelief and alarm.

"You mean... General Lu and the Empress—there is affection between them?"

He paused a long while before nodding once. His expression was conflicted, the weight of loyalty and blood pulling in opposite directions.

"And your brother doesn't know..." she began, then faltered, realizing the danger of even uttering the thought.

"The Empress's heart," he said at last, voice low and careful, "is not for us to speculate on. But if word of this ever escapes—even a whisper—it won't just destroy my brother. It will destroy us all. You know as well as I, there has never been mercy in matters that touch the royal bloodline."

His tone was hushed, as though speaking aloud might invite ruin itself.

Xiao Lingyu's gaze held him for a long moment, then softened.

"I have a way," she said quietly.

He looked at her in surprise. She leaned closer, her eyes clear and steady despite the rising storm around them.

"Go back to your brother," she whispered. "Tell him to stay calm, make no move, and whatever happens, do not act on impulse. I'll find a way to see the Empress myself."

"You?" He stared, half in disbelief. "You can meet her?"

"Of course," Xiao Lingyu said with a faint smile. "Her belly grows by the day. The palace will soon commission new robes for the season and who else but I, the Imperial Merchant, should oversee the work? Entering the palace on business of embroidery is no crime. And I've tailored maternity garments before."

Lu Chou fell silent. For a moment the room held only the sound of their breathing and the soft flicker of the lamp. When he finally spoke again, guilt shadowed his tone.

Seeing his expression dim, she understood at once what weighed on him. She reached out, her fingers finding his, and said gently:

"Don't. I never blamed you. Everything that happened before—I chose it myself. If anyone was dragged into that web unfairly, it was you."

"Xiao Lingyu…" His lips tightened; his hand closed around hers. Her hand was small, cool, and soft, swallowed easily in his palm.

"It's enough that you're still here."

"I have no regrets," she said. "Not about any of it. Especially not about Baor. She's my life's one true fortune."

"Then having you," he replied quietly, "is mine."

She smiled faintly and withdrew her hand.

"Go now. Wait for my word."

He nodded.

"I will. And Xiao Lingyu…" His voice turned low, heavy with emotion. "Thank you."

"Don't thank me yet," she said with a small, knowing smile. "Wait to see if my plan works first."

He lingered for a heartbeat longer, his gaze steady with trust. Then he turned and left, the hem of his robe brushing the threshold like a passing sigh.

When he was gone, Xiao Lingyu stood for a moment before her embroidery frame, watching the candlelight tremble along the threads of gold. Her reflection flickered in the window pane—resolute, serene, and utterly alone.

Outside, the night wind stirred the lilacs again. Their scent crept back into the chamber—faint, bitter, and unforgettably sweet.

And so, it began—

the storm that would soon swallow them all,

* * * * *

The study was dimly lit, its lanterns breathing faint halos into the still air.

Shadows pooled across the shelves, thick with the smell of paper, dust, and wine.

The desk was buried beneath half-open scrolls and overturned cups; amber liquor had long dried on the lacquered surface, leaving behind stains like rust.

The air itself seemed sodden, heavy with the residue of drink and despair.

By the window, Lu Xiu sat sprawled on a low couch, robe undone at the throat, the black fabric creased and wrinkled from long neglect.

His fingers toyed with a cup half-filled with cold wine; each movement was languid, deliberate, as though he needed the rhythm to keep himself from unravelling.

The faint light caught the sharpness of his cheekbones, the darkness beneath his eyes—a face that had once belonged to a soldier, now hollowed by something quieter, more consuming.

Outside, the corridor was empty save for He Qi, who had stood guard for nearly an hour, his brows drawn in silent disapproval. Inside, the silence was so thick it bordered on menace.

Four days had passed since the imperial decree arrived. Only six days remained before departure.

He Qi finally broke the quiet, voice low but edged with unease.

"This can't go on, my lord. If His Majesty asks for you and finds you in this state, who will answer for it?"

From within came a dull sound—glass against wood—and then a soft, derisive laugh.

"No one," Lu Xiu said hoarsely, his words slow, scraping. "No one can make me go."

The last word was bitten off, hard and final.

Before He Qi could reply, the sound of steady boots echoed down the hall. Firm, measured, unhurried.

The door burst open.

Lu Chou stepped in, his gaze sweeping once across the room—disarray, wine, the sagging shadow of his brother—and stopped. His face hardened. He kicked aside a discarded floor cushion and shut the door behind him with a quiet click.

"So," he said, his tone like frost drawn across steel, "is the great General Lu planning to demolish his own house before he leaves?"

Lu Xiu looked up sharply. The retort formed on his lips but died there as Lu Chou's boot met his shin in one swift, merciless strike.

"You're insane—!" he hissed, clutching his leg, his voice breaking between anger and disbelief. "You actually kicked me!"

"You weren't listening," Lu Chou replied coolly, pulling out a chair and sitting with the composure of someone too exhausted to argue. "If I don't hit you, how else will you sober up? I just came from the palace."

The words landed like a stone thrown into still water.

Lu Xiu's voice dropped, low and taut. "The palace? You've heard something?"

"Keep your mouth shut," Lu Chou said flatly. "Then I'll tell you."

The elder brother fell instantly silent, the obedience almost absurd—back straight, eyes alert, waiting as if afraid even a breath might scatter the next words.

Lu Chou exhaled softly, studying him with thinly veiled irritation.

"Xiao Lingyu asked me to tell you to hold yourself together. She's working on a way to see the Empress."

For a moment, Lu Xiu just stared at him, the words sinking in by slow degrees. Then, quietly—almost reverently—he murmured, "She knows?"

"The whole capital knows," Lu Chou said, his voice stripped of emotion. "It's already been proclaimed to the court."

Lu Xiu's fingers tightened around his cup. He didn't drink, just sat there, his knuckles whitening, eyes dimming into something raw and heavy. After a long silence, he lifted his head.

"Lu Chou," he said quietly, the name weighted with something he rarely used: supplication. "Help me. Ask her… ask your lady to find out the truth. I need to know—whose child it is."

Lu Chou blinked once. The back of his neck prickled. "Don't call me that," he muttered. "It's nauseating."

But Lu Xiu wasn't listening anymore. He leaned forward, his voice breaking around the edges.

"If the child is mine…" He stopped, swallowed, then went on, each word scraped from somewhere deep. "If it's mine, I'll take her away. No matter where, I'll go wherever she wishes. I don't care about rank, or war, or honour. The empire can crumble for all I care."

He paused, head bowed, eyes closed as if the words themselves burned. "This life," he said softly, "I've wronged her too deeply."

Lu Chou, who had begun the conversation with all the chill detachment of a magistrate, suddenly found no words. The mockery that rose in his throat dissolved before it reached his tongue.

There was something unbearable about the sight of his brother—a man forged in battle, half undone by a name he would not even speak.

After a long silence, Lu Xiu's voice came again, low and cracked. "Please… tell her, sister-in-law. I beg you."

That single phrase, sister-in-law—landed with the weight of something innocent and unguarded. It disarmed him completely.

Lu Chou looked away. The corners of his mouth twitched; the sigh that followed was half exasperation, half something dangerously close to fondness.

He rose.

"Wait," he said simply.

And without another glance, he turned on his heel and strode toward the door.

He did not look back, did not explain. But as he passed through the corridor, the faintest, unwilling curve lingered at his lips.

That foolish, earnest sister-in-law had struck him deeper than he cared to admit—and for reasons he couldn't name, it left a quiet warmth beneath his ribs that no amount of cold could entirely smother.

Outside, the night wind stirred the lanterns along the eaves, scattering their light like shards of gold across the paving stones.

He walked faster than usual. And though his expression remained as impassive as ever, a trace of that hidden smile still refused to leave his face.

* * * * *

Dusk wavered on the horizon—neither fallen nor whole—while in the depths of the palace, lanterns began to glow like faint stars caught in amber glass.

Xiao Lingyu had waited many days for a chance such as this.

After discreetly placing a few red envelopes in the right hands, she was granted permission to tailor garments for the Empress herself.

With her flawless embroidery and her standing as an Imperial Merchant, the request had passed without question; all appeared to unfold as though ordained.

The embroidery chamber was steeped in fragrance—aloeswood and orchid smoke rising in tender spirals, its triple screens enclosing them in quiet secrecy.

Xiao Lingyu sat with her head bowed, her fingers steady as they drew silver thread through silk, each motion calm and deliberate.

Behind her stood the Empress, Shen Zhaoru, draped only in a robe of pale gauze. Her beauty, once radiant, now carried a fragile translucence; her cheeks were thin, her expression composed yet remote.

From her delicate frame, no one would have guessed she was said to be with child.

"Your Majesty, if you would turn slightly—yes, just so. Here, it should be widened a little," Xiao Lingyu murmured, voice low and respectful, measuring with careful precision.

The Empress complied without protest. Her eyes were lowered, her stillness recalling an old painting in muted tones—so silent one could almost hear the faint rhythm of her breath.

For a long moment, there was only the whisper of thread passing through silk. Then Xiao Lingyu spoke softly, without raising her gaze.

"If Your Majesty has something… to tell General Lu, I can deliver it."

The needle paused.

That single line was as fine and dangerous as the silk she held, slicing open what had been long sealed within the Empress's heart.

"You—?" Shen Zhaoru started, startled into motion, her eyes flashing wide. The words that followed died on her lips.

Xiao Lingyu lifted a finger to her lips, signaling for quiet. Her eyes flicked toward the waiting maids.

At once, the Empress seemed to gather herself. Turning to the attendants, she said evenly, "Leave us. I wish to speak with Madam Xiao alone."

"Yes, Your Majesty." The maids bowed and withdrew, their footsteps fading into the long corridors.

Only when silence returned did the Empress speak again, her voice trembling. "You…?"

Xiao Lingyu understood the question before it was fully formed.

"I am Xiao Lingyu of the Jin Hua establishment," she said calmly. "I came today at the request of Lord Lu."

"Lord Lu?" the Empress repeated, her brows faintly knitting. "You mean—the Vice Minister of Revenue, that man…his… younger brother?"

Xiao Lingyu inclined her head. "Just so."

A flicker of surprise crossed Shen Zhaoru's face, then softened into something like resignation.

"He… is still in the capital?"

"He is," Xiao Lingyu answered gently. "But His Majesty has ordered him to the western frontier. He is to depart within days." A pause, then, more softly, "He would have left already, if not for Your Majesty's condition."

The Empress's composure faltered. Her lashes trembled; moisture gathered at their tips. Then, suddenly, tears fell, soundless but sharp, staining the embroidery silk in her lap.

She turned away, voice small, almost breaking.

"I had already decided to accept my fate. I thought… I could hide the child here, somewhere in the palace, raise it quietly. To have something to remember him by. Just that would have been enough. But…" She swallowed, her tone growing fainter. "The Emperor already knows."

She no longer spoke as an Empress but as a woman stripped bare of titles. Her words carried the fragility of a dream undone, the fear of one who wakes to find the world colder than before.

Xiao Lingyu said nothing. Her expression remained composed, but beneath that calm, a wave of shock and sorrow surged. The Empress's words—were they not an admission?

So it was true. The child belonged to General Lu.

She studied the woman before her—the sovereign of the realm, the very image of grace and dignity—now caught in the same snare she herself had once stumbled into.

Both women bound by love, both crushed by duty. One had bartered her body to save her family; the other had risked a throne to claim a single fragile tenderness.

After a long silence, Xiao Lingyu bowed her head slightly.

"Your Majesty," she murmured, her tone low but firm, "I respect you."

Shen Zhaoru turned back toward her, eyes clouded with grief and a faint, wounded pride. Her reply was quiet, yet carried an authority that brooked no refusal.

"Don't call me that. Call me by my name—Shen Zhaoru."

Xiao Lingyu hesitated, then nodded once. She took the Empress's hand in both of hers, the skin cool as porcelain beneath her touch.

"Lady Shen," she said softly, "there are times when none of us can choose our path. Whatever choice you made—it was still yours. No one else has the right to judge."

The Empress froze; her gaze fixed on Xiao Lingyu as though seeing her for the first time. "You don't think I'm mad?" she asked, almost a whisper.

Xiao Lingyu smiled faintly, a shadow of self-mockery crossing her eyes. "No," she said. "I think you're brave."

And she meant it.

For a moment, she almost laughed at the irony of it all. Once, she had sold her body to bear a child—out of desperation, for survival. And now, here was the most exalted woman in the realm, driven by love to do the same.

One had done it to protect her home.

The other, to preserve a single heartbeat of affection.

The thought left her chest tight, her eyes burning in ways she could not name.

The embroidery chamber fell silent again. Then Shen Zhaoru spoke, her voice thin but steady.

"Tell him… to go. Quickly. And tell him nothing of the child."

Xiao Lingyu looked up, startled. "But—"

"Tell him," the Empress cut in gently but firmly, "that our bond is ended. That fate between us has run its course. From this life to the next, we shall not meet again."

Her lips curved in a faint, wistful smile. "Two hearts once entangled must now unbind. Let love end where the sky begins."

The sound of the needle returned, soft, rhythmic, inevitable.

Xiao Lingyu drew the final measure of silk around the Empress's waist, tying the thread with quiet precision. Her voice came like a sigh.

"Very well. I will deliver your words."

Shen Zhaoru nodded. "Good."

Her face was serene once more, her back straight, her silhouette composed. Only her eyes betrayed her—eyes that gleamed faintly beneath the lamplight, holding within them a sorrow so gentle it could almost be mistaken for grace.

Chapter 95: A Double Blessing

Autumn deepened; the air was crisp; the wind scented faintly with gold.

Yet within the palace walls, festivity bloomed brighter than the season itself—two joyful tidings arrived on the same day, filling the harem with laughter and congratulation.

Her Majesty, Consort Shen Zhaoru, was said to be with child for over a month.

And scarcely had the news spread when another message came from Huixi Palace—Lady Hui, the favoured concubine, too was with child.

Two proclamations of joy in one day; the palace erupted in delight.

Imperial eunuchs carried the Emperor's decree to every hall, voices echoing through corridors lined with glazed tiles: "Twofold happiness descends upon the palace; auspicious fortune fills the air!"

The Empress Dowager ordered a vegetarian banquet to be held at Shou'an Palace for three days, summoning all the consorts and attendants to celebrate the dual blessing.

The Emperor himself was overjoyed: to Consort Shen he bestowed a pair of gold-lotus fragrance boxes said to nourish the foetus; to Lady Hui, a canopy of ice-silk gauze and the attendance of the Imperial Medical Bureau's chief physician.

In the imperial kitchens, the fires burned through the night. Cooks and maids prepared gentle, nourishing dishes—lotus soups, bird's nest congee, sweet jujube broth—while the scent of sandalwood drifted from the Hall of Eternal Spring to the distant gates of the Forbidden City.

Every corridor gleamed with silk; laughter spilled like scattered pearls. It seemed, for a brief and splendid moment, that spring had returned ahead of its time.

Officials across the court submitted memorials of congratulations.

Within the inner palace, seamstresses worked without rest to embroider congratulatory robes and jewelled hairpins; the sound of needles striking silk filled the midnight air, light and rhythmic as falling rain.

Yet beneath the clamour of celebration, beneath the bright silk and gilded words, a question lingered—unspoken but sharp as a blade beneath brocade:

When the time came, which of these women would truly bear the title Mother of the Realm?

Each heart within the palace already carried its own answer.

* * * * *

"She wants me to leave?"

Lu Xiu's voice was as cold as the wind at midnight.

When he finally forced the words out, something inside him seemed to lock in place—his whole body stilled, even his gaze fixed, as though nailed to the spot.

Xiao Lingyu did not avert her eyes. She only nodded once.

"She said… 'This life's affection is spent; our fate fulfilled. Beyond the ends of the earth, we shall never meet again.'"

Silence fell—heavy, absolute.

Lu Chou stood to one side. At those words, he gave a short, brittle laugh—a sound that carried more release than mirth, the kind one makes to let a little of the pain escape.

Leaning against a carved pillar, he watched his elder brother without moving a muscle.

"The Emperor's command is personal," he said, voice clipped and cool. "Do you still think you can refuse?"

Lu Xiu lowered his eyes. For a long while, he said nothing.

Then, softly—almost gently—he laughed.

There was no joy in it. Only the faint absurdity of a man who has bled too long and finally sees how deep the wound runs.

"In that case… fine. I'll go."

The words were simple, flat, but each syllable fell with the weight of a verdict—spoken not only to others, but to himself.

He turned, reached for his cloak, and fastened it with calm, deliberate hands.

"She was right," he murmured. "The bond is broken. The feeling should end as well."

He wanted to ask—Whose child is it?

But the question died before it reached his lips.

If it were his, why would she send him away?

And if it were not, what was left to ask?

A dull ache gathered in his chest, tightening by slow degrees, as though some unseen needle were threading through his heart—stitch by stitch, soundless, merciless—until the pain itself became silence.

At last he spoke, his voice hoarse, stripped of all pretence. "...Thank you."

Then he walked away.

His figure straight as a mountain, his steps so heavy they seemed to grind the stones beneath him.

He neither turned nor spoke again.

And he knew—this parting might be life, or it might be death.

Either way, it was a farewell without a single word left to say.

* * * * *

The late sun hung low, its amber warmth spilling over tiled eaves and white marble balustrades.

Autumn in the palace had ripened to its height—chrysanthemums bloomed in golden profusion, the lingering fragrance of cassia drifted faintly through the air.

A soft wind stirred, and the entire imperial garden shimmered like liquid gold.

The Emperor was in rare good humour.

He wore a dark robe lined with gold, seated in the lakeside pavilion, savoring tea while the reflection of the rippling water played upon his sleeves.

To his right sat Consort Hui, smiling like a flower in full sun; to his left, the Empress Shen Zhaoru, her face calm, her gaze still.

On the jade table lay osmanthus pastries and chilled honey-pear soup—autumn delicacies prepared to please the palate.

Consort Xu Hui leaned sweetly upon the Emperor's arm, her laughter light and effusive.

"Your Majesty, I had thought the flutter in my belly was nothing but a touch of the wind," she said, eyes bright with pride. "Who could have known it was joy taking root? And to share this blessing with Elder Sister—two hearts, two lives—surely Heaven smiles upon us."

Emperor Chen Gen's lips curved into an indulgent smile.

"Auspicious indeed," he said with mellow ease. "Two heirs at once—be it prince or princess, all are cause for joy."

The consort's eyes glowed with delight.

"As long as Your Majesty is pleased, every pain is worth it," she said, her voice lilting with practiced tenderness.

The two spoke back and forth in gentle tones, every gesture one of harmony and affection.

Only the Empress, seated quietly beside them, neither joined nor smiled. She watched their exchange with the faintest tension at her lips—so tight it was nearly bloodless.

Presently, a palace maid entered and knelt.

"Your Majesty, Imperial Physician Liu of the Medical Bureau awaits outside the southern gate. He requests leave to examine Consort Xu Hui."

The Emperor nodded. "Let him wait in the south hall. My dear consort, go on—you must not keep the physician waiting."

Consort Hui rose with a coy smile, bowing gracefully.

"Then this concubine shall obey. May Your Majesty and Her Grace continue to enjoy the view."

She left in a flutter of silken skirts, glancing back thrice before rounding the corridor. Her final smile lingered like perfume before she vanished into the deep shadows of the palace.

Only two remained beneath the pavilion.

The air grew still.

Shen Zhaoru's expression did not change; she looked as though she had merely watched the closing scene of a play. Slowly, she turned her gaze upon the man across from her—her husband, her emperor—and said nothing.

Chen Gen, ever serene, poured her a cup of tea himself.

"Taste it," he said lightly. "A Da Hong Pao—only a few catties are harvested each year."

She did not touch the cup. After a long silence, her voice broke through, low and steady.

"Why," she asked, "did Your Majesty choose to acknowledge that child?"

His eyes narrowed, a trace of mockery flickering behind the calm.

"What else should I have done?" he said. "Announce to the world that the Empress is unchaste? Tell me, where would that leave the face of the Son of Heaven?"

Her hands trembled. "Your Majesty could have ended my life instead— a length of white silk, a cup of poison wine. That would have sufficed. You need not humiliate me."

The Emperor laughed softly.

"Humiliation? Do you think death would save you from disgrace? A hanging empress, guilty of infidelity—would that cleanse your name, or tarnish mine?"

He slammed the porcelain cup down.

The sharp crack split the air; pigeons burst upward from the eaves, scattering into the golden dusk.

"If word spread that the Empress is unchaste," he said, his tone suddenly rough, "what becomes of the imperial dignity? I haven't killed you—not yet—only because of that thing in your womb… perhaps the bastard of the Lu family? Should that scandal reach the court, your entire Shen clan will die paying for your virtue."

Her face drained of colour. Her lips moved, but no sound came.

Chen Gen's fury ebbed as quickly as it had risen. When he spoke again, his voice was calm—too calm—almost kind.

"Be at ease. I've no intention of acting just yet. The northern rebellion has only recently been quelled, and unrest brews again in the west. Soldiers like Lu Xiu are rare; I must keep him useful. So long as he remains of value, you will remain Empress."

The words were mild, almost reasonable—yet each one struck like iron against stone.

It was as if he were speaking of a horse: one still fit to run, not yet ready for slaughter.

Shen Zhaoru's body chilled from crown to heel.

The man before her—the boy she had once known, whose laughter had once warmed her youth—was a stranger now.

She scarcely recognized the face she had once called beloved.

Her voice was hoarse when she whispered, "Then, when he is no longer useful… Your Majesty would have the child killed?"

The Emperor toyed idly with the lid of his teacup, as though discussing the weather.

"In this palace," he said, "so many princes and princesses have died that even the physicians have lost count. What's one more?"

The words were soft. The cruelty in them was infinite.

The Empress straightened, her back rigid as a blade. Her eyes searched his face, desperate for any flicker of humanity.

There was none.

Only the fathomless depth of calculation, and the chill of a heart long since sealed.

Inside her, something stirred—small, fragile—curling tighter, as if the unborn life itself sensed the coldness of the world that awaited it.

The Emperor rose. He brushed his sleeves smooth.

"Come," he said. "We've admired the garden long enough. You need only keep to your duty—nurture the child, and stay silent. Should you grow restless again, my patience will not last."

He left without another glance, his figure receding through the falling light—like a statesman departing a meeting, or an actor stepping off the stage.

Only Shen Zhaoru remained.

The sun had dipped, staining the pavilion in a wash of red gold.

Her face was ashen, her eyes empty.

And when the last light slipped away, a single tear traced down her cheek—soundless, unseen—the quiet fall of something that had already broken.

* * * * *

Late autumn had settled over the Lu residence. Golden leaves drifted through the courtyard, their rustle mingling with the thin whisper of wind and distant rain.

The air was heavy with the scent of cold earth and fallen osmanthus.

That morning, a modest carriage stopped before the vermilion gates.

A steward hurried inside to report, and the Grand Madam, upon hearing his words, rose at once, throwing a thick cloak over her shoulders as she went to the entrance herself.

When she saw the small figure being helped down from the carriage, her steps faltered ever so slightly.

It was a little girl in a pale-yellow jacket.

The hairpin in her dark hair was set askew, and though her eyes were bright, a faint loneliness lingered within them. She looked up at the towering gate—neither crying nor smiling—and only tightened her small fingers around Lu Chou's hand.

"Baor…" the old lady called softly. Her voice carried the gentleness one uses for something fragile.

The child lifted her head.

Before her stood an old woman with snow-white hair and serene grace. Baor's lips curved in a shy smile as she murmured, "Great-Grandmother, hello. Baor has come to see you again."

The Grand Madam bent down until their eyes were level.

"This time," she said tenderly, "don't leave again. From now on, this shall be your home."

Baor's eyes turned red at the rims; she nodded hard, then clutched Lu Chou's hand as they crossed the threshold together.

Inside the main hall, the Minister of Works—Lord Lu—was already waiting. His expression was unreadable but stern. When his gaze fell upon the child, his brows drew together.

"What is the meaning of this?" he asked in a low, deliberate tone.

Lu Chou's reply was calm, almost too calm.

"Baor's mother has been summoned to the palace to oversee the Empress Dowager's birthday robe. She cannot leave her post. I brought the child home—out of worry."

Lord Lu's frown deepened. "And you did not think to consult your mother first?"

Before Chou could answer, the Grand Madam set down her teacup with a soft click.

Her voice was mild but carried the weight of command.

"Since Lu Xiu was dispatched to the Western Frontier three months ago, this house has grown far too cold and silent. It was my wish to bring Baor here. A household this vast can spare a courtyard or two for a child. You needn't trouble yourself further."

The Minister's jaw tightened.

He opened his mouth to object, but one cool glance from his mother silenced him. The words died where they stood.

Baor sensed the tension.

She shrank closer to Lu Chou, her tiny hand clutching the edge of his sleeve, eyes wide with unease.

The Grand Madam noticed.

Her expression softened. Rising, she reached out and took the girl's hand into her own.

"Come," she said with a faint smile. "Let Great-Grandmother show you the back garden. The osmanthus there is still in bloom, and a litter of white kittens was born last week. I think you'll like them."

Baor blinked, then nodded with sudden delight. She turned once toward Lu Chou. He inclined his head.

"Go on," he said quietly. "Whatever Great-Grandmother says, you may believe her."

Hand in hand, the two walked away beneath the corridor eaves.

The old lady's voice drifted back, warm as autumn sunlight.

"This house may be large," she said, "but wherever you are, child—that is where home shall be."

Baor's steps grew lighter, her small face brightening, until even her laughter began to rise among the rustling leaves.

Inside, silence returned.

Lord Lu at last spoke, his tone low and grave.

"Do you understand what this means? To bring a child here, born outside wedlock, before the wedding rites are announced—what will the court think?"

Lu Chou remained composed. "His Majesty has already permitted Lady Xiao Lingyu's presence in the palace. If Baor may reside in her ancestral home, there can be no impropriety."

He paused, then added softly,

"She is not a bastard, Father, nor the child of another.

 Her mother will finish her work on the Empress Dowager's phoenix robe soon enough, and then I will marry her—openly, with the rites due a wife. As for Baor..."

He looked toward the doorway where the faint echo of a child's laughter lingered.

"...she is my blood, my heart's flesh, the pulse beneath my ribs."

The hall fell still.

Outside, the last leaves fell upon the flagstones, and the wind carried their whisper through the silent corridors—like a blessing, or a warning.

Chapter 96: Mutual Admiration

The late autumn in the Imperial Garden was mildly hot.

The wind passed through the pond willows, and yellow leaves fluttered and fell, breaking into circles of ripples upon the water.

The weather was exceedingly fine today.

Chen Gen strolled into the garden, naturally followed by a retinue of court attendants and close officials.

The ground was covered with a thin layer of fine yellow fallen leaves, which rustled softly when stepped upon, imparting a certain sense of unhurried leisure.

Turning around a flower wall, he saw the Consort Hui, accompanied by several daughters of noble families, enjoying tea and entertainment in the waterside pavilion next to a rockery.

The fragrance of tea wafted with the wind, accompanied by soft laughter and whispers.

Before he had even drawn near, everyone in the pavilion simultaneously rose and performed their salute—

"We pay our respects to Your Majesty."

Some performed the salute of married women, others the salute of unmarried maidens, but all moved in unison, their skirts flowing like water.

Just as the group bowed, a young woman in a scarlet dress (blouse and skirt) accidentally stepped on her hem. Her figure swayed, and she tumbled forward, falling directly close to Chen Gen.

Before the attendant guards at his side could react, Chen Gen had instinctively raised his hand to steady her shoulder and arm, his voice steady and unperturbed: "Be careful."

The maiden froze, her eyelashes trembling, and she quickly lowered her head: "I have committed a grave impropriety; this subject deserves death for startling the Sacred Chariot—"

She lifted her head, revealing a delicate and gentle face, fair-skinned with red lips, her eyes, like clear autumn water, filled with panic and shame.

Catching sight of the Emperor's proper and mild expression, her ears turned even redder, and she retreated with great haste.

Chen Gen merely gave a slight nod: "No matter."

He glanced at her with a calm expression, not pausing long, and simply said: "All of you, rise."

Consort Hui stepped forward, and Chen Gen supported her, saying softly: "Your pregnancy must be seven or eight months along now? You and Her Majesty the Empress are due around the same time. Do not walk about aimlessly when there is no need, lest you suffer a mishap."

Liu Hui's face flushed red, and she covered her mouth with a handkerchief, chuckling softly. "The Imperial Physicians all say that frequent walking is better for childbirth. Your Majesty, please rest assured; this Concubine will take good care of herself."

Chen Gen gently patted her arm. "We hold great anticipation for this child of the Consort. It is only right to be more cautious."

"Your Majesty jests. Her Majesty the Empress's term is also nearing, due in another two months. That will be Your Majesty's lawful-son (son of the principal wife)."

Chen Gen's demeanour remained utterly gentle. Seeing this, all the noble maidens present could not help but show looks of envy. This Emperor was not only handsome and distinguished in bearing, but truly a dragon among men—and his kindness towards Consort Hui was beyond reproach.

"Naturally, we regard both with equal importance."

Upon hearing this, Chen Gen appeared utterly gentle, causing all the noble maidens present to display envious looks.

This Emperor was not only handsome but also a dragon among men, and his kindness towards Consort Hui was truly beyond reproach.

"Since that is the case, We still have state duties to attend to and shall take Our leave first."

"We respectfully send off Your Majesty." The group bowed again.

Chen Gen stepped forward to continue, and Chief Attendant Xu, the Grand Eunuch, immediately hastened forward half a pace, bowing and lowering his voice to report at Chen Gen's side: "Your Majesty, the maiden who just now stumbled into your embrace is Jiang Wan'er, the eldest daughter of the Left Censor-in-Chief Jiang Yuanliang. She is seventeen and has always been reputed for both talent and beauty."

Chen Gen's eye corner flickered slightly, but he did not respond.

Seeing his silence, Grand Eunuch Xu continued softly: "The Jiang family is a family of pure, old meritocrats and nobles."

"A noble family's daughter?"

Grand Eunuch Xu became even more deferential. "Her Majesty the Empress serves as the exemplar for the scholarly community. If Your Majesty were now to select another noble maiden from an established family to bring into the Inner Palace, Your Majesty would have both the scholars and the noble houses under your banner. Would this not be splendid?"

He spoke with extreme care, his manner obedient and well-measured, carrying a hint of suggestion.

Chen Gen remained expressionless, merely lightly glancing at the garden scene bathed in the setting sun before them, his tone indifferent: "En."

This "En," neither warm nor cold, was neither a refutation nor a permission, and precisely because of this, it made him unfathomable.

Grand Eunuch Xu heard it and knew what to do in his heart, bowing and stepping back, yet a subtle gleam flashed across his eyes—

This Jiang maiden, perhaps... truly has a chance now. If it comes to pass, it would not be in vain for the person who entrusted him.

* * * * *

The light in the embroidery room was soft, the incense faint. The breeze outside the window ruffled the beaded curtains, casting flickering shadows across the room.

Xiao Lingyu held the measuring tape, taking measurements around the Empress's waist, and said softly: "Shen Zhaoru's body has gained more weight. It is likely growing quickly these days. The waist must be increased by another half inch."

Shen Zhaoru lowered her eyes and smiled softly, placing her fingers over her abdomen, stroking it gently. Yet, the expression in her eyes was momentarily indiscernible; whether it was joy or pain, it was all hidden beneath that gentle curve.

She asked in a low voice: "...Is there news of him?"

Xiao Lingyu paused, making her movements gentler, and slowly replied: "I heard he fought fiercely and won, seemingly disregarding his own life in several battles... the situation on the Western Front is now stable. The court says he is... meritorious."

Shen Zhaoru did not respond, only tightening her fingers, as if trying to grasp something through the thin veil over her belly.

"Child..." she whispered softly, her eyes gently rippling like water: "Your father is a remarkable General..."

The tone, though ostensibly to herself, sounded more like she was confiding in the small life within her abdomen.

No sooner had her voice fallen than her abdomen suddenly moved, like a small fist lightly tapping her palm.

She froze, looking down at her swollen abdomen, her eyes instantly welling up with moisture, yet the corners of her lips slowly curved upwards, a soft and slow smile.

"He heard it," she whispered softly, as if comforting someone, or perhaps comforting herself.

Xiao Lingyu was also startled, then smiled gently, a faint mist also covering her eyes: "This child has a spirit; he takes after his father."

Shen Zhaoru reached out to cover the area where the foetal movement had not yet subsided, murmuring softly: "Do not worry, your mother will wait for him to return... wait well."

At that moment, time seemed to stand still, leaving only the quiet intimacy and deep affection between mother and child, softly falling in the room illuminated by the autumn sun.

Xiao Lingyu looked at her complex yet tender expression, her heart aching, but she merely silently adjusted the Empress's lapel, gently smoothing out the edge of the garment, just as she smoothed over Shen Zhaoru's layers of unspoken anxieties.

* * * * *

The candlelight flickered in the Imperial Study, and yellow silk memorials covered the desk.

The edges of the latest confidential memorial in Chen Gen's hand were slightly curled from where his knuckles had squeezed them.

—Great victory on the Western Front; the enemy's main force was routed, and five hundred thousand prisoners have all been escorted back within the border. In addition, including those who voluntarily surrendered along the way, the troops under Lu Xiu's command have reached a force of one hundred thousand men.

"A hundred thousand..."

He murmured softly, his voice hoarse, yet carrying a not-quite-clear strength.

That was no longer the military strength a minor border general ought to possess.

Chen Gen closed the memorial, his brow still furrowed. His knuckles gently tapped on the document, as if pondering something deeply.

He must grant a reward for this battle. Meritorious service must be rewarded; the iron law could not be violated.

But should these one hundred thousand men be allowed to remain under Lu Xiu's command?

He had not yet reached a conclusion on this point.

"Is he due to return to the Capital soon?" he suddenly asked.

Grand Eunuch Xu quickly stepped forward, answering in a low voice: "Replying to Your Majesty, the principal General of the Western Defence Army set out five days ago. Calculating the itinerary, he should arrive on the outskirts of the Capital within ten days."

Chen Gen gave a cold laugh: "Within ten days?"

He raised his hand and covered the battle report, his knuckles slightly white. After a long moment, he slowly uttered one sentence: "To welcome, or to guard against... he certainly knows how to set a puzzle for Us."

The candlelight on the Imperial desk swayed, as if a wind had risen in his heart at this moment.

Several memorials on the side remained unapproved, a few of which were submitted by the Ministry of Revenue and the Ministry of Rites, concerning disputes between old established families and newly emerging gentry—

In the case of the Secretariat Bureau official, Qin Chi, who was of commoner origin, was promoted, yet jointly impeached by the Zhang family, a member of the old noble houses, on grounds of his low birth and improper conduct.

Another case involved the replacement of a Prefectural Governor; the son of an established family had not served a full month before being accused of corruption by the son of a new gentry family.

These matters, back and forth, never ceased.

"The new gentry and the old families truly make Our head ache with their endless bickering." Chen Gen rubbed his temples, his tone faint, yet revealing an unrestrained annoyance.

"One claims to be the backbone of the pure stream; the other claims the opposition is plagued by hereditary defects. With the entire court arguing back and forth, who truly remembers how much a bag of grain costs the common people?"

He rose abruptly, the hem of his robe billowing, his pace swift.

"Grand Eunuch Xu."

"This subject is present."

"Arrange an official welcome on the outskirts of the Capital for the victorious General of the Western Defence." He paused, the corner of his lips curving into an arc that was neither a smile nor a sneer: "Since General Lu has achieved this victory, We shall reward him with a grand display. Let all those in the court see how We reward meritorious servants."

Grand Eunuch Xu lowered his head in assent, yet a chill subtly rose in his heart.

—Is the Emperor intending to use a single welcoming ceremony to suppress the conflict between the two factions and establish a new order?

No one could be certain.

This was Chen Gen.

He held the universe in his sleeve and concealed the blade within his smile.

"Wait a moment." Chen Gen called back Grand Eunuch Xu, who was about to leave with the command. "Further issue an Edict, commanding Her Majesty the Empress to also proceed to the outskirts of the Capital to greet the victorious army."

"But... Her Ladyship is in her final months, and her body is heavy..."

"It matters not. A soft palanquin will move slowly, that is all." Chen Gen commanded coldly, yet his heart spoke: Lu Xiu, you return to the Capital with one hundred thousand troops, and We must welcome you, but do not forget that the one you love remains in Our grasp. If you make a move, the first to die... will be her!

Chapter 97: What If It Were Her?

The capital's outskirts lay under an autumn sky streaked with drifting cloud—crimson and gold torn thin by wind. Banners rolled in long waves across the parade ground, the fabric snapping like whips. Ten thousand riders stood in formation; armour rang against armour; the air itself seemed to tremble under the returning weight of war.

At the far end, the imperial procession shone—golden canopy, lacquered poles, a palanquin like a moving sun. The Emperor had come in person, with the court in full attendance. Beside the gilded rail, the Empress stood in ceremonial red—true crimson gauze with phoenix plumes worked into the weave, jade pendants chiming faintly at her waist.

Her body was unmistakably heavy with life, well past eight months. She held herself upright, step after measured step, but the wind that lifted the edge of her sleeve also lifted something deeper—something she had pressed down since spring, something that had never died, only been forced quiet.

Far ahead, the Western Army opened like a sea of iron.

From its front line, one man stepped forward.

Gold armour blazed beneath the light. A scarlet plume rose from his helm, streaming behind him like a banner of its own. His pace was steady, unhurried, controlled—so controlled it felt merciless. Each footfall landed on the earth with the certainty of a verdict.

Lu Xiu.

He crossed the distance through ranks that did not move. Soldiers held their breath. Courtiers forgot how to blink. When he reached the base of the golden dais, sunlight struck his breastplate and spilled a hard glare across the square. He did not speak. He did not look aside. He only sank to one knee.

Thud.

Bone met stone. The sound rolled through the hush like thunder breaking across a valley.

Shen Zhaoru flinched so sharply she almost lost her footing. Her fingers tightened on the gilded rail until her knuckles blanched. Her throat burned; a thin haze rose in her eyes. She could not stop it. The water gathered anyway, trembling there like something alive.

Beside her, the Emperor turned.

His voice was warm, careful, perfectly composed—concern shaped into silk.

"My Empress," he asked softly, as though in private, as though the whole world could not hear. "Are you tired again? Has the child been troubling you?"

Every word was gentle. Every word was a blade.

On the steps below, Lu Xiu did not lift his head. He heard each syllable clearly, as though it had been spoken against his ear. His fingers curled within his gauntlets until the joints stood out, tendons taut beneath the metal. Veins rose along the back of his hand—silent rebellion with nowhere to go.

He remained kneeling. He remained still.

Shen Zhaoru could not endure it.

Her breath shuddered once, thin and uneven. The words tore themselves from her throat—hoarse, restrained, shaking despite her effort.

"…General. Please rise."

Soft as a leaf in wind. Yet it carried across armour, banners, and stone steps, reaching him as cleanly as a command.

Lu Xiu lifted his head.

For one brief moment, he looked at her directly.

He should not have. He knew it. She knew it. Yet he did it anyway— one long, quiet, disobedient second.

Her eyes were rimmed red. Her face was pale to the edge of translucence. Exhaustion sat behind her gaze like a bruise. He saw at once how much she had swallowed, how much she had endured without being allowed to speak.

And still she stood at that man's side—phoenix crown, imperial red, above ten thousand kneeling lives.

His mouth moved, as if something might escape.

Nothing did.

He gathered every word back into himself and bowed his head once, low and precise.

"Your servant thanks Her Majesty the Empress."

He rose. He stood at a distance that was close enough to kill and far enough to be called propriety.

Wind rose again. Banners snapped. The Emperor accepted a cup of wine from an attendant; he held one, and extended the other toward Lu Xiu with an even hand, an even face.

"The General has laboured," he said calmly. "Let this cup wash the dust from you and your men. After we return to the palace, We will discuss rewards."

His tone held no wave, no ripple—yet beneath it, the next move was already placed on the board.

Lu Xiu's hands came together at his chest. He hesitated for the length of a single breath, as if weighing whether to accept. Then his gaze slid— only once, only briefly—to the Empress's bloodless face.

That glance decided him.

He took the cup. He lowered his head.

"Your servant thanks Your Majesty for the wine."

Shen Zhaoru could only watch the exchange—two men speaking in clean lines, each line sealed with a meaning no one dared name. Her red skirts stirred on a carpet of yellow leaves. Her eyes blurred. In that moment she understood, with a clarity that tasted like iron:

She was not a wife. Not a queen.

She was a hostage who still had a heartbeat.

The ceremony should have ended there.

The court was already shifting, already exhaling—the trumpet line ready to fall silent, the officials ready to disperse.

Then Lu Xiu moved again.

He stepped forward, one measured pace after another, straight toward the throne. When he reached three paces from the imperial steps, he dropped to his knees a second time.

His voice was low, but it carried—bronze struck hard, ringing clean across the field.

"Your servant's triumph is born of Your Majesty's Heaven-bestowed grace. To receive such favour and praise… I do not dare."

An attendant advanced, bearing a long black-lacquer chest with gilded corners. Its surface swallowed light. It was not a gift-box. It was a coffin for power.

Lu Xiu opened it himself.

Within lay the tiger tally—split metal, carved and weighted, the seal of western command. A token that did not merely signify troops, but held the right to move them: ten thousand lives, ten thousand blades, one order away from slaughter or salvation.

He lifted it with both hands, raised it high above his head, and declared in a voice that struck the air like a war drum:

"Your servant offers up the Tiger Tally of the Western Command. From this day forward, the hundred thousand under my banner shall answer only to the Throne."

The court shuddered.

For a heartbeat, there was no sound at all—not even from the palanquin attendants. Ministers stared as if their tongues had been cut from their mouths. Even the horses seemed to stand quieter.

On the dais, Shen Zhaoru swayed violently. It felt as if the blood in her body had been drained at once. The world tilted. A maid grabbed her arm, hard, to keep her upright.

The Emperor smiled.

His fingers tapped the jade inlay of the rail—slow, deliberate. His eyes were half-lidded, their light unreadable.

"General," he said with gentle ease, "you are too distant with Us. We have been brothers for years. Have I ever doubted you? This tally… you need not do this."

The words were warm. The distance beneath them was colder than steel.

Lu Xiu did not rise.

His knee pressed into stone. His posture was perfect. His refusal was also perfect: not defiance, but insistence in the shape of loyalty.

"Your Majesty is not a ruler who doubts without cause," he said heavily. "But I am not so arrogant as to call myself a pure loyalist by nature. Only by returning this token may I face my own conscience without shame."

He lifted his head and looked up at the man above him.

His eyes were clear.

Too clear—because everything unsaid was being forced into what he did say.

"In the past, I stood beside Your Majesty in the court's hidden wars. The Third Prince's faction was cut down not by noise, but by patience. At that time, I was young, my voice light, my power little. I followed because I believed Your Majesty carried burdens no one else could carry, and because I chose that path without doubt."

He paused, then continued, quieter—each word weighted.

"Now the northwest is pacified. I know I should not continue to hold heavy command. I return it, so that the realm may sleep—and so that I may stand beside Your Majesty in future with no shadow between us. No suspicion. No betrayal."

For an instant, something flickered behind the Emperor's composure—irritation, calculation, a private coldness that did not need to show itself fully.

Then his expression smoothed again.

"Such a gift," he said softly. "You make it difficult for Us to accept."

Lu Xiu's lips curved—not joy, not pride. Something tired. Something almost gentle, and therefore more dangerous.

"I seek nothing else," he said. "Only to keep one person. To grow old with her."

The words fell like ink into still water.

Shen Zhaoru's heart slammed once so hard her vision dimmed. She felt the shock climb her spine, hot and numb all at once. For a breath she could not inhale. She could not even pretend to be calm.

The Emperor turned his head, as if amused by a line of theatre. His smile was spring-light on the surface, winter under the skin.

"Oh?" he asked. "And which family's jewel could make our General cast away command as though it were grass?"

Lu Xiu lowered his gaze.

His voice, when it came, was unnaturally steady—so steady it pressed on the chest like weight.

"…A widow I saved during the march," he said. "She carried a child. After battle, she sheltered me. In sickness, she guarded me. She is gentle, resilient. I have… long since given my heart."

Shen Zhaoru went white.

A widow.

So that was the lie he chose to cut the rope—clean, blunt, merciful, cruel. A lie shaped to protect her by killing what was left of her.

She did not know whether to laugh or vomit.

The Emperor's smile did not change. His gaze drifted, briefly, over the Empress's face—quiet, almost affectionate.

"Then the General is blessed," he said lightly. "Fortune is generous to you."

Lu Xiu bowed deeper, as if he heard only kindness.

"I dare not call myself a gentleman," he replied. "But I understand repayment. I have already pledged myself. I beg Your Majesty to grant it."

The Emperor was silent for a moment, as though considering.

Then he spoke, mild as tea, sharp as metal beneath it.

"You are young, gifted. Countless noble daughters dream of you. If it is repayment you seek, why not return her kindness with gold? With rank?"

Lu Xiu's head lowered further. His humility did not soften the force of his answer.

"Since antiquity, a life-saving debt is repaid with one's person. I have promised her the rest of my life. I cannot dishonour that vow."

A cold laugh slipped from the Emperor—brief, controlled, edged.

He was about to speak—

When Shen Zhaoru's body finally betrayed her.

Her face turned paper-white. Her knees softened. A dark bloom spread fast through layers of crimson silk.

"Your Majesty—" she tried, and her voice vanished.

A scream ripped the air.

"The Empress is bleeding! Quickly—someone!"

The Emperor moved first—long stride, robe flaring. He was at her side in an instant, catching her as she folded.

"Zhaoru!" His voice carried command, and something that sounded like urgency. "Summon the Imperial Physicians. Now!"

And Lu Xiu—

Lu Xiu took one step.

Instinct. Reflex. The body moving before the mind could stop it.

Then he halted.

One step, and no more.

His hands hung at his sides. His fists clenched until the joints whitened. His jaw locked so hard it seemed it might crack. He did not reach for her. He did not call her name. He did not even breathe fully.

He stood there, a single pace away from ruin, and forced himself not to move.

Around them, chaos erupted: attendants shouting, guards splitting the crowd, the Emperor's sleeve dragging through the spreading stain of blood.

Lu Xiu remained fixed in place.

Silent.

As though the only loyalty left to him now was restraint.

And in the cold autumn wind, among drifting leaves and the sharp smell of iron rising into air, the last thread between them—once bright as flame—snapped without sound.

Chapter 98: A Perilous Premature Birth

The Empress had gone into labour before her time.

By the hour she was carried back to the inner palace, the court outside was still in chaos—voices colliding, physicians summoned, silk trains trailing blood.

Yet in the imperial study, all was still. So still, it felt like the hush before a blizzard.

Only the faint clink of porcelain broke the quiet.

The Emperor, Chen Gen, sat motionless behind the long desk, his gaze hidden beneath shadow. After a long silence, he gave a soft, humourless laugh.

"Enough of the performance," he said, voice low and edged. "Tell me, Lu Xiu —what is it you truly want?"

The mask of mild grace had fallen away.

His eyes were sharp as obsidian, the same eyes that once charmed courtiers and cowed rivals. The lines of his hand still bore the pale marks of where he had gripped his wine cup too tightly.

"Ten legions," he continued, his tone calm yet cold. "A hundred thousand men under your command. If you wished to trade them for my throne, they would suffice."

Lu Xiu raised his eyes slowly. When he spoke, his voice was quiet, yet it carried an echo from another lifetime.

"Your Highness," he said.

The old title—Prince, not Emperor—hung in the air like a ghost. It was what he had called him years ago, when Chen Gen was still a cornered heir fighting for survival, and Lu Xiu, a mere bastard son from a noble house had chosen to stake his life on the man everyone else had abandoned, successfully aiding His Highness in dismantling the faction of the Third Prince and securing his position as the Crown Prince.

The memory was a scar reopened, cutting backward through years of blood and victory.

Lu Xiu went on, voice steady, grave: "In those days, this servant pledged his loyalty not for power, but because he believed His Highness would be a ruler for the ages—a sovereign of mercy and truth. I knew little of court or treachery. I had no hunger for rank. I only wished to protect one person and keep her safe all her life."

He paused, the quiet between them thick as ink.

"Now Your Highness has become the Emperor of the kingdom. And I— am still, Your Highness still have my loyalty."

His next words fell slow and deliberate, each one sounding like the strike of a temple bell.

"The hundred thousand soldiers I command are not to buy a kingdom. Not to buy glory."

He drew a breath, meeting the Emperor's gaze with eyes neither defiant nor afraid.

"I ask for one thing only."

Then, softly—

"Your Majesty, will you trade them... for her?"

The room seemed to still again. Even the candlelight stopped flickering.

For the first time that night, Chen Gen's expression wavered. He looked at the man kneeling before him—his brother in war, his rival in faith— and felt the faintest tremor in his chest.

A part of him was moved.

Another part recoiled.

Yes, they had shared battlefields, faced death together when the Third Prince's faction nearly crushed them both. But for a woman—to relinquish command, to beg in her name—this, to Chen Gen, was folly.

"You would have me spare her," he said at last, his voice quieter now, "but tell me, General—how do you intend to protect her?"

Lu Xiu straightened slightly, the light catching the worn edges of his armour.

"It has been arranged," he answered. "Imperial Preceptor Shen and his wife are childless. For the sake of propriety, Lady Shen will adopt her as a daughter from a distant branch of the clan.

Thus, she will remain under their protection—alive, but erased. To the world, she will be only a widow of the Western Frontier, a woman who bears one child."

Chen Gen's laugh was low, thin, and dangerous. "So thorough. You've planned this from the start, haven't you?"

He leaned forward, his tone a blend of mockery and admiration. "You thought today would come. You counted on my temper. You've written the whole play yourself—an Emperor trapped in his own mercy."

Lu Xiu did not flinch. "Your Majesty is a man of great compassion. I dare not presume to test it. I ask only for her peace. If Your Majesty grants it, I will hand over the command myself and serve the Empire until my bones turn to dust. But—"

His voice darkened. "If Your Majesty cannot suffer that I love her, then I will lay down my armour, retire to the fields, and never set foot in court again."

The air thickened, heavy as storm clouds. This gambit was not merely a matter of loyalty; it was a confrontation between personal devotion and destiny. Chen Gen reminded in silent for a long time.

The air thickened, heavy as storm clouds.

For a long while, the Emperor said nothing.

At last, he exhaled—a sound between a sigh and a growl.

"Lu Xiu," he murmured, fingers drumming once on the lacquered desk, "you've always been a strategist. I should have known better than to play this game with you."

His gaze lifted, distant and sharp. "You think I have no choice but to agree?"

A flicker of memory passed behind his eyes—another time, another chamber. When all the world had turned its back on him, when his princely title had been stripped and his allies scattered, there had been only a handful who still came when he called.

Lu Xiu had been one of them.

And now, that same man knelt before him again—not for power, but for a woman.

"Do you still trust me?" the Emperor asked quietly.

Lu Xiu bowed his head.

His answer came low, unshaken:

"I never stopped."

Hurried footsteps shattered the heavy silence within the imperial study.

"Your Majesty—!"

A palace maid fell to her knees, voice quivering.

"The Empress… Her Majesty is in labour. The situation… does not look well."

Before the words even finished, the air itself seemed to sink.

Chen Gen rose sharply, his robes whipping through the air like a surge of wind. He did not speak. He simply turned and strode toward the birthing chambers.

Lu Xiu hesitated—only for the space of a heartbeat—then followed. His brows drew taut, his steps silent and sure.

The two men moved one after another, crossing the imperial corridor. The autumn wind swept through the courtyards, stirring fallen leaves and banners alike.

The flutter of silk sounded eerily like the clash of steel—yet this was no battlefield, only a night where a single life hung by a thread.

Palace servants knelt aside as they passed, too afraid to raise their heads.

Outside the birthing chamber, candle flames quivered. From within came the cries of the midwives, the tearing scream of a woman in agony—each one sharper, more desperate than the last.

It was a sound that stripped the soul bare: the cry of life fighting through pain, a woman's voice trembling on the edge between birth and death.

The Emperor stood still in the courtyard, his face carved from ice, fists clenched at his sides.

He had never seen her suffer like this.

He remembered—vividly—how, years ago, she had stumbled in the imperial garden during a game with the young princes. Her palm had scraped a petal-thin cut, and she had cried as though her heart would break.

Now that same woman bore the pain of life itself—her body torn open, alone amid blood and fear.

Beside him, Lu Xiu said nothing. His gaze fixed upon the closed door, as if staring into a war he could not fight, a battle he had already lost.

Two men stood beneath the same eaves, neither turning to the other, neither able to walk away.

Time froze. Even the air began to crystallize.

Then—

An infant's cry.

High and clear, it pierced the night like lightning across a frozen lake.

The Emperor's body jolted. The tension that had locked his jaw finally broke; a faint smile eased across his lips. For the briefest instant, he seemed almost human again—like a commander after battle, the roar of war receding at last.

He turned to the man beside him, that mountain of iron and silence.

"Congratulations," Chen Gen said softly. "You're a father now."

Lu Xiu's entire body tensed. His pupils contracted, a flash of disbelief breaking through his composure.

"Your Majesty means…"

The Emperor only smiled—thin, unreadable—and said nothing.

For a long moment, Lu Xiu stood frozen. Then he closed his eyes, the sting in his chest burning deeper than any wound. When he inhaled, it was like drawing in a whole season of storm and snow.

From within, the midwife's jubilant cry rang out: "A safe delivery! Both mother and child are well!"

According to custom, the infant's sex would not be announced until the Emperor himself inquired.

The wind outside stilled, holding its breath.

"She made it," Lu Xiu murmured under his breath.

He did not say who he meant. But everyone knew—he was not speaking of the child.

A moment later, the midwife emerged, holding a swaddled bundle. Her face shone with joy, though there was unease in her eyes.

The Emperor leaned slightly forward, looked once, then said calmly, "Take the child to the warming chamber. Send for the imperial physicians—see that both are well cared for."

His gaze lingered on the closed door, his expression shifting like light on water—warm, then cold, unreadable again.

Lu Xiu remained where he was, half his face bathed in candlelight, half lost to shadow.

The wind carried the scent of blood and medicine. His heart tightened—sharp, raw, a pain that left no mark, as if it had been slashed open by a sharp blade. He did not dare ask. He only stood there, silent. ... "Good." The word trembled, rough and low, as though it had been bled out from the deepest part of his heart.

The Emperor heard it. He gave a short laugh—devoid of joy. Then he turned his back and said quietly,

"You've seen enough. You should go."

Lu Xiu lifted his head slightly. His gaze brushed the Emperor's figure, then returned to the door—where his entire soul seemed to anchor.

At last, he bowed deeply.

"Thank you, Your Majesty. This subject… takes his leave."

When he turned away, the wind rose again.

His armour rustled softly—like a distant march fading into the horizon.

And in the wavering lamplight, no one noticed the gleam that slipped from his lashes—shattered light from a heart breaking in silence.

Chapter 99: Reversing Heaven and Earth

Outside, yellow leaves whirled through the air, gilding the courtyard in fragments of autumn. Inside the birthing chamber, the cries of new life had only just begun,

yet the air still throbbed with the tautness of fear and exhaustion, as if the palace itself dared not breathe.

The Emperor's voice, when it came, was calm—warm even—like aged wine poured into a cold cup.

But beneath that gentleness lay something impossible to name: a chill, a quiet authority, and the kind of forgiveness that cuts deeper than anger.

Lu Xiu froze, his fists tightening slightly at his sides. He raised his eyes, lips parting as though to speak—

—but hurried footsteps shattered the fragile calm.

"Your Majesty—!"

An eunuch burst into the courtyard, robes dishevelled, dropping to his knees so hard the tiles rang. Sweat streamed down his temples.

"Your Majesty, Consort Hui… she too—her labour has begun!"

The words struck like a stone breaking water. For one breath, the world went utterly still.

Chen Gen turned his gaze slowly toward the servant.

His eyes revealed nothing—no fury, no surprise—only a brief, glimmering light, gone almost before it appeared.

Then he turned away. Without a word, he began to walk.

His steps were unhurried, steady, yet each carried a weight of frost and finality.

When he reached the steps, he paused. Slowly, he looked back over his shoulder at Lu Xiu.

That glance—silent, fathomless—spoke a thousand things that neither man could ever voice.

Then the Emperor turned once more and left.

Leaves rustled in his wake, spinning down to the marble path.

The wind rose sharp and sudden, cold as the edge of grief. Twilight gathered across the eaves, swallowing colour, swallowing sound.

And Lu Xiu remained alone beneath the falling sky—motionless, wordless, his figure carved against the dusk like a shadow that could not be erased.

The banners above him snapped in the wind, yet he did not move.

All the mountains and rivers of his heart pressed inward, heavy and silent, until even the air seemed to bow beneath their weight.

* * * * *

At dawn, before the palace bells could sound, silence had already fallen upon the Imperial City.

No birds sang. No servants spoke. Even the wind seemed to hold its breath.

Before the golden steps of the Hall of Supreme Harmony, ranks of officials knelt in rows that stretched like dark waves across the jade terrace. The chill of dew soaked through their robes, but none dared to stir.

When the first light touched the eaves, a eunuch's voice broke the stillness—high, trembling, and clear:

"By Heaven's Mandate, His Majesty decrees—

Her Majesty, Empress Shen, delivered a royal son. Yet due to grievous loss of blood, her life could not be saved.

The Emperor grieves beyond measure. Henceforth, court shall be suspended for three days; the realm shall mourn, banners lowered, drums stilled.

But the newborn prince, heaven's blessing upon the dynasty, ensures the line of our ancestors endures. To honour this gift of fate, a general pardon is declared; all crimes beneath exile are forgiven, and the land tax of one year remitted to comfort the people.

As for Consort Hui, though her own child, a princess, was born lifeless, let her now take charge of the royal prince's upbringing, acting as mother in all rites of care and virtue.

Thus decreed."

* * * * *

Each word struck like thunder. The vast court remained deathly still.

Heads bowed, robes whispered. A few aged ministers' eyes glistened red; one raised a sleeve, as though brushing dust, to hide the tremor of grief.

Everyone understood, the decree was not merely about birth and death. It was the closing of one game, and the sealing of another.

At the far end of the ranks, Lu Xiu stood among the lesser officials, dressed in plain court robes.

He neither moved nor spoke, his face calm as stone but within him, a storm pressed tight against the ribs. His fists had clenched before he realized it, the knuckles whitening beneath the sleeves.

When the eunuch's voice fell silent, the quiet returned colder than before.

Beyond the crimson pillars, autumn leaves spun downward through the morning haze; the wind crept beneath the eaves, carrying with it the faint smell of sandalwood and grief.

Lu Xiu slowly lifted his gaze toward the high dais where the decree had been read. The sunlight touched his face, and for a moment, his lips curved—not in sorrow, nor in irony but in something softer.

Relief.

A low, quiet laugh escaped him.

Not a laugh at mercy, nor at fate, nor even at the Emperor's cunning grace—

but at himself.

All the scheming, all the restraint, all the agony he had swallowed like broken glass—

and at last, it had bought this:

She lived.

The child lived.

He had gambled everything, and he had won.

The eunuch's voice rose again, reading the remainder of the decree, words of honour and reward. The Emperor, it said, was moved by his valour in the western and northern campaigns; for his loyalty in returning the Tiger Tally, the realm would remember his merit.

A mansion bestowed.

Gold in thousands.

The title of Grand General of Fushun.

Lu Xiu bent low, every motion measured, voice clear and unwavering:

"Your servant receives the sacred favour."

The sound echoed across the jade terrace, rippling through the rows of kneeling men.

When he straightened, his eyes glimmered faintly. He flexed his fingers, feeling again the solidity of the world—the fragile, precious weight of what he had fought for.

And still, that faint smile lingered on his lips.

Steady.

Resolved.

This time, it was not the smile of a warrior ready to charge, nor of a courtier seeking power.

It was the smile of a man who, at last, had finished the battle of his life— and chosen to lay down his sword.

* * * * *

Deep within the palace grounds, behind the western hall, the courtyard slept beneath drifting bamboo shadows.

Autumn wind moved through the leaves with a faint chill, whispering against the stone lanterns and the empty corridors.

A small palanquin, plain and unadorned, rested in the quiet corner of the garden.

The gauze curtains had not yet been lifted.

Through the faint light one could glimpse a slender figure lying within—pale, still, her breath light as silk, her face calm as if caught between dream and death.

Eunuch Xu bowed low, the weight of the bundle in his arms steady and careful. He stepped forward and presented it.

His voice was low, cautious, wrapped in the soft rustle of his robes.

"The lady General asked for is here," he murmured. "Still unconscious, but her pulse is steady. The child… has been quiet the whole way. Never cried once.

His Majesty bade this servant deliver another message as well—"

Lu Xiu's gaze lifted, sharp beneath the morning sun.

He asked quietly, "Speak plainly, Eunuch Xu. Has the Emperor more to say?"

Xu hesitated, then forced a smile, the kind that sought survival more than favor.

"His Majesty said—'A concubine's son and a widow. A fitting match, wouldn't you say?'"

The words were respectful, yet their weight was barbed—half jest, half warning.

For a moment, silence.

Then Lu Xiu laughed.

It was not loud, not bitter. Just one clear sound that cut through the stillness like sunlight through frost.

He reached out and took the infant into his arms. The baby was swaddled tight, only a tiny face visible—a perfect blossom of warmth against the cold air.

The child slept peacefully, lashes trembling like the wings of a butterfly.

Lu Xiu looked down for a long moment. Then, almost imperceptibly, his expression softened.

And he smiled again.

Not the smile of victory.

Not the smile of mockery.

But the rare, quiet smile of a man who has lost nearly everything—and yet holds, at last, what matters most.

His voice was low when he spoke, carried on the faint rustle of the wind.

"At last," he murmured, "I've won one gamble in this life."

Xu kept his head lowered. The sound of that laugh unsettled him; it was too calm, too final.

Then the general said lightly, "Please trouble yourself, Eunuch Xu, to return a message to His Majesty."

"The Grand General's words shall be delivered."

Lu Xiu raised his eyes. For a heartbeat they caught the sun—hard, gleaming, unreadable. Yet his tone remained courteous, almost gentle.

"Tell His Majesty this," he said. "My congratulations to him, too… He is a father now."

The eunuch froze, his breath catching in his throat.

Lu Xiu turned before another word could be spoken.

The armour at his shoulders caught the light as he walked toward the waiting palanquin, each step measured, steady, resolute.

He drew back the curtain.

A shaft of sunlight slipped through the bamboo leaves, falling across her face—pale, familiar, heartbreakingly still.

He looked at her for a long moment, the child sleeping against his chest, and his voice, when it came, was softer than the autumn wind:

"Zhaoru," he whispered, "I am here, I've finally come to take you home."

* * * * *

Incense curled upward in thin, unbroken spirals. The lamplight swayed faintly, gilding the silence with a dim, honey-coloured glow.

Eunuch Xu entered with light steps, his head bowed low. He knelt before the throne and spoke softly,

"Your Majesty… General Lu has received the woman and the child. All is in order."

Chen Gen did not answer immediately.

He merely lowered his gaze and lifted the teacup between his fingers.

For a moment, the soft clink of porcelain was the only sound.

Then, slowly, his hand stilled.

A faint smile touched his lips—one of those gentle, unreadable smiles that could mean mercy or mockery, no one could tell.

"So," he murmured, "he's gone?"

"Gone, Your Majesty."

The Emperor exhaled, almost in relief. His words came softer than breath, meant for himself rather than any listener.

"Let him go, then. That fool…"

A quiet chuckle escaped him. To trade a hundred thousand men for a single woman. How utterly absurd.

Eunuch Xu bent his head even lower. He knew better than to reply. He backed away, closed the heavy doors, and left the chamber steeped once more in stillness.

The Emperor rose. He walked out beneath the eaves, his robe trailing over the jade tiles, and paused at the top of the steps.

Before him spread the heart of the empire—the white walls, the golden roofs, the courts and halls that trembled beneath his command.

Tonight, they seemed impossibly quiet.

He stood there for a long while, eyes tracing the horizon. His face showed no joy, no sorrow, only a rare and lucid calm.

This empire, he thought, perhaps it is time for a new Madam.

He already held the hearts of the scholars; soon, he would secure the power of the great clans.

Marriage—always the simplest, cleanest, most efficient method.

His thoughts drifted, unbidden, to the Lu brothers.

He remembered how, years ago, when Lu Xiu's elder brother Lu Chou served as his study companion, he would sometimes glimpse the younger Lu from afar.

There had been something fierce in the boy's eyes, a hunger that was not ambition yet not loyalty either.

So, when the chance came to place that same man near his treacherous third brother, he had not hesitated.

Men like Lu Xiu always needed a cause, and once they chose one, they would bleed themselves dry for it.

Still, he had never imagined the general would throw away ten legions for love.

That kind of madness unsettled even an emperor.

A dry laugh escaped him. Fools. Every one of them.

He thought of his own Consort Hui—gentle, quiet, yielding as warm silk. She never fought, never demanded, merely waited for him to turn toward her. She carried his bloodline, tended the embers of his lineage, and asked nothing more.

That, he mused, is how women should be.

The wind rose, stirring the curtain beside him. For the first time in days, his shoulders eased.

He thought back to the day of the triumph—the moment Lu Xiu, before the eyes of the entire court, declared he had pledged himself to a widow.

So the man had planned everything, down to this final exchange.

And he, the Emperor, had played his part to perfection—granting what seemed mercy, claiming what was truly advantage.

"He must have known I would agree," he said aloud, a faint smile curving his lips. "The man knows me too well."

He could not deny a trace of admiration. When the throne had trembled under his third brother's intrigues, all the courtiers had scattered like frightened birds.

Only a handful had stood beside him then.

Lu Xiu was one of them.

Now, the same man had knelt again—not for power, not for glory, but for a woman.

How strange, the Emperor thought. To call that loyalty.

He looked toward the darkening sky. The light had dimmed to the colour of ash; the wind brushed against his cheek like memory.

"You still believe in me," he murmured, recalling the general's final words. "After everything."

He smiled faintly, though his eyes remained cold.

"No, Lu Xiu. It isn't that I am heartless," he said quietly. "It's only that when one reaches this height… who among us ever truly has a choice?"

The last of the incense burned down.

Outside, the autumn wind carried the faint echo of a carriage departing through the northern gate—fading, fading, until even the Emperor could no longer tell whether the sound came from the palace or from somewhere far deeper within his own heart.

Chapter 100: Marrying into a Noble House

The night was deep and the lamp cold, and outside the Qingfeng Courtyard in the Imperial City, a profound stillness reigned.

Grand Eunuch Xu entered through the side gate without a sound, still clad in a narrow-sleeved robe embroidered with gold cloud patterns.

In his hand, he carried a pot of aged rice wine (Daughter's Red), his smile entirely deferential: "This servant ventures to intrude. Was it Lord Lu who summoned this humble servant?"

Lu Chou leaned casually against the small table beneath the eaves, not rising.

He merely lifted his eyes to glance at him, stating calmly: "Eunuch, you attend His Majesty daily now. If a whisper in the ear is delivered with skill, it proves more efficacious than a three-thousand-word memorial."

Grand Eunuch Xu set down the wine pot, revealing a smile of deep meaning: "My Lord speaks with such ease. Yet should the wind blow in the wrong direction, it is no longer a breeze, but a blade—and whose flesh it cuts is not certain."

Lu Chou smiled faintly, his fingertip pushing the wine cup, and said softly: "I have yet to offer my thanks to the Eunuch. Had you not conveyed the timely message: 'The noble houses are deeply rooted and hard to shake, while the new gentry rise with full momentum,' it is likely the Emperor would not have so easily yielded."

Grand Eunuch Xu blinked: "If the Emperor were to hear these words, his countenance would likely turn grim."

"Then do not let him hear it," Lu Chou said, indifferently sipping the rim of his cup. "Chou naturally trusts the Eunuch; thus, I asked for this great favour—to speak a few well-timed words, enabling the Emperor to conceive of the idea himself: to secure the established noble families through marriage to check the rise of the new gentry."

Grand Eunuch Xu gave a theatrical sigh. "Lord Lu almost caused this humble one's death. Had Lord Lu not saved my life back then, this task is one We would not dare to undertake."

Lu Chou raised his eyes to gaze at the deep night in the distance.

His tone gentle yet indisputable: "The momentum of the new gentry was fostered and raised by His Majesty himself. Since the Imperial

Preceptor Shen has now passed, the influence of the scholars will gradually wane. The Emperor's intent to secure the noble families is merely a matter of time. He will ultimately recall that while the scholars of the realm accrue fame for him, who truly is the one capable of unsettling the situation and stabilising the court?"

Grand Eunuch Xu's smile did not diminish, but his expression became more cautious: "Aiya... Lord Lu, how many cunning minds do you possess? I deem eight hundred too few, and every one of them is capable of biting."

Lu Chou laughed softly: "Have you not also survived to this day by relying on two more cunning minds than others?"

Grand Eunuch Xu spread his hands: "This humble one is merely destined to warm the Emperor's shoes and bedding; how dare I compare myself to Your Lordship? However, this scheme of yours is not merely a whisper; it is plainly the lighting of a lamp—intended to incite a collision between the noble families and the new gentry. Should the Emperor accept this gambit, the merit shall be yours, but the fault his. Your blade, Sir, is sufficiently sharp."

Lu Chou picked up the wine in the cup, drained it in one draught, and said faintly: "If the Emperor is a benevolent sovereign, he shall naturally discern what to accept and what to reject; should he be a mediocre man, then so be it."

Grand Eunuch Xu narrowed his eyes at him: "For whom, precisely, are you orchestrating this manoeuvre?"

Lu Chou set down the wine cup, gazing at the sparse shadows in the courtyard, his voice deep, like frost settling on tiled eaves: "For a brother, whom Chou has owed for many years."

Grand Eunuch Xu's expression shifted slightly. He finally sighed, and with a half-smile, half-bowed: "My Lord's path, I fear, will involve three feet of spilt blood. This servant has taken note. As for the whisper in the ear—I shall deliver it with exquisite precision. Consider it the repayment of the Lord's life-saving grace from all those years ago."

* * * * *

The twilight had just descended, and the evening breeze softly brushed the eaves. As Lu Chou stepped into the courtyard, Xiao Lingyu stood beneath the eaves, tidying scraps of fabric.

The afterglow illuminated her profile, the soft light like water, immersing her entire being in a gentle, warm nightscape.

He did not utter a word. He walked forward, gently took her hand, and led her to sit upon the stone bench beneath the long eaves. Outside, the fragrance of osmanthus subtly wafted. Moonlight scattered upon their shoulders, like silver gauze covering snow, tranquil and moving.

"Why have you come again? Did I not say that once the longevity robes were finished in these two days, I would return?"

He said deeply: "I could not wait, and thus I came to seek you."

"And Little Bao? Has she been troubling people seeking me?"

"Occasionally. But with the Old Madam supporting her, the entire Lu Residence allows her to live quite as she pleases."

Hearing this, she smiled: "That is good. Living as she pleases is quite excellent." She paused, her voice light: "Neither you nor I have ever known a moment of living as we pleased in this life... Once this matter is settled, our family of three should also live such days."

He said nothing, only gazing deeply at her, his eyes as tranquil as the night, as if he intended to knead her entire being into his sight and carve her onto his heart.

Xiao Lingyu was about to respond, but suddenly heard him say: "Once this matter concludes, we shall wed."

She froze for a moment, raising her eyes to look at him, her heart trembling slightly.

"You..." Her voice was extremely low; the moment she parted her lips, he gently interrupted her.

"This matter is already under preparation," Lu Chou's tone was gentle yet resolute. "All miscellaneous items have been selected, and the guest lists have been compiled three times. If you lack the time to manage the details, I shall undertake the entire affair. You need only nod your assent—and also, prepare your wedding gown... if you are willing. Otherwise, purchasing one ready-made is also acceptable..."

"What nonsense are you uttering? For the Madam of the Jin Hua Establishment to purchase a wedding gown from another house—what would become of my commercial reputation?" She let out a soft laugh, which lit up in his eyes like scattered stars.

He seemed to realise he had spoken foolishly. "I... merely could not wait."

Xiao Lingyu blushed, turning her gaze away, and murmured softly: "There is no need for such haste..."

He laughed softly, his laughter concealing the tenderness and determination garnered from years of waiting: "It is not hasty. This wedding is already six or seven years overdue. I... could not wait any longer."

His gaze was profound, like a night of wind and snow, yet it held a single, burning thread of light—the light of finally being able to approach her.

She finally met his gaze. In that instant, she saw her own reflection in his eyes, and she also saw the side of him that had shed all armour, gentle only for her.

She lightly parted her red lips, her voice so soft it was almost scattered by the wind, yet clear as a vow—

"Good."

* * * * *

Chime-bells heralded the procession, and the Palace Gates stood wide open. On the ninth day of the first lunar month, the Dowager Empress's Autumnal Longevity birthday was celebrated with a ceremony of unprecedented grandeur and scale.

Before the morning light had broken, red silks were already hung high and coloured banners were like clouds, both inside and outside the Capital.

Lanterns and coloured decorations adorned the streets and alleys. Brocade curtains draped from building eaves down to vermillion gates, and common households affixed gold-rimmed longevity talismans.

The character for longevity illuminated the spring light throughout the city, and the myriad people celebrated together.

Within the Imperial City, the scene was even more splendid: from the Gate of Pure Sound, golden steps and jade stairs were continuously laid out, leading directly to the Longevity Palace.

The steps were strewn with fragrant mud and flowers, their scent carried gently on the wind.

Longevity Mountain stones, transported from the Southern Garden, emitted a fine mist, resembling a gathering of steam and glowing clouds; those walking within seemed to tread in an immortal realm.

The ornaments and vessels in the hall were also of the utmost luxury. Curtains were woven with dragon threads and phoenix filaments, and the canopy suspended a curtain of seven precious jewels.

Flanking the Imperial table were golden basins of longevity peaches, jade carvings of auspicious birds and mythical beasts, Lingzhi fungus, purple ginseng, and century-old panax and deer antlers—all rare treasures contributed from various regions.

All civil and military officials, their ceremonial robes meticulously arrayed, had taken their seats early. Kings, Marquises, Princesses, Commandery Princesses, and the noble ladies of the great families were all present without exception.

The Imperial Consorts also arrived in their grandest attire.

Their ceremonial robes were all embroidered with auspicious clouds, propitious cranes, coiled dragons, and circular phoenixes, their splendour illuminated by the lamplight, breathtakingly magnificent.

Chen Gen personally supported the Dowager Empress as she ascended the Longevity Throne, his expression respectful and intimate.

At his side were Consort Hui and the infant Prince she held in her arms—at that moment, the gaze of the entire court was captured by this 'mother and son' pairing.

The young Prince, clad in a small python robe, his features somewhat resembling Chen Gen's, remained ignorant and silent, yet established an unspoken authority.

Drums and music sounded in unison, and bells and chimes rang out simultaneously. Five hundred youths, clad in feather robes, slowly entered the hall, performing the Dance of Eternal Longevity.

Their movements were dignified and the momentum grand. One hundred palace maids followed, presenting the Tribute to Longevity Scroll, which had been embroidered with ten thousand needles.

The scroll depicted the phoenix dancing high in the heavens, mountains of longevity, and seas of fortune, symbolising eternal peace and long life. The scene was solemn and majestic.

Jade cakes were stacked layer upon layer like mountains, light and shadow flowing across their surfaces. Lingzhi fungus and purple ginseng were arranged on crystal jade plates, emitting a faint, cold shimmer.

The Dowager Empress, her face beaming with smiles, sat upon the Longevity Chair. Clad in golden radiance, her grace remained undiminished, the very embodiment of Imperial nobility.

As the Longevity Banquet reached its climax, a court attendant was suddenly heard announcing loudly:

"Tribute from the Jin Hua Establishment: The Double-Sided, Bi-Coloured Phoenix-Patterned Longevity Robe, respectfully presented to the Dowager Empress!"

The entire assembly stirred slightly, and all eyes turned.

Four youthful seamstresses, their steps steady, were seen each holding a corner of the silk. A bolt of mist-white soft satin slowly unfolded, spread upon the golden steps before the Imperial dais.

Where the light fell obliquely upon the fabric, it displayed a fiery, crimson-gold phoenix; turning into the shadows, it instantly became an ice-blue, cold phoenix. The textures were layered.

The spread phoenix feathers seemed to vibrate faintly; the gold-dust edges were like threads of snow, and cold light shimmered, as if a living creature had spread its wings, ready to soar away.

The crowd collectively held its breath for a moment.

It was, astonishingly, a single, extremely rare heirloom piece: seamless, bi-coloured on both sides.

There was no flaw in the intricate weaving of the fine needlework, and even the tail feathers faintly displayed a light-gathering poise, like flowing rosy clouds, truly resembling a celestial bird hovering in the air.

The Dowager Empress rose up in astonishment, her phoenix eyes shining, and she exclaimed repeatedly: "What a magnificent Garment of the Propitious Phoenix! It is simply the craftsmanship of the heavens and the artistry of the gods! The work of immortals could not surpass this!"

Chen Gen smiled faintly, his gaze passing over the dense crowd, looking towards the woman in red attire standing at the far end of the assembly.

Her black hair was coiled like clouds, and she wore minimal make-up. The brilliance in her eyes and eyebrows could not be hidden—it was precisely Xiao Lingyu.

The name of the Jin Hua Establishment became famous from this one achievement.

No one at the banquet was not astonished by her skill.

The entire court murmured in admiration. Not a single person, not even the habitually conservative old noble families, dared to speak of her 'merchant-woman background,' nor did anyone slight her again.

Even Lu Chou, who sat at the end of the seating arrangement, could not help but smile softly, his knuckles tapping the lid of his cup.

—This fame, she had embroidered it into existence with her own hands, conquering the world.

She required no one to pave the road for her, nor did she need anyone to speak on her behalf.

She, finally—had proven worthy of the name Jin Hua, her reputation shaking the entire dynasty.

Extra chapter 1

The Twin Wedding of Jin Dynasty

The most jubilant day in the capital came at last, a day when two weddings would crown the dawn, and joy itself filled the air.

The city bloomed in red. Silk banners streamed from rooftops, drums thundered through the avenues, and the scent of flowers drifted ten miles outward. Even the Azure Sparrow Tower hung twin scarlet scrolls of double happiness; every household was festooned with lanterns and ribbons. From merchants to nobles, everyone spoke of the same marvel—

"Now this is a true golden age. Heaven itself has bestowed a double blessing."

The first match was General Lu Xiu, the Emperor's appointed groom, wedding Lady Shen Zhaoru, the adopted daughter of the late Imperial Preceptor's household.

The second was Lu Chou, his younger brother, granted marriage by imperial decree to Xiao Lingyu, Madam of Jin Hua Hall, the celebrated merchant house of Jiangnan.

What made the city hum with delight was this—

both brothers wed on the same day, and both brides came bearing children.

Street urchins laughed and called the two little ones "the twin stars of fortune."

"They cry and laugh in harmony," people said, "and together they'll bring luck to their whole clan."

* * * * *

The Wedding Morning

Scarlet banners hung high; bells and drums answered one another; ten miles of crimson procession filled the streets.

Petals rained through the palace gates like blessings from the sky.

Lu Xiu stood tall in embroidered vermilion armour, not court regalia, but it suited him—his bearing still proud, still radiant.

Cradling a tiny girl in his arms, he crossed the threshold beneath the full blaze of day. A faint smile touched his lips as he whispered to his bride,

"The three of us—let's go home."

Shen Zhaoru's wedding gown was woven in Jin Hua's own looms: white silk threaded with molten gold, phoenix feathers unfurling across the hem.

She held the swaddled infant close, turning back with a smile that trembled like light on water.

"This child comes with me as dowry," she said softly. "You must love her—for a lifetime."

Xiu inclined his head, his eyes warm as spring sunlight.

"To gain both mother and child—what more could this life offer?"

Their gazes met. After all their storms and distances, there were no shadows left of politics or deceit—only peace, only gentleness. Even the wind seemed to pause for them.

* * * * *

Within the Lu residence, joy roared like a tide. Lanterns swung from every beam; drums echoed without end.

Baor was dressed like a doll from a painting—

a red silk skirt, two tiny fabric blossoms pinned in her hair. One hand held Xiao Lingyu's sleeve, the other clung to Shen Zhaoru's, her smile radiant as dawn.

"Now both my mamas are brides! Should I call you both sister-in-law?"

Laughter burst from the hall. Even Eunuch Xu doubled over, wheezing between chuckles:

"What a honeyed tongue this child has! No wonder the two households rejoice together."

The Grand Madam Lu listened amid the laughter, tears welling in her eyes. She took her granddaughter's hand and murmured over and over:

"Good, good... This life, at last, is whole."

* * * * *

The Night Banquet

When night fell, the banquet blazed. Candles shimmered; the air swelled with perfume and the rustle of silks.

At the head table sat Lu Chou and Xiao Lingyu, side by side. He poured her wine with uncharacteristic devotion.

"You seldom drink," she teased. "Why so diligent tonight?"

"Because this night," he said, his tone quiet but firm, "is seven years late. I'll not let it pass sober."

Her eyes reddened slightly. She smiled and lifted her cup.

"Then let me be drunk with you—just this once."

At another table, Shen Zhaoru and Lu Xiu sat together. She fed the infant in her arms; he added broth to her bowl without a word. They said nothing at all, yet theirs was the gentlest harmony in the hall.

Then came the Emperor's envoy—Eunuch Xu once more—entering with chests of gold and jade, his voice resounding:

"By imperial decree—'Two generals united in heart; their fortune shall prosper through generations.' Not only are honours bestowed, but the House of Lu is henceforth inscribed among the eternal nobles of the realm!"

The hall erupted in cheers; drums thundered anew.

Xu returned quietly to his corner, whispering to a fellow attendant:

"Two unions—one earned by fate, the other won by love. At last, both found peace. If Heaven has its cycles, perhaps this is what it means."

* * * * *

Later that night, the candles burned low. The wind brushed past the crimson lanterns.

In the courtyard, moonlight spilled like water; beneath the eaves, two couples sat side by side, watching the stars drift over the palace roofs.

"So," Xiao Lingyu mused with a soft laugh, "we've been husband and wife twice now. Isn't that…"

"Fated," Lu Chou finished, his voice steady. "You and I were heaven's design—don't think otherwise."

She leaned lightly against his shoulder.

"Then don't forget," she murmured, "you're carrying both me and Baor on that shoulder of yours."

A little way off, Shen Zhaoru sat beneath the gallery, stroking her daughter's brow. Lu Xiu approached, his tone roughened by emotion:

"I've waited too long for this. Never thought I'd live to see it… For once, Heaven has been kind."

She turned, eyes tender as dusk.

"I don't ask for forever," she whispered, "only that we remember this moment of truth between us—that's enough."

Above them, fireworks burst into bloom. The red light flooded the city; the lanterns of Jin Hua reflected upon the river, forming a golden road of light that flowed from the marketplace to the palace wall—like the Milky Way descended to earth.

That night, the capital shone from end to end. The people sang until dawn.

And in every home, they spoke of the Double Wedding of Prosperity, saying—

"Two lives met, four hearts became a family. One smile erased the dust of the past—beneath crimson veils, every vow was a promise to grow old together."

Extra chapter 2

Ten Maxims for Rising a Daughter - by Chou

It was late spring, warm and tranquil—their second year of marriage.

Lu Chou had received an imperial order to inspect several prefectures in Ruzhou, a journey of more than a month.

On the eve of his departure, Xiao Lingyu found him arranging his travel gear. She asked softly,

"Is there anything still unfinished?"

He looked up at her, calm as always.

"Nothing," he said. "All is in order. Only… Baor is eight years old now."

He paused, then reached behind the writing desk and brought out a slim book bound in plain silk.

"This," he said, handing it to her.

Xiao Lingyu accepted it, curious. On the first page she read, written in firm brushstrokes:

Ten Rules for Raising a Daughter — Recorded by Chou at Qingfeng Court

She blinked in surprise, but before she could speak, he said quietly,

"Do you remember that letter you once left for Baor and me? I never returned the gesture.

Tonight, I'm making it up to you."

His voice was gentle as jade, yet beneath it stirred the faint ache of parting.

She lowered her gaze and opened the book. The handwriting was strong, every stroke deliberate, yet the words themselves were soft as breath:

1. Never betray your own heart.

May her thoughts and choices be her own, free of shame or apology.

2. Speak with care, act with measure—but never from fear.

To know when to hold silence and when to speak truth is a lifelong art.

3. See people clearly, but with compassion.

The world is clouded; may she keep a mind both discerning and kind.

4. Keep promises like jade; never offer them lightly.

Words once given must be lived. Empty vows wound deeper than blades.

5. Hide her brilliance, yet never belittle herself.

She need not always win, nor must she always yield. She is my daughter—

she must trust her own light.

6. Let quietness be her strength, and laughter her edge.

May she be gentle but not weak, her calm concealing steel,

like wind through bamboo, like water guarding a blade.

7. Love others, but guard herself first.

Whomever she gives her heart to, may she always keep her own.

8. Be able to weep, to laugh, to fight, and to retreat.

True strength is not in never crying, but in smiling after the tears.

9. Remember the taste of home.

Home is not in roof or wall, but where the heart rests.

If ever she loses her way, let her recall the hands that once held hers.

10. Be like her mother.

If she grows to be even half of you, I shall have no regrets in this life.

* * * * *

Xiao Lingyu's fingers tightened on the edge of the page. Her lips curved faintly.

She closed the book and looked up at him, teasing softly:

"She's only a child—and a girl at that. Isn't this a little early for such lofty teaching?"

He met her gaze, eyes warm as candlelight.

"She's eight," he said. "At that age I'd already memorized the Analects.

But I'm not as wise as you, nor as thoughtful. So my words grew… long-winded."

She tucked the booklet away, half-mocking, half-moved.

"Still, she's just a little girl. Don't you think this is rather—"

He pondered a moment, then smiled.

"Whether son or daughter, they are our children.

If you will stand beside me, I'll teach her the world of men,

and you'll teach her the world of heart and hands. Between us—she will be complete."

Xiao Lingyu laughed, tears shimmering at the corners of her eyes.

Those ten precepts, she realized, were written not only for Baor,

but for her as well.

As once she had left him words of farewell and trust,

so now he answered—with ink and love.

"You're right," she said softly. "These ten rules work for sons too.

We'll keep them—for next time."

Chou paused.

"Next time?"

She took his hand and placed it gently against her abdomen.

Her voice trembled, smiling through it:

"Tell me… do you hope this one is a son or a daughter?"

He froze—then the meaning struck him. His hand pressed closer, eyes wide.

"What did you say?"

Her smile deepened, calm and radiant.

"You're going to be a father again."

"Truly?" His voice caught, breaking into a laugh of pure joy.

"Xiao Lingyu—that's wonderful!"

He swept her up into his arms and spun her once around.

"Put me down!" she protested, laughing.

"Never!" he answered.

The lamplight trembled; their laughter rippled through the courtyard.

Outside, the spring breeze carried the scent of blossoms,

petals fell like drifting snow, and in their wake lingered

the fragrance of happiness.

Extra chapter 3

The Red Plum Courtyard

The spring sun was mild, the air sweet with falling petals.

In the quiet courtyard, Shen Zhaoru sat upon a stone bench, a book resting open in her hands—yet her gaze never strayed far from the small figure tottering through the garden.

Little Jane, their youngest daughter, clung to the hem of her mother's robe with one hand, and with the other tugged mischievously at the branch of a red plum tree. The blossoms trembled, scattering pale petals into the wind, as though laughing with her.

"Gently," Zhaoru said with a smile. "You'll break the flowers."

But the child only laughed louder, her eyes bending into crescents, her delight setting even the blossoms astir.

From beyond the gate came the soft sound of approaching footsteps.

"Jane—your father's home."

She turned, and there he was: Lu Xiu, not in court robes but in plain attire, sleeves rolled twice at the wrist, as if he had hurried straight from his duties. In his hand he carried a small wooden box, his expression composed yet tinged with anticipation.

"You're back early from court today?" she asked, rising with the child in her arms.

He sat beside her, handing over the box.

"A gift," he said simply.

She arched a brow, lifted the lid—and froze.

Inside lay a gold hairpin, delicate and refined, its tail carved with tiny blossoms set with three pearls. The design was unmistakable: it was exactly the same as the one she had once worn long ago.

"This is…" she began.

"The one you wore that year," he said, voice calm, gentle.

"I remember—at sunset, when we rode together, your hair came loose, the pin slipped.

711

I picked it up and kept it. When I left for the northern campaign, I sent it home with the letters…

but as the years passed, I thought it lost."

He paused, eyes softening as they fell on the glint of gold in her fingers.

"Some weeks ago, the memory returned to me. So I had another made—exactly as before.

Today, with a quiet hour to spare, I thought to bring it back to you."

She tried to laugh, but the sound broke halfway through.

The memory rose like floodwater: the day she had stood before the imperial throne, receiving from the Emperor a broken gold hairpin—his hairpin—brought back from the frontier. That single object had been the proof of his survival, and of their separation. She had smiled then, bowed, and only afterward wept until her sleeves were soaked.

Now the same shape glimmered before her once more, and tears came unbidden.

"Mother… cry?" Jane asked in wonder, reaching a small hand to catch her mother's tears.

Lu Xiu gently took the child into his arm. With his free hand he wiped the wetness from Zhaoru's face, his touch light, his voice low and coaxing.

"Why tears? Aren't we safe and well?"

Then, taking the hairpin, he smoothed a lock of her hair and slipped it back into place, the gesture tender and practiced.

She did not move, simply watched him.

At length, she said softly, her voice hoarse,

"The broken one… I still have it."

He blinked, then laughed quietly.

"So that's where it went. I'd thought it lost."

His smile lingered, but behind it lay a stillness deep as dusk.

"Don't cry anymore," he murmured.

"We've each weathered half a lifetime of wind and storm. To sit here now, in this courtyard, to speak with you, to place this pin once more in your hair—this peace is fortune enough."

His tone was light, yet every word carried weight, like stones laid gently in the heart.

She looked at him, her gaze steady.

"You traded it—for ten armies," she whispered.

Sunlight slipped between them, falling across her hair. The gold pin caught the light, glowing like a spark of the old sun that had once gilded their parting.

"It doesn't matter," he said quietly. "The Emperor would never have let me keep command for long.

Those troops would have been recalled, one way or another. But this pin—I owed you this.

A promise, returned to its rightful place."

In his arms, Jane wriggled and blurted out,

"Papa!"

He laughed at the sound, pressing a kiss to her cheek.

"Come, my little one—let's go see a play."

"A play?" Zhaoru asked, startled. "Why the sudden whim?"

"A new troupe has come from the palace," he said, eyes gleaming.

"I've invited them here for Grandmother's delight. Everyone's waiting."

"And what are they performing?"

He gave a soft chuckle.

"The Romance of the Western Chamber."

Her cheeks flushed. She pushed lightly at his arm.

"Then I'm not going."

"Why not?" He drew her close with a grin.

"That's our story, isn't it?"

"Nonsense."

"How is it nonsense?" he teased, breaking into a half-sung line,

"For love unspeakable, I would cross ten thousand miles…"

She laughed despite herself, covering her face. He joined her laughter, and the evening seemed to soften around them.

Ten years of storm and steel had come to rest in this courtyard of red plum blossoms.

The garden lay calm again—only the flowers swayed in the breeze, their fragrance drifting through the air.

And so, time itself seemed to whisper:

after all the battles, all the vows, all the tears—this peace, this moment, is enough.

Extra chapter 4

Spring Beyond the City Walls

Early spring in the outskirts of the capital, the wind mild, the sunlight gentle.

Shen Zhaoru and Xiao Lingyu had rarely found a day so free. Together they took the children out to the apricot groves for a picnic. Beneath the pale blossoms, laughter shimmered like the breeze through petals.

A short distance away, under the shade of old trees, Lu Chou and Lu Xiu sat across from each other at a stone table. Tea and pastries lay between them; both were dressed in plain attire, their faces calm, though their expressions held a certain quiet tension.

Two-year-old Jane was crouched by the creek, picking up pebbles one by one. Eight-year-old Baor sat at the flower edge, carefully painting a butterfly, each stroke patient and deliberate.

Zhaoru smiled.

"You two," she teased, "why not go watch the children instead of sitting here?"

Chou lifted his gaze toward the little girl by the blossoms, then withdrew it again, replying evenly,

"She prefers to finish her painting before she'll move."

Xiu arched a brow, half amused.

"That daughter of yours grows more like you by the day—measured, precise, as if even her play must follow rules. I swear she was livelier when she was five."

"Better that," Chou returned mildly, "than your little one who tossed stones into her tea cup yesterday."

He paused, as if by accident, and added with deliberate lightness:

"Yesterday Baor recited a passage from The Great Learning. I only taught her once, and she remembered it all."

Xiu's lips quirked.

"Is that so? Mine may be only two, but she can sing already. Even the nightingales can't match her voice."

Chou raised his cup and took a sip of tea, a faint smile touching his mouth.

"Last night, Baor called me Father in her sleep," he said softly.

"She asked that I stay home a few more days. I set aside my memorials without a thought."

Xiu folded his arms, and countered smoothly,

"And what of that? You set down your papers; mine clung to my robe and cried until I carried her off to bed. Not even her mother could coax her quiet."

The words passed between them like polite conversation—

their tones serene, their glances tranquil—

yet each syllable carried the glint of rivalry, sheathed in brotherly courtesy.

Shen Zhaoru bit back her laughter.

Beside her, Xiao Lingyu raised a silk fan to hide her smile and whispered,

"It seems today's contest is not for power, but for daughters."

Zhaoru's gaze followed the two men, who were now solemnly praising their children as if before the court.

"Once," she murmured, "they contended for the empire itself.

Now they compete over whose daughter is cleverer.

I can't tell if that's decline—or progress."

Just then, a small voice rang across the field—

"Papa! Come quick! The butterfly I drew just flew away!"

Lu Chou's expression flickered. He turned and saw a sheet of paper— its butterfly drawing—caught by the wind, curling and fluttering through the air. He rose at once, flicked his long sleeve, and strode over, his voice unusually gentle: "Don't worry. We'll go home and have Mother embroider one for you."

Xiu watched his brother's retreating back, then turned to the creek.

"Jane! Have you gathered enough stones yet?

If so, sing your new song for your Second Uncle!"

716

The child's voice carried back through the grove:

"Only if I get candied haw first!"

At that, both women burst into laughter, doubling over behind their fans.

This quiet little battle of fathers and daughters had no victor, no defeat—only the serenity of ordinary joy.

Two men who had once overturned kingdoms and courts now argued beneath the apricot blossoms about pebbles and verses, their world reduced to sunlight, laughter, and family.

And somehow, that was grander than any triumph they had ever won.

Extra chapter 5

Twenty Years Later

The skies were clear, the air bright with spring.

Two decades had passed beneath the reign of His Majesty Emperor Chen Ken, styled Mingduan Suxu Qixuan, who had united the realm and brought peace to the four seas.

The people said their sovereign was a ruler unseen in a hundred years—wise in strategy, gracious in heart. Yet the peace of his age was not wrought by imperial virtue alone, but also by the two pillars who stood beside the throne: Minister of Revenue Lu Chou and Grand Marshal Lu Xiu.

Civil and military, the brothers stood shoulder to shoulder.

Court wits called them the Twin Jades of the Lu House; scholars inscribed,

"While the Lu brothers serve, the realm shall never fall."

At court, Lu Xiu, now silver at the temples, still wore his battle armour when entering the Council of War. His bearing was as steady as in his youth; the sword at his waist still caught the light. Fifteen years earlier he had reformed the border defences—since then, no tribe dared trespass, and the western kingdoms came year after year to offer tribute.

Lu Chou, by contrast, remained the quiet enigma of the cabinet: austere in manner, unyielding in integrity, a pen sharper than any blade. He oversaw finance and administration, purged corruption without mercy, and was both feared and admired.

The scholars hailed him as First Among the Pure Currents;

the common folk joked,

"If the harvest is good, thank Lord Lu's brush."

The Emperor, who had abolished many titles from the former reign, had elevated only the Lu brothers to first rank—and still, in private, called Chou Brother Lu. Three times each year, he summoned the brothers to a quiet banquet. No politics were spoken, only memories.

They would reminisce about the old days—

the night of rain and weeping,

the cup of wine once thought poisoned,

the confrontation in the imperial study.

"Had I been a suspicious ruler," the Emperor once said with a laugh,

"neither of you would be sitting here today."

Xiu smiled.

"If Your Majesty were truly suspicious, would you have placed that decree—'a concubine's son to wed a widow'—in my own hands?"

Chou said nothing, only lifted his cup. The faint curve of his mouth betrayed a laughter too deep for words.

The Emperor fell quiet, gaze drifting toward the candlelight.

"As for my third brother," he said softly, "I have let him return to his manor. His health has long been frail—he can stir no more storms."

There was no triumph in his tone—only the calm of distance and time.

Xiu nodded, his levity subdued.

"To let go is no small thing. In that, Your Majesty shows the heart of a benevolent king."

Chou remained silent, but his eyes gentled; whatever bitterness had once bound them was now dissolved.

* * * * *

Today, Xiao Lingyu stood as the matron of every guild and atelier in the empire, having revived the artistry of national embroidery. The Xiao family's eldest son, blind from illness, managed the ledgers of Jin Hua Hall. Each evening he sat beneath lamplight with his daughter, listening to storytellers speak of the southern rivers in bloom.

The so-called widow of old—the girl once born to the Shen house, later renamed Shen Zhaoru—was now the head of the Imperial Women's Academy, her virtue rivaling that of any empress.

And the concubine's son?

Now ennobled as a regional prince, commander of three border provinces—his armies vast, his power unchallenged—yet in twenty years he had never crossed his borders once.

The world knew he held the sword, but never drew it.

* * * * *

The storms had long passed.

Beyond the palace walls, willows hung green, flowers opened to the breeze. Children's laughter carried through the lanes.

After court, one often saw three figures walking side by side—the Emperor and the Lu brothers—sometimes joined by two women with their children, visiting old shrines or taking spring outings beyond the city.

The realm was at peace;

the rains came when due;

the people slept without fear.

The old decrees lay yellowed with age, names half-faded.

Those who once bled for the throne had grown grey; new faces filled the hall.

Yet the prosperity of this age rested upon the stone foundations laid in those years of blood and fire.

That spring, the capital's storytellers sang a new ballad that spread from street to street:

"Who stained the golden steps with blood?

Who cast the tiger tally to the wind?

The mountains kept their vow to heroes—

and one eternal sovereign stands among men."

www.ingramcontent.com/pod-product-compliance
Lightning Source LLC
Chambersburg PA
CBHW070332170726
48291CB00001B/21